YOUNG GOODMAN BROWN

Hawthorne's stunning evocation of the ubiquity of evil and depravity.

THE BRIDE COMES TO YELLOW SKY

Stephen Crane's moving story of an alcoholic gunslinger's last fling.

MADAME ZILENSKY AND THE KING OF FINLAND

Carson McCullers' brilliantly humorous portrait of a pathological liar.

A MOTHER'S TALE

James Agee's shattering parable of life, death and the inexorable vise of fate.

THE OLD PEOPLE

William Faulkner's touching story of a young boy's initiation into the mysteries of life.

AND FORTY-FIVE OTHER SHORT MASTERPIECES THAT RUN THE GAMUT OF HUMAN EXPERIENCE AND EMOTION

**50
GREAT
AMERICAN
SHORT STORIES**

50
GREAT
AMERICAN
SHORT STORIES

Edited and with an introduction by
MILTON CRANE

Professor of English Literature
The George Washington University

FOR TOM AND PETER

50 GREAT AMERICAN SHORT STORIES

A Bantam Classic / March 1965
9 printings through June 1971
Bantam Literature edition / April 1972
15 printings through September 1976

ISBN 0-553-10362-8

Library of Congress Catalog Card Number 65-13863

INTRODUCTION

It has frequently been observed that the modern short story is to a striking degree an American creation. Certainly the first important writers in this newest (and also, quite conceivably, oldest) form of fiction were Americans, and the critic who first endeavored to formulate a poetics of the short story, and who gained a worldwide reputation for his own stories, was the American Edgar Allan Poe.

More significant, however, than our desire to plant the American flag on the North Pole of the short story is the fact that American achievements in the short story have commanded international respect and admiration for a century and a half, or as long as the genre may be said to have existed in its modern form. It is not easy to obtain general agreement on the antiquity of the short story, or even on its precise definition. These two problems obviously are linked. If we were to adopt, for example, an abbreviation of Abel Chevalley's definition of the novel (cited by E. M. Forster in his perennially fresh and lively *Aspects of the Novel*): "a fiction in prose of a certain extent (*une fiction en prose d'une certaine étendue*)," then we might be permitted to claim as a short story that most powerful and memorable of all short narratives, the story of King David, Bath-sheba, and the prophet Nathan (II Samuel 11-12). The same is true of the celebrated Milesian tale that has come down to us as "The Widow of Ephesus." But, on the other hand, there are critics who maintain vigorously that these two stories are tales, however excellent, and not short stories in the modern sense. This term they reserve for short fictions dealing principally with the evocation of mood and the revelation of character, as practiced by Chekhov, Joyce, and their followers. By this standard, the tale, as written by Kipling, Guy de Maupassant, or W. Somerset Maugham, is a special literary genre, which employs basically primitive narrative techniques to achieve limited aesthetic effects.

It is not the business of this book to try to render or apply a definitive judgment in this continuing controversy. The short story seems to me sufficiently flexible and eclectic to accommodate both Kipling's tales and Chekhov's vignettes—and, for that matter, Virginia Woolf's impressionistic sketches and Sylvia Townsend Warner's fables. A form that includes "The Snows of Kilimanjaro," "A Municipal Report," "Mme. Tellier's Establishment," "Mario and the Magician," and "The Golden Honeymoon" can hardly be accused of being narrowly restrictive or exclusive. One is tempted to conclude that only so liberal a definition of the short story as that which M. Chevalley proposed for the novel can encompass such bewildering varieties of literary experience.

The present collection attempts to give the reader a comprehensive and representative view of the ways in which Americans have written short stories from the days of Washington Irving to the present. Since 1800 the form has been used by novelists, poets, humorists, satirists, social critics, and reporters. All are represented here. Such familiar stories as Nathaniel Hawthorne's "Young Goodman Brown," Bret Harte's "The Outcasts of Poker Flat," Stephen Crane's "The Bride Comes to Yellow Sky," and Stephen Vincent Benét's "By the Waters of Babylon" have been included, because each seemed uniquely representative of a major aspect of its author's talent. On the other hand, I have chosen certain stories that have rarely, if ever, been reprinted since they were first published. Among them are Edith Wharton's "The Dilettante," Finley Peter Dunne's "Mr. Dooley on the Popularity of Firemen," Charles M. Flandrau's "A Dead Issue" (an extraordinary portrait of a world-famous philosopher as a young man), and James Reid Parker's "The Archimandrite's Niece," for which that great editor the late Harold Ross had a very special regard.

Like every collection of modern American short stories, this book is in part a reflection of the changing character of American magazines, which once provided a rich market for the writer of short stories. Today, the number of magazines that publish serious short stories is sadly diminished. Partly for this reason, *The New Yorker's* domination of the field is now virtually uncontested, and its influence has become unimaginably wide. *The New Yorker* has been so frequently and so excessively criticized in recent years for allegedly imposing stereotypes on the work of gifted young writers that we must in fairness ask: How much poorer would the American short story be today without *The New Yorker*, which for more than a generation has set our standards?

The fifty stories that compose this book mirror the development of American literature, from the gradual discovery of the American mind and nation to the new awareness of an identifiably American imagination. And it is altogether fitting that the short story, with its instantaneous snapshots of life arrested and captured, should have emerged as the characteristic and outstandingly successful form in which this imagination has found expression.

MILTON CRANE

The George Washington University
Washington, D. C.

CONTENTS

Contents

The Adventure of the German Student

BY WASHINGTON IRVING

ON A stormy night, in the tempestuous times of the French Revolution, a young German was returning to his lodgings, at a late hour, across the old part of Paris. The lightning gleamed, and the loud claps of thunder rattled through the lofty narrow streets—but I should first tell you something about this young German.

Gottfried Wolfgang was a young man of good family. He had studied for some time at Göttingen, but being of a visionary and enthusiastic character, he had wandered into those wild and speculative doctrines which have so often bewildered German students. His secluded life, his intense application, and the singular nature of his studies, had an effect on both mind and body. His health was impaired; his imagination diseased. He had been indulging in fanciful speculations on spiritual essences, until, like Swedenborg, he had an ideal world of his own around him. He took up a notion, I do not know from what cause, that there was an evil influence hanging over him; an evil genius or spirit seeking to ensnare him and ensure his perdition. Such an idea working on his melancholy temperament produced the most gloomy effects. He became haggard and desponding. His friends discovered the mental malady preying upon him, and determined that the best cure was a change of scene; he was sent, therefore, to finish his studies amidst the splendors and gayeties of Paris.

Wolfgang arrived at Paris at the breaking out of the revolution. The popular delirium at first caught his enthusiastic mind, and he was captivated by the political and philosophical theories of the day: but the scenes of blood which followed shocked his sensitive nature, disgusted him with society and the world, and made him more than ever a recluse. He shut himself up in a solitary apartment in the *Pays Latin*, the quarter of students. There, in a gloomy street not far from the monastic walls of the Sorbonne, he pursued his favorite

1

speculations. Sometimes he spent hours together in the great libraries of Paris, those catacombs of departed authors, rummaging among their hoards of dusty and obsolete works in quest of food for his unhealthy appetite. He was, in a manner, a literary ghoul, feeding in the charnel-house of decayed literature.

Wolfgang, though solitary and recluse, was of an ardent temperament, but for a time it operated merely upon his imagination. He was too shy and ignorant of the world to make any advances to the fair, but he was a passionate admirer of female beauty, and in his lonely chamber would often lose himself in reveries on forms and faces which he had seen, and his fancy would deck out images of loveliness far surpassing the reality.

While his mind was in this excited and sublimated state, a dream produced an extraordinary effect upon him. It was of a female face of transcendent beauty. So strong was the impression made, that he dreamt of it again and again. It haunted his thoughts by day, his slumbers by night; in fine, he became passionately enamoured of this shadow of a dream. This lasted so long that it became one of those fixed ideas which haunt the minds of melancholy men, and are at times mistaken for madness.

Such was Gottfried Wolfgang, and such his situation at the time I mentioned. He was returning home late one stormy night, through some of the old and gloomy streets of the *Marais*, the ancient part of Paris. The loud claps of thunder rattled among the high houses of the narrow streets. He came to the Place de Grève, the square, where public executions are performed. The lightning quivered about the pinnacles of the ancient Hôtel de Ville, and shed flickering gleams over the open space in front. As Wolfgang was crossing the square, he shrank back with horror at finding himself close by the guillotine. It was the height of the reign of terror, when this dreadful instrument of death stood ever ready, and its scaffold was continually running with the blood of the virtuous and the brave. It had that very day been actively employed in the work of carnage, and there it stood in grim array, amidst a silent and sleeping city, waiting for fresh victims.

Wolfgang's heart sickened within him, and he was turning shuddering from the horrible engine, when he beheld a shadowy form, cowering as it were at the foot of the steps which led up to the scaffold. A succession of vivid flashes of lightning revealed it more distinctly. It was a female figure, dressed in black. She was seated on one of the lower steps of the scaffold, leaning forward, her face hid in her lap; and her long dishevelled tresses hanging to the ground, streaming with the rain which fell in torrents. Wolfgang paused. There was something awful in this solitary monument of woe. The female had the appearance of being above the common order. He knew the times to be full of vicissitude, and that many a fair head, which had once been pillowed on down, now wandered houseless. Perhaps this was some poor mourner whom the dreadful axe had rendered desolate, and who sat here heart-broken on the strand of existence, from which all that was dear to her had been launched into eternity.

He approached, and addressed her in the accents of sympathy. She raised her head and gazed wildly at him. What was his astonishment at beholding, by the bright glare of the lightning, the very face which had haunted him in his dreams. It was pale and disconsolate, but ravishingly beautiful.

Trembling with violent and conflicting emotions, Wolfgang again accosted her. He spoke something of her being exposed at such an hour of the night, and to the fury of such a storm, and offered to conduct her to her friends. She pointed to the guillotine with a gesture of dreadful signification.

"I have no friend on earth!" said she.

"But you have a home," said Wolfgang.

"Yes—in the grave!"

The heart of the student melted at the words.

"If a stranger dare make an offer," said he, "without danger of being misunderstood, I would offer my humble dwelling as a shelter; myself as a devoted friend. I am friendless myself in Paris, and a stranger in the land; but if my life could be of service, it is at your disposal, and should be sacrificed before harm or indignity should come to you."

There was an honest earnestness in the young man's manner that had its effect. His foreign accent, too, was in his favor; it showed him not to be a hackneyed inhabitant of Paris. Indeed, there is an eloquence in true enthusiasm that is not to be doubted. The homeless stranger confided herself implicitly to the protection of the student.

He supported her faltering steps across the Pont Neuf, and by the place where the statue of Henry the Fourth had been overthrown by the populace. The storm had abated, and the thunder rumbled at a distance. All Paris was quiet; that great volcano of human passion slumbered for a while, to gather fresh strength for the next day's eruption. The student conducted his charge through the ancient streets of the *Pays Latin*, and by the dusky walls of the Sorbonne, to the great dingy hotel which he inhabited. The old portress who admitted them stared with surprise at the unusual sight of the melancholy Wolfgang, with a female companion.

On entering his apartment, the student, for the first time, blushed at the scantiness and indifference of his dwelling. He had but one chamber—an old-fashioned saloon—heavily carved, and fantastically furnished with the remains of former magnificence, for it was one of those hotels in the quarter of the Luxembourg palace, which had once belonged to nobility. It was lumbered with books and papers, and all the usual apparatus of a student, and his bed stood in a recess at one end.

When lights were brought, and Wolfgang had a better opportunity of contemplating the stranger, he was more than ever intoxicated by her beauty. Her face was pale, but of a dazzling fairness, set off by a profusion of raven hair that hung clustering about it. Her eyes were large and brilliant, with a singular expression approaching almost to wildness. As far as her black dress permitted her shape to be seen, it was of perfect symmetry. Her whole appearance was highly striking, though she was dressed in the simplest style. The only thing approaching to an ornament which she wore, was a broad black band round her neck, clasped by diamonds.

The perplexity now commenced with the student how to dispose of the helpless being thus thrown upon his protection. He thought of abandoning his chamber to her, and seeking shelter for himself elsewhere. Still he was so fascinated by her charms, there seemed to be such a spell upon his thoughts and senses, that he could not tear himself from her presence. Her manner, too, was singular and unaccountable. She spoke no more of the guillotine. Her grief had abated. The attentions of the student had first won her confidence, and then, apparently, her heart. She was evidently an enthusiast like himself, and enthusiasts soon understand each other.

In the infatuation of the moment, Wolfgang avowed his passion for her. He told her the story of his mysterious dream, and how she had possessed his heart before he had even seen her. She was strangely affected by his recital, and acknowledged to have felt an impulse towards him equally unaccountable. It was the time for wild theory and wild actions. Old prejudices and superstitions were done away; everything was under the sway of the "Goddess of Reason." Among other rubbish of the old times, the forms and ceremonies of marriage began to be considered superfluous bonds for honorable minds. Social compacts were the vogue. Wolfgang was too much of a theorist not to be tainted by the liberal doctrines of the day.

"Why should we separate?" said he: "our hearts are united; in the eye of reason and honor we are as one. What need is there of sordid forms to bind high souls together?"

The stranger listened with emotion: she had evidently received illumination at the same school.

"You have no home nor family," continued he; "let me be everything to you, or rather let us be everything to one another. If form is necessary, form shall be observed—there is my hand. I pledge myself to you forever."

"Forever?" said the stranger, solemnly.

"Forever!" repeated Wolfgang.

The stranger clasped the hand extended to her: "Then I am yours," murmured she, and sank upon his bosom.

The next morning the student left his bride sleeping, and sallied forth at an early hour to seek more spacious apartments suitable to the change in his situation. When he returned, he found the stranger lying with her head hanging over the bed, and one arm thrown over it. He spoke to her, but received no reply. He advanced to awaken her from her uneasy posture. On taking her hand, it was cold—there was no pulsation—her face was pallid and ghastly. In a word, she was a corpse.

Horrified and frantic, he alarmed the house. A scene of confusion ensued. The police was summoned. As the officer of police entered the room, he started back on beholding the corpse.

"Great heaven!" cried he, "how did this woman come here?"

"Do you know anything about her?" said Wolfgang eagerly.

"Do I?" exclaimed the officer: "she was guillotined yesterday."

He stepped forward; undid the black collar round the neck of the corpse, and the head rolled on the floor!

The student burst into a frenzy. "The fiend! the fiend has

gained possession of me!" shrieked he; "I am lost forever."

They tried to soothe him, but in vain. He was possessed with the frightful belief that an evil spirit had reanimated the dead body to ensnare him. He went distracted, and died in a mad-house.

Here the old gentleman with the haunted head finished his narrative.

"And is this really a fact?" said the inquisitive gentleman.

"A fact not to be doubted," replied the other. "I had it from the best authority. The student told it me himself. I saw him in a mad-house in Paris."

Young Goodman Brown

BY NATHANIEL HAWTHORNE

YOUNG GOODMAN BROWN came forth at sunset into the street at Salem village; but put his head back, after crossing the threshold, to exchange a parting kiss with his young wife. And Faith, as the wife was aptly named, thrust her own pretty head into the street, letting the wind play with the pink ribbons of her cap while she called to Goodman Brown.

"Dearest heart," whispered she, softly and rather sadly, when her lips were close to his ear, "prithee put off your journey until sunrise and sleep in your own bed to-night. A lone woman is troubled with such dreams and such thoughts that she's afeard of herself sometimes. Pray tarry with me this night, dear husband, of all nights in the year."

"My love and my Faith," replied young Goodman Brown, "of all nights in the year, this one night must I tarry away from thee. My journey, as thou callest it, forth and back again, must needs be done 'twixt now and sunrise. What, my sweet, pretty wife, dost thou doubt me already, and we but three months married?"

"Then God bless you!" said Faith, with the pink ribbons; "and may you find all well when you come back."

"Amen!" cried Goodman Brown. "Say thy prayers, dear Faith, and go to bed at dusk, and no harm will come to thee."

So they parted; and the young man pursued his way until,

being about to turn the corner by the meeting-house, he looked back and saw the head of Faith still peeping after him with a melancholy air, in spite of her pink ribbons.

"Poor little Faith!" thought he, for his heart smote him. "What a wretch am I to leave her on such an errand! She talks of dreams, too. Methought as she spoke there was trouble in her face, as if a dream had warned her what work is to be done to-night. But no, no; 't would kill her to think it. Well, she's a blessed angel on earth; and after this one night I'll cling to her skirts and follow her to heaven."

With this excellent resolve for the future, Goodman Brown felt himself justified in making more haste on his present evil purpose. He had taken a dreary road, darkened by all the gloomiest trees of the forest, which barely stood aside to let the narrow path creep through, and closed immediately behind. It was all as lonely as could be; and there is this peculiarity in such a solitude, that the traveller knows not who may be concealed by the innumerable trunks and the thick boughs overhead; so that with lonely footsteps he may yet be passing through an unseen multitude.

"There may be a devilish Indian behind every tree," said Goodman Brown to himself; and he glanced fearfully behind him as he added, "What if the devil himself should be at my very elbow!"

His head being turned back, he passed a crook of the road, and, looking forward again, beheld the figure of a man, in grave and decent attire, seated at the foot of an old tree. He arose at Goodman Brown's approach and walked onward side by side with him.

"You are late, Goodman Brown," said he. "The clock of the Old South was striking as I came through Boston, and that is full fifteen minutes agone."

"Faith kept me back a while," replied the young man, with a tremor in his voice, caused by the sudden appearance of his companion, though not wholly unexpected.

It was now deep dusk in the forest, and deepest in that part of it where these two were journeying. As nearly as could be discerned, the second traveller was about fifty years old, apparently in the same rank of life as Goodman Brown, and bearing a considerable resemblance to him, though perhaps more in expression than features. Still they might have been taken for father and son. And yet, though the elder person was as simply clad as the younger, and as simple in manner too, he had an indescribable air of one who knew the world, and who would not have felt abashed at the governor's dinner table or in King William's court, were it possible that his affairs should call him thither. But the only thing about him that could be fixed upon as remarkable was his staff, which bore the likeness of a great black snake, so curiously wrought that it might almost be seen to twist and wriggle itself like a living serpent. This, of course, must have been an ocular deception, assisted by the uncertain light.

"Come, Goodman Brown," cried his fellow-traveller, "this is a dull pace for the beginning of a journey. Take my staff, if you are so soon weary."

"Friend," said the other, exchanging his slow pace for a full stop, "having kept convenant by meeting thee here, it is my purpose now to return whence I came. I have scruples touching the matter thou wot'st of."

"Sayest thou so?" replied he of the serpent, smiling apart. "Let us walk on, nevertheless, reasoning as we go; and if I convince thee not thou shalt turn back. We are but a little way in the forest yet."

"Too far! too far!" exclaimed the goodman, unconsciously resuming his walk. "My father never went into the woods on such an errand, nor his father before him. We have been a race of honest men and good Christians since the days of the martyrs; and shall I be the first of the name of Brown that ever took this path and kept—"

"Such company, thou wouldst say," observed the elder person, interpreting his pause. "Well said, Goodman Brown! I have been as well acquainted with your family as with ever a one among the Puritans; and that's no trifle to say. I helped your grandfather, the constable, when he lashed the Quaker woman so smartly through the streets of Salem; and it was I that brought your father a pitch-pine knot, kindled at my own hearth, to set fire to an Indian village, in King Philip's war. They were my good friends, both; and many a pleasant walk have we had along this path, and returned merrily after midnight. I would fain be friends with you for their sake."

"If it be as thou sayest," replied Goodman Brown, "I marvel they never spoke of these matters; or, verily, I marvel not, seeing that the least rumor of the sort would have driven them from New England. We are a people of prayer, and good works to boot, and abide no such wickedness."

"Wickedness or not," said the traveller with the twisted

staff, "I have a very general acquaintance here in New England. The deacons of many a church have drunk the communion wine with me; the selectmen of divers towns make me their chairman; and a majority of the Great and General Court are firm supporters of my interest. The governor and I, too—But these are state secrets."

"Can this be so?" cried Goodman Brown, with a stare of amazement at his undisturbed companion. "Howbeit, I have nothing to do with the governor and council; they have their own ways, and are no rule for a simple husbandman like me. But, were I to go on with thee, how should I meet the eye of that good old man, our minister, at Salem village? Oh, his voice would make me tremble both Sabbath day and lecture day."

Thus far the elder traveller had listened with due gravity; but now burst into a fit of irrepressible mirth, shaking himself so violently that his snake-like staff actually seemed to wriggle in sympathy.

"Ha! ha! ha!" shouted he again and again; then composing himself, "Well, go on, Goodman Brown, go on; but, prithee, don't kill me with laughing."

"Well, then, to end the matter at once," said Goodman Brown, considerably nettled, "there is my wife, Faith. It would break her dear little heart; and I'd rather break my own."

"Nay, if that be the case," answered the other, "e'en go thy ways, Goodman Brown. I would not for twenty old women like the one hobbling before us that Faith should come to any harm."

As he spoke he pointed his staff at a female figure on the path, in whom Goodman Brown recognized a very pious and exemplary dame, who had taught him his catechism in youth, and was still his moral and spiritual adviser, jointly with the minister and Deacon Gookin.

"A marvel, truly, that Goody Cloyse should be so far in the wilderness at nightfall," said he. "But with your leave, friend, I shall take a cut through the woods until we have left this Christian woman behind. Being a stranger to you, she might ask whom I was consorting with and whither I was going."

"Be it so," said his fellow-traveller. "Betake you the woods, and let me keep the path."

Accordingly the young man turned aside, but took care to watch his companion, who advanced softly along the road until he had come within a staff's length of the old dame. She, meanwhile, was making the best of her way, with singular speed for so aged a woman, and mumbling some indistinct words—a prayer, doubtless—as she went. The traveller put forth his staff and touched her withered neck with what seemed the serpent's tail.

"The devil!" screamed the pious old lady.

"Then Goody Cloyse knows her old friend?" observed the traveller, confronting her and leaning on his writhing stick.

"Ah, forsooth, and is it your worship indeed?" cried the good dame. "Yea, truly is it, and in the very image of my old gossip, Goodman Brown, the grandfather of the silly fellow that now is. But—would your worship believe it?— my broomstick hath strangely disappeared, stolen, as I suspect, by that unhanged witch, Goody Cory, and that, too, when I was all anointed with the juice of smallage, and cinquefoil, and wolf's bane—"

"Mingled with fine wheat and the fat of a new-born babe," said the shape of old Goodman Brown.

"Ah, your worship knows the recipe," cried the old lady, cackling aloud. "So, as I was saying, being all ready for the meeting, and no horse to ride on, I made up my mind to foot it; for they tell me there is a nice young man to be taken into communion to-night. But now your good worship will lend me your arm, and we shall be there in a twinkling."

"That can hardly be," answered her friend. "I may not spare you my arm, Goody Cloyse; but here is my staff, if you will."

So saying, he threw it down at her feet, where, perhaps, it assumed life, being one of the rods which its owner had formerly lent to the Egyptian magi. Of this fact, however, Goodman Brown could not take cognizance. He had cast up his eyes in astonishment, and, looking down again beheld neither Goody Cloyse nor the serpentine staff, but this fellow-traveller alone, who waited for him as calmly as if nothing had happened.

"That old woman taught me my catechism," said the young man; and there was a world of meaning in this simple comment.

They continued to walk onward, while the elder traveller exhorted his companion to make good speed and persevere in the path, discoursing so aptly that his arguments seemed rather to spring up in the bosom of his auditor than to be suggested by himself. As they went, he plucked a branch of maple to serve for a walking stick, and began to strip it of the twigs and little boughs, which were wet with evening dew. The moment his fingers touched them they became strangely withered and dried up as with a week's sunshine. Thus the pair proceeded, at a good free pace, until suddenly, in a gloomy hollow of the road, Goodman Brown sat himself down on the stump of a tree and refused to go any farther.

"Friend," said he, stubbornly, "my mind is made up. Not another step will I budge on this errand. What if a wretched old woman do choose to go to the devil when I thought she was going to heaven: is that any reason why I should quit my dear Faith and go after her?"

"You will think better of this by and by," said his acquaintance, composedly. "Sit here and rest yourself a while; and when you feel like moving again, there is my staff to help you along."

Without more words, he threw his companion the maple stick, and was as speedily out of sight as if he had vanished into the deepening gloom. The young man sat a few moments by the roadside, applauding himself greatly, and thinking with how clear a conscience he should meet the minister in his morning walk, nor shrink from the eye of good old Deacon Gookin. And what calm sleep would be his that very night, which was to have been spent so wickedly, but so purely and sweetly now, in the arms of Faith! Amidst these pleasant and praiseworthy meditations, Goodman Brown heard the tramp of horses along the road, and deemed it advisable to conceal himself within the verge of the forest, conscious of the guilty purpose that had brought him thither, though now so happily turned from it.

On came the hoof tramps and the voices of the riders, two grave old voices, conversing soberly as they drew near. These mingled sounds appeared to pass along the road, within a few yards of the young man's hiding-place; but, owing doubtless to the depth of the gloom at that particular spot, neither the travellers nor their steeds were visible. Though their figures brushed the small boughs by the wayside, it could not be seen that they intercepted, even for a moment, the faint gleam from the strip of bright sky athwart which they must have passed. Goodman Brown alternately crouched and stood on tiptoe, pulling aside the branches and thrusting forth his head as far as he durst without discerning so much as a shadow. It vexed him the more, because he could have sworn, were such a thing possible, that he recognized the voices of the minister and Deacon Gookin, jogging

along quietly, as they were wont to do, when bound to some
ordination or ecclesiastical council. While yet within hearing,
one of the riders stopped to pluck a switch.

"Of the two, reverend sir," said the voice like the deacon's,
"I had rather miss an ordination dinner than to-night's meeting. They tell me that some of our community are to be here
from Falmouth and beyond, and others from Connecticut
and Rhode Island, besides several of the Indian powwows,
who, after their fashion, know almost as much deviltry as the
best of us. Moreover, there is a goodly young woman to be
taken into communion."

"Mighty well, Deacon Gookin!" replied the solemn old
tones of the minister. "Spur up, or we shall be late. Nothing
can be done, you know, until I get on the ground."

The hoofs clattered again; and the voices, talking so
strangely in the empty air, passed on through the forest,
where no church had ever been gathered or solitary Christian prayed. Whither, then, could these holy men be journeying so deep into the heathen wilderness? Young Goodman
Brown caught hold of a tree for support, being ready to sink
down on the ground, faint and overburdened with the heavy
sickness of his heart. He looked up to the sky, doubting
whether there really was a heaven above him. Yet there
was the blue arch, and the stars brightening in it.

"With heaven above and Faith below, I will yet stand
firm against the devil!" cried Goodman Brown.

While he still gazed upward into the deep arch of the
firmament and had lifted his hands to pray, a cloud, though
no wind was stirring, hurried across the zenith and hid the
brightening stars. The blue sky was still visible, except directly overhead, where this black mass of cloud was sweeping swiftly northward. Aloft in the air, as if from the depths
of the cloud, came a confused and doubtful sound of voices.
Once the listener fancied that he could distinguish the accents of towns-people of his own, men and women, both
pious and ungodly, many of whom he had met at the communion table, and had seen others rioting at the tavern. The
next moment, so indistinct were the sounds, he doubted
whether he had heard aught but the murmur of the old
forest, whispering without a wind. Then came a stronger
swell of those familiar tones, heard daily in the sunshine at
Salem village, but never until now from a cloud of night.
There was one voice, of a young woman, uttering lamen-
tations, yet with an uncertain sorrow, and entreating for some

favor, which, perhaps, it would grieve her to obtain; and all the unseen multitude, both saints and sinners, seemed to encourage her onward.

"Faith!" shouted Goodman Brown, in a voice of agony and desperation; and the echoes of the forest mocked him, crying, "Faith! Faith!" as if bewildered wretches were seeking her all through the wilderness.

The cry of grief, rage, and terror was yet piercing the night, when the unhappy husband held his breath for a response. There was a scream, drowned immediately in a louder murmur of voices, fading into far-off laughter, as the dark cloud swept away, leaving the clear and silent sky above Goodman Brown. But something fluttered lightly down through the air and caught on the branch of a tree. The young man seized it, and beheld a pink ribbon.

"My Faith is gone!" cried he, after one stupefied moment. "There is no good on earth; and sin is but a name. Come, devil; for to thee is this world given."

And, maddened with despair, so that he laughed loud and long, did Goodman Brown grasp his staff and set forth again, at such a rate that he seemed to fly along the forest path rather than to walk or run. The road grew wilder and drearier and more faintly traced, and vanished at length, leaving him in the heart of the dark wilderness, still rushing onward with the instinct that guides mortal man to evil. The whole forest was peopled with frightful sounds—the creaking of the trees, the howling of wild beasts, and the yell of Indians; while sometimes the wind tolled like a distant church bell, and sometimes gave a broad roar around the traveller, as if all Nature were laughing him to scorn. But he was himself the chief horror of the scene, and shrank not from its other horrors.

"Ha! ha! ha!" roared Goodman Brown when the wind laughed at him. "Let us hear which will laugh loudest. Think not to frighten me with your deviltry. Come witch, come wizard, come Indian powwow, come devil himself, and here comes Goodman Brown. You may as well fear him as he fear you."

In truth, all through the haunted forest there could be nothing more frightful than the figure of Goodman Brown. On he flew among the black pines, brandishing his staff with frenzied gestures, now giving vent to an inspiration of horrid blasphemy, and now shouting forth such laughter as set all the echoes of the forest laughing like demons around

him. The fiend in his own shape is less hideous than when
he rages in the breast of man. Thus sped the demoniac on his
course, until, quivering among the trees, he saw a red light
before him, as when the felled trunks and branches of a
clearing have been set on fire, and throw up their lurid
blaze against the sky, at the hour of midnight. He paused, in
a lull of the tempest that had driven him onward, and heard
the swell of what seemed a hymn, rolling solemnly from a
distance with the weight of many voices. He knew the tune;
it was a familiar one in the choir of the village meeting-
house. The verse died heavily away, and was lengthened by
a chorus, not of human voices, but of all the sounds of
the benighted wilderness pealing in awful harmony together.
Goodman Brown cried out, and his cry was lost to his own
ear by its unison with the cry of the desert.

In the interval of silence he stole forward until the light
glared full upon his eyes. At one extremity of an open space,
hemmed in by the dark wall of the forest, arose a rock,
bearing some rude, natural resemblance either to an altar or
a pulpit, and surrounded by four blazing pines, their tops
aflame, their stems untouched, like candles at an evening
meeting. The mass of foliage that had overgrown the summit
of the rock was all on fire, blazing high into the night and
fitfully illuminating the whole field. Each pendent twig and
leafy festoon was in a blaze. As the red light arose and fell,
a numerous congregation alternately shone forth, then disappeared in shadow, and again grew, as it were, out of the
darkness, peopling the heart of the solitary woods at once.

"A grave and dark-clad company," quoth Goodman Brown.

In truth they were such. Among them, quivering to and
fro between gloom and splendor, appeared faces that would
be seen next day at the council board of the province, and
others which, Sabbath after Sabbath, looked devoutly
heavenward, and benignantly over the crowded pews, from
the holiest pulpits in the land. Some affirm that the lady of
the governor was there. At least there were high dames well
known to her, and wives of honored husbands, and widows,
a great multitude, and ancient maidens, all of excellent repute, and fair young girls, who trembled lest their mothers
should espy them. Either the sudden gleams of light flashing over the obscure field bedazzled Goodman Brown, or he
recognized a score of the church members of Salem village
famous for their especial sanctity. Good old Deacon Gookin
had arrived, and waited at the skirts of that venerable saint,

his revered pastor. But, irreverently consorting with these grave, reputable, and pious people, these elders of the church, these chaste dames and dewy virgins, there were men of dissolute lives and women of spotted fame, wretches given over to all mean and filthy vice, and suspected even of horrid crimes. It was strange to see that the good shrank not from the wicked, nor were the sinners abashed by the saints. Scattered also among their pale-faced enemies were the Indian priests, or powwows, who had often scared their native forest with more hideous incantations than any known to English witchcraft.

"But where is Faith?" thought Goodman Brown; and, as hope came into his heart, he trembled.

Another verse of the hymn arose, a slow and mournful strain, such as the pious love, but joined to words which expressed all that our nature can conceive of sin, and darkly hinted at far more. Unfathomable to mere mortals is the lore of fiends. Verse after verse was sung; and still the chorus of the desert swelled between like the deepest tone of a mighty organ; and with the final peal of that dreadful anthem there came a sound, as if the roaring wind, the rushing streams, the howling beasts, and every other voice of the unconcerted wilderness were mingling and according with the voice of guilty man in homage to the prince of all. The four blazing pines threw up a loftier flame, and obscurely discovered shapes and visages of horror on the smoke wreaths above the impious assembly. At the same moment the fire on the rock shot redly forth and formed a glowing arch above its base, where now appeared a figure. With reverence be it spoken, the figure bore no slight similitude, both in garb and manner, to some grave divine of the New England churches.

"Bring forth the converts!" cried a voice that echoed through the field and rolled into the forest.

At the word, Goodman Brown stepped forth from the shadow of the trees and approached the congregation, with whom he felt a loathful brotherhood by the sympathy of all that was wicked in his heart. He could have well-nigh sworn that the shape of his own dead father beckoned him to advance, looking downward from a smoke wreath, while a woman, with dim features of despair, threw out her hand to warn him back. Was it his mother? But he had no power to retreat one step, nor to resist, even in thought, when the minister and good old Deacon Gookin seized his arms and led him to the blazing rock. Thither came also the slender form of a veiled female, led between Goody Cloyse, that pious teacher of the catechism, and Martha Carrier, who had received the devil's promise to be queen of hell. A rampant hag was she. And there stood the proselytes beneath the canopy of fire.

"Welcome, my children," said the dark figure, "to the communion of your race. Ye have found thus young your nature and your destiny. My children, look behind you!"

They turned; and flashing forth, as it were, in a sheet of flame, the fiend worshippers were seen; the smile of welcome gleamed darkly on every visage.

"There," resumed the sable form, "are all whom ye have reverenced from youth. Ye deemed them holier than yourselves, and shrank from your own sin, contrasting it with their lives of righteousness and prayerful aspirations heavenward. Yet here are they all in my worshipping assembly. This night it shall be granted you to know their secret deeds: how hoary-bearded elders of the church have whispered wanton words to the young maids of their households; how many a woman, eager for widows' weeds, has given her husband a drink at bedtime and let him sleep his last sleep in her bosom; how beardless youths have made haste to inherit their fathers' wealth; and how fair damsels—blush not, sweet ones—have dug little graves in the garden, and bidden me, the sole guest, to an infant's funeral. By the sympathy of your human hearts for sin ye shall scent out all the places—whether in church, bed-chamber, street, field, or forest—where crime has been committed, and shall exult to behold the whole earth one stain of guilt, one mighty blood spot. Far more than this. It shall be yours to penetrate, in every bosom, the deep mystery of sin, the fountain of all wicked arts, and which inexhaustibly supplies more evil impulses than human power —than my power at its utmost—can make manifest in deeds. And now, my children, look upon each other."

They did so; and, by the blaze of the hell-kindled torches, the wretched man beheld his Faith, and the wife her husband, trembling before that unhallowed altar.

"Lo, there ye stand, my children," said the figure, in a deep and solemn tone, almost sad with its despairing awfulness, as if his once angelic nature could yet mourn for our miserable race. "Depending upon one another's hearts, ye had still hoped that virtue were not all a dream. Now are ye undeceived. Evil is the nature of mankind. Evil must be your only happiness. Welcome again, my children, to the communion of your race."

"Welcome," repeated the fiend worshippers, in one cry of despair and triumph.

And there they stood, the only pair, as it seemed, who were yet hesitating on the verge of wickedness in this dark world. A basin was hollowed, naturally, in a rock. Did it contain water, reddened by the lurid light? or was it blood? or, perchance, a liquid flame? Herein did the shape of evil dip his hand and prepare to lay the mark of baptism upon their foreheads, that they might be partakers of the mystery of sin, more conscious of the secret guilt of others, both in deed and thought, than they could now be of their own. The husband cast one look at his pale wife, and Faith at him. What polluted wretches would the next glance show them to each other, shuddering alike at what they disclosed and what they saw!

"Faith! Faith!" cried the husband, "look up to heaven, and resist the wicked one."

Whether Faith obeyed he knew not. Hardly had he spoken when he found himself amid calm night and solitude, listening to a roar of the wind which died heavily away through the forest. He staggered against the rock, and felt it chill and damp; while a hanging twig, that had been all on fire, besprinkled his cheek with the coldest dew.

The next morning young Goodman Brown came slowly into the street of Salem village, staring around him like a bewildered man. The good old minister was taking a walk along the graveyard to get an appetite for breakfast and meditate his sermon, and bestowed a blessing, as he passed, on Goodman Brown. He shrank from the venerable saint as if to avoid an anathema. Old Deacon Gookin was at domestic worship, and the holy words of his prayer were heard through the open window. "What God doth the wizard pray to?" quoth Goodman Brown. Goody Cloyse, that excellent old Christian, stood in the early sunshine at her own lattice, catechizing a little girl who had brought her a pint of morning's milk. Goodman Brown snatched away the child as from the grasp of the fiend himself. Turning the corner by the meeting-house, he spied the head of Faith, with the pink ribbons, gazing anxiously forth, and bursting into such joy at sight of him that she skipped along the street and almost kissed her husband before the whole village. But Goodman Brown looked sternly and sadly into her face, and passed on without a greeting.

Had Goodman Brown fallen asleep in the forest and only dreamed a wild dream of a witch-meeting?

Be it so if you will; but, alas! it was a dream of evil omen for young Goodman Brown. A stern, a sad, a darkly meditative, a distrustful, if not a desperate man did he become from the night of that fearful dream. On the Sabbath day, when the congregation were singing a holy psalm, he could not listen because an anthem of sin rushed loudly upon his ear and drowned all the blessed strain. When the minister spoke from the pulpit with power and fervid eloquence, and, with his hand on the open Bible, of the sacred truths of our religion, and of saint-like lives and triumphant deaths, and of future bliss or misery unutterable, then did Goodman Brown turn pale, dreading lest the roof should thunder down upon the gray blasphemer and his hearers. Often, awaking suddenly at midnight, he shrank from the bosom of Faith; and at morning or eventide, when the family knelt down at prayer, he scowled and muttered to himself, and gazed sternly at his wife, and turned away. And when he had lived long, and was borne to his grave a hoary corpse, followed by Faith, an aged woman, and children and grandchildren, a goodly procession, besides neighbors not a few, they carved no hopeful verse upon his tombstone, for his dying hour was gloom.

Ms. Found in a Bottle

BY EDGAR ALLAN POE

Qui n'a plus qu'un moment à vivre
N'a plus rien à dissimuler.—Quinault, *Atys*.

OF MY country and of my family I have little to say. Ill usage and length of years have driven me from the one, and estranged me from the other. Hereditary wealth afforded me an education of no common order, and a contemplative turn of mind enabled me to methodise the stories which early study diligently garnered up. Beyond all things, the works of the German moralists gave me a great delight; not from my ill-advised admiration of their eloquent madness, but from the ease with which my habits of rigid thought enabled me to detect their falsities. I have often been reproached with the aridity of my genius; a deficiency of imagination has been imputed to me as a crime; and the Pyrrhonism of my opinions has at all times rendered me notorious. Indeed, a strong relish for physical philosophy has, I fear, tinctured my mind with a very common error of this age—I mean the habit of referring occurrences, even the least susceptible of such reference, to the principles of that science. Upon the whole, no person could be less liable than myself to be led away from the severe precincts of truth by the *ignes fatui* of superstition. I have thought proper to premise thus much, lest the incredible tale I have to tell should be considered rather the raving of a crude imagination, than the positive experience of a mind to which the reveries of fancy have been a dead letter and a nullity.

After many years spent in foreign travel, I sailed in the year 18—, from the port of Batavia, in the rich and populous island of Java, on a voyage to the Archipelago of the Sunda Islands. I went as passenger—having no other inducement than a kind of nervous restlessness which haunted me as a fiend.

Our vessel was a beautiful ship of about four hundred tons, copper-fastened, and built at Bombay of Malabar teak. She was freighted with cotton-wool and oil, from the Lachadive Islands. We had also on board coir, jaggeree, ghee, cocoa-nuts, and a few cases of opium. The stowage was clumsily done, and the vessel consequently crank.

We got under way with a mere breath of wind, and for many days stood along the eastern coast of Java, without any other incident to beguile the monotony of our course than the occasional meeting with some of the small grabs of the Archipelago to which we were bound.

One evening, leaning over the taffrail, I observed a very singular isolated cloud, to the N.W. It was remarkable, as well for its colour, as from its being the first we had seen since our departure from Batavia. I watched it attentively until sunset, when it spread all at once to the eastward and westward, girting in the horizon with a narrow strip of vapour, and looking like a long line of low beach. My notice was soon afterwards attracted by the dusky-red appearance of the moon, and the peculiar character of the sea. The latter was undergoing a rapid change, and the water seemed more than usually transparent. Although I could distinctly see the bottom, yet, heaving the lead, I found the ship in fifteen fathoms. The air now became intolerably hot, and was loaded with spiral exhalations similar to those arising from heated iron. As night came on, every breath of wind died away, and a more entire calm it is impossible to conceive. The flame of a candle burned upon the poop without the least perceptible motion, and a long hair, held between the finger and thumb, hung without the possibility of detecting a vibration. However, as the captain said he could perceive no indication of danger, and as we were drifting in bodily to shore, he ordered the sails to be furled, and the anchor let go. No watch was set, and the crew, consisting principally of Malays, stretched themselves deliberately upon deck. I went below—not without a full presentiment of evil. Indeed, every appearance warranted me in apprehending a simoom. I told the captain my fears; but he paid no attention to what I said, and left me without deigning to give a reply. My uneasiness, however, prevented me from sleeping, and about midnight I went upon deck. As I placed my foot upon the upper step of the companion-ladder, I was startled by a loud, humming noise, like that occasioned by the rapid revolution of a mill-wheel, and before I could ascertain its meaning, I found the ship quivering to its centre. In the next instant, a wilderness of foam hurled us upon our beam-ends, and, rushing over us fore and aft, swept the entire decks from stem to stern.

The extreme fury of the blast proved, in a great measure, the salvation of the ship. Although completely water-logged, yet, as her masts had gone by the board, she rose, after a minute, heavily from the sea, and, staggering awhile beneath the immense pressure of the tempest, finally righted.

By what miracle I escaped destruction, it is impossible to say. Stunned by the shock of the water, I found myself, upon recovery, jammed in between the stern-post and rudder. With great difficulty I gained my feet, and looking dizzily around, was at first struck with the idea of our being among breakers; so terrific, beyond the wildest imagination, was the whirlpool of mountainous and foaming ocean within which we were engulfed. After a while, I heard the voice of an old Swede, who had shipped with us at the moment of leaving port. I hallooed to him with all my strength, and presently he came reeling aft. We soon discovered that we were the sole survivors of the accident. All on deck, with the exception of ourselves, had been swept overboard; the captain and mates must have perished as they slept, for the cabins were deluged with water. Without assistance, we could expect to do little for the security of the ship, and our exertions were at first paralysed by the momentary expectation of going down. Our cable had, of course, parted like pack-thread, at the first breath of the hurricane, or we should have been instantaneously overwhelmed. We scudded with frightful velocity before the sea, and the water made clear breaches over us. The framework of our stern was shattered excessively, and, in almost every respect, we had received considerable injury; but to our extreme joy we found the pumps unchoked, and that we had made no great shifting of our ballast. The main fury of the blast had already blown over, and we apprehended little danger from the violence of the wind; but we looked forward to its total cessation with dismay, well believing, that in our shattered condition, we should inevitably perish in the tremendous swell which would ensue. But this very just apprehension seemed by no means likely to be soon verified. For five entire days and nights—during which our only subsistence was a small quantity of jaggeree, procured with great difficulty from the forecastle—the hulk flew at a rate defying computation, before rapidly succeeding flaws of wind, which without equalling the first violence of the simoom, were still more terrific than any tempest I had before encountered. Our course for the first four days was, with trifling variations, S.E. and by S.; and we must have run down the coast of New Holland. On the fifth day the cold became extreme, although the wind had hauled round a point more to the northward. The sun arose with a sickly yellow lustre, and clambered a very few degrees above the horizon—emitting no decisive light. There were no clouds apparent, yet the wind was upon the increase, and blew with a fitful and unsteady fury. About noon, as nearly as we could guess, our attention was again arrested by the appearance of the sun. It gave out no light, properly so called, but a dull and sullen glow without reflection, as if all its rays were polarised. Just before sinking within the turgid sea, its central fires suddenly went out, as if hurriedly extinguished by some unaccountable power. It was a dim, silver-like rim, alone, as it rushed down the unfathomable ocean.

We waited in vain for the arrival of the sixth day—that day to me has not arrived—to the Swede, never did arrive. Thenceforward we were enshrouded in pitchy darkness, so that we could not have seen an object at twenty paces from the ship. Eternal night continued to envelop us, all unre-

lieved by the phosphoric sea-brilliancy to which we had
been accustomed in the tropics. We observed, too, that, although the tempest continued to rage with unabated violence, there was no longer to be discovered the usual appearance of surf, or foam, which had hitherto attended us. All
around were horror, and thick gloom, and a black sweltering
desert of ebony. Superstitious terror crept by degrees into
the spirit of the old Swede, and my own soul was wrapped
up in silent wonder. We neglected all care of the ship, as
worse than useless, and securing ourselves, as well as possible, to the stump of the mizzen-mast, looked out bitterly
into the world of ocean. We had no means of calculating
time, nor could we form any guess of our situation. We
were, however, well aware of having made farther to the
southward than any previous navigators, and felt great
amazement at not meeting with the usual impediments of ice.
In the meantime every moment threatened to be our last—
every mountainous billow hurried to overwhelm us. The swell
surpassed anything I had imagined possible, and that we
were not instantly buried is a miracle. My companion spoke
of the lightness of our cargo, and reminded me of the excellent qualities of our ship; but I could not help feeling the
utter hopelessness of hope itself, and prepared myself gloomily for that death which I thought nothing could defer beyond an hour, as with every knot of way the ship made, the
swelling of the black stupendous seas became more dismally
appalling. At times we gasped for breath at an elevation
beyond the albatross—at times became dizzy with the velocity
of our descent into some watery hell, where the air grew
stagnant, and no sound disturbed the slumbers of the kraken.

We were at the bottom of one of these abysses, when a
quick scream from my companion broke fearfully upon the
night. "See! see!" cried he, shrieking in my ears, "Almighty
God! see! see!" As he spoke, I became aware of a dull, sullen
glare of red light which streamed down the sides of the vast
chasm where we lay, and threw a fitful brilliancy upon our
deck. Casting my eyes upwards, I beheld a spectacle which
froze the current of my blood. At a terrific height directly
above us, and upon the very verge of the precipitous descent,
hovered a gigantic ship, of perhaps four thousand tons. Although upreared upon the summit of a wave more than a
hundred times her own altitude, her apparent size still exceeded that of any ship of the line or East Indiaman in existence. Her huge hull was of a deep dingy black, unrelieved

by any of the customary carvings of a ship. A single row of
brass cannon protruded from her open ports, and dashed
from their polished surfaces the fires of innumerable battle-
lanterns which swung to and fro about her rigging. But what
mainly inspired us with horror and astonishment, was that
she bore up under a press of sail in the very teeth of that
supernatural sea, and of that ungovernable hurricane. When
we first discovered her, her bows were alone to be seen, as
she rose slowly from the dim and horrible gulf beyond her.
For a moment of intense terror she paused upon the giddy
pinnacle, as if in contemplation of her own sublimity, then
trembled and tottered, and—came down.

At this instant, I know not what sudden self-possession
came over my spirit. Staggering as far aft as I could, I awaited
fearlessly the ruin that was to overwhelm. Our own vessel
was at length ceasing from her struggles, and sinking with
her head to the sea. The shock of the descending mass struck
her, consequently, in that portion of her frame which was
nearly under water, and the inevitable result was to hurl
me, with irresistible violence, upon the rigging of the stranger.

As I fell, the ship hove in stays, and went about; and to
the confusion ensuing I attributed my escape from the notice
of the crew. With little difficulty I made my way, unper-
ceived, to the main hatchway, which was partially open, and
soon found an opportunity of secreting myself in the hold.
Why I did so I can hardly tell. An indefinite sense of awe,
which at first sight of the navigators of the ship had taken
hold of my mind, was perhaps the principle of my concealment. I was unwilling to trust myself with a race of people
who had offered to the cursory glance I had taken, so many
points of vague novelty, doubt, and apprehension. I therefore
thought proper to contrive a hiding-place in the hold. This
I did by removing a small portion of the shifting-boards, in
such a manner as to afford me a convenient retreat between
the huge timbers of the ship.

I had scarcely completed my work, when a footstep in the
hold forced me to make use of it. A man passed by my place
of concealment with a feeble and unsteady gait. I could not
see his face, but had an opportunity of observing his general appearance. There was about it an evidence of great
age and infirmity. His knees tottered beneath a load of years,
and his entire frame quivered under the burthen. He muttered to himself, in a low broken tone, some words of a

language which I could not understand, and groped in a corner among a pile of singular-looking instruments, and decayed charts of navigation. His manner was a wild mixture of the peevishness of second childhood and the solemn dignity of a god. He at length went on deck, and I saw him no more.

A feeling, for which I have no name, has taken possession of my soul—a sensation which will admit of no analysis, to which the lessons of bygone time are inadequate, and for which I fear futurity itself will offer me no key. To a mind constituted like my own, the latter consideration is an evil. I shall never—I know that I shall never—be satisfied with regard to the nature of my conceptions. Yet it is not wonderful that these conceptions are indefinite, since they have their origin in sources so utterly novel. A new sense—a new entity is added to my soul.

It is long since I first trod the deck of this terrible ship, and the rays of my destiny are, I think, gathering to a focus. Incomprehensible men! Wrapped up in meditations of a kind which I cannot divine, they pass me by unnoticed. Concealment is utter folly on my part, for the people *will not* see. It was but just now that I passed directly before the eyes of the mate; it was no long while ago that I ventured into the captain's own private cabin, and took thence the materials with which I write, and have written. I shall from time to time continue this journal. It is true that I may not find an opportunity of transmitting it to the world, but I will not fail to make the endeavour. At the last moment I will enclose the MS. in a bottle, and cast it within the sea.

An incident has occurred which has given me new room for meditation. Are such things the operation of ungoverned chance? I had ventured upon deck and thrown myself down, without attracting any notice, among a pile of ratlin-stuff and old sails, in the bottom of the yawl. While musing upon the singularity of my fate, I unwittingly daubed with a tar-brush the edges of a neatly-folded studding-sail which lay near me on a barrel. The studding-sail is now bent upon the ship, and the thoughtless touches of the brush are spread out into the word DISCOVERY.

I have made many observations lately upon the structure of the vessel. Although well armed, she is not, I think, a ship

of war. Her rigging, build, and general equipment, all negative a supposition of this kind. What she *is not,* I can easily
perceive; what she *is,* I fear it is impossible to say. I know
not how it is, but in scrutinising her strange model and singular cast of spars, her huge size and overgrown suits of
canvas, her severely simple bow and antiquated stern, there
will occasionally flash across my mind a sensation of familiar
things, and there is always mixed up with such indistinct
shadows of recollection, an unaccountable memory of old
foreign chronicles and ages long ago.

I have been looking at the timbers of the ship. She is built
of a material to which I am a stranger. There is a peculiar
character about the wood which strikes me as rendering it
unfit for the purpose to which it has been applied. I mean its
extreme *porousness,* considered independently of the worm-
eaten condition which is a consequence of navigation in these
seas, and apart from the rottenness attendant upon age. It
will appear, perhaps, an observation somewhat over-curious,
but this wood would have every characteristic of Spanish oak,
if Spanish oak were distended by any unnatural means.

In reading the above sentence, a curious apothegm of an
old weather-beaten Dutch navigator comes full upon my
recollection. "It is as sure," he was wont to say, when any
doubt was entertained of his veracity, "as sure as there is a
sea where the ship itself will grow in bulk like the living
body of the seaman."

About an hour ago I made bold to trust myself among a
group of the crew. They paid me no manner of attention,
and, although I stood in the very midst of them all, seemed
utterly unconscious of my presence. Like the one I had at
first seen in the hold, they all bore about them the marks of a
hoary old age. Their knees trembled with infirmity; their
shoulders were bent double with decrepitude; their shriv-
elled skins rattled in the wind; their voices were low, tremulous, and broken; their eyes glistened with the rheum of
years; and their grey hairs streamed terribly in the tempest.
Around them, on every part of the deck, lay scattered mathe-
matical instruments of the most quaint and obsolete construction.

I mentioned, some time ago, the bending of a studding-
sail. From that period, the ship, being thrown dead off the

wind, has continued her terrific course due south, with every rag of canvas packed upon her, from her truck to her lower studding-sail booms, and rolling every moment her top-gallant yard-arms into the most appalling hell of water which it can enter into the mind of man to imagine. I have just left the deck, where I find it impossible to maintain a footing, although the crew seem to experience little inconvenience. It appears to me a miracle of miracles that our enormous bulk is not swallowed up at once and for ever. We are surely doomed to hover continually upon the brink of eternity, without taking a final plunge into the abyss. From billows a thousand times more stupendous than any I have ever seen, we glide away with the facility of the arrowy sea-gull; and the colossal waters rear their heads above us like demons of the deep, but like demons confined to simple threats, and forbidden to destroy. I am led to attribute these frequent escapes to the only natural cause which can account for such effect. I must suppose the ship to be within the influence of some strong current, or impetuous under-tow.

I have seen the captain face to face, and in his own cabin—but, as I expected, he paid me no attention. Although in his appearance there is, to a casual observer, nothing which might bespeak him more or less than man, still a feeling of irrepressible reverence and awe mingled with the sensation of wonder with which I regarded him. In stature, he is nearly my own height; that is, about five feet eight inches. He is of a well-knit and compact frame of body, neither robust nor remarkable otherwise. But it is the singularity of the expression which reigns upon the face—it is the intense, the wonderful, the thrilling evidence of old age so utter, so extreme, which excites within my spirit a sense—a sentiment ineffable. His forehead, although little wrinkled, seems to bear upon it the stamp of a myriad of years. His grey hairs are records of the past, and his greyer eyes are sibyls of the future. The cabin floor was thickly strewn with strange, iron-clasped folios, and mouldering instruments of science, and obsolete long-forgotten charts. His head was bowed down upon his hands, and he pored, with a fiery, unquiet eye, over a paper which I took to be a commission, and which, at all events, bore the signature of a monarch. He muttered to himself—as did the first seaman whom I saw in the hold—some low peevish syllables of a foreign tongue;

and although the speaker was close at my elbow, his voice seemed to reach my ears from the distance of a mile.

The ship and all in it are imbued with the spirit of Eld. The crew glide to and fro like the ghosts of buried centuries; their eyes have an eager and uneasy meaning; and when their fingers fall athwart my path in the wild glare of the battle-lanterns, I feel as I have never felt before, although I have been all my life a dealer in antiquities, and have imbibed the shadows of fallen columns at Balbec, and Tadmor, and Persepolis, until my very soul has become a ruin.

When I look around me, I feel ashamed of my former apprehensions. If I trembled at the blast which has hitherto attended us, shall I not stand aghast at a warring of wind and ocean, to convey any idea of which, the words tornado and simoom are trivial and ineffective? All in the immediate vicinity of the ship is the blackness of eternal night, and a chaos of foamless water; but, about a league on either side of us, may be seen, indistinctly, and at intervals, stupendous ramparts of ice, towering away into the desolate sky, and looking like the walls of the universe.

As I imagined, the ship proves to be in a current—if that appellation can properly be given to a tide which, howling and shrieking by the white ice, thunders on to the southward with a velocity like the headlong dashing of a cataract.

To conceive the horror of my sensations is, I presume, utterly impossible; yet a curiosity to penetrate the mysteries of these awful regions predominates even over my despair, and will reconcile me to the most hideous aspect of death. It is evident that we are hurrying onwards to some exciting knowledge—some never-to-be-imparted secret, whose attainment is destruction. Perhaps this current leads us to the southern pole itself. It must be confessed that a supposition apparently so wild has every probability in its favour.

The crew pace the deck with unquiet and tremulous step; but there is upon their countenance an expression more of the eagerness of hope than of the apathy of despair.

In the meantime the wind is still in our poop, and, as we carry a crowd of canvas, the ship is at times lifted bodily from out the sea! Oh, horror upon horror!—the ice opens suddenly to the right, and to the left, and we are whirling dizzily, in immense concentric circles, round and round the borders of a gigantic amphitheatre, the summit of whose walls is lost in the darkness and the distance. But little time will be left me to ponder upon my destiny! The circles rapidly grow small—we are plunging madly within the grasp of the whirlpool—and amid a roaring, and bellowing, and thundering of ocean and tempest, the ship is quivering—O God! and ——going down!

Note.—The "MS. Found in a Bottle" was originally published in 1831; and it was not until many years afterwards that I became acquainted with the maps of Mercator, in which the ocean is represented as rushing, by four mouths, into the (northern) Polar Gulf, to be absorbed into the bowels of the earth; the Pole itself being represented by a black rock, towering to a prodigious height.

The Fiddler

BY HERMAN MELVILLE

So MY poem is damned, and immortal fame is not for me! I am nobody forever and ever. Intolerable fate!

Snatching my hat, I dashed down the criticism, and rushed out into Broadway, where enthusiastic throngs were crowding to a circus in a side-street near by, very recently started, and famous for a capital clown.

Presently my old friend Standard rather boisterously accosted me.

"Well met, Helmstone, my boy! Ah! what's the matter? Haven't been committing murder? Ain't flying justice? You look wild!"

"You have seen it, then?" said I, of course referring to the criticism.

"Oh yes; I was there at the morning performance. Great clown, I assure you. But here comes Hautboy. Hautboy—Helmstone."

Without having time or inclination to resent so mortifying a mistake, I was instantly soothed as I gazed on the face of the new acquaintance so unceremoniously introduced. His person was short and full, with a juvenile, animated cast to it. His complexion rurally ruddy; his eye sincere, cheery, and gray. His hair alone betrayed that he was not an overgrown boy. From his hair I set him down as forty or more.

"Come, Standard," he gleefully cried to my friend, "are you not going to the circus? The clown is inimitable, they say. Come; Mr. Helmstone, too—come both; and circus over, we'll take a nice stew and punch at Taylor's."

The sterling content, good humor, and extraordinary ruddy, sincere expression of this most singular new acquaintance acted upon me like magic. It seemed mere loyalty to human nature to accept an invitation from so unmistakably kind and honest a heart.

During the circus performance I kept my eye more on Hautboy than on the celebrated clown. Hautboy was the sight for me. Such genuine enjoyment as his struck me to the soul with a sense of the reality of the thing called happiness. The jokes of the clown he seemed to roll under his tongue as ripe magnum bonums. Now the foot, now the hand, was employed to attest his grateful applause. If any hit more than ordinary, he turned upon Standard and me to see if his rare pleasure was shared. In a man of forty I saw a boy of twelve; and this too without the slightest abatement of my respect. Because all was so honest and natural, every expression and attitude so graceful with genuine good-nature, that the marvelous juvenility of Hautboy assumed a sort of divine and immortal air, like that of some forever youthful god of Greece.

But much as I gazed upon Hautboy, and much as I admired his air, yet that desperate mood in which I had first rushed from the house had not so entirely departed as not to molest me with momentary returns. But from these relapses I would rouse myself, and swiftly glance round the broad amphitheatre of eagerly interested and all-applauding human faces. Hark! claps, thumps, deafening huzzas; the vast assembly seemed frantic with acclamation; and what, mused I, has caused all this? Why, the clown only comically grinned with one of his extra grins.

Then I repeated in my mind that sublime passage in my poem, in which Cleothemes the Argive vindicates the justice of the war. Aye, aye, thought I to myself, did I now leap into the ring there, and repeat that identical passage, nay, enact the whole tragic poem before them, would they applaud the poet as they applaud the clown? No! They would

hoot me, and call me doting or mad. Then what does this
prove? Your infatuation or their insensibility? Perhaps both;
but indubitably the first. But why wail? Do you seek admiration from the admirers of a buffoon? Call to mind the saying
of the Athenian, who, when the people vociferously applauded in the forum, asked his friend in a whisper what foolish
thing had he said?

Again my eye swept the circus, and fell on the ruddy radiance of the countenance of Hautboy. But its clear honest
cheeriness disdained my disdain. My intolerant pride was
rebuked. And yet Hautboy dreamed not what magic reproof
to a soul like mine sat on his laughing brow. At the very
instant I felt the dart of the censure, his eye twinkled, his
hand waved, his voice was lifted in jubilant delight at another joke of the inexhaustible clown.

Circus over, we went to Taylor's. Among crowds of others,
we sat down to our stews and punches at one of the small
marble tables. Hautboy sat opposite to me. Though greatly
subdued from its former hilarity, his face still shone with
gladness. But added to this was a quality not so prominent
before: a certain serene expression of leisurely, deep good
sense. Good sense and good humor in him joined hands.
As the conversation proceeded between the brisk Standard
and him—for I said little or nothing—I was more and more
struck with the excellent judgment he evinced. In most of his
remarks upon a variety of topics Hautboy seemed intuitively
to hit the exact line between enthusiasm and apathy. It was
plain that while Hautboy saw the world pretty much as it
was, yet he did not theoretically espouse its bright side
nor its dark side. Rejecting all solutions, he but acknowledged
facts. What was sad in the world he did not superficially
gainsay; what was glad in it he did not cynically slur; and all
which was to him personally enjoyable, he gratefully took
to his heart. It was plain, then—so it seemed at that moment,
at least—that his extraordinary cheerfulness did not arise
either from deficiency of feeling or thought.

Suddenly remembering an engagement, he took up his
hat, bowed pleasantly, and left us.

"Well, Helmstone," said Standard, inaudibly drumming on
the slab, "what do you think of your new acquaintance?"

The two last words tingled with a peculiar and novel significance.

"New acquaintance indeed," echoed I. "Standard, I owe
you a thousand thanks for introducing me to one of the most

singular men I have ever seen. It needed the optical sight of such a man to believe in the possibility of his existence."

"You rather like him, then," said Standard, with ironical dryness.

"I hugely love and admire him, Standard. I wish I were Hautboy."

"Ah? That's a pity, now. There's only one Hautboy in the world."

This last remark set me to pondering again, and somehow it revived my dark mood.

"His wonderful cheerfulness, I suppose," said I, sneering with spleen, "originates not less in a felicitous fortune than in a felicitous temper. His great good sense is apparent; but great good sense may exist without sublime endowments. Nay, I take it, in certain cases, that good sense is simply owing to the absence of those. Much more, cheerfulness. Unpossessed of genius, Hautboy is eternally blessed."

"Ah? You would not think him an extraordinary genius, then?"

"Genius? What! such a short, fat fellow a genius! Genius, like Cassius, is lank."

"Ah? But could you not fancy that Hautboy might formerly have had genius, but luckily getting rid of it, at last fatted up?"

"For a genius to get rid of his genius is as impossible as for a man in the galloping consumption to get rid of that."

"Ah? You speak very decidedly."

"Yes, Standard," cried I, increasing in spleen, "your cheery Hautboy, after all, is no pattern, no lesson for you and me. With average abilities; opinions clear, because circumscribed; passions docile, because they are feeble; a temper hilarious, because he was born to it—how can your Hautboy be made a reasonable example to a heady fellow like you, or an ambitious dreamer like me? Nothing tempts him beyond common limit; in himself he has nothing to restrain. By constitution he is exempted from all moral harm. Could ambition but prick him; had he but once heard applause, or endured contempt, a very different man would your Hautboy be. Acquiescent and calm from the cradle to the grave, he obviously slides through the crowd."

"Ah?"

"Why do you say *Ah* to me so strangely whenever I speak?"

"Did you ever hear of Master Betty?"

"The great English prodigy, who long ago ousted the Siddons and the Kembles from Drury Lane, and made the whole town run mad with acclamation?"

"The same," said Standard, once more inaudibly drumming on the slab.

I looked at him perplexed. He seemed to be holding the master-key of our theme in mysterious reserve; seemed to be throwing out his Master Betty, too, to puzzle me only the more.

"What under heaven can Master Betty, the great genius and prodigy, an English boy twelve years old, have to do with the poor commonplace plodder, Hautboy, an American of forty?"

"Oh, nothing in the least. I don't imagine that they ever saw each other. Besides, Master Betty must be dead and buried long ere this."

"Then why cross the ocean, and rifle the grave to drag his remains into this living discussion?"

"Absent-mindedness, I suppose. I humbly beg pardon. Proceed with your observations on Hautboy. You think he never had genius, quite too contented, and happy and fat for that—ah? You think him no pattern for men in general? affording no lesson of value to neglected merit, genius ignored, or impotent presumption rebuked?—all of which three amount to much the same thing. You admire his cheerfulness, while scorning his commonplace soul. Poor Hautboy, how sad that your very cheerfulness should, by a byblow, bring you despite!"

"I don't say I scorn him; you are unjust. I simply declare that he is no pattern for me."

A sudden noise at my side attracted my ear. Turning, I saw Hautboy again, who very blithely reseated himself on the chair he had left.

"I was behind time with my engagement," said Hautboy, "so thought I would run back and rejoin you. But come, you have sat long enough here. Let us go to my rooms. It is only a five minutes' walk."

"If you will promise to fiddle for us, we will," said Standard.

Fiddle! thought I—he's a jiggumbob *fiddler*, then? No wonder genius declines to measure its pace to a fiddler's bow. My spleen was very strong on me now.

"I will gladly fiddle you your fill," replied Hautboy to Standard. "Come on."

In a few minutes we found ourselves in the fifth story of a sort of storehouse, in a lateral street to Broadway. It was curiously furnished with all sorts of odd furniture which seemed to have been obtained, piece by piece, at auctions of old-fashioned household stuff. But all was charmingly clean and cozy.

Pressed by Standard, Hautboy forthwith got out his dented old fiddle and, sitting down on a tall rickety stool, played away right merrily at "Yankee Doodle" and other off-handed, dashing, and disdainfully care-free airs. But common as were the tunes, I was transfixed by something miraculously superior in the style. Sitting there on the old stool, his rusty hat sideways cocked on his head, one foot dangling adrift, he plied the bow of an enchanter. All my moody discontent, every vestige of peevishness, fled. My whole splenetic soul capitulated to the magical fiddle.

"Something of an Orpheus, ah?" said Standard, archly nudging me beneath the left rib.

"And I, the charmed Bruin," murmured I.

The fiddle ceased. Once more, with redoubled curiosity, I gazed upon the easy, indifferent Hautboy. But he entirely baffled inquisition.

When, leaving him, Standard and I were in the street once more, I earnestly conjured him to tell me who, in sober truth, this marvelous Hautboy was.

"Why, haven't you seen him? And didn't you yourself lay his whole anatomy open on the marble slab at Taylor's? What more can you possibly learn? Doubtless, your own masterly insight has already put you in possession of all."

"You mock me, Standard. There is some mystery here. Tell me, I entreat you, who is Hautboy?"

"An extraordinary genius, Helmstone," said Standard, with sudden ardor, "who in boyhood drained the whole flagon of glory; whose going from city to city was a going from triumph to triumph. One who has been an object of wonder to the wisest, been caressed by the loveliest, received the open homage of thousands on thousands of the rabble. But to-day he walks Broadway and no man knows him. With you and me, the elbow of the hurrying clerk, and the pole of the remorseless omnibus, shove him. He who has a hundred times been crowned with laurels, now wears, as you see, a bunged beaver. Once fortune poured showers of gold into his lap, as showers of laurel leaves upon his brow. To-day, from house to house he hies, teaching fiddling for a living. Crammed

once with fame, he is now hilarious without it. *With* genius
and *without* fame, he is happier than a king. More a prodigy
now than ever."

"His true name?"

"Let me whisper it in your ear."

"What! Oh, Standard, myself, as a child, have shouted
myself hoarse applauding that very name in the theatre."

"I have heard your poem was not very handsomely received," said Standard, now suddenly shifting the subject.

"Not a word of that, for Heaven's sake!" cried I. "If Cicero,
traveling in the East, found sympathetic solace for his grief
in beholding the arid overthrow of a once gorgeous city, shall
not my petty affair be as nothing, when I behold in Hautboy
the vine and the rose climbing the shattered shafts of his
tumbled temple of Fame?"

Next day I tore all my manuscripts, bought me a fiddle,
and went to take regular lessons of Hautboy.

What Was It?

BY FITZ-JAMES O'BRIEN

It is, I confess, with considerable diffidence that I approach
the strange narrative which I am about to relate. The events
which I purpose detailing are of so extraordinary a character
that I am quite prepared to meet with an unusual amount of
incredulity and scorn. I accept all such beforehand. I have, I
trust, the literary courage to face unbelief. I have, after mature consideration, resolved to narrate, in as simple and
straightforward a manner as I can compass, some facts that
passed under my observation, in the month of July last, and
which, in the annals of the mysteries of physical science,
are wholly unparalleled.

I live at No. — Twenty-sixth Street, in New York. The house
is in some respects a curious one. It has enjoyed for the last
two years the reputation of being haunted. It is a large and
stately residence, surrounded by what was once a garden,
but which is now only a green enclosure used for bleaching
clothes. The dry basin of what has been a fountain, and a
few fruit trees ragged and unpruned, indicate that this spot

in past days was a pleasant, shady retreat, filled with fruits and flowers and the sweet murmur of waters.

The house is very spacious. A hall of noble size leads to a large spiral staircase winding through its centre, while the various apartments are of imposing dimensions. It was built some fifteen or twenty years since by Mr. A——, the well-known New York merchant, who five years ago threw the commercial world into convulsions by a stupendous bank fraud. Mr. A——, as everyone knows, escaped to Europe, and died not long after, of a broken heart. Almost immediately after the news of his decease reached this country and was verified, the report spread in Twenty-sixth Street that No.— was haunted. Legal measures had dispossessed the widow of its former owner, and it was inhabited merely by a caretaker and his wife, placed there by the house agent into whose hands it had passed for purposes of renting or sale. These people declared that they were troubled with unnatural noises. Doors were opened without any visible agency. The remnants of furniture scattered through the various rooms, were, during the night, piled one upon the other by unknown hands. Invisible feet passed up and down the stairs in broad daylight, accompanied by the rustle of unseen silk dresses, and the gliding of viewless hands along the massive balusters. The caretaker and his wife declared they would live there no longer. The house agent laughed, dismissed them, and put others in their place. The noises and supernatural manifestations continued. The neighborhood caught up the story, and the house remained untenanted for three years. Several persons negotiated for it; but, somehow, always before the bargain was closed they heard the unpleasant rumors and declined to treat any further.

It was in this state of things that my landlady, who at that time kept a boarding-house in Bleecker Street, and who wished to move further up town, conceived the bold idea of renting No. — Twenty-sixth Street. Happening to have in her house rather a plucky and philosophical set of boarders, she laid her scheme before us, stating candidly everything she had heard respecting the ghostly qualities of the establishment to which she wished to remove us. With the exception of two timid persons—a sea-captain and a returned Californian, who immediately gave notice that they would leave —all of Mrs. Moffat's guests declared that they would accompany her in her chivalric incursion into the abode of spirits.

Our removal was effected in the month of May, and we were charmed with our new residence. The portion of Twenty-sixth Street where our house is situated, between Seventh and Eighth Avenues, is one of the pleasantest localities in New York. The gardens back of the houses, running down nearly to the Hudson, form, in the summer time, a perfect avenue of verdure. The air is pure and invigorating, sweeping, as it does, straight across the river from the Weehawken heights, and even the ragged garden which surrounded the house, although displaying on washing days rather too much clothesline, still gave us a piece of greensward to look at, and a cool retreat in the summer evenings, where we smoked our cigars in the dusk, and watched the fireflies flashing their dark lanterns in the long grass.

Of course we had no sooner established ourselves at No. — than we began to expect the ghosts. We absolutely awaited their advent with eagerness. Our dinner conversation was supernatural. One of the boarders, who had purchased Mrs. Crowe's "Night Side of Nature" for his own private delectation, was regarded as a public enemy by the entire household for not having bought twenty copies. The man led a life of supreme wretchedness while he was reading this volume. A system of espionage was established, of which he was the victim. If he incautiously laid the book down for an instant and left the room, it was immediately seized and read aloud in secret places to a select few. I found myself a person of immense importance, it having leaked out that I was tolerably well versed in the history of supernaturalism, and had once written a story the foundation of which was a ghost. If a table or a wainscot panel happened to warp when we were assembled in the large drawing-room, there was an instant silence, and every one was prepared for an immediate clanking of chains and a spectral form.

After a month of psychological excitement, it was with the utmost dissatisfaction that we were forced to acknowledge that nothing in the remotest degree approaching the supernatural had manifested itself. Once the black butler asseverated that his candle had been blown out by some invisible agency while he was undressing himself for the night; but as I had more than once discovered this colored gentleman in a condition when one candle must have appeared to him like two, I thought it possible that, by going a step further in his potations, he might have reversed this phenomenon, and seen no candle at all where he ought to have beheld one.

Things were in this state when an incident took place so awful and inexplicable in its character that my reason fairly reels at the bare memory of the occurrence. It was the tenth of July. After dinner was over I repaired, with my friend Dr. Hammond, to the garden to smoke my evening pipe. Independent of certain mental sympathies which existed between the Doctor and myself, we were linked together by a vice. We both smoked opium. We knew each other's secret, and respected it. We enjoyed together that wonderful expansion of thought, that marvellous intensifying of the perceptive faculties, that boundless feeling of existence when we seem to have points of contact with the whole universe—in short, that unimaginable spiritual bliss, which I would not surrender for a throne, and which I hope you, reader, will never—never taste.

Those hours of opium happiness which the Doctor and I spent together in secret were regulated with a scientific accuracy. We did not blindly smoke the drug of paradise, and leave our dreams to chance. While smoking, we carefully steered our conversation through the brightest and calmest channels of thought. We talked of the East, and endeavored to recall the magical panorama of its glowing scenery. We criticised the most sensuous poets—those who painted life ruddy with health, brimming with passion, happy in the possession of youth and strength and beauty. If we talked of Shakespeare's "Tempest," we lingered over Ariel, and avoided Caliban. Like the Guebers, we turned our faces to the east, and saw only the sunny side of the world.

This skillful coloring of our train of thought produced in our subsequent visions a corresponding tone. The splendors of Arabian fairyland dyed our dreams. We paced that narrow strip of grass with the tread and port of kings. The song of the *rana arborea*, while he clung to the bark of the ragged plum tree, sounded like the strains of divine musicians. Houses, walls, and streets melted like rain clouds, and vistas of unimaginable glory stretched away before us. It was a rapturous companionship. We enjoyed the vast delight more perfectly because, even in our most ecstatic moments, we were conscious of each other's presence. Our pleasures, while individual, were still twin, vibrating and moving in musical accord.

On the evening in question, the tenth of July, the Doctor and myself drifted into an unusually metaphysical mood. We lit our large meerschaums, filled with fine Turkish tobacco, in the core of which burned a little black nut of opium, that, like the nut in the fairy tale, held within its narrow limits wonders beyond the reach of kings; we paced to and fro, conversing. A strange perversity dominated the currents of our thought. They would *not* flow through the sun-lit channels into which we strove to divert them. For some unaccountable reason, they constantly diverged into dark and lonesome beds, where a continual gloom brooded. It was in vain that, after our old fashion, we flung ourselves on the shores of the East, and talked of its gay bazaars, of the splendors of the time of Haroun, of harems and golden palaces. Black afreets continually arose from the depths of our talk, and expanded, like the one the fisherman released from the copper vessel, until they blotted everything bright from our vision. Insensibly, we yielded to the occult force that swayed us, and indulged in gloomy speculation. We had talked some time upon the proneness of the human mind to mysticism, and the almost universal love of the terrible when Hammond suddenly said to me, "What do you consider to be the greatest element of terror?"

The question puzzled me. That many things were terrible, I knew. Stumbling over a corpse in the dark; beholding, as I once did, a woman floating down a deep and rapid river, with wildly lifted arms, and awful, upturned face, uttering, as she drifted, shrieks that rent one's heart, while we, the spectators, stood frozen at a window which overhung the river at a height of sixty feet, unable to make the slightest effort to save her, but dumbly watching her last supreme agony and her disappearance. A shattered wreck, with no life visible, encountered floating listlessly on the ocean, is a terrible object, for it suggests a huge terror, the proportions of which are veiled. But it now struck me, for the first time, that there must be one great and ruling embodiment of fear—a King of Terrors, to which all others must succumb. What might it be? To what train of circumstances would it owe its existence?

"I confess, Hammond," I replied to my friend, "I never considered the subject before. That there must be one Something more terrible than any other thing, I feel. I cannot attempt, however, even the most vague definition."

"I am somewhat like you, Harry," he answered. "I feel

my capacity to experience a terror greater than anything yet conceived by the human mind—something combining in fearful and unnatural amalgamation hitherto supposed incompatible elements. The calling of the voices in Brockden Brown's novel of 'Wieland' is awful; so is the picture of the Dweller of the Threshold, in Bulwer's 'Zanoni'; but," he added, shaking his head gloomily, "there is something more horrible still than these."

"Look here, Hammond," I rejoined, "let us drop this kind of talk, for heaven's sake! We shall suffer for it, depend on it."

"I don't know what's the matter with me to-night," he replied, "but my brain is running upon all sorts of weird and awful thoughts. I feel as if I could write a story like Hoffman, to-night, if I were only master of a literary style."

"Well, if we are going to be Hoffmanesque in our talk, I'm off to bed. Opium and nightmares should never be brought together. How sultry it is! Good-night, Hammond."

"Good-night, Harry. Pleasant dreams to you."

"To you, gloomy wretch, afreets, ghouls, and enchanters."

We parted, and each sought his respective chamber. I undressed quickly and got into bed, taking with me, according to my usual custom, a book, over which I generally read myself to sleep. I opened the volume as soon as I had laid my head upon the pillow, and instantly flung it to the other side of the room. It was Goudon's "History of Monsters," a curious French work, which I had lately imported from Paris, but which, in the state of mind I had then reached, was anything but an agreeable companion. I resolved to go to sleep at once; so, turning down my gas until nothing but a little blue point of light glimmered on the top of the tube, I composed myself to rest.

The room was in total darkness. The atom of gas that still remained alight did not illuminate a distance of three inches round the burner. I desperately drew my arm across my eyes, as if to shut out even the darkness, and tried to think of nothing. It was in vain. The confounded themes touched on by Hammond in the garden kept obtruding themselves on my brain. I battled against them. I erected ramparts of would-be blankness of intellect to keep them out. They still crowded upon me. While I was lying still as a corpse, hoping that by a perfect physical inaction I should hasten mental repose, an awful incident occurred. A Something dropped, as it seemed, from the ceiling, plumb upon my chest, and the next instant I felt two bony hands encircling my throat, endeavoring to choke me.

I am no coward, and am possessed of considerable physical strength. The suddenness of the attack, instead of stunning me, strung every nerve to its highest tension. My body acted from instinct, before my brain had time to realize the terrors of my position. In an instant I wound two muscular arms around the creature, and squeezed it, with all the strength of despair, against my chest. In a few seconds the bony hands that had fastened on my throat loosened their hold, and I was free to breathe once more. Then commenced a struggle of awful intensity. Immersed in the most profound darkness, totally ignorant of the nature of the Thing by which I was so suddenly attacked, finding my grasp slipping every moment, by reason, it seemed to me, of the entire nakedness of my assailant, bitten with sharp teeth in the shoulder, neck, and chest, having every moment to protect my throat against a pair of sinewy, agile hands, which my utmost efforts could not confine—these were a combination of circumstances to combat which required all the strength, skill, and courage that I possessed.

At last, after a silent, deadly, exhausting struggle, I got my assailant under by a series of incredible efforts of strength. Once pinned, with my knee on what I made out to be its chest, I knew that I was victor. I rested for a moment to breathe. I heard the creature beneath me panting in the darkness, and felt the violent throbbing of a heart. It was apparently as exhausted as I was; that was one comfort. At this moment I remembered that I usually placed under my pillow, before going to bed, a large yellow silk pocket handkerchief. I felt for it instantly; it was there. In a few seconds more I had, after a fashion, pinioned the creature's arms.

I now felt tolerably secure. There was nothing more to be done but to turn on the gas, and, having first seen what my midnight assailant was like, arouse the household. I will confess to being actuated by a certain pride in not giving the alarm before; I wished to make the capture alone and unaided.

Never losing my hold for an instant, I slipped from the bed to the floor, dragging my captive with me. I had but a few steps to make to reach the gas burner; these I made with the greatest caution, holding the creature in a grip like a vise. At last I got within arm's length of the tiny speck of blue light which told me where the gas burner lay. Quick as lightning I released my grasp with one hand and let on the full flood of light. Then I turned to look at my captive.

I cannot even attempt to give any definition of my sensations the instant after I turned on the gas. I suppose I must have shrieked with terror, for in less than a minute afterward my room was crowded with the inmates of the house. I shudder now as I think of that awful moment. *I saw nothing!* Yes; I had one arm firmly clasped round a breathing, panting, corporeal shape, my other hand gripped with all its strength a throat as warm, and apparently fleshly, as my own; and yet, with this living substance in my grasp, with its body pressed against my own, and all in the bright glare of a large jet of gas, I absolutely beheld nothing! Not even an outline—a vapor!

I do not, even at this hour, realize the situation in which I found myself. I cannot recall the astounding incident thoroughly. Imagination in vain tries to compass the awful paradox.

It breathed. I felt its warm breath upon my cheek. It struggled fiercely. It had hands. They clutched me. Its skin was smooth, like my own. There it lay, pressed close up against me, solid as stone—and yet utterly invisible!

I wonder that I did not faint or go mad on the instant. Some wonderful instinct must have sustained me; for, absolutely, in place of loosening my hold on the terrible Enigma, I seemed to gain an additional strength in my moment of horror, and tightened my grasp with such wonderful force that I felt the creature shivering with agony.

Just then Hammond entered my room at the head of the household. As soon as he beheld my face—which, I suppose, must have been an awful sight to look at—he hastened forward, crying, "Great heaven, Harry! what has happened?"

"Hammond! Hammond!" I cried, "come here. O, this is awful! I have been attacked in bed by something or other, which I have hold of; but I can't see it—I can't see it!"

Hammond, doubtless struck by the unfeigned horror expressed in my countenance, made one or two steps forward with an anxious yet puzzled expression. A very audible titter burst from the remainder of my visitors. This suppressed laughter made me furious. To laugh at a human

being in my position! It was the worst species of cruelty.
Now, I can understand why the appearance of a man struggling violently, as it would seem, with an airy nothing, and
calling for assistance against a vision, should have appeared ludicrous. *Then,* so great was my rage against the
mocking crowd that had I the power I would have stricken
them dead where they stood.

"Hammond! Hammond!" I cried again, despairingly, "for
God's sake come to me. I can hold the—the Thing but a short
while longer. It is overpowering me. Help me! Help me!"

"Harry," whispered Hammond, approaching me, "you have
been smoking too much opium."

"I swear to you, Hammond, that this is no vision," I
answered, in the same low tone. "Don't you see how it shakes
my whole frame with its struggles? If you don't believe me,
convince yourself. Feel it—touch it."

Hammond advanced and laid his hand in the spot I indicated. A wild cry of horror burst from him. He had felt it!

In a moment he had discovered somewhere in my room a
long piece of cord, and was the next instant winding it
and knotting it about the body of the unseen being that I
clasped in my arms.

"Harry," he said, in a hoarse, agitated voice, for, though
he preserved his presence of mind, he was deeply moved,
"Harry, it's all safe now. You may let go, old fellow, if
you're tired. The Thing can't move."

I was utterly exhausted, and I gladly loosed my hold.

Hammond stood holding the ends of the cord that bound
the Invisible, twisted round his hand, while before him,
self-supporting as it were, he beheld a rope laced and inter-
laced, and stretching tightly around a vacant space. I never
saw a man look so thoroughly stricken with awe. Nevertheless his face expressed all the courage and determination
which I knew him to possess. His lips, although white,
were set firmly, and one could perceive at a glance that, although stricken with fear, he was not daunted.

The confusion that ensued among the guests of the house
who were witnesses of this extraordinary scene between
Hammond and myself—who beheld the pantomime of binding this struggling Something—who beheld me almost sinking
from physical exhaustion when my task of jailer was over—
the confusion and terror that took possession of the bystanders, when they saw all this, was beyond description.
The weaker ones fled from the apartment. The few who re-

mained clustered near the door and could not be induced to approach Hammond and his Charge. Still incredulity broke out through their terror. They had not the courage to satisfy themselves, and yet they doubted. It was in vain that I begged of some of the men to come near and convince themselves by touch of the existence in that room of a living being which was invisible. They were incredulous, but did not dare to undeceive themselves. How could a solid, living, breathing body be invisible, they asked. My reply was this. I gave a sign to Hammond, and both of us—conquering our fearful repugnance to touch the invisible creature—lifted it from the ground, manacled as it was, and took it to my bed. Its weight was about that of a boy of fourteen.

"Now, my friends," I said, as Hammond and myself held the creature suspended over the bed, "I can give you self-evident proof that here is a solid, ponderable body, which, nevertheless, you cannot see. Be good enough to watch the surface of the bed attentively."

I was astonished at my own courage in treating this strange event so calmly; but I had recovered from my first terror, and felt a sort of scientific pride in the affair, which dominated every other feeling.

The eyes of the bystanders were immediately fixed on my bed. At a given signal Hammond and I let the creature fall. There was the dull sound of a heavy body alighting on a soft mass. The timbers of the bed creaked. A deep impression marked itself distinctly on the pillow, and on the bed itself. The crowd who witnessed this gave a low cry, and rushed from the room. Hammond and I were left alone with our Mystery.

We remained silent for some time, listening to the low, irregular breathing of the creature on the bed, and watching the rustle of the bedclothes as it impotently struggled to free itself from confinement. Then Hammond spoke.

"Harry, this is awful."

"Ay, awful."

"But not unaccountable."

"Not unaccountable! What do you mean? Such a thing has never occurred since the birth of the world. I know not what to think, Hammond. God grant that I am not mad, and that this is not an insane fantasy!"

"Let us reason a little, Harry. Here is a solid body which we touch, but which we cannot see. The fact is so unusual that it strikes us with terror. Is there no parallel, though,

for such a phenomenon? Take a piece of pure glass. It is
tangible and transparent. A certain chemical coarseness is
all that prevents its being so entirely transparent as to be
totally invisible. It is not *theoretically impossible*, mind you,
to make a glass which shall not reflect a single ray of light—
a glass so pure and homogeneous in its atoms that the rays
from the sun will pass through it as they do through the air,
refracted but not reflected. We do not see the air, and yet we
feel it."

"That's all very well, Hammond, but these are inanimate
substances. Glass does not breathe, air does not breathe.
This thing has a heart that palpitates—a will that moves it—
lungs that play and inspire and respire."

"You forget the phenomena of which we have so often
heard of late," answered the Doctor, gravely. "At the meetings called 'spirit circles,' invisible hands have been thrust
into the hands of those persons round the table—warm,
fleshly hands that seemed to pulsate with mortal life."

"What? Do you think, then, that this thing is—"

"I don't know what it is," was the solemn reply; "but
please the gods I will, with your assistance, thoroughly in-
vestigate it."

We watched together, smoking many pipes, all night long,
by the bedside of the unearthly being that tossed and panted
until it was apparently wearied out. Then we learned by the
low, regular breathing that it slept.

The next morning the house was all astir. The boarders
congregated on the landing outside my room, and Hammond
and myself were lions. We had to answer a thousand questions as to the state of our extraordinary prisoner, for as yet
not one person in the house except ourselves could be induced to set foot in the apartment.

The creature was awake. This was evidenced by the convulsive manner in which the bedclothes were moved in its
effort to escape. There was something truly terrible in beholding, as it were, those second-hand indications of the terrible writhings and agonized struggles for liberty which
themselves were invisible.

Hammond and myself had racked our brains during the
long night to discover some means by which we might realize the shape and general appearance of the Enigma. As well
as we could make out by passing our hands over the creature's form, its outlines and lineaments were human. There
was a mouth; a round, smooth head without hair; a nose,

which, however, was little elevated above the cheeks; and its hands and feet felt like those of a boy. At first we thought of placing the being on a smooth surface and tracing its outline with chalk, as shoemakers trace the outline of the foot. This plan was given up as being of no value. Such an outline would give not the slightest idea of its conformation.

A happy thought struck me. We would take a cast of it in plaster of Paris. This would give us the solid figure, and satisfy all our wishes. But how to do it? The movements of the creature would disturb the setting of the plastic covering, and distort the mould. Another thought. Why not give it chloroform? It had respiratory organs—that was evident by its breathing. Once reduced to a state of insensibility, we could do with it what we would. Doctor X—— was sent for; and after the worthy physician had recovered from the first shock of amazement, he proceeded to administer the chloroform. In three minutes afterward we were enabled to remove the fetters from the creature's body, and a modeller was busily engaged in covering the invisible form with the moist clay. In five minutes more we had a mould, and before evening a rough facsimile of the Mystery. It was shaped like a man—distorted, uncouth, and horrible, but still a man. It was small, not over four feet and some inches in height, and its limbs revealed a muscular development that was unparalleled. Its face surpassed in hideousness anything I had ever seen. Gustave Doré, or Callot, or Tony Johannot never conceived anything so horrible. There is a face in one of the latter's illustrations to *Un Voyage où il vous plaira*, which somewhat approaches the countenance of this creature, but does not equal it. It was the physiognomy of what I should fancy a ghoul might be. It looked as if it was capable of feeding on human flesh.

Having satisfied our curiosity, and bound everyone in the house to secrecy, it became a question what was to be done with our Enigma? It was impossible that we should keep such a horror in our house; it was equally impossible that such an awful being should be let loose upon the world. I confess that I would have gladly voted for the creature's destruction. But who would shoulder the responsibility? Who would undertake the execution of this horrible semblance of a human being? Day after day this question was deliberated gravely. The boarders all left the house. Mrs. Moffat was in despair, and threatened Hammond and myself with all sorts of legal penalties if we did not remove the Horror. Our answer was, "We will go if you like, but we decline taking this creature with us. Remove it yourself if you please. It appeared in your house. On you the responsibility rests." To this there was, of course, no answer. Mrs. Moffat could not obtain for love or money a person who would even approach the Mystery.

The most singular part of the affair was that we were entirely ignorant of what the creature habitually fed on. Everything in the way of nutriment that we could think of was placed before it, but was never touched. It was awful to stand by, day after day, and see the clothes toss, and hear the hard breathing, and know that it was starving.

Ten, twelve days, a fortnight passed, and it still lived. The pulsations of the heart, however, were daily growing fainter, and had now nearly ceased. It was evident that the creature was dying for want of sustenance. While this terrible life struggle was going on, I felt miserable. I could not sleep. Horrible as the creature was, it was pitiful to think of the pangs it was suffering.

At last it died. Hammond and I found it cold and stiff one morning in the bed. The heart had ceased to beat, the lungs to inspire. We hastened to bury it in the garden. It was a strange funeral, the dropping of that viewless corpse into the damp hole. The cast of its form I gave to Doctor X——, who keeps it in his museum in Tenth Street.

As I am on the eve of a long journey from which I may not return, I have drawn up this narrative of an event the most singular that has ever come to my knowledge.

Luck*

BY MARK TWAIN
(Samuel Langhorne Clemens)

IT WAS at a banquet in London in honor of one of the two or three conspicuously illustrious English military names of this generation. For reasons which will presently appear, I will withhold his real name and titles and call him Lieuten-

---

* This is not a fancy sketch. I got it from a clergyman who was an instructor at Woolwich forty years ago, and who vouched for its truth. M.T.

ant-General Lord Arthur Scoresby, Y.C., K.C.B., etc., etc., etc. What a fascination there is in a renowned name! There sat the man, in actual flesh, whom I had heard of so many thousands of times since that day, thirty years before, when his name shot suddenly to the zenith from a Crimean battle-field, to remain forever celebrated. It was food and drink to me to look, and look, and look at that demi-god; scanning, searching, noting: the quietness, the reserve, the noble gravity of his countenance; the simple honesty that expressed itself all over him; the sweet unconsciousness of his great-ness—unconsciousness of the hundreds of admiring eyes fastened upon him, unconsciousness of the deep, loving, sincere worship welling out of the breasts of those people and flowing toward him.

The clergyman at my left was an old acquaintance of mine—clergyman now, but had spent the first half of his life in the camp and field and as an instructor in the military school at Woolwich. Just at the moment I have been talking about a veiled and singular light glimmered in his eyes and he leaned down and muttered confidently to me—indicating the hero of the banquet with a gesture:

"Privately—he's an absolute fool."

This verdict was a great surprise to me. If its subject had been Napoleon, or Socrates, or Solomon, my astonishment could not have been greater. Two things I was well aware of: that the Reverend was a man of strict veracity and that his judgment of men was good. Therefore I knew, beyond doubt or question, that the world was mistaken about this hero: he *was* a fool. So I meant to find out, at a convenient moment, how the Reverend, all solitary and alone, had discovered the secret.

Some days later the opportunity came, and this is what the Reverend told me:

About forty years ago I was an instructor in the military academy at Woolwich. I was present in one of the sections when young Scoresby underwent his preliminary examination. I was touched to the quick with pity, for the rest of the class answered up brightly and handsomely, while he—why, dear me, he didn't know *anything*, so to speak. He was evidently good, and sweet, and lovable, and guileless; and so it was exceedingly painful to see him stand there, as serene as a graven image, and deliver himself of answers which were veritably miraculous for stupidity and ignorance. All the compassion in me was aroused in his behalf. I said to myself, when he comes to be examined again he will be flung over, of course; so it will be simply a harmless act of charity to ease his fall as much as I can. I took him aside and found that he knew a little of Cæsar's history; and as he didn't know anything else, I went to work and drilled him like a galley-slave on a certain line of stock questions concerning Cæsar which I knew would be used. If you'll believe me, he went through with flying colors on examination day! He went through on that purely superficial "cram," and got compliments too, while others, who knew a thousand times more than he, got plucked. By some strangely lucky accident—an accident not likely to happen twice in a century—he was asked no question outside of the narrow limits of his drill.

It was stupefying. Well, all through his course I stood by him, with something of the sentiment which a mother feels for a crippled child; and he always saved himself—just by miracle, apparently.

Now, of course, the thing that would expose him and kill him at last was mathematics. I resolved to make his death as easy as I could; so I drilled him and crammed him, and crammed him and drilled him, just on the line of questions which the examiners would be most likely to use, and then launched him on his fate. Well, sir, try to conceive of the result: to my consternation, he took the first prize! And with it he got a perfect ovation in the way of compliments.

Sleep? There was no more sleep for me for a week. My conscience tortured me day and night. What I had done I had done purely through charity, and only to ease the poor youth's fall. I never had dreamed of any such preposterous results as the thing that had happened. I felt as guilty and miserable as Frankenstein. Here was a wooden-head whom I had put in the way of glittering promotions and prodigious responsibilities, and but one thing could happen: he and his responsibilities would all go to ruin together at the first opportunity.

The Crimean War had just broken out. Of course there had to be a war, I said to myself. We couldn't have peace and give this donkey a chance to die before he is found out. I waited for the earthquake. It came. And it made me reel when it did come. He was actually gazetted to a captaincy in a marching regiment! Better men grow old and gray in the service before they climb to a sublimity like that. And who could ever have foreseen that they would go and put such a load of responsibility on such green and inadequate shoulders? I could just barely have stood it if they had made him a cornet; but a captain—think of it! I thought my hair would turn white.

Consider what I did—I who so loved repose and inaction. I said to myself, I am responsible to the country for this, and I must go along with him and protect the country against him as far as I can. So I took my poor little capital that I had saved up through years of work and grinding economy, and went with a sigh and bought a cornetcy in his regiment, and away we went to the field.

And there—oh, dear, it was awful. Blunders?—why he never did anything *but* blunder. But, you see, nobody was in the fellow's secret. Everybody had him focused wrong, and necessarily misinterpreted his performance every time. Consequently they took his idiotic blunders for inspirations of genius. They did, honestly! His mildest blunders were enough to make a man in his right mind cry; and they did make me cry—and rage and rave, too, privately. And the thing that kept me always in a sweat of apprehension was the fact that every fresh blunder he made increased the luster of his reputation! I kept saying to myself, he'll get so high that when discovery does finally come it will be like the sun falling out of the sky.

He went right along, up from grade to grade, over the dead bodies of his superiors, until at last, in the hottest moment of the battle of —— down went our colonel, and my heart jumped into my mouth, for Scoresby was next in rank! Now for it, said I; we'll all land in Sheol in ten minutes, sure.

The battle was awfully hot; the allies were steadily giving way all over the field. Our regiment occupied a position that was vital; a blunder now must be destruction. At this crucial moment, what does this immortal fool do but detach the regiment from its place and order a charge over a neighboring hill where there wasn't a suggestion of an enemy! "There you go!" I said to myself; "this *is* the end at last."

And away we did go, and were over the shoulder of the hill before the insane movement could be discovered and stopped. And what did we find? An entire and unsuspected Russian army in reserve! And what happened? We were eaten up? That is necessarily what would have happened in ninety-nine cases out of a hundred. But no, those Russians argued that no single regiment would come browsing around there at such a time. It must be the entire English army, and that the sly Russian game was detected and blocked; so they

turned tail, and away they went, pell-mell, over the hill
and down into the field, in wild confusion, and we after
them; they themselves broke the solid Russian center in the
field, and tore through, and in no time there was the most
tremendous rout you ever saw, and the defeat of the allies
was turned into a sweeping and splendid victory! Marshal
Canrobert looked on, dizzy with astonishment, admiration,
and delight; and sent right off for Scoresby, and hugged him,
and decorated him on the field in presence of all the armies!

And what was Scoresby's blunder that time? Merely the
mistaking his right hand for his left—that was all. An order
had come to him to fall back and support our right; and,
instead, he fell *forward* and went over the hill to the left.
But the name he won that day as a marvelous military genius
filled the world with his glory, and that glory will never fade
while history books last.

He is just as good and sweet and lovable and unpretending
as a man can be, but he doesn't know enough to come in
when it rains. Now that is absolutely true. He is the suprem-
est ass in the universe; and until half an hour ago nobody
knew it but himself and me. He has been pursued, day by
day and year by year, by a most phenomenal and astonishing
luckiness. He has been a shining soldier in all our wars for a
generation; he has littered his whole military life with blunders, and yet has never committed one that didn't make him
a knight or a baronet or a lord or something. Look at his
breast; why, he is just clothed in domestic and foreign
decorations. Well, sir, every one of them is the record of
some shouting stupidity or other; and, taken together, they
are proof that the very best thing in all this world that can
befall a man is to be born lucky. I say again, as I said at
the banquet, Scoresby's an absolute fool.

The Outcasts of Poker Flat

BY FRANCIS BRET HARTE

As Mr. John Oakhurst, gambler, stepped into the main street
of Poker Flat on the morning of the twenty-third of November, 1850, he was conscious of a change in its moral
atmosphere since the preceding night. Two or three men,

conversing earnestly together, ceased as he approached, and exchanged significant glances. There was a Sabbath lull in the air, which, in a settlement unused to Sabbath influences, looked ominous.

Mr. Oakhurst's calm, handsome face betrayed small concern of these indications. Whether he was conscious of any predisposing cause, was another question. "I reckon they're after somebody," he reflected; "likely it's me." He returned to his pocket the handkerchief with which he had been whipping away the red dust of Poker Flat from his neat boots, and quietly discharged his mind of any further conjecture.

In point of fact, Poker Flat was "after somebody." It had lately suffered the loss of several thousand dollars, two valuable horses, and a prominent citizen. It was experiencing a spasm of virtuous reaction, quite as lawless and ungovernable as any of the acts that had provoked it. A secret committee had determined to rid the town of all improper persons. This was done permanently in regard of two men who were then hanging from the boughs of a sycamore in the gulch, and temporarily in the banishment of certain other objectionable characters. I regret to say that some of these were ladies. It is but due to the sex, however, to state that their impropriety was professional, and it was only in such easily established standards of evil that Poker Flat ventured to sit in judgment.

Mr. Oakhurst was right in supposing that he was included in this category. A few of the committee had urged hanging him as a possible example, and a sure method of reimbursing themselves from his pockets of the sums he had won from them. "It's agin justice," said Jim Wheeler, "to let this yer young man from Roaring Camp—an entire stranger—carry away our money." But a crude sentiment of equity residing in the breasts of those who had been fortunate enough to win from Mr. Oakhurst overruled this narrower local prejudice.

Mr. Oakhurst received his sentence with philosophic calmness, none the less coolly that he was aware of the hesitation of his judges. He was too much of a gambler not to accept Fate. With him life was at best an uncertain game, and he recognized the usual percentage in favor of the dealer.

A body of armed men accompanied the deported wickedness of Poker Flat to the outskirts of the settlement. Besides Mr. Oakhurst, who was known to be a coolly desperate man, and for whose intimidation the armed escort was intended, the expatriated party consisted of a young woman familiarly known as "The Duchess"; another, who had gained the infelicitous title of "Mother Shipton"; and "Uncle Billy," a suspected sluice-robber and confirmed drunkard. The cavalcade provoked no comments from the spectators, nor was any word uttered by the escort. Only, when the gulch which marked the uttermost limit of Poker Flat was reached, the leader spoke briefly and to the point. The exiles were forbidden to return at the peril of their lives.

As the escort disappeared, their pent-up feelings found vent in a few hysterical tears from the Duchess, some bad language from Mother Shipton, and a Parthian volley of expletives from Uncle Billy. The philosophic Oakhurst alone remained still. He listened calmly to Mother Shipton's desire to cut somebody's heart out, to the repeated statements of the Duchess that she would die on the road, and to the alarming oaths that seemed to be bumped out of Uncle Billy as he rode forward. With the easy good humor characteristic of his class, he insisted upon exchanging his own riding-horse, Five Spot, for the sorry mule which the Duchess rode. But even this act did not draw the party into any closer sympathy. The young woman readjusted her somewhat draggled plumes with a feeble, faded coquetry; Mother Shipton eyed the possessor of Five Spot with malevolence, and Uncle Billy included the whole party in one sweeping anathema.

The road to Sandy Bar—a camp that, not having as yet experienced the regenerating influences of Poker Flat, consequently seemed to offer some invitation to the emigrants— lay over a steep mountain range. It was distant a day's severe journey. In that advanced season, the party soon passed out of the moist, temperate regions of the foothills into the dry, cold, bracing air of the Sierras. The trail was narrow and difficult. At noon the Duchess, rolling out of her saddle upon the ground, declared her intention of going no farther, and the party halted.

The spot was singularly wild and impressive. A wooded amphitheater, surrounded on three sides by precipitous cliffs of naked granite, sloped gently toward the crest of another precipice that overlooked the valley. It was undoubtedly the most suitable spot for a camp, had camping been advisable. But Mr. Oakhurst knew that scarcely half the journey to Sandy Bar was accomplished, and the party were not equipped or provisioned for delay. This fact he pointed out to his companions curtly, with a philosophic commentary on the folly of "throwing up their hand before the game was played out." But they were furnished with liquor, which in this emergency stood them in place of food, fuel, rest, and prescience. In spite of his remonstrances, it was not long before they were more or less under its influence. Uncle Billy passed rapidly from a bellicose state into one of stupor, the Duchess became maudlin, and Mother Shipton snored. Mr. Oakhurst alone remained erect, leaning against a rock, calmly surveying them.

Mr. Oakhurst did not drink. It interfered with a profession which required coolness, impassiveness, and presence of mind, and, in his own language, he "couldn't afford it." As he gazed at his recumbent fellow-exiles, the loneliness begotten of his pariah-trade, his habits of life, his very vices, for the first time seriously oppressed him. He bestirred himself in dusting his black clothes, washing his hands and face, and other acts characteristic of his studiously neat habits, and for a moment forgot his annoyance. The thought of deserting his weaker and more pitiable companions never perhaps occurred to him. Yet he could not help feeling the want of that excitement which, singularly enough, was most conducive to the calm equanimity for which he was notorious. He looked at the gloomy walls that rose a thousand feet sheer above the circling pines around him; at the sky, ominously clouded; at the valley below, already deepening into shadow. And, doing so, suddenly he heard his own name called.

A horseman slowly ascended the trail. In the fresh, open face of the new-comer Mr. Oakhurst recognized Tom Simson, otherwise known as "The Innocent" of Sandy Bar. He had met him some months before over a "little game," and had, with perfect equanimity, won the entire fortune—amounting to some forty dollars—of that guileless youth. After the game was finished, Mr. Oakhurst drew the youthful speculator behind the door and thus addressed him: "Tommy, you're a good little man, but you can't gamble worth a cent. Don't try it over again." He then handed him his money back, pushed him gently from the room, and so made a devoted slave of Tom Simson.

There was a remembrance of this in his boyish and enthusiastic greeting of Mr. Oakhurst. He had started, he said, to go to Poker Flat to seek his fortune. "Alone?" No, not

exactly alone; in fact—a giggle—he had run away with Piney
Woods. Didn't Mr. Oakhurst remember Piney? She that used
to wait on the table at the Temperance House? They had
been engaged a long time, but old Jake Woods had objected, and so they had run away, and were going to Poker
Flat to be married, and here they were. And they were tired
out, and how lucky it was they had found a place to camp
and company. All this the Innocent delivered rapidly, while
Piney—a stout, comely damsel of fifteen—emerged from behind the pine-tree, where she had been blushing unseen,
and rode to the side of her lover.

Mr. Oakhurst seldom troubled himself with sentiment, still
less with propriety; but he had a vague idea that the situation
was not felicitous. He retained, however, his presence of
mind sufficiently to kick Uncle Billy, who was about to
say something, and Uncle Billy was sober enough to recognize in Mr. Oakhurst's kick a superior power that would not
bear trifling. He then endeavored to dissuade Tom Simson
from delaying further, but in vain. He even pointed out the
fact that there was no provision, nor means of making a
camp. But, unluckily, the Innocent met this objection by
assuring the party that he was provided with an extra mule
loaded with provisions, and by the discovery of a rude attempt at a log-house near the trail. "Piney can stay with Mrs.
Oakhurst," said the Innocent, pointing to the Duchess, "and
I can shift for myself."

Nothing but Mr. Oakhurst's admonishing foot saved Uncle
Billy from bursting into a roar of laughter. As it was, he felt
compelled to retire up the canyon until he could recover his
gravity. There he confided the joke to the tall pine-trees, with
many slaps of his leg, contortions of his face, and the usual
profanity. But when he returned to the party, he found
them seated by a fire—for the air had grown strangely chill
and the sky overcast—in apparently amicable conversation.
Piney was actually talking in an impulsive, girlish fashion
to the Duchess, who was listening with an interest and
animation she had not shown for many days. The Innocent
was holding forth, apparently with equal effect, to Mr.
Oakhurst and Mother Shipton, who was actually relaxing into
amiability. "Is this yer a d—d picnic?" said Uncle Billy, with
inward scorn, as he surveyed the sylvan group, the glancing
fire-light, and the tethered animals in the foreground. Suddenly an idea mingled with the alcoholic fumes that disturbed his brain. It was apparently of a jocular nature, for

he felt impelled to slap his leg again and cram his fist into his mouth.

As the shadows crept slowly up the mountain, a slight breeze rocked the tops of the pine-trees, and moaned through their long and gloomy aisles. The ruined cabin, patched and covered with pine boughs, was set apart for the ladies. As the lovers parted, they unaffectedly exchanged a kiss, so honest and sincere that it might have been heard above the swaying pines. The frail Duchess and the malevolent Mother Shipton were probably too stunned to remark upon this last evidence of simplicity, and so turned without a word to the hut. The fire was replenished, the men lay down before the door, and in a few minutes were asleep.

Mr. Oakhurst was a light sleeper. Toward morning he awoke benumbed and cold. As he stirred the dying fire, the wind, which was now blowing strongly, brought to his cheek that which caused the blood to leave it—snow!

He started to his feet with the intention of awakening the sleepers, for there was no time to lose. But turning to where Uncle Billy had been lying, he found him gone. A suspicion leaped to his brain and a curse to his lips. He ran to the spot where the mules had been tethered; they were no longer there. The tracks were already rapidly disappearing in the snow.

The momentary excitement brought Mr. Oakhurst back to the fire with his usual calm. He did not waken the sleepers. The Innocent slumbered peacefully, with a smile on his good humored, freckled face; the virgin Piney slept beside her frailer sisters as sweetly as though attended by celestial guardians, and Mr. Oakhurst, drawing his blanket over his shoulders, stroked his mustachios and waited for the dawn. It came slowly in the whirling mist of snowflakes, that dazzled and confused the eye. What could be seen of the landscape appeared magically changed. He looked over the valley, and summed up the present and future in two words—"Snowed in!"

A careful inventory of the provisions, which, fortunately for the party, had been stored within the hut, and so escaped the felonious fingers of Uncle Billy, disclosed the fact that with care and prudence they might last ten days longer. "That is," said Mr. Oakhurst, *sotto voce* to the Innocent, "if you're willing to board us. If you ain't—and perhaps you'd better not—you can wait till Uncle Billy gets back with provisions." For some occult reason, Mr. Oakhurst could not

bring himself to disclose Uncle Billy's rascality, and so offered the hypothesis that he had wandered from the camp and
had accidentally stampeded the animals. He dropped a
warning to the Duchess and Mother Shipton, who of course
knew the facts of their associate's defection. "They'll find
out the truth about us *all*, when they find out anything," he
added, significantly, "and there's no good frightening them
now."

Tom Simson not only put all his worldly store at the disposal of Mr. Oakhurst, but seemed to enjoy the prospect of
their enforced seclusion. "We'll have a good camp for a
week, and then the snow'll melt, and we'll all go back together." The cheerful gayety of the young man and Mr.
Oakhurst's calm infected the others. The Innocent, with the
aid of pine boughs, extemporized a thatch for the roofless
cabin, and the Duchess directed Piney in the rearrange-
ment of the interior with a taste and tact that opened the
blue eyes of that provincial maiden to their fullest extent.

"I reckon now you're used to fine things at Poker Flat,"
said Piney. The Duchess turned away sharply to conceal
something that reddened her cheek through its professional
tint, and Mother Shipton requested Piney not to "chatter."
But when Mr. Oakhurst returned from a weary search for the
trail, he heard the sound of happy laughter echoed from the
rocks. He stopped in some alarm, and his thoughts first
naturally reverted to the whisky, which he had prudently
cached. "And yet it don't somehow sound like whisky,"
said the gambler. It was not until he caught sight of the
blazing fire through the still blinding storm, and the group
around it, that he settled to the conviction that it was "square
fun."

Whether Mr. Oakhurst had *cached* his cards with the
whisky as something debarred the free access of the community, I cannot say. It was certain that, in Mother Shipton's
words, he "didn't say cards once" during the evening. Haply
the time was beguiled by an accordion, produced somewhat ostentatiously by Tom Simson, from his pack. Not-
withstanding some difficulties attending the manipulation of
this instrument, Piney Woods managed to pluck several re-
luctant melodies from its keys, to an accompaniment by
the Innocent on a pair of bone castinets. But the crowning
festivity of the evening was reached in a rude camp-meeting
hymn, which the lovers, joining hands, sang with great
earnestness and vociferation. I fear that a certain defiant

tone and Covenanter's swing to its chorus, rather than any devotional quality, caused it speedily to infect the others, who at last joined in the refrain:

> I'm proud to live in the service of the Lord,
> And I'm bound to die in His army.

The pines rocked, the storm eddied and whirled above the miserable group, and the flames of their altar leaped heavenward, as if in token of the vow.

At midnight the storm abated, the rolling clouds parted, and the stars glittered keenly above the sleeping camp. Mr. Oakhurst, whose professional habits had enabled him to live on the smallest possible amount of sleep, in dividing the watch with Tom Simson, somehow managed to take upon himself the greater part of that duty. He excused himself to the Innocent, by saying that he had "often been a week without sleep." "Doing what?" asked Tom. "Poker!" replied Oakhurst, sententiously, "when a man gets a streak of luck—nigger-luck—he don't get tired. The luck gives in first. Luck," continued the gambler, reflectively, "is a mighty queer thing. All you know about it for certain is that it's bound to change. And it's finding out when it's going to change that makes you. We've had a streak of bad luck since we left Poker Flat—you come along, and slap you get into it, too. If you can hold your cards right along you're all right. For," added the gambler, with cheerful irrelevance,

> "I'm proud to live in the service of the Lord,
> And I'm bound to die in His army."

The third day came, and the sun, looking through the white-curtained valley, saw the outcasts divide their slowly decreasing store of provisions for the morning meal. It was one of the peculiarities of that mountain climate that its rays diffused a kindly warmth over the wintry landscape, as if in regretful commiseration of the past. But it revealed drift on drift of snow piled high around the hut; a hopeless, uncharted, trackless sea of white lying below the rocky shores to which the castaways still clung. Through the marvelously clear air, the smoke of the pastoral village of Poker Flat rose miles away. Mother Shipton saw it, and from a remote pinnacle of her rocky fastness, hurled in that direction a final malediction. It was her last vituperative at-

tempt, and perhaps for that reason was invested with a
certain degree of sublimity. It did her good, she privately informed the Duchess. "Just to go out there and cuss, and
see." She then set herself to the task of amusing "the child,"
as she and the Duchess were pleased to call Piney. Piney
was no chicken, but it was a soothing and ingenious theory
of the pair thus to account for the fact that she didn't swear
and wasn't improper.

When night crept up again through the gorges, the reedy
notes of the accordion rose and fell in fitful spasms and long-
drawn gasps by the flickering camp-fire. But music failed to
fill entirely the aching void left by insufficient food, and a
new diversion was proposed by Piney—story-telling. Neither
Mr. Oakhurst nor his female companions caring to relate
their personal experiences, this plan would have failed, too,
but for the Innocent. Some months before he had chanced
upon a stray copy of Mr. Pope's ingenious translation of the
Iliad. He now proposed to narrate the principal incidents of
that poem—having thoroughly mastered the argument and
fairly forgotten the words—in the current vernacular of
Sandy Bar. And so for the rest of that night the Homeric
demigods again walked the earth. Trojan bully and wily
Greek wrestled in the winds, and the great pines in the
canyon seemed to bow to the wrath of the son of Peleus.
Mr. Oakhurst listened with quiet satisfaction. Most especially
was he interested in the fate of "Ash-heels," as the Innocent
persisted in denominating the "swift-footed Achilles."

So with small food and much of Homer and the accordion,
a week passed over the heads of the outcasts. The sun again
forsook them, and again from leaden skies the snowflakes
were sifted over the land. Day by day closer around them
drew the snowy circle, until at last they looked from their
prison over drifted walls of dazzling white, that towered
twenty feet above their heads. It became more and more
difficult to replenish their fires, even from the fallen trees
beside them, now half-hidden in the drifts. And yet no one
complained. The lovers turned from the dreary prospect and
looked into each other's eyes, and were happy. Mr. Oakhurst
settled himself coolly to the losing game before him. The
Duchess, more cheerful than she had been, assumed the
care of Piney. Only Mother Shipton—once the strongest of
the party—seemed to sicken and fade. At midnight on the
tenth day she called Oakhurst to her side. "I'm going," she
said, in a voice of querulous weakness, "but don't say any-

thing about it. Don't waken the kids. Take the bundle from under my head and open it." Mr. Oakhurst did so. It contained Mother Shipton's rations for the last week, untouched. "Give 'em to the child," she said, pointing to the sleeping Piney. "You've starved yourself," said the gambler. "That's what they call it," said the woman, querulously, as she lay down again, and, turning her face to the wall, passed quietly away.

The accordion and the bones were put aside that day, and Homer was forgotten. When the body of Mother Shipton had been committed to the snow, Mr. Oakhurst took the Innocent aside, and showed him a pair of snowshoes, which he had fashioned from the old pack-saddle. "There's one chance in a hundred to save her yet," he said, pointing to Piney; "but it's there," he added, pointing toward Poker Flat. "If you can reach there in two days she's safe." "And you?" asked Tom Simson. "I'll stay here," was the curt reply.

The lovers parted with a long embrace. "You are not going, too?" said the Duchess, as she saw Mr. Oakhurst apparently waiting to accompany him. "As far as the canyon," he replied. He turned suddenly, and kissed the Duchess, leaving her pallid face aflame, and her trembling limbs rigid with amazement.

Night came, but not Mr. Oakhurst. It brought the storm again and the whirling snow. Then the Duchess, feeding the fire, found that some one had quietly piled beside the hut enough fuel to last a few days longer. The tears rose to her eyes, but she hid them from Piney.

The women slept but little. In the morning, looking into each other's faces, they read their fate. Neither spoke; but Piney, accepting the position of the stronger, drew near and placed her arm around the Duchess's waist. They kept this attitude for the rest of the day. That night the storm reached its greatest fury, and, rending asunder the protecting pines, invaded the very hut.

Toward morning they found themselves unable to feed the fire, which gradually died away. As the embers slowly blackened, the Duchess crept closer to Piney, and broke the silence of many hours: "Piney, can you pray?" "No, dear," said Piney, simply. The Duchess without knowing exactly why, felt relieved, and, putting her head upon Piney's shoulder, spoke no more. And so reclining, the younger and purer pillowing the head of her soiled sister upon her virgin breast, they fell asleep.

The wind lulled as if it feared to waken them. Feathery drifts of snow, shaken from the long pine boughs, flew like white-winged birds, and settled about them as they slept. The moon through the rifted clouds looked down upon what had been the camp. But all human stain, all trace of earthly travail, was hidden beneath the spotless mantle mercifully flung from above.

They slept all that day and the next, nor did they waken when voices and footsteps broke the silence of the camp. And when pitying fingers brushed the snow from their wan faces, you could scarcely have told from the equal peace that dwelt upon them, which was she that had sinned. Even the Law of Poker Flat recognized this, and turned away, leaving them still locked in each other's arms.

But at the head of the gulch, on one of the largest pine trees, they found the deuce of clubs pinned to the bark with a bowie knife. It bore the following, written in pencil, in a firm hand:

✝

BENEATH THIS TREE
LIES THE BODY
OF
JOHN OAKHURST,
WHO STRUCK A STREAK OF BAD LUCK
ON THE 23D OF NOVEMBER, 1850,
AND
HANDED IN HIS CHECKS
ON THE 7TH OF DECEMBER, 1850.

✝

And pulseless and cold, with a Derringer by his side and a bullet in his heart, though still calm as in life, beneath the snow lay he who was at once the strongest and yet the weakest of the outcasts of Poker Flat.

The Damned Thing

BY AMBROSE BIERCE

ONE DOES NOT ALWAYS EAT
WHAT IS ON THE TABLE

I

BY THE light of a tallow candle which had been placed on
one end of a rough table a man was reading something
written in a book. It was an old account book, greatly
worn; and the writing was not, apparently, very legible, for
the man sometimes held the page close to the flame of the
candle to get a stronger light on it. The shadow of the book
would then throw into obscurity a half of the room, darkening a number of faces and figures; for besides the reader,
eight other men were present. Seven of them sat against the
rough log walls, silent, motionless, and the room being
small, not very far from the table. By extending an arm any
one of them could have touched the eighth man, who lay
on the table, face upward, partly covered by a sheet, his arms
at his sides. He was dead.

The man with the book was not reading aloud, and no
one spoke; all seemed to be waiting for something to occur;
the dead man only was without expectation. From the blank
darkness outside came in, through the aperture that served
for a window, all the ever unfamiliar noises of night in the
wilderness—the long nameless note of a distant coyote; the
stilly pulsing thrill of tireless insects in trees; strange cries of
night birds, so different from those of the birds of day;
the drone of great blundering beetles, and all that mysterious chorus of small sounds that seem always to have been
but half heard when they have suddenly ceased, as if
conscious of an indiscretion. But nothing of all this was noted
in that company; its members were not overmuch addicted
to idle interest in matters of no practical importance; that
was obvious in every line of their rugged faces—obvious
even in the dim light of the single candle. They were evidently men of the vicinity—farmers and woodsmen.

The person reading was a trifle different; one would have

said of him that he was of the world, worldly, albeit there
was that in his attire which attested a certain fellowship
with the organisms of his environment. His coat would
hardly have passed muster in San Francisco; his foot-gear
was not of urban origin, and the hat that lay by him on
the floor (he was the only one uncovered) was such that if
one had considered it as an article of mere personal adornment he would have missed its meaning. In countenance the
man was rather prepossessing, with just a hint of stern-
ness; though that he may have assumed or cultivated, as
appropriate to one in authority. For he was a coroner. It was
by virtue of his office that he had possession of the book in
which he was reading; it had been found among the dead
man's effects—in his cabin, where the inquest was now
taking place.

When the coroner had finished reading he put the book
into his breast pocket. At that moment the door was pushed
open and a young man entered. He, clearly, was not of
mountain birth and breeding: he was clad as those who
dwell in cities. His clothing was dusty, however, as from
travel. He had, in fact, been riding hard to attend the inquest.

The coroner nodded; no one else greeted him.

"We have waited for you," said the coroner. "It is necessary to have done with this business to-night."

The young man smiled. "I am sorry to have kept you,"
he said. "I went away, not to evade your summons, but to
post to my newspaper an account of what I suppose I am
called back to relate."

The coroner smiled.

"The account that you posted to your newspaper," he
said, "differs, probably, from that which you will give here
under oath."

"That," replied the other, rather hotly and with a visible
flush, "is as you please. I used manifold paper and have a
copy of what I sent. It was not written as news, for it is incredible, but as fiction. It may go as a part of my testimony
under oath."

"But you say it is incredible."

"That is nothing to you, sir, if I also swear that it is true."

The coroner was silent for a time, his eyes upon the
floor. The men about the sides of the cabin talked in
whispers, but seldom withdrew their gaze from the face of

the corpse. Presently the coroner lifted his eyes and said: "We will resume the inquest."

The men removed their hats. The witness was sworn.

"What is your name?" the coroner asked.

"William Harker."

"Age?"

"Twenty-seven."

"You knew the deceased, Hugh Morgan?"

"Yes."

"You were with him when he died?"

"Near him."

"How did that happen—your presence, I mean?"

"I was visiting him at this place to shoot and fish. A part of my purpose, however, was to study him and his odd, solitary way of life. He seemed a good model for a character in fiction. I sometimes write stories."

"I sometimes read them."

"Thank you."

"Stories in general—not yours."

Some of the jurors laughed. Against a sombre background humor shows high lights. Soldiers in the intervals of battle laugh easily, and a jest in the death chamber conquers by surprise.

"Relate the circumstances of this man's death," said the coroner. "You may use any notes or memoranda that you please."

The witness understood. Pulling a manuscript from his breast pocket he held it near the candle and turning the leaves until he found the passage that he wanted began to read.

II

WHAT MAY HAPPEN IN A FIELD OF WILD OATS

". . . The sun had hardly risen when we left the house. We were looking for quail, each with a shotgun, but we had only one dog. Morgan said that our best ground was beyond a certain ridge that he pointed out, and we crossed it by a trail through the *chaparral*. On the other side was comparatively level ground, thickly covered with wild oats. As we emerged from the *chaparral* Morgan was but a few yards in advance. Suddenly we heard, at a little distance to our right and partly in front, a noise as of some animal thrashing about in the bushes, which we could see were violently agitated.

" 'We've started a deer,' I said. 'I wish we had brought a rifle.'

"Morgan, who had stopped and was intently watching the agitated *chaparral,* said nothing, but had cocked both barrels of his gun and was holding it in readiness to aim. I thought him a trifle excited, which surprised me, for he had a reputation for exceptional coolness, even in moments of sudden and imminent peril.

" 'O, come,' I said. 'You are not going to fill up a deer with quail-shot, are you?'

"Still he did not reply; but catching a sight of his face as he turned it slightly toward me I was struck by the intensity of his look. Then I understood that we had serious business in hand and my first conjecture was that we had 'jumped' a grizzly. I advanced to Morgan's side, cocking my piece as I moved.

"The bushes were now quiet and the sounds had ceased, but Morgan was as attentive to the place as before.

" 'What is it? What the devil is it?' I asked.

" 'That Damned Thing!' he replied, without turning his head. His voice was husky and unnatural. He trembled visibly.

"I was about to speak further, when I observed the wild oats near the place of the disturbance moving in the most inexplicable way. I can hardly describe it. It seemed as if stirred by a streak of wind, which not only bent it, but pressed it down—crushed it so that it did not rise; and this movement was slowly prolonging itself directly toward us.

"Nothing that I had ever seen had affected me so strangely as this unfamiliar and unaccountable phenomenon, yet I am unable to recall any sense of fear. I remember—and tell it here because, singularly enough, I recollected it then—that once in looking carelessly out of an open window I momentarily mistook a small tree close at hand for one of a group of larger trees at a little distance away. It looked the same size as the others, but being more distinctly and sharply defined in mass and detail seemed out of harmony with them. It was a mere falsification of the law of aërial perspective, but it startled, almost terrified me. We so rely upon the orderly operation of familiar natural laws that any seeming suspension of them is noted as a menace to our safety, a warning of unthinkable calamity. So now the apparently causeless movement of the herbage and the slow, undeviating approach of the line of disturbance were distinctly disquieting. My companion appeared actually frightened, and I could hardly credit my senses when I saw him suddenly throw his gun to his shoulder and fire both barrels at the agitated grain! Before the smoke of the discharge had cleared away I heard a loud savage cry—a scream like that of a wild animal—and flinging his gun upon the ground Morgan sprang away and ran swiftly from the spot. At the same instant I was thrown violently to the ground by the impact of something unseen in the smoke—some soft, heavy substance that seemed thrown against me with great force.

"Before I could get upon my feet and recover my gun, which seemed to have been struck from my hands, I heard Morgan crying out as if in mortal agony, and mingling with his cries were such hoarse, savage sounds as one hears from fighting dogs. Inexpressibly terrified, I struggled to my feet and looked in the direction of Morgan's retreat; and may Heaven in mercy spare me from another sight like that! At a distance of less than thirty yards was my friend, down upon one knee, his head thrown back at a frightful angle, hatless, his long hair in disorder and his whole body in violent movement from side to side, backward and forward. His right arm was lifted and seemed to lack the hand—at least, I could see none. The other arm was invisible. At times, as my memory now reports this extraordinary scene, I could discern but a part of his body; it was as if he had been partly blotted out—I cannot otherwise express it—then a shifting of his position would bring it all into view again.

"All this must have occurred within a few seconds, yet in that time Morgan assumed all the postures of a determined wrestler vanquished by superior weight and strength. I saw nothing but him, and him not always distinctly. During the entire incident his shouts and curses were heard, as if through an enveloping uproar of such sounds of rage and fury as I had never heard from the throat of man or brute!

"For a moment only I stood irresolute, then throwing down my gun I ran forward to my friend's assistance. I had a vague belief that he was suffering from a fit, or some form of convulsion. Before I could reach his side he was down and quiet. All sounds had ceased, but with a feeling of such terror as even these awful events had not inspired I now saw again the mysterious movement of the wild oats, prolonging itself from the trampled area about the prostrate man to-

ward the edge of a wood. It was only when it had reached
the wood that I was able to withdraw my eyes and look at my
companion. He was dead."

III

A MAN THOUGH NAKED MAY BE IN RAGS

The coroner rose from his seat and stood beside the
dead man. Lifting an edge of the sheet he pulled it away, ex-
posing the entire body, altogether naked and showing in the
candle-light a claylike yellow. It had, however, broad macu-
lations of bluish black, obviously caused by extravasated
blood from contusions. The chest and sides looked as if they
had been beaten with a bludgeon. There were dreadful
lacerations; the skin was torn in strips and shreds.

The coroner moved round to the end of the table and undid a silk handkerchief which had been passed under the
chin and knotted on the top of the head. When the handkerchief was drawn away it exposed what had been the
throat. Some of the jurors who had risen to get a better view
repented their curiosity and turned away their faces. Witness
Harker went to the open window and leaned out across the
sill, faint and sick. Dropping the handkerchief upon the
dead man's neck the coroner stepped to an angle of the
room and from a pile of clothing produced one garment after
another, each of which he held up a moment for inspection.
All were torn, and stiff with blood. The jurors did not make
a closer inspection. They seemed rather uninterested. They
had, in truth, seen all this before; the only thing that was
new to them being Harker's testimony.

"Gentlemen," the coroner said, "we have no more evidence, I think. Your duty has been already explained to you;
if there is nothing you wish to ask you may go outside and
consider your verdict."

The foreman rose—a tall, bearded man of sixty, coarsely
clad.

"I should like to ask one question, Mr. Coroner," he said.
"What asylum did this yer last witness escape from?"

"Mr. Harker," said the coroner, gravely and tranquilly,
"from what asylum did you last escape?"

Harker flushed crimson again, but said nothing, and the
seven jurors rose and solemnly filed out of the cabin.

"If you have done insulting me, sir," said Harker, as soon as he and the officer were left alone with the dead man, "I suppose I am at liberty to go?"

"Yes."

Harker started to leave, but paused, with his hand on the door latch. The habit of his profession was strong in him—stronger than his sense of personal dignity. He turned about and said:

"The book that you have there—I recognize it as Morgan's diary. You seemed greatly interested in it; you read in it while I was testifying. May I see it? The public would like——"

"The book will cut no figure in this matter," replied the official, slipping it into his coat pocket; "all the entries in it were made before the writer's death."

As Harker passed out of the house the jury reëntered and stood about the table, on which the now covered corpse showed under the sheet with sharp definition. The foreman seated himself near the candle, produced from his breast pocket a pencil and scrap of paper and wrote rather laboriously the following verdict, which with various degrees of effort all signed:

"We, the jury, do find that the remains come to their death at the hands of a mountain lion, but some of us thinks, all the same, they had fits."

IV

AN EXPLANATION FROM THE TOMB

In the diary of the late Hugh Morgan are certain interesting entries having, possibly, a scientific value as suggestions. At the inquest upon his body the book was not put in evidence; possibly the coroner thought it not worth while to confuse the jury. The date of the first of the entries mentioned cannot be ascertained; the upper part of the leaf is torn away; the part of the entry remaining follows:

". . . would run in a half-circle, keeping his head turned always toward the centre, and again he would stand still, barking furiously. At last he ran away into the brush as fast as he could go. I thought at first that he had gone mad, but on returning to the house found no other alteration in his manner than what was obviously due to fear of punishment.

"Can a dog see with his nose? Do odors impress some cerebral centre with images of the thing that emitted them? . . .

"Sept. 2.—Looking at the stars last night as they rose above the crest of the ridge east of the house, I observed them successively disappear—from left to right. Each was eclipsed but an instant, and only a few at the same time, but along the entire length of the ridge all that were within a degree or two of the crest were blotted out. It was as if something had passed along between me and them; but I could not see it, and the stars were not thick enough to define its outline. Ugh! I don't like this." . . .

Several weeks' entries are missing, three leaves being torn from the book.

"Sept. 27.—It has been about here again—I find evidences of its presence every day. I watched again all last night in the same cover, gun in hand, double-charged with buckshot. In the morning the fresh footprints were there, as before. Yet I would have sworn that I did not sleep—indeed, I hardly sleep at all. It is terrible, insupportable! If these amazing experiences are real I shall go mad; if they are fanciful I am mad already.

"Oct. 3.—I shall not go—it shall not drive me away. No, this is *my* house, *my* land. God hates a coward. . . .

"Oct. 5.—I can stand it no longer; I have invited Harker to pass a few weeks with me—he has a level head. I can judge from his manner if he thinks me mad.

"Oct. 7.—I have the solution of the mystery; it came to me last night—suddenly, as by revelation. How simple—how terribly simple!

"There are sounds that we cannot hear. At either end of the scale are notes that stir no chord of that imperfect instrument, the human ear. They are too high or too grave. I have observed a flock of blackbirds occupying an entire tree-top—the tops of several trees—and all in full song. Suddenly—in a moment—at absolutely the same instant—all spring into the air and fly away. How? They could not all see one another—whole tree-tops intervened. At no point could a leader have been visible to all. There must have been a signal of warning or command, high and shrill above the din, but by me unheard. I have observed, too, the same simultaneous flight when all were silent, among not only blackbirds, but other birds—quail, for example, widely separated by bushes—even on opposite sides of a hill.

"It is known to seamen that a school of whales basking or sporting on the surface of the ocean, miles apart, with the convexity of the earth between, will sometimes dive at the same instant—all gone out of sight in a moment. The signal has been sounded—too grave for the ear of the sailor at the masthead and his comrades on the deck—who nevertheless feel its vibrations in the ship as the stones of a cathedral are stirred by the bass of the organ.

"As with sounds, so with colors. At each end of the solar spectrum the chemist can detect the presence of what are known as 'actinic' rays. They represent colors—integral colors in the composition of light—which we are unable to discern. The human eye is an imperfect instrument; its range is but a few octaves of the real 'chromatic scale.' I am not mad; there are colors that we cannot see.

"And, God help me! the Damned Thing is of such a color!"

The Two Faces

BY HENRY JAMES

THE SERVANT, who, in spite of his sealed stamped look, appeared to have his reasons, stood there for instruction in a manner not quite usual after announcing the name. Mrs. Grantham, however, took it up—"Lord Gwyther?"—with a quick surprise that for an instant justified him even to the small scintilla in the glance she gave her companion, which might have had exactly the sense of the butler's hesitation. This companion, a shortish fairish youngish man, clean-shaven and keen-eyed, had, with a promptitude that would have struck an observer—which the butler indeed was—sprung to his feet and moved to the chimney-piece, though his hostess herself meanwhile managed not otherwise to stir. "Well?" she said as for the visitor to advance; which she immediately followed with a sharper "He's not there?"

"Shall I show him up, ma'am?"

"But of course!" The point of his doubt made her at last rise for impatience, and Bates, before leaving the room, might still have caught the achieved irony of her appeal to the gentleman into whose communion with her he had broken.

"Why in the world not—? What a way—!" she exclaimed as Sutton felt beside his cheek the passage of her eyes to the glass behind him.

"He wasn't sure you'd see any one."

"I don't see 'any one,' but I see individuals."

"That's just it—and sometimes you don't see them."

"Do you mean ever because of *you?*" she asked as she touched into place a tendril of hair. "That's just his impertinence, as to which I shall speak to him."

"Don't," said Shirley Sutton. "Never notice anything."

"That's nice advice from you," she laughed, "who notice everything!"

"Ah but I speak of nothing."

She looked at him a moment. "You're still more impertinent than Bates. You'll please not budge," she went on.

"Really? I must sit him out?" he continued as, after a minute, she had not again spoken—only glancing about, while she changed her place, partly for another look at the glass and partly to see if she could improve her seat. What she felt was rather more than, clever and charming though she was, she could hide. "If you're wondering how you seem I can tell you. Awfully cool and easy."

She gave him another stare. She was beautiful and conscious. "And if you're wondering how *you* seem—"

"Oh I'm not!" he laughed from before the fire. "I always perfectly know."

"How you seem," she retorted, "is as if you didn't!"

Once more for a little he watched her. "You're looking lovely for him—extraordinarily lovely, within the marked limits of your range. But that's enough. Don't be clever."

"Then who *will* be?"

"There you are!" he sighed with amusement.

"Do you know him?" she asked as, through the door left open by Bates, they heard steps on the landing.

Sutton had to think an instant, and produced a "No" just as Lord Gwyther was again announced, which gave an unexpectedness to the greeting offered him a moment later by this personage—a young man, stout and smooth and fresh, but not at all shy, who, after the happiest rapid passage with Mrs. Grantham, put out a hand with a straight free "How d' ye do?"

"Mr. Shirley Sutton," Mrs. Grantham explained.

"Oh yes," said her second visitor quite as if he knew; which, as he couldn't have known, had for her first the interest of confirming a perception that his lordship would be—no, not at all, in general, embarrassed, only was now exceptionally and especially agitated. As it is, for that matter, with Sutton's total impression that we are particularly and almost exclusively concerned, it may be further mentioned that he was not less clear as to the really handsome way in which the young man kept himself together and little by little—though with all proper aid indeed—finally found his feet. All sorts of things, for the twenty minutes, occurred to Sutton, though one of them was certainly not that it would, after all, be better he should go. One of them was that their hostess was doing it in perfection—simply, easily, kindly, yet with something the least bit queer in her wonderful eyes; another was that if he had been recognised without the least ground it was through a tension of nerves on the part of his fellow guest that produced inconsequent motions; still another was that, even had departure been indicated, he would positively have felt dissuasion in the rare promise of the scene. This was in especial after Lord Gwyther not only had announced that he was now married, but had mentioned that he wished to bring his wife to Mrs. Grantham for the benefit so certain to be derived. It was the passage immediately produced by that speech that provoked in Sutton the intensity, as it were, of his arrest. He already knew of the marriage as well as Mrs. Grantham herself, and as well also as he knew of some other things; and this gave him doubtless the better measure of what took place before him and the keener consciousness of the quick look that, at a marked moment—though it was not absolutely meant for him any more than for his companion—Mrs. Grantham let him catch.

She smiled, but it had a gravity. "I think, you know, you ought to have told me before."

"Do you mean when I first got engaged? Well, it all took place so far away, and we really told, at home, so few people."

Oh there might have been reasons; but it had not been quite right. "You were married at Stuttgart? That wasn't too far for *my* interest, at least, to reach."

"Awfully kind of you—and of course one knew you *would* be kind. But it wasn't at Stuttgart; it was over there, but quite in the country. We should have managed it in England but that her mother naturally wished to be present, yet wasn't in health to come. So it was really, you see, a sort of little hole-and-corner German affair."

This didn't in the least check Mrs. Grantham's claim, but it started a slight anxiety. "Will she be—a—then German?"

Sutton knew her to know perfectly what Lady Gwyther would "be," but he had by this time, while their friend explained, his independent interest. "Oh dear no! My father-in-law has never parted with the proud birthright of a Briton. But his wife, you see, holds an estate in Würtemberg from *her* mother, Countess Kremnitz, on which, with the awful condition of his English property, you know, they've found it for years a tremendous saving to live. So that though Valda was luckily born at home she has practically spent her life over there."

"Oh I see." Then, after a slight pause, "Is Valda her pretty name?" Mrs. Grantham asked.

"Well," said the young man, only wishing, in his candour, it was clear, to be drawn out—"well, she has, in the manner of her mother's people, about thirteen; but that's the one we generally use."

Mrs. Grantham waited but an instant. "Then may *I* generally use it?"

"It would be too charming of you; and nothing would give her—as I assure you nothing would give *me*—greater pleasure." Lord Gwyther quite glowed with the thought.

"Then I think that instead of coming alone you might have brought her to see me."

"It's exactly what," he instantly replied, "I came to ask your leave to do." He explained that for the moment Lady Gwyther was not in town, having as soon as she arrived gone down to Torquay to put in a few days with one of her aunts, also her godmother, to whom she was an object of great interest. She had seen no one yet, and no one—not that *that* mattered—had seen her; she knew nothing whatever of London and was awfully frightened at facing it and at what (however little) might be expected of her. "She wants some one," he said, "some one who knows the whole thing, don't you see? and who's thoroughly kind and clever, as you would be, if I may say so, to take her by the hand." It was at this point and on these words that the eyes of Lord Gwyther's two auditors inevitably and wonderfully met. But there was nothing in the way he kept it up to show he caught the encounter. "She wants, if I may tell you so, a real friend for the great labyrinth; and asking myself what I could do to make things ready for her, and who would be absolutely the best woman in London—"

"You thought naturally of *me?*" Mrs. Grantham had listened with no sign but the faint flash just noted; now, however, she gave him the full light of her expressive face—which immediately brought Shirley Sutton, looking at his watch, once more to his feet.

"She *is* the best woman in London!" He addressed himself with a laugh to the other visitor, but offered his hand in farewell to their hostess.

"You're going?"

"I must," he said without scruple.

"Then we do meet at dinner?"

"I hope so." On which, to take leave, he returned with interest to Lord Gwyther the friendly clutch he had a short time before received.

II

They did meet at dinner, and if they were not, as it happened, side by side, they made that up afterwards in the happiest angle of a drawing-room that offered both shine and shadow and that was positively much appreciated, in the circle in which they moved, for the favourable "corners" created by its shrewd mistress. Mrs. Grantham's face, charged with something produced in it by Lord Gwyther's visit, had been with him so constantly for the previous hours that, when she instantly challenged him on his "treatment" of her in the afternoon, he was on the point of naming it as his reason for not having remained with her. Something new had quickly come into her beauty; he couldn't as yet have said what, nor whether on the whole to its advantage or its loss. Till he should see this clearer, at any rate he would say nothing; so that he found with sufficient presence of mind a better excuse. If in short he had in defiance of her particular request left her alone with Lord Gwyther it was simply because the situation had suddenly turned so exciting that he had fairly feared the contagion of it—the temptation of its making him, most improperly, put in his word.

They could now talk of these things at their ease. Other couples, ensconced and scattered, enjoyed the same privilege, and Sutton had more and more the profit, such as it was, of feeling that his interest in Mrs. Grantham had become—what was the luxury of so high a social code—an acknowledged and protected relation. He knew his London well enough to know that he was on the way to be regarded as her main source of consolation for the trick Lord Gwyther had several months before publicly played her. Many persons had not held that, by the high social code in question, his lordship could have "reserved the right" to turn up that way, from one day to another, engaged to be married. For himself London took, with its short cuts and its cheap psychology, an immense deal for granted. To his own sense he was never—could in the nature of things never be—any man's "successor." Just what had constituted the predecessorship of other men was apparently that they had been able to make up their mind. He, worse luck, was at the mercy of her face, and more than ever at the mercy of it now, which meant moreover not that it made a slave of him, but that it made, disconcertingly, a sceptic. It was the absolute perfection of the handsome, but things had a way of coming into it. "I felt," he said, "that you were there together at a point at which you had a right to the ease the absence of a listener would give. I was sure that when you made me promise to stay you hadn't guessed—"

"That he could possibly have come to me on such an extraordinary errand? No, of course I hadn't guessed. Who *would*? But didn't you see how little I was upset by it?"

Sutton demurred. Then with a smile: "I think *he* saw how little."

"You yourself didn't then?"

He again held back, but not, after all, to answer. "He was wonderful, wasn't he?"

"I think he was," she returned after a moment. To which she added: "Why did he pretend that way he knew you?"

"He didn't pretend. He somehow felt on the spot that I was 'in it.'" Sutton had found this afterwards and found it to represent a reality. "It was an effusion of cheer and hope. He was so glad to see me there and to find you happy."

"Happy?"

"Happy. Aren't you?"

"Because of *you*?"

"Well—according to the impression he received as he came in."

"That was sudden then," she asked, "and unexpected?"

Her companion thought. "Prepared in some degree, but confirmed by the sight of us, there together, so awfully jolly and sociable over your fire."

Mrs. Grantham turned this round. "If he knew I was

'happy' then—which, by the way, is none of his business, nor of yours either—why in the world did he come?"

"Well, for good manners, and for his idea," said Sutton.

She took it in, appearing to have no hardness of rancour that could bar discussion. "Do you mean by his idea his proposal that I should grandmother his wife? And if you do is the proposal your reason for calling him wonderful?"

Sutton laughed. "Pray what's yours?" As this was a question, however, that she took her time to answer or not to answer—only appearing interested for a moment in a combination that had formed itself on the other side of the room—he presently went on. "What's *his*?—that would seem to be the point. His, I mean, for having decided on the extraordinary step of throwing his little wife, bound hands and feet, into your arms. Intelligent as you are, and with these three or four hours to have thought it over, I yet don't see how that can fail still to mystify you."

She continued to watch their opposite neighbours. " 'Little,' you call her. Is she so very small?"

"Tiny, tiny—she *must* be; as different as possible in every way—of necessity—from you. They always *are* the opposite pole, you know," said Shirley Sutton.

She glanced at him now. "You strike me as of an impudence—!"

"No, no. I only like to make it out with you."

She looked away again and after a little went on. "I'm sure she's charming, and only hope one isn't to gather he's already tired of her."

"Not a bit! He's tremendously in love, and he'll remain so."

"So much the better. And if it's a question," said Mrs. Grantham, "of one's doing what one can for her, he has only, as I told him when you had gone, to give me the chance."

"Good! So he *is* to commit her to you?"

"You use extraordinary expressions, but it's settled that he brings her."

"And you'll really and truly help her?"

"Really and truly?" said Mrs. Grantham with her eyes again on him. "Why not? For what do you take me?"

"Ah isn't that just what I still have the discomfort, every day I live, of asking myself?"

She had made, as she spoke, a movement to rise, which, as if she was tired of his tone, his last words appeared to determine. But, also getting up, he held her, when they were on their feet, long enough to hear the rest of what he had to say. "If you do help her, you know, you'll show him you've understood."

"Understood what?"

"Why, his idea—the deep acute train of reasoning that has led him to take, as one may say, the bull by the horns; to reflect that as you might, as you probably *would*, in any case, get at her, he plays the wise game, as well as the bold one, by treating your generosity as a real thing and placing himself publicly under an obligation to you."

Mrs. Grantham showed not only that she had listened, but that she had for an instant considered. "What is it you elegantly describe as my getting 'at' her?"

"He takes his risk, but puts you, you see, on your honour."

She thought a moment more. "What profundities indeed then over the simplest of matters! And if your idea is," she went on, "that if I do help her I shall show him I've understood them, so it will be that if I don't—"

"You'll show him"—Sutton took her up—"that you haven't? Precisely. But in spite of not wanting to appear to have understood *too* much—"

"I may still be depended on to do what I can? Quite certainly. You'll see what I may still be depended on to do." And she moved away.

III

It was not, doubtless, that there had been anything in their rather sharp separation at that moment to sustain or prolong the interruption; yet it definitely befell that, circumstances aiding, they practically failed to meet again before the great party at Burbeck. This occasion was to gather in some thirty persons from a certain Friday to the following Monday, and it was on the Friday that Sutton went down. He had known in advance that Mrs. Grantham was to be there, and this perhaps, during the interval of hindrance, had helped him a little to be patient. He had before him the certitude of a real full cup—two days brimming over with the sight of her. He found, however, on his arrival that she was not yet in the field, and presently learned that her place would be in a small contingent that was to join the party on the morrow. This knowledge he extracted from Miss Banker, who was always the first to present herself at any gathering that was to enjoy her, and whom moreover—partly on that very account—the wary not less than the speculative were apt to hold themselves well-advised to engage with at as early as possible a stage of the business. She was stout red rich mature universal—a massive much-fingered volume, alphabetical wonderful indexed, that opened of itself at the right place. She opened for Sutton instinctively at G——, which happened to be remarkably convenient. "What she's really waiting over for is to bring down Lady Gwyther."

"Ah the Gwythers are coming?"

"Yes; caught, through Mrs. Grantham, just in time. *She'll* be the feature—every one wants to see her."

Speculation and wariness met and combined at this moment in Shirley Sutton. "Do you mean—a—Mrs. Grantham?"

"Dear no! Poor little Lady Gwyther, who, but just arrived in England, appears now literally for the first time in her life in any society whatever, and whom (don't you know the extraordinary story? you ought to—*you!*) she, of all people, has so wonderfully taken up. It will be quite—here—as if she were 'presenting' her."

Sutton of course took in more things than even appeared. "I never know what I ought to know; I only know, inveterately, what I oughtn't. So what *is* the extraordinary story?"

"You really haven't heard?"

"Really," he replied without winking.

"It happened indeed but the other day," said Miss Banker, "yet every one's already wondering. Gwyther has thrown his wife on her mercy—but I won't believe you if you pretend to me you don't know why he shouldn't."

Sutton asked himself then what he *could* pretend. "Do you mean because she's merciless?"

She hesitated. "If you don't know perhaps I oughtn't to tell you."

He liked Miss Banker and found just the right tone to plead. "*Do* tell me."

"Well," she sighed, "it will be your own fault—! They have been such friends that there could have been but one name for the crudity of his original *procédé*. When I was a girl we used to call it throwing over. They call it in French to *lâcher*. But I refer not so much to the act itself as to the manner of it, though you may say indeed of course that there's in such cases after all only one manner. Least said soonest mended."

Sutton seemed to wonder. "Oh he said too much?"

"He said nothing. That was it."

Sutton kept it up. "But was *what?*"

"Why, what she must, like any woman in her shoes, have felt to be his perfidy. He simply went and *did* it—took to himself this child, that is, without the preliminary of a scandal or a rupture—before she could turn round."

"I follow you. But it would appear from what you say that she *has* turned round now."

"Well," Miss Banker laughed, "we shall see for ourselves how far. It will be what every one will try to see."

"Oh then we've work cut out!" And Sutton certainly felt that he himself had—an impression that lost nothing from a further talk with Miss Banker in the course of a short stroll in the grounds with her the next day. He spoke as one who had now considered many things.

"Did I understand from you yesterday that Lady Gwyther's a 'child'?"

"Nobody knows. It's prodigious the way she has managed."

"The way Lady Gwyther has—?"

"No, the way May Grantham has kept her till this hour in her pocket."

He was quick at his watch. "Do you mean by 'this hour' that they're due now?"

"Not till tea. All the others arrive together in time for that." Miss Banker had clearly, since the previous day, filled in gaps and become, as it were, revised and enlarged. "She'll have kept a cat from seeing her, so as to produce her entirely herself."

"Well," Sutton mused, "that will have been a very noble sort of return—"

"For Gwyther's behaviour? Very. Yet I feel creepy."

"Creepy?"

"Because so much depends for the girl—in the way of the right start or the wrong start—on the signs and omens of this first appearance. It's a great house and a great occasion, and we're assembled here, it strikes me, very much as the Roman mob at the circus used to be to see the next Christian maiden brought out to the tigers."

"Oh if she *is* a Christian maiden—!" Sutton murmured. But he stopped at what his imagination called up.

It perhaps fed that faculty a little that Miss Banker had the effect of making out that Mrs. Grantham might individually be, in any case, something of a Roman matron. "She has kept her in the dark so that we may only take her from her hand. She'll have formed her for us."

"In so few days?"

"Well, she'll have prepared her—decked her for the sacrifice with ribbons and flowers."

"Ah if you only mean that she'll have taken her to her dressmaker—!" And it came to Sutton, at once as a new light and as a check, almost, to anxiety, that this was all poor Gwyther, mistrustful probably of a taste formed by Stuttgart, might have desired of their friend.

There were usually at Burbeck many things taking place at once; so that wherever else, on such occasions, tea might be served, it went forward with matchless pomp, weather permitting, on a shaded stretch of one of the terraces and in presence of one of the prospects. Shirley Sutton, moving, as the afternoon waned, more restlessly about and mingling in dispersed groups only to find they had nothing to keep him quiet, came upon it as he turned a corner of the house— saw it seated there in all its state. It might be said that at Burbeck it was, like everything else, made the most of. It constituted immediately, with multiplied tables and glittering plate, with rugs and cushions and ices and fruit and wonderful porcelain and beautiful women, a scene of splendour, almost an incident of grand opera. One of the beautiful women might quite have been expected to rise with a gold cup and a celebrated song.

One of them did rise, as happened, while Sutton drew near, and he found himself a moment later seeing nothing and nobody but Mrs. Grantham. They met on the terrace, just away from the others, and the movement in which he had the effect of arresting her might have been that of withdrawal. He quickly saw, however, that if she had been about to pass into the house it was only on some errand—to get something or to call some one—that would immediately have restored her to her public. It somehow struck him on the spot—and more than ever yet, though the impression was not wholly new to him—that she felt herself a figure for the forefront of the stage and indeed would have been recognised by any one at a glance as the *prima donna assoluta*. She caused, in fact, during the few minutes he stood talking to her, an extraordinary series of waves to roll extraordinarily fast over his sense, not the least mark of the matter being that the appearance with which it

ended was again the one with which it had begun. "The
face—the face," as he kept dumbly repeating; that was at
last, as at first, all he could clearly see. She had a perfection
resplendent, but what in the world had it done, this perfection, to her beauty? It was her beauty doubtless that
looked out at him, but it was into something else that, as
their eyes met, he strangely found himself looking.

It was as if something had happened in consequence of
which she had changed, and there was that in this swift
perception that made him glance eagerly about for Lady
Gwyther. But as he took in the recruited group—identities
of the hour added to those of the previous twenty-four—he
saw, among his recognitions, one of which was the husband
of the person missing, that Lady Gwyther was not there.
Nothing in the whole business was more singular than his
consciousness that, as he came back to his interlocutress
after the nods and smiles and hand-waves he had launched,
she knew what had been his thought. She knew for whom
he had looked without success; but why should this knowledge visibly have hardened and sharpened her, and precisely
at a moment when she was unprecedentedly magnificent?
The indefinable apprehension that had somewhat sunk after
his second talk with Miss Banker and then had perversely
risen again—this nameless anxiety now produced on him, with
a sudden sharper pinch, the effect of a great suspense.
The action of that, in turn, was to show him that he hadn't
yet fully known how much he had at stake on a final view.
It was revealed to him for the first time that he "really
cared" whether Mrs. Grantham were a safe nature. It was
too ridiculous by what a thread it hung, but something was
certainly in the air that would definitely tell him.

What was in the air descended the next moment to
earth. He turned round as he caught the expression with
which her eyes attached themselves to something that approached. A little person, very young and very much
dressed, had come out of the house, and the expression in
Mrs. Grantham's eyes was that of the artist confronted with
her work and interested, even to impatience, in the judge-
ment of others. The little person drew nearer, and though
Sutton's companion, without looking at him now, gave it a
name and met it, he had jumped for himself at certitude.
He saw many things—too many, and they appeared to be
feathers, frills, excrescences of silk and lace—massed together
and conflicting, and after a moment also saw struggling out

of them a small face that struck him as either scared or sick. Then, with his eyes again returning to Mrs. Grantham, he saw another.

He had no more talk with Miss Banker till late that evening—an evening during which he had felt himself too noticeably silent; but something had passed between this pair, across dinner-table and drawing-room, without speech, and when they at last found words it was in the needed ease of a quiet end of the long, lighted gallery, where she opened again at the very paragraph.

"You were right—that *was* it. She did the only thing that, at such short notice, she *could* do. She took her to her dressmaker."

Sutton, with his back to the reach of the gallery, had, as if to banish a vision, buried his eyes for a minute in his hands. "And oh the face—the face!"

"Which?" Miss Banker asked.

"Whichever one looks at."

"But May Grantham's glorious. She has turned herself out—"

"With a splendour of taste and a sense of effect, eh? Yes." Sutton showed he saw far.

"She *has* the sense of effect. The sense of effect as exhibited in Lady Gwyther's clothes—!" was something Miss Banker failed of words to express. "Everybody's overwhelmed. Here, you know, that sort of thing's grave. The poor creature's lost."

"Lost?"

"Since on the first impression, as we said, so much depends. The first impression's made—oh made! I defy her now ever to unmake it. Her husband, who's proud, won't like her the better for it. And I don't see," Miss Banker went on, "that her prettiness *was* enough—a mere little feverish frightened freshness; what *did* he see in her?—to be so blasted. It has been done with an atrocity of art—"

"That supposes the dressmaker then also a devil?"

"Oh your London women and their dressmakers!" Miss Banker laughed.

"But the face—the face!" Sutton woefully repeated.

"May's?"

"The little girl's. It's exquisite."

"Exquisite?"

"For unimaginable pathos."

"Oh!" Miss Banker dropped.

"She has at last begun to see." Sutton showed again how far *he* saw. "It glimmers upon her innocence, she makes it dimly out—what has been done with her. She's even worse this evening—the way, my eye, she looked at dinner!—than when she came. Yes"—he was confident—"it has dawned (how couldn't it, out of all of you?) and she knows."

"She ought to have known before!" Miss Banker intelligently sighed.

"No; she wouldn't in that case have been so beautiful."

"Beautiful?" cried Miss Banker; "overloaded like a monkey in a show!"

"The face, yes; which goes to the heart. It's that that makes it," said Shirley Sutton. "And it's that"—he thought it out—"that makes the other."

"I see. Conscious?"

"Horrible!"

"You take it hard," said Miss Banker.

Lord Gwyther, just before she spoke, had come in sight and now was near them. Sutton on this, appearing to wish to avoid him, reached, before answering his companion's observation, a door that opened close at hand. "So hard," he replied from that point, "that I shall be off tomorrow morning."

"And not see the rest?" she called after him.

But he had already gone, and Lord Gwyther, arriving, amiably took up her question. "The rest of what?"

Miss Banker looked him well in the eyes. "Of Mrs. Grantham's clothes."

A New England Nun

BY MARY E. WILKINS FREEMAN

IT WAS late in the afternoon, and the light was waning. There was a difference in the look of the tree shadows out in the yard. Somewhere in the distance cows were lowing and a little bell was tinkling; now and then a farm-wagon tilted by, and the dust flew; some blue-shirted laborers with shovels over their shoulders plodded past; little swarms of flies were dancing up and down before the people's faces in the soft air. There seemed to be a gentle stir arising over everything for the mere sake of subsidence —a very premonition of rest and hush and night.

This soft diurnal commotion was over Louisa Ellis also. She had been peacefully sewing at her sitting-room window all the afternoon. Now she quilted her needle carefully into her work, which she folded precisely, and laid in a basket with her thimble and thread and scissors. Louisa Ellis could not remember that ever in her life she had mislaid one of these little feminine appurtenances, which had become, from long use and constant association, a very part of her personality.

Louisa tied a green apron round her waist, and got out a flat straw hat with a green ribbon. Then she went into the garden with a little blue crockery bowl, to pick some currants for her tea. After the currants were picked she sat on the back doorstep and stemmed them, collecting the stems carefully in her apron, and afterward throwing them into the hen-coop. She looked sharply at the grass beside the step to see if any had fallen there.

Louisa was slow and still in her movements; it took her a long time to prepare her tea; but when ready it was set forth with as much grace as if she had been a veritable guest to her own self. The little square table stood exactly in the center of the kitchen, and was covered with a starched linen cloth whose border pattern of flowers glistened. Louisa had a damask napkin on her tea-tray, where were arranged a cut-glass tumbler full of teaspoons, a silver cream-pitcher, a china sugar-bowl, and one pink china cup and saucer. Louisa used china every day—something which none of her neighbors did. They whispered about it among themselves. Their daily tables were laid with common crockery, their sets of best china stayed in the parlor closet, and Louisa Ellis was no richer nor better bred than they. Still she would use the china. She had for her supper a glass dish full of sugared currants, a plate of little cakes, and one of light white biscuits. Also a leaf or two of lettuce, which she cut up daintily. Louisa was very fond of lettuce, which she raised to perfection in her little garden. She ate quite heartily, though in a delicate, pecking way; it seemed almost surprising that any considerable bulk of the food should vanish.

After tea she filled a plate with nicely baked thin corn-cakes, and carried them out into the backyard.

"Caesar!" she called. "Caesar! Caesar!"

There was a little rush, and the clank of a chain, and a large yellow-and-white dog appeared at the door of his tiny hut, which was half hidden among the tall grasses and flowers. Louisa patted him and gave him the corn-cakes. Then she returned to the house and washed the tea-things, polishing the china carefully. The twilight had deepened; the chorus of the frogs floated in at the open window wonderfully loud and shrill, and once in a while a long sharp drone from a tree-toad pierced it. Louisa took off her green gingham apron, disclosing a shorter one of pink-and-white print. She lighted her lamp, and sat down again with her sewing.

In about half an hour Joe Dagget came. She heard his heavy step on the walk, and rose and took off her pink-and-white apron. Under that was still another—white linen with a little cambric edging on the bottom; that was Louisa's company apron: She never wore it without her calico sewing-apron over it unless she had a guest. She had barely folded the pink-and-white one with methodical haste and laid it in a table-drawer when the door opened and Joe Dagget entered.

He seemed to fill up the whole room. A little yellow canary that had been asleep in his green cage at the south window woke up and fluttered wildly, beating his little yellow wings against the wires. He always did so when Joe Dagget came into the room.

"Good-evening," said Louisa. She extended her hand with a kind of solemn cordiality.

"Good-evening, Louisa," returned the man, in a loud voice.

She placed a chair for him, and they sat facing each other, with the table between them. He sat bolt-upright, toeing out his heavy feet squarely, glancing with a good-humored uneasiness around the room. She sat gently erect, folding her slender hands in her white-linen lap.

"Been a pleasant day," remarked Dagget.

"Real pleasant," Louisa assented, softly. "Have you been haying?" she asked, after a little while.

"Yes, I've been haying all day, down in the ten-acre lot. Pretty hot work."

"It must be."

"Yes, it's pretty hot work in the sun."

"Is your mother well today?"

"Yes, mother's pretty well."

"I suppose Lily Dyer's with her now?"

Dagget colored. "Yes, she's with her," he answered, slowly.

He was not very young, but there was a boyish look about his large face. Louisa was not quite as old as he, her face was fairer and smoother, but she gave people the impression of being older.

"I suppose she's a good deal of help to your mother," she said, further.

"I guess she is; I don't know how mother'd get along without her," said Dagget, with a sort of embarrassed warmth.

"She looks like a real capable girl. She's pretty-looking too," remarked Louisa.

"Yes, she is pretty fair-looking."

Presently Dagget began fingering the books on the table. There was a square red autograph album, and a Young Lady's Gift-Book which had belonged to Louisa's mother. He took them up one after the other and opened them; then laid them down again, the album on the Gift-Book.

Louisa kept eying them with mild uneasiness. Finally she rose and changed the position of the books, putting the album underneath. That was the way they had been arranged in the first place.

Dagget gave an awkward little laugh. "Now what difference did it make which book was on top?" said he.

Louisa looked at him with a deprecating smile. "I always keep them that way," murmured she.

"You do beat everything," said Dagget, trying to laugh again. His large face was flushed.

He remained about an hour longer, then rose to take leave. Going out, he stumbled over a rug, and, trying to recover himself, hit Louisa's work-basket on the table, and knocked it on the floor.

He looked at Louisa, then at the rolling spools; he ducked himself awkwardly toward them, but she stopped him. "Never mind," said she; "I'll pick them up after you're gone."

She spoke with a mild stiffness. Either she was a little disturbed, or his nervousness affected her, and made her seem constrained in her effort to reassure him.

When Joe Dagget was outside he drew in the sweet evening air with a sigh, and felt much as an innocent and perfectly well-intentioned bear might after his exit from a china shop.

Louisa, on her part, felt much as the kind-hearted, long-

suffering owner of the china shop might have done after
the exit of the bear.

She tied on the pink, then the green apron, picked up
all the scattered treasures and replaced them in her work-
basket, and straightened the rug. Then she set the lamp on
the floor, and began sharply examining the carpet. She
even rubbed her fingers over it, and looked at them.

"He's tracked in a good deal of dust," she murmured. "I
thought he must have."

Louisa got a dustpan and brush, and swept Joe Dagget's
track carefully.

If he could have known it, it would have increased his
perplexity and uneasiness, although it would not have
disturbed his loyalty in the least. He came twice a week to
see Louisa Ellis, and every time, sitting there in her delicately
sweet room, he felt as if surrounded by a hedge of lace.
He was afraid to stir lest he should put a clumsy foot or
hand through the fairy web, and he had always the consciousness that Louisa was watching fearfully lest he
should.

Still the lace and Louisa commanded perforce his perfect
respect and patience and loyalty. They were to be married in a month, after a singular courtship which had lasted
for a matter of fifteen years. For fourteen out of the fifteen
years the two had not once seen each other, and they
had seldom exchanged letters. Joe had been all those
years in Australia, where he had gone to make his fortune,
and where he had stayed until he made it. He would have
stayed fifty years if it had taken so long, and come home
feeble and tottering, or never come home at all, to marry
Louisa.

But the fortune had been made in the fourteen years,
and he had come home now to marry the woman who had
been patiently and unquestioningly waiting for him all that
time.

Shortly after they were engaged he had announced to
Louisa his determination to strike out into new fields, and
secure a competency before they should be married. She
had listened and assented with the sweet serenity which
never failed her, not even when her lover set forth on that
long and uncertain journey. Joe, buoyed up as he was by
his sturdy determination, broke down a little at the last,
but Louisa kissed him with a mild blush, and said good-
by.

"It won't be for long," poor Joe had said, huskily; but it was for fourteen years.

In that length of time much had happened. Louisa's mother and brother had died, and she was all alone in the world. But greatest happening of all—a subtle happening which both were too simple to understand—Louisa's feet had turned into a path, smooth maybe under a calm, serene sky, but so straight and unswerving that it could only meet a check at her grave, and so narrow that there was no room for anyone at her side.

Louisa's first emotion when Joe Dagget came home (he had not apprised her of his coming) was consternation, although she would not admit it to herself, and he never dreamed of it. Fifteen years ago she had been in love with him—at least she considered herself to be. Just at that time, gently acquiescing with and falling into the natural drift of girlhood, she had seen marriage ahead as a reasonable feature and a probable desirability of life. She had listened with calm docility to her mother's views upon the subject. Her mother was remarkable for her cool sense and sweet, even temperament. She talked wisely to her daughter when Joe Dagget presented himself, and Louisa accepted him with no hesitation. He was the first lover she had ever had.

She had been faithful to him all these years. She had never dreamed of the possibility of marrying anyone else. Her life, especially for the last seven years, had been full of a pleasant peace, she had never felt discontented nor impatient over her lover's absence; still she had always looked foward to his return and their marriage as the inevitable conclusion of things. However, she had fallen into a way of placing it so far in the future that it was almost equal to placing it over the boundaries of another life.

When Joe came she had been expecting him, and expecting to be married for fourteen years, but she was as much surprised and taken aback as if she had never thought of it.

Joe's consternation came later. He eyed Louisa with an instant confirmation of his old admiration. She had changed but little. She still kept her pretty manner and soft grace, and was, he considered, every whit as attractive as ever. As for himself, his stint was done; he had turned his face away from fortune-seeking, and the old winds of romance whistled as loud and sweet as ever through his ears. All the song which he had been wont to hear in them was

Louisa; he had for a long time a loyal belief that he heard it still, but finally it seemed to him that although the winds sang always that one song, it had another name. But for Louisa the wind had never more than murmured; now it had gone down, and everything was still. She listened for a little while with half-wistful attention; then she turned quietly away and went to work on her wedding-clothes.

Joe had made some extensive and quite magnificent alterations in his house. It was the old homestead; the newly married couple would live there, for Joe could not desert his mother, who refused to leave her old home. So Louisa must leave hers. Every morning, rising and going about among her neat maidenly possessions, she felt as one looking her last upon the faces of dear friends. It was true that in a measure she could take them with her, but, robbed of their old environments, they would appear in such new guises that they would almost cease to be themselves. Then there were some peculiar features of her happy solitary life which she would probably be obliged to relinquish altogether. Sterner tasks than these graceful but half-needless ones would probably devolve upon her. There would be a large house to care for; there would be company to entertain; there would be Joe's rigorous and feeble old mother to wait upon; and it would be contrary to all thrifty village traditions for her to keep more than one servant. Louisa had a little still, and she used to occupy herself pleasantly in summer weather with distilling the sweet and aromatic essences from roses and peppermint and spearmint. By-and-by her still must be laid away. Her store of essences was already considerable, and there would be no time for her to distil for the mere pleasure of it. Then Joe's mother would think it foolishness; she had already hinted her opinion in the matter. Louise dearly loved to sew a linen seam, not always for use, but for the simple, mild pleasure which she took in it. She would have been loath to confess how more than once she had ripped a seam from the mere delight of sewing it together again. Sitting at her window during long sweet afternoons, drawing her needle gently through the dainty fabric, she was peace itself. But there was small chance of such foolish comfort in the future. Joe's mother, domineering, shrewd old matron that she was even in her old age, and very likely even Joe himself, with his honest masculine rudeness, would laugh and frown down all these pretty but senseless old-maiden ways.

Louisa had almost the enthusiasm of an artist over the mere order and cleanliness of her solitary home. She had throbs of genuine triumph at the sight of the window-panes which she had polished until they shone like jewels. She gloated gently over her orderly bureau-drawers, with their exquisitely folded contents redolent with lavender and sweet clover and very purity. Could she be sure of the endurance of even this? She had visions, so startling that she half repudiated them as indelicate, of coarse masculine belongings strewn about in endless litter; of dust and disorder arising necessarily from a coarse masculine presence in the midst of all this delicate harmony.

Among her forebodings of disturbance, not the least was with regard to Caesar. Caesar was a veritable hermit of a dog. For the greater part of his life he had dwelt in his secluded hut, shut out from the society of his kind and all innocent canine joys. Never had Caesar since his early youth watched at a woodchuck's hole; never had he known the delights of a stray bone at a neighbor's kitchen door. And it was all on account of a sin committed when hardly out of his puppyhood. No one knew the possible depth of remorse of which this mild-visaged, altogether innocent-looking old dog might be capable; but whether or not he had encountered remorse, he had encountered a full measure of righteous retribution. Old Caesar seldom lifted up his voice in a growl or a bark; he was fat and sleepy; there were yellow rings which looked like spectacles around his dim old eyes; but there was a neighbor who bore on his hand the imprint of several of Caesar's sharp, white, youthful teeth, and for that he had lived at the end of a chain, all alone in a little hut, for fourteen years. The neighbor, who was choleric and smarting with the pain of his wound, had demanded either Caesar's death or complete ostracism. So Louisa's brother, to whom the dog had belonged, had built him his little kennel and tied him up. It was now fourteen years since, in a flood of youthful spirits, he had inflicted that memorable bite, and with the exception of short excursions, always at the end of the chain, under the strict guardianship of his master or Louisa, the old dog had remained a close prisoner. It is doubtful if, with his limited ambition, he took much pride in the fact, but it is certain that he was possessed of considerable cheap fame. He was regarded by all the children in the village and by many adults as a very monster of ferocity. St. George's dragon

could hardly have surpassed in evil repute Louisa Ellis's
old yellow dog. Mothers charged their children with solemn
emphasis not to go too near to him, and the children listened and believed greedily, with a fascinated appetite for
terror, and ran by Louisa's house stealthily, with many side-
long and backward glances at the terrible dog. If perchance he sounded a hoarse bark, there was a panic.
Wayfarers chancing into Louisa's yard eyed him with respect, and inquired if the chain were stout. Caesar at
large might have seemed a very ordinary dog, and excited
no comment whatever; chained, his reputation overshadowed
him, so that he lost his own proper outlines and looked
darkly vague and enormous. Joe Dagget, however, with his
good-humored sense and shrewdness, saw him as he was.
He strode valiantly up to him and patted him on the head,
in spite of Louisa's soft clamor of warning, and even attempted to set him loose. Louisa grew so alarmed that he
desisted, but kept announcing his opinion in the matter
quite forcibly at intervals. "There ain't a better-natured dog
in town," he would say, "and it's downright cruel to keep
him tied up there. Some day I'm going to take him out."

Louisa had very little hope that he would not, one
of these days, when their interests and possessions
should be more completely fused in one. She pictured to
herself Caesar on the rampage through the quiet and
unguarded village. She saw innocent children bleeding in his path. She was herself very fond of the old
dog, because he had belonged to her dead brother, and he
was always very gentle with her; still she had great faith
in his ferocity. She always warned people not to go too
near him. She fed him on ascetic fare of corn-mush and
cakes, and never fired his dangerous temper with heating
and sanguinary diet of flesh and bones. Louisa looked at
the old dog munching his simple fare, and thought of her
approaching marriage and trembled. Still no anticipation
of disorder and confusion in lieu of sweet peace and harmony, no forebodings of Caesar on the rampage, no wild
fluttering of her little yellow canary, were sufficient to turn
her a hair's breadth. Joe Dagget had been fond of her and
working for her all these years. It was not for her, whatever came to pass, to prove untrue and break his heart.
She put the exquisite little stitches into her wedding-gar-
ments, and the time went on until it was only a week be-

fore her wedding-day. It was a Tuesday evening, and the wedding was to be a week from Wednesday.

There was a full moon that night. About nine o'clock Louisa strolled down the road a little way. There were harvest-fields on either hand, bordered by low stone walls. Luxuriant clumps of bushes grew beside the wall, and trees—wild cherry and old apple trees—at intervals. Presently Louisa sat down on the wall and looked about her with mildly sorrowful reflectiveness. Tall shrubs of blueberry and meadow-sweet, all woven together and tangled with black-berry vines and horsebriers, shut her in on either side. She had a little clear space between them. Opposite her, on the other side of the road, was a spreading tree; the moon shone between its boughs, and the leaves twinkled like silver. The road was bespread with a beautiful shifting dapple of silver and shadow; the air was full of a mysterious sweetness. "I wonder if it's wild grapes?" murmured Louisa. She sat there some time. She was just thinking of rising, when she heard footsteps and low voices, and remained quiet. It was a lonely place, and she felt a little timid. She thought she would keep still in the shadow and let the persons, whoever they might be, pass her.

But just before they reached her the voices ceased, and the footsteps. She understood that their owners had also found seats upon the stone wall. She was wondering if she could not steal away unobserved, when the voice broke the stillness. It was Joe Dagget's. She sat still and listened.

The voice was announced by a loud sigh, which was as familiar as itself. "Well," said Dagget, "you've made up your mind, then, I suppose?"

"Yes," returned another voice; "I'm going day after to-morrow."

"That's Lily Dyer," thought Louisa to herself. The voice embodied itself in her mind. She saw a girl tall and full-figured, with a firm, fair face, looking fairer and firmer in the moonlight, her strong yellow hair braided in a close knot. A girl full of a calm rustic strength and bloom, with a masterful way which might have beseemed a princess. Lily Dyer was a favorite with the village folk; she had just the qualities to arouse the admiration. She was good and hand-some and smart. Louisa had often heard her praises sounded.

"Well," said Joe Dagget, "I ain't got a word to say."

"I don't know what you could say," returned Lily Dyer.

"Not a word to say," repeated Joe, drawing out the words heavily. Then there was a silence. "I ain't sorry," he began at last, "that that happened yesterday—that we kind of let on how we felt to each other. I guess it's just as well we knew. Of course, I can't do anything any different. I'm going right on an' get married next week. I ain't going back on a woman that's waited for me fourteen years, an' break her heart."

"If you should jilt her tomorrow, I wouldn't have you," spoke up the girl, with sudden vehemence.

"Well, I ain't going to give you the chance," said he; "but I don't believe you would, either."

"You'd see I wouldn't. Honor's honor, an' right's right. An' I'd never think anything of any man that went against 'em for me or any other girl; you'd find that out, Joe Dagget."

"Well, you'll find out fast enough that I ain't going against 'em for you or any other girl," returned he. Their voices sounded almost as if they were angry with each other. Louisa was listening eagerly.

"I'm sorry you feel as if you must go away," said Joe, "but I don't know but it's best."

"Of course it's best. I hope you and I have got common-sense."

"Well, I suppose you're right." Suddenly Joe's voice got an undertone of tenderness. "Say, Lily," said he, "I'll get along well enough myself, but I can't bear to think— You don't suppose you're going to fret much over it?"

"I guess you'll find out I sha'n't fret much over a married man."

"Well, I hope you won't—I hope you won't, Lily. God knows I do. And—I hope—one of these days—you'll—come across somebody else—"

"I don't see any reason why I shouldn't." Suddenly her tone changed. She spoke in a sweet, clear voice, so loud that she could have been heard across the street. "No, Joe Dagget," said she, "I'll never marry any other man as long as I live. I've got good sense, an' I ain't going to break my heart nor make a fool of myself; but I'm never going to be married, you can be sure of that. I ain't that sort of a girl to feel this way twice."

Louisa heard an exclamation and a soft commotion behind the bushes; then Lily spoke again—the voice sounded as if she had risen. "This must be put a stop to," said she. "We've stayed here long enough. I'm going home."

Louisa sat there in a daze, listening to their retreating steps. After a while she got up and slunk softly home herself. The next day she did her housework methodically; that was as much a matter of course as breathing; but she did not sew on her wedding-clothes. She sat at her window and meditated. In the evening Joe came. Louisa Ellis had never known that she had any diplomacy in her, but when she came to look for it that night she found it, although meek of its kind, among her little feminine weapons. Even now she could hardly believe that she had heard aright, and that she would not do Joe a terrible injury should she break her troth-plight. She wanted to sound him without betraying too soon her own inclinations in the matter. She did it successfully, and they finally came to an understanding; but it was a difficult thing, for he was as afraid of betraying himself as she.

She never mentioned Lily Dyer. She simply said that while she had no cause of complaint against him, she had lived so long in one way that she shrank from making a change.

"Well, I never shrank, Louisa," said Dagget. "I'm going to be honest enough to say that I think maybe it's better this way; but if you'd wanted to keep on, I'd have stuck to you till my dying day. I hope you know that."

"Yes, I do," said she.

That night she and Joe parted more tenderly than they had done for a long time. Standing in the door, holding each other's hands, a last great wave of regretful memory swept over them.

"Well, this ain't the way we've thought it was all going to end, is it, Louisa?" said Joe.

She shook her head. There was a little quiver on her placid face.

"You let me know if there's ever anything I can do for you," said he. "I ain't ever going to forget you, Louisa." Then he kissed her, and went down the path. Louisa, all alone by herself that night, wept a little, she hardly knew why; but the next morning, on waking, she felt like a queen who, after fearing lest her domain be wrested away from her, sees it firmly insured in her possession.

Now the tall weeds and grasses might cluster around Caesar's little hermit hut, the snow might fall on its roof year in and year out, but he never would go on a rampage through the unguarded village. Now the little canary might

turn itself into a peaceful yellow ball night after night, and
have no need to wake and flutter with wild terror against
its bars. Louisa could sew linen seams, and distil roses, and
dust and polish and fold away in lavender, as long as she
listed. That afternoon she sat with her needlework at the
window, and felt fairly steeped in peace. Lily Dyer, tall and
erect and blooming, went past; but she felt no qualm. If
Louisa Ellis had sold her birthright she did not know it, the
taste of the pottage was so delicious, and had been her sole
satisfaction for so long. Serenity and placid narrowness had
become to her as the birthright itself. She gazed ahead
through a long reach of future days strung together like pearls
in a rosary, every one like the others, and all smooth and
flawless and innocent, and her heart went up in thankful-
ness. Outside was the fervid summer afternoon; the air was
filled with the sounds of the busy harvest of men and birds
and bees; there were halloos, metallic clatterings, sweet
calls, and long hummings. Louisa sat, prayerfully numbering
her days, like an uncloistered nun.

The Courting of Sister Wisby

BY SARAH ORNE JEWETT

ALL THE morning there had been an increasing temptation
to take an outdoor holiday, and early in the afternoon the
temptation outgrew my power of resistance. A far away pasture on the long southwestern slope of a high hill was per-
sistently present to my mind, yet there seemed to be no particular reason why I should think of it. I was not sure that
I wanted anything from the pasture, and there was no sign,
except the temptation, that the pasture wanted anything of
me. But I was on the farther side of as many as three fences
before I stopped to think again where I was going, and why.

There is no use in trying to tell another person about that
afternoon unless he distinctly remembers weather exactly
like it. No number of details concerning an Arctic ice
blockade will give a single shiver to a child of the tropics.
This was one of those perfect New England days in late
summer, when the spirit of autumn takes a first stealthy
flight, like a spy, through the ripening countryside, and,

with feigned sympathy for those who droop with August heat, puts her cool cloak of bracing air about leaf and flower and human shoulders. Every living thing grows suddenly cheerful and strong; it is only when you catch sight of a horror-stricken little maple in swampy soil—a little maple that has second-sight and fore-knowledge of coming disaster to her race—only then does a distrust of autumn's friendliness dim your joyful satisfaction.

In the midwinter there is always a day when one has the first foretaste of spring; in late August there is a morning when the air is for the first time autumn-like. Perhaps it is a hint to the squirrels to get in their first supplies for the winter hoards, or a reminder that summer will soon end, and everybody had better make the most of it. We are always looking forward to the passing and ending of winter, but when summer is here it seems as if summer must always last. As I went across the fields that day, I found myself half lamenting that the world must fade again, even that the best of her budding and bloom was only a preparation for another springtime, for an awakening beyond the coming winter's sleep.

The sun was slightly veiled; there was a chattering group of birds, which had gathered for a conference about their early migration. Yet, oddly enough, I heard the voice of a belated bobolink, and presently saw him rise from the grass and hover leisurely, while he sang a brief tune. He was much behind time if he were still a housekeeper; but as for the other birds who listened, they cared only for their own notes. An old crow went sagging by, and gave a croak at his despised neighbor, just as a black reviewer croaked at Keats —so hard it is to be just to one's contemporaries. The bobolink was indeed singing out of season, and it was impossible to say whether he really belonged most to this summer or to the next. He might have been delayed on his northward journey; at any rate, he had a light heart now, to judge from his song, and I wished that I could ask him a few questions— how he liked being the last man among the bobolinks, and where he had taken singing lessons in the South.

Presently I left the lower fields, and took a path that led higher, where I could look beyond the village to the northern country mountainward. Here the sweet fern grew thick and fragrant, and I also found myself heedlessly treading on pennyroyal. Nearby, in a field corner, I long ago made a most comfortable seat by putting a stray piece of board and bit of rail across the angle of the fences. I have spent many a delightful hour there, in the shade and shelter of a young pitch pine and a wild cherry tree, with a lovely outlook toward the village, just far enough away beyond the green slopes and tall elms of the lower meadows. But that day I still had the feeling of being outward bound, and did not turn aside nor linger. The high pasture land grew more and more enticing.

I stopped to pick some blackberries that twinkled at me like beads among their dry vines, and two or three yellow-birds fluttered up from the leaves of a thistle and then came back again, as if they had complacently discovered that I was only an overgrown yellowbird, in strange disguise but perfectly harmless. They made me feel as if I were an intruder, though they did not offer to peck at me, and we parted company very soon. It was good to stand at last on the great shoulder of the hill. The wind was coming in from the sea, there was a fine fragrance from the pines, and the air grew sweeter every moment. I took new pleasure in the thought that in a piece of wild pasture land like this one may get closest to Nature, and subsist upon what she gives of her own free will. There have been no drudging, heavy-shod ploughmen to overturn the soil, and vex it into yielding artificial crops. Here one has to take just what Nature is pleased to give, whether one is a yellowbird or a human being. It is very good entertainment for a summer wayfarer, and I am asking my reader now to share the winter provision which I harvested that day. Let us hope that the small birds are also faring well after their fashion, but I give them an anxious thought while the snow goes hurrying in long waves across the buried fields, this windy winter night.

I next went farther down the hill, and got a drink of fresh cool water from the brook, and pulled a tender sheaf of sweet flag beside it. The mossy old fence just beyond was the last barrier between me and the pasture which had sent an invisible messenger earlier in the day, but I saw that somebody else had come first to the rendezvous: there was a brown gingham cape-bonnet and a sprigged shoulder-shawl bobbing up and down, a little way off among the junipers. I had taken such uncommon pleasure in being alone that I instantly felt a sense of disappointment; then a warm glow of pleasant satisfaction rebuked my selfishness. This could be no one but dear old Mrs. Goodsoe, the friend of my

childhood and fond dependence of my maturer years. I
had not seen her for many weeks, but here she was, out on
one of her famous campaigns for herbs, or perhaps just
returning from a blueberrying expedition. I approached
with care, so as not to startle the gingham bonnet; but she
heard the rustle of the bushes against my dress, and looked
up quickly, as she knelt, bending over the turf. In that position she was hardly taller than the luxuriant junipers themselves.

"I'm a-gittin' in my mulleins," she said briskly, "an' I've
been thinking o' you these twenty times since I come out o'
the house. I begun to believe you must ha' forgot me at
last."

"I have been away from home," I explained. "Why don't
you get in your pennyroyal too? There's a great plantation
of it beyond the next fence but one."

"Pennyr'yall" repeated the dear little old woman, with an
air of compassion for inferior knowledge; "'tain't the right
time, darlin'. Pennyr'yal's too rank now. But for mulleins
this day is prime. I've got a dreadful graspin' fit for 'em
this year; seems if I must be goin' to need 'em extry. I feel
like the squirrels must when they know a hard winter's
comin'." And Mrs. Goodsoe bent over her work again, while
I stood by and watched her carefully cut the best full-
grown leaves with a clumsy pair of scissors, which might
have served through at least half a century of herb-gather-
ing. They were fastened to her apron strings by a long piece
of list.

"I'm going to take my jack-knife and help you," I suggested, with some fear of refusal. "I just passed a flourishing
family of six or seven heads that must have been growing
on purpose for you."

"Now be keerful, dear heart," was the anxious response;
"choose 'em well. There's odds in mulleins same's there is
in angels. Take a plant that's all run up to stalk, and there
ain't but little goodness in the leaves. This one I'm at now
must ha' been stepped on by some creatur and blighted of
its bloom, and the leaves is han'some! When I was small
I used to have a notion that Adam an' Eve must ha' took
mulleins fer their winter wear. Ain't they just like flannel,
for all the world? I've had experience, and I know there's
plenty of sickness might be saved to folks if they'd quit horse-
radish and such fiery, exasperating things, and use mullein
drarves in proper season. Now I shall spread these an' dry

'em nice on my spare floor in the garrit, an' come to steam
'em for use along in the winter there'll be the valley of the
whole summer's goodness in 'em, sartin." And she snipped
away with the dull scissors while I listened respectfully,
and took great pains to have my part of the harvest present
a good appearance.

"This is most too dry a head," she added presently, a little
out of breath. "There! I can tell you there's win'rows o'
young doctors, bilin' over with book-larnin', that is truly ignorant of what to do for the sick, or how to p'int out those
paths that well people foller toward sickness. Book-fools
I call 'em, them young men, an' some on 'em never'll live
to know much better, if they git to be Methuselahs. In my
time every middle-aged woman who had brought up a family had some proper ideas of dealin' with complaints. I
won't say but there was some fools amongst *them*, but I'd
rather take my chances, unless they'd forsook herbs and
gone to dealin' with patent stuff. Now my mother really did
sense the use of herbs and roots. I never see anybody that
come up to her. She was a meek-looking woman, but very
understandin', mother was."

"Then that's where you learned so much yourself, Mrs.
Goodsoe," I ventured to say.

"Bless your heart, I don't hold a candle to her; 'tis but
little I can recall of what she used to say. No, her larnin'
died with her," said my friend, in a self-deprecating tone.
"Why, there was as many as twenty kinds of roots alone that
she used to keep by her, that I forgot the use of; an' I'm
sure I shouldn't know where to find the most of 'em, any.
There was an herb"—*airb* she called it—"an herb called
Pennsylvany; and she used to think everything of nobleliver-
wort, but I never could seem to get the right effects from it,
as she could. Though I don't know as she ever really did use
masterwort where somethin' else wouldn't ha' served. She
had a cousin married out in Pennsylvany that used to take
pains to get it to her every year or two, and so she felt
'twas important to have it. Some set more by such things as
come from a distance, but I rec'lect mother always used to
maintain that folks was meant to be doctored with the stuff
that grew right about 'em; 'twas sufficient, an' so ordered.
That was before the whole population took to livin' on
wheels, the way they do now. 'Twas never my idee that
we was meant to know what's goin' on all over the world

to once. There's goin' to be some sort of a set-back one o' these days, with these telegraphs an' things, an' letters comin' every hand's turn, and folks leavin' their proper work to answer 'em. I may not live to see it. 'Twas allowed to be difficult for folks to git about in old times, or to git word across the country, and they stood in their lot an' place, and weren't all just alike, either, same as pine-spills."

We were kneeling side by side now, as if in penitence for the march of progress, but we laughed as we turned to look at each other.

"Do you think it did much good when everybody brewed a cracked quart mug of herb-tea?" I asked, walking away on my knees to a new mullein.

"I've always lifted my voice against the practice, far's I could," declared Mrs. Goodsoe; "an' I won't deal out none o' the herbs I save for no such nonsense. There was three houses along our road—I call no names—where you couldn't go into the livin' room without findin' a mess o' herb-tea drorin' on the stove or side o' the fireplace, winter or summer, sick or well. One was thoroughwut, one would be camomile, and the other, like as not, yellow dock; but they all used to put in a little new rum to git out the goodness, or keep it from spilin'." (Mrs. Goodsoe favored me with a knowing smile.) "Land, how mother used to laugh! But, poor creatures, they had to work hard, and I guess it never done 'em a mite o' harm; they was all good herbs. I wish you could hear the quawkin' there used to be when they was indulged with a real case o' sickness. Everybody would collect from far an' near; you'd see 'em coming along the road and across the pastures then; everybody clamorin' that nothin' would do no kind o' good but her choice o' teas or drarves to the feet. I wonder there was a babe lived to grow up in the whole lower part o' the town; an' if nothin' else 'peared to ail 'em, word was passed about that 'twas likely Mis' So-and-So's last young one was goin' to be foolish. Land, how they'd gather! I know one day the doctor come to Widder Peck's and the house was crammed so't he could scercely git inside the door; and he says, just as polite, 'Do send for some of the neighbors!' as if there wa'n't a soul to turn to, right or left. You'd ought to seen 'em begin to scatter."

"But don't you think the cars and telegraphs have given people more to interest them, Mrs. Goodsoe? Don't you be-

lieve people's lives were narrower then, and more taken up
with little things?" I asked, unwisely, being a product of
modern times.

"Not one mite, dear," said my companion stoutly. "There
was as big thoughts then as there is now; these times was
born o' them. The difference is in folks themselves; but
now, instead o' doin' their own housekeepin' and watchin'
their own neighbors—though that was carried to excess—
they git word that a niece's child is ailin' the other side o'
Massachusetts, and they drop everything and git on their
best clothes, and off they jiggit in the cars. 'Tis a bad
sign when folks wear out their best clothes faster 'n they do
their everyday ones. The other side o' Massachusetts has
got to look after itself by rights. An' besides that, Sunday-
keepin's all gone out o' fashion. Some lays it to one thing
an' some another, but some o' them old ministers that
folks are all a-sighin' for did preach a lot o' stoff that wa'n't
nothin' but chaff; 'twa'n't the word o' God out o' either
Old Testament or New. But everybody went to meetin'
and heard it, and come home, and was set to fightin' with
their next door neighbor over it. Now I'm a believer, and I
try to live a Christian life, but I'd as soon hear a surveyor's
book read out, figgers an' all, as try to get any simple
truth out o' most sermons. It's them as is most to blame."

"What was the matter that day at Widow Peck's?" I hastened to ask, for I knew by experience that the good, clear
minded soul beside me was apt to grow unduly vexed
and distressed when she contemplated the state of religious
teaching.

"Why, there wa'n't nothin' the matter, only a gal o' Miss
Peck's had met with a dis'pintment and had gone into
screechin' fits. 'Twas a rovin' creatur that had come along
hayin' time, and he'd gone off an' forsook her betwixt two
days; nobody ever knew what become of him. Them Pecks
was 'Good Lord, anybody!' kind o' gals, an took up with
whoever they could get. One of 'em married Heron, the
Irishman; they lived in that little house that was burnt this
summer, over on the edge o' the plains. He was a good-
hearted creatur, with a laughin' eye and a clever word for
everybody. He was the first Irishman that ever came this
way, and we was all for gettin' a look at him, when he first
used to go by. Mother's folks was what they call Scotch-
Irish, though; there was an old race of 'em settled about
here. They could foretell events, some on 'em, and had sec-

ond-sight. I know folks used to say mother's grandmother had them gifts, but mother was never free to speak about it to us. She remembered her well, too."

"I suppose that you mean old Jim Heron, who was such a famous fiddler?" I asked with great interest, for I am always delighted to know more about that rustic hero, parochial Orpheus that he must have been!

"Now, dear heart, I suppose you don't remember him, do you?" replied Mrs. Goodsoe, earnestly. "Fiddle! He'd about break your heart with them tunes of his, or else set your heels flyin' up the floor in a jig, though you was minister o' the First Parish and all wound up for a funeral prayer. I tell ye there win't no tunes sounds like them used to. It used to seem to me summer nights when I was comin' along the plains road, and he set by the window playin', as if there was a bewitched human creatur in that old red fiddle o' his. He could make it sound just like a woman's voice tellin' somethin' over and over, as if folks could help her out o' her sorrows if she could only make 'em understand. I've set by the stone wall and cried as if my heart was broke, and dear knows it wa'n't in them days. How he would twirl off them jigs and dance tunes! He used to make somethin' han'some out of 'em in fall an' winter, playin' at huskins and dancin' parties; but he was unstiddy by spells, as he got along in years, and never knew what it was to be forehanded. Everybody felt bad when he died; you couldn't help likin' the creatur. He'd got the gift—that's all you could say about it.

"There was a Mis' Jerry Foss, that lived over by the brook bridge, on the plains road, that had lost her husband early, and was left with three chil'n. She set the world by 'em, and was a real pleasant, ambitious little woman, and was workin' on as best she could with that little farm, when there come a rage o' scarlet fever, and her boy and two girls was swept off and laid dead within the same week. Everyone o' the neighbors did what they could, but she'd had no sleep since they was taken sick, and after the funeral she set there just like a piece o' marble, and would only shake her head when you spoke to her. They all thought her reason would go; and 'twould certain, if she couldn't have shed tears. An' one o' the neighbors—'twas like mother's sense, but it might have been somebody else—spoke o' Jim Heron. Mother an' one or two o' the women that knew her best was in the house with her. 'Twas right in the edge o' the woods and some of us younger ones was over by the wall on the other side of the road where there was a couple of old willows—I remember just how the brook damp felt—and we kept quiet's we could, and some other folks come along down the road, and stood waitin' on the little bridge, hopin' somebody'd come out, I suppose, and they'd git news. Everybody was wrought up, and felt a good deal for her, you know. By an' by Jim Heron come stealin' right out o' the shadows an' set down on the doorstep, an' 'twas a good while before we heard a sound; then, oh, dear me! 'twas what the whole neighborhood felt for that mother all spoke in the notes, an' they told me afterwards that Mis' Foss's face changed in a minute, and she come right over 'n got into my mother's lap—she was a little woman—an' laid her head down, and there she cried herself into a blessed sleep. After awhile one o' the other women stole out an' told the folks, and we all went home. He only played that one tune.

"But there!" resumed Mrs. Goodsoe, after a silence, during which my eyes were filled with tears. "His wife always complained that the fiddle made her nervous. She never 'peared to think nothin' o' poor Heron after she'd once got him."

"That's often the way," I said, with harsh cynicism, though I had no guilty person in my mind at the moment; and we went straying off, not very far apart, up through the pasture. Mrs. Goodsoe cautioned me that we must not get so far off that we could not get back the same day. The sunshine began to feel very hot on our backs, and we both turned toward the shade. We had already collected a large bundle of mullein leaves, which were carefully laid into a clean, calico apron, held together by the four corners, and proudly carried by me, though my companion regarded them with anxious eyes. We sat down together at the edge of the pine woods, and Mrs. Goodsoe proceeded to fan herself with her limp cape-bonnet.

"I declare, how hot it is! The east wind's all gone again," she said. "It felt so cool this forenoon that I overburdened myself with as thick a petticoat as any I've got. I'm despri't afeared of having a chill, now that I ain't so young as once. I hate to be housed up."

"It's only August, after all," I assured her unnecessarily, confirming my statement by taking two peaches out of my pocket, and laying them side by side on the brown pine needles between us.

"Dear sakes alive!" exclaimed the old lady, with evident pleasure. "Where did you get them, now? Doesn't anything taste twice better out-o'-doors? I ain't had such a peach for years. Do le's keep the stones, an' I'll plant 'em; it only takes four years for a peach pit to come to bearing, an' I guess I'm good for four years, 'thout I meet with some accident."

I could not help agreeing, or taking a fond look at the thin little figure, and her winkled brown face and kind, twinkling eyes. She looked as if she had properly dried herself, by mistake, with some of her mullein leaves, and was likely to keep her goodness, and to last the longer in consequence. There never was a truer, simple-hearted soul made out of the old-fashioned country dust than Mrs. Goodsoe. I thought, as I looked away from her across the wide country, that nobody was left in any of the farmhouses so original, so full of rural wisdom and reminiscence, so really able and dependable, as she. And nobody had made better use of her time in a world foolish enough to sometimes undervalue medicinal herbs.

When we had eaten our peaches we still sat under the pines, and I was not without pride when I had poked about in the ground with a little twig, and displayed to my crony a long fine root, bright yellow to the eye, and a wholesome bitter to the taste.

"Yis, dear, goldthread," she assented indulgently. "Seems to me there's more of it than anything except grass an' hardtack. Good for canker, but no better than two or three other things I can call to mind; but I always lay in a good wisp of it, for old times' sake. Now, I want to know why you should ha' bit it, and took away all the taste o' your nice peach? I was just thinkin' what a han'some entertainment we've had. I've got so I 'sociate certain things with certain folks, and goldthread was somethin' Lizy Wisby couldn't keep house without, no ways whatever. I believe she took so much it kind o' puckered her disposition."

"Lizy Wisby?" I repeated inquiringly.

"You knew her, if ever, by the name of Mis' Deacon Brimblecom," answered my friend, as if this were only a brief preface to further information, so I waited with respectful expectation. Mrs. Goodsoe had grown tired out in the sun, and a good story would be an excuse for sufficient rest. It was a most lovely place where we sat, halfway up the long hillside; for my part, I was perfectly contented and happy. "You've often heard of Deacon Brimblecom?" she asked, as if a great deal depended upon his being properly introduced.

"I remember him," said I. "They called him Deacon Brimfull, you know, and he used to go about with a witch-hazel branch to show people where to dig wells."

"That's the one," said Mrs. Goodsoe, laughing. "I didn't know's you could go so far back. I'm always divided between whether you can remember everything I can, or are only a babe in arms."

"I have a dim recollection of there being something strange about their marriage," I suggested, after a pause, which began to appear dangerous. I was so much afraid the subject would be changed.

"I can tell you all about it," I was quickly answered. "Deacon Brimblecom was very pious accordin' to his lights in his early years. He lived way back in the country then, and there come a rovin' preacher along, and set everybody up that way all by the ears. I've heard the old folks talk it over, but I forget most of his doctrine, except some of his followers was persuaded they could dwell among the angels while yet on airth, and this Deacon Brimfull, as you call him, felt sure he was called by the voice of a spirit bride. So he left a good, deservin' wife he had, an' four children, and built him a new house over to the other side of the land he'd had from his father. They didn't take much pains with the buildin', because they expected to be translated before long, and then the spirit brides and·them folks was goin' to appear and divide up the airth amongst 'em, and the world's folks and on-believers was goin' to serve 'em or be sent to torments. They had meetin's about in the schoolhouses, an' all sorts o' goin's on; some on 'em went crazy, but the deacon held on to what wits he had, an' by an' by the spirit bride didn't turn out to be much of a housekeeper, an' he had always been used to good livin', so he sneaked home ag'in. One o' mother's sisters married up to Ash Hill, where it all took place; that's how I come to have the particulars."

"Then how did he come to find his Eliza Wisby?" I inquired. "Do tell me the whole story; you've got mullein leaves enough."

"There's all yesterday's at home, if I haven't," replied Mrs. Goodsoe. "The way he come a-courtin' o' Sister Wisby was this: she went a-courtin' o' him.

"There was a spell he lived to home, and then his poor wife died, and he had a spirit bride in good earnest, an' the child'n was placed about with his folks and hers, for they was both out o' good families; and I don't know what come over him, but he had another pious fit that looked for all the world like the real thing. He hadn't no family cares, and he lived with his brother's folks, and turned his land in with theirs. He used to travel to every meetin' an' conference that was within reach of his old sorrel hoss's feeble legs; he j'ined the Christian Baptists that was just in their early prime, and he was a great exhorter, and got to be called deacon, though I guess he wa'n't deacon, 'less it was for a spare hand when deacon times was scarcer'n usual. An' one time there was a four-days' protracted meetin' to the church in the lower part of the town. 'Twas a real solemn time; somethin' more'n usual was goin' forward, an' they collected from the whole country round. Women folks liked it, an' the men too; it give 'em a change, an' they was quartered round free, same as conference folks now. Some on 'em, for a joke, sent Silas Brimblecom up to Lizy Wisby's, though she'd give out she couldn't accommodate nobody, because of expectin' her cousin's folks. Everybody knew 'twas a lie; she was amazin' close considerin' she had plenty to do with. There was a streak that wa'n't just right somewheres in Lizy's wits, I always thought. She was very kind in case o' sickness, I'll say that for her.

"You know where the house is, over there on what they call Windy Hill? There the deacon went, all unsuspectin', and 'stead o' Lizy's resentin' of him she put in her own hoss, and they come back together to evenin' meetin'. She was prominent among the sect herself, an' he bawled and talked, and she bawled and talked, an' took up more'n the time allotted in the exercises, just as if they was showin' off to each what they was able to do at expoundin'. Everybody was laughin' at 'em after the meetin' broke up, and that next day an' the next, an' all through, they was constant, and seemed to be havin' a beautiful occasion. Lizy had always give out she scorned the men, but when she got a chance at a particular one 'twas altogether different, and the deacon seemed to please her somehow or 'nother, and— There! you don't want to listen to this old stuff that's past an' gone?"

"Oh, yes, I do," said I.

"I run on like a clock that's onset her striking hand," said

Mrs. Goodsoe mildly. "Sometimes my kitchen timepiece goes on half the forenoon, and I says to myself the day before yesterday I would let it be a warnin', and keep it in mind for a check on my own speech. The next news that was heard was that the deacon an' Lizy—well, opinions differed which of 'em had spoke first, but them fools settled it before the protracted meetin' was over, and give away their hearts before he started for home. They considered 'twould be wise, though, considerin' their short acquaintance, to take one another on trial a spell; 'twas Lizy's notion, and she asked him why he wouldn't come over and stop with her till spring, and then, if both continued to like, they could git married any time 'twas convenient. Lizy, she come and talked it over with mother, and mother disliked to offend her, but she spoke pretty plain; and Lizy felt hurt, an' thought they was showin' excellent judgment, so much harm come from hasty unions and folks comin' to a realizin' sense of each other's failin's when 'twas too late.

"So one day our folks saw Deacon Brimfull a-ridin' by with a gre't coopful of hens in the back o' his wagon, and bundles o' stuff tied to top and hitched to the exes underneath; and he riz a hymn just as he passed the house, and was speedin' the old sorrel with a willer switch. 'Twas most Thanksgivin' time, an' sooner'n she expected him. New Year's was the time she set; but he thought he'd come while the roads was fit for wheels. They was out to meetin' together Thanksgivin' Day, an' that used to be a gre't season for marryin'; so the young folks nudged each other, and some on 'em ventured to speak to the couple as they come down the aisle. Lizy carried it off real well; she wa'n't afraid o' what nobody said or thought, and so home they went. They'd got out her yaller sleigh and her hoss; she never would ride after the deacon's poor old creatur, and I believe it died long o' the winter from stiffenin' up.

"Yes," said Mrs. Goodsoe, emphatically, after we had silently considered the situation for a short space of time, "yes, there was consider'ble talk, now I tell you! The raskil boys pestered 'em just about to death for a while. They used to collect up there an' rap on the winders, and they'd turn out all the deacon's hens 'long at nine o'clock o' night, and chase 'em all over the dingle; an' one night they even lugged the pig right out o' the sty, and shoved it into the back entry, an' run for their lives. They'd stuffed its mouth full o' somethin,' so it couldn't squeal till it got there. There

wa'n't a sign o' nobody to be seen when Lizy hasted out
with the light, and she an' the deacon had to persuade the
creatur back as best they could; 'twas a cold night, and they
said it took 'em till towards mornin'. You see the deacon
was just the kind of a man that a hog wouldn't budge for;
it takes a masterful man to deal with a hog. Well, there
was no end to the works nor the talk, but Lizy left 'em
pretty much alone. She did 'pear kind of dignified about it,
I must say!"

"And then, were they married in the spring?"

"I was tryin' to remember whether it was just before
Fast Day or just after," responded my friend, with a careful
look at the sun, which was nearer the west than either of
us had noticed. "I think likely 'twas along in the last o' April,
anyway some of us looked out o' the window one Monday
mornin' early, and says, 'For goodness' sake! Lizy's sent the
deacon home again!' His old sorrel havin' passed away, he
was ridin' in Ezry Welsh's hoss-cart, with his hen-coop and
more bundles than he had when he come, and looked as
meechin' as ever you see. Ezry was drivin', and he let a
glance fly swiftly round to see if any of us was lookin'
out; an' then I declare if he didn't have the malice to turn
right in towards the barn, where he see my oldest brother,
Joshuay, an' says he real natural, 'Joshuay, just step out
with your wrench. I believe I hear my kingbolt rattlin'
kind o' loose.' Brother, he went out an' took in the sitooation,
an' the deacon bowed kind of stiff. Joshuay was so full o'
laugh, and Ezry Welsh, that they couldn't look one another
in the face. There wa'n't nothing ailed the kingbolt, you
know, an' when Josh riz up he says, 'Goin' up country
for a spell, Mr. Brimblecom?'

"'I be,' says the deacon, lookin' dreadful mortified and
cast down.

"'Ain't things turned out well with you an' Sister Wisby?'
says Joshuay. 'You had ought to remember that the woman
is the weaker vessel.'

"'Hang her, let her carry less sail, then!' the deacon bu'st
out, and he stood right up an' shook his fist there by the
hen-coop, he was so mad; an' Ezry's hoss was a young creatur, an' started up and set the deacon right over backwards
into the chips. We didn't know but he'd broke his neck;
but when he see the women folks runnin' out he jumped
up quick as a cat, an' clim into the cart, an' off they went.
Ezry said he told him that he couldn't git along with Lizy,

she was so fractious in thundery weather; if there was a rumble in the daytime she must go right to bed an' screech, and 'twas night she must git right up an' go an' call him out of a sound sleep. But everybody knew he'd never gone home unless she'd sent him.

"Somehow they made it up ag'in, him an' Lizy, and she had him back. She's been countin' all along on not havin' to hire nobidy to work about the gardin' an' so on, an' she said she wa'nt' goin' to let him have a whole winter's board for nothin'. So the old hens was moved back, and they was married right off fair an' square, an' I don't know but they got along well as most folks. He brought his youngest girl down to live with 'em after a while, an' she was a real treasure to Lizy; everybody spoke well o' Phœbe Brimblecom. The deacon got over his pious fit, and there was consider'ble work in him if you kept right after him. He was an amazin' cider-drinker, and he airnt the name you know him by in his latter days. Lizy never trusted him with nothin', but she kep' him well. She left everything she owned to Phœbe, when she died, 'cept somethin' to satisfy the law. There, they're all gone now; seems to me sometimes, when I get thinkin', as if I'd lived a thousand years!"

I laughed, but I found Mrs. Goodsoe's thoughts had taken a serious turn.

"There, I come by some old graves down here in the lower edge of the pasture," she said as we rose to go. "I couldn't help thinking how I should like to be laid right out in the pasture ground, when my time comes; it looked sort o' comfortable, and I have ranged these slopes so many summers. Seems as if I could see right up through the turf and tell when the weather was pleasant, and get the goodness o' the sweet fern. Now, dear, just hand me my apernful o' mulleins out o' the shade. I hope you won't come to need none this winter, but I'll dry some special for you."

"I'm going by the road," said I, "or else by the path across the meaows, so I will walk as far as the house with you. Aren't you pleased with my company?" for she demurred at my going the least bit out of the way.

So we strolled towards the little gray house, with our plunder of mullein leaves slung on a stick which we carried between us. Of course I went in to make a call, as if I had not seen my hostess before; she is the last maker of muster-gingerbread, and before I came away I was kindly measured for a pair of mittens.

"You'll be sure to come an' see them two peach trees after I get 'em well growin'?" Mrs. Goodsoe called after me when I had said good-by, and was almost out of hearing down the road.

The Dilettante

BY EDITH WHARTON

IT WAS on an impulse hardly needing the arguments he found himself advancing in its favour, that Thursdale, on his way to the club, turned as usual into Mrs. Vervain's street.

The "as usual" was his own qualification of the act; a convenient way of bridging the interval—in days and other sequences—that lay between this visit and the last. It was characteristic of him that he instinctively excluded his call two days earlier, with Ruth Gaynor, from the list of his visits to Mrs. Vervain: the special conditions attending it had made it no more like a visit to Mrs. Vervain than an engraved dinner invitation is like a personal letter. Yet it was to talk over his call with Miss Gaynor that he was now returning to the scene of that episode; and it was because Mrs. Vervain could be trusted to handle the talking over as skilfully as the interview itself that, at her corner, he had felt the dilettante's irresistible craving to take a last look at a work of art that was passing out of his possession.

On the whole, he knew no one better fitted to deal with the unexpected than Mrs. Vervain. She excelled in the rare art of taking things for granted, and Thursdale felt a pardonable pride in the thought that she owed her excellence to his training. Early in his career Thursdale had made the mistake, at the outset of his acquaintance with a lady, of telling her that he loved her and exacting the same avowal in return. The latter part of that episode had been like the long walk back from a picnic, when one has to carry all the crockery one has finished using: it was the last time Thursdale ever allowed himself to be encumbered with the débris of a feast. He thus incidentally learned that the privilege of loving her is one of the least favours that a charming woman can accord; and in seeking to avoid the pitfalls of sentiment he had developed a science of evasion in which the woman of the moment became a mere implement of the game. He owed a great deal of delicate enjoyment to the cultivation of this art. The perils from which it had been his refuge became naïvely harmless: was it possible that he who now took his easy way along the levels had once preferred to gasp on the raw heights of emotion? Youth is a high-coloured season; but he had the satisfaction of feeling that he had entered earlier than most into that *chiaro-oscuro* of sensation where every half-tone has its value.

As a promoter of this pleasure no one he had known was comparable to Mrs. Vervain. He had taught a good many women not to betray their feelings, but he had never before had such fine material to work in. She had been surprisingly crude when he first knew her; capable of making the most awkward inferences, of plunging through thin ice, of recklessly undressing her emotions; but she had acquired, under the discipline of his reticences and evasions, a skill almost equal to his own, and perhaps more remarkable in that it involved keeping time with any tune he played and reading at sight some uncommonly difficult passages.

It had taken Thursdale seven years to form this fine talent; but the result justified the effort. At the crucial moment she had been perfect: her way of greeting Miss Gaynor had made him regret that he had announced his engagement by letter. It was an evasion that confessed a difficulty; a deviation implying an obstacle, where, by common consent, it was agreed to see none; it betrayed, in short, a lack of confidence in the completeness of his method. It had been his pride never to put himself in a position which had to be quitted, as it were, by the back door; but here, as he perceived, the main portals would have opened for him of their own accord. All this, and much more, he read in the finished naturalness with which Mrs. Vervain had met Miss Gaynor. He had never seen a better piece of work: there was no over-eagerness, no suspicious warmth, above all (and this gave her art the grace of a natural quality) there were none of those damnable implications whereby a woman, in welcoming her friend's betrothed, may keep him on pins and needles while she laps the lady in complacency. So masterly a performance, indeed, hardly needed the offset of Miss Gaynor's door-step words—"To be so kind to me, how she must have liked you!"—though he caught himself wishing it lay within the bounds of fitness to transmit them, as a final tribute, to the one woman he knew who was unfailingly certain to enjoy a good thing. It was perhaps the one drawback to his new situation that it might develop good things which it would be impossible to hand on to Margaret Vervain.

The fact that he had made the mistake of underrating his friend's powers, the consciousness that his writing must have betrayed his distrust of her efficiency, seemed an added reason for turning down her street instead of going on to the club. He would show her that he knew how to value her; he would ask her to achieve with him a feat infinitely rarer and more delicate than the one he had appeared to avoid. Incidentally, he would also dispose of the interval of time before dinner: ever since he had seen Miss Gaynor off, an hour earlier, on her return journey to Buffalo, he had been wondering how he should put in the rest of the afternoon. It was absurd, how he missed the girl. . . . Yes, that was it: the desire to talk about her was, after all, at the bottom of his impulse to call on Mrs. Vervain! It was absurd, if you like—but it was delightfully rejuvenating. He could recall the time when he had been afraid of being obvious: now he felt that this return to the primitive emotions might be as restorative as a holiday in the Canadian woods. And it was precisely by the girl's candour, her directness, her lack of complications, that he was taken. The sense that she might say something rash at any moment was positively exhilarating: if she had thrown her arms about him at the station he would not have given a thought to his crumpled dignity. It surprised Thursdale to find what freshness of heart he brought to the adventure; and though his sense of irony prevented his ascribing his intactness to any conscious purpose, he could but rejoice in the fact that his sentimental economies had left him such a large surplus to draw upon.

Mrs. Vervain was at home—as usual. When one visits the cemetery one expects to find the angel on the tombstone, and it struck Thursdale as another proof of his friend's good taste that she had been in no undue haste to change her habits. The whole house appeared to count on his coming; the footman took his hat and overcoat as naturally as though there had been no lapse in his visits; and the drawing-room at once enveloped him in that atmosphere of tacit intelligence which Mrs. Vervain imparted to her very furniture.

It was a surprise that, in this general harmony of circumstances, Mrs. Vervain should herself sound the first false note.

"You?" she exclaimed; and the book she held slipped from her hand.

It was crude, certainly; unless it were a touch of the finest art. The difficulty of classifying it disturbed Thursdale's balance.

"Why not?" he said, restoring the book. "Isn't it my hour?" And as she made no answer, he added gently, "Unless it's some one else's?"

She laid the book aside and sank back into her chair. "Mine, merely," she said.

"I hope that doesn't mean that you're unwilling to share it?"

"With you? By no means. You're welcome to my last crust."

He looked at her reproachfully. "Do you call this the last?"

She smiled as he dropped into the seat across the hearth. "It's a way of giving it more flavour!"

He returned the smile. "A visit to you doesn't need such condiments."

She took this with just the right measure of retrospective amusement.

"Ah, but I want to put into this one a very special taste," she confessed.

Her smile was so confident, so reassuring, that it lulled him into the imprudence of saying: "Why should you want it to be different from what was always so perfectly right?"

She hesitated. "Doesn't the fact that it's the last constitute a difference?"

"The last—my visit to you?"

"Oh, metaphorically, I mean—there's a break in the continuity."

Decidedly, she was pressing too hard: unlearning his arts already!

"I don't recognise it," he said. "Unless you make me—" he added, with a note that slightly stirred her attitude of languid attention.

She turned to him with grave eyes. "You recognise no difference whatever?"

"None—except an added link in the chain."

"An added link?"

"In having one more thing to like you for—your letting Miss Gaynor see why I had already so many." He flattered himself that this turn had taken the least hint of fatuity from the phrase.

Mrs. Vervain sank into her former easy pose. "Was it that you came for?" she asked, almost gaily.

"If it is necessary to have a reason—that was one."

"To talk to me about Miss Gaynor?"

"To tell you how she talks about you."

"That will be very interesting—especially if you have seen her since her second visit to me."

"Her second visit?" Thursdale pushed his chair back with a start and moved to another. "She came to see you again?"

"This morning, yes—by appointment."

He continued to look at her blankly. "You sent for her?"

"I didn't have to—she wrote and asked me last night. But no doubt you have seen her since."

Thursdale sat silent. He was trying to separate his words from his thoughts, but they still clung together inextricably. "I saw her off just now at the station."

"And she didn't tell you that she had been here again?"

"There was hardly time, I suppose—there were people about—" he floundered.

"Ah, she'll write, then."

He regained his composure. "Of course she'll write: very often, I hope. You know I'm absurdly in love," he cried audaciously.

She tilted her head back, looking up at him as he leaned against the chimney-piece. He had leaned there so often that the attitude touched a pulse which set up a throbbing in her throat. "Oh, my poor Thursdale!" she murmured.

"I suppose it's rather ridiculous," he owned; and as she remained silent, he added, with a sudden break—"Or have you another reason for pitying me?"

Her answer was another question. "Have you been back to your rooms since you left her?"

"Since I left her at the station? I came straight here."

"Ah, yes—you *could:* there was no reason—" Her words passed into a silent musing.

Thursdale moved nervously nearer. "You said you had something to tell me?"

"Perhaps I had better let her do so. There may be a letter at your rooms."

"A letter? What do you mean? A letter from *her*? What has happened?"

His paleness shook her, and she raised a hand of reassurance. "Nothing has happened—perhaps that is just the worst of it. You always *hated*, you know," she added incoherently, "to have things happen: you never would let them."

"And now—?"

"Well, that was what she came here for: I supposed you had guessed. To know if anything had happened."

"Had happened?" He gazed at her slowly. "Between you and me?" he said with a rush of light.

The words were so much cruder than any that had ever passed between them, that the colour rose to her face; but she held his startled gaze.

"You know girls are not quite as unsophisticated as they used to be. Are you surprised that such an idea should occur to her?"

His own colour answered hers: it was the only reply that came to him.

Mrs. Vervain went on smoothly: "I supposed it might have struck you that there were times when we presented that appearance."

He made an impatient gesture. "A man's past is his own!"

"Perhaps—it certainly never belongs to the woman who has shared it. But one learns such truths only by experience; and Miss Gaynor is naturally inexperienced."

"Of course—but—supposing her act a natural one—" he floundered lamentably among his innuendoes—"I still don't see—how there was anything—"

"Anything to take hold of? There wasn't—"

"Well, then—?" escaped him, in undisguised satisfaction; but as she did not complete the sentence he went on with a faltering laugh: "She can hardly object to the existence of a mere friendship between us!"

"But she does," said Mrs. Vervain.

Thursdale stood perplexed. He had seen, on the previous day, no trace of jealousy or resentment in his betrothed: he could still hear the candid ring of the girl's praise of Mrs. Vervain. If she were such an abyss of insincerity as to dissemble distrust under such frankness, she must at least

be more subtle than to bring her doubts to her rival for
solution. The situation seemed one through which one could
no longer move in a penumbra, and he let in a burst of
light with the direct query: "Won't you explain what you
mean?"

Mrs. Vervain sat silent, not provokingly, as though to
prolong his distress, but as if, in the attenuated phraseology
he had taught her, it was difficult to find words robust
enough to meet his challenge. It was the first time he had
ever asked her to explain anything; and she had lived so
long in dread of offering elucidations which were not
wanted, that she seemed unable to produce one on the spot.

At last she said slowly: "She came to find out if you
were really free."

Thursdale coloured again. "Free?" he stammered, with a
sense of physical disgust at contact with such crassness.

"Yes—if I had quite done with you." She smiled in recovered security. "It seems she likes clear outlines; she has a
passion for definitions."

"Yes—well?" he said, wincing at the echo of his own
subtlety.

"Well—and when I told her that you had never belonged
to me, she wanted me to define *my* status—to know exactly
where I had stood all along."

Thursdale sat gazing at her intently; his hand was not
yet on the clue. "And even when you had told her that—"

"Even when I had told her that I had had no status—
that I had never stood anywhere, in any sense she meant,"
said Mrs. Vervain, slowly—"even then she wasn't satisfied,
it seems."

He uttered an uneasy exclamation. "She didn't believe
you, you mean?"

"I mean that she *did* believe me: too thoroughly."

"Well, then—in God's name, what did she want?"

"Something more—those were the words she used."

"Something more? Between—between you and me? Is it
a conundrum?" He laughed awkwardly.

"Girls are not what they were in my day; they are no
longer forbidden to contemplate the relation of the sexes."

"So it seems!" he commented. "But since, in this case,
there wasn't any—" he broke off, catching the dawn of a
revelation in her gaze.

"That's just it. The unpardonable offence has been—in
our not offending."

He flung himself down despairingly. "I give it up! —What did you tell her?" he burst out with sudden crudeness.

"The exact truth. If I had only known," she broke off with a beseeching tenderness, "won't you believe that I would still have lied for you?"

"Lied for me? Why on earth should you have lied for either of us?"

"To save you—to hide you from her to the last! As I've hidden you from myself all these years!" She stood up with a sudden tragic import in her movement. "You believe me capable of that, don't you? If I had only guessed—but I have never known a girl like her; she had the truth out of me with a spring."

"The truth that you and I had never—"

"Had never—never in all these years! Oh, she knew why —she measured us both in a flash. She didn't suspect me of having haggled with you—her words pelted me like hail. 'He just took what he wanted—sifted and sorted you to suit his taste. Burnt out the gold and left a heap of cinders. And you let him—you let yourself be cut in bits'—she mixed her metaphors a little—'be cut in bits, and used or discarded, while all the while every drop of blood in you belonged to him! But he's Shylock—he's Shylock—and you have bled to death of the pound of flesh he has cut off you.' But she despises me the most, you know—far the most—" Mrs. Vervain ended.

The words fell strangely on the scented stillness of the room: they seemed out of harmony with its setting of afternoon intimacy, the kind of intimacy on which, at any moment, a visitor might intrude without perceptibly lowering the atmosphere. It was as though a grand opera-singer had strained the acoustics of a private music-room.

Thursdale stood up, facing his hostess. Half the room was between them, but they seemed to stare close at each other now that the veils of reticence and ambiguity had fallen.

His first words were characteristic: "She *does* despise me, then?" he exclaimed.

"She thinks the pound of flesh you took was a little too near the heart."

He was excessively pale. "Please tell me exactly what she said of me."

"She did not speak much of you: she is proud. But I

gather that while she understands love or indifference, her eyes have never been opened to the many intermediate shades of feeling. At any rate, she expressed an unwillingness to be taken with reservations—she thinks you would have loved her better if you had loved some one else first. The point of view is original—she insists on a man with a past!"

"Oh, a past—if she's serious—I could rake up a past!" he said with a laugh.

"So I suggested: but she has her eyes on this particular portion of it. She insists on making it a test case. She wanted to know what you had done to me; and before I could guess her drift I blundered into telling her."

Thursdale drew a difficult breath. "I never supposed—your revenge is complete," he said slowly.

He heard a little gasp in her throat. "My revenge? When I sent for you to warn you—to save you from being surprised as *I* was surprised?"

"You're very good—but it's rather late to talk of saving me." He held out his hand in the mechanical gesture of leave-taking.

"How you must care!—for I never saw you so dull," was her answer. "Don't you see that it's not too late for me to help you?" And as he continued to stare, she brought out sublimely: "Take the rest—in imagination! Let it at least be of that much use to you. Tell her I lied to her—she's too ready to believe it! And so, after all, in a sense, I sha'n't have been wasted."

His stare hung on her, widening to a kind of wonder. She gave the look back brightly, unblushingly, as though the expedient were too simple to need oblique approaches. It was extraordinary how a few words had swept them from an atmosphere of the most complex dissimulations to this contact of naked souls.

It was not in Thursdale to expand with the pressure of fate; but something in him cracked with it, and the rift let in new light. He went up to his friend and took her hand.

"You would do it—you would do it!"

She looked at him, smiling, but her hand shook.

"Good-bye," he said, kissing it.

"Good-bye? You are going—?"

"To get my letter."

"Your letter? The letter won't matter, if you will only do what I ask."

He returned her gaze. "I might, I suppose, without being

out of character. Only, don't you see that if your plan helped me it could only harm her?"

"Harm *her?*"

"To sacrifice you wouldn't make me different. I shall go on being what I have always been—sifting and sorting, as she calls it. Do you want my punishment to fall on *her?*"

She looked at him long and deeply. "Ah, if I had to choose between you—!"

"You would let her take her chance? But I can't, you see. I must take my punishment alone."

She drew her hand away, sighing. "Oh, there will be no punishment for either of you."

"For either of us? There will be the reading of her letter for me."

She shook her head with a slight laugh. "There will be no letter."

Thursdale faced about from the threshold with fresh life in his look. "No letter? You don't mean—"

"I mean that she's been with you since I saw her—she's seen you and heard your voice. If there *is* a letter, she has recalled it—from the first station, by telegraph."

He turned back to the door, forcing an answer to her smile. "But in the meanwhile I shall have read it," he said.

The door closed on him, and she hid her eyes from the dreadful emptiness of the room.

Masters of Arts

BY O. HENRY
(William Sydney Porter)

A TWO-INCH stub of a blue pencil was the wand with which Keogh performed the preliminary acts of his magic. So, with this he covered paper with diagrams and figures while he waited for the United States of America to send down to Coralio a successor to Atwood, resigned.

The new scheme that his mind had conceived, his stout heart indorsed, and his blue pencil corroborated, was laid around the characteristics and human frailties of the new president of Anchuria. These characteristics, and the situation out of which Keogh hoped to wrest a golden tribute, deserve chronicling contributive to the clear order of events.

President Losada—many called him Dictator—was a man whose genius would have made him conspicuous even among Anglo-Saxons, had not that genius been intermixed with other traits that were petty and subversive. He had some of the lofty patriotism of Washington (the man he most admired), the force of Napoleon, and much of the wisdom of the sages. These characteristics might have justified him in the assumption of the title of "The Illustrious Liberator," had they not been accompanied by a stupendous and amazing vanity that kept him in the less worthy ranks of the dictators.

Yet he did his country great service. With a mighty grasp he shook it nearly free from the shackles of ignorance and sloth and the vermin that fed upon it, and all but made it a power in the council of nations. He established schools and hospitals, built roads, bridges, railroads and palaces, and bestowed generous subsidies upon the arts and sciences. He was the absolute despot and the idol of his people. The wealth of the country poured into his hands. Other presidents had been rapacious without reason. Losada amassed enormous wealth, but his people had their share of the benefits.

The joint in his armour was his insatiate passion for monuments and tokens commemorating his glory. In every town he caused to be erected statues of himself bearing legends in praise of his greatness. In the walls of every public edifice, tablets were fixed reciting his splendour and the gratitude of his subjects. His statuettes and portraits were scattered throughout the land in every house and hut. One of the sycophants in his court painted him as St. John, with a halo and a train of attendants in full uniform. Losada saw nothing incongruous in this picture, and had it hung in a church in the capital. He ordered from a French sculptor a marble group including himself with Napoleon, Alexander the Great, and one or two others whom he deemed worthy of the honour.

He ransacked Europe for decorations, employing policy, money and intrigue to cajole the orders he coveted from kings and rulers. On state occasions his breast was covered from shoulder to shoulder with crosses, stars, golden roses, medals and ribbons. It was said that the man who could contrive for him a new decoration, or invent some new method of extolling his greatness, might plunge a hand deep into the treasury.

This was the man upon whom Billy Keogh had his eye. The gentle buccaneer had observed the rain of favours that fell upon those who ministered to the president's vanities, and he did not deem it his duty to hoist his umbrella against the scattering drops of liquid fortune.

In a few weeks the new consul arrived, releasing Keogh from his temporary duties. He was a young man fresh from college, who lived for botany alone. The consulate at Coralio gave him the opportunity to study tropical flora. He wore smoked glasses, and carried a green umbrella. He filled the cool, back porch of the consulate with plants and specimens so that space for a bottle and chair was not to be found. Keogh gazed on him sadly, but without rancour, and began to pack his gripsack. For his new plot against stagnation along the Spanish Main required of him a voyage overseas.

Soon came the *Karlsefin* again—she of the trampish habits—gleaning a cargo of cocoanuts for a speculative descent upon the New York market. Keogh was booked for a passage on the return trip.

"Yes, I'm going to New York," he explained to the group of his countrymen that had gathered on the beach to see him off. "But I'll be back before you miss me. I've undertaken the art education of this piebald country, and I'm not the man to desert it while it's in the early throes of tintypes."

With this mysterious declaration of his intentions Keogh boarded the *Karlsefin*.

Ten days later, shivering, with the collar of his thin coat turned high, he burst into the studio of Carolus White at the top of a tall building in Tenth Street, New York City.

Carolus White was smoking a cigarette and frying sausages over an oil stove. He was only twenty-three, and had noble theories about art.

"Billy Keogh!" exclaimed White, extending the hand that was not busy with the frying pan. "From what part of the uncivilized world, I wonder!"

"Hello, Carry," said Keogh, dragging forward a stool, and holding his fingers close to the stove. "I'm glad I found you so soon. I've been looking for you all day in the directories and art galleries. The free-lunch man on the corner told me where you were, quick. I was sure you'd be painting pictures yet."

Keogh glanced about the studio with the shrewd eye of a connoisseur in business.

"Yes, you can do it," he declared, with many gentle nods of his head. "That big one in the corner with the angels and green clouds and band-wagon is just the sort of thing we want. What would you call that, Carry—scene from Coney Island, ain't it?"

"That," said White, "I had intended to call 'The Translation of Elijah,' but you may be nearer right than I am."

"Name doesn't matter," said Keogh, largely; "it's the frame and the varieties of paint that does the trick. Now, I can tell you in a minute what I want. I've come on a little voyage of two thousand miles to take you in with me on a scheme. I thought of you as soon as the scheme showed itself to me. How would you like to go back with me and paint a picture? Ninety days for the trip, and five thousand dollars for the job."

"Cereal food or hair-tonic posters?" asked White.

"It isn't an ad."

"What kind of a picture is it to be?"

"It's a long story," said Keogh.

"Go ahead with it. If you don't mind, while you talk I'll just keep my eye on these sausages. Let 'em get one shade deeper than a Vandyke brown and you spoil 'em."

Keogh explained his project. They were to return to Coralio, where White was to pose as a distinguished American portrait painter who was touring in the tropics as a relaxation from his arduous and remunerative professional labours. It was not an unreasonable hope, even to those who trod in the beaten paths of business, that an artist with so much prestige might secure a commission to perpetuate upon canvas the lineaments of the president, and secure a share of the *pesos* that were raining upon the caterers to his weaknesses.

Keogh had set his price at ten thousand dollars. Artists had been paid more for portraits. He and White were to share the expenses of the trip, and divide the possible profits. Thus he laid the scheme before White, whom he had known in the West before one declared for Art and the other became a Bedouin.

Before long the two machinators abandoned the rigour of the bare studio for a snug corner of a café. There they sat far into the night, with old envelopes and Keogh's stub of blue pencil between them.

At twelve o'clock White doubled up in his chair, with his chin on his fist, and shut his eyes at the unbeautiful wall-paper.

"I'll go you, Billy," he said, in the quiet tones of decision. "I've got two or three hundred saved up for sausages and rent; and I'll take the chance with you. Five thousand! It will give me two years in Paris and one in Italy. I'll begin to pack to-morrow."

"You'll begin in ten minutes," said Keogh. "It's to-morrow now. The *Karlsefin* starts back at four P.M. Come on to your painting shop, and I'll help you."

For five months in the year Coralio is the Newport of Anchuria. Then only does the town possess life. From November to March it is practically the seat of government. The president with his official family sojourns there; and society follows him. The pleasure-loving people make the season one long holiday of amusement and rejoicing. *Fiestas*, balls, games, sea bathing, processions and small theatres contribute to their enjoyment. The famous Swiss band from the capital plays in the little plaza every evening, while the fourteen carriages and vehicles in the town circle in funereal but complacent procession. Indians from the interior mountains, looking like prehistoric stone idols, come down to peddle their handiwork in the streets. The people throng the narrow ways, a chattering, happy, careless stream of buoyant humanity. Preposterous children rigged out with the shortest of ballet skirts and gilt wings, howl, underfoot, among the effervescent crowds. Especially is the arrival of the presidential party, at the opening of the season, attended with pomp, show and patriotic demonstrations of enthusiasm and delight.

When Keogh and White reached their destination, on the return trip of the *Karlsefin*, the gay winter season was well begun. As they stepped upon the beach they could hear the band playing in the plaza. The village maidens, with fire-flies already fixed in their dark locks, were gliding, bare-foot and coy-eyed, along the paths. Dandies in white linen, swinging their canes, were beginning their seductive strolls. The air was full of human essence, of artificial entice-ment, of coquetry, indolence, pleasure—the man-made sense of existence.

The first two or three days after their arrival were spent in preliminaries. Keogh escorted the artist about town, introducing him to the little circle of English-speaking residents and pulling whatever wires he could to effect the spreading of White's fame as a painter. And then Keogh planned a more spectacular demonstration of the idea he wished to keep before the public.

He and White engaged rooms in the Hotel de los Estranjeros. The two were clad in new suits of immaculate duck, with American straw hats, and carried canes of remarkable uniqueness and inutility. Few caballeros in Coralio—even the gorgeously uniformed officers of the Anchurian army—were as conspicuous for ease and elegance of demeanour as Keogh and his friend, the great American painter, Señor White.

White set up his easel on the beach and made striking sketches of the mountain and sea views. The native population formed at his rear in a vast, chattering semicircle to watch his work. Keogh, with his care for details, had arranged for himself a pose which he carried out with fidelity. His rôle was that of friend to the great artist, a man of affairs and leisure. The visible emblem of his position was a pocket camera.

"For branding the man who owns it," said he, "a genteel dilettante with a bank account and an easy conscience, a steam-yacht ain't in it with a camera. You see a man doing nothing but loafing around making snap-shots, and you know right away he reads up well in 'Bradstreet.' You notice these old millionaire boys—soon as they get through taking everything else in sight they go to taking photographs. People are more impressed by a kodak than they are by a title or a four-carat scarf-pin." So Keogh strolled blandly about Coralio, snapping the scenery and the shrinking señoritas, while White posed conspicuously in the higher regions of art.

Two weeks after their arrival, the scheme began to bear fruit. An aide-de-camp of the president drove to the hotel in a dashing victoria. The president desired that Señor White come to the Casa Morena for an informal interview.

Keogh gripped his pipe tightly between his teeth. "Not a cent less than ten thousand," he said to the artist—"remember the price. And in gold or its equivalent—don't let him stick you with this bargain-counter stuff they call money here."

"Perhaps it isn't that he wants," said White.

"Get out!" said Keogh, with splendid confidence. "I know

what he wants. He wants his picture painted by the celebrated young American painter and filibuster now sojourn-
ing in his down-trodden country. Off you go."

The victoria sped away with the artist. Keogh walked up
and down, puffing great clouds of smoke from his pipe, and
waited. In an hour the victoria swept again to the door of
the hotel, deposited White, and vanished. The artist dashed
up the stairs, three at a step. Keogh stopped smoking, and
became a silent interrogation point.

"Landed," exclaimed White, with his boyish face flushed
with elation. "Billy, you are a wonder. He wants a picture.
I'll tell you all about it. By Heavens! that dictator chap
is a corker! He's a dictator clear down to his finger-ends.
He's a kind of combination of Julius Cæsar, Lucifer and
Chauncey Depew done in sepia. Polite and grim—that's his
way. The room I saw him in was about ten acres big, and
looked like a Mississippi steamboat with its gilding and
mirrors and white paint. He talks English better than I can
ever hope to. The matter of the price came up. I mentioned
ten thousand. I expected him to call the guard and have
me taken out and shot. He didn't move an eyelash. He
just waved one of his chestnut hands in a careless way,
and said, 'Whatever you say.' I am to go back to-morrow
and discuss with him the details of the picture."

Keogh hung his head. Self-abasement was easy to read in
his downcast countenance.

"I'm failing, Carry," he said, sorrowfully. "I'm not fit to
handle these man's-size schemes any longer. Peddling oranges
in a push-cart is about the suitable graft for me. When I
said ten thousand, I swear I thought I had sized up that
brown man's limit to within two cents. He'd have melted
down for fifteen thousand just as easy. Say—Carry—you'll
see old man Keogh safe in some nice, quiet idiot asylum,
won't you, if he makes a break like that again?"

The Casa Morena, although only one story in height, was
a building of brown stone, luxurious as a palace in its interior. It stood on a low hill in a walled garden of splendid
tropical flora at the upper edge of Coralio. The next day
the president's carriage came again for the artist. Keogh
went out for a walk along the beach, where he and his
"picture box" were now familiar sights. When he returned
to the hotel White was sitting in a steamer-chair on the
balcony.

"Well," said Keogh, "did you and His Nibs decide on the kind of a chromo he wants?"

White got up and walked back and forth on the balcony a few times. Then he stopped, and laughed strangely. His face was flushed, and his eyes were bright with a kind of angry amusement.

"Look here, Billy," he said, somewhat roughly, "when you first came to me in my studio and mentioned a picture, I thought you wanted a Smashed Oats or a Hair Tonic poster painted on a range of mountains or the side of a continent. Well, either of those jobs would have been Art in its highest form compared to the one you've steered me against. I can't paint that picture, Billy. You've got to let me out. Let me try to tell you what that barbarian wants. He had it all planned out and even a sketch made of his idea. The old boy doesn't draw badly at all. But, ye goddesses of Art! listen to the monstrosity he expects me to paint. He wants himself in the centre of the canvas, of course. He is to be painted as Jupiter sitting on Olympus, with the clouds at his feet. At one side of him stands George Washington, in full regimentals, with his hand on the president's shoulder. An angel with outstretched wings hovers overhead, and is placing a laurel wreath on the president's head, crowning him—Queen of the May, I suppose. In the background is to be cannon, more angels and soldiers. The man who would paint that picture would have to have the soul of a dog, and would deserve to go down into oblivion without even a tin can tied to his tail to sound his memory."

Little beads of moisture crept out all over Billy Keogh's brow. The stub of his blue pencil had not figured out a contingency like this. The machinery of his plan had run with flattering smoothness until now. He dragged another chair upon the balcony, and got White back to his seat. He lit his pipe with apparent calm.

"Now, sonny," he said, with gentle grimness, "you and me will have an Art to Art talk. You've got your art and I've got mine. Yours is the real Pierian stuff that turns up its nose at bock-beer signs and oleographs of the Old Mill. Mine's the art of Business. This was my scheme, and it worked out like two-and-two. Paint that president man as Old King Cole, or Venus, or a landscape, or a fresco, or a bunch of lilies, or anything he thinks he looks like. But get the paint on the canvas and collect the spoils. You

wouldn't throw me down, Carry, at this stage of the game.
Think of that ten thousand."

"I can't help thinking of it," said White, "and that's what
hurts. I'm tempted to throw every ideal I ever had down in
the mire, and steep my soul in infamy by painting that
picture. That five thousand meant three years of foreign
study to me, and I'd almost sell my soul for that."

"Now it ain't as bad as that," said Keogh, soothingly. "It's
a business proposition. It's so much paint and time against
money. I don't fall in with your idea that that picture
would so everlastingly jolt the art side of the question. George
Washington was all right, you know, and nobody could say
a word against the angel. I don't think so bad of that group.
If you was to give Jupiter a pair of epaulets and a sword,
and kind of work the clouds around to look like a black-
berry patch, it wouldn't make such a bad battle scene. Why,
if we hadn't already settled on the price, he ought to pay
an extra thousand for Washington, and the angel ought
to raise it five hundred."

"You don't understand, Billy," said White, with an uneasy
laugh. "Some of us fellows who try to paint have big notions about Art. I wanted to paint a picture some day that
people would stand before and forget that it was made of
paint. I wanted it to creep into them like a bar of music
and mushroom there like a soft bullet. And I wanted 'em
to go away and ask, 'What else has he done?' And I didn't
want 'em to find a thing; not a portrait nor a magazine
cover nor an illustration nor a drawing of a girl—nothing but
the picture. That's why I've lived on fried sausages, and
tried to keep true to myself. I persuaded myself to do this
portrait for the chance it might give me to study abroad.
But this howling, screaming caricature! Good Lord! can't
you see how it is?"

"Sure," said Keogh, as tenderly as he would have spoken
to a child, and he laid a long forefinger on White's knee.
"I see. It's bad to have your art all slugged up like that.
I know. You wanted to paint a big thing like the panorama
of the battle of Gettysburg. But let me kalsomine you a
little mental sketch to consider. Up to date we're out
$385.50 on this scheme. Our capital took every cent both
of us could raise. We've got about enough left to get back
to New York on. I need my share of that ten thousand. I
want to work a copper deal in Idaho, and make a hundred
thousand. That's the business end of the thing. Come down

off your art perch, Carry, and let's land that hatful of
dollars."

"Billy," said White, with an effort, "I'll try. I won't say
I'll do it, but I'll try. I'll go at it, and put it through if
I can."

"That's business," said Keogh, heartily. "Good boy! Now,
here's another thing—rush that picture—crowd it through as
quick as you can. Get a couple of boys to help you mix
the paint if necessary. I've picked up some pointers around
town. The people here are beginning to get sick of Mr.
President. They say he's been too free with concessions;
and they accuse him of trying to make a dicker with England to sell out the country. We want that picture done
and paid for before there's any row."

In the great *patio* of Casa Morena, the president caused
to be stretched a huge canvas. Under this White set up
his temporary studio. For two hours each day the great man
sat to him.

White worked faithfully. But, as the work progressed, he
had seasons of bitter scorn, of infinite self-contempt, of sullen
gloom and sardonic gaiety. Keogh, with the patience of a
great general, soothed, coaxed, argued—kept him at the picture.

At the end of a month White announced that the picture
was completed—Jupiter, Washington, angels, clouds, cannon
and all. His face was pale and his mouth drawn straight
when he told Keogh. He said the president was much pleased
with it. It was to be hung in the National Gallery of
Statesmen and Heroes. The artist had been requested to
return to Casa Morena on the following day to receive pay-
ment. At the appointed time he left the hotel, silent under
his friend's joyful talk of their success.

An hour later he walked into the room where Keogh was
waiting, threw his hat on the floor, and sat upon the table.

"Billy," he said, in strained and labouring tones, "I've a
little money out West in a small business that my brother
is running. It's what I've been living on while I've been
studying art. I'll draw out my share and pay you back
what you've lost on this scheme."

"Lost!" exclaimed Keogh, jumping up. "Didn't you get
paid for the picture?"

"Yes, I got paid," said White. "But just now there isn't
any picture, and there isn't any pay. If you care to hear
about it, here are the edifying details. The president and

I were looking at the painting. His secretary brought a bank
draft on New York for ten thousand dollars and handed it
to me. The moment I touched it I went wild. I tore it into
little pieces and threw them on the floor. A workman was
repainting the pillars inside the *patio*. A bucket of his paint
happened to be convenient. I picked up his brush and slapped
a quart of blue paint all over that ten-thousand-dollar nightmare. I bowed, and walked out. The president didn't move
or speak. That was one time he was taken by surprise. It's
tough on you, Billy, but I couldn't help it."

There seemed to be excitement in Coralio. Outside there
was a confused, rising murmur pierced by high-pitched cries.
"*Bajo el traidor—Muerte el traidor!*" were the words they
seemed to form.

"Listen to that!" exclaimed White, bitterly; "I know that
much Spanish. They're shouting, 'Down with the traitor!'
I heard them before. I felt that they meant me. I was a
traitor to Art. The picture had to go."

"'Down with the blank fool' would have suited your case
better," said Keogh, with fiery emphasis. "You tear up ten
thousand dollars like an old rag because the way you've
spread on five dollars' worth of paint hurts your conscience.
Next time I pick a side-partner in a scheme the man has
got to go before a notary and swear he never even heard
the word 'ideal' mentioned."

Keogh strode from the room, white-hot. White paid little
attention to his resentment. The scorn of Billy Keogh seemed
a trifling thing beside the greater self-scorn he had escaped.

In Coralio the excitement waxed. An outburst was imminent. The cause of this demonstration of displeasure was
the presence in the town of a big, pink-cheeked Englishman, who, it was said, was an agent of his government
come to clinch the bargain by which the president placed
his people in the hands of a foreign power. It was charged
that not only had he given away priceless concessions, but
that the public debt was to be transferred into the hands of
the English, and the custom-houses turned over to them as
a guarantee. The long-enduring people had determined to
make their protest felt.

On that night, in Coralio and in other towns, their ire
found vent. Yelling mobs, mercurial but dangerous, roamed
the streets. They overthrew the great bronze statue of the
president that stood in the centre of the plaza, and hacked
it to shapeless pieces. They tore from public buildings the

tablets set there proclaiming the glory of the "Illustrious Liberator." His pictures in the government offices were demolished. The mobs even attacked the Casa Morena, but were driven away by the military, which remained faithful to the executive. All the night terror reigned.

The greatness of Losada was shown by the fact that by noon the next day order was restored, and he was still absolute. He issued proclamations denying positively that any negotiation of any kind had been entered into with England. Sir Stafford Vaughn, the pink-cheeked Englishman, also declared in placards and in public print that his presence there had no international significance. He was a traveller without guile. In fact (so he stated), he had not even spoken with the president or been in his presence since his arrival.

During this disturbance, White was preparing for his homeward voyage in the steamship that was to sail within two or three days. About noon, Keogh, the restless, took his camera out with the hope of speeding the lagging hours. The town was now as quiet as if peace had never departed from her perch on the red-tiled roofs.

About the middle of the afternoon, Keogh hurried back to the hotel with something decidedly special in his air. He retired to the little room where he developed his pictures.

Later on he came out to White on the balcony, with a luminous, grim, predatory smile on his face.

"Do you know what that is?" he asked, holding up a 4 x 5 photograph mounted on cardboard.

"Snap-shot of a señorita sitting in the sand—alliteration unintentional," guessed White, lazily.

"Wrong," said Keogh with shining eyes. "It's a slung-shot. It's a can of dynamite. It's a gold mine. It's a sight-draft on your president man for twenty thousand dollars—yes, sir —twenty thousand this time, and no spoiling the picture. No ethics of art in the way. Art! You with your smelly little tubes! I've got you skinned to death with a kodak. Take a look at that."

White took the picture in his hand, and gave a long whistle.

"Jove!" he exclaimed, "but wouldn't that stir up a row in town if you let it be seen. How in the world did you get it, Billy?"

"You know that high wall around the president man's back garden? I was up there trying to get a bird's-eye of the town. I happened to notice a chink in the wall where a stone and a lot of plaster had slid out. Thinks I, I'll take a peep through to see how Mr. President's cabbages are growing. The first thing I saw was him and this Sir Englishman sitting at a little table about twenty feet away. They had the table all spread over with documents, and they were hobnobbing over them as thick as two pirates. 'Twas a nice corner of the garden, all private and shady with palms and orange trees, and they had a pail of champagne set by handy in the grass. I knew then was the time for me to make my big hit in Art. So I raised the machine up to the crack, and pressed the button. Just as I did so them old boys shook hands on the deal—you see they took that way in the picture."

Keogh put on his coat and hat.

"What are you doing to do with it?" asked White.

"Me," said Keogh in a hurt tone, "why, I'm going to tie a pink ribbon to it and hang it on the what-not, of course. I'm surprised at you. But while I'm out you just try to figure out what gingercake potentate would be most likely to want to buy this work of art for his private collection—just to keep it out of circulation."

The sunset was reddening the tops of the cocoanut palms when Billy Keogh came back from Casa Morena. He nodded to the artist's questioning gaze; and lay down on a cot with his hands under the back of his head.

"I saw him. He paid the money like a little man. They didn't want to let me in at first. I told 'em it was important. Yes, that president man is on the plenty-able list. He's got a beautiful business system about the way he uses his brains. All I had to do was to hold up the photograph so he could see it, and name the price. He just smiled, and walked over to a safe and got the cash. Twenty one-thousand-dollar brand-new United States Treasury notes he laid on the table, like I'd pay out a dollar and a quarter. Fine notes, too—they crackled with a sound like burning the brush off a ten-acre lot."

"Let's try the feel of one," said White, curiously. "I never saw a thousand-dollar bill." Keogh did not immediately respond.

"Carry," he said, in an absent-minded way, "you think a heap of your art, don't you?"

"More," said White, frankly, "than has been for the financial good of myself and my friends."

"I thought you were a fool the other day," went on Keogh, quietly, "and I'm not sure now that you wasn't. But if you was, so am I. I've been in some funny deals, Carry, but I've always managed to scramble fair, and match my brains and capital against the other fellow's. But when it comes to—well, when you've got the other fellow cinched, and the screws on him, and he's got to put up—why, it don't strike me as being a man's game. They've got a name for it, you know; it's—confound you, don't you understand. A fellow feels—it's something like that blamed art of yours—he—well, I tore that photograph up and laid the pieces on that stack of money and shoved the whole business back across the table. 'Excuse me, Mr. Losada,' I said, 'but I guess I've made a mistake in the price. You get the photo for nothing.' Now, Carry, you get out the pencil, and we'll do some more figuring. I'd like to save enough out of our capital for you to have some fried sausages in your joint when you get back to New York."

Effie Whittlesy

BY GEORGE ADE

MRS. WALLACE assisted her husband to remove his overcoat and put her warm palms against his red and wind-beaten cheeks.

"I have good news," said she.

"Another bargain sale?"

"Pshaw, no! A new girl, and I really believe she's a jewel. She isn't young or good-looking, and when I asked her if she wanted any nights off she said she wouldn't go out after dark for anything in the world. What do you think of that?"

"That's too good to be true."

"No, it isn't. Wait and see her. She came here from the intelligence office about two o'clock and said she was willing to 'lick right in.' You wouldn't know the kitchen. She has it as clean as a pin."

"What nationality?"

"None—that is, she's a home product. She's from the country—and *green!* But she's a good soul, I'm sure. As soon as I looked at her, I just felt sure that we could trust her."

"Well, I hope so. If she is all that you say, why, for
goodness sake give her any pay she wants—put lace curtains in her room and subscribe for all the story papers on
the market."

"Bless you, I don't believe she'd read them. Every time
I've looked into the kitchen she's been working like a Trojan
and singing 'Beulah Land.' "

"Oh, she sings, does she? I knew there'd be some draw-
backs."

"You won't mind that. We can keep the doors closed."

The dinner-table was set in tempting cleanliness. Mrs.
Wallace surveyed the arrangement of glass and silver and
gave a nod of approval and relief. Then she touched the
bell and in a moment the new servant entered.

She was a tall woman who had said her last farewell to
girlhood.

Then a very strange thing happened.

Mr. Wallace turned to look at the new girl and his eyes
enlarged. He gazed at her as if fascinated either by cap or
freckles. An expression of wonderment came to his face and
he said, "Well, by George!"

The girl had come very near the table when she took the
first overt glance at him. Why did the tureen sway in her
hands? She smiled in a frightened way and hurriedly set
the tureen on the table.

Mr. Wallace was not long undecided, but during that moment of hesitancy the panorama of his life was rolled backward. He had been reared in the democracy of a small
community, and the democratic spirit came uppermost.

"This isn't Effie Whittlesy?" said he.

"For the land's sake!" she exclaimed, backing away, and
this was a virtual confession.

"You don't know me."

"Well, if it ain't Ed Wallace!"

Would that words were ample to tell how Mrs. Wallace
settled back in her chair blinking first at her husband and
then at the new girl, vainly trying to understand what it
meant.

She saw Mr. Wallace reach awkwardly across the table
and shake hands with the new girl and then she found
voice to gasp, "Of all things!"

Mr. Wallace was confused and without a policy. He was
wavering between his formal duty as an employer and his

natural regard for an old friend. Anyway, it occurred to him that an explanation would be timely.

"This is Effie Whittlesy from Brainerd," said he. "I used to go to school with her. She's been at our house often. I haven't seen her for—I didn't know you were in Chicago," turning to Effie.

"Well, Ed Wallace, you could knock me down with a feather," said Effie, who still stood in a flustered attitude a few paces back from the table. "I had no more idee when I heard the name Wallace that it'd be you, though knowin', of course, you was up here. Wallace is such a common name I never give it a second thought. But the minute I seen you—law! I knew who it was, well enough."

"I thought you were still at Brainerd," said Mr. Wallace, after a pause.

"I left there a year ago November, and come to visit Mort's people. I s'pose you know that Mort has a position with the street-car company. He's doin' *so* well. I didn't want to be no burden on him, so I started out on my own hook, seein' that there was no use of goin' back to Brainerd to slave for two dollars a week. I had a good place with Mr. Sanders, the railroad man on the North Side, but I left becuz they wanted me to serve liquor. I'd about as soon handle a toad as a bottle of beer. Liquor was the ruination of Jesse. He's gone to the dogs—been off with a circus somewheres for two years."

"The family's all broken up, eh!" asked Mr. Wallace.

"Gone to the four winds since mother died. Of course you know that Lora married Huntford Thomas and is livin' on the old Murphy place. They're doin' about as well as you could expect, with Huntford as lazy as he is."

"Yes? That's good," said Mr. Wallace.

Was this an old settlers' reunion or a quiet family dinner? The soup had been waiting.

Mrs. Wallace came into the breach.

"That will be all for the present, Effie," said she.

Effie gave a startled "Oh!" and vanished into the kitchen.

"It means," said Mr. Wallace, "that we were children together, made mud pies in the same puddle and sat next to each other in the old schoolhouse at Brainerd. She is a Whittlesy. Everybody in Brainerd knew the Whittlesys. Large family, all poor as church mice, but sociable—and freckled. Effie's a good girl."

"Effie! *Effie!* And she called you Ed!"

"My dear, there are no misters in Brainerd. Why shouldn't she call me Ed! She never heard me called anything else."

"She'll have to call you something else here. You tell her so."

"Now, don't ask me to put on any airs with one of the Whittlesys, because they know me from away back. Effie has seen me licked at school. She has been at our house, almost like one of the family, when mother was sick and needed another girl. If my memory serves me right, I've taken her to singing-school and exhibitions. So I'm in no position to lord it over, and I wouldn't do it any way. I'd hate to have her go back to Brainerd and report that she met me here in Chicago and I was too stuck up to remember old times and requested her to address me as 'Mister Wallace.' Now, you never lived in a small town."

"No, I never enjoyed that privilege," said Mrs. Wallace, dryly.

"Well, it is a privilege in some respects, but it carries certain penalties with it, too. It's a very poor schooling for a fellow who wants to be a snob."

"I would call it snobbishness to correct a servant who addresses me by my first name. 'Ed' indeed! Why, I never dared to call you that."

"No, you never lived in Brainerd."

"And you say you used to take her to singing-school?"

"Yes, ma'am—twenty years ago, in Brainerd. You're not surprised, are you? You knew when you married me that I was a child of the soil, who worked his way through college and came to the city in a suit of store clothes. I'll admit that my past does not exactly qualify me for the Four Hundred, but it will be great if I ever get into politics."

"I don't object to your having a past, but I was just thinking how pleasant it will be when we give a dinner-party to have her come in and address you as 'Ed.'"

Mr. Wallace patted the tablecloth cheerily with both hands and laughed.

"I really don't believe you'd care," said Mrs. Wallace.

"Effie isn't going to demoralize the household," he said, consolingly. "Down in Brainerd we may be a little slack on the by-laws of etiquette, but we can learn in time."

Mrs. Wallace touched the bell and Effie returned.

As she brought in the second course, Mr. Wallace deliberately encouraged her by an amiable smile, and she asked, "Do you get the Brainerd papers?"

"Yes—every week."

"There's been a good deal of sickness down there this winter. Lora wrote to me that your uncle Joe had been kind o' poorly."

"I think he's up and around again."

"That's good."

And she edged back to the kitchen.

With the change for dessert she ventured to say: "Mort was wonderin' about you the other day. He said he hadn't saw you for a long time. My! You've got a nice house here."

After dinner Mrs. Wallace published her edict. Effie would have to go. Mr. Wallace positively forbade the "strong talking-to" which his wife advocated. He said it was better that Effie should go, but she must be sent away gently and diplomatically.

Effie was "doing up" the dishes when Mr. Wallace lounged into the kitchen and began a roundabout talk. His wife, seated in the front room, heard the prolonged murmur. Ed and Effie were going over the family histories of Brainerd and recalling incidents that may have related to mud pies or school exhibitions.

Mrs. Wallace had been a Twombley, of Baltimore, and no Twombley, with relatives in Virginia, could humiliate herself into rivalry with a kitchen girl, or dream of such a thing, so why should Mrs. Wallace be uneasy and constantly wonder what Ed and Effie were talking about?

Mrs. Wallace was faint from loss of pride. The night before they had dined with the Gages. Mr. Wallace, a picture of distinction in his evening clothes, had shown himself the bright light of the seven who sat at the table. She had been proud of him. Twenty-four hours later a servant emerges from the kitchen and hails him as "Ed"!

The low talk in the kitchen continued. Mrs. Wallace had a feverish longing to tiptoe down that way and listen, or else go into the kitchen, sweepingly, and with a few succinct commands, set Miss Whittlesy back into her menial station. But she knew that Mr. Wallace would misinterpret any such move and probably taunt her with joking references to her "jealousy," so she forbore.

Mr. Wallace, with an unlighted cigar in his mouth (Effie had forbidden him to smoke in the kitchen), leaned in the doorway and waited to give the conversation a turn.

At last he said: "Effie, why don't you go down and visit Lora for a month or so? She'd be glad to see you."

"I know, Ed, but I ain't a Rockefeller to lay off work a month at a time an' go around visitin' my relations. I'd like to well enough—but—"

"Oh pshaw! I can get you a ticket to Brainerd tomorrow and it won't cost you anything down there."

"No, it ain't Chicago, that's a fact. A dollar goes a good ways down there. But what'll your wife do? She told me to-day she'd had an awful time gettin' any help."

"Well—to tell you the truth, Effie, you see—you're an old friend of mine and I don't like the idea of your being here in my house as a—well, as a hired girl."

"No, I guess I'm a servant now. I used to be a hired girl when I worked for your ma, but now I'm a servant. I don't see as it makes any difference what you call me, as long as the work's the same."

"You understand what I mean, don't you? Any time you come here to my house I want you to come as an old acquaintance—a visitor, not a servant."

"Ed Wallace, don't be foolish. I'd as soon work for you as anyone, and a good deal sooner."

"I know, but I wouldn't like to see my wife giving orders to an old friend, as you are. You understand, don't you?"

"I don't know. I'll quit if you say so."

"Tut! tut! I'll get you that ticket and you can start for Brainerd tomorrow. Promise me, now."

"I'll go, and tickled enough, if that's the way you look at it."

"And if you come back, I can get you a dozen places to work."

Next evening Effie departed by carriage, although protesting against the luxury.

"Ed Wallace," she said, pausing in the hallway, "they never will believe me when I tell it in Brainerd."

"Give them my best and tell them I'm about the same as ever."

"I'll do that. Good-by."

"Good-by."

Mrs. Wallace, watching from the window, saw Effie disappear into the carriage.

"Thank goodness," said she.

"Yes," said Mr. Wallace, to whom the whole episode had

been like a cheering beverage, "I've invited her to call when she comes back."

"To call—here?"

"Most assuredly. I told her you'd be delighted to see her at any time."

"The idea! Did you invite her, really?"

"Of course I did! And I'm reasonably certain that she'll come."

"What shall I do?"

"I think you can manage it, even if you never did live in Brainerd."

Then the revulsion came and Mrs. Wallace, with a return of pride in her husband, said she would try.

Mr. Dooley on the Popularity of Firemen

BY FINLEY PETER DUNNE

"I KNOWED a man be th' name iv Clancy wanst, Jawn. He was fr'm th' County May-o, but a good man f'r all that; an', whin he'd growed to be a big, sthrappin' fellow, he wint on to th' fire departmint. They'se an Irishman 'r two on th' fire departmint an' in th' army, too, Jawn, though ye'd think be hearin' some talk they was all runnin' prim'ries an' thryin' to be cinthral comitymen. So ye wud. Ye niver hear iv thim on'y whin they die; an' thin, murther, what funerals they have!

"Well, this Clancy wint on th' fire departmint, an' they give him a place in thruck twinty-three. All th' r-road was proud iv him, an' faith he was proud iv himsilf. He r-rode free on th' sthreet ca-ars, an' was th' champeen hand-ball player f'r miles around. Ye shud see him goin' down th' sthreet, with his blue shirt an' his blue coat with th' buttons on it, an' his cap on his ear. But ne'er a cap or coat'd he wear whin they was a fire. He might be shiv'rin' be the stove in th' ingine house with a buffalo robe over his head; but, whin th' gong sthruck, 'twas off with coat an' cap an' buffalo robe, an' out come me brave Clancy, bare-headed an' bare hand, dhrivin' with wan line an' spillin' th' hose cart on wan wheel at ivry jump iv the horse. Did anny wan iver see a fireman with his coat on or a polisman with his off? Why, wanst, whin Clancy was standin' up f'r Grogan's eighth, his soon come runnin' in to tell him they was a fire in Vogel's packin' house. He dhropped th' kid at Father Kelly's feet, an' whipped off his long coat an' wint tearin' f'r th' dure, kickin' over th' poorbox an' buttin' ol' Mis' O'Neill that'd come in to say th' stations. 'Twas lucky 'twas wan iv th' Grogans. They're a fine family f'r falls. Jawn Grogan was wurrukin' on th' top iv Metzri an' O'Connell's brewery wanst, with a man be th' name iv Dorsey. He slipped an' fell wan hundherd feet. Whin they come to see if he was dead, he got up, an' says he: 'Lave me at him.' 'At who?' says they. 'He's dliryous,' they says. 'At Dorsey,' says Grogan. 'He thripped me.' So it didn't hurt Grogan's eighth to fall four 'r five feet.

"Well, Clancy wint to fires an' fires. Whin th' big organ facthry burnt, he carrid th' hose up to th' fourth story an' he come up fr'm th' brick an' boards an' saluted th' chief. 'Clancy,' says th' chief, 'ye betther go over an' get a dhrink.' He did so, Jawn. I heerd it. An' Clancy was that proud!

"Whin th' Hogan flats on Halsted Sthreet took fire, they got all th' people out but wan; an' she was a woman asleep on th' fourth flure. 'Who'll go up?' says Bill Musham. 'Sure, sir,' says Clancy, 'I'll go'; an' up he wint. His captain was a man be th' name iv O'Connell, fr'm th' County Kerry; an' he had his fut on th' ladder whin Clancy started. Well, th' good man wint into th' smoke, with his wife faintin' down below. 'He'll be kilt,' says his brother. 'Ye don't know him,' says Bill Musham. An' sure enough, win ivry wan'd give him up, out comes me brave Clancy, as black as a turk, with th' girl in his arms. Th' others wint up like monkeys, but he shtud wavin' thim off, an' come down th' ladder face forward. 'Where'd ye larn that?' says Bill Musham. 'I seen a man do it at th' Lyceem whin I was a kid,' says Clancy. 'Was it all right?' 'I'll have ye up before th' ol' man,' says Bill Musham. 'I'll teach ye to come down a laddher as if ye was in a quadhrille, ye horse-stealin', ham-sthringin' May-o man,' he says. But he didn't. Clancy wint over to see his wife. 'O Mike,' says she, ' 'twas fine,' she says. 'But why d'ye take th' risk?' she says. 'Did ye see th' captain?' he says with a scowl. 'He wanted to go. Did ye think I'd follow a Kerry man with all th' ward lukkin' on?' he says.

"Well, so he wint dhrivin' th' hose-cart on wan wheel, an' jumpin' whin he heerd a man so much as hit a glass to make it ring. All th' people looked up to him, an' th' kids followed him down th' sthreet; an' 'twas th' gr-reatest priv'lige f'r anny wan f'r to play dominos with him near th' joker. But about a year ago he come in to see me, an' says he, 'Well, I'm goin' to quit.' 'Why,' says I, 'ye'er a young man yet,' I says. 'Faith,' he says, 'look at me hair,' he says,—'young heart, ol' head. I've been at it these twenty year, an' th' good woman's wantin' to see more iv me thin blowin' into a saucer iv coffee,' he says. 'I'm goin' to quit,' he says, 'on'y I want to see wan more good fire,' he says. 'A rale good ol' hot wan,' he says, 'with th' win' blowin' f'r it an' a good dhraft in th' ili-vator-shaft, an' about two stories, with pitcher-frames an' gasoline an' excelsior, an' to hear th' chief yellin': "Play 'way, sivinteen. What th' hell an' damnation are ye standin' aroun' with that pipe f'r? Is this a fire 'r a dam livin' pitcher? I'll break ivry man iv eighteen, four, six, an' chem'cal five to-morrah mornin' befure breakfast." Oh,' he says, bringin' his fist down, 'wan more, an' I'll quit.'

"An' he did, Jawn. Th' day th' Carpenter Brothers' box-factory burnt. 'Twas wan iv thim big, fine-lookin' buildings that pious men built out iv celluloid an' plasther iv Paris. An' Clancy was wan iv th' men undher whin th' wall fell. I see thim bringin' him home; an' th' little woman met him at th' dure, rumplin' her apron in her hands."

The Bride Comes to Yellow Sky

BY STEPHEN CRANE

I

THE GREAT Pullman was whirling onward with such dignity of motion that a glance from the window seemed simply to prove that the plains of Texas were pouring eastward. Vast flats of green grass, dull-hued spaces of mesquit and cactus, little groups of frame houses, woods of light and tender trees, all were sweeping into the east, sweeping over the horizon, a precipice.

A newly married pair had boarded this coach at San Antonio. The man's face was reddened from many days in the wind and sun, and a direct result of his new black clothes was that his brick-coloured hands were constantly performing in a most conscious fashion. From time to time he looked down respectfully at his attire. He sat with a hand on each knee, like a man waiting in a barber's shop. The glances he devoted to other passengers were furtive and shy.

The bride was not pretty, nor was she very young. She wore a dress of blue cashmere, with small reservations of velvet here and there, and with steel buttons abounding. She continually twisted her head to regard her puff sleeves, very stiff, straight, and high. They embarrassed her. It was quite apparent that she had cooked, and that she expected to cook, dutifully. The blushes caused by the careless scrutiny of some passengers as she had entered the car were strange to see upon this plain, under-class countenance, which was drawn in placid, almost emotionless lines.

They were evidently very happy. "Ever been in a parlour-car before?" he asked, smiling with delight.

"No," she answered; "I never was. It's fine, ain't it?"

"Great! And then after a while we'll go forward to the diner, and get a big lay-out. Finest meal in the world. Charge a dollar."

"Oh, do they?" cried the bride. "Charge a dollar? Why, that's too much—for us—ain't it, Jack?"

"Not this trip, anyhow," he answered bravely. "We're going to go the whole thing."

Later he explained to her about the trains. "You see, it's a thousand miles from one end of Texas to the other; and this train runs right across it, and never stops but four times." He had the pride of an owner. He pointed out to her the dazzling fittings of the coach; and in truth her eyes opened wider as she contemplated the sea-green figured velvet, the shining brass, silver, and glass, the wood that gleamed as darkly brilliant as the surface of a pool of oil. At one end a bronze figure sturdily held a support for a separated chamber, and at convenient places on the ceiling were frescoes in olive and silver.

To the minds of the pair, their surroundings reflected the glory of their marriage that morning in San Antonio; this was the environment of their new estate; and the man's face in particular beamed with an elation that made him appear ridiculous to the negro porter. This individual at times surveyed them from afar with an amused and superior grin. On other occasions he bullied them with skill in ways that did not make it exactly plain to them that they were being bullied. He subtly used all the manners of the most unconquer-

able kind of snobbery. He oppressed them; but of his op-
pression they had small knowledge, and they speedily forgot
that infrequently a number of travellers covered them with
stares of derisive enjoyment. Historically there was supposed
to be something infinitely humorous in their situation.

"We are due in Yellow Sky at 3:42," he said, looking tenderly into her eyes.

"Oh, are we?" she said, as if she had not been aware of it.
To evince surprise at her husband's statement was part of her
wifely amiability. She took from a pocket a little silver
watch; and as she held it before her, and stared at it with a
frown of attention, the new husband's face shone.

"I bought it in San Anton' from a friend of mine," he told
her gleefully.

"It's seventeen minutes past twelve," she said, looking up
at him with a kind of shy and clumsy coquetry. A passenger,
noting this play, grew excessively sardonic, and winked at
himself in one of the numerous mirrors.

At last they went to the dining-car. Two rows of negro
waiters, in glowing white suits, surveyed their entrance with
the interest, and also the equanimity, of men who had been
forewarned. The pair fell to the lot of a waiter who happened to feel pleasure in steering them through their
meal. He viewed them with the manner of a fatherly pilot,
his countenance radiated with benevolence. The patron-
age, entwined with the ordinary deference, was not plain to
them. And yet, as they returned to their coach, they showed
in their faces a sense of escape.

To the left, miles down a long purple slope, was a little
ribbon of mist where moved the keening Rio Grande.
The train was approaching it at an angle, and the apex was
Yellow Sky. Presently it was apparent that, as the distance
from Yellow Sky grew shorter, the husband became com-
mensurately restless. His brick-red hands were more insistent in their prominence. Occasionally he was even
rather absent-minded and far-away when the bride leaned
forward and addressed him.

As a matter of truth, Jack Potter was beginning to find the
shadow of a deed weigh upon him like a leaden slab. He,
the town marshal of Yellow Sky, a man known, liked, and
feared in his corner, a prominent person, had gone to San
Antonio to meet a girl he believed he loved, and there, after
the usual prayers, had actually induced her to marry him,
without consulting Yellow Sky for any part of the transac-

tion. He was now bringing his bride before an innocent and unsuspecting community.

Of course people in Yellow Sky married as it pleased them, in accordance with a general custom; but such was Potter's thought of his duty to his friends, or of their idea of his duty, or of an unspoken form which does not control men in these matters, that he felt he was heinous. He had committed an extraordinary crime. Face to face with this girl in San Antonio, and spurred by his sharp impulse, he had gone headlong over all the social hedges. At San Antonio he was like a man hidden in the dark. A knife to sever any friendly duty, any form, was easy to his hand in that remote city. But the hour of Yellow Sky—the hour of daylight—was approaching.

He knew full well that his marriage was an important thing to his town. It could only be exceeded by the burning of the new hotel. His friends could not forgive him. Frequently he had reflected on the advisability of telling them by telegraph, but a new cowardice had been upon him. He feared to do it. And now the train was hurrying him toward a scene of amazement, glee, and reproach. He glanced out of the window at the line of haze swinging slowly in toward the train.

Yellow Sky had a kind of brass band, which played painfully, to the delight of the populace. He laughed without heart as he thought of it. If the citizens could dream of his prospective arrival with his bride, they would parade the band at the station and escort them, amid cheers and laughing congratulations, to his adobe home.

He resolved that he would use all the devices of speed and plainscraft in making the journey from the station to his house. Once within that safe citadel, he could issue some sort of vocal bulletin, and then not go among the citizens until they had time to wear off a little of their enthusiasm.

The bride looked anxiously at him. "What's worrying you, Jack?"

He laughed again. "I'm not worrying, girl; I'm only thinking of Yellow Sky."

She flushed in comprehension.

A sense of mutual guilt invaded their minds and developed a finer tenderness. They looked at each other with eyes softly aglow. But Potter often laughed the same nervous laugh; the flush upon the bride's face seemed quite permanent.

The traitor to the feelings of Yellow Sky narrowly watched the speeding landscape. "We're nearly there," he said.

Presently the porter came and announced the proximity of Potter's home. He held a brush in his hand, and, with all his airy superiority gone, he brushed Potter's new clothes as the latter slowly turned this way and that way. Potter fumbled out a coin and gave it to the porter, as he had seen others do. It was a heavy and muscle-bound business, as that of a man shoeing his first horse.

The porter took their bag, and as the train began to slow they moved forward to the hooded platform of the car. Presently the two engines and their long string of coaches rushed into the station of Yellow Sky.

"They have to take water here," said Potter, from a constricted throat and in mournful cadence, as one announcing death. Before the train stopped his eye had swept the length of the platform, and he was glad and astonished to see there was none upon it but the station-agent, who, with a slightly hurried and anxious air, was walking toward the water-tanks. When the train had halted, the porter alighted first, and placed in position a little temporary step.

"Come on, girl," said Potter, hoarsely. As he helped her down they each laughed on a false note. He took the bag from the negro, and bade his wife cling to his arm. As they slunk rapidly away, his hang-dog glance perceived that they were unloading the two trunks, and also that the station-agent, far ahead near the baggage-car, had turned and was running toward him, making gestures. He laughed, and groaned as he laughed, when he noted the first effect of his marital bliss upon Yellow Sky. He gripped his wife's arm firmly to his side, and they fled. Behind them the porter stood, chuckling fatuously.

II

The California express on the Southern Railway was due at Yellow Sky in twenty-one minutes. There were six men at the bar of the Weary Gentleman saloon. One was a drummer who talked a great deal and rapidly; three were Texans who did not care to talk at that time; and two were Mexican sheepherders, who did not talk as a general practice in the Weary Gentleman saloon. The barkeeper's dog lay on the board walk that crossed in front of the door. His head was on his paws, and he glanced drowsily here and there with the constant vigilance of a dog that is kicked on occasion. Across the sandy street were some vivid green grass-plots, so wonderful in appearance, amid the sands that burned near them in a blazing sun, that they caused a doubt in the mind. They exactly resembled the grass mats used to represent lawns on the stage. At the cooler end of the railway station, a man without a coat sat in a tilted chair and smoked his pipe. The fresh-cut bank of the Rio Grande circled near the town, and there could be seen beyond it a great plum-coloured plain of mesquit.

Save for the busy drummer and his companions in the saloon, Yellow Sky was dozing. The new-comer leaned gracefully upon the bar, and recited many tales with the confidence of a bard who has come upon a new field.

"—and at the moment that the old man fell downstairs with the bureau in his arms, the old woman was coming up with two scuttles of coal, and of course—"

The drummer's tale was interrupted by a young man who suddenly appeared in the open door. He cried: "Scratchy Wilson's drunk, and has turned loose with both hands." The two Mexicans at once set down their glasses and faded out of the rear entrance of the saloon.

The drummer, innocent and jocular, answered: "All right, old man. S'pose he has? Come in and have a drink, anyhow."

But the information had made such an obvious cleft in every skull in the room that the drummer was obliged to see its importance. All had become instantly solemn. "Say," said he, mystified, "what is this?" His three companions made the introductory gesture of eloquent speech; but the young man at the door forestalled them.

"It means, my friend," he answered, as he came into the saloon, "that for the next two hours this town won't be a health resort."

The barkeeper went to the door, and locked and barred it; reaching out of the window, he pulled in heavy wooden shutters, and barred them. Immediately a solemn, chapel-like gloom was upon the place. The drummer was looking from one to another.

"But say," he cried, "what is this, anyhow? You don't mean there is going to be a gun-fight?"

"Don't know whether there'll be a fight or not," answered one man, grimly; "but there'll be some shootin'—some good shootin'."

The young man who had warned them waved his hand. "Oh, there'll be a fight fast enough, if any one wants it. Anybody can get a fight out there in the street. There's a fight just waiting."

The drummer seemed to be swayed between the interest of a foreigner and a perception of personal danger.

"What did you say his name was?" he asked.

"Scratchy Wilson," they answered in chorus.

"And will he kill anybody? What are you going to do? Does this happen often? Does he rampage around like this once a week or so? Can he break in at that door?"

"No; he can't break down that door," replied the bar-keeper. "He's tried it three times. But when he comes you'd better lay down on the floor, stranger. He's dead sure to shoot at it, and a bullet may come through."

Thereafter the drummer kept a strict eye upon the door. The time had not yet been called for him to hug the floor, but, as a minor precaution, he sidled near to the wall. "Will he kill anybody?" he said again.

The man laughed low and scornfully at the question.

"He's out to shoot, and he's out for trouble. Don't see any good in experimentin' with him."

"But what do you do in a case like this? What do you do?"

A man responded: "Why, he and Jack Potter—"

"But," in chorus the other men interrupted, "Jack Potter's in San Anton'."

"Well, who is he? What's he got to do with it?"

"Oh, he's the town marshal. He goes out and fights Scratchy when he gets on one of these tears."

"Wow!" said the drummer, mopping his brow. "Nice job he's got."

The voices had toned away to mere whisperings. The drummer wished to ask further questions, which were born of an increasing anxiety and bewilderment; but when he attempted them, the men merely looked at him in irritation and motioned him to remain silent. A tense waiting hush was upon them. In the deep shadows of the room their eyes shone as they listened for sounds from the street. One man made three gestures at the barkeeper; and the latter, moving like a ghost, handed him a glass and a bottle. The man poured a full glass of whisky, and set down the bottle noiselessly. He gulped the whisky in a swallow, and turned again toward the door in immovable silence. The drummer saw that the barkeeper, without a sound, had taken a Winchester from beneath the bar. Later he saw this individual beckoning to him, so he tiptoed across the room.

"You better come with me back of the bar."

"No, thanks," said the drummer, perspiring; "I'd rather be where I can make a break for the back door."

Whereupon the man of bottles made a kindly but peremptory gesture. The drummer obeyed it, and, finding himself seated on a box with his head below the level of the bar, balm was laid upon his soul at sight of various zinc and copper fittings that bore a resemblance to armour-plate. The barkeeper took a seat comfortably upon an adjacent box.

"You see," he whispered, "this here Scratchy Wilson is a wonder with a gun—a perfect wonder; and when he goes on the war-trail, we hunt our holes—naturally. He's about the last one of the old gang that used to hang out along the river here. He's a terror when he's drunk. When he's sober he's all right—kind of simple—wouldn't hurt a fly—nicest fellow in town. But when he's drunk—whool!"

There were periods of stillness. "I wish Jack Potter was back from San Anton'," said the barkeeper. "He shot Wilson up once—in the leg—and he would sail in and pull out the kinks in this thing."

Presently they heard from a distance the sound of a shot, followed by three wild yowls. It instantly removed a bond from the men in the darkened saloon. There was a shuffling of feet. They looked at each other. "Here he comes," they said.

III

A man in a maroon-coloured flannel shirt, which had been purchased for purposes of decoration, and made principally by some Jewish women on the East Side of New York, rounded a corner and walked into the middle of the main street of Yellow Sky. In either hand the man held a long, heavy, blue-black revolver. Often he yelled, and these cries rang through a semblance of a deserted village, shrilly flying over the roofs in a volume that seemed to have no relation to the ordinary vocal strength of a man. It was as if the surrounding stillness formed the arch of a tomb over of silence. And his boots had red tops with gilded imprints, of the kind beloved in winter by little sledding boys on the hillsides of New England.

him. These cries of ferocious challenge rang against walls

The man's face flamed in a rage begot of whisky. His eyes, rolling, and yet keen for ambush, hunted the still doorways and windows. He walked with the creeping movement of the midnight cat. As it occurred to him, he roared menacing information. The long revolvers in his hands were as easy as straws; they were moved with an electric swiftness. The little fingers of each hand played sometimes in a musician's way. Plain from the low collar of the shirt, the cords of his neck straightened and sank, straightened and sank, as passion moved him. The only sounds were his terrible invitations. The calm adobes preserved their demeanour at the passing of this small thing in the middle of the street.

There was no offer of fight—no offer of fight. The man called to the sky. There were no attractions. He bellowed and fumed and swayed his revolvers here and everywhere.

The dog of the barkeeper of the Weary Gentleman saloon had not appreciated the advance of events. He yet lay dozing in front of his master's door. At sight of the dog, the man paused and raised his revolver humorously. At sight of the man, the dog sprang up and walked diagonally away, with a sullen head, and growling. The man yelled, and the dog broke into a gallop. As it was about to enter an alley, there was a loud noise, a whistling, and something spat the ground directly before it. The dog screamed, and, wheeling in terror, galloped headlong in a new direction. Again there was a noise, a whistling, and sand was kicked viciously before it. Fear-stricken, the dog turned and flurried like an animal in a pen. The man stood laughing, his weapons at his hips.

Ultimately the man was attracted by the closed door of the Weary Gentleman saloon. He went to it and, hammering with a revolver, demanded drink.

The door remaining imperturbable, he picked a bit of paper from the walk, and nailed it to the framework with a knife. He then turned his back contemptuously upon this popular resort and, walking to the opposite side of the street and spinning there on his heel quickly and lithely, fired at the bit of paper. He missed it by a half-inch. He swore at himself, and went away. Later he comfortably fusilladed the windows of his most intimate friend. The man was playing with this town; it was a toy for him.

But still there was no offer of fight. The name of Jack Potter, his ancient antagonist, entered his mind, and he concluded that it would be a glad thing if he should go to Potter's house, and by bombardment induce him to come out and fight. He moved in the direction of his desire, chanting Apache scalp-music.

When he arrived at it, Potter's house presented the same still front as had the other adobes. Taking up a strategic position, the man howled a challenge. But this house regarded him as might a great stone god. It gave no sign. After a decent wait, the man howled further challenges, mingling with them wonderful epithets.

Presently there came the spectacle of a man churning himself into deepest rage over the immobility of a house. He fumed at it as the winter wind attacks a prairie cabin in the North. To the distance there should have gone the sound of a tumult like the fighting of two hundred Mexicans. As necessity bade him, he paused for breath or to reload his revolvers.

IV

Potter and his bride walked sheepishly and with speed. Sometimes they laughed together shamefacedly and low.

"Next corner, dear," he said finally.

They put forth the efforts of a pair walking bowed against a strong wind. Potter was about to raise a finger to point the first appearance of the new home when, as they circled the corner, they came face to face with a man in a maroon-coloured shirt, who was feverishly pushing cartridges into a large revolver. Upon the instant the man dropped his revolver to the ground and, like lightning, whipped another from its holster. The second weapon was aimed at the bridegroom's chest.

There was a silence. Potter's mouth seemed to be merely a grave for his tongue. He exhibited an instinct to at once loosen his arm from the woman's grip, and he dropped the bag to the sand. As for the bride, her face had gone as yellow as old cloth. She was a slave to hideous rites, gazing at the apparitional snake.

The two men faced each other at a distance of three paces. He of the revolver smiled with a new and quiet ferocity.

"Tried to sneak up on me," he said. "Tried to sneak up on me!" His eyes grew more baleful. As Potter made a slight movement, the man thrust his revolver venomously forward. "No; don't you do it, Jack Potter. Don't you move a finger toward a gun just yet. Don't you move an eyelash. The time has come for me to settle with you, and I'm goin' to do it my own way, and loaf along with no interferin'. So if you don't want a gun bent on you, just mind what I tell you."

Potter looked at his enemy. "I ain't got a gun on me, Scratchy," he said. "Honest, I ain't." He was stiffening and steadying, but yet somewhere at the back of his mind a vision of the Pullman floated: the sea-green figured velvet, the shining brass, silver, and glass, the wood that gleamed as darkly brilliant as the surface of a pool of oil—all the glory of the marriage, the environment of the new estate. "You know I fight when it comes to fighting, Scratchy Wilson; but I ain't got a gun on me. You'll have to do all the shootin' yourself."

His enemy's face went livid. He stepped forward, and lashed his weapon to and fro before Potter's chest. "Don't you tell me you ain't got no gun on you, you whelp. Don't tell me no lie like that. There ain't a man in Texas ever seen you without no gun. Don't take me for no kid.". His eyes blazed with light, and his throat worked like a pump.

"I ain't takin' you for no kid," answered Potter. His heels had not moved an inch backward. "I'm takin' you for a damn fool. I tell you I ain't got a gun, and I ain't. If you're goin' to shoot me up, you better begin now; you'll never get a chance like this again."

So much enforced reasoning had told on Wilson's rage; he was calmer. "If you ain't got a gun, why ain't you got a gun?" he sneered. "Been to Sunday-school?"

"I ain't got a gun because I've just come from San Anton' with my wife. I'm married," said Potter. "And if I'd thought there was going to be any galoots like you prowling around when I brought my wife home, I'd had a gun, and don't you forget it."

"Married!" said Scratchy, not at all comprehending.

"Yes, married. I'm married," said Potter, distinctly.

"Married?" said Scratchy. Seemingly for the first time, he saw the drooping, drowning woman at the other man's side. "No!" he said. He was like a creature allowed a glimpse of another world. He moved a pace backward, and his arm, with the revolver, dropped to his side. "Is this the lady?" he asked.

"Yes; this is the lady," answered Potter.

There was another period of silence.

"Well," said Wilson at last, slowly, "I s'pose it's all off now."

"It's all off if you say so, Scratchy. You know I didn't make the trouble." Potter lifted his valise.

"Well, I 'low it's off, Jack," said Wilson. He was looking at the ground. "Married!" He was not a student of chivalry; it was merely that in the presence of this foreign condition he was a simple child of the earlier plains. He picked up his starboard revolver, and, placing both weapons in their holsters, he went away. His feet made funnel-shaped tracks in the heavy sand.

A Dead Issue

BY CHARLES M. FLANDRAU

MARCUS THORN, instructor in Harvard University, was thirty-two years old on the twentieth of June. He looked thirty-five, and felt about a hundred. When he got out of bed on his birthday morning, and pattered into the vestibule for his mail, the date at the top of the Crimson recalled the first of these unpleasant truths to him. His mirror—it was one of those detestable folding mirrors in three sections—enabled him to examine his bald spot with pitiless ease, reproduced his profile some forty-five times in quick succession, and made it possible for him to see all the way round himself several times at once. It was this devilish invention that revealed fact number two to Mr. Thorn, while he was brushing his hair and tying his necktie. One plus two equalled three, as usual, and Thorn felt old and unhappy. But he didn't linger over his dressing to philosophise on the evanescence of youth; he didn't even murmur,—

> "Alas for hourly change! Alas for all
> The loves that from his hand proud youth lets fall,
> Even as the beads of a told rosary."

He could do that sort of thing very well; he had been doing it steadily for five months. But this morning, the reality of the situation—impressed upon him by the date of his birth

—led him to adopt more practical measures. What he actually did, was to disarrange his hair a little on top,—fluff it up to make it look more,—and press it down toward his temples to remove the appearance of having too much complexion for the size of his head. Then he went out to breakfast.

Thorn's birthday had fallen, ironically, on one of those rainwashed, blue-and-gold days when "all nature rejoices." The whitest of clouds were drifting across the bluest of skies when the instructor walked out into the Yard; the elms rustled gently in the delicate June haze, and the robins hopped across the yellow paths, freshly sanded, and screamed in the sparkling grass. All nature rejoiced, and in so doing got very much on Thorn's nerves. When he reached his club, he was a most excellent person not to breakfast with.

It was early—half-past eight—and no one except Prescott, a sophomore, and Wynne, a junior, had dropped in as yet. Wynne, with his spectacles on, was sitting in the chair he always sat in at that hour, reading the morning paper. Thorn knew that he would read it through from beginning to end, carefully put his spectacles back in their case, and then go to the piano and play the "Blue Danube." By that time his eggs and coffee would be served. Wynne did this every morning, and the instructor, who at the beginning of the year had regarded the boy's methodical habits at the club as "quaint,"—suggestive, somehow, of the first chapter of "Pendennis,"—felt this morning that the "Blue Danube" before breakfast would be in the nature of a last straw. Prescott, looking as fresh and clean as the morning, was laughing over an illustrated funny paper. He merely nodded to Thorn, although the instructor hadn't breakfasted there for many months, and called him across to enjoy something. Thorn glanced at the paper and smiled feebly.

"I don't see how you can do it at this hour," he said; "I would as soon drink flat champagne." Prescott understood but vaguely what the man was talking about, yet he didn't appear disturbed or anxious for enlightenment.

"I'll have my breakfast on the piazza," Thorn said to the steward who answered his ring. Then he walked nervously out of the room.

From the piazza he could look over a tangled barrier of lilac bushes and trellised grapevines into an old-fashioned garden. A slim lady in a white dress and a broad brimmed hat that hid her face was cutting nasturtiums and humming placidly to herself. Thorn thought she was a young girl,

until she turned and revealed the fact that she was not a
young girl—that she was about his own age. This seemed
to annoy him in much the same way that the robins and
Wynne and the funny paper had, for he threw himself into
a low steamer-chair where he wouldn't have to look at the
woman, and gave himself up to a sort of luxurious melancholy.

In October, nine months before, Thorn had appeared one
evening in the doorway of the club dining-room after a
more or less continuous absence of eight years from Cambridge. It was the night before college opened, and the
dining-room was crowded. For an instant there was an uproar of confused greetings; then Haydock and Ellis and
Sears Wolcott and Wynne—the only ones Thorn knew—
pushed back from the table and went forward to shake hands
with him. Of the nine or ten boys still left at the table by
this proceeding, those whose backs were turned to the new
arrival stopped eating and waited without looking around,
to be introduced to the owner of the unfamiliar voice. Their
companions opposite paused too; some of them laid their
napkins on the table. They, however, could glance up and
see that the newcomer was a dark man of thirty years or
more. They supposed, correctly, that he was an "old graduate" and a member of the club.

"You don't know any of these people, do you?" said Haydock, taking him by the arm; "what a devil of a time you've
been away from this place."

"I know that that's a Prescott," laughed the graduate. In
his quick survey of the table, while the others had been welcoming him back, his eyes had rested a moment on a big
fellow with light hair. Everybody laughed, because it really
was a Prescott and all Prescotts were simply more or less
happy replicas of all other Prescotts. "I know your brothers,"
said the graduate, shaking hands with the boy, who had
risen.

"It's Mr. Thorn." Haydock made this announcement loud
enough to be heard by the crowd. He introduced every one,
prefixing "Mr." to the names of the first few, but changing
to given and even nicknames before completing the circuit
of the table. The humour of some of these last,—"Dink,"
"Pink," and "Mary," for instance,—lost sight of in long
established usage, suggested itself anew; and the fellows
laughed again as they made a place for Thorn at the crowded
table.

"It's six years, isn't it?" Haydock asked politely. The others had begun to babble cheerfully again of their own affairs.

"Six! I wish it were; it's eight," answered Thorn. "Eight since I left college. But of course I've been here two or three times since,—just long enough to make me unhappy at having to go back to Europe again."

"And now you're a great, haughty Ph.D. person, an 'Officer of Instruction and Government,' announced in the prospectus to teach in two courses," mused Ellis, admiringly. "How do you like the idea?"

"It's very good to be back," said Thorn. He looked about the familiar room with a contented smile, while the steward bustled in and out to supply him with the apparatus of dining.

It was, indeed, good to be back. The satisfaction deepened and broadened with every moment. It was good to be again in the town, the house, the room that, during his life abroad, he had grown to look upon more as "home" than any place in the world; good to come back and find that the place had changed so little; good, for instance, when he ordered a bottle of beer, to have it brought to him in his own mug, with his name and class cut in the pewter,—just as if he had never been away at all. This was but one of innumerable little things that made Thorn feel that at last he was where he belonged; that he had stepped into his old background; that it still fitted. The fellows, of course, were recent acquisitions—all of them. Even his four acquaintances had entered college long since his own time. But the crowd, except that it seemed to him a gathering decidedly younger than his contemporaries had been at the same age, was in no way strange to him. There were the same general types of young men up and down the table, and at both ends, that he had known in his day. They were discussing the same topics, in the same tones and inflections, that had made the dinner-table lively in the eighties,—which was not surprising when he considered that certain families belong to certain clubs at Harvard almost as a matter of course, and that some of the boys at the table were the brothers and cousins of his own classmates. He realised, with a glow of sentiment, that he had returned to his own people after years of absence in foreign lands; a performance whose emotional value was not decreased for Thorn by the conviction, just then, that his own people were better bred, and better

looking, and better dressed than any he had met elsewhere.
As he looked about at his civilised surroundings, and took
in, from the general chatter, fragments of talk,—breezy and
cosmopolitan with incidents of the vacation just ended,—he
considered his gratification worth the time he had been
spending among the fuzzy young gentlemen of a German
university.

Thorn, like many another college antiquity, might have
been the occasion of a mutual feeling of constraint had he
descended upon this undergraduate meal in the indefinite
capacity of "an old graduate." The ease with which he filled
his place at the table, and the effortless civility that
acknowledged his presence there, were largely due to his
never having allowed his interest in the life of the club
to wane during his years away from it. He knew the sort
of men the place had gone in for, and, in many instances,
their names as well. Some of his own, classmates—glad, no
doubt, of so congenial an item for their occasional European
letters—had never failed to write him, in diverting detail,
of the great Christmas and spring dinners. And they, in
turn, had often read extracts from Thorn's letters to them,
when called on to speak at these festivities. More than once
the graduate had sent, from the other side of the world,
some doggerel verses, a sketch to be used as a dinner-
card, or a trifling addition to the club's library or dining-
room. Haydock and Ellis and Wolcott and Wynne he had
met at various times abroad. He had made a point of
hunting them up and getting to know them, with the result
that his interest had succeeded in preserving his identity;
he was not unknown to the youngest member of the club.
If they didn't actually know him, they at least knew of him.
Even this crust is sweet to the returned graduate whose
age is just far enough removed from either end of life's
measure to make it intrinsically unimportant.

"What courses do you give?" It was the big Prescott, sitting opposite, who asked this. The effort involved a change
of colour.

"You'd better look out, or you'll have Pink in your class
the first thing you know," some one called, in a voice of
warning, from the other end of the table.

"Yes; he's on the lookout for snaps," said some one else.

"Then he'd better stay away from my lectures," answered
Thorn, smiling across at Prescott, who blushed some more at
this sudden convergence of attention on himself. "They say

that new instructors always mark hard—just to show off."

"I had you on my list before I knew who you were," announced another. "I thought the course looked interesting; you'll have to let me through."

"Swipe! swipe!" came in a chorus from around the table. This bantering attitude toward his official position pleased Thorn, perhaps, more than anything else. It flattered and reassured him as to the impression his personality made on younger—much younger—men. He almost saw in himself the solution of the perennial problem of "How to bring about a closer sympathy between instructor and student."

After dinner Haydock and Ellis took him from room to room, and showed him the new table, the new rugs, the new books, *ex dono* this, that, and the other member. In the library, he came across one of his own sketches, prettily framed. Some of his verses had been carefully pasted into the club scrap-book. Ellis and Haydock turned to his class photograph in the album, and laughed. It was not until long afterwards that he wondered if they had done so because the picture had not yet begun to lose its hair. When they had seen everything from the kitchen to the attic, they went back to the big room where the fellows were drinking their coffee and smoking. Others had come in in the interval; they were condoling gaily with those already arrived, on the hard luck of having to be in Cambridge once more. Thorn stood with his back to the fireplace, and observed them.

It was anything but a representative collection of college men. There were athletes, it was true,—Prescott was one, —and men who helped edit the college papers, and men who stood high in their studies, and others who didn't stand anywhere, talking and chaffing in that room. But it was characteristic of the life of the college that these varied distinctions had in no way served to bring the fellows together there. That Ellis would, without doubt, graduate with a *magna*, perhaps a *summa cum laude*, was a matter of interest to no one but Ellis. That Prescott had played admirable football on Soldiers' Field the year before, and would shortly do it again, made Prescott indispensable to the Eleven, perhaps, but it didn't in the least enhance his value to the club. In fact, it kept him away so much, and sent him to bed so early, that his skill at the game was, at times, almost deplored. That Haydock once in a while contributed verses of more than ordinary merit to the "Monthly" and "Advocate" had nearly kept him out of the club altogether. It was the one thing against him,—he had to live it down. On the whole, the club, like all of the five small clubs at Harvard whose influence is the most powerful, the farthest reaching influence in the undergraduate life of the place, rather prided itself in not being a reward for either the meritorious or the energetic. It was composed of young men drawn from the same station in life, the similarity of whose past associations and experience, in addition to whatever natural attractions they possessed, rendered them mutually agreeable. The system was scarcely broadening, but it was very delightful. And as the graduate stood there watching the fellows—brown and exuberant after the long vacation—come and go, discussing, comparing, or simply fooling, but always frankly absorbed in themselves and one another, he could not help thinking that however much such institutions had helped to enfeeble the class spirit of days gone by, they had a rather exquisite, if less diffusive spirit of their own. He liked the liveliness of the place, the broad, simple terms of intimacy on which every one seemed to be with every one else, the freedom of speech and action. Not that he had any desire to bombard people with sofa-cushions, as Sears Wolcott happened to be doing at that instant, or even to lie on his back in the middle of the centre-table with his head under the lamp, and read the "Transcript," as some one else had done most of the evening; but he enjoyed the environment that made such things possible and unobjectionable.

"I must make a point of coming here a great deal," reflected Thorn.

The next day college opened. More men enrolled in Thorn's class that afternoon than he thought would be attracted by the subject he was announced to lecture in on that day of the week. Among all the students who straggled, during the hour, into the bare recitation-room at the top of Sever, the only ones whose individualities were distinct enough to impress themselves on Thorn's unpractised memory, were a negro, a stained ivory statuette of a creature from Japan, a middle-aged gentleman with a misplaced trust in the efficacy of a flowing sandy beard for concealing an absence of collar and necktie, Prescott, and Haydock. Prescott surprised him. There was a crowd around the desk when he appeared, and Thorn didn't get a chance to speak to him; but he was pleased to have the boy enrol in his course,—more pleased somehow than if there had been any known intellectual reason for his having done such a thing; more pleased, for instance, than he was when Haydock strolled in a moment or two later, although he knew that the senior would get from his teachings whatever there was in them. Haydock was the last to arrive before the hour ended. Thorn gathered up his pack of enrolment cards, and the two left the noisy building together.

"Prescott enrolled just a minute or two before you did," said Thorn, as they walked across the Yard. He was a vain man in a quiet way.

"Yes," answered Haydock drily, "he said your course came at a convenient hour," he didn't add that, from what he knew of Prescott, complications might, under the circumstances, be looked for.

"Shall I see you at dinner?" Thorn asked before they separated.

"Oh, are you going to eat at the club?" Haydock had wondered the night before how much the man would frequent the place.

"Why, yes, I thought I would—for a time at least." No other arrangement had ever occurred to Thorn.

"That's good—I'm glad," said the senior; he asked himself, as he walked away, why truthful people managed to lie so easily and so often in the course of a day. As a matter of fact, he was vaguely sorry for what Thorn had just told him. Haydock didn't object to the instructor. Had his opinion been asked, he would have said, with truth, that he liked the man. For Thorn was intelligent, and what Haydock called "house broken," and the two had once spent a pleasant week together in Germany. It was not inhospitality, but a disturbed sense of the fitness of things that made Haydock regret Thorn's apparent intention of becoming so intimate with his juniors. The instructor's place, Haydock told himself, was with his academic colleagues, at the Colonial Club—or wherever it was that they ate.

Thorn did dine with the undergraduates that night, and on many nights following. It was a privilege he enjoyed for a time exceedingly. It amused him, and, after the first few weeks of his new life in Cambridge, he craved amusement. For in spite of the work he did for the college—the preparing and delivering of lectures, the reading and marking of various written tasks, and the enlightening, during consultation hours, of long haired, long winded seekers after truth, whose cold, insistent passion for the literal almost crazed him—

he was often profoundly bored. He had not been away from
Cambridge long enough to outlive the conviction, acquired
in his Freshman year, that the residents of that suburb
would prove unexhilarating if in a moment of inadvertence
he should ever chance to meet any of them. But he had
been too long an exile to retain a very satisfactory grasp on
contemporary Boston. Of course he hunted up some of his
classmates he had known well. Most of them were men of
affairs in a way that was as yet small enough to make them
seem to Thorn aggressively full of purpose. They were
all glad to see him. Some of them asked him to luncheon in
town at hours that proved inconvenient to one living in Cambridge; some of them had wives, and asked him to call on
them. He did so, and found them to be nice women. But this
he had suspected before. Two of his classmates were rich
beyond the dreams of industry. They toiled not, and might
have been diverting if they hadn't—both of them—happened to be unspeakably dull men. For one reason or another, he found it impossible to see his friends often enough
to get into any but a very lame sort of step with their lives.
Thorn's occasional meetings with them left him melancholy,
sceptical as to the depth of their natures and his own, cynical
as to the worth of college friendships—friendships that had
depended, for their warmth, so entirely on propinquity—on
the occasion. His most absorbing topics of conversation with
the men he had once known—his closest ties—were after all
issues very trivial and very dead. Dinner with a classmate he grew to look on as either suicide, or a post mortem.

It was the club with its fifteen or twenty undergraduate
members that went far at first toward satisfying his idle
moments. Dead issues, other than the personal traditions
that added colour and atmosphere to the every day life
of the place, were given no welcome there. The thrill of the
fleeting present was enough. The life Thorn saw there was,
as far as he could tell, more than complete with the healthy
joy of eating and drinking, of going to the play, of getting hot
and dirty and tired over athletics, and cool and clean and
hungry again afterwards. The instructor was entranced by its
innocence—its unconscious contentment. It was so unlike his
own life of recent years, he told himself; it was so "physical." He liked to stop at the club late in the winter afternoons, after a brisk walk on Brattle Street. There was always
a crowd around the fire at that hour, and no room that he
could remember that ever seemed so full of warmth and

sympathy as the big room where the fellows sat, at five o'clock on a winter's day, with the curtains drawn and the light of the fire flickering up the dark walls and across the ceiling. He often dropped in at midnight, or even later. The place was rarely quite deserted. Returned "theatre bees" came there to scramble eggs and drink beer, instead of tarrying with the mob at the Victoria or the Adams House. In the chill of the small hours, a herdic load of boys from some dance in town would often stream in to gossip and get warm, or to give the driver a drink after the long cold drive across the bridge. And Thorn, who had not been disposed to gather up and cling to the dropped threads of his old interests, who was not wedded to his work, who was not sufficient unto himself, enjoyed it all thoroughly, unreservedly —for a time.

For a time only. For as the winter wore on, the inevitable happened—or rather the expected didn't happen, which is pretty much the same thing after all. Thorn, observant, analytical, and—where he himself was not concerned—clever, grew to know the fellows better than they knew themselves. Before he had lived among them three months, he had appreciated their respective temperaments, he had taken the measure of their ambitions and limitations, he had catalogued their likes and dislikes, he had pigeon-holed their weaknesses and illuminated their virtues. Day after day, night after night, consciously and unconsciously, he had observed them in what was probably the frankest, simplest intercourse of their lives. And he knew them.

But they didn't know him. Nor did it ever occur to them that they wanted to or could. They were not seeking the maturer companionship Thorn had to give; they were not seeking much of anything. They took life as they found it near at hand, and Thorn was far, very far away. For them, the niche he occupied could have been filled by any gentleman of thirty-two with a kind interest in them and an affection for the club. To him, they were everything that made the world, as he knew it just then, interesting and beautiful. Youth, energy, cleanliness were the trinity Thorn worshipped. And they were young, strong, and undefiled. Yet, after the first pleasure at being back had left him, Thorn was not a happy man, although he had not then begun to tell himself so.

The seemingly unimportant question presented by his own name began to worry him a little as the weeks passed

into months. First names and the absurd sounds men had
answered to from babyhood were naturally in common use
at the club. Thorn dropped into the way of them easily, as
a matter of course. Not to have done so would, in time, have
become impossible. The fellows would have thought it
strange—formal. Yet the name of "Marcus" was rarely
heard there. Haydock, once in a while, called him that, after
due premeditation. Sears Wolcott occasionally used it by
way of a joke—as if he were taking an impertinent liberty,
and rather enjoyed doing it. But none of the other men ever
did. On no occasion had any one said "Marcus" absent-
mindedly, and then looked embarrassed, as Thorn had hoped
might happen. It hurt him a little always to be called
"Thorn;" to be appealed to in the capacity of "Mr. Thorn," as
he sometimes was by the younger members, positively annoyed him. Prescott was the most incorrigible in this respect.
He had come from one of those fitting schools where all
speech between master and pupil is carried on to a mo-
notonous chant of "Yes, sir," "No, sir," and "I think so, sir."
He had ideas, or rather habits,—for Prescott's ideas were few,
—of deference to those whose mission it was to assist in his
education that Thorn found almost impossible to displace.
For a long time—until the graduate laughed and asked him
not to—he prefixed the distasteful "Mr." to Thorn's name.
Then, for as long again, he refrained markedly from calling
him anything. One afternoon he came into the club where the
instructor was alone, writing a letter, and after fussing for a
time among the magazines on the table, he managed to
say,—

"Thorn, do you know whether Sears has been here since
luncheon?"

Thorn didn't know and he didn't care, but had Prescott
handed him an appointment to an assistant professor's chair,
instead of having robbed him a little of what dignity he
possessed, he would not have been so elated by half. Prescott continued to call him "Thorn" after that, but always
with apparent effort,—as if aware that in doing it he was not
living quite up to his principles. This trouble with his name
might have served Thorn as an indication of what his position actually was in the tiny world he longed so much to be
part of once more. But he was not a clever man where he
himself was concerned.

Little things hurt him constantly without opening his eyes.
For instance, it rarely occurred to the fellows that the instruc-

tor might care to join them in any of their hastily planned expeditions to town after dinner. Not that he was ostracised; he was simply overlooked. When he did go to the theatre, he bought the tickets himself, and asked Prescott or Sears, or some of them, to go with him. The occasion invariably lacked the charm of spontaneity. When he invited any of them to dine with him in town, as he often did, they went, if they hadn't anything else to do, and seemed to enjoy their dinner. But to Thorn these feasts were a series of disappointments. He always got up from the table with a sense of having failed in something. What? He didn't know—he couldn't have told. He was like a man who shoots carefully at nothing, and then feels badly because he hits it. He persisted in loitering along sunny lanes, and growing melancholy because they led nowhere. It was Sears Wolcott who took even the zest of anticipation out of Thorn's little dinners in town, by saying to the graduate one evening,—

"What's the point of going to the Victoria for dinner? It's less trouble, and a damned sight livelier, to eat out here." Sears had what Haydock called, "that disagreeable habit of hitting promiscuously from the shoulder." The reaction on Thorn of all this was at last a dawning suspicion of his own unimportance. By the time the midyear examinations came, he felt somehow as if he were "losing ground;" he hadn't reached the point yet of realising that he never had had any. He used to throw down his work in a fit of depression and consult his three-sided mirror apprehensively.

The big Prescott, however, became the real problem, around which the others were as mere corollaries. It was he who managed, in his "artless Japanese way," as the fellows used to call it, to crystallise the situation, to bring it to a pass where Thorn's rather unmanly sentimentality found itself confronted by something more definite and disturbing than merely the vanishing point of youth. Prescott accomplished this very simply, by doing the poorest kind of work— no work at all, in fact—in the course he was taking from Thorn. Barely, and by the grace of the instructor, had he scraped through the first examination in November. Since then he had rested calmly, like a great monolith, on his laurels. He went to Thorn's lectures only after intervals of absence that made his going at all a farce. He ignored the written work of the course, and the reports on outside reading, with magnificent completeness. Altogether, he behaved as he wouldn't have behaved had he ever for a moment con-

sidered Thorn in any light other than that of an instructor,
an officer of the college, a creature to whom deference—servility, almost—was due when he was compelled to talk to
him, but to whom all obligation ended there. His attitude
was not an unusual one among college "men" who have not
outgrown the school idea, but the attendant circumstances
were. For Thorn's concern over Prescott's indifference to the
course was aroused by a strong personal attachment, one in
which an ordinary professorial interest had nothing to do.
He smarted at his failure to attract the boy sufficiently to
draw him to his lectures; yet he looked with a sort of panic
toward the approaching day when he should be obliged,
in all conscience, to flunk him in the midyear examination. He admired Prescott, as little, intelligent men sometimes
do admire big, stupid ones. He idealised him, and even went
the length, one afternoon when taking a walk with Haydock,
of telling the senior that under Prescott's restful, olympic
exterior he thought there lurked a soul. To which Haydock
had answered with asperity, "Well, I hope so, I'm sure,"
and let the subject drop. Later in the walk, Haydock announced, irrelevantly, and with a good deal of vigour, that if
he ever made or inherited millions, he would establish a
chair in the university, call it the "Haydock Professorship of
Common Sense," and respectfully suggest to the President
and Faculty that the course be made compulsory.

Thorn would have spoken to the soulful Prescott,—told
him gently that he didn't seem to be quite in sympathy with
the work of the course,—if Prescott had condescended to go
to his lectures in the six or seven weeks between the end of
the Christmas recess and the examination period. But Prescott
cut Tuesday, Thursday, and Saturday, at half-past two
o'clock, with a regularity that, considered as regularity, was
admirable. Toward the last, he did drop in every now and
then, sit near the door, and slip out again before the hour
was ended. This was just after he had been summoned by
the Recorder to the Office for "cutting." Thorn never got a
chance to speak to him. He might have approached the boy
at the club; but the instructor shrank from taking advantage
of his connection with that place to make a delicate official duty possible. He had all along avoided "shop" there
so elaborately,—had made so light of it when the subject
had come up,—that he couldn't bring himself at that late
day to arise, viper like, from the hearthstone and smite. A
note of warning would have to be light, facetious, and con-

sequently without value, in order not to prove a very false and uncalled for note indeed. The ready cooperation of the Dean, Thorn refrained from calling on; he was far from wishing to get Prescott into difficulties.

By the time the examination day arrived, the instructor was in a state of turmoil that in ordinary circumstances would have been excessive and absurd. In the case of Thorn, it was half pathetic, half contemptible. He knew that in spite of Prescott's soul (a superabundance of soul is, as a matter of fact, a positive hindrance in passing examinations),—the boy would do wretchedly. To give him an E—the lowest possible mark, always excepting, of course, the jocose and sarcastic F—would be to bring upon him Prescott's everlasting anger and "despision." Of this Thorn was sure. Furthermore, the mark would not tend to make the instructor wildly popular at the club; for although everybody was willing to concede that Prescott was not a person of brilliant mental attainments, he was very much beloved. One hears a good deal about the "rough justice of boys." Thorn knew that such a thing existed, and did not doubt but that, in theory, he would be upheld by the members of the club if he gave Prescott an E, and brought the heavy hand of the Office down on him. But the justice of boys, he reflected, was, after all, rough; it would acknowledge his right to flunk Prescott, perhaps, and, without doubt, hate him cordially for doing it. Thorn's aversion to being hated was almost morbid.

If, on the other hand, he let the boy through,—gave him, say, the undeserved and highly respectable mark of C,— well, that would be tampering dishonestly with the standards of the college, gross injustice to the rest of the students, injurious to the self-respect of the instructor, and a great many other objectionable things, too numerous to mention. Altogether, Thorn was in a "state of mind." He began to understand something of the fine line that separates instructor from instructed, on whose other side neither may trespass.

When at length the morning of the examination had come and gone, and Thorn was in his own room at his desk with the neat bundle of blue-covered books before him, in which the examinations are written, it was easy enough to make up his mind. He knew that the question of flunking or passing Prescott admitted of no arguments whatever. The boy's work in the course failed to present the tiniest loophole in the way of "extenuating circumstances," and Prescott had capped the climax of his past record that morning by staying in the examination-room just an hour and a quarter of the three hours he was supposed to be there. That alone was equivalent to failure in a man of Prescott's denseness. Not to give Prescott a simple and unadorned E would be holding the pettiest of personal interests higher than one's duty to the college. There was no other way of looking at it. And Thorn, whose mind was perfectly clear on this point, deliberately extricated Prescott's book from the blue pile on his desk, dropped it carelessly—without opening it—into the glowing coals of his fireplace, and entered the boy's midyear mark in the records as C.

No lectures are given in the college during the midyears. Men who are fortunate enough to finish their examinations early in the period can run away to New York, to the country, to Old Point Comfort, to almost anywhere that isn't Cambridge, and recuperate. Haydock went South. Ellis and Wynne tried a walking trip in the Berkshire Hills, and, after two days' floundering in the mud, waded to the nearest train for a city. Boston men went to Boston—except Sears Wolcott and Prescott, who disappeared to some wild and inaccessible New England hamlet to snow-shoe or spear fish or shoot rabbits; no one could with authority say which, as the two had veiled their preparations in mystery. So it happened that Thorn didn't see Prescott for more than a week after he had marked his book. In the mean time he had become used to the idea of having done it according to a somewhat unconventional system—to put it charitably. He passed much of the time in which the fellows were away, alone; for the few who went to the club, went there with note-books under their arms and preoccupied expressions in their eyes. They kept a sharp look-out for unexpected manœuvres on the part of the clock, and had a general air of having to be in some place else very soon. Thorn, thrown on his own resources, had a mild experience of what Cambridge can be without a crowd to play with, and came to the conclusion that, for his own interest and pleasure in life, he had done wisely in not incurring Prescott's ill-will and startling the club in the new rôle of hardhearted, uncompromising pedagogue. The insignificant part he played in the lives of the undergraduates was far from satisfying; but it was the sort of half a loaf one doesn't willingly throw away. By the time Prescott came back, Thorn had so wholly accepted his own view of the case that he was totally unprepared for the way in which the boy took the news of his mark. He met Prescott in the Yard the morning college opened again, and stopped to speak to him. He wouldn't have referred to the examination—it was enough to know that the little crisis had passed—had not Prescott, blushing uneasily, and looking over Thorn's shoulder at something across the Yard, said,—

"I don't suppose you were very much surprised at the way I did in the exam, were you?"

"It might have been better," answered Thorn, seriously. "I hope you will do better the second half year. But then, it might have been worse; your mark was C."

Prescott looked at him, a quizzical, startled look; and then realising that Thorn was serious, that there had been nothing of the sarcastic in his tone or manner, he laughed rudely in the instructor's face.

"I beg your pardon," he said, as politely as he could, with his eyes still full of wonder and laughter; "I had no idea I did so well." He turned abruptly and walked away. Thorn would have felt offended, if he hadn't all at once been exceedingly scared. Prescott's manner was extraordinary for one who, as a rule, took everything as it came, calmly, unquestioningly. His face and his laugh had expressed anything but ordinary satisfaction at not having failed. There was something behind that unwonted astonishment, something more than mere surprise at having received what was, after all, a mediocre mark. Thorn had mixed enough with human kind to be aware that no man living is ever very much surprised in his heart of hearts to have his humble efforts in any direction given grade C. Men like Prescott, who know but little of the subjects they are examined in, usually try to compose vague answers that may, like the oracles, be interpreted according to the mood of him who reads them. No matter how general or how few Prescott's answers had been— Thorn stopped suddenly in the middle of the path. The explanation that had come to him took hold of him, and like a tightened rein drew him up short. Prescott had written nothing. The pages of his blue book had left the examination-room as virgin white as when they had been brought in and placed on the desk by the proctor. There was no other explanation possible, and the instructor tingled all over with the horrid sensation of being an unspeakable fool. He turned quickly to go to University Hall; he meant to have Prescott's mark changed at once. But

Prescott, at that moment, was bounding up the steps of University, two at a time. He was undoubtedly on his way to the Office to verify what Thorn had just told him. Thorn walked rapidly to his entry in Holworthy, although he had just come from there. Then, with short, nervous steps, he turned back again, left the Yard, and hurried in aimless haste up North Avenue. He had been an ass,—a bungling, awful ass,—he told himself over and over again. And that was about as coherent a meditation as Mr. Thorn was able to indulge in for some time. Once the idea of pretending that he had made a mistake did suggest itself for a moment; but that struck him as wild, impossible. It would have merely resulted in forcing the Office to regard him as stupid and careless, and, should embarrassing questions arise, he no longer had Prescott's book with which to clear himself. More than that, it would give Prescott reason to believe him an underhand trickster. The boy now knew him to be an example of brazen partiality; there was no point in incurring even harsher criticism. Thorn tried to convince himself, as he hurried along the straight, hideous highway, that perhaps, he was wrong,—that Prescott hadn't handed in a perfectly blank book. If only he could have been sure of that, he would have risked the bland assertion that the boy had stumbled on more or less intelligent answers to the examination questions, without perhaps knowing it himself. This, practically, was the tone he had meant to adopt all along. But he couldn't be sure, and, unfortunately, the only person who could give information as to what was or wasn't in the book, was Prescott. But Prescott had given information of the most direct and convincing kind. That astounded look and impertinent laugh had as much as said:—

"Well, old swipe, what's your little game? What do you expect to get by giving a good mark to a man who wasn't able to answer a single question?" And Thorn knew it. At first he was alarmed at what he had done. He could easily see how such a performance, if known, might stand in the light of his reappointment to teach in the college, even if it didn't eject him at once. But before he returned to his room, after walking miles, he scarcely knew where, fear had entirely given way to shame,—an over-powering shame that actually made the man sick at his stomach. It wasn't as if he had committed a man's fault in a world of men where he would be comfortably judged and damned by a tribunal he respected about as much as he respected himself. He had turned himself inside out before the clear eyes of a lot of boys, whose dealings with themselves and one another were like so many shafts of white light in an unrefracting medium. He had let them know what a weak, characterless, poor thing he was, by holding himself open to a bribe, showing himself willing to exchange, for the leavings of their friendships, something he was bound in honour to give only when earned, prostituting his profession that they might continue to like him a little, tolerate his presence among them. And he was one whom the college had honoured by judging worthy to stand up before young men and teach them. It was really very sickening.

Thorn couldn't bring himself to go near the club for some days. He knew, however, as well as if he had been present, what had probably happened there in the meanwhile. Prescott had told Haydock and Wolcott, and very likely some of the others, the story of his examination. They had laughed at first, as if it had been a good joke in which Prescott had come out decidedly ahead; then Haydock had said something—Thorn could hear him saying it—that put the matter in a pitilessly true light, and the others had agreed with him. They usually did in the end. It took all the "nerve" Thorn had to show himself again.

But when he had summoned up enough courage to drop in at the club late one evening, he found every one's manner toward him pretty much as it always had been; yet he could tell instinctively, as he sat there, who had and who hadn't heard Prescott's little anecdote. Wolcott knew; he called Thorn, "Marcus," with unnecessary gusto, and once or twice laughed his peculiarly irritating laugh when there was nothing, as far as Thorn could see, to laugh at. Haydock knew; Thorn winced under the cool speculative stare of the senior's grey eyes. Wynne knew; although Thorn had no more specific reason for believing so, than that the boy seemed rather more formidably bespectacled than usual. Several of the younger fellows also knew; Thorn knew that they knew; he couldn't stand it. When the front door slammed after him on his way back to his room, he told himself that, as far as he was concerned, it had slammed for the last time.

He was very nearly right. He would have had to be a pachyderm compared to which the "blood sweating behemoth of Holy Writ" is a mere satin-skinned invalid, in order to have brazened out the rest of the year on the old basis.

He couldn't go to the club and converse on base-ball and
the "musical glasses," knowing that the fellows with whom
he was talking were probably weighing the pros and cons of
taking his courses next year, and getting creditable marks in
them, without doing a stroke of work. He couldn't face
that "rough justice of boys" that would sanction the fellows
making use of him, and considering him a pretty poor
thing, at the same time. So he stayed away; he didn't go
near the place through March and April and May. When his
work didn't call him elsewhere, he stayed in his room and
attempted to live the life of a scholar,—an existence for
which he was in every conceivable way unfitted. For a time
he studied hard out of books; but the most profitable knowledge he acquired in his solitude was the great deal he
learned about himself. He tried to write. He had always
thought it in him to "write something," if he ever should
find the necessary leisure. But the play he began amounted
to no more than a harmless pretext for discoursing in a dis-
illusioned strain on Life and Art in the many letters he
wrote to people he had known abroad,—people, for whom,
all at once, he conceived a feeling of intimacy that no
doubt surprised them when they received his letters. His
volume of essays was never actually written, but the fact
that he was hard at work on it served well as an answer
to:—

"Why the devil don't we ever see you at the club now-
adays?"

For the fellows asked him that, of course, when he met
them in the Yard or in the electric cars; and Haydock tarried
once or twice after his lecture and hoped politely that he
was coming to the next club dinner. He wasn't at the next
club dinner, however, nor the next, nor the next. Haydock
stopped reminding him of them. The club had gradually
ceased to have any but a spectacular interest for Thorn.
His part at a dinner there would be—and, since his return,
always had been—that of decorous audience in the stalls,
watching a sprightly farce. The club didn't insist on an audience, so Thorn's meetings with its members were few.
He saw Haydock and Prescott, in a purely official way, more
than any of them. Strangely enough, Prescott seemed to be
trying to do better in Thorn's course. He came to the lectures as regularly as he had avoided them before the midyears. He handed in written work of such ingenious unin-

telligence that there was no question in Thorn's mind as to the boy's having conscientiously evolved it unaided. The instructor liked the spirit of Prescott's efforts, although it was a perpetual "rubbing in," of the memory of his own indiscretion; it displayed a pretty understanding of *noblesse oblige.*

The second half year was long and dreary and good for Thorn. It set him down hard,—so hard that when he collected himself and began to look about him once more, he knew precisely where he was—which was something he hadn't known until then. He was thirty-two years old; he looked thirty-five, and he felt a hundred, to begin with. He wasn't an undergraduate, and he hadn't been one for a good many years. He still felt that he loved youth and sympathised with its every phase,—from its mindless gambolings to its preposterous maturity. But he knew now that it was with the love and sympathy of one who had lost it. He had learned, too, that when it goes, it bids one a cavalier adieu, and takes with it what one has come to regard as one's rights,— like a saucy house-maid departing with the spoons. He knew that he had no rights; he had forfeited them by losing some of his hair. He wouldn't get any of them back again until he had lost all of it. He was the merest speck on the horizon of the fellows whom he had, earlier in the year, tried to know on a basis of equality,—a speck too far away, too microscopic even to annoy them. If he had only known it all along, he told himself, how different his year might have been. He wouldn't have squandered the first four months of it, for one thing, in a stupid insistence on a relation that must of necessity be artificial—unsatisfying. He wouldn't have spent the last five of it in coming to his senses. He wouldn't have misused all of it in burning—or at least in allowing to fall into a precarious state of unrepair—the bridges that led back to the friends of his own age and time.

"I have learned more than I have taught, this year," thought Thorn.

To-day was Thorn's birthday. Impelled by a tender, tepid feeling of self-pity the instructor had come once more to the club to look at it and say good-bye before leaving Cambridge. He would have liked to breakfast on the piazza and suffer luxuriously alone. But just at the moment he was beginning to feel most deeply, Sears Wolcott appeared at the open French window, and said he was "Going to eat out there in the landscape too." So Thorn, in spite of himself, had to revive.

"What did you think of the Pudding show last night?" began Sears. Talk with him usually meant leading questions and their simplest answers.

"It was very amusing—very well done," said Thorn. What was the use, he asked himself, of drawing a cow-eyed stare from Wolcott by saying what he really thought—that Strawberry Night at the Pudding had been "exuberant," "noisy," "intensely young."

"I saw you after it was over," Sears went on; "why didn't you buck up with the old grads around the piano? You looked lonely."

"I was lonely," answered Thorn, truthfully this time.

"Where were your classmates? There was a big crowd out."

"My classmates? Oh, they were there, I suppose. I haven't seen much of them this year."

Wolcott's next question was:—

"Why the devil can't we have better strawberries at this club, I wonder? Where's the granulated sugar? They know I never eat this damned face powder on anything." He called loudly for the steward, and Thorn went on with his breakfast in silence. After Sears had been appeased with granulated sugar, he asked:—

"Going to be here next year?"

"I've been reappointed; but I think I shall live in town. Why do you ask?"

"Oh, nothing—I was thinking I might take your courses. What mark is Prescott going to get for the year?"

Thorn looked up to meet Wolcott's eyes unflinchingly; but the boy was deeply absorbed in studying the little air bubbles on the surface of his coffee.

"I don't know what mark he'll get. I haven't looked at his book yet," said Thorn. Sears remarked "Oh!" and laughed as he submerged the bubbles with a spoon. It was unlike him not to have said, "You do go through the formality of reading his books then?"

Prescott and Wynne joined them. They chattered gaily with Wolcott about nothing out there on the piazza, and watched the slim lady on the other side of the nodding lilac bushes cut nasturtiums. Thorn listened to them, and looked at them, and liked them; but he couldn't be one of them, even for the moment. He couldn't babble unpremeditatedly about nothing, because he had forgotten how it was done. So, in a little while, he got up to leave them. He had to mark some examination books and pack his trunks and go abroad, he told them. He said good-bye to Prescott and Wolcott and Wynne and some others who had come in while they were at breakfast, and hoped they would have "a good summer." They hoped the same to him.

As he strolled back to his room with the sounds of their voices in his ears, but with no memory of what they had been saying, he wondered if, after all, they hadn't from the very first bored him just a little; if his unhappiness—his sense of failure when he talked to young people—didn't come from the fact that they commended themselves to his affections rather than to his intellect. Thorn was a vain man in a quiet way.

Prescott's final examination book certainly didn't commend itself to his intellect. It was long, and conscientious, and quite incorrect from cover to cover. The instructor left it until the last. He almost missed his train in deciding upon its mark.

The Lost Phoebe

BY THEODORE DREISER

THEY LIVED together in a part of the country which was not so prosperous as it had once been, about three miles from one of those towns that, instead of increasing in population, is steadily decreasing. The territory was not very thickly settled; perhaps a house every other mile or so, with large acres of corn- and wheatland and fallow fields that at odd seasons had been sown to timothy and clover. Their particular house was part log and part frame, the log portion being the old original home of Henry's grandfather. The new portion, of now rain-beaten, time-worn slabs, through which the wind squeaked in the chinks at times, and which several overshadowing elms and a butternut tree made picturesque and reminiscently pathetic, but a little damp, was erected by Henry when he was twenty-one and just married.

That was forty-eight years before. The furniture inside,

like the house outside, was old and mildewy and reminiscent of an earlier day. You have seen the what-not of cherry wood, perhaps, with spiral legs and fluted top. It was there. The old-fashioned four-poster bed, with its ball-like protuberances and deep curving incisions, was there also, a sadly alienated descendant of an early Jacobean ancestor. The bureau of cherry was also high and wide and solidly built, but faded-looking, and with a musty odor. The rag carpet that underlay all these sturdy examples of enduring furniture was a weak, faded, lead and pink colored affair woven by Phœbe Ann's own hands, when she was fifteen years younger than she was when she died. The creaky wooden loom on which it had been done now stood like a dusty bony skeleton, along with a broken rocking-chair, a worm-eaten clothes press—Heavens knows how old—a lime-stained bench that had once been used to keep flowers on outside the door, and other decrepit factors of household utility, in an east room that was a lean-to against this so-called main portion. All sorts of other broken-down furniture were about this place; an antiquated clothes-horse, cracked in two of its ribs; a broken mirror in an old cherry frame, which had fallen from a nail and cracked itself three days before their youngest son, Jerry, died; an extension hat-rack, which once had had porcelain knobs on the ends of its pegs; and a sewing machine, long since outdone in its clumsy mechanism by rivals of a newer generation.

The orchard to the east of the house was full of gnarled old apple trees, worm eaten as to trunks and branches, and fully ornamented with green and white lichens, so that it had a sad, greenish-white, silvery effect in moonlight. The low outhouses, which had once housed chickens, a horse or two, a cow, and several pigs, were covered with patches of moss as to their roof, and the sides had been free of paint for so long that they were blackish-gray as to color, and a little spongy. The picket fence in front, with its gate squeaky and askew, and the side fences of the stake-and-rider type were in an equally run-down condition. As a matter of fact, they had aged synchronously with the persons who lived here, old Henry Reifsneider and his wife Phœbe Ann.

They had lived here, these two, ever since their marriage, forty-eight years before, and Henry had lived here before that from his childhood up. His father and mother, well along in years when he was a boy, had invited him to bring his wife here when he had first fallen in love and decided to marry; and he had done so. His father and mother were the companions of himself and his wife for ten years after they were married, when both died; and then Henry and Phœbe were left with their five children growing lustily apace. But all sorts of things had happened since then. Of the seven children, all told, that had been born to them, three had died; one girl had gone to Kansas; one boy had gone to Sioux Falls, never even to be heard of after; another boy had gone to Washington; and the last girl lived five counties away in the same State, but was so burdened with cares of her own that she rarely gave them a thought. Time and a commonplace home life that had never been attractive had weaned them thoroughly, so that, wherever they were, they gave little thought as to how it might be with their father and mother.

Old Henry Reifsnider and his wife Phœbe were a loving couple. You perhaps know how it is with simple natures that fasten themselves like lichens on the stones of circumstance and weather their days to a crumbling conclusion. The great world sounds widely, but it has no call for them. They have no soaring intellect. The orchard, the meadow, the corn-field, the pig-pen, and the chicken-lot measure the range of their human activities. When the wheat is headed it is reaped and threshed; when the corn is browned and frosted it is cut and shocked; when the timothy is in full head it is cut, and the hay-cock erected. After that comes winter, with the hauling of grain to market, the sawing and splitting of wood, the simple chores of fire-building, meal-getting, occasional repairing, and visiting. Beyond these and the changes of weather—the snows, the rains, and the fair days—there are no immediate, significant things. All the rest of life is a far-off, clamorous phantasmagoria, flickering like Northern lights in the night, and sounding as faintly as cow-bells tinkling in the distance.

Old Henry and his wife Phœbe were as fond of each other as it is possible for two old people to be who have nothing else in this life to be fond of. He was a thin old man, seventy when she died, a queer, crotchety person with coarse gray-black hair and beard, quite straggly and unkempt. He looked at you out of dull, fishy, watery eyes that had deep-brown crow's-feet at the sides. His clothes, like the clothes of many farmers, were aged and angular and baggy, standing out at the pockets, not fitting about the neck, protuberant and

worn at elbow and knee. Phœbe Ann was thin and shapeless,
a very umbrella of a woman, clad in shabby black, and with
a black bonnet for her best wear. As time had passed, and
they had only themselves to look after, their movements had
become slower and slower, their activities fewer and fewer.
The annual keep of pigs had been reduced from five to one
grunting porker, and the single horse which Henry now retained was a sleepy animal, not over-nourished and not very
clean. The chickens, of which formerly there was a large
flock, had almost disappeared, owing to ferrets, foxes,
and the lack of proper care, which produces disease. The
former healthy garden was now a straggling memory of itself, and the vines and flowerbeds that formerly ornamented
the windows and dooryard had now become choking thick-
ets. A will had been made which divided the small tax-
eaten property equally among the remaining four, so that it
was really of no interest to any of them. Yet these two lived
together in peace and sympathy, only that now and then old
Henry would become unduly cranky, complaining almost
invariably that something had been neglected or mislaid
which was of no importance at all.

"Phœbe, where's my corn knife? You ain't never minded
to let my things alone no more."

"Now you hush, Henry," his wife would caution him in a
cracked and squeaky voice. "If you don't, I'll leave yuh. I'll
git up and walk out of here some day, and then where would
y' be? Y' ain't got anybody but me to look after yuh, so yuh
just behave yourself. Your corn knife's on the mantel where
it's allus been unless you've gone an' put it summers else."

Old Henry, who knew his wife would never leave him
under any circumstances, used to speculate at times as to
what he would do if she were to die. That was the one leaving that he really feared. As he climbed on the chair at night
to wind the old, long-pendulumed, double-weighted clock,
or went finally to the front and the back door to see that they
were safely shut in, it was a comfort to know that Phœbe
was there, properly ensconsed on her side of the bed, and
that if he stirred restlessly in the night, she would be there
to ask what he wanted.

"Now, Henry, do lie still! You're as restless as a chicken."

"Well, I can't sleep, Phœbe."

"Well, yuh needn't roll so, anyhow. Yuh kin let me sleep."

This usually reduced him to a state of somnolent ease. If
she wanted a pail of water, it was a grumbling pleasure for

him to get it; and if she did rise first to build the fires, he saw that the wood was cut and placed within easy reach. They divided this simple world nicely between them.

As the years had gone on, however, fewer and fewer people had called. They were well-known for a distance of as much as ten square miles as old Mr. and Mrs. Reifsneider, honest, moderately Christian, but too old to be really interesting any longer. The writing of letters had become an almost impossible burden too difficult to continue or even negotiate via others, although an occasional letter still did arrive from the daughter in Pemberton County. Now and then some old friend stopped with a pie or cake or a roasted chicken or duck, or merely to see that they were well; but even these kindly minded visits were no longer frequent.

One day in the early spring of her sixty-fourth year Mrs. Reifsneider took sick, and from a low fever passed into some indefinable ailment which, because of her age, was no longer curable. Old Henry drove to Swinnerton, the neighboring town, and procured a doctor. Some friends called, and the immediate care of her was taken off his hands. Then one chill spring night she died, and old Henry, in a fog of sorrow and uncertainty, followed her body to the nearest graveyard, an unattractive space with a few pines growing in it. Although he might have gone to the daughter in Pemberton or sent for her, it was really too much trouble and he was too weary and fixed. It was suggested to him at once by one friend and another that he come to stay with them awhile, but he did not see fit. He was so old and so fixed in his notions and so accustomed to the exact surroundings he had known all his days, that he could not think of leaving. He wanted to remain near where they had put his Phœbe; and the fact that he would have to live alone did not trouble him in the least. The living children were notified and the care of him offered if he would leave, but he would not.

"I kin make a shift for myself," he continually announced to old Dr. Morrow, who had attended his wife in this case. "I kin cook a little, and, besides, it don't take much more'n coffee an' bread in the mornin's to satisfy me. I'll get along now well enough. Yuh just let me be." And after many pleadings and proffers of advice, with supplies of coffee and bacon and baked bread duly offered and accepted, he was left to himself. For a while he sat idly outside his door brooding in the spring sun. He tried to revive his interest in farming, and to keep himself busy and free from thought by

looking after the fields, which of late had been much neglected. It was a gloomy thing to come in of an evening, however, or in the afternoon, and find no shadow of Phœbe
where everything suggested her. By degrees he put a few of
her things away. At night he sat beside his lamp and read in
the papers that were left him occasionally or in a Bible that
he had neglected for years, but he could get little solace
from these things. Mostly he held his hand over his
mouth and looked at the floor as he sat and thought of what
had become of her, and how soon he himself would die.
He made a great business of making his coffee in the morning and frying himself a little bacon at night; but his appetite was gone. The shell in which he had been housed so
long seemed vacant, and its shadows were suggestive of im-
medicable griefs. So he lived quite dolefully for five long
months, and then a change began.

It was one night, after he had looked after the front and
the back door, wound the clock, blown out the light, and
gone through all the selfsame motions that he had indulged in for years, that he went to bed not so much to sleep
as to think. It was a moonlight night. The green-lichen-cov-
ered orchard just outside and to be seen from his bed where
he now lay was a silvery affair, sweetly spectral. The moon
shone through the east windows, throwing the pattern of
the panes on the wooden floor, and making the old furniture, to which he was accustomed, stand out dimly in the
room. As usual he had been thinking of Phœbe and the
years when they had been young together, and of the
children who had gone, and the poor shift he was making
of his present days. The house was coming to be in a very
bad state indeed. The bedclothes were in disorder and not
clean, for he made a wretched shift of washing. It was a terror to him. The roof leaked, causing things, some of them,
to remain damp for weeks at a time, but he was getting into
that brooding state where he would accept anything rather
than exert himself. He preferred to pace slowly to and fro or
to sit and think.

By twelve o'clock of this particular night he was asleep,
however, and by two had waked again. The moon by this
time had shifted to a position on the western side of the
house, and it now shone in through the windows of the living-room and those of the kitchen beyond. A certain combination of furniture—a chair near a table with his coat on
it, the half-open kitchen door casting a shadow, and the po-

sition of a lamp near a paper—gave him an exact representation of Phœbe leaning over the table as he had often seen her do in life. It gave him a great start. Could it be she—or her ghost? He had scarcely ever believed in spirits; and still—. He looked at her fixedly in the feeble half-light, his old hair tingling oddly at the roots, and then sat up. The figure did not move. He put his thin legs out of the bed and sat looking at her, wondering if this could really be Phœbe. They had talked of ghosts often in their lifetime, of apparitions and omens; but they had never agreed that such things could be. It had never been a part of his wife's creed that she could have a spirit that could return to walk the earth. Her afterworld was quite a different affair, a vague heaven, no less, from which the righteous did not trouble to return. Yet here she was now, bending over the table in her black skirt and gray shawl, her pale profile outlined against the moonlight.

"Phœbe," he called, thrilling from head to toe, and putting out one bony hand, "have yuh come back?"

The figure did not stir, and he arose and walked uncertainly to the door, looking at it fixedly the while. As he drew near, however, the apparition resolved itself into its primal content—his old coat over the high backed chair, the lamp by the paper, the half-open door.

"Well," he said to himself, his mouth open, "I thought shore I saw her." And he ran his hand strangely and vaguely through his hair, the while his nervous tension relaxed. Vanished as it had, it gave him the idea that she might return.

Another night, because of this first illusion, and because his mind was now constantly on her and he was old, he looked out of the window that was nearest his bed and commanded a hen-coop and pig-pen and a part of the wagonshed, and there, a faint mist exuding from the damp of the ground, he thought he saw her again. It was one of those little wisps of mist, one of those faint exhalations of the earth that rise in a cool night after a warm day, and flicker like small white cypresses of fog before they disappear. In life it had been a custom of hers to cross this lot from her kitchen door to the pig-pen to throw in any scrap that was left from her cooking, and here she was again. He sat up and watched it strangely, doubtfully, because of his previous experience, but inclined, because of the nervous titillation that passed over his body, to believe that spirits really were, and that Phœbe, who would be concerned because of his lonely state, must be thinking about him, and hence returning. What other way would she have? How otherwise could she express herself? It would be within the province of her charity so to do, and like her loving interest in him. He quivered and watched it eagerly; but, a faint breath of air stirring, it wound away toward the fence and disappeared.

A third night, as he was actually dreaming, some ten days later, she came to his bedside and put her hand on his head.

"Poor Henry!" she said. "It's too bad."

He roused out of his sleep, actually to see her, he thought, moving from his bedroom into the one living room, her figure a shadowy mass of black. The weak straining of his eyes caused little points of light to flicker about the outlines of her form. He arose, greatly astonished, walked the floor in the cool room, convinced that Phœbe was coming back to him. If he only thought sufficiently, if he made it perfectly clear by his feeling that he needed her greatly, she would come back, this kindly wife, and tell him what to do. She would perhaps be with him much of the time, in the night, anyhow; and that would make him less lonely, this state more endurable.

In age and with the feeble it is not such a far cry from the subtleties of illusion to actual hallucination, and in due time this transition was made for Henry. Night after night he waited, expecting her return. Once in his weird mood he thought he saw a pale light moving about the room, and another time he thought he saw her walking in the orchard after dark. It was one morning when the details of his lonely state were virtually unendurable that he woke with the thought that she was not dead. How he had arrived at this conclusion it is hard to say. His mind had gone. In its place was a fixed illusion. He and Phœbe had had a senseless quarrel. He had reproached her for not leaving his pipe where he was accustomed to find it, and she had left. It was an aberrated fulfillment of her old jesting threat that if he did not behave himself she would leave him.

"I guess I could find yuh ag'in," he had always said. But her cackling threat had always been:

"Yuh'll not find me if I ever leave yuh. I guess I kin git some place where yuh can't find me."

This morning when he arose he did not think to build the fire in the customary way or to grind his coffee and cut his bread, as was his wont, but solely to meditate as to where he should search for her and how he should induce her to come back. Recently the one horse had been dispensed with because he found it cumbersome and beyond his needs. He took down his soft crush hat after he had dressed himself, a new glint of interest and determination in his eye, and taking his black crook cane from behind the door, where he had always placed it, started out briskly to look for her among the nearest neighbors. His old shoes clumped soundly in the dust as he walked, and his gray-black locks, now grown rather long, straggled out in a dramatic fringe or halo from under his hat. His short coat stirred busily as he walked, and his hands and face were peaked and pale.

"Why, hello, Henry! Where're yuh goin' this mornin'?" inquired Farmer Dodge, who, hauling a load of wheat to market, encountered him on the public road. He had not seen the aged farmer in months, not since his wife's death, and he wondered now, seeing him looking so spry.

"Yuh ain't seen Phœbe, have yuh?" inquired the old man, looking up quizzically.

"Phœbe who?" inquired Farmer Dodge, not for the moment connecting the name with Henry's dead wife.

"Why, my wife Phœbe, o' course. Who do yuh s'pose I mean?" He stared up with a pathetic sharpness of glance from under his shaggy, gray eyebrows.

"Wall, I'll swan, Henry, yuh ain't jokin', are yuh?" said the solid Dodge, a pursy man, with a smooth, hard, red face. "It can't be your wife yuh're talkin' about. She's dead."

"Dead! Shucks!" retorted the demented Reifsneider. "She left me early this mornin', while I was sleepin'. She allus got up to build the fire, but she's gone now. We had a little spat last night, an' I guess that's the reason. But I guess I kin find her. She's gone over to Matilda Race's, that's where she's gone."

He started briskly up the road, leaving the amazed Dodge to stare in wonder after him.

"Well, I'll be switched!" he said aloud to himself. "He's clean out'n his head. The poor old feller's been livin' down there till he's gone outen his mind. I'll have to notify the authorities." And he flicked his whip with great enthusiasm. "Geddap!" he said, and was off.

Reifsneider met no one else in this poorly populated region until he reached the whitewashed fence of Matilda Race and her husband three miles away. He had passed several other houses en route, but these not being within the range of his illusion were not considered. His wife, who had known Matilda well, must be here. He opened the picket-gate which guarded the walk, and stamped briskly up to the door.

"Why, Mr. Reifsneider," exclaimed old Matilda herself, a stout woman, looking out of the door in answer to his knock, "what brings yuh here this mornin'?"

"Is Phœbe here?" he demanded eagerly.

"Phœbe who? What Phœbe?" replied Mrs. Race, curious as to this sudden development of energy on his part.

"Why, my Phœbe, o' course. My wife Phœbe. Who do yuh s'pose? Ain't she here now?"

"Lawsy me!" exclaimed Mrs. Race, opening her mouth. "Yuh pore man! So you're clean out'n your mind now. Yuh come right in and sit down. I'll git yuh a cup o' coffee. O' course your wife ain't here; but yuh come in an' sit down. I'll find her fer yuh after a while. I know where she is."

The old farmer's eyes softened, and he entered. He was so thin and pale a specimen, pantalooned and patriarchal, that he aroused Mrs. Race's extremest sympathy as he took off his hat and laid it on his knees, quite softly and mildly.

"We had a quarrel last night, an' she left me," he volunteered.

"Laws! laws!" sighed Mrs. Race, there being no one present with whom to share her astonishment as she went to her kitchen. "The pore man! Now somebody's just got to look after him. He can't be allowed to run around the country this way lookin' for his dead wife. It's turrible."

She boiled him a pot of coffee and brought in some of her new-baked bread and fresh butter. She set out some of her best jam and put a couple of eggs to boil, lying wholeheartedly the while.

"Now yuh stay right there, Uncle Henry, till Jake comes in, an' I'll send him to look for Phœbe. I think it's more'n likely she's over to Swinnerton with some o' her friends. Anyhow, we'll find her. Now yuh just drink this coffee an' eat this bread. Yuh must be tired. Yuh've had a long walk this mornin'." Her idea was to take counsel with Jake, "her man," and perhaps have him notify the authorities.

She bustled about, meditating on the uncertainties of life, while old Reifsneider thrummed on the rim of his hat with his pale fingers and later ate abstractedly of what she offered. His mind was on his wife, however, and since she was not here, or did not appear, it wandered vaguely away to a family by the name of Murray, miles away in another direction. He decided after a time that he would not wait for Jack Race to hunt his wife but would seek her for himself. He must be on, and urge her to come back.

"Well, I'll be goin'," he said, getting up and looking strangely about him. "I guess she didn't come here after all. She went over to the Murrays, I guess. I'll not wait any longer, Mis' Race. There's a lot to do over to the house today." And out he marched in the face of her protests taking to the dusty road again in the warm spring sun, his cane striking the earth as he went.

It was two hours later that this pale figure of a man appeared in the Murrays' doorway, dusty, perspiring, eager. He had tramped all of five miles, and it was noon. An amazed husband and wife of sixty heard his strange query, and realized also that he was mad. They begged him to stay to dinner, intending to notify the authorities later and see what could be done; but though he stayed to partake of a little something, he did not stay long, and was off again to another distant farmhouse, his idea of many things to do and his need of Phoebe impelling him. So it went for that day and the next and the next, the circle of his inquiry ever widening.

The process by which a character assumes the significance of being peculiar, his antics weird, yet harmless, in such a community is often involute and pathetic. This day, as has been said, saw Reifsneider at other doors, eagerly asking his unnatural question, and leaving a trail of amazement, sympathy, and pity in his wake. Although the authorities were informed—the county sheriff, no less—it was not deemed advisable to take him into custody; for when those who knew old Henry, and had for so long, reflected on the condition of the county insane asylum, a place which, because of the poverty of the district, was of staggering aberration and sickening environment, it was decided to let him remain at large; for, strange to relate, it was found on investigation that at night he returned peaceably enough to his lonesome domicile there to discover whether his wife had returned, and to brood in loneliness until the morning. Who would lock up a thin, eager, seeking old man with iron-gray hair and an attitude of kindly, innocent inquiry, particularly when he was well known for a past of only kindly servitude and reliability? Those who had known him best rather agreed that he should be allowed to roam at large. He could do no harm. There were many who were willing to help him as to food, old clothes, the odds and ends of his daily life—at least at first.

His figure after a time became not so much a commonplace
as an accepted curiosity, and the replies, "Why, no, Henry; I
ain't see her," or "No, Henry; she ain't been here today,"
more customary.

For several years thereafter then he was an odd figure in
the sun and rain, on dusty roads and muddy ones, encountered occasionally in strange and unexpected places, pursuing his endless search. Undernourishment, after a time, although the neighbors and those who knew his history gladly
contributed from their store, affected his body; for he
walked much and ate little. The longer he roamed the public
highway in this manner, the deeper became his strange hallucination; and finding it harder and harder to return from
his more and more distant pilgrimages, he finally began taking a few utensils with him from his home, making a
small package of them, in order that he might not be compelled to return. In an old tin coffee-pot of large size he
placed a small tin cup, a knife, fork, and spoon, some salt
and pepper, and to the outside of it, by a string forced
through a pierced hole, he fastened a plate, which could be
released, and which was his woodland table. It was no trouble
for him to secure the little food that he needed, and with a
strange, almost religious dignity, he had no hesitation in asking for that much. By degrees his hair became longer and
longer, his once black hat became an earthen brown, and his
clothes threadbare and dusty.

For all of three years he walked, and none knew how wide
were his perambulations, nor how he survived the storms
and cold. They could not see him, with homely rural understanding and forethought, sheltering himself in haycocks, or
by the sides of cattle, whose warm bodies protected him from
the cold, and whose dull understandings were not opposed
to his harmless presence. Overhanging rocks and trees kept
him at times from the rain, and a friendly hay-loft or corn-
crib was not above his humble consideration.

The involute progression of hallucination is strange. From
asking at doors and being constantly rebuffed or denied, he
finally came to the conclusion that although his Phœbe
might not be in any of the houses at the doors of which he
inquired, she might nevertheless be within the sound of his
voice. And so, from patient inquiry, he began to call sad, occasional cries, that ever and anon walked the quiet land-
scapes and ragged hill regions, and set to echoing to his thin
"O-o-o Phœbe! O-o-o Phœbe!" It had a pathetic, albeit in-

sane, ring, and many a farmer or plowboy came to know it even from afar and say, "There goes old Reifsneider."

Another thing that puzzled him greatly after a time and after many hundreds of inquiries was, when he no longer had any particular door-yard in view and no special inquiry to make, which way to go. These cross-roads, which occasionally led in four or even six directions, came after a time to puzzle him. But to solve this knotty problem, which became more and more of a puzzle, there came to his aid another hallucination. Phœbe's spirit or some power of the air or wind or nature would tell him. If he stood at the center of the parting of the ways, closed his eyes, turned thrice about, and called "O-o-o Phœbe!" twice, and then threw his cane straight before him, that would surely indicate which way to go, for Phœbe, or one of these mystic powers would surely govern its direction and fall! In whichever direction it went, even though, as was not infrequently the case, it took him back along the path he had already come, or across fields, he was not so far gone in his mind but that he gave himself ample time to search before he called again. Also the hallucination seemed to persist that at some time he would surely find her. There were hours when his feet were sore, and his limbs weary, when he would stop in the heat to wipe his seamed brow, or in the cold to beat his arms. Sometimes, after throwing away his cane, and finding it indicating the direction from which he had just come, he would shake his head wearily and philosophically, as if contemplating the unbelievable or an untoward fate, and then start briskly off. His strange figure came finally to be known in the farthest reaches of three or four counties. Old Reifsneider was a pathetic character. His fame was wide.

Near a little town called Watersville, in Green County, perhaps four miles from that minor center of human activity, there was a place or precipice locally known as the Red Cliff, a sheer wall of red sandstone, perhaps a hundred feet high, which raised its sharp face for half a mile or more about the fruitful cornfields and orchards that lay beneath, and which was surmounted by a thick grove of trees. The slope that slowly led up to it from the opposite side was covered by a rank growth of beech, hickory, and ash, through which threaded a number of wagon-tracks crossing at various angles. In fair weather it had become old Reifsneider's habit, so inured was he by now to the open, to make his bed in some such patch of trees as this, to fry his bacon or boil his

eggs at the foot of some tree, before laying himself down
for the night. Occasionally, so light and inconsequential was
his sleep, he would walk at night. More often, the moonlight
or some sudden wind stirring in the trees or a reconnoitering animal arousing him, he would sit up and think, or pur-
sue his quest in the moonlight or the dark, a strange, unnatural, half wild, half savage-looking but utterly harmless creature, calling at lonely road crossings, staring at dark
and shuttered houses, and wondering where, where Phœbe
could really be.

That particular lull that comes in the systole-diastole of
this earthly ball at two o'clock in the morning invariably
aroused him, and though he might not go any farther he
would sit up and contemplate the darkness or the stars, wondering. Sometimes in the strange processes of his mind he
would fancy that he saw moving among the trees the figure
of his lost wife, and then he would get up to follow, taking
his utensils, always on a string, and his cane. If she seemed to
evade him too easily he would run, or plead, or, suddenly
losing track of the fancied figure, stand awed or disappointed,
grieving for the moment over the almost insurmountable difficulties of his search.

It was in the seventh year of these hopeless peregrina-
tions, in the dawn of a similar springtime to that in which
his wife had died, that he came at last one night to the vicinity of this selfsame patch that crowned the rise to the Red
Cliff. His far-flung cane, used as a divining-rod at the
last cross-roads, had brought him hither. He had walked
many, many miles. It was after ten o'clock at night, and he
was very weary. Long wandering and little eating had left
him but a shadow of his former self. It was a question now
not so much of physical strength but of spiritual endurance
which kept him up. He had scarcely eaten this day, and now,
exhausted, he set himself down in the dark to rest and possibly to sleep.

Curiously on this occasion a strange suggestion of the
presence of his wife surrounded him. It would not be long
now, he counseled with himself, although the long months
had brought him nothing, until he should see her, talk to her.
He fell asleep after a time, his head on his knees. At midnight the moon began to rise, and at two in the morning, his
wakeful hour, was a large silver disk shining through the
trees to the east. He opened his eyes when the radiance became strong, making a silver pattern at his feet and lighting

the woods with strange lusters and silvery, shadowy forms. As usual, his old notion that his wife must be near occurred to him on this occasion, and he looked about him with a speculative, anticipatory eye. What was it that moved in the distant shadows along the path by which he had entered—a pale, flickering will-o'-the-wisp that bobbed gracefully among the trees and riveted his expectant gaze? Moonlight and shadows combined to give it a strange form and a stranger reality, this fluttering of bog-fire or dancing of wandering fireflies. Was it truly his lost Phœbe? By a circuitous route it passed about him, and in his fevered state he fancied that he could see the very eyes of her, not as she was when he last saw her in the black dress and shawl, but now a strangely younger Phœbe, gayer, sweeter, the one whom he had known years before as a girl. Old Reifsneider got up. He had been expecting and dreaming of this hour all these years, and now as he saw the feeble light dancing lightly before him he peered at it questioningly, one thin hand in his gray hair.

Of a sudden there came to him now for the first time in many years the full charm of her girlish figure as he had known it in boyhood, the pleasing, sympathetic smile, the brown hair, the blue sash she had once worn about her waist at a picnic, her gay, graceful movements. He walked around the base of the tree, straining with his eyes, forgetting for once his cane and utensils, and following eagerly after. On she moved before him, a will-o'-the-wisp of the spring, a little flame above her head, and it seemed as though among the small saplings of ash and beech and the thick trunks of hickory and elm that she signaled with a young, a lightsome hand.

"Oh, Phœbe! Phœbe!" he called. "Have yuh really come? Have yuh really answered me?" And hurrying faster, he fell once, scrambling lamely to his feet, only to see the light in the distance dancing illusively on. On and on he hurried until he was fairly running, brushing his ragged arms against the trees striking his hands and face against impeding twigs. His hat was gone, his lungs were breathless, his reason quite astray, when coming to the edge of the cliff he saw her below among a silvery bed of apple trees now blooming in the spring.

"Oh, Phœbe!" he called. "Oh, Phœbe! Oh, no, don't leave me!" And feeling the lure of a world where love was young and Phœbe, as this vision presented her, a delightful epitome of their quondam youth, he gave a gay cry of "Oh, wait, Phœbe!" and leaped.

Some farmer-boys, reconnoitering this region of bounty and prospect some few days afterward, found first the tin utensils tied together under the tree where he had left them, and then later at the foot of the cliff, pale, broken, but elate, a molded smile of peace and delight upon his lips, his body. His old hat was discovered lying under some low-growing saplings, the twigs of which had held it back. No one of all the simple population knew how eagerly and joyously he had found his lost mate.

Father Is Firm with His Ailments

BY CLARENCE DAY

FATHER GOT annoyed at us when we didn't stay well. He usually stayed well himself and he expected us to be like him, and not faint and slump on his hands and thus add to his burdens.

He was fearless about disease. He despised it. All this talk about germs, he said, was merely newfangled nonsense. He said that when he was a boy there had been no germs that he knew of. Perhaps invisible insects existed, but what of it? He was as healthy as they were. "If any damned germs want to have a try at me," he said, "bring 'em on."

From Father's point of view, Mother didn't know how to handle an ailment. He admired her most of the time and thought there was nobody like her; he often said to us boys, "Your mother is a wonderful woman;" but he always seemed to disapprove of her when she was ill.

Mother went to bed, for instance, at such times. Yet she didn't make noises. Father heard a little gasping moan sometimes, but she didn't want him to hear even that. Consequently he was sure she wasn't suffering. There was nothing to indicate it, he said.

The worse she felt, the less she ever said about it, and the harder it was for him to believe that there was anything really wrong with her. "He says he can't see why I stay in bed so long," she once wrote to me, when I was away, "but this colitis is a mean affair which keeps one perfectly flat. The doctor told him yesterday the meaning of colitis, but he said he 'had never heard of the damned thing, thank God.' He feels very abused that he should be 'so upset by people with queer things the matter with them and doctors all over the place.'" (Mother underlined the word "people.")

Even Mother's colds made him fretful. Whenever she had one, she kept going as long as she could, pottering about her room looking white and tired, with a shawl round her shoulders. But sometimes she had to give up and crawl into her bed.

Father pished and poohed to himself about this, and muttered that it was silly. He said Mother was perfectly healthy. When people thought they were ill, he declared it didn't mean that there was anything the matter with them, it was merely a sign of weak character. He often told Mother how weak it was to give in to an ailment, but every time he tried to strengthen her character in this respect, he said she seemed to resent it. He never remembered to try except when she could hardly hold her head up. From his point of view, though, that was the very time that she needed his help.

He needed hers, too, or not exactly her help but her company, and he never hesitated to say so. When she was ill, he felt lost.

He usually came up from his office at about five or six. The first thing he did was to look around the house to find Mother. It made his home feel queer and empty to him when she wasn't there.

One night about six o'clock he opened the door of her bedroom. There was no light except for a struggling little fire which flickered and sank in the grate. A smell of witch-hazel was in the air, mixed with spirits of camphor. On the bed, huddled up under an afghan, Mother lay still, in the dark.

"Are you there, Vinnie?" Father said, in a voice even louder than usual because of his not being sure.

Mother moaned, "Go away."

"What?" he asked, in astonishment.

"Go away. Oh, go 'way."

"Damnation!" he said, marching out.

"Clare!"

"What is it?"

"Won't you *ple-e-ease* shut my door again!"

Father ground his teeth and shut it with such a bang that it made Mother jump.

He told himself she had nothing the matter with her. She'd be all right in the morning. He ate a good dinner. Being lonely, he added an extra glass of claret and some toasted crackers and cheese. He had such a long and dull evening that he smoked two extra cigars.

After breakfast the next morning, he went to her bedroom again. The fire was out. Two worn old slippers lay on a chair. The gray daylight was cheerless. Father stood at the foot of Mother's bed, looking disconsolately at her because she wasn't well yet. He had no one to laugh at or quarrel with; his features were lumpy with gloom.

"What is it?" Mother asked in a whisper, opening her weary eyes.

"Nothing," he said loudly. "Nothing."

"Well, for mercy's sake, don't come in here looking like that, Clare," Mother begged.

"What do you mean? Looking like what?"

"Oh, go away!" Mother shrieked. "When people are sick, they like to see a smile or something. I never will get well if you stand there and stare at me that way! And shut my door quietly this time. And let me alone."

Outside her door, when I asked him how Mother was, he said with a chuckle: "She's all right again. She isn't out of bed yet, but she sounds much better this morning."

Father's own experiences in a sick-room had been very few. When he was in his early thirties, he had an attack of gout which lasted three weeks. From that time until he was seventy-four and had pneumonia, he had no other serious illnesses. He said illnesses were mostly imaginary and he didn't believe in them.

He even declared that his pneumonia was imaginary. "It's only some idea of that doctor's," he said. "Nothing the matter with me but a cold." Our regular physician had died, and this new man and two trained nurses had all they could do, at first, to keep Father in bed.

The new doctor had pale-blue eyes, a slight build, and a way of inwardly smiling at the persons he talked to. He had a strong will in crises, and he was one of the ablest physicians in town. Mother had chosen him, however, chiefly because she liked one of his female cousins.

When Father got worse, the doctor kept warning him

that it really *was* pneumonia, and that if he wouldn't be tractable, he might not get over it—especially at seventy-four.

Father lay in bed glowering at him and said: "I didn't send for you, sir. You needn't stand there and tell me what you want me to do. I know all about doctors. They think they know a damned lot. But they don't. Give your pills and things to Mrs. Day—she believes in them. That's all I have to say. There's no need to continue this discussion. There's the door, sir. Goodbye."

But somehow the discussion kept on, and much to his surprise Father at last became convinced he was ill. The doctor, leaving him alone in his bedroom to digest the bad news, came out in the hall, anxious and tired, to have a few words with Mother. As they stood outside Father's door whispering quietly, they heard his voice from within. Apparently, now that he knew he was in trouble, his thoughts had turned to his God. "Have mercy!" they heard him shouting indignantly. "I say have mercy, damn it!"

Any sufferings that Father ever had he attributed solely to God. Naturally, he never thought for a moment that God could mean him to suffer. He couldn't imagine God's wishing to punish him either, for his conscience was clear. His explanation seemed to be that God was clumsy, not to say muddle-headed.

However, in spite of God and the doctor, Father got over pneumonia, just as, some forty years before, he had got over his gout. Only, in conquering his gout, he had had the help of a cane and a masseur called Old Lowndes.

While the gout was besieging him, Father sat in a big chair by the fire with his bad foot on a stool, armed with a cane which he kept constantly ready. Not that he used the cane to walk with. When he walked, he hopped around on his other foot, uttering strong howls of fury. But he valued his cane highly, and needed it, too, as a war club. He threatened the whole family with it. When visitors entered the room he brandished it fiercely at them, to keep them away from his toe.

Old Lowndes was allowed to approach nearer than others, but he was warned that if he made any mistakes that cane would come down on his head. Father felt there was no knowing what harm Lowndes might have done if he hadn't shaken his cane at him and made him take care.

As it was, owing largely to this useful stick, Father got well.

This experience convinced him that any disease could be conquered by firmness.

When he had a cold, his method of dealing with it was to try to clear it out by main force, either by violently blowing his nose or, still better, by sneezing. Mother didn't like him to sneeze, he did it with such a roar. She said she could feel it half across the room, and she was sure it was catching. Father said this was nonsense. He said his sneezes were healthy. And presently we'd hear a hearty, triumphant blast as he sneezed again.

Aside from colds, which he had very seldom, his only foes were sick headaches. He said headaches only came from eating, however. Hence a man who knew enough to stop eating could always get rid of one that way. It took time to starve it out thoroughly. It might take several hours. But as soon as it was gone, he could eat again and enjoy his cigar.

When one of these headaches started, Father lay down and shut his eyes tight and yelled. The severity of a headache could be judged by the volume of sound he put forth. His idea seemed to be to show the headache that he was just as strong as it was, and stronger. When a headache and he went to bed together, they were a noisy pair.

Father's code required him to be game, I suppose. He never spoke. or thought of having a code; he wasn't that sort of person; but he denounced men whose standards were low, as to gameness or anything else. It didn't occur to him to conceal his sufferings, however; when he had any pains, he expressed them as fully as he knew how. His way of being brave was not to keep still but to keep on fighting the headache.

Mother used to beg him to be quiet at night, even if he did have a headache, and not wake up the whole house. He never paid the slightest attention to such a request. When she said, "Please don't groan so much, Clare," he'd look at her in disgust, as though he were a warrior being asked to stifle his battle-cries.

One evening he found Mother worrying because Aunt Emma was ill with some disease that was then epidemic.

"Oh, pooh!" Father said. "Nothing the matter with Emma. You can trust people to get any ailment whatever that's fashionable. They hear of a lot of other people having it, and the first thing you know they get scared and think they have it themselves. Then they go to bed, and send for the doctor. The doctor! All poppycock."

"Well, but Clare dear, if you were in charge of them, what would you do instead?"

"Cheer 'em up, that's the way to cure 'em."

"How would you cheer them up, darling?" Mother asked doubtfully.

"I? I'd tell 'em, *'Bah!'* "

Death in the Woods

BY SHERWOOD ANDERSON

SHE WAS an old woman and lived on a farm near the town in which I lived. All country and small-town people have seen such old women, but no one knows much about them. Such an old woman comes into town driving an old worn-out horse or she comes afoot carrying a basket. She may own a few hens and have eggs to sell. She brings them in a basket and takes them to a grocer. There she trades them in. She gets some salt pork and some beans. Then she gets a pound or two of sugar and some flour.

Afterwards she goes to the butcher's and asks for some dog-meat. She may spend ten or fifteen cents, but when she does she asks for something. Formerly the butchers gave liver to any one who wanted to carry it away. In our family we were always having it. Once one of my brothers got a whole cow's liver at the slaughter-house near the fairgrounds in our town. We had it until we were sick of it. It never cost a cent. I have hated the thought of it ever since.

The old farm woman got some liver and a soup-bone. She never visited with any one, and as soon as she got what she wanted she lit out for home. It made quite a load for such an old body. No one gave her a lift. People drive right down a road and never notice an old woman like that.

There was such an old woman who used to come into town past our house one Summer and Fall when I was a

young boy and was sick with what was called inflammatory
rheumatism. She went home later carrying a heavy pack on
her back. Two or three large gaunt-looking dogs followed
at her heels.

The old woman was nothing special. She was one of the
nameless ones that hardly any one knows, but she got into
my thoughts. I have just suddenly now, after all these years,
remembered her and what happened. It is a story. Her name
was Grimes, and she lived with her husband and son in a
small unpainted house on the bank of a small creek four
miles from town.

The husband and son were a tough lot. Although the
son was but twenty-one, he had already served a term in
jail. It was whispered about that the woman's husband stole
horses and ran them off to some other county. Now and
then, when a horse turned up missing, the man had also
disappeared. No one ever caught him. Once, when I was
loafing at Tom Whitehead's livery-barn, the man came there
and sat on the bench in front. Two or three other men
were there, but no one spoke to him. He sat for a few
minutes and then got up and went away. When he was
leaving he turned around and stared at the men. There
was a look of defiance in his eyes. "Well, I have tried to
be friendly. You don't want to talk to me. It has been so
wherever I have gone in this town. If, some day, one of
your fine horses turns up missing, well, then what?" He
did not say anything actually. "I'd like to bust one of you
on the jaw," was about what his eyes said. I remember
how the look in his eyes made me shiver.

The old man belonged to a family that had had money
once. His name was Jake Grimes. It all comes back clearly
now. His father, John Grimes, had owned a sawmill when
the country was new, and had made money. Then he got
to drinking and running after women. When he died there
wasn't much left.

Jake blew in the rest. Pretty soon there wasn't any more
lumber to cut and his land was nearly all gone.

He got his wife off a German farmer, for whom he went
to work one June day in the wheat harvest. She was a
young thing then and scared to death. You see, the farmer
was up to something with the girl—she was, I think, a
bound girl and his wife had her suspicions. She took it out
on the girl when the man wasn't around. Then, when the
wife had to go off to town for supplies, the farmer got

after her. She told young Jake that nothing really ever happened, but he didn't know whether to believe it or not.

He got her pretty easy himself, the first time he was out with her. He wouldn't have married her if the German farmer hadn't tried to tell him where to get off. He got her to go riding with him in his buggy one night when he was threshing on the place, and then he came for her the next Sunday night.

She managed to get out of the house without her employer's seeing, but when she was getting into the buggy he showed up. It was almost dark, and he just popped up suddenly at the horse's head. He grabbed the horse by the bridle and Jake got out his buggy-whip.

They had it out all right! The German was a tough one. Maybe he didn't care whether his wife knew or not. Jake hit him over the face and shoulders with the buggy-whip, but the horse got to acting up and he had to get out.

Then the two men went for it. The girl didn't see it. The horse started to run away and went nearly a mile down the road before the girl got him stopped. Then she managed to tie him to a tree beside the road. (I wonder how I know all this. It must have stuck in my mind from small-town tales when I was a boy.) Jake found her there after he got through with the German. She was huddled up in the buggy seat, crying, scared to death. She told Jake a lot of stuff, how the German had tried to get her, how he chased her once into the barn, how another time, when they happened to be alone in the house together, he tore her dress open clear down the front. The German, she said, might have got her that time if he hadn't heard his old woman drive in at the gate. She had been off to town for supplies. Well, she would be putting the horse in the barn. The German managed to sneak off to the fields without his wife seeing. He told the girl he would kill her if she told. What could she do? She told a lie about ripping her dress in the barn when she was feeding the stock. I remember now that she was a bound girl and did not know where her father and mother were. Maybe she did not have any father. You know what I mean.

Such bound children were often enough cruelly treated. They were children who had no parents, slaves really. There were very few orphan homes then. They were legally bound into some home. It was a matter of pure luck how it came out.

II

She married Jake and had a son and daughter, but the daughter died.

Then she settled down to feed stock. That was her job. At the German's place she had cooked the food for the German and his wife. The wife was a strong woman with big hips and worked most of the time in the fields with her husband. She fed them and fed the cows in the barn, fed the pigs, the horses and the chickens. Every moment of every day, as a young girl, was spent feeding something.

Then she married Jake Grimes and he had to be fed. She was a slight thing, and when she had been married for three or four years, and after the two children were born, her slender shoulders became stooped.

Jake always had a lot of big dogs around the house, that stood near the unused sawmill near the creek. He was always trading horses when he wasn't stealing something and had a lot of poor bony ones about. Also he kept three or four pigs and a cow. They were all pastured in the few acres left of the Grimes place and Jake did little enough work.

He went into debt for a threshing outfit and ran it for several years, but it did not pay. People did not trust him. They were afraid he would steal the grain at night. He had to go a long way off to get work and it cost too much to get there. In the Winter he hunted and cut a little firewood, to be sold in some nearby town. When the son grew up he was just like the father. They got drunk together. If there wasn't anything to eat in the house when they came home the old man gave his old woman a cut over the head. She had a few chickens of her own and had to kill one of them in a hurry. When they were all killed she wouldn't have any eggs to sell when she went to town, and then what would she do?

She had to scheme all her life about getting things fed, getting the pigs fed so they would grow fat and could be butchered in the Fall. When they were butchered her husband took most of the meat off to town and sold it. If he did not do it first the boy did. They fought sometimes and when they fought the old woman stood aside trembling.

She had got the habit of silence anyway—that was fixed. Sometimes, when she began to look old—she wasn't forty yet—and when the husband and son were both off, trading horses or drinking or hunting or stealing, she went around the house and the barnyard muttering to herself.

How was she going to get everything fed?—that was her problem. The dogs had to be fed. There wasn't enough hay in the barn for the horses and the cow. If she didn't feed the chickens how could they lay eggs? Without eggs to sell how could she get things in town, things she had to have to keep the life of the farm going? Thank heaven, she did not have to feed her husband—in a certain way. That hadn't lasted long after their marriage and after the babies came. Where he went on his long trips she did not know. Sometimes he was gone from home for weeks, and after the boy grew up they went off together.

They left everything at home for her to manage and she had no money. She knew no one. No one ever talked to her in town. When it was Winter she had to gather sticks of wood for her fire, had to try to keep the stock fed with very little grain.

The stock in the barn cried to her hungrily, the dogs followed her about. In the Winter the hens laid few enough eggs. They huddled in the corners of the barn and she kept watching them. If a hen lays an egg in the barn in the Winter and you do not find it, it freezes and breaks.

One day in Winter the old woman went off to town with a few eggs and the dogs followed her. She did not get started until nearly three o'clock and the snow was heavy. She hadn't been feeling very well for several days and so she went muttering along, scantily clad, her shoulders stooped. She had an old grain bag in which she carried her eggs, tucked away down in the bottom. There weren't many of them, but in Winter the price of eggs is up. She would get a little meat in exchange for the eggs, some salt pork, a little sugar, and some coffee perhaps. It might be the butcher would give her a piece of liver.

When she had got to town and was trading in her eggs the dogs lay by the door outside. She did pretty well, got the things she needed, more than she had hoped. Then she went to the butcher and he gave her some liver and some dog-meat.

It was the first time any one had spoken to her in a friendly way for a long time. The butcher was alone in his shop when she came in and was annoyed by the thought of such a sick-looking old woman out on such a day. It was bitter cold and the snow, that had let up during the afternoon, was falling again. The butcher said something about her husband and her son, swore at them, and the old woman stared at him, a look of mild surprise in her eyes as he talked. He said that if either the husband or the son were going to get any of the liver or the heavy bones with scraps of meat hanging to them that he had put into the grain bag, he'd see him starve first.

Starve, eh? Well, things had to be fed. Men had to be fed, and the horses that weren't any good but maybe could be traded off, and the poor thin cow that hadn't given any milk for three months.

Horses, cows, pigs, dogs, men.

III

The old woman had to get back before darkness came if she could. The dogs followed at her heels, sniffing at the heavy grain bag she had fastened on her back. When she got to the edge of town she stopped by a fence and tied the bag on her back with a piece of rope she had carried in her dress-pocket for just that purpose. That was an easier way to carry it. Her arms ached. It was hard when she had to crawl over fences and once she fell over and landed in the snow. The dogs went frisking about. She had to struggle to get to her feet again, but she made it. The point of climbing over the fences was that there was a short cut over a hill and through a woods. She might have gone around by the road, but it was a mile farther that way. She was afraid she couldn't make it. And then, besides, the stock had to fed. There was a little hay left and a little corn. Perhaps her husband and son would bring some home when they came. They had driven off in the only buggy the Grimes family had, a rickety thing, a rickety horse hitched to the buggy, two other rickety horses led by halters. They were going to trade horses, get a little money if they could. They might come home drunk. It would be well to have something in the house when they came back.

The son had an affair on with a woman at the county seat, fifteen miles away. She was a rough enough woman, a tough one. Once, in the Summer, the son had brought her to the house. Both she and the son had been drinking. Jake Grimes was away and the son and his woman ordered the old woman about like a servant. She didn't mind much;

she was used to it. Whatever happened she never said anything. That was her way of getting along. She had managed that way when she was a young girl at the German's and ever since she had married Jake. That time her son brought his woman to the house they stayed all night, sleeping together just as though they were married. It hadn't shocked the old woman, not much. She had got past being shocked early in life.

With the pack on her back she went painfully along across an open field, wading in the deep snow, and got into the woods.

There was a path, but it was hard to follow. Just beyond the top of the hill, where the woods was thickest, there was a small clearing. Had some one once thought of building a house there? The clearing was as large as a building lot in town, large enough for a house and a garden. The path ran along the side of the clearing, and when she got there the old woman sat down to rest at the foot of a tree.

It was a foolish thing to do. When she got herself placed, the pack against the tree's trunk, it was nice, but what about getting up again? She worried about that for a moment and then quietly closed her eyes.

She must have slept for a time. When you are about so cold you can't get any colder. The afternoon grew a little warmer and the snow came thicker than ever. Then after a time the weather cleared. The moon even came out.

There were four Grimes dogs that had followed Mrs. Grimes into town, all tall gaunt fellows. Such men as Jake Grimes and his son always keep just such dogs. They kick and abuse them, but they stay. The Grimes dogs, in order to keep from starving, had to do a lot of foraging for themselves, and they had been at it while the old woman slept with her back to the tree at the side of the clearing. They had been chasing rabbits in the woods and in adjoining fields and in their ranging had picked up three other farm dogs.

After a time all the dogs came back to the clearing. They were excited about something. Such nights, cold and clear and with a moon, do things to dogs. It may be that some old instinct, come down from the time when they were wolves and ranged the woods in packs on Winter nights, comes back into them.

The dogs in the clearing, before the old woman, had caught two or three rabbits and their immediate hunger had

been satisfied. They began to play, running in circles in
the clearing. Round and round they ran, each dog's nose
at the tail of the next dog. In the clearing, under the snow-
laden trees and under the wintry moon they made a strange
picture, running thus silently, in a circle their running had
beaten in the soft snow. The dogs made no sound. They
ran around and around in the circle.

It may have been that the old woman saw them doing
that before she died. She may have awakened once or twice
and looked at the strange sight with dim old eyes.

She wouldn't be very cold now, just drowsy. Life hangs
on a long time. Perhaps the old woman was out of her
head. She may have dreamed of her girlhood, at the German's, and before that, when she was a child and before
her mother lit out and left her.

Her dreams couldn't have been very pleasant. Not many
pleasant things had happened to her. Now and then one
of the Grimes dogs left the running circle and came to
stand before her. The dog thrust his face close to her face.
His red tongue was hanging out.

The running of the dogs may have been a kind of death
ceremony. It may have been that the primitive instinct of
the wolf, having been aroused in the dogs by the night
and the running, made them somehow afraid.

"Now we are no longer wolves. We are dogs, the servants
of men. Keep alive, man! When man dies we becomes
wolves again."

When one of the dogs came to where the old woman sat
with her back against the tree and thrust his nose close to
her face he seemed satisfied and went back to run with the
pack. All the Grimes dogs did it at some time during the
evening, before she died. I knew all about it afterward,
when I grew to be a man, because once in a woods in
Illinois, on another Winter night, I saw a pack of dogs act
just like that. The dogs were waiting for me to die as they
had waited for the old woman that night when I was a
child, but when it happened to me I was a young man
and had no intention whatever of dying.

The old woman died softly and quietly. When she was
dead and when one of the Grimes dogs had come to her
and had found her dead all the dogs stopped running.

They gathered about her.

Well, she was dead now. She had fed the Grimes dogs
when she was alive, what about now?

There was the pack on her back, the grain bag containing the piece of salt pork, the liver the butcher had given her, the dog-meat, the soup bones. The butcher in town, having been suddenly overcome with a feeling of pity, had loaded her grain bag heavily. It had been a big haul for the old woman.

It was a big haul for the dogs now.

IV

One of the Grimes dogs sprang suddenly out from among the others and began worrying the pack on the old woman's back. Had the dogs really been wolves that one would have been the leader of the pack. What he did, all the others did.

All of them sank their teeth into the grain bag the old woman had fastened with ropes to her back.

They dragged the old woman's body out into the open clearing. The worn-out dress was quickly torn from her shoulders. When she was found, a day or two later, the dress had been torn from her body clear to the hips, but the dogs had not touched her body. They had got the meat out of the grain bag, that was all. Her body was frozen stiff when it was found, and the shoulders were so narrow and the body so slight that in death it looked like the body of some charming young girl.

Such things happened in towns of the Middle West, on farms near town, when I was a boy. A hunter out after rabbits found the old woman's body and did not touch it. Something, the beaten round path in the little snow-covered clearing, the silence of the place, the place where the dogs had worried the body trying to pull the grain bag away or tear it open—something startled the man and he hurried off to town.

I was in Main street with one of my brothers who was town newsboy and who was taking the afternoon papers to the stores. It was almost night.

The hunter came into a grocery and told his story. Then he went to a hardware-shop and into a drugstore. Men began to gather on the sidewalks. Then they started out along the road to the place in the woods.

My brother should have gone on about his business of distributing papers but he didn't. Every one was going to the woods. The undertaker went and the town marshal. Several men got on a dray and rode out to where the path left the road and went into the woods, but the horses weren't very sharply shod and slid about on the slippery roads. They made no better time than those of us who walked.

The town marshal was a large man whose leg had been injured in the Civil War. He carried a heavy cane and limped rapidly along the road. My brother and I followed at his heels, and as we went other men and boys joined the crowd.

It had grown dark by the time we got to where the old woman had left the road but the moon had come out. The marshal was thinking there might have been a murder. He kept asking the hunter questions. The hunter went along with his gun across his shoulders, a dog following at his heels. It isn't often a rabbit hunter has a chance to be so conspicuous. He was taking full advantage of it, leading the procession with the town marshal. "I didn't see any wounds. She was a beautiful young girl. Her face was buried in the snow. No, I didn't know her." As a matter of fact, the hunter had not looked closely at the body. He had been frightened. She might have been murdered and some one might spring out from behind a tree and murder him. In a woods, in the late afternoon, when the trees are all bare and there is white snow on the ground, when all is silent, something creepy steals over the mind and body. If something strange or uncanny has happened in the neighborhood all you think about is getting away from there as fast as you can.

The crowd of men and boys had got to where the old woman had crossed the field and went, following the marshal and the hunter, up the slight incline and into the woods.

My brother and I were silent. He had his bundle of papers in a bag slung across his shoulder. When he got back to town he would have to go on distributing his papers before he went home to supper. If I went along, as he had no doubt already determined I should, we would both be late. Either mother or our older sister would have to warm our supper.

Well, we would have something to tell. A boy did not get such a chance very often. It was lucky we just happened to go into the grocery when the hunter came in. The hunter was a country fellow. Neither of us had ever seen him before.

Now the crowd of men and boys had got to the clearing.

Darkness comes quickly on such Winter nights, but the full moon made everything clear. My brother and I stood near the tree, beneath which the old woman had died.

She did not look old, lying there in that light, frozen and still. One of the men turned her over in the snow and I saw everything. My body trembled with some strange mystical feeling and so did my brother's. It might have been the cold.

Neither of us had ever seen a woman's body before. It may have been the snow, clinging to the frozen flesh, that made it look so white and lovely, so like marble. No woman had come with the party from town; but one of the men, he was the town blacksmith, took off his overcoat and spread it over her. Then he gathered her into his arms and started off to town, all the others following silently. At that time no one knew who she was.

V

I had seen everything, had seen the oval in the snow, like a miniature race-track, where the dogs had run, had seen how the men were mystified, had seen the white bare young-looking shoulders, had heard the whispered comments of the men.

The men were simply mystified. They took the body to the undertaker's, and when the blacksmith, the hunter, the marshal and several others had got inside they closed the door. If father had been there perhaps he could have got in, but we boys couldn't.

I went with my brother to distribute the rest of his papers and when we got home it was my brother who told the story.

I kept silent and went to bed early. It may have been I was not satisfied with the way he told it.

Later, in the town, I must have heard other fragments of the old woman's story. She was recognized the next day and there was an investigation.

The husband and son were found somewhere and brought to town and there was an attempt to connect them with the woman's death, but it did not work. They had perfect enough alibis.

However, the town was against them. They had to get out. Where they went I never heard.

I remember only the picture there in the forest, the men

standing about, the naked girlish-looking figure, face down in the snow, the tracks made by the running dogs and the clear cold Winter sky above. White fragments of clouds were drifting across the sky. They went racing across the little open space among the trees.

The scene in the forest had become for me, without my knowing it, the foundation for the real story I am now trying to tell. The fragments, you see, had to be picked up slowly, long afterwards.

Things happened. When I was a young man I worked on the farm of a German. The hired-girl was afraid of her employer. The farmer's wife hated her.

I saw things at that place. Once later, I had a half-uncanny, mystical adventure with dogs in an Illinois forest on a clear, moon-lit Winter night. When I was a schoolboy, and on a Summer day, I went with a boy friend out along a creek some miles from town and came to the house where the old woman had lived. No one had lived in the house since her death. The doors were broken from the hinges; the window lights were all broken. As the boy and I stood in the road outside, two dogs, just roving farm dogs no doubt, came running around the corner of the house. The dogs were tall, gaunt fellows and came down to the fence and glared through at us, standing in the road.

The whole thing, the story of the old woman's death, was to me as I grew older like music heard from far off. The notes had to be picked up slowly one at a time. Something had to be understood.

The woman who died was one destined to feed animal life. Anyway, that is all she ever did. She was feeding animal life before she was born, as a child, as a young woman working on the farm of the German, after she married, when she grew old and, when she died. She fed animal life in cows, in chickens, in pigs, in horses, in dogs, in men. Her daughter had died in childhood and with her one son she had no articulate relations. On the night when she died she was hurrying homeward, bearing on her body food for animal life.

She died in the clearing in the woods and even after her death continued feeding animal life.

You see it is likely that, when my brother told the story, that night when we got home and my mother and sister sat listening, I did not think he got the point. He was too young and so was I. A thing so complete has its own beauty.

I shall not try to emphasize the point. I am only explaining why I was dissatisfied then and have been ever since. I speak of that only that you may understand why I have been impelled to try to tell the simple story over again.

To Build a Fire

BY JACK LONDON

DAY HAD broken cold and gray, exceedingly cold and gray, when the man turned aside from the main Yukon trail and climbed the high earth-bank, where a dim and little-traveled trail led eastward through the fat spruce timberland. It was a steep bank, and he paused for breath at the top, excusing the act to himself by looking at his watch. It was nine o'clock. There was no sun nor hint of sun, though there was not a cloud in the sky. It was a clear day, and yet there seemed an intangible pall over the face of things, a subtle gloom that made the day dark, and that was due to the absence of sun. This fact did not worry the man. He was used to the lack of sun. It had been days since he had seen the sun, and he knew that a few more days must pass before that cheerful orb, due south, would just peep above the skyline and dip immediately from view.

The man flung a look back along the way he had come. The Yukon lay a mile wide and hidden under three feet of ice. On top of this ice were as many feet of snow. It was all pure white, rolling in gentle, undulations where the ice-jams of the freeze-up had formed. North and south, as far as his eye could see, it was unbroken white, save for a dark hair-line that curved and twisted from around the spruce-covered island to the south, and that curved and twisted away into the north, where it disappeared behind another spruce-covered island. This dark hair-line was the trail—the main trail—that led south five hundred miles to the Chilcoot Pass, Dyea, and salt water; and that led north seventy miles to Dawson, and still on to the north a thousand miles to Nulato, and finally to St. Michael on Bering Sea, a thousand miles and half a thousand more.

But all this—the mysterious, far-reaching hair-line trail, the absence of sun from the sky, the tremendous cold, and the strangeness and weirdness of it all—made no impression on the man. It was not because he was long used to it. He was a newcomer in the land, a *chechaquo*, and this was his first winter. The trouble with him was that he was without imagination. He was quick and alert in the things of life, but only in the things, and not in the significances. Fifty degrees below zero meant eighty-odd degrees of frost. Such fact impressed him as being cold and uncomfortable, and that was all. It did not lead him to meditate upon his frailty as a creature of temperature, and upon man's frailty in general, able only to live within certain narrow limits of heat and cold; and from there on it did not lead him to the conjectural field of immortality and man's place in the universe. Fifty degrees below zero stood for a bite of frost that hurt and that must be guarded against by the use of mittens, ear-flaps, warm moccasins, and thick socks. Fifty degrees below zero was to him just precisely fifty degrees below zero. That there should be anything more to it than that was a thought that never entered his head.

As he turned to go on, he spat speculatively. There was a sharp, explosive crackle that startled him. He spat again. And again, in the air, before it could fall to the snow, the spittle crackled. He knew that at fifty below spittle crackled on the snow, but this spittle had crackled in the air. Undoubtedly it was colder than fifty below—how much colder he did not know. But the temperature did not matter. He was bound for the old claim on the left fork of Henderson Creek, where the boys were already. They had come over across the divide from the Indian Creek country, while he had come the roundabout way to take a look at the possibilities of getting out logs in the spring from the islands in the Yukon. He would be in to camp by six o'clock; a bit after dark, it was true, but the boys would be there, a fire would be going, and a hot supper would be ready. As for lunch, he pressed his hand against the protruding bundle under his jacket. It was also under his shirt, wrapped up in a handkerchief and lying against the naked skin. It was the only way to keep the biscuits from freezing. He smiled agreeably to himself as he thought of those biscuits, each cut open and sopped in bacon grease, and each enclosing a generous slice of fried bacon.

He plunged in among the big spruce trees. The trail was faint. A foot of snow had fallen since the last sled had passed over, and he was glad he was without a sled, traveling light. In fact, he carried nothing but the lunch wrapped in the handkerchief. He was surprised, however, at the cold. It certainly was cold, he concluded, as he rubbed his numb nose and cheek-bones with his mittened hand. He was a warm-whiskered man, but the hair on his face did not protect the high cheek-bones and the eager nose that thrust itself aggressively into the frosty air.

At the man's heels trotted a dog, a big native husky, the proper wolf-dog, gray-coated and without any visible or temperamental difference from its brother, the wild wolf. The animal was depressed by the tremendous cold. It knew that it was no time for traveling. Its instinct told it a truer tale than was told to the man by the man's judgment. In reality, it was not merely colder than fifty below zero; it was colder than sixty below, than seventy below. It was seventy-five below zero. Since the freezing point is thirty-two above zero, it meant that one hundred and seven degrees of frost obtained. The dog did not know anything about thermometers. Possibly in its brain there was no sharp consciousness of a condition of very cold such as was in the man's brain. But the brute had its instinct. It experienced a vague but menacing apprehension that subdued it and made it slink along at the man's heels, and that made it question eagerly every unwonted movement of the man as if expecting him to go into camp or to seek shelter somewhere and build a fire. The dog had learned fire, and it wanted fire, or else to burrow under the snow and cuddle its warmth away from the air.

The frozen moisture of its breathing had settled on its fur in a fine powder of frost, and especially were its jowls, muzzle, and eyelashes whitened by its crystalled breath. The man's red beard and mustache were likewise frosted, but more solidly, the deposit taking the form of ice and increasing with every warm, moist breath he exhaled. Also, the man was chewing tobacco, and the muzzle of ice held his lips so rigidly that he was unable to clear his chin when he expelled the juice. The result was that a crystal beard of the color and solidity of amber was increasing its length on his chin. If he fell down it would shatter itself, like glass, into brittle fragments. But he did not mind the appendage. It was the penalty all tobacco-chewers paid in that country, and he had been out before in two cold snaps. They had not been so cold as this, he knew, but by the

spirit thermometer at Sixty Mile he knew they had been
registered at fifty below and at fifty-five.

He held on through the level stretch of woods for several miles, crossed a wide flat of nigger-heads, and dropped
down a bank to the frozen bed of a small stream. This was
Henderson Creek, and he knew he was ten miles from the
forks. He looked at his watch. It was ten o'clock. He was
making four miles an hour, and he calculated that he would
arrive at the forks at half-past twelve. He decided to cele-
brate that event by eating his lunch there.

The dog dropped in again at his heels, with a tail drooping discouragement, as the man swung along the creek-
bed. The furrow of the old sled-trail was plainly visible, but
a dozen inches of snow covered the marks of the last run-
ners. In a month no man had come up or down that silent
creek. The man held steadily on. He was not much given
to thinking, and just then particularly he had nothing to
think about save that he would eat lunch at the forks and
that at six o'clock he would be in camp with the boys.
There was nobody to talk to; and, had there been, speech
would have been impossible because of the ice-muzzle on
his mouth. So he continued monotonously to chew tobacco
and to increase the length of his amber beard.

Once in a while the thought reiterated itself that it was
very cold and that he had never experienced such cold.
As he walked along he rubbed his cheek-bones and nose
with the back of his mittened hand. He did this automatically, now and again changing hands. But rub as he would,
the instant he stopped his cheek-bones went numb, and the
following instant the end of his nose went numb. He was
sure to frost his cheeks; he knew that, and experienced a
pang of regret that he had not devised a nose-strap of the
sort Bud wore in cold snaps. Such a strap passed across
the cheeks, as well, and saved them. But it didn't matter
much, after all. What were frosted cheeks? A bit painful,
that was all; they were never serious.

Empty as the man's mind was of thoughts, he was keenly
observant, and he noticed the changes in the creek, the
curves and bends and timber-jams, and always he sharply
noted where he placed his feet. Once, coming around a bend,
he shied abruptly, like a startled horse, curved away from
the place where he had been walking, and retreated several paces back along the trail. The creek he knew was
frozen clear to the bottom,—no creek could contain water

in that arctic winter,—but he knew also that there were springs that bubbled out from the hillsides and ran along under the snow and on top the ice of the creek. He knew that the coldest snaps never froze these springs, and he knew likewise their danger. They were traps. They hid pools of water under the snow that might be three inches deep, or three feet. Sometimes a skin of ice half an inch thick covered them, and in turn was covered by the snow. Sometimes there were alternate layers of water and ice-skin, so that when one broke through he kept on breaking through for a while, sometimes wetting himself to the waist.

That was why he had shied in such panic. He had felt the give under his feet and heard the crackle of a snow-hidden ice-skin. And to get his feet wet in such a temperature meant trouble and danger. At the very least it meant delay, for he would be forced to stop and build a fire, and under its protection to bare his feet while he dried his socks and moccasins. He stood and studied the creek-bed and its banks, and decided that the flow of water came from the right. He reflected a while, rubbing his nose and cheeks, then skirted to the left, stepping gingerly and testing the footing for each step. Once clear of the danger, he took a fresh chew of tobacco and swung along at his four-mile gait.

In the course of the next two hours he came upon several similar traps. Usually the snow above the hidden pools had a sunken, candied appearance that advertised the danger. Once again, however, he had a close call; and once, suspecting danger, he compelled the dog to go on in front. The dog did not want to go. It hung back until the man shoved it forward, and then it went quickly across the white, unbroken surface. Suddenly it broke through, floundered to one side, and got away to firmer footing. It had wet its forefeet and legs, and almost immediately the water that clung to it turned to ice. It made quick efforts to lick the ice off its legs, then dropped down in the snow and began to bite out the ice that had formed between the toes. This was a matter of instinct. To permit the ice to remain would mean sore feet. It did not know this, it merely obeyed the mysterious prompting that arose from the deep crypts of its being. But the man knew, having achieved a judgment on the subject, and he removed the mitten from his right hand and helped tear out the ice-particles. He did not expose his fingers more than a minute, and was astonished at the swift numbness that smote them. It certainly was cold. He pulled on the mitten hastily, and beat the hand savagely across his chest.

At twelve o'clock the day was at its brightest. Yet the sun was too far south on its winter journey to clear the horizon. The bulge of the earth intervened between it and Henderson Creek, where the man walked under a clear sky at noon and cast no shadow. At half-past twelve, to the minute, he arrived at the forks of the creek. He was pleased at the speed he had made. If he kept it up, he would certainly be with the boys by six. He unbuttoned his jacket and shirt and drew forth his lunch. The action consumed no more than a quarter of a minute, yet in that brief moment the numbness laid hold of the exposed fingers. He did not put the mitten on, but, instead struck the fingers a dozen sharp smashes against his leg. Then he sat down on a snow-covered log to eat. The sting that followed upon the striking of his fingers against his leg ceased so quickly that he was startled. He had had no chance to take a bite of biscuit. He struck the fingers repeatedly and returned them to the mitten, baring the other hand for the purpose of eating. He tried to take a mouthful, but the ice-muzzle prevented. He had forgotten to build a fire and thaw out. He chuckled at his foolishness, and as he chuckled he noted the numbness creeping into the exposed fingers. Also, he noted that the stinging which had first come to his toes when he sat down was already passing away. He wondered whether the toes were warm or numb. He moved them inside the moccasins and decided that they were numb.

He pulled the mitten on hurriedly and stood up. He was a bit frightened. He stamped up and down until the stinging returned into the feet. It certainly was cold, was his thought. That man from Sulphur Creek had spoken the truth when telling how cold it sometimes got in the country. And he had laughed at him at the time! That showed one must not be too sure of things. There was no mistake about it, it *was* cold. He strode up and down, stamping his feet and threshing his arms, until reassured by the returning warmth. Then he got out matches and proceeded to make a fire. From the undergrowth, where high water of the previous spring had lodged a supply of seasoned twigs, he got his firewood. Working carefully from a small beginning, he soon had a roaring fire, over which he thawed the ice from his face and in the protection of which he ate his biscuits. For the moment the cold of space was outwitted. The dog took satisfaction in the fire, stretching out close enough for warmth and far enough away to escape being singed.

When the man had finished, he filled his pipe and took his comfortable time over a smoke. Then he pulled on his mittens, settled the earflaps of his cap firmly about his ears, and took the creek trail up the left fork. The dog was disappointed and yearned back toward the fire. This man did not know cold. Possibly all the generations of his ancestry had been ignorant of cold, of real cold, of cold one hundred and seven degrees below freezing point. But the dog knew; all its ancestry knew, and it had inherited the knowledge. And it knew that it was not good to walk abroad in such fearful cold. It was the time to lie snug in a hole in the snow and wait for a curtain of cloud to be drawn across the face of outer space whence this cold came. On the other hand, there was no keen intimacy between the dog and the man. The one was the toil-slave of the other, and the only caresses it had ever received were the caresses of the whip-lash and of harsh and menacing throat-sounds that threatened the whiplash. So the dog made no effort to communicate its apprehension to the man. It was not concerned in the welfare of the man; it was for its own sake that it yearned back toward the fire. But the man whistled, and spoke to it with the sound of whiplashes, and the dog swung in at the man's heel and followed after.

The man took a chew of tobacco and proceeded to start a new amber beard. Also, his moist breath quickly powdered with white his mustache, eyebrows, and lashes. There did not seem to be so many springs on the left fork of the Henderson, and for half an hour the man saw no signs of any. And then it happened. At a place where there were no signs, where the soft, unbroken snow seemed to advertise solidity beneath, the man broke through. It was not deep. He wet himself halfway to the knees before he floundered out to the firm crust.

He was angry, and cursed his luck aloud. He had hoped to get into camp with the boys at six o'clock, and this would delay him an hour, for he would have to build a fire and dry out his foot-gear. This was imperative at that low temperature—he knew that much; and he turned aside to the bank, which he climbed. On top, tangled in the underbrush about the trunks of several small spruce trees, was a high-water deposit of dry firewood—sticks and twigs, principally, but also larger portions of seasoned branches and fine, dry, last-year's grasses. He threw down several large pieces on top of the snow. This served for a foundation and prevented the young flame from drowning itself in the snow it otherwise would melt. The flame he got by touching a match to a small shred of birch bark that he took from his pocket. This burned even more readily than paper. Placing it on the foundation, he fed the young flame with wisps of dry grass and with the tiniest dry twigs.

He worked slowly and carefully, keenly aware of his danger. Gradually, as the flame grew stronger, he increased the size of the twigs with which he fed it. He squatted in the snow, pulling the twigs out from their entanglement in the brush and feeding directly to the flame. He knew there must be no failure. When it is seventy-five below zero, a man must not fail in his first attempt to build a fire—that is, if his feet are wet. If his feet are dry, and he fails, he can run along the trail for half a mile and restore his circulation. But the circulation of wet and freezing feet cannot be restored by running when it is seventy-five below. No matter how fast he runs, the wet feet will freeze the harder.

All this the man knew. The old-timer on Sulphur Creek had told him about it the previous fall, and now he was appreciating the advice. Already all sensation had gone out of his feet. To build the fire he had been forced to remove his mittens, and the fingers had quickly gone numb. His pace of four miles an hour had kept his heart pumping blood to the surface of his body and to all the extremities. But the instant he stopped, the action of the pump eased down. The cold of space smote the unprotected tip of the planet, and he, being on that unprotected tip, received the full force of the blow. The blood of his body recoiled before it. The blood was alive, like the dog, and like the dog it wanted to hide away and cover itself up from the fearful cold. So long as he walked four miles an hour, he pumped that blood, will-nilly, to the surface; but now it ebbed away and sank down into the recesses of his body. The extremities were the first to feel its absence. His wet feet froze the faster, and his exposed fingers numbed the faster, though they had not yet begun to freeze. Nose and cheeks were already freezing, while the skin of all his body chilled as it lost its blood.

But he was safe. Toes and nose and cheeks would be only

touched by the frost, for the fire was beginning to burn with strength. He was feeding it with twigs the size of his finger. In another minute he would be able to feed it with branches the size of his wrist, and then he could remove his wet foot-gear, and, while it dried, he could keep his naked feet warm by the fire, rubbing them at first, of course, with snow. The fire was a success. He was safe. He remembered the advice of the old-timer on Sulphur Creek, and smiled. The old-timer had been very serious in laying down the law that no man must travel alone in the Klondike after fifty below. Well, here he was; he had had the accident; he was alone; and he had saved himself. Those old-timers were rather womanish, some of them, he thought. All a man had to do was to keep his head; and he was all right. Any man who was a man could travel alone. But it was surprising, the rapidity with which his cheeks and nose were freezing. And he had not thought his fingers could go lifeless in so short a time. Lifeless they were, for he could scarcely make them move together to grip a twig, and they seemed remote from his body and from him. When he touched a twig, he had to look and see whether or not he had hold of it. The wires were pretty well down between him and his finger-ends.

All of which counted for little. There was the fire, snapping and crackling and promising life with every dancing flame. He started to untie his moccasins. They were coated with ice; the thick German socks were like sheaths of iron halfway to the knees; and the moccasin strings were like rods of steel all twisted and knotted as by some conflagration. For a moment he tugged with his numb fingers, then, realizing the folly of it, he drew his sheath-knife.

But before he could cut the strings, it happened. It was his own fault or, rather, his mistake. He should not have built the fire under the spruce tree. He should have built it in the open. But it had been easier to pull the twigs from the brush and drop them directly on the fire. Now the tree under which he had done this carried a weight of snow on its boughs. No wind had blown for weeks, and each bough was fully freighted. Each time he had pulled a twig he had communicated a slight agitation to the tree—an imperceptible agitation, so far as he was concerned, but an agitation sufficient to bring about the disaster. High up in the tree one bough capsized its load of snow. This fell on the boughs beneath, capsizing them. This process continued,

spreading out and involving the whole tree. It grew like
an avalanche, and it descended without warning upon the
man and the fire, and the fire was blotted out! Where it
had burned was a mantle of fresh and disordered snow.

The man was shocked. It was as though he had just
heard his own sentence of death. For a moment he sat
and stared at the spot where the fire had been. Then he
grew very calm. Perhaps the old-timer on Sulphur Creek
was right. If he had only had a trail-mate he would have
been in no danger now. The trail-mate could have built the
fire. Well, it was up to him to build the fire over again,
and this second time there must be no failure. Even if he
succeeded, he would most likely lose some toes. His feet
must be badly frozen by now, and there would be some
time before the second fire was ready.

Such were his thoughts, but he did not sit and think
them. He was busy all the time they were passing through
his mind. He made a new foundation for a fire, this time
in the open, where no treacherous tree could blot it out.
Next, he gathered dry grasses and tiny twigs from the
high-water flotsam. He could not bring his fingers together
to pull them out, but he was able to gather them by the
handful. In this way he got many rotten twigs and bits of
green moss that were undesirable, but it was the best he
could do. He worked methodically, even collecting an arm-
ful of the larger branches to be used later when the fire
gathered strength. And all the while the dog sat and
watched him, a certain yearning wistfulness in its eyes, for
it looked upon him as the fire-provider, and the fire was
slow in coming.

When all was ready, the man reached in his pocket for
a second piece of birch bark. He knew the bark was there,
and, though he could not feel it with his fingers, he
could hear its crisp rustling as he fumbled for it. Try as he
would, he could not clutch hold of it. And all the time,
in his consciousness, was the knowledge that each instant
his feet were freezing. This thought tended to put him in a
panic, but he fought against it and kept calm. He pulled
on his mittens with his teeth, and threshed his arms back
and forth, beating his hands with all his might against his
sides. He did this sitting down, and he stood up to do it;
and all the while the dog sat in the snow, its wolf-brush
of a tail curled around warmly over its forefeet, its sharp
wolf-ears pricked forward intently as it watched the man.

And the man, as he beat and threshed with his arms and hands, felt a great surge of envy as he regarded the creature that was warm and secure in its natural covering.

After a time he was aware of the first far-away signals of sensation in his beaten fingers. The faint tingling grew stronger till it evolved into a stinging ache that was excruciating, but which the man hailed with satisfaction. He stripped the mitten from his right hand and fetched forth the birch bark. The exposed fingers were quickly going numb again. Next he brought out his bunch of sulphur matches. But the tremendous cold had already driven the life out of his fingers. In his effort to separate one match from the others, the whole bunch fell in the snow. He tried to pick it out of the snow, but failed. The dead fingers could neither touch nor clutch. He was very careful. He drove the thought of his freezing feet, and nose, and cheeks, out of his mind, devoting his whole soul to the matches. He watched, using the sense of vision in place of touch, and when he saw his fingers on each side the bunch, he closed them—that is, he willed to close them, for the wires were down, and the fingers did not obey. He pulled the mitten on the right hand, and beat it fiercely against his knee. Then, with both mittened hands, he scooped the bunch of matches, along with much snow, into his lap. Yet he was no better off.

After some manipulation he managed to get the bunch between the heels of his mittened hands. In this fashion he carried it to his mouth. The ice crackled and snapped when by a violent effort he opened his mouth. He drew the lower jaw in, curled the upper lip out of the way, and scraped the bunch with his upper teeth in order to separate a match. He succeeded in getting one, which he dropped on his lap. He was no better off. He could not pick it up. Then he devised a way. He picked it up in his teeth and scratched it on his leg. Twenty times he scratched before he succeeded in lighting it. As it flamed he held it with his teeth to the birch bark. But the burning brimstone went up his nostrils and into his lungs, causing him to cough spasmodically. The match fell into the snow and went out.

The old-timer on Sulphur Creek was right, he thought in the moment of controlled despair that ensued: after fifty below, a man should travel with a partner. He beat his hands, but failed in exciting any sensation. Suddenly he bared both hands, removing the mittens with his teeth. He

caught the whole bunch between the heels of his hands.
His arm-muscles not being frozen enabled him to press the
hand-heels tightly against the matches. Then he scratched
the bunch along his leg. It flared into flame, seventy sulphur matches at once! There was no wind to blow them
out. He kept his head to one side to escape the strangling
fumes, and held the blazing bunch to the birch bark. As
he so held it, he became aware of sensation in his hand.
His flesh was burning. He could smell it. Deep down below
the surface he could feel it. The sensation developed into
pain that grew acute. And still he endured it, holding the
flame of the matches clumsily to the bark that would
not light readily because his own burning hands were in
the way, absorbing most of the flame.

At last, when he could endure no more, he jerked his
hands apart. The blazing matches fell sizzling into the
snow, but the birch bark was alight. He began laying dry
grasses and the tiniest twigs on the flame. He could not pick
and choose, for he had to lift the fuel between the heels of
his hands. Small pieces of rotten wood and green moss
clung to the twigs, and he bit them off as well as he could
with his teeth. He cherished the flame carefully and awkwardly. It meant life, and it must not perish. The withdrawal of blood from the surface of his body now made
him begin to shiver, and he grew more awkward. A large
piece of green moss fell squarely on the little fire. He tried
to poke it out with his fingers, but his shivering frame
made him poke too far, and he disrupted the nucleus of the
little fire, the burning grasses and tiny twigs separating
and scattering. He tried to poke them together again, but in
spite of the tenseness of the effort, his shivering got away
with him, and the twigs were hopelessly scattered. Each
twig gushed a puff of smoke and went out. The fire-provider
had failed. As he looked apathetically about him, his eyes
chanced on the dog, sitting across the ruins of the fire
from him, in the snow, making restless, hunching movements, slightly lifting one forefoot and then the other,
shifting its weight back and forth on them with wistful
eagerness.

The sight of the dog put a wild idea into his head. He
remembered the tale of the man, caught in a blizzard,
who killed a steer and crawled inside the carcass, and so
was saved. He would kill the dog and bury his hands in
the warm body until the numbness went out of them.

Then he could build another fire. He spoke to the dog, calling it to him; but in his voice was a strange note of fear that frightened the animal, who had never known the man to speak in such way before. Something was the matter, and its suspicious nature sensed danger—it knew not what danger, but somewhere, somehow, in its brain arose an apprehension of the man. It flattened its ears down at the sound of the man's voice, and its restless, hunching movements and the liftings and shiftings of its forefeet became more pronounced; but it would not come to the man. He got on his hands and knees and crawled toward the dog. This unusual posture again excited suspicion, and the animal sidled mincingly away.

The man sat up in the snow for a moment and struggled for calmness. Then he pulled on his mittens, by means of his teeth, and got upon his feet. He glanced down at first in order to assure himself that he was really standing up, for the absence of sensation in his feet left him unrelated to the earth. His erect position in itself started to drive the webs of suspicion from the dog's mind; and when he spoke peremptorily, with the sound of whiplashes in his voice, the dog rendered its customary allegiance and came to him. As it came within reaching distance, the man lost his control. His arms flashed out to the dog, and he experienced genuine surprise when he discovered that his hands could not clutch, that there was neither bend nor feeling in the fingers. He had forgotten for the moment that they were frozen and that they were freezing more and more. All this happened quickly, and before the animal could get away, he encircled its body with his arms. He sat down in the snow, and in this fashion held the dog, while it snarled and whined and struggled.

But it was all he could do, hold its body encircled in his arms and sit there. He realized that he could not kill the dog. There was no way to do it. With his helpless hands he could neither draw nor hold his sheath-knife nor throttle the animal. He released it, and it plunged wildly away, with tail between its legs, and still snarling. It halted forty feet away and surveyed him curiously, with ears sharply pricked forward. The man looked down at his hands in order to locate them, and found them hanging on the ends of his arms. It struck him as curious that one should have to use his eyes in order to find out where his hands were. He began threshing his arms back and forth, beating the

mittened hands against his sides. He did this for five minutes, violently, and his heart pumped enough blood up to
the surface to put a stop to his shivering. But no sensation was aroused in the hands. He had an impression that
they hung like weights on the ends of his arms, but when
he tried to run the impression down, he could not find it.

A certain fear of death, dull and oppressive, came to him.
This fear quickly became poignant as he realized that it
was no longer a mere matter of freezing his fingers and
toes, or of losing his hands and feet, but that it was a
matter of life and death with the chances against him.
This threw him into a panic, and he turned and ran up the
creek-bed along the old, dim trail. The dog joined in behind and kept up with him. He ran blindly, without intention, in fear such as he had never known in his life.
Slowly, as he plowed and floundered through the snow,
he began to see things again,—the banks of the creeks, the
old timber-jams, the leafless aspens, and the sky. The running made him feel better. He did not shiver. Maybe, if he
ran on, his feet would thaw out; and, anyway, if he ran
far enough, he would reach camp and the boys. Without
doubt he would lose some fingers and toes and some of
his face; but the boys would take care of him, and save
the rest of him when he got there. And at the same time
there was another thought in his mind that said he would
never get to the camp and the boys; that it was too many
miles away, that the freezing had too great a start on
him, and that he would soon be stiff and dead. This
thought he kept in the background and refused to consider.
Sometimes it pushed itself forward and demanded to be
heard, but he thrust it back and strove to think of other
things.

It struck him as curious that he could run at all on feet
so frozen that he could not feel them when they struck
the earth and took the weight of his body. He seemed
to himself to skim along above the surface, and to have no
connection with the earth. Somewhere he had once seen
a winged Mercury, and he wondered if Mercury felt as he
felt when skimming over the earth.

His theory of running until he reached camp and the
boys had one flaw in it: he lacked the endurance. Several
times he stumbled, and finally he tottered, crumpled up,
and fell. When he tried to rise, he failed. He must sit and
rest, he decided, and next time he would merely walk and

keep on going. As he sat and regained his breath, he noted that he was feeling quite warm and comfortable. He was not shivering, and it even seemed that a warm glow had come to his chest and trunk. And yet, when he touched his nose or cheeks, there was no sensation. Running would not thaw them out. Nor would it thaw out his hands and feet. Then the thought came to him that the frozen portions of his body must be extending. He tried to keep this thought down, to forget it, to think of something else; he was aware of the panicky feeling that it caused, and he was afraid of the panic. But the thought asserted itself, and persisted, until it produced a vision of his body totally frozen. This was too much, and he made another wild run along the trail. Once he slowed down to a walk, but the thought of the freezing extending itself made him run again.

And all the time the dog ran with him, at his heels. When he fell down a second time, it curled its tail over its fore-feet and sat in front of him, facing him, curiously eager and intent. The warmth and security of the animal angered him, and he cursed it till it flattened down its ears appeasingly. This time the shivering came more quickly upon the man. He was losing in his battle with the frost. It was creeping into his body from all sides. The thought of it drove him on, but he ran no more than a hundred feet, when he staggered and pitched headlong. It was his last panic. When he had recovered his breath and control, he sat up and entertained in his mind the conception of meeting death with dignity. However, the conception did not come to him in such terms. His idea of it was that he had been making a fool of himself, running around like a chicken with its head cut off—such was the simile that occurred to him. Well, he was bound to freeze anyway, and he might as well take it decently. With this new-found peace of mind came the first glimmerings of drowsiness. A good idea, he thought, to sleep off to death. It was like taking an anaesthetic. Freezing was not so bad as people thought. There were lots worse ways to die.

He pictured the boys finding his body next day. Suddenly he found himself with them, coming along the trail and looking for himself. And, still with them, he came around a turn in the trail and found himself lying in the snow. He did not belong with himself any more, for even then he was out of himself, standing with the boys and looking at himself in the snow. It certainly was cold, was his thought.

When he got back to the States he could tell the folks what real cold was. He drifted on from this to a vision of the old-timer on Sulphur Creek. He could see him quite clearly, warm and comfortable, and smoking a pipe.

"You were right, old hoss; you were right," the man mumbled to the old-timer of Sulphur Creek.

Then the man drowsed off into what seemed to him the most comfortable and satisfying sleep he had ever known. The dog sat facing him and waiting. The brief day drew to a close in a long, slow twilight. There were no signs of a fire to be made, and, besides, never in the dog's experience had it known a man to sit like that in the snow and make no fire. As the twilight drew on, its eager yearning for the fire mastered it, and with a great lifting and shifting of forefeet, it whined softly, then flattened its ears down in anticipation of being chidden by the man. But the man remained silent. Later, the dog whined loudly. And still later it crept close to the man and caught the scent of death. This made the animal bristle and back away. A little longer it delayed, howling under the stars that leaped and danced and shone brightly in the cold sky. Then it turned and trotted up the trail in the direction of the camp it knew, where were the other food-providers and fire-providers.

The Use of Force

BY WILLIAM CARLOS WILLIAMS

THEY WERE new patients to me, all I had was the name, Olson. Please come down as soon as you can, my daughter is very sick.

When I arrived I was met by the mother, a big startled looking woman, very clean and apologetic who merely said, Is this the doctor? and let me in. In the back, she added. You must excuse us, doctor, we have her in the kitchen where it is warm. It is very damp here sometimes.

The child was fully dressed and sitting on her father's lap near the kitchen table. He tried to get up, but I motioned for him not to bother, took off my overcoat and started to look things over. I could see that they were all very nervous, eyeing me up and down distrustfully. As often, in such cases, they weren't telling me more than they had to, it was up to me to tell them; that's why they were spending three dollars on me.

The child was fairly eating me up with her cold, steady eyes, and no expression to her face whatever. She did not move and seemed, inwardly, quiet; an unusually attractive little thing, and as strong as a heifer in appearance. But her face was flushed, she was breathing rapidly, and I realized that she had a high fever. She had magnificent blonde hair, in profusion. One of those picture children often reproduced in advertising leaflets and the photogravure sections of the Sunday papers.

She's had a fever for three days, began the father and we don't know what it comes from. My wife has given her things, you know, like people do, but it don't do no good. And there's been a lot of sickness around. So we tho't you'd better look her over and tell us what is the matter.

As doctors often do I took a trial shot at it as a point of departure. Had she had a sore throat?

Both parents answered me together, No . . . No, she says her throat don't hurt her.

Does your throat hurt you? added the mother to the child. But the little girl's expression didn't change nor did she move her eyes from my face.

Have you looked?

I tried to, said the mother, but I couldn't see.

As it happens we had been having a number of cases of dipththeria in the school to which this child went during that month and we were all, quite apparently, thinking of that, though no one had as yet spoken of the thing.

Well, I said, suppose we take a look at the throat first. I smiled in my best professional manner and asking for the child's first name I said, come on, Mathilda, open your mouth and let's take a look at your throat.

Nothing doing.

Aw, come on, I coaxed, just open your mouth wide and let me take a look. Look, I said opening both hands wide, I haven't anything in my hands. Just open up and let me see.

Such a nice man, put in the mother. Look how kind he is to you. Come on, do what he tells you to. He won't hurt you.

At that I ground my teeth in disgust. If only they wouldn't

use the word "hurt" I might be able to get somewhere. But I did not allow myself to be hurried or disturbed but speaking quietly and slowly I approached the child again.

As I moved my chair a little nearer suddenly with one catlike movement both her hands clawed instinctively for my eyes and she almost reached them too. In fact she knocked my glasses flying and they fell, though unbroken, several feet away from me on the kitchen floor.

Both the mother and father almost turned themselves inside out in embarrassment and apology. You bad girl, said the mother, taking her and shaking her by one arm. Look what you've done. The nice man . . .

For heaven's sake, I broke in. Don't call me a nice man to her. I'm here to look at her throat on the chance that she might have dipththeria and possibly die of it. But that's nothing to her. Look here, I said to the child, we're going to look at your throat. You're old enough to understand what I'm saying. Will you open it now by yourself or shall we have to open it for you?

Not a move. Even her expression hadn't changed. Her breaths however were coming faster and faster. Then the battle began. I had to do it. I had to have a throat culture for her own protection. But first I told the parents that it was entirely up to them. I explained the danger but said that I would not insist on a throat examination so long as they would take the responsibility.

If you don't do what the doctor says you'll have to go to the hospital, the mother admonished her severely.

Oh yeah? I had to smile to myself. After all, I had already fallen in love with the savage brat, the parents were contemptible to me. In the ensuing struggle they grew more and more abject, crushed, exhausted while she surely rose to magnificent heights of insane fury of effort bred of her terror of me.

The father tried his best, and he was a big man but the fact that she was his daughter, his shame at her behavior and his dread of hurting her made him release her just at the critical moment several times when I had almost achieved success, till I wanted to kill him. But his dread also that she might have diphtheria made him tell me to go on, go on though he himself was almost fainting, while the mother moved back and forth behind us raising and lowering her hands in an agony of apprehension.

Put her in front of you on your lap, I ordered, and held both her wrists.

But as soon as he did the child let out a scream. Don't, you're hurting me. Let go of my hands. Let them go I tell you. Then she shrieked terrifyingly, hysterically. Stop it! Stop it! You're killing me!

Do you think she can stand it, doctor! said the mother.

You get out, said the husband to his wife. Do you want her to die of diphtheria?

Come on now, hold her, I said.

Then I grasped the child's head with my left hand and tried to get the wooden tongue depressor between her teeth. She fought, with clenched teeth, desperately! But now I also had grown furious—at a child. I tried to hold myself down but I couldn't. I know how to expose a throat for inspection. And I did my best. When finally I got the wooden spatula behind the last teeth and just the point of it into the mouth cavity, she opened up for an instant but before I could see anything she came down again and gripping the wooden blade between her molars she reduced it to splinters before I could get it out again.

Aren't you ashamed to act like that in front of the doctor?

Get me a smooth-handled spoon of some sort, I told the mother. We're going through this. The child's mouth was already bleeding. Her tongue was cut and she was screaming in wild hysterical shrieks. Perhaps I should have desisted and come back in an hour or more. No doubt it would have been better. But I have seen at least two children lying dead in bed of neglect in such cases, and feeling that I must get a diagnosis now or never I went at it again. But the worst of it was that I too had got beyond reason. I could have torn the child apart in my own fury and enjoyed it. It was a pleasure to attack her. My face was burning with it.

The damned little brat must be protected against her own idiocy, one says to one's self at such times. Others must be protected against her. It is a social necessity. And all these things are true. But a blind fury, a feeling of adult shame, bred of a longing for muscular release are the operatives. One goes on to the end.

In a final unreasoning assault I overpowered the child's neck and jaws. I forced the heavy silver spoon back of her teeth and down her throat till she gagged. And there it was—both tonsils covered with membrane. She had fought valiantly to keep me from knowing her secret. She had been hiding that sore throat for three days at least and lying to her parents in order to escape just such an outcome as this.

Now truly she *was* furious. She had been on the defensive before but now she attacked. Tried to get off her father's lap and fly at me while tears of defeat blinded her eyes.

Old Folks' Christmas

BY RING W. LARDNER

TOM AND Grace Carter sat in their living-room on Christmas Eve, sometimes talking, sometimes pretending to read and all the time thinking things they didn't want to think. Their two children, Junior, aged nineteen, and Grace, two years younger, had come home that day from their schools for the Christmas vacation. Junior was in his first year at the university and Grace attending a boarding-school that would fit her for college.

I won't call them Grace and Junior any more, though that is the way they had been christened. Junior had changed his name to Ted and Grace was now Caroline, and thus they insisted on being addressed, even by their parents. This was one of the things Tom and Grace the elder were thinking of as they sat in their living-room Christmas Eve.

Other university freshmen who had lived here had returned on the twenty-first, the day when the vacation was supposed to begin. Ted had telegraphed that he would be three days late owing to a special examination which, if he passed it, would lighten the terrific burden of the next term. He had arrived at home looking so pale, heavy-eyed and shaky that his mother doubted the wisdom of the concentrated mental effort, while his father secretly hoped the stuff had been non-poisonous and would not have lasting effects. Caroline, too, had been behind schedule, explaining that her laundry had gone astray and she had not dared trust others to trace it for her.

Grace and Tom had attempted, with fair success, to conceal their disappointment over this delayed home-coming and had continued with their preparations for a Christmas that would thrill their children and consequently themselves. They had bought an imposing lot of presents, costing twice or three times as much as had been Tom's father's annual income when Tom was Ted's age, or Tom's own income a year ago, before General Motors' acceptance of his new weather-proof paint had enabled him to buy this suburban home and luxuries such as his own parents and Grace's had never dreamed of, and to give Ted and Caroline advantages that he and Grace had perforce gone without.

Behind the closed door of the music-room was the elaborately decked tree. The piano and piano bench and the floor around the tree were covered with beribboned packages of all sizes, shapes and weights, one of them addressed to Tom, another to Grace, a few to the servants and the rest to Ted and Caroline. A huge box contained a sealskin coat for Caroline, a coat that had cost as much as the Carters had formerly paid a year for rent. Even more expensive was a "set" of jewelry consisting of an opal brooch, a bracelet of opals and gold filigree, and an opal ring surrounded by diamonds.

Grace always had preferred opals to any other stone, but now that she could afford them, some inhibition prevented her from buying them for herself; she could enjoy them much more adorning her pretty daughter. There were boxes of silk stockings, lingerie, gloves and handkerchiefs. And for Ted, a three-hundred-dollar watch, a de-luxe edition of Balzac, an expensive bag of shiny, new steel-shafted golf-clubs and the last word in portable phonographs.

But the big surprise for the boy was locked in the garage, a black Gorham sedan, a model more up to date and better-looking than Tom's own year-old car that stood beside it. Ted could use it during the vacation if the mild weather continued and could look forward to driving it around home next spring and summer, there being a rule at the university forbidding undergraduates the possession or use of private automobiles.

Every year for sixteen years, since Ted was three and Caroline one, it had been the Christmas Eve custom of the Carter's to hang up their children's stockings and fill them with inexpensive toys. Tom and Grace had thought it would

be fun to continue the custom this year; the contents of
the stockings—a mechanical negro dancing doll, music-boxes,
a kitten that meowed when you pressed a spot on her
back, et cetera—would make the "kids" laugh. And one of
Grace's first pronouncements to her returned offspring was
that they must go to bed early so Santa Claus would not
be frightened away.

But it seemed they couldn't promise to make it so terribly early. They both had long-standing dates in town. Caroline was going to dinner and a play with Beatrice Murdock
and Beatrice's nineteen-year-old brother Paul. The latter
would call for her in his car at half past six. Ted had
accepted an invitation to see the hockey match with two
classmates, Herb Castle and Bernard King. He wanted to
take his father's Gorham, but Tom told him untruthfully
that the foot-brake was not working; Ted must be kept
out of the garage till tomorrow morning.

Ted and Caroline had taken naps in the afternoon and
gone off together in Paul Murdock's stylish roadster, giving
their word that they would be back by midnight or a little
later and that tomorrow night they would stay home.

And now their mother and father were sitting up for
them, because the stockings could not be filled and hung
till they were safely in bed, and also because trying
to go to sleep is a painful and hopeless business when
you are kind of jumpy.

"What time is it?" asked Grace, looking up from the
third page of a book that she had begun to "read" soon
after dinner.

"Half past two," said her husband. (He had answered
the same question every fifteen or twenty minutes since
midnight.)

"You don't suppose anything could have happened?"
said Grace.

"We'd have heard if there had," said Tom.

"It isn't likely, of course," said Grace, "but they might
have had an accident some place where nobody was there
to report it or telephone or anything. We don't know what
kind of a driver the Murdock boy is."

"He's Ted's age. Boys that age may be inclined to drive
too fast, but they drive pretty well."

"How do you know?"

"Well, I've watched some of them drive."

"Yes, but not all of them."

"I doubt whether anybody in the world has seen every nineteen-year-old boy drive."

"Boys these days seem so kind of irresponsible."

"Oh, don't worry! They probably met some of their young friends and stopped for a bite to eat or something." Tom got up and walked to the window with studied carelessness. "It's a pretty night," he said. "You can see every star in the sky."

But he wasn't looking at the stars. He was looking down the road for headlights. There were none in sight and after a few moments he returned to his chair.

"What time is it?" asked Grace.

"Twenty-two of," he said.

"Of what?"

"Of three."

"Your watch must have stopped. Nearly an hour ago you told me it was half past two."

"My watch is all right. You probably dozed off."

"I haven't closed my eyes."

"Well, it's time you did. Why don't you go to bed?"

"Why don't *you?*"

"I'm not sleepy."

"Neither am I. But honestly, Tom, it's silly for you to stay up. I'm just doing it so I can fix the stockings, and because I feel so wakeful. But there's no use of your losing your sleep."

"I couldn't sleep a wink till they're home."

"That's foolishness! There's nothing to worry about. They're just having a good time. You were young once yourself."

"That's just it! When I was young, I was young." He picked up his paper and tried to get interested in the shipping news.

"What time is it?" asked Grace.

"Five minutes of three."

"Maybe they're staying at the Murdocks' all night."

"They'd have let us know."

"They were afraid to wake us up, telephoning."

At three-twenty a car stopped at the front gate.

"There they are!"

"I told you there was nothing to worry about."

Tom went to the window. He could just discern the outlines of the Murdock boy's roadster, whose lighting system seemed to have broken down.

"He hasn't any lights," said Tom. "Maybe I'd better go out and see if I can fix them."

"No, don't!" said Grace sharply. "He can fix them himself. He's just saving them while he stands still."

"Why don't they come in?"

"They're probably making plans."

"They can make them in here. I'll go out and tell them we're still up."

"No, don't!" said Grace as before, and Tom obediently remained at the window.

It was nearly four when the car lights flashed on and the car drove away. Caroline walked into the house and stared dazedly at her parents.

"Heavens! What are you doing up?"

Tom was about to say something, but Grace forestalled him.

"We were talking over old Christmases," she said. "Is it very late?"

"I haven't any idea," said Caroline.

"Where is Ted?"

"Isn't he home? I haven't seen him since we dropped him at the hockey place."

"Well, you go right to bed," said her mother. "You must be worn out."

"I am, kind of. We danced after the play. What time is breakfast?"

"Eight o'clock."

"Oh, Mother, can't you make it nine?"

"I guess so. You used to want to get up early on Christmas."

"I know, but——"

"Who brought you home?" asked Tom.

"Why, Paul Murdock—and Beatrice."

"You look rumpled."

"They made me sit in the 'rumple' seat."

She laughed at her joke, said good night and went upstairs. She had not come even within hand-shaking distance of her father and mother.

"The Murdocks," said Tom, "must have great manners, making their guest ride in that uncomfortable seat."

Grace was silent.

"You go to bed, too," said Tom. "I'll wait for Ted."

"You couldn't fix the stockings."

"I won't try. We'll have time for that in the morning; I mean, later in the morning."

"I'm not going to bed till you do," said Grace.

"All right, we'll both go. Ted ought not to be long now. I suppose his friends will bring him home. We'll hear him when he comes in."

There was no chance not to hear him when, at ten minutes before six, he came in. He had done his Christmas shopping late and brought home a package.

Grace was downstairs again at half past seven, telling the servants breakfast would be postponed till nine. She nailed the stockings beside the fireplace, went into the music-room to see that nothing had been disturbed and removed Ted's hat and overcoat from where he had carefully hung them on the hall floor.

Tom appeared a little before nine and suggested that the children ought to be awakened.

"I'll wake them," said Grace, and went upstairs. She opened Ted's door, looked, and softly closed it again. She entered her daughter's room and found Caroline semiconscious.

"Do I have to get up now? Honestly I can't eat anything. If you could just have Molla bring me some coffee. Ted and I are both invited to the Murdock's for breakfast at half past twelve, and I could sleep for another hour or two."

"But dearie, don't you know we have Christmas dinner at one?"

"It's a shame, Mother, but I thought of course our dinner would be at night."

"Don't you want to see your presents?"

"Certainly I do, but can't they wait?"

Grace was about to go to the kitchen to tell the cook that dinner would be at seven instead of one, but she remembered having promised Signe the afternoon and evening off, as a cold, light supper would be all anyone wanted after the heavy midday meal.

Tom and Grace breakfasted alone and once more sat in the living-room, talking, thinking and pretending to read.

"You ought to speak to Caroline," said Tom.

"I will, but not today. It's Christmas."

"And I intend to say a few words to Ted."

"Yes, dear, you must. But not today."

"I suppose they'll be out again tonight."

"No, they promised to stay home. We'll have a nice cozy evening."

"Don't bet too much on that," said Tom.

At noon the "children" made their entrance and responded to their parents' salutations with almost the proper warmth. Ted declined a cup of coffee and he and Caroline apologized for making a "breakfast" date at the Murdocks'.

"Sis and I both thought you'd be having dinner at seven, as usual."

"We've always had it at one o'clock on Christmas," said Tom.

"I'd forgotten it was Christmas," said Ted.

"Well, those stockings ought to remind you."

Ted and Caroline looked at the bulging stockings.

"Isn't there a tree?" asked Caroline.

"Of course," said her mother. "But the stockings come first."

"We've only a little time," said Caroline. "We'll be terribly late as it is. So can't we see the tree now?"

"I guess so," said Grace, and led the way into the music-room.

The servants were summoned and the tree stared at and admired.

"You must open your presents," said Grace to her daughter.

"I can't open them all now," said Caroline. "Tell me which is special."

The cover was removed from the huge box and Grace held up the coat.

"Oh, Mother!" said Caroline. "A sealskin coat!"

"Put it on," said her father.

"Not now. We haven't time."

"Then look at this!" said Grace, and opened the case of jewels.

"Oh, Mother! Opals!" said Caroline.

"They're my favorite stone," said Grace quietly.

"If nobody minds," said Ted, "I'll postpone my personal investigation till we get back. I know I'll like everything you've given me. But if we have no car in working order, I've got to call a taxi and catch a train."

"You can drive in," said his father.

"Did you fix the brake?"

"I think it's all right. Come up to the garage and we'll see."

Ted got his hat and coat and kissed his mother good-by.

"Mother," he said, "I know you'll forgive me for not having any presents for you and Dad. I was so rushed the last three days at school. And I thought I'd have time to shop a little when we got in yesterday, but I was in too much of a hurry to be home. Last night, everything was closed."

"Don't worry," said Grace. "Christmas is for young people. Dad and I have everything we want."

The servants had found their gifts and disappeared, expressing effusive Scandinavian thanks.

Caroline and her mother were left alone.

"Mother, where did the coat come from?"

"Lloyd and Henry's."

"They keep all kinds of furs, don't they?"

"Yes."

"Would you mind horribly if I exchanged this?"

"Certainly not, dear. You pick out anything you like, and if it's a little more expensive, it won't make any difference. We can go in town tomorrow or next day. But don't you want to wear your opals to the Murdocks'?"

"I don't believe so. They might get lost or something. And I'm not—well, I'm not so crazy about——"

"I think they can be exchanged, too," said Grace. "You run along now and get ready to start."

Caroline obeyed with alacrity, and Grace spent a welcome moment by herself.

Tom opened the garage door.

"Why, you've got two cars!" said Ted.

"The new one isn't mine," said Tom.

"Whose is it?"

"Yours. It's the new model."

"Dad, that's wonderful! But it looks just like the old one."

"Well, the old one's pretty good. Just the same, yours is better. You'll find that out when you drive it. Hop in and get started. I had her filled with gas."

"I think I'd rather drive the old one."

"Why?"

"Well, what I really wanted, Dad, was a Barnes sport roadster, something like Paul Murdock's, only a different color scheme. And if I don't drive this Gorham at all, maybe you could get them to take it back or make some kind of a deal with the Barnes people."

Tom didn't speak till he was sure of his voice. Then: "All right, son. Take my car and I'll see what can be done about yours."

Caroline, waiting for Ted, remembered something and called to her mother. "Here's what I got for you and Dad," she said. "It's two tickets to 'Jolly Jane,' the play I saw last night. You'll love it!"

"When are they for?" asked Grace.

"Tonight," said Caroline.

"But dearie," said her mother, "we don't want to go out tonight, when you promised to stay home."

"We'll keep our promise," said Caroline, "but the Murdocks may drop in and bring some friends and we'll dance and there'll be music. And Ted and I both thought you'd rather be away somewhere so our noise wouldn't disturb you."

"It was sweet of you to do this," said her mother, "but your father and I don't mind noise as long as you're enjoying yourselves."

"It's time anyway that you and Dad had a treat."

"The real treat," said Grace, "would be to spend a quiet evening here with just you two."

"The Murdocks practically invited themselves and I couldn't say no after they'd been so nice to me. And honestly, Mother, you'll love this play!"

"Will you be home for supper?"

"I'm pretty sure we will, but if we're a little late, don't you and Dad wait for us. Take the seven-twenty so you won't miss anything. The first act is really the best. We probably won't be hungry, but have Signe leave something out for us in case we are."

Tom and Grace sat down to the elaborate Christmas dinner and didn't make much impression on it. Even if they had had any appetite, the sixteen-pound turkey would have looked almost like new when they had eaten their fill. Conversation was intermittent and related chiefly to Signe's excellence as a cook and the mildness of the weather. Children and Christmas were barely touched on.

Tom merely suggested that on account of its being a holiday and their having theatre tickets, they ought to take the six-ten and eat supper at the Metropole. His wife said no; Ted and Caroline might come home and be disappointed at not finding them. Tom seemed about to make some re-mark, but changed his mind.

The afternoon was the longest Grace had ever known. The children were still absent at seven and she and Tom taxied to the train. Neither talked much on the way to town. As for the play, which Grace was sure to love, it turned out to be a rehash of "Cradle Snatchers" and "Sex," retaining the worst features of each.

When it was over, Tom said: "Now I'm inviting you to the Cove Club. You didn't eat any breakfast or dinner or supper and I can't have you starving to death on a feast-day. Besides, I'm thirsty as well as hungry."

They ordered the special *table d'hôte* and struggled hard to get away with it. Tom drank six high-balls, but they failed to produce the usual effect of making him jovial. Grace had one highball and some kind of cordial that gave her a warm, contented feeling for a moment. But the warmth and contentment left her before the train was half way home.

The living-room looked as if Von Kluck's army had just passed through. Ted and Caroline had kept their promise up to a certain point. They had spent part of the evening at home, and the Murdocks must have brought all their own friends and everybody else's, judging from the results. The tables and floors were strewn with empty glasses, ashes and cigaret stubs. The stockings had been torn off their nails and wrecked contents were all over the place. Two sizable holes had been burnt in Grace's favorite rug.

Tom took his wife by the arm and led her into the music-room.

"You never took the trouble to open your own present," he said.

"And I think there's one for you, too," said Grace. "They didn't come in here," she added, "so I guess there wasn't much dancing or music."

Tom found his gift from Grace, a set of diamond studs and cuff buttons for festive wear. Grace's present from him was an opal ring.

"Oh, Tom!" she said.

"We'll have to go out somewhere tomorrow night, so I can break these in," said Tom.

"Well, if we do that, we'd better get a good night's rest."

"I'll beat you upstairs," said Tom.

Silent Snow, Secret Snow

BY CONRAD AIKEN

JUST WHY it should have happened, or why it should have happened just when it did, he could not, of course, possibly have said; nor perhaps could it even have occurred to him to ask. The thing was above all a secret, something to be preciously concealed from Mother and Father; and to that very fact it owed an enormous part of its deliciousness. It was like a peculiarly beautiful trinket to be carried unmentioned in one's trouser-pocket—a rare stamp, an old coin, a few tiny gold links found trodden out of shape on the path in the park, a pebble of carnelian, a sea shell distinguishable from all others by an unusual spot or stripe—and, as if it were anyone of these, he carried around with him everywhere a warm and persistent and increasingly beautiful sense of possession. Nor was it only a sense of possession—it was also a sense of protection. It was as if, in some delightful way, his secret gave him a fortress, a wall behind which he could retreat into heavenly seclusion. This was almost the first thing he had noticed about it—apart from the oddness of the thing itself—and it was this that now again, for the fiftieth time, occurred to him, as he sat in the little schoolroom. It was the half hour for geography. Miss Buell was revolving with one finger, slowly, a huge terrestrial globe which had been placed on her desk. The green and yellow continents passed and repassed, questions were asked and answered, and now the little girl in front of him, Deirdre, who had a funny little constellation of freckles on the back of her neck, exactly like the Big Dipper, was standing up and telling Miss Buell that the equator was the line that ran round the middle.

Miss Buell's face, which was old and grayish and kindly, with gray stiff curls beside the cheeks, and eyes that swam very brightly, like little minnows, behind thick glasses, wrinkled itself into a complication of amusements.

"Ah! I see. The earth is wearing a belt, or a sash. Or someone drew a line round it!"

"Oh, no—not that—I mean—"

In the general laughter, he did not share, or only a very little. He was thinking about the Arctic and Antarctic regions, which of course, on the globe, were white. Miss Buell was now telling them about the tropics, the jungles, the steamy heat of equatorial swamps, where the birds and butterflies, and even the snakes, were like living jewels. As he listened to these things, he was already, with a pleasant sense of half-effort, putting his secret between himself and the words. Was it really an effort at all? For effort implied something voluntary, and perhaps even something one did not especially want; whereas this was distinctly pleasant, and came almost of its own accord. All he needed to do was to think of that morning, the first one, and then of all the others—

But it was all so absurdly simple! It had amounted to so little. It was nothing, just an idea—and just why it should have become so wonderful, so permanent, was a mystery— a very pleasant one, to be sure, but also, in an amusing way, foolish. However, without ceasing to listen to Miss Buell, who had now moved up to the north temperate zones, he deliberately invited his memory of the first morning. It was only a moment or two after he had waked up—or perhaps the moment itself. But was there, to be exact, an exact moment? Was one awake all at once? or was it gradual? Anyway, it was after he had stretched a lazy hand up towards the headrail, and yawned, and then relaxed again among his warm covers, all the more grateful on a December morning, that the thing had happened. Suddenly, for no reason, he had thought of the postman, he remembered the postman. Perhaps there was nothing so odd in that. After all, he heard the postman almost every morning in his life—his heavy boots could be heard clumping round the corner at the top of the little cobbled hill-street, and then, progressively nearer, progressively louder, the double knock at each door, the crossings and re-crossings of the street, till finally the clumsy steps came stumbling across to the very door, and the tremendous knock came which shook the house itself.

(Miss Buell was saying "Vast wheat-growing areas in North America and Siberia."

Dierdre had for the moment placed her left hand across the back of her neck.)

But on this particular morning, the first morning, as he

lay there with his eyes closed, he had for some reason
waited for the postman. He wanted to hear him come
round the corner. And that was precisely the joke—he never
did. He never came. He never had come—*round the corner*
—again. For when at last the steps *were* heard, they had
already, he was quite sure, come a little down the hill, to
the first house; and even so, the steps were curiously different—they were softer, they had a new secrecy about
them, they were muffled and indistinct; and while the
rhythm of them was the same, it now said a new thing—
it said peace, it said remoteness, it said cold, it said
sleep. And he had understood the situation at once—nothing could have seemed simpler—there had been snow in the
night, such as all winter he had been longing for; and it
was this which had rendered the postman's first footsteps
inaudible, and the later ones faint. Of course! How lovely!
And even now it must be snowing—it was going to be a
snowy day—the long white ragged lines were drifting and
sifting across the street, across the faces of the old houses,
whispering and hushing, making little triangles of white
in the corners between cobblestones, seething a little
when the wind blew them over the ground to a drifted
corner; and so it would be all day, getting deeper and
deeper and silenter and silenter.

(Miss Buell was saying "Land of perpetual snow.")

All this time, of course (while he lay in bed), he had
kept his eyes closed, listening to the nearer progress of
the postman, the muffled footsteps thumping and slipping
on the snow-sheathed cobbles; and all the other sounds—
the double knocks, a frosty far-off voice or two, a bell
ringing thinly and softly as if under a sheet of ice—had the
same slightly abstracted quality, as if removed by one degree from actuality—as if everything in the world had
been insulated by snow. But when at last, pleased, he
opened his eyes, and turned them towards the window, to
see for himself this long-desired and now so clearly
imagined miracle—what he saw instead was brilliant sunlight on a roof; and when, astonished, he jumped out of bed
and stared down into the street, expecting to see the
cobbles obliterated by the snow, he saw nothing but the
bare bright cobbles themselves.

Queer, the effect this extraordinary surprise had had upon
him—all the following morning he had kept with him a

sense as of snow falling about him, a secret screen of new snow between himself and the world. If he had not dreamed such a thing—and how could he have dreamed it while awake?—how else could one explain it? In any case, the delusion had been so vivid as to affect his entire behavior. He could not now remember whether it was on the first or the second morning—or was it even the third?—that his mother had drawn attention to some oddness in his manner.

"But my darling—" she had said at the breakfast table—"what has come over you? You don't seem to be listening. . . ."

And how often that very thing had happened since!

(Miss Buell was now asking if anyone knew the difference between the North Pole and the Magnetic Pole. Deirdre was holding up her flickering brown hand, and he could see the four white dimples that marked the knuckles.)

Perhaps it hadn't been either the second or third morning—or even the fourth or fifth. How could he be sure? How could he be sure just when the delicious *progress* had become clear? Just when it had really *begun?* The intervals weren't very precise. . . . All he now knew was, that at some point or other—perhaps the second day, perhaps the sixth—he had noticed that the presence of the snow was a little more insistent, the sound of it clearer; and, conversely, the sound of the postman's footsteps more indistinct. Not only could he not hear the steps come round the corner, he could not even hear them at the first house. It was below the first house that he heard them; and then, a few days later, it was below the second house that he heard them; and a few days later again, below the third. Gradually, gradually, the snow was becoming heavier, the sound of its seething louder, the cobblestones more and more muffled. When he found, each morning, on going to the window, after the ritual of listening that the roofs and cobbles were as bare as ever, it made no difference. This was, after all, only what he had expected. It was even what pleased him, what rewarded him: the thing was his own, belonged to no one else. No one else knew about it, not even his mother and father. There, outside, were the bare cobbles; and here, inside, was the snow. Snow growing heavier each day, muffling the world, hiding the ugly, and deadening increasingly—above all—the steps of the postman.

"But my darling—" she had said at the luncheon table—

"what has come over you? You don't seem to listen when people speak to you. That's the third time I've asked you to pass your plate. . . ."

How was one to explain this to Mother? or to Father? There was, of course, nothing to be done about it: nothing. All one could do was to laugh embarrassedly, pretend to be a little ashamed, apologize, and take a sudden and somewhat disingenuous interest in what was being done or said. The cat had stayed out all night. He had a curious swelling on his left cheek—perhaps somebody had kicked him, or a stone had struck him. Mrs. Kempton was or was not coming to tea. The house was going to be house cleaned, or "turned out," on Wednesday instead of Friday. A new lamp was provided for his evening work—perhaps it was eyestrain which accounted for this new and so peculiar vagueness of his—Mother was looking at him with amusement as she said this, but with something else as well. A new lamp? A new lamp. Yes Mother, No Mother, Yes Mother. School is going very well. The geometry is very easy. The history is very dull. The geography is very interesting—particularly when it takes one to the North Pole. Why the North Pole? Oh, well, it would be fun to be an explorer. Another Peary or Scott or Shackleton. And then abruptly he found his interest in the talk at an end, stared at the pudding on his plate, listened, waited, and began once more—ah how heavenly, too, the first beginnings—to hear or feel—for could he actually hear it?—the silent snow, the secret snow.

(Miss Buell was telling them about the search for the Northwest Passage, about Hendrik Hudson, the Half Moon.)

This had been, indeed, the only distressing feature of the new experience: the fact that it so increasingly had brought him into a kind of mute misunderstanding, or even conflict, with his father and mother. It was as if he were trying to lead a double life. On the one hand he had to be Paul Hasleman, and keep up the appearance of being that person—dress, wash, and answer intelligently when spoken to—; on the other, he had to explore this new world which had been opened to him. Nor could there be the slightest doubt—not the slightest—that the new world was the profounder and more wonderful of the two. It was irresistible. It was miraculous. Its beauty was simply beyond anything—beyond speech as beyond thought—utterly incommunicable. But how then, between the two worlds, of which he was thus constantly aware, was he to keep a balance? One must get up, one must go to breakfast, one must talk with Mother, go to school, do one's lessons—and, in all this, try not to appear too much of a fool. But if all the while one was also trying to extract the full deliciousness of another and quite separate existence, one which could not easily (if at all) be spoken of—how was one to manage? How was one to explain? Would it be safe to explain? Would it be absurd? Would it merely mean that he would get into some obscure kind of trouble?

These thoughts came and went, came and went, as softly and secretly as the snow; they were not precisely a disturbance, perhaps they were even a pleasure; he liked to have them; their presence was something palpable, something he could stroke with his hand, without closing his eyes, and without ceasing to see Miss Buell and the school room and the globe and the freckles on Deirdre's neck; neverthelsss he did in a sense cease to see, or to see the obvious external world, and substituted for this vision of snow, the sound of snow, and the slow, almost soundless, approach of the postman. Yesterday, it had been only at the sixth house that the postman had become audible; the snow was much deeper now, it was falling more swiftly and heavily, the sound of its seething was more distinct, more soothing, more persistent. And this morning, it had been—as nearly as he could figure—just above the seventh house—perhaps only a step or two above: at most, he had heard two or three footsteps before the knock had sounded. . . . And with each such narrowing of the sphere, each nearer approach of the limit at which the postman was first audible, it was odd how sharply was increased the amount of illusion which had to be carried into the ordinary business of daily life. Each day, it was harder to get out of bed, to go to the window, to look out at the—as always—perfectly empty and snowless street. Each day it was more difficult to go through the perfunctory motions of greeting Mother and Father at breakfast, to reply to their questions, to put his books together and go to school. And at school, how extraordinarily hard to conduct with success simultaneously the public life and the life that was secret. There were times when he longed—positively ached—to tell everyone about it—to burst out with it—only to be checked almost at once by a far-off feeling as of some faint absurdity which was inherent in it—but *was* it absurd?—and more importantly by a sense of mysterious power in his very secrecy. Yes: it must be kept secret. That, more and more, became clear. At whatever cost to himself, whatever pain to others—

(Miss Buell looked straight at him, smiling, and said, "Perhaps we'll ask Paul. I'm sure Paul will come out of his daydream long enough to be able to tell us. Won't you, Paul." He rose slowly from his chair, resting one hand on the brightly varnished desk, and deliberately stared through the snow towards the blackboard. It was an effort, but it was amusing to make it. "Yes," he said slowly, "it was what we now call the Hudson River. This he thought to be the Northwest Passage. He was disappointed." He sat down again, and as he did so Deirdre half turned in her chair and gave him a shy smile, of approval and admiration.)

At whatever pain to others.

This part of it was very puzzling, very puzzling. Mother was very nice, and so was Father. Yes, that was all true enough. He wanted to be nice to them, to tell them everything—and yet, was it really wrong of him to want to have a secret place of his own?

At bedtime, the night before, Mother had said, "If this goes on, my lad, we'll have to see a doctor, we will! We can't have our boy—" But what was it she had said? "Live in another world"? "Live so far away"? The word "far" had been in it, he was sure, and then Mother had taken up a magazine again and laughed a little, but with an expression which wasn't mirthful. He had felt sorry for her. . . .

The bell rang for dismissal. The sound came to him through long curved parallels of falling snow. He saw Deirdre rise, and had himself risen almost as soon—but not quite as soon—as she.

II

On the walk homeward, which was timeless, it pleased him to see through the accompaniment, or counterpoint, of snow, the items of mere externality on his way. There were many kinds of bricks in the sidewalks, and laid in many kinds of pattern. The garden walls too were various, some of wooden palings, some of plaster, some of stone. Twigs of bushes leaned over the walls; the little hard green winterbuds of lilac, on gray stems, sheathed and fat; other branches very thin and fine and black and dessicated. Dirty sparrows huddled in the bushes, as dull in color as dead fruit left in leafless trees. A single starling creaked on a weather vane. In the gutter, beside a drain, was a scrap of torn and dirty newspaper, caught in a little delta of filth: the word ECZEMA appeared in large capitals, and below it was a letter from Mrs. Amelia D. Cravath, 2100 Pine Street, Fort Worth, Texas, to the effect that after being a sufferer for years she had been cured by Caley's Ointment. In the little delta, beside the fan-shaped and deeply runneled continent of brown mud, were lost twigs, descended from their parent trees, dead matches, a rusty horse-chestnut burr, a small concentration of sparkling gravel on the lip of the sewer, a fragment of eggshell, a streak of yellow sawdust which had been wet and was now dry and congealed, a brown pebble, and a broken feather. Further on was a cement sidewalk, ruled into geometrical parallelograms, with a brass inlay at one end commemorating the contractors who had laid it, and, halfway across, an irregular and random series of dog-tracks, immortalized in synthetic stone. He knew these well, and always stepped on them; to cover the little hollows with his own foot had always been a queer pleasure; today he did it once more, but perfunctorily and detachedly, all the while thinking of something else. That was a dog, a long time ago, who had made a mistake and walked on the cement while it was still wet. He had probably wagged his tail, but that hadn't been recorded. Now, Paul Hasleman, aged twelve, on his way home from school, crossed the same river, which in the meantime had frozen into rock. Homeward through the snow, the snow falling in bright sunshine. Homeward?

Then came the gateway with the two posts surmounted by egg-shaped stones which had been cunningly balanced on their ends, as if by Columbus, and mortared in the very act of balance: a source of perpetual wonder. On the brick wall just beyond, the letter H had been stenciled, presumably for some purpose. H? H.

The green hydrant, with a little green-painted chain attached to the brass screw-cap.

The elm tree, with the great gray wound in the bark, kidney-shaped, into which he always put his hand—to feel the cold but living wood. The injury, he had been sure, was due to the gnawings of a tethered horse. But now it deserved only a passing palm, a merely tolerant eye. There were more important things. Miracles. Beyond the thoughts

of trees, mere elms. Beyond the thoughts of sidewalks, mere
stone, mere brick, mere cement. Beyond the thoughts even
of his own shoes, which trod these sidewalks obediently,
bearing a burden—far above—of elaborate mystery. He
watched them. They were not very well polished; he had
neglected them, for a very good reason: they were
one of the many parts of the increasing difficulty of the
daily return to daily life, the morning struggle. To get
up, having at last opened one's eyes, to go to the window,
and discover no snow, to wash, to dress, to descend the
curving stairs to breakfast—

At whatever pain to others, nevertheless, one must persevere in severance, since the incommunicability of the
experience demanded it. It was desirable of course to be
kind to Mother and Father, especially as they seemed to be
worried, but it was also desirable to be resolute. If they
should decide—as appeared likely—to consult the doctor, Doctor Howells, and have Paul inspected, his heart listened to
through a kind of dictaphone, his lungs, his stomach—
well, that was all right. He would go through with it. He
would give them answer for question, too—perhaps such answers as they hadn't expected? No. That would never do.
For the secret world must, at all costs, be preserved.

The bird-house in the apple-tree was empty—it was the
wrong time of year for wrens. The little round black door had
lost its pleasure. The wrens were enjoying other houses,
other nests, remoter trees. But this too was a notion which he
only vaguely and grazingly entertained—as if, for the moment, he merely touched an edge of it; there was something further on, which was already assuming a sharper
importance; something which already teased at the corners
of his eyes, teasing also at the corner of his mind. It
was funny to think that he so wanted this, so awaited it—
and yet found himself enjoying this momentary dalliance
with the bird-house, as if for a quite deliberate postpone-
ment and enhancement of the approaching pleasure. He
was aware of his delay, of his smiling and detached and
now almost uncomprehending gaze at the little bird-house;
he knew what he was going to look at next: it was his own
little cobbled hill-street, his own house, the little river at
the bottom of the hill, the grocer's shop with the cardboard
man in the window—and now, thinking of all this, he turned
his head, still smiling, and looking quickly right and left
through the snow-laden sunlight.

And the mist of snow, as he had foreseen, was still on it—a ghost of snow falling in the bright sunlight, softly and steadily floating and turning and pausing, soundlessly meeting the snow that covered, as with a transparent mirage, the bare bright cobbles. He loved it—he stood still and loved it. Its beauty was paralyzing—beyond all words, all experience, all dream. No fairy-story he had ever read could be compared with it—none had ever given him this extraordinary combination of ethereal loveliness with a something else, unnameable, which was just faintly and deliciously terrifying. What was this thing? As he thought of it, he looked upward toward his own bedroom window, which was open—and it was as if he looked straight into the room and saw himself lying half awake in his bed. There he was—at this very instant he was still perhaps actually there—more truly there than standing here at the edge of the cobbled hill-street, with one hand lifted to shade his eyes against the snow-sun. Had he indeed ever left his room, in all this time? since that very first morning? Was the whole progress still being enacted there, was it still the same morning, and himself not yet wholly awake? And even now, had the postman not yet come round the corner? . . .

This idea amused him, and automatically, as he thought of it, he turned his head and looked toward the top of the hill. There was, of course, nothing there—nothing and no one. The street was empty and quiet. And all the more because of its emptiness it occurred to him to count the houses—a thing which, oddly enough, he hadn't before thought of doing. Of course, he had known there weren't many—many, that is, on his own side of the street, which were the ones that figured in the postman's progress—but nevertheless it came to him as something of a shock to find that there were precisely *six*, above his own house—his own house was the seventh.

Six!

Astonished, he looked at his own house—looked at the door, on which was the number thirteen—and then realized that the whole thing was exactly and logically and absurdly what he ought to have known. Just the same, the realization gave him abruptly, and even a little frighteningly, a sense of hurry. He was being hurried—he was being rushed. For—he knit his brows—he couldn't be mistaken—it was just above the *seventh* house, his *own* house, that the postman had first been audible this very morning. But in that case—in that case—did it mean that tomorrow he would hear nothing? The knock he had heard must have been the knock of their own door. Did it mean—and this was an idea which gave him a really extraordinary feeling of surprise—that he would never hear the postman again?—that tomorrow morning the postman would already have passed the house, in a snow by then so deep as to render his footsteps completely inaudible? That he would have made his approach down the snow-filled street so soundlessly, so secretly, that he, Paul Hasleman, there lying in bed, would not have waked in time, or, waking, would have heard nothing?

But how could that be? Unless even the knocker should be muffled in the snow—frozen tight, perhaps? . . . But in that case—

A vague feeling of disappointment came over him; a vague sadness, as if he felt himself deprived of something which he had long looked forward to, something much prized. After all this, all this beautiful progress, the slow delicious advance of the postman through the silent and secret snow, the knock creeping closer each day, and the footsteps nearer, the audible compass of the world thus daily narrowed, narrowed, narrowed, as the snow soothingly and beautifully encroached and deepened, after all this, was he to be defrauded of the one thing he had so wanted —to be able to count, as it were, the last two or three solemn footsteps, as they finally approached his own door? Was it all going to happen, at the end, so suddenly? or indeed, had it already happened? with no slow and subtle gradations of menace, in which he could luxuriate?

He gazed upward again, toward his own window which flashed in the sun: and this time almost with a feeling that it would be better if he *were* still in bed, in that room; for in that case this must still be the first morning, and there would be six more mornings to come—or, for that matter, seven or eight or nine—how could he be sure?—or even more.

III

After supper, the inquisition began. He stood before the doctor, under the lamp, and submitted silently to the usual thumpings and tappings.

"Now will you please say 'Ah!'?"

"Ah!"

"Now again please, if you don't mind."

"Ah."

"Say it slowly, and hold it if you can—"

"Ah-h-h-h-h-h—"

"Good."

How silly all this was. As if it had anything to do with his throat! Or his heart or lungs!

Relaxing his mouth, of which the corners, after all this absurd stretching, felt uncomfortable, he avoided the doctor's eyes, and stared towards the fireplace, past his mother's feet (in gray slippers) which projected from the green chair, and his father's feet (in brown slippers) which stood neatly side by side on the hearth rug.

"Hm. There is certainly nothing wrong there . . ."

He felt the doctor's eyes fixed upon him, and, as if merely to be polite, returned the look, but with a feeling of justifiable evasiveness.

"Now, young man, tell me,—do you feel all right?"

"Yes, sir, quite all right."

"No headaches? no dizziness?"

"No, I don't think so."

"Let me see. Let's get a book, if you don't mind—yes, thank you, that will do splendidly—and now, Paul, if you'll just read it, holding it as you would normally hold it—"

He took the book and read:

"And another praise have I to tell for this the city our mother, the gift of a great god, a glory of the land most high; the might of horses, the might of young horses, the might of the sea. . . . For thou, son of Cronus, our lord Poseidon, hast throned herein this pride, since in these roads first thou didst show forth the curb that cures the rage of steeds. And the shapely oar, apt to men's hands, hath a wondrous speed on the brine, following the hundred-footed Nereids. . . . O land that art praised above all lands, now is it for thee to make those bright praises seen in deeds."

He stopped, tentatively, and lowered the heavy book.

"No—as I thought—there is certainly no superficial sign of eye-strain."

Silence thronged the room, and he was aware of the focused scrutiny of the three people who confronted him. . . .

"We could have his eyes examined—but I believe it is
something else."

"What could it be?" This was his father's voice.

"It's only this curious absent-minded—" This was his
mother's voice.

In the presence of the doctor, they both seemed irritating-
ly apologetic.

"I believe it is something else. Now Paul—I would like
very much to ask you a question or two. You will answer
them, won't you—you know I'm an old, old friend of yours,
eh? That's right! . . ."

His back was thumped twice by the doctor's fat fist,—
then the doctor was grinning at him with false amiability,
while with one finger-nail he was scratching the top button of his waistcoat. Beyond the doctor's shoulder was the
fire, the fingers of flame making light prestidigitation against
the sooty fireback, the soft sound of their random flutter the
only sound.

"I would like to know—is there anything that worries
you?"

The doctor was again smiling, his eyelids low against the
little black pupils, in each of which was a tiny white bead
of light. Why answer him? why answer him at all? "At whatever pain to others"—but it was all a nuisance, this necessity
for resistance, this necessity for attention: it was as if one
had been stood up on a brilliantly lighted stage, under a great
round blaze of spotlight; as if one were merely a trained
seal, or a performing dog, or a fish, dipped out of an aquar-
ium and held up by the tail. It would serve them right
if he were merely to bark or growl. And meanwhile, to miss
these last few precious hours, these hours of which every
minute was more beautiful than the last, more menacing—? He still looked, as if from a great distance, at the
beads of light in the doctor's eyes, at the fixed false smile,
and then, beyond, once more at his mother's slippers, his
father's slippers, the soft flutter of the fire. Even here, even
amongst these hostile presences, and in this arranged light,
he could see the snow, he could hear it—it was in the corners of the room, where the shadow was deepest, under the
sofa, behind the half-opened door which led to the dining
room. It was gentler here, softer, its seethe the quietest of
whispers, as if, in deference to a drawing room, it had quite
deliberately put on its "manners"; it kept itself out of sight,

obliterated itself, but distinctly with an air of saying, "Ah, but just wait! Wait till we are alone together! Then I will begin to tell you something new! Something white! something cold! something sleepy! something of cease, and peace, and the long bright curve of space! Tell them to go away. Banish them. Refuse to speak. Leave them, go upstairs to your room, turn out the light and get into bed—I will go with you, I will be waiting for you, I will tell you a better story than Little Kay of the Skates, or The Snow Ghost—I will surround your bed, I will close the windows, pile a deep drift against the door, so that none will ever again be able to enter. Speak to them! . . ." It seemed as if the little hissing voice came from a slow white spiral of falling flakes in the corner by the front window—but he could not be sure. He felt himself smiling, then, and said to the doctor, but without looking at him, looking beyond him still—

"Oh, no, I think not—"

"But are you sure, my boy?"

His father's voice came softly and coldly then—the familiar voice of silken warning. . . .

"You needn't answer at once, Paul—remember we're trying to help you—think it over and be quite sure, won't you?"

He felt himself smiling again, at the notion of being quite sure. What a joke! As if he weren't so sure that reassurance was no longer necessary, and all this cross-examination a ridiculous farce, a grotesque parody! What could they know about it? These gross intelligences, these humdrum minds so bound to the usual, the ordinary? Impossible to tell them about it! Why, even now, even now, with the proof so abundant, so formidable, so imminent, so appallingly present here in this very room, could they believe it?—could even his mother believe it? No—it was only too plain that if anything were said about it, the merest hint given, they would be incredulous—they would laugh—they would say "Absurd!"—think things about him which weren't true. . . .

"Why no, I'm not worried—why should I be?"

He looked then straight at the doctor's low-lidded eyes, looked from one of them to the other, from one bead of light to the other, and gave a little laugh.

The doctor seemed to be disconcerted by this. He drew

back in his chair, resting a fat white hand on either knee. The smile faded slowly from his face.

"Well, Paul!" he said, and paused gravely, "I'm afraid you don't take this quite seriously enough. I think you perhaps don't quite realize—don't quite realize—" He took a deep quick breath, and turned, as if helplessly, at a loss for words, to the others. But Mother and Father were both silent—no help was forthcoming.

"You must surely know, be aware, that you have not been quite yourself, of late? don't you know that? . . ."

It was amusing to watch the doctor's renewed attempt at a smile, a queer disorganized look, as of confidential embarrassment.

"I feel all right, sir," he said, and again gave the little laugh.

"And we're trying to help you." The doctor's tone sharpened.

"Yes sir, I know. But why? I'm all right. I'm just *thinking*, that's all."

His mother made a quick movement forward, resting a hand on the back of the doctor's chair.

"Thinking?" she said. "But my dear, about what?"

This was a direct challenge—and would have to be directly met. But before he met it, he looked again into the corner by the door, as if for reassurance. He smiled again at what he saw, at what he heard. The little spiral was still there, still softly whirling, like the ghost of a white kitten chasing the ghost of a white tail, and making as it did so the faintest of whispers. It was all right! If only he could remain firm, everything was going to be all right.

"Oh, about anything, about nothing,—*you* know the way you do!"

"You mean—day-dreaming?"

"Oh, no—thinking!"

"But thinking about *what*?"

"Anything."

He laughed a third time—but this time, happening to glance upward towards his mother's face, he was appalled at the effect his laughter seemed to have upon her. Her mouth had opened in an expression of horror. . . . This was too bad! Unfortunate! He had known it would cause pain, of course—but he hadn't expected it to be quite so bad as this. Perhaps—perhaps if he just gave them a tiny gleaming hint—?

"About the snow," he said.

"What on earth!" This was his father's voice. The brown slippers came a step nearer on the hearth-rug.

"But, my dear, what do you mean!" This was his mother's voice.

The doctor merely stared.

"Just *snow*, that's all. I like to think about it."

"Tell us about it, my boy."

"But that's all it is. There's nothing to tell. *You* know what snow is?"

This he said almost angrily, for he felt that they were trying to corner him. He turned sideways so as no longer to face the doctor, and the better to see the inch of blackness between the window-sill and the lowered curtain,—the cold inch of beckoning and delicious night. At once he felt better, more assured.

"Mother—can I go to bed, now, please? I've got a headache."

"But I thought you said—"

"It's just come. It's all these questions—! Can I, Mother?"

"You can go as soon as the doctor has finished."

"Don't you think this thing ought to be gone into thoroughly, and *now*?" This was Father's voice. The brown slippers again came a step nearer, the voice was the well-known "punishment" voice, resonant and cruel.

"Oh, what's the use, Norman—"

Quite suddenly, everyone was silent. And without precisely facing them, nevertheless he was aware that all three of them were watching him with an extraordinary intensity—staring hard at him—as if he had done something monstrous, or was himself some kind of monster. He could hear the soft irregular flutter of the flames; the cluck-click-cluck-click of the clock; far and faint, two sudden spurts of laughter from the kitchen, as quickly cut off as begun; a murmur of water in the pipes; and then, the silence seemed to deepen, to spread out, to become world-long and world-wide, to become timeless and shapeless, and to center inevitably and rightly, with a slow and sleepy but enormous concentration of all power, on the beginning of a new sound. What this new sound was going to be, he knew perfectly well. It might begin with a hiss, but it would end with a roar—there was no time to lose—he must escape. It mustn't happen here—

Without another word, he turned and ran up the stairs.

IV

Not a moment too soon. The darkness was coming in long
white waves. A prolonged sibilance filled the night—a great
seamless seethe of wild influence went abruptly across it—
a cold low humming shook the windows. He shut the door
and flung off his clothes in the dark. The bare black floor
was like a little raft tossed in waves of snow, almost overwhelmed, washed under whitely, up again, smothered in
curled billows of feather. The snow was laughing: it spoke
from all sides at once: it pressed closer to him as he ran
and jumped exulting into his bed.

"Listen to us!" it said. "Listen! We have come to tell you
the story we told you about. You remember? Lie down.
Shut your eyes, now—you will no longer see much—in this
white darkness who could see, or want to see? We will
take the place of everything. . . . Listen—"

A beautiful varying dance of snow began at the front
of the room, came forward and then retreated, flattened
out toward the floor, then rose fountain-like to the ceiling,
swayed, recruited itself from a new stream of flakes which
poured laughing in through the humming window, advanced
again, lifted long white arms. It said peace, it said remoteness, it said cold—it said—

But then a gash of horrible light fell brutally across the
room from the opening door—the snow drew back hissing—
something alien had come into the room—something hostile.
This thing rushed at him, clutched at him, shook him—
and he was not merely horrified, he was filled with such a
loathing as he had never known. What was this? this cruel
disturbance? this act of anger and hate? It was as if he
had to reach up a hand toward another world for any understanding of it,—an effort of which he was only barely capable. But of that other world he still remembered just enough
to know the exorcising words. They tore themselves from
his other life suddenly—

"Mother! Mother! Go away! I hate you!"

And with that effort, everything was solved, everything
became all right: the seamless hiss advanced once more,
the long white wavering lines rose and fell like enormous
whispering sea-waves, the whisper becoming louder, the
laughter more numerous.

"Listen!" it said. "We'll tell you the last, the most beauti-

ful and secret story—shut your eyes—it is a very small story—
a story that gets smaller and smaller—it comes inward instead of opening like a flower—it is a flower becoming a
seed—a little cold seed—do you hear? we are leaning closer
to you—"

The hiss was now becoming a roar—the whole world was
a vast moving screen of snow—but even now it said peace,
it said remoteness, it said cold, it said sleep.

By the Waters of Babylon

BY STEPHEN VINCENT BENÉT

THE NORTH and the west and the south are good hunting
ground, but it is forbidden to go east. It is forbidden to go
to any of the Dead Places except to search for metal and
then he who touches the metal must be a priest or the
son of a priest. Afterwards, both the man and the metal
must be purified. These are the rules and the laws; they
are well made. It is forbidden to cross the great river and
look upon the place that was the Place of the Gods—this is
most strictly forbidden. We do not even say its name
though we know its name. It is there that spirits live, and
demons—it is there that there are the ashes of the Great
Burning. These things are forbidden—they have been forbidden since the beginning of time.

My father is a priest; I am the son of a priest. I have
been in the Dead Places near us, with my father—at first, I
was afraid. When my father went into the house to search
for the metal, I stood by the door and my heart felt small
and weak. It was a dead man's house, a spirit house. It
did not have the smell of man, though there were old
bones in a corner. But it is not fitting that a priest's son
should show fear. I looked at the bones in the shadow and
kept my voice still.

Then my father came out with the metal—a good, strong
piece. He looked at me with both eyes but I had not run
away. He gave me the metal to hold—I took it and did not
die. So he knew that I was truly his son and would be a
priest in my time. That was when I was very young—
nevertheless, my brothers would not have done it, though

they are good hunters. After that, they gave me the good piece of meat and the warm corner of the fire. My father watched over me—he was glad that I should be a priest. But when I boasted or wept without a reason, he punished me more strictly than my brothers. That was right.

After a time, I myself was allowed to go into the dead houses and search for metal. So I learned the ways of those houses—and if I saw bones, I was no longer afraid. The bones are light and old—sometimes they will fall into dust if you touch them. But that is a great sin.

I was taught the chants and the spells—I was taught how to stop the running of blood from a wound and many secrets. A priest must know many secrets—that was what my father said.

If the hunters think we do all things by chants and spells, they may believe so—it does not hurt them. I was taught how to read in the old books and how to make the old writings—that was hard and took a long time. My knowledge made me happy—it was like a fire in my heart. Most of all, I liked to hear of the Old Days and the stories of the gods. I asked myself many questions that I could not answer, but it was good to ask them. At night, I would lie awake and listen to the wind—it seemed to me that it was the voice of the gods as they flew through the air.

We are not ignorant like the Forest People—our women spin wool on the wheel, our priests wear a white robe. We do not eat grubs from the trees, we have not forgotten the old writings, although they are hard to understand. Nevertheless, my knowledge and my lack of knowledge burned in me—I wished to know more. When I was a man at last, I came to my father and said, "It is time for me to go on my journey. Give me your leave."

He looked at me for a long time, stroking his beard, then he said at last, "Yes. It is time." That night, in the house of the priesthood, I asked for and received purification. My body hurt but my spirit was a cool stone. It was my father himself who questioned me about my dreams.

He bade me look into the smoke of the fire and see—I saw and told what I saw. It was what I have always seen—a river, and, beyond it, a great Dead Place and in it the gods walking. I have always thought about that. His eyes were stern when I told him—he was no longer my father but a priest. He said, "This is a strong dream."

"It is mine," I said, while the smoke waved and my head

felt light. They were singing the Star song in the outer chamber and it was like the buzzing of bees in my head.

He asked me how the gods were dressed and I told him how they were dressed. We know how they were dressed from the book, but I saw them as if they were before me. When I had finished, he threw the sticks three times and studied them as they fell.

"This is a very strong dream," he said. "It may eat you up."

"I am not afraid," I said and looked at him with both eyes. My voice sounded thin in my ears but that was because of the smoke.

He touched me on the breast and the forehead. He gave me the bow and the three arrows.

"Take them," he said. "It is forbidden to travel east. It is forbidden to cross the river. It is forbidden to go to the Place of the Gods. All these things are forbidden."

"All these things are forbidden," I said, but it was my voice that spoke and not my spirit. He looked at me again.

"My son," he said. "Once I had young dreams. If your dreams do not eat you up, you may be a great priest. If they eat you, you are still my son. Now go on your journey."

I went fasting, as is the law. My body hurt but not my heart. When the dawn came, I was out of sight of the village. I prayed and purified myself, waiting for a sign. The sign was an eagle. It flew east.

Sometimes signs are sent by bad spirits. I waited again on the flat rock, fasting, taking no food. I was very still—I could feel the sky above me and the earth beneath. I waited till the sun was beginning to sink. Then three deer passed in the valley going east—they did not mind me or see me. There was a white fawn with them—a very great sign.

I followed them, at a distance, waiting for what would happen. My heart was troubled about going east, yet I knew that I must go. My head hummed with my fasting—I did not even see the panther spring upon the white fawn. But, before I knew it, the bow was in my hand. I shouted and the panther lifted his head from the fawn. It is not easy to kill a panther with one arrow but the arrow went through his eye and into his brain. He died as he tried to spring —he rolled over, tearing at the ground. Then I knew I was meant to go east—I knew that was my journey. When the night came, I made my fire and roasted meat.

It is eight suns' journey to the east and a man passes by many Dead Places. The Forest People are afraid of them but I am not. Once I made my fire on the edge of a Dead Place at night and, next morning, in the dead house, I found a good knife, little rusted. That was small to what came afterward but it made my heart feel big. Always when I looked for game, it was in front of my arrow, and twice I passed hunting parties of the Forest People without their knowing. So I knew my magic was strong and my journey clean, in spite of the law.

Toward the setting of the eighth sun, I came to the banks of the great river. It was half-a-day's journey after I had left the god-road—we do not use the god-roads now for they are falling apart into great blocks of stone, and the forest is safer going. A long way off, I had seen the water through trees but the trees were thick. At last, I came out upon an open place at the top of a cliff. There was the great river below, like a giant in the sun. It is very long, very wide. It could eat all the streams we know and still be thirsty. Its name is Ou-dis-sun, the Sacred, the Long. No man of my tribe had seen it, not even my father, the priest. It was magic and I prayed.

Then I raised my eyes and looked south. It was there, the Place of the Gods.

How can I tell what it was like—you do not know. It was there, in the red light, and they were too big to be houses. It was there with the red light upon it, mighty and ruined. I knew that in another moment the gods would see me. I covered my eyes with my hands and crept back into the forest.

Surely, that was enough to do, and live. Surely it was enough to spend the night upon the cliff. The Forest People themselves do not come near. Yet, all through the night, I knew that I should have to cross the river and walk in the places of the gods, although the gods ate me up. My magic did not help me at all and yet there was a fire in my bowels, a fire in my mind. When the sun rose, I thought, "My journey has been clean. Now I will go home from my journey." But, even as I thought so, I knew I could not. If I went to the Place of the Gods, I would surely die, but, if I did not go, I could never be at peace with my spirit again. It is better to lose one's life than one's spirit, if one is a priest and the son of a priest.

Nevertheless, as I made the raft, the tears ran out of my

eyes. The Forest People could have killed me without fight, if they had come upon me then, but they did not come. When the raft was made, I said the sayings for the dead and painted myself for death. My heart was cold as a frog and my knees like water, but the burning in my mind would not let me have peace. As I pushed the raft from the shore, I began my death song—I had the right. It was a fine song.

"I am John, son of John," I sang. "My people are the Hill
    People. They are the men.
I go into the Dead Places but I am not slain.
I take the metal from the Dead Places but I am not blasted.
I travel upon the god-roads and am not afraid. E-yah! I
    have killed the panther, I have killed the fawn!
E-yah! I have come to the great river. No man has come
    there before.
It is forbidden to go east, but I have gone, forbidden to
    go on the great river, but I am there.
Open your hearts, you spirits, and hear my song.
    Now I go to the Place of the Gods, I shall not return.
My body is painted for death and my limbs weak, but my
    heart is big as I go to the Place of the Gods!"

All the same, when I came to the Place of the Gods, I was afraid, afraid. The current of the great river is very strong—it gripped my raft with its hands. That was magic, for the river itself is wide and calm. I could feel evil spirits about me, in the bright morning; I could feel their breath on my neck as I was swept down the stream. Never have I been so much alone—I tried to think of my knowledge, but it was a squirrel's heap of winter nuts. There was no strength in my knowledge any more and I felt small and naked as a new-hatched bird—alone upon the great river, the servant of the gods.

Yet, after a while, my eyes were opened and I saw. I saw both banks of the river—I saw that once there had been god-roads across it, though now they were broken and fallen like broken vines. Very great they were, and wonderful and broken—broken in the time of the Great Burning when the fire fell out of the sky. And always the current took me nearer to the Place of the Gods, and the huge ruins rose before my eyes.

I do not know the customs of rivers—we are the People of

the Hills. I tried to guide my raft with the pole but it spun around. I thought the river meant to take me past the Place of the Gods and out into the Bitter Water of the legends. I grew angry then—my heart felt strong. I said aloud, "I am a priest and the son of a priest!" The gods heard me—they showed me how to paddle with the pole on one side of the raft. The current changed itself—I drew near to the Place of the Gods.

When I was very near, my raft struck and turned over. I can swim in our lakes—I swam to the shore. There was a great spike of rusted metal sticking out into the river— I hauled myself up upon it and sat there, panting. I had saved my bow and two arrows and the knife I found in the Dead Place but that was all. My raft went whirling downstream toward the Bitter Water. I looked after it, and thought if it had trod me under, at least I would be safely dead. Nevertheless, when I had dried my bowstring and re-strung it, I walked forward to the Place of the Gods.

It felt like ground underfoot; it did not burn me. It is not true what some of the tales say, that the ground there burns forever, for I have been there. Here and there were the marks and stains of the Great Burning, on the ruins, that is true. But they were old marks and old stains. It is not true either, what some of our priests say, that it is an island covered with fogs and enchantments. It is not. It is a great Dead Place—greater than any Dead Place we know. Everywhere in it there are god-roads, though most are cracked and broken. Everywhere there are the ruins of the high towers of the gods.

How shall I tell what I saw? I went carefully, my strung bow in my hand, my skin ready for danger. There should have been the wailings of spirits and the shrieks of demons, but there were not. It was very silent and sunny where I had landed—the wind and the rain and the birds that drop seeds had done their work—the grass grew in the cracks of the broken stone. It is a fair island—no wonder the gods built there. If I had come there, a god, I also would have built.

How shall I tell what I saw? The towers are not all broken —here and there one still stands, like a great tree in a forest, and the birds nest high. But the towers themselves look blind, for the gods are gone. I saw a fish-hawk, catching fish in the river. I saw a little dance of white butter-flies over a great heap of broken stones and columns. I went there and looked about me—there was a carved stone with cut-letters, broken in half. I can read letters but I could not understand these. They said UBTREAS. There was also the shattered image of a man or a god. It had been made of white stone and he wore his hair tied back like a woman's. His name was ASHING, as I read on the cracked half of a stone. I thought it wise to pray to ASHING, though I do not know that god.

How shall I tell what I saw? There was no smell of man left, on stone or metal. Nor were there many trees in that wilderness of stone. There are many pigeons, nesting and dropping in the towers—the gods must have loved them, or, perhaps, they used them for sacrifices. There are wild cats that roam the god-roads, green-eyed, unafraid of man. At night they wail like demons but they are not demons. The wild dogs are more dangerous, for they hunt in a pack, but them I did not meet till later. Everywhere there are the carved stones, carved with magical numbers or words.

I went north—I did not try to hide myself. When a god or a demon saw me, then I would die, but meanwhile I was no longer afraid. My hunger for knowledge burned in me—there was so much that I could not understand. After a while, I knew that my belly was hungry. I could have hunted for my meat, but I did not hunt. It is known that the gods did not hunt as we do—they got their food from enchanted boxes and jars. Sometimes these are still found in the Dead Places—once, when I was a child and foolish, I opened such a jar and tasted it and found the food sweet. But my father found out and punished me for it strictly, for, often, that food is death. Now, though, I had long gone past what was forbidden, and I entered the likeliest towers, looking for the food of the gods.

I found it at last in the ruins of a great temple in the mid-city. A mighty temple it must have been, for the roof was painted like the sky at night with its stars—that much I could see, though the colors were faint and dim. It went down into great caves and tunnels—perhaps they kept their slaves there. But when I started to climb down, I heard the squeaking of rats, so I did not go—rats are unclean, and there must have been many tribes of them, from the squeaking. But near there, I found food, in the heart of a ruin, behind a door that still opened. I ate only the fruits from the jars—they had a very sweet taste. There was drink, too, in bottles of glass—the drink of the gods was strong and made my head swim. After I had eaten and drunk, I slept on the top of a stone, my bow at my side.

When I woke, the sun was low. Looking down from where I lay, I saw a dog sitting on his haunches. His tongue was hanging out of his mouth; he looked as if he were laughing. He was a big dog, with a gray-brown coat, as big as a wolf. I sprang up and shouted at him but he did not move— he just sat there as if he were laughing. I did not like that. When I reached for a stone to throw, he moved swiftly out of the way of the stone. He was not afraid of me; he looked at me as if I were meat. No doubt I could have killed him with an arrow, but I did not know if there were others. Moreover, night was falling.

I looked about me—not far away there was a great, broken god-road, leading north. The towers were high enough, but not so high, and while many of the dead-houses were wrecked, there were some that stood. I went toward this god-road, keeping to the heights of the ruins, while the dog followed. When I had reached the god-road, I saw that there were others behind him. If I had slept later, they would have come upon me asleep and torn out my throat. As it was, they were sure enough of me; they did not hurry. When I went into the dead-house, they kept watch at the entrance—doubtless they thought they would have a fine hunt. But a dog cannot open a door and I knew, from the books, that the gods did not like to live on the ground but on high.

I had just found a door I could open when the dogs decided to rush. Ha! They were surprised when I shut the door in their faces—it was a good door, of strong metal. I could hear their foolish baying beyond it but I did not stop to answer them. I was in darkness—I found stairs and climbed. There were many stairs, turning around till my head was dizzy. At the top was another door—I found the knob and opened it. I was in a long small chamber—on one side of it was a bronze door that could not be opened, for it had no handle. Perhaps there was a magic word to open it but I did not have the word. I turned to the door in the opposite side of the wall. The lock of it was broken and I opened it and went in.

Within, there was a place of great riches. The god who lived there must have been a powerful god. The first room was a small ante-room—I waited there for some time, tell-

ing the spirits of the place that I came in peace and not as
a robber. When it seemed to me that they had had time to
hear me, I went on. Ah, what riches! Few, even, of the windows had been broken—it was all as it had been. The great
windows that looked over the city had not been broken at
all though they were dusty and streaked with many years.
There were coverings on the floors, the colors not greatly
faded, and the chairs were soft and deep. There were pictures upon the walls, very strange, very wonderful—I remember one of a bunch of flowers in a jar—if you came
close to it, you could see nothing but bits of color, but if
you stood away from it, the flowers might have been picked
yesterday. It made my heart feel strange to look at this
picture—and to look at the figure of a bird, in some hard
clay, on a table and see it so like our birds. Everywhere
there were books and writings, many in tongues that I
could not read. The god who lived there must have been
a wise god and full of knowledge. I felt I had right there,
as I sought knowledge also.

Nevertheless, it was strange. There was a washing-place
but no water—perhaps the gods washed in air. There was a
cooking place but no wood, and though there was a machine to cook food, there was no place to put fire in it.
Nor were there candles or lamps—there were things that
looked like lamps but they had neither oil nor wick. All
these things were magic, but I touched them and lived—
the magic had gone out of them. Let me tell one thing to
show. In the washing-place, a thing said "Hot" but it was
not hot to the touch—another thing said "Cold" but it was
not cold. This must have been a strong magic but the magic
was gone. I do not understand—they had ways—I wish that
I knew.

It was close and dry and dusty in their house of the gods.
I have said the magic was gone but that is not true—it
had gone from the magic things but it had not gone from
the place. I felt the spirits about me, weighing upon me.
Nor had I ever slept in a Dead Place before—and yet, tonight,
I must sleep there. When I thought of it, my tongue felt
dry in my throat, in spite of my wish for knowledge. Almost I would have gone down again and faced the dogs, but
I did not.

I had not gone through all the rooms when the darkness
fell. When it fell, I went back to the big room looking
over the city and made fire. There was a place to make fire

and a box with wood in it, though I do not think they cooked there. I wrapped myself in a floor-covering and slept in front of the fire—I was very tired.

Now I tell what is very strong magic. I woke in the midst of the night. When I woke, the fire had gone out and I was cold. It seemed to me that all around me there were whisperings and voices. I closed my eyes to shut them out. Some will say that I slept again, but I do not think that I slept. I could feel the spirits drawing my spirit out of my body as a fish is drawn on a line.

Why should I lie about it? I am a priest and the son of a priest. If there are spirits, as they say, in the small Dead Places near us, what spirits must there not be in that great Place of the Gods? And would not they wish to speak? After such long years? I know that I felt myself drawn as a fish is drawn on a line. I had stepped out of my body—I could see my body asleep in front of the cold fire, but it was not I. I was drawn to look out upon the city of the gods.

It should have been dark, for it was night, but it was not dark. Everywhere there were lights—lines of light—circles and blurs of light—ten thousand torches would not have been the same. The sky itself was alight—you could barely see the stars for the glow in the sky. I thought to myself "This is strong magic" and trembled. There was a roaring in my ears like the rushing of rivers. Then my eyes grew used to the light and my ears to the sound. I knew that I was seeing the city as it had been when the gods were alive.

That was a sight indeed—yes, that was a sight: I could not have seen it in the body—my body would have died. Everywhere went the gods, on foot and in chariots—there were gods beyond number and counting and their chariots blocked the streets. They had turned night to day for their pleasure—they did not sleep with the sun. The noise of their coming and going was the noise of the many waters. It was magic what they could do—it was magic what they did.

I looked out of another window—the great vines of their bridges were mended and the god-roads went east and west. Restless, restless, were the gods and always in motion! They burrowed tunnels under rivers—they flew in the air. With unbelievable tools they did giant works—no part of the earth was safe from them, for, if they wished for a thing, they summoned it from the other side of the world. And always, as they labored and rested, as they feasted and made love, there was a drum in their ears—the pulse of the giant city, beating and beating like a man's heart.

Were they happy? What is happiness to the gods? They were great, they were mighty, they were wonderful and terrible. As I looked upon them and their magic, I felt like a child—but a little more, it seemed to me, and they would pull down the moon from the sky. I saw them with wisdom beyond wisdom and knowledge beyond knowledge. And yet not all they did was well done—even I could see that—and yet their wisdom could not but grow until all was peace.

Then I saw their fate come upon them and that was terrible past speech. It came upon them as they walked the streets of their city. I have been in the fights with the Forest People—I have seen men die. But this was not like that. When gods war with gods, they use weapons we do not know. It was fire falling out of the sky and a mist that poisoned. It was the time of the Great Burning and the Destruction. They ran about like ants in the streets of their city—poor gods, poor gods! Then the towers began to fall. A few escaped—yes, a few. The legends tell it. But, even after the city had become a Dead Place, for many years the poison was still in the ground. I saw it happen, I saw the last of them die. It was darkness over the broken city and I wept.

All this, I saw. I saw it as I have told it, though not in the body. When I woke in the morning, I was hungry, but I did not think first of my hunger for my heart was perplexed and confused. I knew the reason for the Dead Places but I did not see why it had happened. It seemed to me it should not have happened, with all the magic they had. I went through the house looking for an answer. There was so much in the house I could not understand—and yet I am a priest and the son of a priest. It was like being on one side of the great river, at night, with no light to show the way.

Then I saw the dead god. He was sitting in his chair, by the window, in a room I had not entered before and, for the first moment, I thought that he was alive. Then I saw the skin on the back of his hand—it was like dry leather. The room was shut, hot and dry—no doubt that had kept him as he was. At first I was afraid to approach him—then the fear left me. He was sitting looking out over the city—he was dressed in the clothes of the gods. His age was neither

young nor old—I could not tell his age. But there was
wisdom in his face and great sadness. You could see that
he would have not run away. He had sat at his window,
watching his city die—then he himself had died. But it is
better to lose one's life than one's spirit—and you could
see from the face that his spirit had not been lost. I knew,
that, if I touched him, he would fall into dust—and yet, there
was something unconquered in the face.

That is all of my story, for then I knew he was a man—I
knew then that they had been men, neither gods nor
demons. It is a great knowledge, hard to tell and believe.
They were men—they went a dark road, but they were men.
I had no fear after that—I had no fear going home, though
twice I fought off the dogs and once I was hunted for two
days by the Forest People. When I saw my father again,
I prayed and was purified. He touched my lips and my
breast, he said, "You went away a boy. You come back a
man and a priest." I said, "Father, they were men! I have
been in the Place of the Gods and seen it! Now slay
me, if it is the law—but still I know they were men."

He looked at me out of both eyes. He said, "The law is not
always the same shape—you have done what you have done.
I could not have done it my time, but you come after me.
Tell!"

I told and he listened. After that, I wished to tell all the
people but he showed me otherwise. He said, "Truth is a
hard deer to hunt. If you eat too much truth at once, you
may die of the truth. It was not idly that our fathers forbade
the Dead Places." He was right—it is better the truth should
come little by little. I have learned that, being a priest. Perhaps, in the old days, they ate knowledge too fast.

Nevertheless, we make a beginning. It is not for the
metal alone we go to the Dead Places now—there are
the books and the writings. They are hard to learn. And
the magic tools are broken—but we can look at them and
wonder. At least, we make a beginning. And, when I am
chief priest we shall go beyond the great river. We shall
go to the Place of the Gods—the place newyork—not one
man but a company. We shall look for the images of the
gods and find the god ASHING and the others—the gods
Lincoln and Biltmore and Moses. But they were men who
built the city, not gods or demons. They were men. I remember the dead man's face. They were men who were
here before us. We must build again.

Soldiers of the Republic

BY DOROTHY PARKER

THAT SUNDAY afternoon we sat with the Swedish girl in the big café in Valencia. We had vermouth in thick goblets, each with a cube of honeycombed gray ice in it. The waiter was so proud of that ice he could hardly bear to leave the glasses on the table, and thus part from it forever. He went to his duty—all over the room they were clapping their hands and hissing to draw his attention—but he looked back over his shoulder.

It was dark outside, the quick, new dark that leaps down without dusk on the day; but, because there were no lights in the streets, it seemed as set and as old as midnight. So you wondered that all the babies were still up. There were babies everywhere in the café, babies serious without solemnity and interested in a tolerant way in their surroundings.

At the table next ours, there was a notably small one; maybe six months old. Its father, a little man in a big uniform that dragged his shoulders down, held it carefully on his knee. It was doing nothing whatever, yet he and his thin young wife, whose belly was already big again under her sleazy dress, sat watching it in a sort of ecstasy of admiration, while their coffee cooled in front of them. The baby was in Sunday white; its dress was patched so delicately that you would have thought the fabric whole had not the patches varied in their shades of whiteness. In its hair was a bow of new blue ribbon, tied with absolute balance of loops and ends. The ribbon was of no use; there was not enough hair to require restraint. The bow was sheerly an adornment, a calculated bit of dash.

"Oh, for God's sake, stop that!" I said to myself. "All right, so it's got a piece of blue ribbon on its hair. All right, so its mother went without eating so it could look pretty when its father came home on leave. All right, so it's her business, and none of yours. All right, so what have you got to cry about?"

The big, dim room was crowded and lively. That morning there had been a bombing from the air, the more horrible for broad daylight. But nobody in the café sat tense and strained, nobody desperately forced forgetfulness. They drank coffee or bottled lemonade, in the pleasant, earned ease of Sunday afternoon, chatting of small, gay matters, all talking at once, all hearing and answering.

There were many soldiers in the room, in what appeared to be the uniforms of twenty different armies until you saw that the variety lay in the differing ways the cloth had worn or faded. Only a few of them had been wounded; here and there you saw one stepping gingerly, leaning on a crutch or two canes, but so far on toward recovery that his face had color. There were many men, too, in civilian clothes—some of them soldiers home on leave, some of them governmental workers, some of them anybody's guess. There were plump, comfortable wives, active with paper fans, and old women as quiet as their grandchildren. There were many pretty girls and some beauties, of whom you did not remark, "There's a charming Spanish type," but said, "What a beautiful girl!" The women's clothes were not new, and their material was too humble ever to have warranted skillful cutting.

"It's funny," I said to the Swedish girl, "how when nobody in a place is best-dressed, you don't notice that everybody isn't."

"Please?" the Swedish girl said.

No one, save an occasional soldier, wore a hat. When we had first come to Valencia, I lived in a state of puzzled pain as to why everybody on the streets laughed at me. It was not because "West End Avenue" was writ across my face as if left there by a customs officer's chalked scrawl. They like Americans in Valencia, where they have seen good ones—the doctors who left their practices and came to help, the calm young nurses, the men of the International Brigade. But when I walked forth, men and women courteously laid their hands across their splitting faces and little children, too innocent for dissembling, doubled with glee and pointed and cried, "*Olé!*" Then, pretty late, I made my discovery, and left my hat off; and there was laughter no longer. It was not one of those comic hats, either; it was just a hat.

The café filled to overflow, and I left our table to speak to a friend across the room. When I came back to the table, six soldiers were sitting there. They were crowded in, and I scraped past them to my chair. They looked tired and dusty and little, the way that the newly dead look little, and the first things you saw about them were the tendons in their necks. I felt like a prize sow.

They were all in conversation with the Swedish girl. She has Spanish, French, German, anything in Scandinavian, Italian, and English. When she has a moment for regret, she sighs that her Dutch is so rusty she can no longer speak it, only read it, and the same is true of her Rumanian.

They had told her, she told us, that they were at the end of forty-eight hours' leave from the trenches, and, for their holiday, they had all pooled their money for cigarettes, and something had gone wrong, and the cigarettes had never come through to them. I had a pack of American cigarettes—in Spain rubies are as nothing to them—and I brought it out, and by nods and smiles and a sort of breast stroke, made it understood that I was offering it to those six men yearning for tobacco. When they saw what I meant, each one of them rose and shook my hand. Darling of me to share my cigarettes with the men on their way back to the trenches. Little Lady Bountiful. The prize sow.

Each one lit his cigarette with a contrivance of yellow rope that stank when afire and was also used, the Swedish girl translated, for igniting grenades. Each one received what he had ordered, a glass of coffee, and each one murmured appreciatively over the tiny cornucopia of coarse sugar that accompanied it. Then they talked.

They talked through the Swedish girl, but they did to us that thing we all do when we speak our own language to one who has no knowledge of it. They looked us square in the face, and spoke slowly, and pronounced their words with elaborate movements of their lips. Then, as their stories came, they poured them at us so vehemently, so emphatically that they were sure we must understand. They were so convinced we would understand that we were ashamed for not understanding.

But the Swedish girl told us. They were all farmers and farmers' sons, from a district so poor that you try not to remember there is that kind of poverty. Their village was next that one where the old men and the sick men and the women and children had gone, on a holiday, to the bull-ring; and the planes had come over and dropped bombs on the bullring, and the old men and the sick men and the women and the children were more than two hundred.

They had all, the six of them, been in the war for over a year, and most of that time they had been in the trenches.

Four of them were married. One had one child, two had three children, one had five. They had not had word from their families since they had left for the front. There had been no communication; two of them had learned to write from men fighting next them in the trench, but they had not dared to write home. They belonged to a union, and union men, of course, are put to death if taken. The village where their families lived had been captured, and if your wife gets a letter from a union man, who knows but they'll shoot her for the connection?

They told about how they had not heard from their families for more than a year. They did not tell it gallantly or whimsically or stoically. They told it as if— Well, look. You have been in the trenches, fighting, for a year. You have heard nothing of your wife and your children. They do not know if you are dead or alive or blinded. You do not know where they are, or if they are. You must talk to somebody. That is the way they told about it.

One of them, some six months before, had heard of his wife and his three children—they had such beautiful eyes, he said—from a brother-in-law in France. They were all alive then, he was told, and had a bowl of beans a day. But his wife had not complained of the food, he heard. What had troubled her was that she had no thread to mend the children's ragged clothes. So that troubled him, too.

"She has no thread," he kept telling us. "My wife has no thread to mend with. No thread."

We sat there, and listened to what the Swedish girl told us they were saying. Suddenly one of them looked at the clock, and then there was excitement. They jumped up, as a man, and there were calls for the waiter and rapid talk with him, and each of them shook the hand of each of us. We went through more swimming motions to explain to them that they were to take the rest of the cigarettes— fourteen cigarettes for six soldiers to take to war—and then they shook our hands again. Then all of us said *"Salud!"* as many times as could be for six of them and three of us, and then they filed out of the café, the six of them, tired and dusty and little, as men of a mighty horde are little.

Only the Swedish girl talked, after they had gone. The Swedish girl has been in Spain since the start of the war. She has nursed splintered men, and she has carried stretchers into the trenches and, heavier laden, back to the hospital. She has seen and heard too much to be knocked into silence.

Presently it was time to go, and the Swedish girl raised her hands above her head and clapped them twice together to summon the waiter. He came, but he only shook his head and his hand, and moved away.

The soldiers had paid for our drinks.

Mr. Preble Gets Rid of His Wife

BY JAMES THURBER

MR. PREBLE was a plump middle-aged lawyer in Scarsdale. He used to kid with his stenographer about running away with him. "Let's run away together," he would say, during a pause in dictation. "All righty," she would say.

One rainy Monday afternoon, Mr. Preble was more serious about it than usual.

"Let's run away together," said Mr. Preble.

"All righty," said his stenographer. Mr. Preble jingled the keys in his pocket and looked out the window.

"My wife would be glad to get rid of me," he said.

"Would she give you a divorce?" asked the stenographer.

"I don't suppose so," he said. The stenographer laughed.

"You'd have to get rid of your wife," she said.

Mr. Preble was unusually silent at dinner that night. About half an hour after coffee, he spoke without looking up from his paper.

"Let's go down in the cellar," Mr. Preble said to his wife.

"What for?" she said, not looking up from her book.

"Oh, I don't know," he said. "We never go down in the cellar any more. The way we used to."

"We never did go down in the cellar that I remember," said Mrs. Preble. "I could rest easy the balance of my life if I never went down in the cellar." Mr. Preble was silent for several minutes.

"Supposing I said it meant a whole lot to me," began Mr. Preble.

"What's come over you?" his wife demanded. "It's cold down there and there is absolutely nothing to do."

"We could pick up pieces of coal," said Mr. Preble. "We might get up some kind of a game with pieces of coal."

"I don't want to," said his wife. "Anyway, I'm reading."

"Listen," said Mr. Preble, rising and walking up and down. "Why won't you come down in the cellar? You can read down there, as far as that goes."

"There isn't a good enough light down there," she said, "and anyway, I'm not going to go down in the cellar. You may as well make up your mind to that."

"Gee whiz!" said Mr. Preble, kicking at the edge of a rug. "Other people's wives go down in the cellar. Why is it you never want to do anything? I come home worn out from the office and you won't even go down in the cellar with me. God knows it isn't very far—it isn't as if I was asking you to go to the movies or some place."

"I don't want to *go!*" shouted Mrs. Preble. Mr. Preble sat down on the edge of a davenport.

"All right, all *right,*" he said. He picked up the newspaper again. "I wish you'd let me tell you more about it. It's—kind of a surprise."

"Will you quit harping on that subject?" asked Mrs. Preble.

"Listen," said Mr. Preble, leaping to his feet. "I might as well tell you the truth instead of beating around the bush. I want to get rid of you so I can marry my stenographer. Is there anything especially wrong about that? People do it every day. Love is something you can't control—"

"We've been all over that," said Mrs. Preble. "I'm not going to go all over that again."

"I just wanted you to know how things are," said Mr. Preble. "But you have to take everything so literally. Good Lord, do you suppose I really wanted to go down there and make up some silly game with pieces of coal?"

"I never believed that for a minute," said Mrs. Preble. "I knew all along you wanted to get me down there and bury me."

"You can say that now—after I told you," said Mr. Preble. "But it would never have occurred to you if I hadn't."

"You didn't tell me; I got it out of you," said Mrs. Preble. "Anyway, I'm always two steps ahead of what you're thinking."

"You're never within a mile of what I'm thinking," said Mr. Preble.

"Is that so? I knew you wanted to bury me the minute you set foot in this house tonight." Mrs. Preble held him with a glare.

"Now that's just plain damn exaggeration," said Mr. Preble, considerably annoyed. "You knew nothing of the sort. As a matter of fact, I never thought of it till just a few minutes ago."

"It was in the back of your mind," said Mrs. Preble. "I suppose this filing woman put you up to it."

"You needn't get sarcastic," said Mr. Preble. "I have plenty of people to file without having her file. She doesn't know anything about this. She isn't in on it. I was going to tell her you had gone to visit some friends and fell over a cliff. She wants me to get a divorce."

"That's a laugh," said Mrs. Preble. "*That's* a laugh. You may bury me, but you'll never get a divorce."

"She knows that! I told her that," said Mr. Preble. "I mean—I told I'd never get a divorce."

"Oh, you probably told her about burying me, too," said Mrs. Preble.

"That's not true," said Mr. Preble, with dignity. "That's between you and me. I was never going to tell a soul."

"You'd blab it to the whole world; don't tell me," said Mrs. Preble. "I know you." Mr. Preble puffed at his cigar.

"I wish you were buried now and it was all over with," he said.

"Don't you suppose you would get caught, you crazy thing?" she said. "They always get caught. Why don't you go to bed? You're just getting yourself worked up over nothing."

"I'm not going to bed," said Mr. Preble. "I'm going to bury you in the cellar. I've got my mind made up to it. I don't know how I could make it any plainer."

"Listen," cried Mrs. Preble, throwing her book down, "will you be satisfied and shut up if I go down in the cellar? Can I have a little peace if I go down in the cellar? Will you let me alone then?"

"Yes," said Mr. Preble. "But you spoil it by taking that attitude."

"Sure, sure, I always spoil everything. I stop reading right in the middle of a chapter. I'll never know how the story comes out—but that's nothing to you."

"Did I make you start reading the book?" asked Mr. Preble. He opened the cellar door. "Here, you go first."

"Brrr," said Mrs. Preble, starting down the steps. "It's *cold* down here! You *would* think of this, at this time of year! Any other husband would have buried his wife in the summer."

"You can't arrange these things just whenever you want to," said Mr. Preble. "I didn't fall in love with this girl till late fall."

"Anybody else would have fallen in love with her long before that. She's been around for years. Why is it you always let other men get in ahead of you? Mercy, but it's dirty down here! What have you got there?"

"I was going to hit you over the head with this shovel," said Mr. Preble.

"You were, huh?" said Mrs. Preble. "Well, get that out of your mind. Do you want to leave a great big clue right here in the middle of everything where the first detective that comes snooping around will find it? Go out in the street and find some piece of iron or something— something that doesn't belong to you."

"Oh, all right," said Mr. Preble. "But there won't be any piece of iron in the street. Women always expect to pick up a piece of iron anywhere."

"If you look in the right place you'll find it," said Mrs. Preble. "And don't be gone long. Don't you dare stop in at the cigar store. I'm not going to stand down here in this cold cellar all night and freeze."

"All right," said Mr. Preble. "I'll hurry."

"And shut that *door* behind you!" she screamed after him. "Where were you born—in a barn?"

Cluney McFarrar's Hardtack

BY JOHN MC NULTY

THE ONLY trouble with this coffee pot around a Hundred and Sixty-eighth Street is it's practically one whole war behind the times. Dozens of guys who go in there off the

Fifth Avenue buses are old Sixty-ninth men and they keep some track of the war in the *News* every morning. But no sooner do they talk ten minutes about this war than back they hop into the other war because it is still more familiar to them. The result was they got this war into France before it really got there. They're always talking about Looney-ville—that was a spot in France in the other war—and about LaFurty Millon, they call it, that was also in the other war.

They're bus drivers and conductors on the buses, and this coffee pot is a hangout for them. Sometimes they get talking the other war and they get carried away by their own talk so that once in a while it makes quite a story they tell, in its own way. The other day it was Cluney Mc-Farrar talking. He just finished up work on the Burma Road line, they call it, because it's the Number Two that goes through Harlem.

Cluney McFarrar was a sergeant in the Sixty-ninth and it is practically a miracle how he weaves around in traffic with that big bus, considering the right arm he got. It was hit by a machine gun in a wheat field and later on he developed a thing in it called osteomyelitis. He knows the medical name for it because he heard the doctors in the hospitals talking about it a million times. But osteomyelitis or no osteomyelitis, he can jockey that bus around O.K., and not only that but with his bum arm he can maneuver the door open and shut in traffic in the twinkle of an eye, so that he can spit tobacco into the street as he goes along. One conductor that works with him says McFarrar is a marvel of timing, opening and shutting the door for this purpose.

This day, a couple days ago, McFarrar finished on the Burma Road, had a slug or two in a place next door to this coffee pot, then came in for coffee and to sit around talking. One thing led to another and McFarrar told about one time in a woods in France—still back a whole war, into 1918.

"There was no more trenches than a rabbit," McFarrar said, "because it was July, around that sometime, and we were chasing them but still plenty of our fellers getting killed. You don't know really what's happening in a war like that until a couple years later when you come home and read in a slow-written book just what the hell was going on that time, like for instance the day I'm talking about.

"We couldn't go up the road, so we were going ahead the best we could through a woods, the woods on both sides the road. They were shelling the road so you couldn't go up it.

"Guys would see Germans here and there ahead of them in the woods, so the way you'd have to do is stand behind a tree and fire a few, then run up and get behind another tree like the goddam Indians they used to have here in this country, except the only Indians most of us knew was those cop-shooters and wild men used to be around the West Side, Tenth Avenyuh and around there.

"That was the best way to do it, behind trees, everybody separated, but it's hell to keep soldiers separated. Or deployed, if you want to call it that. The toughest thing a sergeant has to do is keep the troops spread out, because as soon as there's shooting, they bunch up, usually around the sergeant, which'd make a fine target out of him.

"We kept separated pretty good through that woods, though, going ahead a little at a time. I come across McElroy, from Eight Avenyuh, behind one tree, smoking his pipe and shooting one shot after the other. He says to me when I bunched behind the same tree, 'Have you got a match, McFarrar? This pipe keeps going out, and I ought to hold up a minute for a smoke anyway. The bolt of this rifle is getting hot, so help me God.'

"All that has no bearing on what I was going to say, I mean about the hardtack. Well, after I left McElroy and ran for another tree ahead a little bit and McElroy found *himself* another tree, I saw something out of the corner of my eye while I was running up to this other tree.

"What I saw was a nice new can of hardtack lying there, and jeez, was I hungry. I forgot to say the chow wagons didn't get up, and everybody was hungry. And there was this can of hardtack some poor guy dropped. He was dead near it. I had to run past it, but I never saw anything so clear as that hardtack.

"So when I got behind the tree I says to myself, 'I'll come back and get that hardtack if I ever live through this day.' And to make sure where I was, I mean where the hardtack was, I took a good look around. I looked up at how the trees set with regards to the road, and how if a man was walking on the road he could look in and tell this part of the woods exactly. Like distinguishing marks, I mean, that you'd see from the road, how the trees grew and the like of that. 'If it's the last thing I ever do, I'll get that hardtack tonight,' I says to myself.

"Well, the day come to an end, and us maybe two miles ahead of where McElroy and me was behind the tree and the hardtack was."

Then McFarrar said they had a funny thing about that other war, compared to this war they got now. He said in some ways that other war was a union war, like. In some places, anyway, it seemed to have regular hours.

"Near this woods was one of those places where the war kept regular hours," McFarrar went on. "It seemed to stop almost altogether at night, even before night. What you might call twilight, it stopped, only the way I remember it, this twilight come at pretty near ten o'clock. Not dark yet, only getting gray and birds going to bed in the trees.

"The birds were funny. I remember them because when everything come to a halt and I was still alive for the end of that day, I says to myself, 'Now I'll go back and get the hardtack.' And I started all alone back down the road. They wasn't shelling it any more, because whether it seems logical or not, the war come to a stop, I tell you, right about that hour. Not a stop for good I don't mean, but a stop for that day. And I walked back down the road toward the place where the hardtack was. Jeez, I was hungry—no chow wagons yet.

"About the birds. While I was walking back the road, I could hear them loud and busy, getting ready for the night. Banging and shooting sounds all the day, and there were the birds singing or at least talking, at this kind of twilight, as if nothing happened. It seemed funny, and it was that quiet I could hear my feet scrunching the gravel down the road.

"Of course I kept glancing into the woods, so I wouldn't pass where the hardtack was. It got silenter and silenter except for the birds, and gradually they started to shut up and it got a little darker, only not what you'd call dark. For some reason there was nobody on the road but me. The stuff like camions and chow wagons wouldn't come up until real black dark.

"There was beginning to be a little smell from the woods. They were the quietest woods I ever seen then, even though they was certainly noisy all that day we just pulled through.

"I come to the place I marked in my mind's eye, and my

stomach give a jump because I knew the hardtack was right in there. Honest to God, I was near starved. I stood a minute in the road and checked up. I wanted to make sure by the shape of the trees I was right and that was the place. And I started to go into the woods after the hardtack.

"Then the silence come over me. Every bird quit all to once. My feet stopped going into the woods. It come over me how in there was all the guys, some of them I knew, would never come out of those woods again. Some of them from New York. Most of them, you might say, because don't forget this was the Sixty-ninth. I thought how they'd never walk around on the New York streets any more, Ninety-sixth or anywhere, and not ever get get drunk in New York on Saturday night the way you do. And on top of all that, this silence I got to explain to you but I can't.

"And that was the last step I took toward that hardtack when I thought all that. I turned around and went up the road again.

"I couldn't have gone in those woods if there was Fig Newtons in there."

The Darkness of the Night

BY ROBERT M. COATES

THE CAFÉ was a small one, just west of Sixth Avenue, on Greenwich. It was a Villagey sort of place, full of women sitting with their legs crossed high on the red leather stools in front of the bar and men crowded around them, and one reason Fred and Flora had taken to meeting there was that they had never seen anyone they knew, or even anyone from the neighborhood who might have known them. When Fred pushed the door open around nine o'clock on that Saturday night, things were going full swing, with people lined two and three deep at the bar and clustered around the tables, and the air dense with smoke and excitement.

For a moment it baffled him, coming in from the quiet street outside, but even before he could find his bearings he had that feeling he often had when he was keeping a date with Flora, that she was already there somewhere and watching him. It was a curious feeling, and it was so strong that sometimes when it turned out wrong and he arrived first at their meeting place, it would still be with him, enough to make it seem that she must already know what he was doing and thinking about, and he would find himself talking to her, in his mind of course, and when she finally appeared she would just be there, and that would be the only difference.

This time, though, he wasn't mistaken. He was a tall man, blond, with a broad, heavy face and small, solemn blue eyes, and it took him a half-minute or so to sort out the scene before him. Then he saw her. She was sitting at a table in the far corner of the room, a half-finished glass of beer before her and her elbow on the table beside it, her head resting on her hand and the hand slid so far up her cheek that the fingers shoved her short-cut brown hair up in a little fluffy plume above her head. Her face was turned toward the door, and when their eyes met she didn't smile or wave; she just watched him, pivoting her head on her hand to keep him in view as he pushed through the crowd and dropped into the seat opposite her.

"Gee, Flora, I'm sorry," he said. "I'm late."

"It don't matter," she said. She had a small, pointed face and large brown eyes. Tonight, he noticed, her face looked pale.

"You know how it is up there now," he said. "I told you. The night crew comes on at six, like always. But now they got a stunt with the day crew. We got to tend counter till eight, and then it's up to us to clean up the steam tables, fixing up for the supper dishes, before we knock off. So by the time I go home and get changed and all and come down here . . ." She was still sitting with her head propped on her hand, looking up at him, and the steadiness of her gaze made him feel uncomfortable. "Nine o'clock," he said. "I guess I ain't so very late, maybe."

"It don't matter." Suddenly she smiled up at him. "I don't mind waiting."

As soon as she smiled, Fred's face brightened too. "Well," he said, "what you having?"

"A beer."

"Yeah, I know. But you're about through with that. How about something stronger?"

She glanced down at her glass and then up at him and nodded.

"Rye?" Fred asked.

"O.K."

Fred signalled to a waiter. "Rye-and-soda," he said. "Two." He and Flora sat looking at each other a little awkwardly, smiling, till the waiter came back with the drinks. When he had gone, Fred leaned forward and picked up his glass. "Well," he said, "how was it today?"

"Oh, all right," she said. "You know, Saturdays. He came home. All he'd had was a couple of drinks. And he brought in some beer." Always when she started talking about her husband, Fred would get a feeling of hot, helpless anger, so hot and so deep inside him that it was almost a physical pain. But he could never help asking. He could feel the anger rising inside him now and his face growing red with it. Flora didn't notice. She was sitting with her head bent down, watching the ice bob around in the glass as she stirred her drink. "He drunk most of the beer," she went on, "and then we had dinner. And then, when he seen I was going out, he asked where, and I said to my Cousin Annie's. And he said—" She broke off and glanced up at him. "Ah, Fred. It's so foolish."

"What's foolish?" He had been only half listening, and with the rest of his mind he had been trying to imagine what it had been like in the apartment, her cooking the meal and setting the table and the other one sitting there, drinking his beer and watching her, telling her what he wanted, owning her. For a moment he couldn't get back to what she was saying. "What's foolish?" he repeated.

"What we're doing. What we're thinking about." She had eyes that could convey more kinds of emotion than any other woman's he had ever seen, and now she was looking at him with so weary and hopeless an expression that it dismayed him. "Why don't you just go?" she was saying. "Why don't you just leave me?"

"I couldn't do that, Flora. You know that." She had let one hand fall on the table and he reached forward and seized it, and he must have squeezed it too hard, for she gave a little yank and a cry. Fred was fleetingly conscious that someone had laughed, and he glanced up and saw a red-faced man in the group at the next table looking over at him. "They're doing all right, it would seem," the man said, grinning knowingly. Fred met the man's eye and then turned back to Flora. "What you don't realize," he said in a lower voice, "is a good counterman can get jobs anywhere. There's lunchrooms everywhere, and the setup is always the same. And the fellows are always drifting. I could take you to Buffalo, or out to Detroit, or even further. We could go anywhere. I could make a living." He was still holding her hand, but she had let it go loose inside his and after a while he released it. The waiter was there again, picking up their empty glasses. "Two more rye-and-sodas," Fred said.

She shook her head at him sadly. "I couldn't," she said. "Fred, I've told you. Wherever we went, it would be a shame to me. Wherever you took me."

"Nobody would ask any questions. We'd be Mr. and Mrs. to them, and who'd ever think to ask different?"

"'Till death do us part,'" she quoted. "I take things like that serious, Fred. You can't move me."

"You could get a divorce."

"On what grounds? He ain't been unfaithful, has he? He's a good provider."

They had argued this way before, and always it had come out the same. Always, too, Fred had got angry. "Well, God, then!" he said.

Flora faced him with an expression almost of triumph on her face. "Like I said," she retorted. "Just leave me. You could get other girls to go off with you like that, maybe, but not me." She leaned back slowly, drawing her hand away till it slipped off the edge of the table into her lap. For a while, without speaking, they sat staring at each other; the look of triumph faded from her eyes and a hurt look came into them, and for a moment they were welling with tears. Then—she was leaning back now, with her head resting against the dark wood that formed the back of the seats against the wall—a kind of caressingness filled them; for a while neither she nor Fred said anything, and in the silence they couldn't help hearing the talk that was going on at the next table. "Well, the old lady just looked at the kid and kept on stirring," a man in a dark-blue suit was saying. "'I don't know where he is,' says she. 'All I know is he's never around when you want him.'" When the man had finished speaking, a girl in a gray tailored coat and a short black skirt gave a whoop and pushed herself back in her chair so hard that she almost lost balance. She grabbed at the red-faced man's

arm to steady herself. "Oh, God!" she cried. "What a
simply crazy story! Eddie, where do you get them?" The
red-faced man was laughing too. "Now, listen," he said.
"Let me tell one." Flora gave a little sigh. "Ah, Fred," she
said. "People can have such good times, can't they?"

"Only us," Fred said.

"Only us."

"We could have good times, too."

She shook her head slowly at him, not speaking. "Look,"
the red-faced man was saying, "this one's an Irish one, and
you ought to know the accent to really put it over. But it
seems there was a snowstorm in Ireland . . ." Flora giggled
suddenly. "You know, Fred," she said. "I busted a light
bulb yesterday."

Fred stared at her, puzzled. "A light bulb?"

"Yes. You know, a light bulb. It was out in the kitchen
over the sink, and it had burned out, so yesterday I thought
I would change it. And then, when I was screwing it out,
it dropped, bang, into the sink. It smashed into a thousand pieces. Really, Fred, I bet if you'd count them . . ."
She stopped for a second, looking at him. They were yelling again at the next table and Fred couldn't keep from
grinning; he couldn't help thinking there was a joke in
what Flora was saying, too. "Right near where the stew
was," she went on. She had leaned forward a little, and
there was something in her voice that made Fred stop
grinning. For an instant his heart and his breathing stopped
too. "The stew I was putting some vegetables in," she said.
"For his supper. And I couldn't help thinking . . ." She
had opened her purse and was fishing around in it. She
pulled out a newspaper clipping. "Fred, did you notice
this? Because I was reading it in the *News* just before
I started fixing that bulb."

The clipping was a small one, and it was date-lined some
place in Ohio. Fred could hardly read it, but it told in a
half-jokingly way how a woman had confessed feeding
her husband almost the whole of two beer bottles, broken
up, before the glass had killed him. Fred's hand shook a
little as he laid the clipping down. Then he picked it up
again, squeezed it carefully into a ball, and dropped it under
the table. They had talked of such things before. "Taking
life's a crime, too," he said.

Flora didn't argue. She had watched him while he
crumpled the paper and threw it away. Now, without a

word, she lowered her head and sat looking down at the table between them. Fred leaned closer. "And what you don't think of," he said, "is if you read about that in the papers, it shows she didn't get away with it, don't it?" She still didn't answer. They were sitting with their heads almost touching now, and as she bent forward, the V of her dress fell away from her body—not far, but enough so that he could see, as she breathed, the soft upper part of her breasts shrink away inside the opening and then rise again, steadily and firmly. Somehow, the sight didn't excite him as it might have done; instead, it filled him with a feeling of awe at her frailty, and of wonder at the obscure mechanism of her body, and with a queer, shaken feeling of shame that he should be faced with it now. He would have liked to look away, but he couldn't, and as he sat there staring she leaned back and looked up at him. "Well, anyway," she said, "I got to be going."

"Why? It's early yet."

"Think so?" she said. "Maybe he won't."

"What's he got to do with it?" Fred demanded.

"Ah, Fred," she said, "do I have to tell you? What's a man like him want of a woman, anyways? What's he marry her for? You ain't a child, are you?" Fred felt a great lump rise up in his throat and stick there. He reached over to grab her hand, and then he remembered what had happened the last time he had done that, and glanced quickly at the next table. The four who were there were all pretty drunk by now and none of them was bothering much about what went on around them. The girl in the tailored suit, he noticed, was leaning against the red-faced man's chest, her face so close to his that their lips almost touched as they talked. Nevertheless, Fred folded his hand over Flora's carefully. "He told me he'd wait up for me," she said. "He'll be waiting."

"But listen, Flora," Fred said. "You don't have to. If you really don't want to."

She was shaking her head, her eyes solemn. "No, Fred," she said. "You don't realize. And when it's a wife's duty." She pulled her hand free and picked up her purse. Then she sat looking at him, waiting for him to call the waiter. "Well," she said, "that's what I got to look forward to now." She didn't give him much chance to say anything more. The waiter, coming past, dropped the check on their table, and she got up immediately. By the time Fred had paid

it, she was already halfway to the door. He started to
follow her and then stopped. "Wait!" he called, and turned
back to the table.

The waiter had picked up their glasses and gone, and
the table was vacant. Quickly, Fred bent down and began
searching the floor underneath. As he did so, he felt a
hand grip his shoulder. It made him jump a little, but
when he looked up he saw it was only the red-faced man,
peering down at him. "What's the matter, friend?" the
man asked unsteadily. "Lose something?" Fred's hand had
already closed on the wadded clipping. He jerked his shoulder free and shoved himself to his feet. "No," he said,
but there was so much noise in the place that he couldn't
be sure the man heard him. "It's O.K. Never mind." He
saw the man staring at him, puzzled and a little resentful.
Flora was just going out the door.

She was waiting for him outside. "I got this," he said
as soon as he saw her, and he opened his hand to show
her the clipping. She glanced at it and then up at him,
but she didn't say anything. It was as if she wasn't interested, and when he started walking down toward West
Tenth Street she paced along beside him quietly. He had
had a moment of panic back there, arguing with that drunk,
and he still wasn't over it; he discovered that he was
breathing hard and fast. "You don't want to leave things
like that lying around," he told her. Still she didn't speak.
They walked to the corner of Tenth and turned west. There
was a rustle of cars going up and down Seventh Avenue,
and a sprinkling of people along the sidewalks, but mostly
the streets were quiet. The day's heat was thinning away
and a cool evening calm was replacing it; when they
crossed Seventh, the block that stretched to West Fourth
Street was almost deserted.

The block after that was hers. They crossed West Fourth
Street. Flora still walked silently, almost docilely, beside
him, but when they crossed the street, to Fred it was as if
they had entered another air, higher, lighter, more urgent;
his quick breathing came back and with it a feeling of
haste. Ahead he could see the two granite columns and
the heavy porch cornice that made her apartment house
different from the others. It was only a few dozen steps
away, and when he saw it so close he couldn't help think-

ing of the time he had wasted, not settling his mind, not deciding, in the blocks before.

Or rather, even now, he wasn't thinking; what began going through his mind was not thought but waves of emotion, and these were so swift in their passage that they hardly meant more than mere words pictorialized. Fear, parting, love, death, disappointment, horror—these presented themselves to his mind in a jumble of sensation, and beneath them all was a feeling that he was being hurried, that a decision was being forced on him. What that decision was he still couldn't think, but the feeling was so strong that he almost cried out with it. If he could only stop, stand still for a moment, think quietly; if she would only just stop being there, walking silently beside him, leaving everything up to him. . . . They had reached the sidewalk in front of her apartment house. It came almost with the sweetness of a reprieve when she said, "Fred, let's walk on." She was looking pleadingly up at him. "To the corner. Shall we?"

They walked on to the corner of Bleecker. There was a bakery on the opposite corner and this was lighted, but all the other shop fronts at the intersection—the bookstore, the market, the Salvation Army store beside which they were standing—were closed and dark. All up and down Bleecker, all up and down Tenth, not a soul was moving. They stood a moment, looking at each other. "Well, now I go back," she said. "You go on to the subway. You go on uptown." She paused. "Goodbye, Fred."

"Goodbye?" he said.

"I've been thinking," she said. "All the while we were walking. It's better that way. I won't be seeing you any more, Fred."

He stared down at her. In the light of the street lamp above them he could see her features, pale and sharp, but he couldn't make out her expression or what she was thinking. There was no clue for him there, but suddenly it came to him that he had enough determination for both of them. It was time for him to decide. Almost roughly, he seized her arm at the elbow. Under the light summer dress, the skin felt soft and cool. "Listen, now," he said. "You may be seeing a lot of me." He felt strong and calm and purposeful. "I'm coming back with you," he said.

"Listen, now," he said. He was walking her back along West Tenth again. There was ease in his mind now, and

peace. "You go up to him. See, now, you go up to him.
And tell him there's a man in the vestibule. There's a man
been annoying people, and he made a grab at you as you
came in and you had to run for it. When he comes down,
I'll be waiting for him."

She was walking lightly along beside him. She was walking so swiftly and so freely that he almost had to run
to keep up with her. But the speed only gave him pleasure.
"But supposing he don't come down, Fred?" she said.
Her voice was low and excited. "He's in bed now, anyway.
He'll be sleeping. And even if he wasn't, the most that
he'd do would be call the janitor."

It crossed Fred's mind that something she had said before had been different. In his mind he had had a different picture. He had pictured the other one waiting up
for her. But maybe he had misunderstood, and anyway it
didn't matter. "Well, then, listen," he said. The fact that
he'd had to alter his plans didn't shake his confidence;
to find that he could change them so quickly and surely,
as need arose, only added to his feeling of power and
confidence. They were in the vestibule now, and she had
her bag open, getting out the key. "I'll come up with
you, then," he said. She turned the key and the door
swung open. She was filled with a haste as furious as his
own. She stepped first into the dark hall inside and he followed her. "I'll be right there with you," he said.

"That's better." They were speaking in whispers now.

"Well, then. Where'll he be?"

"In the bedroom, for sure. And most likely he'll be asleep.
He's had plenty beers. I took care of that."

"Where's the bedroom?"

"In back, on the court. I'll show you. Ah, Fred," she
said. He couldn't see her. For a while, as they stood apart
in the dark hallway, he couldn't feel her, either; it was as
if she wasn't there, and a kind of uncertainty took hold
of him. "I'll need something," he said. "I can't do it with
my bare fists." But even as he spoke, her hand touched his
and then, having located him, her body met his in a rush;
for a moment she lay against him, and from somewhere
out of the darkness her lips reached his in a long, strong
kiss. As her body lay against his, he could feel it quivering,
but it was not the shaking of nervousness or of fear; it
was like the tight, taut quivering of a string or a wire that has
been stretched to the singing point. "Ah, the bastard!" she

said. Her arm had gone round his neck, and her face was so close that when she spoke he could feel the brush of her lips against his own. "The low, sneaking, snivelling bastard! With his pawing, his pleading. Coming home to me there, and then begging. There's my shears," she said. He could feel her arm tighten on his neck, and then contact vanished. The next thing he felt was her fingers closing over his hand. "There's my dressmaking shears. They're out on the dining-room table, right in front of the door. I'd know where they were, even in the dark." The hand was tugging at his now, leading him toward the stairs.

"Come on," she said.

The Old People

BY WILLIAM FAULKNER

1.

AT FIRST there was nothing. There was the faint, cold, steady rain, the gray and constant light of the late November dawn, with the voices of the hounds converging somewhere in it and toward them. Then Sam Fathers, standing just behind the boy as he had been standing when the boy shot his first running rabbit with his first gun and almost with the first load it ever carried, touched his shoulder and he began to shake, not with any cold. Then the buck was there. He did not come into sight; he was just there, looking not like a ghost but as if all of light were condensed in him and he were the source of it, not only moving in it but disseminating it, already running, seen first as you always see the deer, in that split second after he has already seen you, already slanting away in that first soaring bound, the antlers even in that dim light looking like a small rocking-chair balanced on his head.

"Now," Sam Fathers said, "shoot quick, and slow."

The boy did not remember that shot at all. He would live to be eighty, as his father and his father's twin brother and their father in his turn had lived to be, but he would never hear that shot nor remember even the shock of the gun-butt. He didn't even remember what he did with the gun afterward. He was running. Then he was standing over the buck where it lay on the wet earth still in the attitude of speed and not looking at all dead, standing over it shaking and jerking, with Sam Fathers beside him again, extending the knife. "Don't walk up to him in front," Sam said. "If he aint dead, he will cut you all to pieces with his feet. Walk up to him from behind and take him by the horn first, so you can hold his head down until you can jump away. Then slip your other hand down and hook your fingers in his nostrils."

The boy did that—drew the head back and the throat taut and drew Sam Fathers' knife across the throat and Sam stooped and dipped his hands in the hot smoking blood and wiped them back and forth across the boy's face. Then Sam's horn rang in the wet gray woods and again and again; there was a boiling wave of dogs about them, with Tennie's Jim and Boon Hogganbeck whipping them back after each had had a taste of the blood, then the men, the true hunters—Walter Ewell whose rifle never missed, and Major de Spain and old General Compson and the boy's cousin, McCaslin Edmonds, grandson of his father's sister, sixteen years his senior and, since both he and McCaslin were only children and the boy's father had been nearing seventy when he was born, more his brother than his cousin and more his father than either—sitting their horses and looking down at them: at the old man of seventy who had been a negro for two generations now but whose face and bearing were still those of the Chickasaw chief who had been his father; and the white boy of twelve with the prints of the bloody hands on his face, who had nothing to do but stand straight and not let the trembling show.

"Did he do all right, Sam?" his cousin McCaslin said.

"He done all right," Sam Fathers said.

They were the white boy, marked forever, and the old dark man sired on both sides by savage kings, who had marked him, whose bloody hands had merely formally consecrated him to that which, under the man's tutelage, he had already accepted, humbly and joyfully, with abnegation and with pride too; the hands, the touch, the first worthy blood which he had been found at last worthy to draw, joining him and the man forever, so that the man would continue to live past the boy's seventy years and then eighty years, long after the man himself had entered the earth as chiefs and kings entered it;—the child, not yet a man,

whose grandfather had lived in the same country and in
almost the same manner as the boy himself would grow up
to live, leaving his descendants in the land in his turn
as his grandfather had done, and the old man past seventy
whose grandfathers had owned the land long before the
white men ever saw it and who had vanished from it now
with all their kind, what of blood they left behind them
running now in another race and for a while even in bondage
and now drawing toward the end of its alien and irrevocable
course, barren, since Sam Fathers had no children.

His father was Ikkemotubbe himself, who had named
himself Doom. Sam told the boy about that—how Ikkemotubbe, old Issetibbeha's sister's son, had run away to New
Orleans in his youth and returned seven years later with
a French companion calling himself the Chevalier Soeur-
Blonde de Vitry, who must have been the Ikkemotubbe
of his family too and who was already addressing Ikkemotubbe as *Du Homme;*—returned, came home again, with
his foreign Aramis and the quadroon slave woman who was
to be Sam's mother, and a gold-laced hat and coat and
a wicker wine-hamper containing a litter of month-old puppies and a gold snuff-box filled with a white powder resem-
bling fine sugar. And how he was met at the River landing
by three or four companions of his bachelor youth, and
while the light of a smoking torch gleamed on the glittering braid of the hat and coat Doom squatted in the mud
of the land and took one of the puppies from the hamper
and put a pinch of the white powder on its tongue and
the puppy died before the one who was holding it could
cast it away. And how they returned to the Plantation
where Issetibbeha, dead now, had been succeeded by his
son, Doom's fat cousin Moketubbe, and the next day Moketubbe's eight-year-old son died suddenly and that afternoon,
in the presence of Moketubbe and most of the others (the
People, Sam Fathers called them) Doom produced another
puppy from the wine-hamper and put a pinch of the white
powder on its tongue and Moketubbe abdicated and Doom
became in fact The Man which his French friend already
called him. And how on the day after that, during the ceremony of accession, Doom pronounced a marriage between
the pregnant quadroon and one of the slave men which
he just inherited (that was how Sam Fathers got his
name, which in Chickasaw had been Had-Two-Fathers)

and two years later sold the man and woman and the child who was his own son to his white neighbor, Carothers Mc-Caslin.

That was seventy years ago. The Sam Fathers whom the boy knew was already sixty—a man not tall, squat rather, almost sedentary, flabby-looking though he actually was not, with hair like a horse's mane which even at seventy showed no trace of white and a face which showed no age until he smiled, whose only visible trace of negro blood was a slight dullness of the hair and the fingernails, and something else which you did notice about the eyes, which you noticed because it was not always there, only in repose and not always then—something not in their shape nor pigment but in their expression, and the boy's cousin McCaslin told him what that was: not the heritage of Ham, not the mark of servitude but of bondage; the knowledge that for a while that part of his blood had been the blood of slaves. "Like an old lion or a bear in a cage," McCaslin said. "He was born in the cage and has been in it all his life; he knows nothing else. Then he smells something. It might be anything, any breeze blowing past anything and then into his nostrils. But there for a second was the hot sand or the cane-brake that he never even saw himself, might not even know if he did see it and probably does know he couldn't hold his own with it if he got back to it. But that's not what he smells then. It was the cage he smelled. He hadn't smelled the cage until that minute. Then the hot sand or the brake blew into his nostrils and blew away, and all he could smell was the cage. That's what makes his eyes look like that."

"Then let him go!" the boy cried. "Let him go!"

His cousin laughed shortly. Then he stopped laughing, making the sound that is. It had never been laughing. "His cage aint McCaslins," he said. "He was a wild man. When he was born, all his blood on both sides, except the little white part, knew things that had been tamed out of our blood so long ago that we have not only forgotten them, we have to live together in herds to protect ourselves from our own sources. He was the direct son not only of a warrior but of a chief. Then he grew up and began to learn things, and all of a sudden one day he found out that he had been betrayed, the blood of the warriors and chiefs had been betrayed. Not by his father," he added quickly. "He probably never held it against old Doom for selling him and his mother into slavery, because he probably believed the damage was already done before then and it was the same warriors' and chiefs' blood in him and Doom both that was betrayed through the black blood which his mother gave him. Not betrayed by the black blood and not wilfully betrayed by his mother, but betrayed by her all the same, who had bequeathed him not only the blood of slaves but even a little of the very blood which had enslaved it; himself his own battleground, the scene of his own vanquishment and the mausoleum of his defeat. His cage aint us," McCaslin said. "Did you ever know anybody yet, even your father and Uncle Buddy, that ever told him to do or not do anything that he ever paid any attention to?"

That was true. The boy first remembered him as sitting in the door of the plantation blacksmith-shop, where he sharpened plow-points and mended tools and even did rough carpenter-work when he was not in the woods. And sometimes, even when the woods had not drawn him, even with the shop cluttered with work which the farm waited on, Sam would sit there, doing nothing at all for half a day or a whole one, and no man, neither the boy's father and twin uncle in their day nor his cousin McCaslin after he became practical though not yet titular master, ever to say to him, "I want this finished by sundown" or "why wasn't this done yesterday?" And once each year, in the late fall, in November, the boy would watch the wagon, the hooped canvas top erected now, being loaded—the food, hams and sausage from the smokehouse, coffee and flour and molasses from the commissary, a whole beef killed just last night for the dogs until there would be meat in camp, the crate containing the dogs themselves, then the bedding, the guns, the horns and lanterns and axes, and his cousin McCaslin and Sam Fathers in their hunting clothes would mount to the seat and with Tennie's Jim sitting on the dog-crate they would drive away to Jefferson, to join Major de Spain and General Compson and Boon Hogganbeck and Walter Ewell and go into the big bottom of the Tallahatchie where the deer and bear were, to be gone two weeks. But before the wagon was even loaded the boy would find that he could watch no longer. He would go away, running almost, to stand behind the corner where he could not see the wagon and nobody could see him, not crying, holding himself rigid except for the trembling, whispering to himself: "Soon now. Soon now. Just three more years" (or two

more or one more) "and I will be ten. Then Cass said I
can go."

White man's work, when Sam did work. Because he did
nothing else: farmed no alloted acres of his own, as the
other ex-slaves of old Carothers McCaslin did, performed
no field-work for daily wages as the younger and newer
negroes did—and the boy never knew just how that had
been settled between Sam and old Carothers, or perhaps
with old Carothers' twin sons after him. For, although Sam
lived among the negroes, in a cabin among the other cabins
in the quarters, and consorted with negroes (what of consorting with anyone Sam did after the boy got big enough
to walk alone from the house to the blacksmith-shop and
then to carry a gun) and dressed like them and talked
like them and even went with them to the negro church
now and then, he was still the son of that Chickasaw chief
and the negroes knew it. And, it seemed to the boy, not
only negroes. Boon Hogganbeck's grandmother had been a
Chickasaw woman too, and although the blood had run
white since and Boon was a white man, it was not chief's
blood. To the boy at least, the difference was apparent immediately you saw Boon and Sam together, and even
Boon seemed to know it was there—even Boon, to whom in
his tradition it had never occurred that anyone might be
better born than himself. A man might be smarter, he admitted that, or richer (luckier, he called it) but not better
born. Boon was a mastiff, absolutely faithful, dividing his
fidelity equally between Major de Spain and the boy's cousin
McCaslin, absolutely dependent for his very bread and dividing that impartially too between Major de Spain and Mc-
Caslin, hardy, generous, courageous enough, a slave to all
the appetites and almost unratiocinative. In the boy's eyes
at least it was Sam Fathers, the negro, who bore himself
not only toward his cousin McCaslin and Major de Spain
but toward all white men, with gravity and dignity and without servility or recourse to that impenetrable wall of ready
and easy mirth which negroes sustain between themselves
and white men, bearing himself toward his cousin McCaslin not only as one man to another but as an older man to
a younger.

He taught the boy the woods, to hunt, when to shoot
and when not to shoot, when to kill and when not to kill,
and better, what to do with it afterward. Then he would talk
to the boy, the two of them sitting beneath the close fierce

stars on a summer hilltop while they waited for the hounds to bring the fox back within hearing, or beside a fire in the November or December woods while the dogs worked out a coon's trail along the creek, or fireless in the pitch dark and heavy dew of April mornings while they squatted beneath a turkey-roost. The boy would never question him; Sam did not react to questions. The boy would just wait and then listen and Sam would begin, talking about the old days and the People whom he had not had time ever to know and so could not remember (he did not remember ever having seen his father's face), and in place of whom the other race into which his blood had run supplied him with no substitute.

And as he talked about those old times and those dead and vanished men of another race from either that the boy knew, gradually to the boy those old times would cease to be old times and would become a part of the boy's present, not only as if they had happened yesterday but as if they were still happening, the men who walked through them actually walking in breath and air and casting an actual shadow on the earth they had not quitted. And more: as if some of them had not happened yet but would occur tomorrow, until at last it would seem to the boy that he himself had not come into existence yet, that none of his race nor the other subject race which his people had brought with them into the land had come here yet; that although it had been his grandfather's and then his father's and uncle's and was now his cousin's and someday would be his own land which he and Sam hunted over, their hold upon it actually was as trivial and without reality as the now faded and archaic script in the chancery book in Jefferson which allocated it to them and that it was he, the boy, who was the guest here and Sam Father's voice the mouthpiece of the host.

Until three years ago there had been two of them, the other a full-blood Chickasaw, in a sense even more incredibly lost than Sam Fathers. He called himself Jobaker, as if it were one word. Nobody knew his history at all. He was a hermit, living in a foul little shack at the forks of the creek five miles from the plantation and about that far from any other habitation. He was a market hunter and fisherman and he consorted with nobody, black or white; no negro would even cross his path and no man dared approach his hut except Sam. And perhaps once a month the boy would find them in Sam's shop—two old men squatting on their heels on the dirt floor, talking in a mixture of negroid English and flat hill dialect and now and then a phrase of that old tongue which as time went on and the boy squatted there too listening, he began to learn. Then Jobaker died. That is, nobody had seen him in some time. Then one morning Sam was missing, nobody, not even the boy, knew when nor where, until that night when some negroes hunting in the creek bottom saw the sudden burst of flame and approached. It was Jobaker's hut, but before they got anywhere near it, someone shot at them from the shadows beyond it. It was Sam who fired, but nobody ever found Jobaker's grave.

The next morning, sitting at breakfast with his cousin, the boy saw Sam pass the dining-room window and he remembered then that never in his life before had he seen Sam nearer the house than the blacksmith-shop. He stopped eating even; he sat there and he and his cousin both heard the voices from beyond the pantry door, then the door opened and Sam entered, carrying his hat in his hand but without knocking as anyone else on the place except a house servant would have done, entered just far enough for the door to close behind him and stood looking at neither of them—the Indian face above the nigger clothes, looking at something over their heads or at something not even in the room.

"I want to go," he said. "I want to go to the Big Bottom to live."

"To live?" the boy's cousin said.

"At Major de Spain's and your camp, where you go to hunt," Sam said. "I could take care of it for you all while you aint there. I will build me a little house in the woods, if you rather I didn't stay in the big one."

"What about Isaac here?" his cousin said. "How will you get away from him? Are you going to take him with you?" But still Sam looked at neither of them, standing just inside the room with that face which showed nothing, which showed that he was an old man only when it smiled.

"I want to go," he said. "Let me go."

"Yes," the cousin said quietly. "Of course. I'll fix it with Major de Spain. You want to go soon?"

"I'm going now," Sam said. He went out. And that was all. The boy was nine then; it seemed perfectly natural that nobody, not even his cousin McCaslin, should argue with Sam. Also, since he was nine now, he could understand that Sam could leave him and their days and nights in the woods together without any wrench. He believed that he and Sam both knew that this was not only temporary but that the exigencies of his maturing, of that for which Sam had been training him all his life some day to dedicate himself, required it. They had settled that one night last summer while they listened to the hounds bringing a fox back up the creek valley; now the boy discerned in that very talk under the high, fierce August stars a presage, a warning, of this moment today. "I done taught you all there is of this settled country," Sam said. "You can hunt it good as I can now. You are ready for the Big Bottom now, for bear and deer. Hunter's meat," he said. "Next year you will be ten. You will write your age in two numbers and you will be ready to become a man. Your pa" (Sam always referred to the boy's cousin as his father, establishing even before the boy's orphanhood did that relation between them not of the ward to his guardian and kinsman and chief and head of his blood, but of the child to the man who sired his flesh and his thinking too.) "promised you can go with us then." So the boy could understand Sam's going. But he couldn't understand why now, in March, six months before the moon for hunting.

"If Jobaker's dead like they say," he said, "and Sam hasn't got anybody but us at all kin to him, why does he want to go to the Big Bottom now, when it will be six months before we get there?"

"Maybe that's what he wants," McCaslin said. "Maybe he wants to get away from you a little while."

But that was all right. McCaslin and other grown people often said things like that and he paid no attention to them, just as he paid no attention to Sam saying he wanted to go the Big Bottom to live. After all, he would have to live there for six months, because there would be no use in going at all if he was going to turn right around and come back. And, as Sam himself had told him, he already knew all about hunting in this settled country that Sam or anybody else could teach him. So it would be all right. Summer, then the bright days after the first frost, then the cold and himself on the wagon with McCaslin this time and the moment would come and he would draw the blood, the big blood which would make him a man, a hunter, and Sam would come back home with them and he too would have outgrown the child's pursuit of rabbits and 'possums.

Then he too would make one before the winter fire, talking
of the old hunts and the hunts to come as hunters talked.

So Sam departed. He owned so little that he could carry it.
He walked. He would neither let McCaslin send him in
the wagon, nor take a mule to ride. No one saw him go even.
He was just gone one morning, the cabin which had
never had very much in it, vacant and empty, the shop
in which there never had been very much done, standing
idle. Then November came at last, and now the boy made
one—himself and his cousin McCaslin and Tennie's Jim,
and Major de Spain and General Compson and Walter Ewell and Boon and old Uncle Ash to do the cooking, waiting
for them in Jefferson with the other wagon, and the surrey
in which he and McCaslin and General Compson and Major
de Spain would ride.

Sam was waiting at the camp to meet them. If he was
glad to see them, he did not show it. And if, when they
broke camp two weeks later to return home, he was sorry
to see them go, he did not show that either. Because he did
not come back with them. It was only the boy who returned, returning solitary and alone to the settled familiar
land, to follow for eleven months the childish business of
rabbits and such while he waited to go back, having brought
with him, even from his brief first sojourn, an unforgettable
sense of the big woods—not a quality dangerous or particularly inimical, but profound, sentient, gigantic and
brooding, amid which he had been permitted to go to and
fro at will, unscathed, why he knew not, but dwarfed and,
until he had drawn honorably blood worthy of being drawn,
alien.

Then November, and they would come back. Each morning Sam would take the boy out to the stand allotted him.
It would be one of the poorer stands of course, since he
was only ten and eleven and twelve and he had never
even seen a deer running yet. But they would stand there,
Sam a little behind him and without a gun himself, as he
had been standing when the boy shot the running rabbit
when he was eight years old. They would stand there in
the November dawns, and after a while they would hear
the dogs. Sometimes the chase would sweep up and past
quite close, belling and invisible; once they heard the
two heavy reports of Boon Hogganbeck's old gun with
which he had never killed anything larger than a squirrel

and that sitting, and twice they heard the flat unreverberant clap of Walter Ewell's rifle, following which you did not even wait to hear his horn.

"I'll never get a shot," the boy said. "I'll never kill one."

"Yes you will," Sam said. "You wait. You'll be a hunter. You'll be a man."

But Sam wouldn't come out. They would leave him there. He would come as far as the road where the surrey waited, to take the riding horses back, and that was all. The men would ride the horses and Uncle Ash and Tennie's Jim and the boy would follow in the wagon with Sam, with the camp equipment and the trophies, the meat, the heads, the antlers, the good ones, the wagon winding on among the tremendous gums and cypresses and oaks where no axe save that of the hunter had ever sounded, between the impenetrable walls of cane and brier—the two changing yet constant walls just beyond which the wilderness whose mark he had brought away forever on his spirit even from that first two weeks seemed to lean, stooping a little, watching them and listening, not quite inimical because they were too small, even those such as Walter and Major de Spain and old General Compson who had killed many deer and bear, their sojourn too brief and too harmless to excite to that, but just brooding, secret, tremendous, almost inattentive.

Then they would emerge, they would be out of it, the line as sharp as the demarcation of a doored wall. Suddenly skeleton cotton- and corn-fields would flow away on either hand, gaunt and motionless beneath the gray rain; there would be a house, barns, fences, where the hand of man had clawed for an instant, holding, the wall of the wilderness behind them now, tremendous and still and seemingly impenetrable in the gray and fading light, the very tiny orifice through which they had emerged apparently swallowed up. The surrey would be waiting, his cousin McCaslin and Major de Spain and General Compson and Walter and Boon dismounted beside it. Then Sam would get down from the wagon and mount one of the horses and, with the others on a rope behind him for a while against that tall and secret wall, growing smaller and smaller against it, never looking back. Then he would enter it, returning to what the boy believed, and thought that his cousin McCaslin believed, was his loneliness and solitude.

2.

So the instant came. He pulled trigger and Sam Fathers marked his face with the hot blood which he had spilled and he ceased to be a child and became a hunter and a man. It was the last day. They broke camp that afternoon and went out, his cousin and Major de Spain and General Compson and Boon on the horses, Walter Ewell and the negroes in the wagon with him and Sam and his hide and antlers. There could have been (and were) other trophies in the wagon. But for him they did not exist, just as for all practical purposes he and Sam Fathers were still alone together as they had been that morning. The wagon wound and jolted between the slow and shifting yet constant walls from beyond and above which the wilderness watched them pass, less than inimical now and never to be inimical again since the buck still and forever leaped, the shaking gun-barrels coming constantly and forever steady at last, crashing, and still out of his instant of immortality the buck sprang, forever immortal;—the wagon jolting and bouncing on, the moment of the buck, the shot, Sam Fathers and himself and the blood with which Sam had marked him forever one with the wilderness which had accepted him since Sam said that he had done all right, when suddenly Sam reined back and stopped the wagon and they all heard the unmistakable and unforgettable sound of a deer breaking cover.

Then Boon shouted from beyond the bend of the trail and while they sat motionless in the halted wagon, Walter and the boy already reaching for their guns, Boon came galloping back, flopping his mule with his hat, his face wild and amazed as he shouted down at them. Then the other riders came around the bend, also spurring.

"Get the dogs!" Boon cried. "Get the dogs! If he had a nub on his head, he had fourteen points! Laying right there by the road in that pawpaw thicket! If I'd a knowed he was there, I could have cut his throat with my pocket knife!"

"Maybe that's why he run," Walter said. "He saw you never had your gun." He was already out of the wagon with his rifle. Then the boy was out too with his gun, and the other riders came up and Boon got off his mule somehow and was scrabbling and clawing among the duffel in the wagon, still shouting, "Get the dogs! Get the dogs!" And it seemed to the boy too that it would take them forever to decide what to do—the old men in whom the blood ran cold and slow, in whom during the intervening years between them and himself the blood had become a different and colder substance from that which ran in him and even in Boon and Walter.

"What about it, Sam?" Major de Spain said. "Could the dogs bring him back?"

"We wont need the dogs," Sam said. "If he dont hear the dogs behind him, he will circle back in here about sundown to bed."

"All right," Major de Spain said. "You boys take the horses. We'll go on out to the road in the wagon and wait there." He and General Compson and McCaslin got into the wagon and Boon and Walter and Sam and the boy mounted the horses and turned back and out of the trail. Sam led them for an hour through the gray and unmarked afternoon whose light was little different from what it had been at dawn and which would become darkness without any graduation between. Then Sam stopped them.

"This is far enough," he said. "He'll be coming upwind, and he dont want to smell the mules." They tied the mounts in a thicket. Sam led them on foot now, unpathed through the markless afternoon, the boy pressing close behind him, the two others, or so it seemed to the boy, on his heels. But they were not. Twice Sam turned his head slightly and spoke back to him across his shoulder, still walking: "You got time. We'll get there fore he does."

So he tried to go slower. He tried deliberately to decelerate the dizzy rushing of time in which the buck which he had not even seen was moving, which it seemed to him must be carrying the buck farther and farther and more and more irretrievably away from them even though there were no dogs behind him now to make him run, even though, according to Sam, he must have completed his circle now and was heading back toward them. They went on; it could have been another hour or twice that or less than half, the boy could not have said. Then they were on a ridge. He had never been in here before and he could not see that it was a ridge. He just knew that the earth had risen slightly because the underbrush had thinned a little, the ground sloping invisibly away toward a dense wall of cane. Sam stopped. "That is it," he said. He spoke to Walter and Boon: "Follow this ridge and you will come to two crossings. You will see the tracks. If he crosses, it will be at one of these three."

Walter looked about for a moment. "I know it," he said. "I've even seen your deer. I was in here last Monday. He aint nothing but a yearling."

"A yearling?" Boon said. He was panting from the walking. His face still looked a little wild. "If the one I saw was any yearling, I'm still in kindergarden."

"Then I must have seen a rabbit," Walter said. "I always heard you quit school altogether two years before the first grade."

Boon glared at Walter. "If you dont want to shoot him, get out of the way," he said. "Set down somewhere. By God, I——"

"Aint nobody going to shoot him standing here," Sam said quietly.

"Sam's right," Walter said. He moved, slanting the worn, silver-colored barrel of his rifle downward to walk with it again. "A little more moving and a little more quiet too. Five miles is still Hogganbeck range, even if we wasn't downwind." They went on. The boy could still hear Boon talking, though presently that ceased too. Then once more he and Sam stood motionless together against a tremendous pin oak in a little thicket, and again there was nothing. There was only the soaring and sombre solitude in the dim light, there was the thin murmur of the faint cold rain which had not ceased all day. Then, as if it had waited for them to find their positions and become still, the wilderness breathed again. It seemed to lean inward above them, above himself and Sam and Walter and Boon in their separate lurking-places, tremendous, attentive, impartial and omniscient, the buck moving in it somewhere, not running yet since he had not been pursued, not frightened yet and never fearsome but just alert also as they were alert, perhaps already circling back, perhaps quite near, perhaps conscious also of the eye of the ancient immortal Umpire. Because he was just twelve then, and that morning something had happened to him: in less than a second he had ceased forever to be the child he was yesterday. Or perhaps that made no difference, perhaps even a city-bred man, let alone a child, could not have understood it; perhaps only a country-bred one could comprehend loving the life he spills. He began to shake again.

"I'm glad it's started now," he whispered. He did not

move to speak; only his lips shaped the expiring words: "Then it will be gone when I raise the gun——"

Nor did Sam. "Hush," he said.

"Is he that near?" the boy whispered. "Do you think——"

"Hush," Sam said. So he hushed. But he could not stop the shaking. He did not try, because he knew it would go away when he needed the steadiness—had not Sam Fathers already consecrated and absolved him from weakness and regret too?—not from love and pity for all which lived and ran and then ceased to live in a second in the very midst of splendor and speed, but from weakness and regret. So they stood motionless, breathing deep and quiet and steady. If there had been any sun, it would be near to setting now; there was a condensing, a densifying, of what he had thought was the gray and unchanging light until he realised suddenly that it was his own breathing, his heart, his blood—something, all things, and that Sam Fathers had marked him indeed, not as a mere hunter, but with something Sam had had in his turn of his vanished and forgotten people. He stopped breathing then; there was only his heart, his blood, and in the following silence the wilderness ceased to breathe also, leaning, stooping overhead with its breath held, tremendous and impartial and waiting. Then the shaking stopped too, as he had known it would, and he drew back the two heavy hammers of the gun.

Then it had passed. It was over. The solitude did not breathe again yet; it had merely stopped watching him and was looking somewhere else, even turning its back on him, looking on away up the ridge at another point, and the boy knew as well as if he had seen him that the buck had come to the edge of the cane and had either seen or scented them and faded back into it. But the solitude did not breathe again. It should have suspired again then but it did not. It was still facing, watching, what it had been watching and it was not here, not where he and Sam stood; rigid, not breathing himself, he thought, cried *No! No!*, knowing already that it was too late, thinking with the old despair of two and three years ago: *I'll never get a shot.* Then he heard it—the flat single clap of Walter Ewell's rifle which never missed. Then the mellow sound of the horn came down the ridge and something went out of him and he knew then he had never expected to get the shot at all.

"I reckon that's it," he said. "Walter got him." He had

raised the gun slightly without knowing it. He lowered it again and had lowered one of the hammers and was already moving out of the thicket when Sam spoke.

"Wait."

"Wait?" the boy cried. And he would remember that— how he turned upon Sam in the truculence of a boy's grief over the missed opportunity, the missed buck. "What for? Dont you hear that horn?"

And he would remember how Sam was standing. Sam had not moved. He was not tall, squat rather and broad, and the boy had been growing fast for the past year or so and there was not much difference between them in height, yet Sam was looking over the boy's head and up the ridge toward the sound of the horn and the boy knew that Sam did not even see him; that Sam knew he was still there beside him but he did not see the boy. Then the boy saw the buck. It was coming down the ridge, as if it were walking out of the very sound of the horn which related its death. It was not running, it was walking, tremendous, unhurried, slanting and tilting its head to pass the antlers through the undergrowth, and the boy standing with Sam beside him now instead of behind him as Sam always stood, and the gun still partly aimed and one of the hammers still cocked.

Then it saw them. And still it did not begin to run. It just stopped for an instant, taller than any man, looking at them; then its muscles suppled, gathered. It did not even alter its course, not fleeing, not even running, just moving with that winged and effortless ease with which deer move, passing within twenty feet of them, its head high and the eye not proud and not haughty but just full and wild and unafraid, and Sam standing beside the boy now, his right arm raised at full length, palm-outward, speaking in that tongue which the boy had learned from listening to him and Joe Baker in the blacksmith shop, while up the ridge Walter Ewell's horn was still blowing them in to a dead buck.

"Oleh, Chief," Sam said. "Grandfather."

When they reached Walter, he was standing with his back toward them, quite still, bemused almost, looking down at his feet. He didn't look up at all.

"Come here, Sam," he said quietly. When they reached him he still did not look up, standing above a little spike buck which had still been a fawn last spring. "He was so little I pretty near let him go," Walter said. "But just look at the track he was making. It's pretty near big as a cow's. If there were any more tracks here besides the ones he is laying in, I would swear there was another buck here that I never even saw."

3.

It was dark when they reached the road where the surrey waited. It was turning cold, the rain had stopped, and the sky was beginning to blow clear. His cousin and Major de Spain and General Compson had a fire going. "Did you get him?" Major de Spain said.

"Got a good-sized swamp-rabbit with spike horns," Walter said. He slid the little buck down from his mule. The boy's cousin McCaslin looked at it.

"Nobody saw the big one?" he said.

"I dont even believe Boon saw it," Walter said. "He probably jumped somebody's straw cow in that thicket." Boon started cursing, swearing at Walter and at Sam for not getting the dogs in the first place and at the buck and all.

"Never mind," Major de Spain said. "He'll be here for us next fall. Let's get started home."

It was after midnight when they let Walter out at his gate two miles from Jefferson and later still when they took General Compson to his house and then returned to Major de Spain's, where he and McCaslin would spend the rest of the night, since it was still seventeen miles home. It was cold, the sky was clear now; there would be a heavy frost by sunup and the ground was already frozen beneath the horses' feet and the wheels and beneath their own feet as they crossed Major de Spain's yard and entered the house, the warm dark house, feeling their way up the dark stairs until Major de Spain found a candle and lit it, and into the strange room and the big deep bed, the still cold sheets until they began to warm to their bodies and at last the shaking stopped and suddenly he was telling McCaslin about it while McCaslin listened, quietly until he had finished. "You dont believe it," the boy said. "I know you dont——"

"Why not?" McCaslin said. "Think of all that has happened here, on this earth. All the blood hot and strong for living, pleasuring, that has soaked back into it. For grieving and suffering too, of course, but still getting something out of it for all that, getting a lot out of it, because after all you dont have to continue to bear what you believe is suffering; you can always choose to stop that, put an end to that.

And even suffering and grieving is better than nothing; there is only one thing worse than not being alive, and that's shame. But you cant be alive forever, and you always wear out life long before you have exhausted the possibilities of living. And all that must be somewhere; all that could not have been invented and created just to be thrown away. And the earth is shallow; there is not a great deal of it before you come to the rock. And the earth dont want to just keep things, hoard them; it wants to use them again. Look at the seed, the acorns, at what happens even to carrion when you try to bury it: it refuses too, seethes and struggles too until it reaches light and air again, hunting the sun still. And they—" the boy saw his hand in silhouette for a moment against the window beyond which, accustomed to the darkness now, he could see sky where the scoured and icy stars glittered "— they dont want it, need it. Besides, what would it want, it-self, knocking around out there, when it never had enough time about the earth as it was, when there is plenty of room about the earth, plenty of places still unchanged from what they were when the blood used and pleasured in them while it was still blood?"

"But we want them," the boy said. "We want them too. There is plenty of room for us and them too."

"That's right," McCaslin said. "Suppose they dont have substance, cant cast a shadow——"

"But I saw it!" the boy cried. "I saw him!"

"Steady," McCaslin said. For an instant his hand touched the boy's flank beneath the covers. "Steady. I know you did. So did I. Sam took me in there once after I killed my first deer."

Grapes for Monsieur Cape

BY LUDWIG BEMELMANS

I was a commis de rang in Monsieur Victor's domain for several months, during which I met some remarkable peo-ple but none more remarkable than the maître d'hôtel whom the others sometimes called "Beau Maxime" because he was so ugly, and sometimes "Useless." Maxime was a bankrupt hotelkeeper from Paris. His ugliness was almost decorative; he had arthritis, and could hardly see out over the two cocoa-colored hammocks of wrinkles that hung under his smeary eyes. He had his station on the dining-room balcony where he could walk up and down with his cane and his beard and see himself reflected in the mirror.

He was a great trouble to the chefs de rang, the commis, and the kitchen because he took the guests' orders down wrong, forgot things, dictated orders upside down; his hand was too shaky to write, he held the menu up against his face and read it through a lorgnette.

When guests had eaten, smoked, and talked, and there was still no sign of a tip for him, a kind of hysteria would come over Beau Maxime. He became part of the table then. With heavy breath, he moved glasses about, took away a sugar bowl, dusted off a few breadcrumbs with the edge of his menu. Then he would leave for a while, but not for long, and the chicanery would start all over again. Again he moved the glasses back to where they were before; his eyelids twitched as he looked at the people; he brought a clean napkin to cover up a little coffee stain, he took away a vacant chair. If still nothing had happened, he bent to the guest's ear and asked if everything had been all right.

He mumbled as the guests started to leave, and watched them in the mirror and outside of it with a kind of despair in his face and hands, as if in a minute it would be too late to keep something terrible from happening. He kept behind them, pulled out their chairs, and bowed, and if again nothing happened, then he played his last card. He hung his stick on the banister, the service table, or over the back of a chair, and ran after them. He had a glove in his pocket, which he kept for just such purposes; he pulled this glove out and, in the center of the Jade Lounge, asked if they had forgotten it. Sometimes this worked; they would say no, but give him his dollar, and then he climbed back to the restaurant and up to his balcony.

He ate unbelievable amounts of food. The maîtres d'hôtel had luncheon and dinner before the guests, a very bad arrangement. They should be fed afterwards; a man who has just filled himself cannot recommend things well, he is asleep on his feet and makes unpleasant noises. But, as a matter of fact, they did also eat afterwards.

On the stations where the chefs and commis had their service tables, which contained extra plates, silver, napkins, vinegar, oil, ketchup bottles, and mustard pots, there were

also electric heaters. On these heaters the commis put all
the food that was left over after his chef had served the
guests. After the guests had left, the commis took the food
down to the employees' dining-room, where the chef de
rang and his commis, sitting across from each other, shared
it. With these meals they usually had a bottle of wine,
bought underhand, and since the portions were liberal, and
the food excellent, and too much of everything was ordered,
the men ate very well and of the best, that is all of them
did except the chefs and commis on Beau Maxime's station.

For after each serving he visited all the service tables on
his station, of which there were three, and carefully lifted
the covers of the casseroles, stirred around in them with a
fork, fished out wings of capons, little tender foie gras
dumplings, pieces of truffle, cocks' combs. Then he sent a
commis for soup plates and, while the poor chef and the
commis stared at him, he filled one of the plates with the
very best of their left-overs. He grunted while he did this,
his eyes shone and almost fell into the pots. For his second
soup plate he would take a lobster claw, tilt the casserole to
get the fine sauce for it, add some rice. In the third plate
might go a little curry. When he had enough, one of the
commis whom he had robbed, a pale little French boy, had
to take the plate upstairs to the captains' dining-room. (On
the stairway, when no one could see him, the commis carefully spat into all three plates.) Beau Maxime followed, a
long French bread under his arm as if it were an umbrella.

Up there, he ate slowly, then moved his chair over to
the window. From this third-floor window one could see over
the curtains and into the fitting-room of a corsetière on the
second floor of the building across the street, where, in the
afternoon, fat women undressed to try on corsets. Beau
Maxime took off his shoes and put his feet on a pile of
used napkins that were put there to be counted later. He
watched the scene for an hour and then fell asleep. A bus-
boy cleared away the dishes and reset the table for the dinner of the maître d'hôtel, which was served at five-thirty.
Maxime woke up in time for that, put on his shoes, and
turned around, to eat.

He was the worst, this Beau Maxime, but all maîtres
d'hôtel love to eat. They lean over sideboards, behind high
screens, to stuff something quickly away. They are especially fond of little fried things which they can pick up from

hot dishes as the commis bring them up from the kitchen, such easily disposed of things as whitebait, oyster crabs, fried scallops, frogs' legs, and fried potatoes. They have learned to eat so that their cheeks and jaws do not move; they can eat in the middle of the dining-room and no one know it.

One of the maîtres d'hôtel in the Splendide, a very good-looking one, had a front tooth missing, it was being repaired. At one very busy luncheon he took a green olive from a tray behind the screen on one of his service tables. Just then he was called to a table; the publisher Frank Munsey wanted to order the rest of his luncheon while he waited for his soup to cool. Mr. Munsey looked over the card that was handed him and decided on some *tête de veau en tortue*. As the maître d'hôtel repeated this, with its many T's, the olive pit shot out through the hole in his teeth and landed in Mr. Munsey's soup.

Fortunately the publisher was bent over talking to someone at the next table and saw nothing. The maître d'hôtel nervously asked if he could not take the soup back and get something hotter, but Mr. Munsey, a very much feared guest, said he had been waiting for it to cool, it was just about right now.

But there is a way out of such difficulties, a technique of upset and confusion, often employed in dangerous situations with hard clients. The maître d'hôtel first instructs the chef de rang and the commis; there is a small quick meeting—then excitement, noise, shouting, a waving in the face of bills of fare, some pushing, and one, two, three, the soup is gone. All this happens while the maître d'hôtel is a few tables away, so that the client can call him to complain. He comes, is surprised, and calls the waiter names: "Specimen of an idiot, where is the soup of Monsieur Munsey?" "Ah, pardon—I thought—" "You should not think, stupid one! Ah, Monsieur Munsey, pardon, pardon." The soup is back on the table after the commis, behind the screen, has fished the olive pit out with his fingers. For the rest of the meal the guest has perfect service, and when he leaves, the maître d'hôtel says once more: "So sorry about the soup," and for this he gets sometimes one, two, or five dollars, but never from Mr. Munsey.

But then, this maître d'hôtel was luckier than the one who had his station on the balcony diagonally across from

Maxime's. He was a restless, hoppy Frenchman whose body was forever bending into the shape of compliments. He walked mostly backwards, like a crab, pulling customers from the door to his station. When he had nothing else to do, he made little pirouettes, looked at himself in a corner of the mirror, quickly, birdlike in gesture, tugged at his sleeves, pushed a handkerchief into his cuff. Old guests whom he knew from the Paris Splendide he greeted with both arms up in the air, wiggling to the door with dancing paces, with smiles of joy on his face. He had been in America only three weeks when I met him.

He had a trick of showing the anatomy of the kitchen on his own body. With his palm held flat as the blade of a carving knife, he traced the shape of a breast of guinea hen from under his arm to the lapel of his dress coat and down to his ribs. Lifting his leg up to the level of the table, he showed on it the cut of meat that was used for an *ossi bughi à la milanaise*. When speaking of fish, he again used his palm, laying it flat if the talk was of sole, and with the other hand he cut filets therefrom. He made a good deal of money, for many people love this theater.

One did not. She was the wife of a steel man, who was also a judge. She was old and ugly; her dresses were like the robes of a stout priest, they fell flat from a plateau of flesh under her chin and covered a tub filled with fat. Stomach, legs, and breasts were pressed together in this volume so one could not see where they began and ended. Out of the shoulders came two arms, red and thick, coarse-skinned, with common hands. The feet were in tight shoes.

From her hat there usually hung a veil; when the veil was lifted, it revealed a face that had the texture of an old pocketbook; on its worn-out corners rested the ends of a mouth, that was closed to with a snap. Gray, carmine, and purple veins covered her face, and patches of its skin would jump as does the skin on the flanks of horses when flies come near them. Her ears were thick bunches on one disorderly shape that included face, neck, and shoulders.

She had to stop for breath at every step when she came up the short, decorative stairway of the restaurant. She would stop to hold onto the banister, to groan and take hold of herself, and she would look around as if for help, as if angry, yet not what the word helpless means.

Behind her, baldheaded and quiet, walked the Steel Judge, mostly in light gray clothes and with a face that was old,

Japanese, and cigar-colored. Madame always referred to him as "The Judge."

Large compliments went to them from the man who opened the door of their car on the sidewalk, from Monsieur Victor on the stairway, from all the maîtres d'hôtel, the chefs de rang, the commis, the musicians, from the last coat-room girl. For they were very liberal, and gave a small fortune away at Christmas time.

Madame also brought with her on every visit her own butler. He carried her own wine cooler and at large parties arrived with a second man to supplement his supply of the champagne she liked. The judge and his wife were invited to the very best parties, but no matter at whose table she sat, Madame insisted on her own champagne.

She laughed with the sound of a wild bird, a screech, that filled the large oval dining-room with its "Kwaaa, kaaa, kwaaaaa," and she laughed most in the company of her friends, two women who were always with her when she came alone—one who was equally fearful and dressed with the same costly despair, the wife of some street-car magnate; and the second intimate, a woman with traces of gentility, a face that once must have been nice, who could not see, squinted, and had an Italian villa in Long Island, but a political husband with a red nose. They called themselves, when speaking of anything they would do together, "We Girls."

These three arrived one day when the only free table good enough, at which they could be seated immediately and without trouble, was on the edge of the balcony, in front of the mirror, on the station of the hoppy Frenchman. He bowed and scraped, danced and pirouetted, and pulled out their chairs. They sat down, and Madame complained, as she often did, about the fact that the menu was printed in French.

"What is," she asked the maître d'hôtel, "what is an *escalope de veau à l'ancienne?*"

He lifted his leg and with a flat hand showed her from what part of the animal the cutlet came. That was easy, but *veau* was difficult. He thought about the problem for a minute with many grimaces, and then smiled. He bent down, made a cute figure, and put his face close to the hat to say that he did not know the *américain* word for *veau,* but that he would try to explain.

"You have a son, Madame?"

"No," she said.

"Well, we assume you have a son, Madame."

"So what?"

"You, Madame, are *vache*, your son is *veau*. *Escalope de veau* is a cutlet of son of cow."

She laughed her terrible laugh again, called for Monsieur Victor and said:

"Fire that son of a bitch."

Everyone in the hotel was saying: "Monsieur Cape is coming, Monsieur Cape is coming from England." There was much cleaning up and shining, and everybody seemed to be afraid of Monsieur Cape. For Monsieur Cape was the president of our company. His offices were in London, and from there he always went on his rounds first to Paris, where the company had another big hotel, then across to Rio de Janeiro and Havana, where the company also had restaurants, and finally to the Splendide.

Serafini told me that from Thursday on I would be on duty every morning at seven, with clean collar, brushed hair, shined shoes, and fingernails in shape, to serve Monsieur Cape's breakfast; and that, he added, was "a great honor."

At last the great man arrived, was received with much bowing and scraping, and was installed in the Adam Suite, one of the private apartments, our most palatial accommodations. It was a completely isolated duplex home with its own salon, dining-room, staircase, and back service-entrance. Up the latter, every morning, I brought breakfast to him and his niece. For he had brought a very beautiful niece with him, a girl with blue eyes and ash-blond hair. He had many nieces, the chambermaid told me; this was the fifth one, and always a different one came with him from England, and the maid closed one eye when she said that.

In bed Mr. Cape was very small and not much bigger when he got up. He had a red face with a small beard at the bottom, which made it look like a radish upside down. He talked very little and walked back and forth, playing with the keys in his pocket and looking at the floor, like Uncle Hans. One of the first things he did whenever he came from England was to go to the coatroom of the restaurant, where there was a beautiful Irish girl, take her arm, go behind a sea-green drapery with her, and there whisper a joke into her ear. Unlike the nieces, it was always the same joke.

For his breakfast I had to go down into the kitchen and first of all order a basket of fruit from an old Frenchman in charge of them. The fruit was kept in the innermost and coldest refrigerator of a series of three, one inside the other. I gave the old Frenchman a slip on which I had written: *"Un Panier de Fruit,"* and under this, underscored with two thick lines: *"Pour Monsieur Cape."*

It always took a lot of time. The old man searched for the keys, unlocked each refrigerator in turn, skewered the slip on a long bent needle that hung over his desk, and said to himself several times: *"Un panier de fruit, pour Monsieur Cape."* When we were inside, he held the fruit up to his eyes, placed it in the basket, and rearranged it several times to get the right Fruit Basket feeling.

When all was built up to his satisfaction, he placed a bunch of grapes on top, a big beautiful Belgian hothouse bunch with fat grapes that were so closely pressed together that some of them had square sides. These grapes came six bunches to a box, in a bed of ground cork and soft tissue paper. Then, in the open spaces around the grapes, the old Frenchman put a few more figs and plums, and finally he straightened out and said: *"Voilà, mon petit, un panier de fruit pour Monsieur Cape."*

I carried the basket of fruit carefully upstairs. In the warm air outside of the icebox a film of water in tiny beads set on all the fruit; the plums were most beautiful that way. Fruit should always be served so, from out of the cold.

On my first trip up, I also took with me a fingerbowl, a pair of silver shears for the grapes, and the linen. Then I went down again, by the private staircase, through the reception room of the apartment, out the door to the hotel corridor, down with the service elevator, across the pantry, and down into the kitchen. On the second trip up, I brought the orange juice for the niece, the porridge, and the tea. For everything I had to write slips with "POUR MONSIEUR CAPE" underlined.

After I had carried all this upstairs, I sat in the salon and waited until Monsieur Cape rang. The little alcohol flames burned under the silver kettle—he made his own tea —and under the porridge which stood in a dish of hot water. For the toast I had to run down a third time while Monsieur Cape ate his fruit. It was a job nobody liked.

It took a long time for him to wake up. I started with the basket of fruit at seven-thirty and busied myself with this breakfast until about nine-thirty, because, while I was there, no one could call me away for any other duty. On the desk in the salon were the accounts of the hotel. I read them every morning; much was in red ink; it did not seem to be a very profitable hotel. Uncle Hans's hotels were much better paying. After I had read the accounts and the English funny papers, there was nothing to do.

I started on the first day to eat a few of the grapes on the Belgian hothouse bunch. The bunch got to look bad on one side, so I turned it around. But still Monsieur Cape did not ring, and I ate more on the good side. Then the bunch was altogether bad-looking; it was impossible to serve it to anyone and so I finished it and put some figs in its place. From then on I ate a bunch of grapes every morning.

Soon after I had eaten the grapes, a door would open and I would hear a little swish of nightgown and soft steps. That was the niece going to her own bedroom. Then another door would open and close and soon the little bell would ring and Monsieur Cape got his breakfast. The niece would come in and say "Good morning" to me and to the uncle, and then she would sit on the side of the bed and help him prepare his tea. When I bent over, I could smell her hair and see that she was very young and firm and beautiful.

When I took the dishes down and brought the basket back to the icebox, it was about nine-thirty and the first chef was in his office, through the window of which he could see me pass and hand the basket back to the old man.

The first chef was, of course, also a Frenchman, but he was tall and, unlike most cooks and most Frenchmen, very quiet and self-controlled. One had to stand close to him to hear what he said, for he never raised his voice, not even in the greatest luncheon rush, when dishes clattered and the cooks were red in the face and excited and everybody ran and shouted. He was very saving for the hotel and he knew the contents of all his iceboxes. He also knew about the fruit and the basket for Mr. Cape and, of course, about the grapes.

When I came back with the basket, he always stepped to the door and looked at it, and said quietly: "They are costly, these grapes of Belgium." I wrote out a slip then, for *"Une grappe de raisin de Belgique,"* and for whatever other fruit had been used up, and the old man took it in exchange for the slip I had given him before for the whole basket. The first slip was torn up, and the slip for the grapes was collected by the accounting department with all the others and billed, but of course the president of the company had everything free and never received a bill.

All this went along very nicely for weeks. In the morning I served Monsieur Cape and in the evening worked in the wind-swept roof garden, overlooking the city from the thirty-second floor. There was a foyer on it with little tables and a large buffet that was made of tin containers filled with ice and with a little fountain in its center.

About six o'clock I had to be up there and help arrange cold dishes on the ice: large salmons in parsley and lemons, glacéd pheasants, poussins in aspic, cold bœuf à la mode, galantines of capon, hors d'œuvres, saucissons d'Arles, sauce verte, mayonnaise, beautifully decorated salads, strawberry tarts with whipped cream, compotes—many fine, good things. The first chef supervised all this and watched out that nothing disappeared.

On a very hot evening Monsieur Cape and his niece came and waited for their dinner guests in the chairs in front of the buffet. In a little while Monsieur Cape was walking back and forth, with his hands in his pockets playing with his keys. The chef had not seen Monsieur Cape since his arrival and he bowed and smiled. The guests were arriving now and engaging Monsieur Cape in conversation as they walked away from the buffet, and I thought everything was going to turn out all right. But the chef walked in front of them, and Monsieur Cape shook hands with him and introduced him to his guests. The air became thick, and though the chef spoke so quietly, I could hear him say: "Monsieur Cape loves the Belgian hothouse grapes I send up every morning, yes?"

"What Belgian hothouse grapes?" asked Monsieur Cape.

I did not hear any more because I went out quickly with some plates.

The chef sent for me, he held my arm so tight it hurt, and he said quietly: "*Sacré voleur!* It is shameful, such a young man of good family as you are! You will never be allowed to serve Monsieur Cape again."

A Man of the World

BY ERNEST HEMINGWAY

THE BLIND man knew the sounds of all the different machines in the saloon. I don't know how long it took him to learn the sounds of the machines but it must have taken him quite a time because he only worked one saloon at a time. He worked two towns though and he would start out of The Flats along after it was good and dark on his way up to Jessup. He'd stop by the side of the road when he heard a car coming and their lights would pick him up and either they would stop and give him a ride or they wouldn't and would go on by on the icy road. It would depend on how they were loaded and whether there were women in the car because the blind man smelled plenty strong and especially in winter. But someone would always stop for him because he was a blind man.

Everybody knew him and they called him Blindy which is a good name for a blind man in that part of the country, and the name of the saloon that he threw his trade to was The Pilot. Right next to it was another saloon, also with gambling and a dining room, that was called The Index. Both of these were the names of mountains and they were both good saloons with old-days bars and the gambling was about the same in one as in the other except you ate better in The Pilot probably, although you got a better sizzling steak at The Index. Then The Index was open all night long and got the early morning trade and from daylight until ten o'clock in the morning the drinks were on the house. They were the only saloons in Jessup and they did not have to do that kind of thing. But that was the way they were.

Blindy probably preferred The Pilot because the machines were right along the left-hand wall as you came in and faced the bar. This gave him better control over them than he would have had at The Index where they were scattered on account it was a bigger place with more room. On this night it was really cold outside and he came in with icicles on his mustache and small pus icicles out of both eyes and he didn't look really very good. Even his smell was froze but that wasn't for very long and he started to put out almost as soon as the door was shut. It was always hard for me to look at him but I was looking at him carefully because I knew he always rode and I didn't see how he would be frozen up so bad. Finally I asked him.

"Where you walk from, Blindy?"

"Willie Sawyer put me out of his car down below the railway bridge. There weren't no more cars come and I walked in."

"What did he put you afoot for?" somebody asked.

"Said I smelled too bad."

Someone had pulled the handle on a machine and Blindy started listening to the whirr. It came up nothing. "Any dudes playing?" he asked me.

"Can't you hear?"

"Not yet."

"No dudes, Blindy, and it's a Wednesday."

"I know what night it is. Don't start telling me what night it is."

Blindy went down the line of machines feeling in all of them to see if anything had been left in the cups by mistake. Naturally there wasn't anything, but that was the first part of his pitch. He came back to the bar where we were and Al Chaney asked him to have a drink.

"No," Blindy said. "I got to be careful on those roads."

"What you mean those roads?" somebody asked him. "You only go on one road. Between here and The Flats."

"I been on lots of roads," Blindy said. "And any time I may have to take off and go on more."

Somebody hit on a machine but it wasn't any heavy hit. Blindy moved on it just the same. It was a quarter machine and the young fellow who was playing it gave him a quarter sort of reluctantly. Blindy felt it before he put it in his pocket.

"Thank you," he said. "You'll never miss it."

The young fellow said, "Nice to know that," and put a quarter back in the machine and pulled down again.

He hit again but this time pretty good and he scooped in the quarters and gave a quarter to Blindy.

"Thanks," Blindy said. "You're doing fine."

"Tonight's my night," the young fellow who was playing said.

"Your night is my night," Blindy said and the young fellow went on playing but he wasn't doing any good any more and Blindy was so strong standing by him and he looked so awful and finally the fellow quit playing and came over to the bar. Blindy had run him out but he had no way of noticing it because the fellow didn't say anything, so Blindy just checked the machines again with his hand and stood there waiting for someone else to come in and make a play.

There wasn't any play at the wheel nor at the crap table and at the poker game there were just gamblers sitting there and cutting each other up. It was a quiet evening on a week night in town and there wasn't any excitement. The place was not making a nickel except at the bar. But at the bar it was pleasant and the place had been nice until Blindy had come in. Now everybody was figuring they might as well go next door to The Index or else cut out and go home.

"What will yours be, Tom?" Frank the bartender asked me. "This is on the house."

"I was figuring on shoving."

"Have one first then."

"The same with ditch," I said. Frank asked the young fellow, who was wearing heavy Oregon Cities and a black hat and was shaved clean and had a snow-burned face, what he would drink and the young fellow took the same. The whisky was Old Forester.

I nodded to him and raised my drink and we both sipped at the drinks. Blindy was down at the far end of the machines. I think he figured maybe no one would come in if they saw him at the door. Not that he was self-conscious.

"How did that man lose his sight?" the young fellow asked me.

"I wouldn't know," I told him.

"In a fight," Frank told him.

"Him fight?" the stranger said. He shook his head.

"Yeah," Frank said. "He got that high voice out of the same fight. Tell him, Tom."

"I never heard of it."

"No. You wouldn't of," Frank said. "Of course not. You wasn't here, I suppose. Mister, it was a night about as cold as tonight. Maybe colder. It was a quick fight too. I didn't see the start of it. Then they come fighting out of the door of The Index. Blackie, him that's Blindy now, and this other boy Willie Sawyer, and they were slugging and kneeing and gouging and biting and I see one of Blackie's eyes hanging down on his cheek. They were fighting on the ice of the road with the snow all banked up and the light from this door and The Index door, and Hollis Sands was right behind Willie Sawyer who was gouging for the eye and Hollis kept hollering, 'Bite it off! Bite it off just like it was a grape!' Blackie was biting onto Willie Sawyer's face and he had a good holt and it give way with a jerk and then he had another good holt and they were down on the ice now and Willie Sawyer was gouging him to make him let go and then Blackie gave a yell like you've never heard. Worse than when they cut a boar."

Blindy had come up opposite us and we smelled him and turned around.

"'Bite it off just like it was a grape,'" he said in his high-pitched voice and looked at us, moving his head up and down. "That was the left eye. He got the other one without no advice. Then he stomped me when I couldn't see. That was the bad part." He patted himself.

"I could fight good then," he said. "But he got the eye before I knew even what was happening. He got it with a lucky gouge. Well," Blindy said without any rancor, "that put a stop to my fighting days."

"Give Blackie a drink," I said to Frank.

"Blindy's the name, Tom. I earned that name. You seen me earn it. That's the same fellow who put me adrift down the road tonight. Fellow bit the eye. We ain't never made friends."

"What did you do to him?" the stranger asked.

"Oh you'll see him around," Blindy said. "You'll recognize him any time you see him. I'll let it come as a surprise."

"You don't want to see him," I told the stranger.

"You know that's one of the reasons I'd like to see sometimes," Blindy said. "I'd like to just have one good look at him."

"You know what he looks like," Frank told him. "You went up and put your hands on his face once."

"Did it again tonight too," Blindy said happily. "That's why he put me out of the car. He ain't got no sense of humor at all. I told him on a cold night like this he'd ought to bundle up so the whole inside of his face wouldn't catch cold. He didn't even think that was funny. You know that Willie Sawyer he'll never be a man of the world."

"Blackie, you have one on the house," Frank said. "I can't drive you home because I only live just down the road. But you can sleep in the back of the place."

"That's mighty good of you, Frank. Only just don't call me Blackie. I'm not Blackie any more. Blindy's my name."

"Have a drink, Blindy."

"Yes, sir," Blindy said. His hand reached out and found the glass and he raised it accurately to the three of us.

"That Willie Sawyer," he said. "Probably alone home by himself. That Willie Sawyer he don't know how to have any fun at all."

The Hour of Letdown

BY E. B. WHITE

WHEN THE man came in, carrying the machine, most of us looked up from our drinks, because we had never seen anything like it before. The man set the thing down on top of the bar near the beerpulls. It took up an ungodly amount of room and you could see the bartender didn't like it any too well, having this big, ugly-looking gadget parked right there.

"Two rye-and-water," the man said.

The bartender went on puddling an Old-Fashioned that he was working on, but he was obviously turning over the request in his mind.

"You want a double?" he asked, after a bit.

"No," said the man. "Two rye-and-water, please." He stared straight at the bartender, not exactly unfriendly but on the other hand not affirmatively friendly.

Many years of catering to the kind of people that come into saloons had provided the bartender with an adjustable mind. Nevertheless, he did not adjust readily to this fellow, and he did not like the machine—that was sure. He picked up a live cigarette that was idling on the edge of the cash register, took a drag out of it, and returned it thoughtfully. Then he poured two shots of rye whiskey, drew two glasses of water, and shoved the drinks in front of the man. People were watching. When something a little out of the ordinary takes place at a bar, the sense of it spreads quickly all along the line and pulls the customers together.

The man gave no sign of being the center of attention. He laid a five-dollar bill down on the bar. Then he drank one of the ryes and chased it with water. He picked up the other rye, opened a small vent in the machine (it was like an oil cup) and poured the whiskey in, and then poured the water in.

The bartender watched grimly. "Not funny," he said in an even voice. "And furthermore, your companion takes up too much room. Why'n you put it over on that bench by the door, make more room here."

"There's plenty of room for everyone here," replied the man.

"I ain't amused," said the bartender. "Put the goddam thing over near the door like I say. Nobody will touch it."

The man smiled. "You should have seen it this afternoon," he said. "It was magnificent. Today was the third day of the tournament. Imagine it—three days of continuous brainwork! And against the top players in the country, too. Early in the game it gained an advantage; then for two hours it exploited the advantage brilliantly, ending with the opponent's king backed in a corner. The sudden capture of a knight, the neutralization of a bishop, and it was all over. You know how much money it won, all told, in three days of playing chess?"

"How much?" asked the bartender.

"Five thousand dollars," said the man. "Now it wants to let down, wants to get a little drunk."

The bartender ran his towel vaguely over some wet spots. "Take it somewheres else and get it drunk there!" he said firmly. "I got enough troubles."

The man shook his head and smiled. "No, we like it here." He pointed at the empty glasses. "Do this again, will you, please?"

The bartender slowly shook his head. He seemed dazed but dogged. "You stow the thing away," he ordered. "I'm not ladling out whiskey for jokestersmiths."

" 'Jokesmiths,' " said the machine. "The word is 'jokesmiths.' "

A few feet down the bar, a customer who was on his third highball seemed ready to participate in this conversation to which we had all been listening so attentively. He was a middle-aged man. His necktie was pulled down away from his collar, and he had eased the collar by unbuttoning it. He had pretty nearly finished his third drink, and the alcohol tended to make him throw his support in with the underprivileged and the thirsty.

"If the machine wants another drink, give it another drink," he said to the bartender. "Let's not have haggling."

The fellow with the machine turned to his new-found friend and gravely raised his hand to his temple, giving him a salute of gratitude and fellowship. He addressed his next remark to him, as though deliberately snubbing the bartender.

"You know how it is when you're all fagged out mentally, how you want a drink?"

"Certainly do," replied the friend. "Most natural thing in the world."

There was a stir all along the bar, some seeming to side with the bartender, others with the machine group. A tall, gloomy man standing next to me spoke up.

"Another whiskey sour, Bill," he said. "And go easy on the lemon juice."

"Picric acid," said the machine, sullenly. "They don't use lemon juice in these places."

"That does it!" said the bartender, smacking his hand on the bar. "Will you put that thing away or else beat it out of here. I ain't in the mood, I tell you. I got this saloon to run and I don't want lip from a mechanical brain or whatever the hell you've got there."

The man ignored this ultimatum. He addressed his friend, whose glass was now empty.

"It's not just that it's all tuckered out after three days of chess," he said amiably. "You know another reason it wants a drink?"

"No," said the friend. "Why?"

"It cheated," said the man.

At this remark, the machine chuckled. One of its arms dipped slightly, and a light glowed in a dial.

The friend frowned. He looked as though his dignity had been hurt, as though his trust had been misplaced. "Nobody can cheat at chess," he said. "Simpossible. In chess, everything is open and above the board. The nature of the game of chess is such that cheating is impossible."

"That's what I used to think, too," said the man. "But there *is* a way."

"Well, it doesn't surprise me any," put in the bartender. "The first time I laid my eyes on that crummy thing I spotted it for a crook."

"Two rye-and-water," said the man.

"You can't have the whiskey," said the bartender. He glared at the mechanical brain. "How do I know it ain't drunk already?"

"That's simple. Ask it something," said the man.

The customers shifted and stared into the mirror. We were all in this thing now, up to our necks. We waited. It was the bartender's move.

"Ask it what? Such as?" said the bartender.

"Makes no difference. Pick a couple big figures, ask it to multiply them together. You couldn't multiply big figures together if you were drunk, could you?"

The machine shook slightly, as though making internal preparations.

"Ten thousand eight hundred and sixty-two, multiply it by ninety-nine," said the bartender, viciously. We could tell that he was throwing in the two nines to make it hard.

The machine flickered. One of its tubes spat, and a hand changed position, jerkily.

"One million seventy-five thousand three hundred and thirty-eight," said the machine.

Not a glass was raised all along the bar. People just stared gloomily into the mirror; some of us studied our own faces, others took carom shots at the man and the machine.

Finally, a youngish, mathematically minded customer got out a piece of paper and a pencil and went into retirement. "It works out," he reported, after some minutes of calculating. "You can't say the machine is drunk!"

Everyone now glared at the bartender. Reluctantly he poured two shots of rye, drew two glasses of water. The man drank his drink. Then he fed the machine its drink. The machine's light grew fainter. One of its cranky little arms wilted.

For a while the saloon simmered along like a ship at sea in calm weather. Every one of us seemed to be trying to digest the situation, with the help of liquor. Quite a few glasses were refilled. Most of us sought help in the mirror—the court of last appeal.

The fellow with the unbuttoned collar settled his score. He walked stiffly over and stood between the man and the machine. He put one arm around the man, the other arm around the machine. "Let's get out of here and go to a good place," he said.

The machine glowed slightly. It seemed to be a little drunk now.

"All right," said the man. "That suits me fine. I've got my car outside."

He settled for the drinks and put down a tip. Quietly and a trifle uncertainly he tucked the machine under his arm, and he and his companion of the night walked to the door and out into the street.

The bartender stared fixedly, then resumed his light house-keeping. "So he's got his car outside," he said, with heavy sarcasm. "Now isn't that nice!"

A customer at the end of the bar near the door left his drink, stepped to the window, parted the curtains, and looked out. He watched for a moment, then returned to his place and addressed the bartender. "It's even nicer than you think," he said. "It's a Cadillac. And which one of the three of them d'ya think is doing the driving?"

The Resting Place

BY OLIVER LA FARGE

THE POSSIBILITY that Dr. Hillebrand was developing klepto-mania caused a good deal of pleasure among his younger colleagues—that is, the entire personnel of the Department of Anthropology, including its director, Walter Klibben. It was not that anybody really disliked the old boy. That would have been hard to do, for he was coöperative and gentle, and his humor was mild; he was perhaps the greatest living authority on Southwestern archeology, and broadly learned in the general science of anthropology; and he was a man who delighted in the success of others.

Dr. Hillebrand was the last surviving member of a group of men who had made the Department of Anthropology fa-mous in the earlier part of the twentieth century. His ideas were old-fashioned; to Walter Klibben, who at forty was very much the young comer, and to the men he had gathered about him, Dr. Hillebrand's presence, clothed with authority, was as incongruous as that of a small, mild brontosaurus would be in a modern farmyard.

On the other hand, no one living had a finer archeological technique. Added to this was a curious intuition, which caused him to dig in unexpected places and come up with striking finds—the kind of thing that delights donors and trustees, such as the largest unbroken Mesa Verde black-on-white jar known up to that time, the famous Biltabito Cache of turquoise and shell objects, discovered two years before and not yet on exhibition, and, only the previous year, the mural decorations at Painted Mask Ruin. The mural, of which as yet only a small part had been uncovered, compared favorably with the murals found at Awatovi and Kawaika-a by the Peabody Museum, but was several centuries older. Moreover, in the part already exposed there was an identifiable katchina mask, unique and conclusive evidence that the katchina cult dated back to long before the white man came. This meant, Dr. Klibben foresaw gloomily, that once again all available funds for publication would be tied up by the old coot's material.

The trustees loved him. Several years ago, he had reached the age of retirement and they had waived the usual limitation in his case. He was curator of the museum, a position only slightly less important than that of director, and he occupied the Kleinman Chair in American Archeology. This was an endowed position paying several thousand a year more than Klibben's own professorship.

Dr. Hillebrand's occupancy of these positions, on top of his near monopoly of publication money, was the rub. He blocked everything. If only the old relic would become emeritus, the younger men could move up. Klibben had it all worked out. There would be the Kleinman Chair for himself, and McDonnell could accede to his professorship. He would leave Steinberg an associate, but make him curator. Thus, Steinberg and McDonnell would have it in mind that the curatorship always might be transferred to McDonnell as the man with senior status, which would keep them both on their toes. At least one assistant professor could, in due course, be made an associate, and young George Franklin, Klibben's own prized student, could be promoted from instructor to assistant. It all fitted together and reinforced his own position. Then, given free access to funds for monographs and papers . . .

But Dr. Hillebrand showed no signs of retiring. It was not that he needed the money from his two positions; he was a bachelor and something of an ascetic, and much of his salary he put into his own expeditions. He loved to teach, he said —and his students liked him. He loved his museum; in fact, he was daffy about it, pottering around in it until late at night. Well, let him retire, and he could still teach a course or two if he wanted; he could still potter, but Klibben could run his Department as he wished, as it ought to be run.

Since there seemed no hope that the old man would give

out physically in the near future, Klibben had begun looking for symptoms of mental failure. There was, for instance,
the illogical way in which Dr. Hillebrand often decided just
where to run a trench or dig a posthole. As Steinberg
once remarked, it was as if he were guided by an ouija
board. Unfortunately, this eccentricity produced splendid results.

Then, sometimes Hillebrand would say to his students,
"Now, let us imagine—" and proceed to indulge in surprising
reconstructions of the daily life and religion of the ancient
cliff dwellers, going far beyond the available evidence. The
director had put Franklin onto that, because the young man
had worked on Hopi and Zuñi ceremonial. Franklin reported that the old boy always made it clear that these
reconstructions were not science, and, further, Franklin said
that they were remarkably shrewd and had given him some
helpful new insights into aspects of modern Indians' religion.

The possibility of kleptomania was something else again.
The evidence—insufficient so far—concerned the rich Biltabito
Cache, which Dr. Hillebrand himself was enumerating, cata-
loguing, and describing, mostly evenings, when the museum
was closed. He was the only one who knew exactly how
many objects had been in the find, but it did look as if
some of it might now be missing. There was also what the
night watchman thought he had seen. And then there was
that one turquoise bead—but no proof it had come from
that source, of course—that McDonnell had found on the floor
near the cast of the Quiriguá stela, just inside the entrance
to the museum.

The thefts—if there had been any—had taken place in
April and early May, when everyone was thinking of the end
of the college year and the summer's field trips. A short
time later, and quite by accident, Klibben learned from an
associate professor of ornithology that old Hillebrand had obtained from him a number of feathers, which he said he
wanted for repairing his collection of katchina dolls. Among
them were parrot and macaw feathers, and the fluffy feathers
from the breast of an eagle.

Klibben's field was not the American Southwest, but any
American anthropologist would have been able to draw an
obvious conclusion; turquoise, shell, and feathers of those
sorts were components of ritual offerings among the modern
Hopis and Zuñis, and possibly their ancestors, among whose
remains Dr. Hillebrand had carried on his life-work. Dr.

Klibben began to suspect—or hope—that the old man was succumbing to mental weakness far more serious than would be evidenced by the mere stealing of a few bits of turquoise and shell.

The Director made tactful inquiries at the genetics field laboratory to see if the old man had been seeking corn pollen, another component of the ritual offerings, and found that there the question of the evolution of *Zea maiz* in the Southwest was related to the larger and much vexed question of the origin and domestication of that important New World plant, so interesting to archeologists, botanists, and geneticists. Dr. Hillebrand had been collecting specimens of ancient corn from archeological sites for a long time—ears, cobs, and grains extending over two millenniums or more, and other parts of the plant, including some fragments of tassels. It was, Klibben thought, the kind of niggling little detail you would expect to find Hillebrand spending good time on. Dr. Hillebrand had been turning his specimens over to the plant and heredity boys, who were delighted to have them. They, in turn, had followed this up by obtaining—for comparison—seed of modern Pueblo Indian, Navajo, and Hopi corn, and planting it. It was natural enough, then, that from time to time Dr. Hillebrand should take specimens of seed and pollen home to study on his own. It might be clear as day to Klibben that the old boy had gone gaga to the point of making ritual offerings to the gods of the cliff dwellings; he still had nothing that would convince a strongly pro-Hillebrand board of trustees.

Even so, the situation was hopeful. Klibben suggested to the night watchman that, out of concern for Professor Hillebrand's health, he keep a special eye on the Professor's afterhours activities in the museum. Come June, he would arrange for Franklin—with his Southwestern interests, Franklin was the logical choice—to go along on Hillebrand's expedition and see what he could see.

Franklin took the assignment willingly, by no means unaware of the possible advantages to himself should the old man be retired. The archeologist accepted the addition of the young man to his staff with equanimity. He remarked that Franklin's knowledge of Pueblo daily life would be helpful in interpreting what might be uncovered, while a better grounding in Southwestern prehistory would add depth to the young man's ethnographic perceptions. Right after commence-

ment, they set out for the Navajo country of Arizona, accompanied by two undergraduate and four graduate students.

At Farmington, in New Mexico, they picked up the university's truck and station wagon, and Hillebrand's own field
car, a Model A Ford as archaic as its owner. In view of
the man's income, Franklin thought, his hanging on to the
thing was one more oddity, an item that could be added
to many others to help prove Klibben's case. At Farmington,
too, they took on a cook and general helper. Dr. Hillebrand's work was generously financed, quite apart from what
went into it from his own earnings.

The party bounced over the horrifying road past the Four
Corners and around the north end of Beautiful Mountain,
into the Chinlee Valley, then southward and westward until,
after having taken a day and a half to drive about two
hundred miles, they reached the cliffs against which stood
Painted Mask Ruin. The principal aim of the current summer's work was to excavate the decorated kiva in detail,
test another kiva, and make further, standard excavations
in the ruin as a whole.

By the end of a week, the work was going nicely. Dr.
Hillebrand put Franklin, as the senior scientist under him,
in charge of the work in the painted kiva. Franklin knew
perfectly well that he was deficient in the required techniques; he would, in fact, be dependent upon his first
assistant, Philip Fleming, who was just short of his Ph.D.
Fleming had worked in that kiva the previous season, had
spent three earlier seasons with Dr. Hillebrand, and was
regarded by him as the most promising of the many who
had worked under him. There was real affection between the
two men.

Two of the other graduate students were well qualified
to run a simple dig for themselves. One was put in charge
of the untouched second kiva, the other of a trench cutting
into the general mass of the ruin from the north. Franklin
felt uncomfortably supernumerary, but he recognized that
that was an advantage in pursuing his main purpose of
keeping a close watch on the expedition's director.

After supper on the evening of the eighth day, Dr. Hillebrand announced rather shyly that he would be gone for
about four days, "to follow an old custom you all know
about." The younger men smiled. Franklin kept a blank face
to cover his quickened interest.

This was a famous, or notorious, eccentricity of the old

man's, and one in which Drs. Klibben, McDonnell, and the rest put great hope. Every year, early in the season, Dr. Hillebrand went alone to a ruin he had excavated early in his career. There was some uncertainty as to just where the ruin was; it was believed to be one known to the Navajos as Tsekaiye Kin. No one knew what he did there. He said he found the surroundings and the solitude invaluable for thinking out the task in hand. It was usually not long after his return from it that he would announce his decision to dig in such-and-such a spot, and proceed to uncover the painted kiva, or the Kettle Cave fetishes, or the Kin Hatsosi blanket, or some other notable find.

If Franklin could slip away in the station wagon and follow the old man, he might get just the information he wanted. So far, Dr. Hillebrand's activities on the expedition had evidenced nothing but his great competence. If the old man ever performed mad antique rites with stolen specimens, it would be at his secret place of meditation. Perhaps he got up and danced to the ancient gods. One might be able to sneak a photo . . .

Dr. Hillebrand said, "I shan't be gone long. Meantime, of course, Dr. Franklin will be in charge." He turned directly to his junior. "George, there are several things on which you must keep a close watch. If you will look at these diagrams—and you, too, Phil . . ."

Franklin and Fleming sat down beside him. Dr. Hillebrand expounded. Whether the ancient devil had done it intentionally or not, Franklin saw that he was neatly hooked. In the face of the delicacy and the probable outcome of the next few days' work, he could not possibly make an excuse for absenting himself when the head of the expedition was also absent.

Dr. Hillebrand took off early the next morning in his throbbing Model A. He carried with him a Spartan minimum of food and bedding. It was good to be alone once more in the long-loved reaches of the Navajo country. The car drove well. He still used it because, short of a jeep, nothing newer had the clearance to take him where he wanted to go.

He drove slowly, for he was at the age when knowledge and skill must replace strength, and getting stuck would be serious. When he was fifty, he reflected, he would have reached T'iiz Hatsosi Canyon from this year's camp in under four hours; when he was thirty, if it had been possible to travel this country in a car, he would have made even greater speed, and as like as not ended by getting lost. He reached the open farming area outside the place where T'iiz Hatsosi sliced into the great mesa to the south. There were nearly twice as many hogans to be seen as when he had first come here; several of them were square and equipped with windows, and by some of them cars were parked. Everything was changing, but these were good people still, although not as genial and hospitable as their grandparents had been when he first packed in.

He entered the narrow mouth of T'iiz Hatsosi Canyon in the late afternoon, and by the exercise of consummate skill drove some four miles up it. At that point, it was somewhat wider than elsewhere, slightly under two hundred feet across at the bottom. The heavy grazing that had so damaged all the Navajos' land had had some effect here. There was less grass than there used to be—but then, he reflected, he had no horses to graze—and the bed of the wash was more deeply eroded, and here and there sharp gullies led into it from the sides.

Still, the cottonwoods grew between the occasional stream and the high, warmly golden-buff cliffs. Except at noon, there was shade, and the quality of privacy, almost of secrecy, remained. In the west wall was the wide strip of white rocks from which the little ruin took its name, Tsekaiye Kin, leading the eye to the long ledge above which the cliff arched like a scallop shell, and upon which stood the ancient habitations. The lip of the ledge was about twenty feet above the level of the canyon, and approachable by a talus slope that was not too hard to negotiate. Some small evergreens grew at the corners of the ledge. From the ground, the settlement did not seem as if it had been empty for centuries, but rather as if its occupants at the moment happened not to be visible. The small black rectangle of doorways and three tiny squares of windows made him feel, as they had done over forty years ago, as if the little settlement were watching him.

South of the far end of the ledge, and at the level of the canyon floor, was the spring. Water seeped richly through a crack in the rock a few feet above the ground and flowed down over rock to form a pool at the base. The wet golden-brown stone glistened; small water growths clung to crevices. In the pool itself, there was cress, and around it moss and grass rich enough to make a few feet of turf.

Here Dr. Hillebrand deposited his bedroll and his food. He estimated that he had better than two hours of daylight left. He cut himself a supply of firewood. Then he took a package out of his coffeepot. The package was wrapped in an old piece of buckskin. With this in hand, he climbed up the slope to the ruin.

The sense of peace had begun once he was out of sight of the camp at Painted Mask Ruin. It had grown when he entered T'iiz Hatsosi Canyon; it had become stronger when he stepped out of the car and glimpsed through the cotton-woods his little village, with its fourteen rooms. By the spring, it had become stronger yet, and mixed with a nostalgia of past times that was sweetly painful, like a memory of an old and good lost love. These feelings were set aside as he addressed himself to the task of climbing, which was not entirely simple; then they returned fourfold when he was in the ruin. Here he had worked alone, a green young man with a shiny new Doctor's degree, a boy-man not unlike young Fleming. Here he had discovered what it was like to step into a room that still had its roof intact, and see the marks of the smoke from the household fire, the loom ties still in place in the ceiling and floor, the broken cooking pot still in the corner.

He paid his respects to that chamber—Room 4-B; stood in the small, open, central area; then went to the roofless, irregular oval of the kiva. All by himself he had dug it out.

Could Dr. Franklin have been there then, spying unseen, he would have been most happy. From under a stone that appeared firmly embedded in the clay flooring Dr. Hillebrand took an ancient, crude stone pipe fitted with a recent willow stem. He filled it with tobacco, performed curious motions as he lit it, and puffed smoke in the six directions. Then he climbed out of the kiva on the inner side and went behind the double row of habitations, to the darker area under the convex curve of the wall at the back of the cave, the floor of which was a mixture of earth and rubbish. Two smallish, rounded stones about three feet apart inconspicuously marked a place. Sitting by it on a convenient ledge of rock, he puffed at the pipe again; then he opened the buckskin package and proceeded to make an offering of ancient turquoise beads, white and red shell, black stone, feathers and down, and corn pollen.

Sitting back comfortably, he said, "Well, here I am again." The answer did not come from the ground, in which the bones of the speaker reposed, but from a point in space, as if he were sitting opposite Dr. Hillebrand. "Welcome, old friend. Thank you for the gifts; their smell is pleasing to us all."

"I don't know whether I can bring you any more," the archeologist said. "I can buy new things, of course, but getting the old ones is becoming difficult. They are watching me."

"It is not necessary," the voice answered. "We are rich in the spirits of things such as these, and our grandchildren on earth still offer them to us. It has been rather for your benefit that I have had you bringing them, and I think that that training has served its purpose."

"You relieve me." Then, with a note of anxiety, "That doesn't mean that I have to stop visiting you?"

"Not at all. And, by the way, there is a very handsome jar with a quantity of beans of an early variety in it where you are digging now. It was left behind by accident when the people before the ones who built the painted kiva moved out. It belonged to a woman called Bluebird Tailfeather. Her small child ran off and was lost just as they were moving, and by the time she found him, the war chief was impatient. However, we can come back to that later. I can see that you have something on your mind."

"I'm lonely," Dr. Hillebrand said simply. "My real friends are all gone. There are a lot of people I get on nicely with, but no one left I love—that is, above the ground—and you are the only one below the ground I seem to be able to reach. I— I'd like to take your remains back with me, and then we could talk nights."

"I would not like that."

"Then of course I won't."

"I was sure of that. Your country is strange to me, and travelling back and forth would be a lot of effort. What I saw that time I visited you was alien to me; it would be to you, too, I think. It won't be long, I believe, before I am relieved of attachment to my bones entirely, but if you moved them now, it would be annoying. You take that burial you carried home ten years ago—old Rabbit Stick. He says you treat him well and have given him the smell of ceremonial jewels whenever you could, but sometimes he arrives quite worn out from his journey."

"Rabbit Stick," Dr. Hillebrand mused. "I wondered if there were not someone there. He has never spoken to me."

"He couldn't. He was just an ordinary Reed Clan man. But he is grateful to you for the offerings, because they have given him the strength he needed. As you know, I can speak with you because I was the Sun's Forehead, and there was the good luck that you were thinking and feeling in the right way when you approached me. But tell me, don't the young men who learn from you keep you company?"

"Yes. There is one now who is like a son to me. But then they have learned, and they go away. The men in between, who have become chiefs, you might say, in my Department, have no use for me. They want to make me emeritus—that is, put me on a pension, take over my authority and my rewards, and set me where I could give advice and they could ignore it. They have new ways, and they despise mine. So now they are watching me. They have sent a young man out this time just to watch me. They call him a student of the ways of your grandchildren; he spent six weeks at Zuñi once, and when even he could see that the people didn't like him, he went and put in the rest of the summer at Oraibi."

"New Oraibi or Old Oraibi?" the Sun's Forehead asked.

"New Oraibi."

The chief snorted.

"So, having also read some books, he thinks he is an ethnographer, only he calls himself a cultural anthropologist. And he is out here to try to find proof that my mind is failing." He smiled. "They'd certainly think so if they saw me sitting here talking to empty air."

The Sun's Forehead chuckled.

"They certainly would. They wouldn't be able to hear me, you know." Then his voice became serious again. "That always happens, I think. It happened to me. They wanted to do things differently, when I had at last come to the point at which an Old Man talked to me. I reached it in old age—not young, as you did. They could not take my title, but they wanted to handle my duties for me, bring me enough food to live on, hear my advice and not listen to it. Struggling against them became wearying and distasteful, so finally I decided to go under. At the age I had reached—about your age—it is easy to do."

"And now you say that you are about to be detached from your bones entirely? You are reaching the next stage?"

"Let us say that I begin to hope. Our life is beautiful,

but for a hundred years or so now I have been longing for the next, and I begin to hope."

"How does it happen? Or is it wrong for me to know?"

"You may know. You are good, and you keep your secrets, as our wise men always did. You will see a man who has become young, handsome, and full of light. When we dance, he dances with great beauty; his singing is beautiful, and you feel as if it were creating life. Then one time when the katchinas themselves are dancing before us—not masks, you understand, the katchinas themselves—you can't find him among the watchers. Then you seem to recognize him, there among the sacred people, dancing like them. Then you think that the next time our grandchildren on the earth put on the masks and dance, that one, whom you knew as a spirit striving to purify himself, who used to tell you about his days on the earth, will be there. With his own eyes he will see our grandchildren and bless them." The chief's voice trailed off, as though the longing for what he was describing deprived him of words.

"To see the katchinas themselves dancing," Dr. Hillebrand mused. "Not the masks, but what the masks stand for . . . That would keep me happy for centuries. But then, I could not join your people. I was never initiated. I'd be plain silly trying to dance with them. It's not for me."

"For over forty years I have been initiating you," the Sun's Forehead said. "As for dancing—you will no longer be in that old body. You will not be dancing with those fragile, rheumatic bones. There is room for you in our country. Why don't you come over? Just lie down in that crevice back there and make up your mind."

"You know," Dr. Hillebrand said, "I think I will."

Both the Kleinman Professor of American Archeology and the spirit who once had been the Sun's Forehead for the settlements in the neighborhood of T'iiz Hatsosi were thoroughly unworldly. It had not occurred to either of them that within six days after Dr. Hillebrand had left camp Dr. George Franklin would organize a search for him, and that four days later his body would be found where he had died of, apparently, heart failure. Above all, it had not occurred to them that his body would be taken home and buried with proper pomp in the appropriate cemetery. (But Philip Fleming, close to tears, resolutely overlooked the scattering of turquoise and shell in the rubbish between the crevice and the kiva.)

Dr. Hillebrand found himself among people as alien to him as they had been to the Sun's Forehead. They seemed to be gaunt from the total lack of offerings, and the means by which they should purify and advance themselves to where they could leave this life for the next, which he believed to be the final one, were confused. He realized that his spirit was burdened with much dross, and that it would be a long time before he could gather the strength to attempt a journey to the country of his friend.

His portrait, in academic gown and hood, was painted posthumously and hung in the entrance of the museum, to one side of the stela from Quiriguá and facing the reproduction of the famous Painted Kiva mural. Dr. Klibben adroitly handled the promotions and emoluments that fell under his control. Philip Fleming won his Ph.D. with honor, and was promptly offered a splendid position at Harvard. Moved by he knew not what drive, and following one or two other actions he had performed to his own surprise, Fleming went to Dr. Hillebrand's grave, for a gesture of respect and thanks.

It had seemed to him inappropriate to bring any flowers. Instead, as he sat by the grave, with small motions of his hands he sprinkled over it some bits of turquoise and shell he had held out from a necklace he had unearthed, and followed them with a pinch of pollen given him by a Navajo. Suddenly his face registered utter astonishment; then careful listening.

The following season, Fleming returned to Painted Mask Ruin by agreement with Dr. Klibben, who was delighted to get his Department entirely out of Southwestern archeology. There he ran a trench that led right into a magnificent polychrome pot containing a store of beans of high botanical interest.

Within a few years, he stopped visiting the grave, but he was sentimentalist enough to make a pilgrimage all alone to Tsekaiye Kin at the beginning of each field season. It was jokingly said among his confreres that there he communed with the spirit of old Hillebrand. Certainly he seemed to have inherited that legendary figure's gift for making spectacular finds.

The Touch of Nutmeg Makes It

BY JOHN COLLIER

A DOZEN big firms subsidize our mineralogical institute, and most of them keep at least one man permanently on research there. The library has the intimate and smoky atmosphere of a club. Logan and I had been there longest and had the two tables in the big window bay. Against the wall, just at the edge of the bay, where the light was bad, was a small table which was left for newcomers or transients.

One morning a new man was sitting at this table. It was not necessary to look at the books he had taken from the shelves to know that he was on statistics rather than formulae. He had one of those skull-like faces on which the skin seems stretched painfully tight. These are almost a hallmark of the statistician. His mouth was intensely disciplined but became convulsive at the least relaxation. His hands were the focal point of a minor morbidity. When he had occasion to stretch them both out together—to shift an open book, for example—he would stare at them for a full minute at a time. At such times the convulsive action of his mouth muscles was particularly marked.

The newcomer crouched low over his table when anyone passed behind his chair, as if trying to decrease the likelihood of contact. Presently he took out a cigarette, but his eye fell on the "No smoking" sign, which was universally disregarded, and he returned the cigarette to its pack. At midmorning he dissolved a tablet in a glass of water. I guessed at a long-standing anxiety neurosis.

I mentioned this to Logan at lunchtime. He said, "The poor guy certainly looks as miserable as a wet cat."

I am never repelled or chilled, as many people are, by the cheerless self-centredness of the nervous or the unhappy. Logan, who has less curiosity, has a superabundance of good nature. We watched this man sitting in his solitary cell of depression for several days while the pleasant camaraderie of the library flowed all around him. Then, without further discussion, we asked him to lunch with us.

He took the invitation in the typical neurotic fashion,

seeming to weigh half-a-dozen shadowy objections before he accepted it. However, he came along, and before the meal was over he confirmed my suspicion that he had been starving for company but was too tied-up to make any move toward it. We had already found out his name, of course— J. Chapman Reid—and that he worked for the Walls Tyman Corporation. He named a string of towns he had lived in at one time or another, and told us that he came originally from Georgia. That was all the information he offered. He opened up very noticeably when the talk turned on general matters, and occasionally showed signs of having an intense and painful wit, which is the sort I like best. He was pathetically grateful for the casual invitation. He thanked us when we got up from the table, again as we emerged from the restaurant, and yet again on the threshold of the library. This made it all the more natural to suggest a quiet evening together sometime soon.

During the next few weeks we saw a good deal of J. Chapman Reid and found him a very agreeable companion. I have a great weakness for these dry, reserved characters who once or twice an evening come out with a vivid, penetrating remark that shows there is a volcanic core smouldering away at high pressure underneath. We might even have become friends if Reid himself hadn't prevented this final step, less by his reserve, which I took to be part of his nature, than by his unnecessary gratitude. He made no effusive speeches—he was not that type—but a lost dog has no need of words to show his dependence and his appreciation. It was clear our company was everything to J. Chapman Reid.

One day Nathan Trimble, a friend of Logan's, looked in at the library. He was a newspaperman and was killing an hour while waiting for a train connection. He sat on Logan's table facing the window, with his back to the rest of the room. I went round and talked to him and Logan. It was just about time for Trimble to leave when Reid came in and sat down at his table. Trimble happened to look around, and he and Reid saw each other.

I was watching Reid. After the first startled stare, he did not even glance at the visitor. He sat quite still for a minute or so, his head dropping lower and lower in little jerks, as if someone was pushing it down. Then he got up and walked out of the library.

"By God!" said Trimble. "Do you know who that is? Do you know who you've got there?"

"No," said we. "Who?"

"Jason C. Reid."

"Jason C.?" I said. "No, it's J. Chapman. Oh, yes, I see. So what?"

"Why, for God's sake, don't you read the news? Don't you remember the Pittsburgh cleaver murder?"

"No," said I.

"Wait a minute," said Logan. "About a year or so ago, was it? I read something."

"Damn it!" said Trimble. "It was a front-page sensation. This guy was tried for it. They said he hacked a pal of his pretty nearly to pieces. I saw the body. Never seen such a mess in my life. Fantastic! Horrible!"

"However," said I, "it would appear this fellow didn't do it. Presumably he wasn't convicted."

"They tried to pin it on him," said Trimble, "but they couldn't. It looked hellish bad, I must say. Alone together. No trace of any outsider. But no motive. I don't know. I just don't know. I covered the trial. I was in court every day, but I couldn't make up my mind about the guy. Don't leave any meat cleavers round this library, that's all."

With that, he bade us goodbye. I looked at Logan. Logan looked at me. "I don't believe it," said Logan. "I don't believe he did it."

"I don't wonder his nerves are eating him," said I.

"No," said Logan. "It must be damnable. And now it's followed him here, and he knows it."

"We'll let him know, somehow," said I, "that we're not even interested enough to look up the newspaper files."

"Good idea," said Logan.

A little later Reid came in again, his movements showing signs of intense control. He came over to where we were sitting. "Would you prefer to cancel our arrangement for to-night?" said he. "I think it would be better if we cancelled it. I shall ask my firm to transfer me again. I——"

"Hold on," said Logan. "Who said so? Not us."

"Didn't he tell you?" said Reid. "Of course he did."

"He said you were tried," said I. "And he said you were acquitted. That's good enough for us."

"You're still acquitted," said Logan. "And the date's on. And we *won't* talk."

"Oh!" said Reid. "Oh!"

"Forget it," said Logan, returning to his papers.

I took Reid by the shoulder and gave him a friendly shove in the direction of his table. We avoided looking at him for the rest of the afternoon.

That night, when we met for dinner, we were naturally a little self-conscious. Reid probably felt it. "Look here," he said when we had finished eating, "would either of you mind if we skipped the movie tonight?"

"It's O.K. by me," said Logan. "Shall we go to Chancey's?"

"No," said Reid, "I want you to come somewhere where we can talk. Come up to my place."

"Just as you like," said I. "It's not necessary."

"Yes it is," said Reid. "We may as well get it over."

He was in a painfully nervous state, so we consented and went up to his apartment, where we had never been before. It was a single room with a pull-down bed and a bathroom and kitchenette opening off it. Though Reid had now been in town over two months, there was absolutely no sign that he was living there at all. It might have been a room hired for the uncomfortable conversation of this one night.

We sat down, but Reid immediately got up again and stood between us, in front of the imitation fireplace.

"I should like to say nothing about what happened today," he began. "I should like to ignore it and let it be forgotten. But it can't be forgotten.

"It's no use telling me you won't think about it," said he. "Of course you'll think about it. Everyone did back there. The firm sent me to Cleveland. It became known there, too. Everyone was thinking about it, whispering about it, wondering.

"You see, it would be rather more exciting if the fellow *was* guilty after all, wouldn't it?

"In a way, I'm glad this has come out. With you two, I mean. Most people—I don't want them to know anything. You two—you've been decent to me—I want you to know all about it. All.

"I came up from Georgia to Pittsburgh, was there for ten years with the Walls Tyman people. While there I met —I met Earle Wilson. He came from Georgia, too, and we became very great friends. I've never been one to go about much. Earle was not only my best friend: he was almost my only friend.

"Very well. Earle's job with our company was a better paid one than mine. He was able to afford a small house just beyond the fringe of the town. I used to drive out there two or three evenings a week. We spent the evenings very quietly. I want you to understand that I was quite at home in the house. There was no host-and-guest atmosphere about it. If I felt sleepy, I'd make no bones about going upstairs and stretching out on a bed and taking a nap for half an hour. There's nothing so extraordinary about that, is there?"

"No, nothing extraordinary about that," said Logan.

"Some people seemed to think there was," said Reid. "Well, one night I went out there after work. We ate, we sat about a bit, we played a game of checkers. He mixed a couple of drinks, then I mixed a couple. Normal enough, isn't it?"

"It certainly is," said Logan.

"I was tired," said Reid. "I felt heavy. I said I'd go upstairs and stretch out for half an hour. That always puts me right. So I went up.

"I sleep heavily, very heavily, for half an hour, then I'm all right. This time I seemed to be dreaming, a sort of nightmare. I thought I was in an air raid somewhere, and heard Earle's voice calling me, but I didn't wake, not until the usual half-hour was up anyway.

"I went downstairs. The room below was dark. I called out to Earle and started across from the stairs toward the light switch. Halfway across, I tripped over something—it turned out to be the floor lamp, which had fallen over, and I went down, and I fell flat on him.

"I knew he was dead. I got up and found the light. He was lying there. He looked as if he had been attacked by a madman. He was cut to pieces, almost. God!

"I got hold of the phone at once and called the police. Naturally. While they were coming, I looked round. But first of all I just walked about, dazed. It seems I must have gone up into the bedroom again. I've got no recollection of that, but they found a smear of blood on the pillow. Of course, I was covered with it. Absolutely covered; I'd fallen on him. You can understand a man being dazed, can't you? You can understand him going upstairs, even, and not remembering it? Can't you?"

"I certainly can," said Logan.

"It seems very natural," said I.

"They thought they had trapped me over that," said Reid. "They said so to my face. The idiots! Well, I remember looking around, and I saw what it had been done with. Earle had a great equipment of cutlery in his kitchen. One of our firm's subsidiaries was in that line. One of the things was a meat cleaver, the sort of thing you see usually in a butcher's shop. It was there on the carpet.

"Well, the police came. I told them all I could. Earle was a quiet fellow. He had no enemies. Does *anyone* have that sort of enemy? I thought it must be some maniac. Nothing was missing. It wasn't robbery, unless some half-crazy tramp had got in and been too scared in the end to take anything.

"Whoever it was had made a very clean getaway. Too clean for the police. And too clean for me. They looked for fingerprints, and they couldn't find any.

"They have an endless routine in this sort of thing. I won't bore you with every single detail. It seemed their routine wasn't good enough—the fellow was too clever for them. But of course they wanted an arrest. So they indicted me.

"Their case was nothing but a negative one. God knows how they thought it could succeed. Perhaps they didn't think so. But, you see, if they could build up a strong presumptive case, and I only got off because of a hung jury—well, that's different from having to admit they couldn't find hair or hide of the real murderer.

"What was the evidence against me? That they couldn't find traces of anyone else! That's evidence of their own damned inefficiency, that's all. Does a man murder his best friend for nothing? Could they find any reason, any motive? They were trying to find some woman first of all. They have the mentality of a ten-cent magazine. They combed our money affairs. They even tried to smell out some subversive tieup. God, if you knew what it was to be confronted with faces out of a comic strip and with minds that match the faces! If ever you are charged with murder, hang yourself in your cell the first night.

"In the end they settled on our game of checkers. Our poor, harmless game of checkers! We talked all the while we were playing, you know, and sometimes even forgot whose turn it was to move next. I suppose there are people who can go berserk in a dispute over a childish game, but to me that's something utterly incomprehensible. Can *you* understand a man murdering his friend over a game? I can't. As a matter of fact, I remember we had to start this game over again, not once but twice—first when Earle mixed the drinks, and then when I mixed them. Each time we forgot who was to move. However, they fixed on that. They had to find some shadow of a motive, and that was the best they could do.

"Of course, my lawyer tore it to shreds. By the mercy of God there'd been quite a craze at the works for playing checkers at lunchtime. So he soon found half-a-dozen men to swear that neither Earle nor I ever played the game seriously enough to get het up about it.

"They had no other motive to put forward. Absolutely none. Both our lives were simple, ordinary, humdrum, and open as a book. What was their case? They couldn't find what they were paid to find. For that, they proposed to send a man to the death cell. Can you beat that?"

"It sounds pretty damnable," said I.

"Yes," said he passionately. "Damnable is the word. They got what they were after—the jury voted nine to three for acquittal, which saved the faces of the police. There was plenty of room for a hint that they were on the right track all the time. You can imagine what my life has been since! If you ever get into that sort of mess, my friends, hang yourselves the first night, in your cell."

"Don't talk like that," said Logan. "Look here, you've had a bad time. Damned bad. But what the hell? It's over. You're here now."

"And we're here," said I. "If that helps any."

"Helps?" said he. "God, if you could ever guess how it helped! I'll never be able to tell you. I'm no good at that sort of thing. See, I drag you here, the only human beings who've treated me decently, and I pour all this stuff out and don't offer you a drink, even. Never mind, I'll give you one now—a drink you'll like."

"I could certainly swallow a highball," said Logan.

"You shall have something better than that," said Reid, moving toward the kitchenette. "We have a little specialty down in our corner of Georgia. Only it's got to be fixed properly. Wait just a minute."

He disappeared through the door, and we heard corks being drawn and a great clatter of pouring and mixing. While this went on, he was still talking through the doorway. "I'm glad I brought you up here," he said. "I'm glad I put the whole thing to you. You don't know what it means —to be believed, understood by God! I feel I'm alive again."

He emerged with three brimming glasses on a tray. "Try this," he said proudly.

"To the days ahead!" said Logan, as we raised our glasses.

We drank and raised our eyebrows in appreciation. The drink seemed to be a sort of variant of sherry flip, with a heavy sprinkling of nutmeg.

"You like it?" cried Reid eagerly. "There's not many people know the recipe for that drink, and fewer still can make it well. There are one or two bastard versions which some damned fools mix up—a disgrace to Georgia. I could—I could pour the mess over their heads. Wait a minute. You're men of discernment. Yes, by God, you are! You shall decide for yourselves."

With that, he darted back into the kitchenette and rattled his bottles more furiously than before, still talking to us disjointedly, praising the orthodox version of his drink, and damning all imitations.

"Now, here you are," said he, appearing with the tray loaded with drinks very much like the first but rather differently garnished. "These abortions have mace and ginger on the top instead of nutmeg. Take them. Drink them. Spit them out on the carpet if you want to. I'll mix some more of the real thing to take the taste out of your mouth. Just try them. Just tell me what you think of a barbarian who could insist that *that* was a Georgian flip. Go on. Tell me."

We sipped. There was no considerable difference. However, we replied as was expected of us.

"What do you think, Logan?" said I. "The first has it, beyond doubt."

"Beyond doubt," said Logan. "The first is the real thing."

"Yes," said Reid, his face livid and his eyes blazing like live coals. "And *that* is hogwash. The man who calls *that* a Georgian flip is not fit to mix bootblacking. It hasn't the nutmeg. The touch of nutmeg makes it. A man who'd leave out the nutmeg——! I could——!"

He put out both his hands to lift the tray, and his eyes fell on them. He sat very still, staring at them.

The Harness

BY JOHN STEINBECK

PETER RANDALL was one of the most highly respected farmers of Monterey County. Once, before he was to make a little speech at a Masonic convention, the brother who introduced him referred to him as an example for young Masons of California to emulate. He was nearing fifty; his manner was grave and restrained, and he wore a carefully tended beard. From every gathering he reaped the authority that belongs to the bearded man. Peter's eyes were grave, too; blue and grave almost to the point of sorrowfulness. People knew there was force in him, but force held caged. Sometimes, for no apparent reason, his eyes grew sullen and mean, like the eyes of a bad dog; but that look soon passed, and the restraint and probity came back into his face. He was tall and broad. He held his shoulders back as though they were braced, and he sucked in his stomach like a soldier. Inasmuch as farmers are usually slouchy men, Peter gained an added respect because of his posture.

Concerning Peter's wife, Emma, people generally agreed that it was hard to see how such a little skin-and-bones woman could go on living, particularly when she was sick most of the time. She weighed eighty-seven pounds. At forty-five, her face was as wrinkled and brown as that of an old, old woman, but her dark eyes were feverish with a determination to live. She was a proud woman, who complained very little. Her father had been a thirty-third degree Mason and Worshipful Master of the Grand Lodge of California. Before he died he had taken a great deal of interest in Peter's Masonic career.

Once a year Peter went away for a week, leaving his wife alone on the farm. To neighbors who called to keep her company she invariably explained, "He's away on a business trip."

Each time Peter returned from a business trip, Emma was ailing for a month or two, and this was hard on Peter, for Emma did her own work and refused to hire a girl. When she was ill, Peter had to do the housework.

The Randall ranch lay across the Salinas River, next to the foothills. It was an ideal balance of bottom and upland. Forty-five acres of rich level soil brought from the cream of the county by the river in old times and spread out as flat as a board; and eighty acres of gentle upland for hay and orchard. The white farmhouse was as neat and restrained as its owners. The immediate yard was fenced, and in the garden, under Emma's direction, Peter raised button dahlias and immortelles, carnations and pinks.

From the front porch one could look down over the flat to the river with its sheath of willows and cottonwoods, and across the river to the beet fields, and past the fields to the bulbous dome of the Salinas courthouse. Often in the afternoon Emma sat in a rocking-chair on the front porch, until the breeze drove her in. She knitted constantly, looking up now and then to watch Peter working on the flat or in the orchard, or on the slope below the house.

The Randall ranch was no more encumbered with mortgage than any of the others in the valley. The crops, judiciously chosen and carefully tended, paid the interest, made a reasonable living and left a few hundred dollars every year toward paying off the principal. It was no wonder that Peter Randall was respected by his neighbors, and that his seldom spoken words were given attention even when they were about the weather or the way things were going. Let Peter say, "I'm going to kill a pig Saturday," and nearly every one of his hearers went home and killed a pig on Saturday. They didn't know why, but if Peter Randall was going to kill a pig, it seemed like a good, safe, conservative thing to do.

Peter and Emma were married for twenty-one years. They collected a houseful of good furniture, a number of framed pictures, vases of all shapes, and books of a sturdy type. Emma had no children. The house was unscarred, uncarved, unchalked. On the front and back porches footscrapers and thick cocoa-fiber mats kept dirt out of the house.

In the intervals between her illnesses, Emma saw to it that the house was kept up. The hinges of doors and cupboards were oiled, and no screws were gone from the catches. The furniture and woodwork were freshly varnished once a year. Repairs were usually made after Peter came home from his yearly business trips.

Whenever the word went around among the farms that

Emma was sick again, the neighbors waylaid the doctor as he drove by on the river road.

"Oh, I guess she'll be all right," he answered their questions. "She'll have to stay in bed for a couple of weeks."

The good neighbors took cakes to the Randall farm, and they tiptoed into the sickroom, where the little skinny bird of a woman lay in a tremendous walnut bed. She looked at them with her bright little dark eyes.

"Wouldn't you like the curtains up a little, dear?" they asked.

"No, thank you. The light worries my eyes."

"Is there anything we can do for you?"

"No, thank you. Peter does for me very well."

"Just remember, if there's anything you think of—"

Emma was such a tight woman. There was nothing you could do for her when she was ill, except to take pies and cakes to Peter. Peter would be in the kitchen, wearing a neat, clean apron. He would be filling a hot water bottle or making junket.

And so, one fall, when the news traveled that Emma was down, the farm-wives baked for Peter and prepared to make their usual visits.

Mrs. Chappell, the next farm neighbor, stood on the river road when the doctor drove by. "How's Emma Randall, doctor?"

"I don't think she's so very well, Mrs. Chappell. I think she's a pretty sick woman."

Because to Dr. Marn anyone who wasn't actually a corpse was well on the road to recovery, the word went about among the farms that Emma Randall was going to die.

It was a long, terrible illness. Peter himself gave enemas and carried bedpans. The doctor's suggestion that a nurse be employed met only beady, fierce refusal in the eyes of the patient; and, ill as she was, her demands were respected. Peter fed her and bathed her, and made up the great walnut bed. The bedroom curtains remained drawn.

It was two months before the dark, sharp bird eyes veiled, and the sharp mind retired into unconsciousness. And only then did a nurse come to the house. Peter was lean and sick himself, not far from collapse. The neighbors brought him cakes and pies, and found them uneaten in the kitchen when they called again.

Mrs. Chappell was in the house with Peter the afternoon Emma died. Peter became hysterical immediately. Mrs.

Chappell telephoned the doctor, and then she called her husband to come and help her, for Peter was wailing like a crazy man, and beating his bearded cheeks with his fists. Ed Chappell was ashamed when he saw him.

Peter's beard was wet with his tears. His loud sobbing could be heard throughout the house. Sometimes he sat by the bed and covered his head with a pillow, and sometimes he paced the floor of the bedroom bellowing like a calf. When Ed Chappell self-consciously put a hand on his shoulder and said, "Come on, Peter, come on, now," in a helpless voice, Peter shook his hand off. The doctor drove out and signed the certificate.

When the undertaker came, they had a devil of a time with Peter. He was half mad. He fought them when they tried to take the body away. It was only after Ed Chappell and the undertaker held him down while the doctor stuck him with a hypodermic, that they were able to remove Emma.

The morphine didn't put Peter to sleep. He sat hunched in the corner, breathing heavily and staring at the floor.

"Who's going to stay with him?" the doctor asked. "Miss Jack?" to the nurse.

"I couldn't handle him, doctor, not alone."

"Will you stay, Chappell?"

"Sure, I'll stay."

"Well, look. Here are some triple bromides. If he gets going again, give him one of these. And if they don't work, here's some sodium amytal. One of these capsules will calm him down."

Before they went away, they helped the stupefied Peter into the sitting-room and laid him gently down on a sofa. Ed Chappell sat in an easy-chair and watched him. The bromides and a glass of water were on the table beside him.

The little sitting-room was clean and dusted. Only that morning Peter had swept the floor with pieces of damp newspaper. Ed built a little fire in the grate, and put on a couple of pieces of oak when the flames were well started. The dark had come early. A light rain spattered against the windows when the wind drove it. Ed trimmed the kerosene lamps and turned the flames low. In the grate the blaze snapped and crackled and the flames curled like hair over the oak. For a long time Ed sat in his easy-chair watching Peter where he lay drugged on the couch. At last Ed dozed off to sleep.

It was about ten o'clock when he awakened. He started up

and looked toward the sofa. Peter was sitting up, looking at him. Ed's hand went out toward the bromide bottle, but Peter shook his head.

"No need to give me anything, Ed. I guess the doctor slugged me pretty hard, didn't he? I feel all right now, only a little dopey."

"If you'll just take one of these, you'll get some sleep."

"I don't want sleep." He fingered his draggled beard and then stood up. "I'll go out and wash my face, then I'll feel better."

Ed heard him running water in the kitchen. In a moment he came back into the living-room, still drying his face on a towel. Peter was smiling curiously. It was an expression Ed had never seen on him before, a quizzical, wondering smile. "I guess I kind of broke loose when she died, didn't I?" Peter said.

"Well—yes, you carried on some."

"It seemed like something snapped inside of me," Peter explained. "Something like a suspender strap. It made me all come apart. I'm all right, now, though."

Ed looked down at the floor and saw a little brown spider crawling, and stretched out his foot and stomped it.

Peter asked suddenly, "Do you believe in an after-life?"

Ed Chappell squirmed. He didn't like to talk about such things, for to talk about them was to bring them up in his mind and think about them. "Well, yes. I suppose if you come right down to it, I do."

"Do you believe that somebody that's—passed on—can look down and see what we're doing?"

"Oh, I don't know as I'd go that far—I don't know."

Peter went on as though he were talking to himself. "Even if she could see me, and I didn't do what she wanted, she ought to feel good because I did it when she was here. It ought to please her that she made a good man of me. If I wasn't a good man when she wasn't here, that'd prove she did it all, wouldn't it? I was a good man, wasn't I, Ed?"

"What do you mean, 'was'?"

"Well, except for one week a year I was good. I don't know what I'll do now. . . ." His face grew angry. "Except one thing." He stood up and stripped off his coat and his shirt. Over his underwear there was a web harness that pulled his shoulders back. He unhooked the harness and threw it off. Then he dropped his trousers, disclosing a wide elastic belt. He shucked this off over his feet, and then he scratched his stomach luxuriously before he put on his clothes again. He smiled at Ed, the strange, wondering smile, again. "I don't know how she got me to do things, but she did. She didn't seem to boss me, but she always made me do things. You know, I don't think I believe in an after-life. When she was alive, even when she was sick, I had to do things she wanted, but just the minute she died, it was—why like that harness coming off! I couldn't stand it. It was all over, I'm going to have to get used to going without that harness." He shook his finger in Ed's direction. "My stomach's going to stick out," he said positively. "I'm going to let it stick out. Why, I'm fifty years old."

Ed didn't like that. He wanted to get away. This sort of thing wasn't very decent. "If you'll just take one of these, you'll get some sleep," he said weakly.

Peter had not put his coat on. He was sitting on the sofa in an open shirt. "I don't want to sleep. I want to talk. I guess I'll have to put that belt and harness on for the funeral, but after that I'm going to burn them. Listen, I've got a bottle of whiskey in the barn. I'll go get it."

"Oh no," Ed protested quickly. "I couldn't drink now, not at a time like this."

Peter stood up. "Well, I could. You can sit and watch me if you want. I tell you, it's all over." He went out the door, leaving Ed Chappell unhappy and scandalized. It was only a moment before he was back. He started talking as he came through the doorway with the whiskey. "I only got one thing in my life, those trips. Emma was a pretty bright woman. She knew I'd've gone crazy if I didn't get away once a year. God, how she worked on my conscience when I came back!" His voice lowered confidentially. "You know what I did on those trips?"

Ed's eyes were wide open now. Here was a man he didn't know, and he was becoming fascinated. He took the glass of whiskey when it was handed to him. "No, what did you do?"

Peter gulped his drink and coughed, and wiped his mouth with his hand. "I got drunk," he said. "I went to fancy houses in San Francisco. I was drunk for a week, and I went to a fancy house every night." He poured his glass full again. "I guess Emma knew, but she never said anything. I'd've busted if I hadn't got away."

Ed Chappell sipped his whiskey gingerly. "She always said you went on business."

Peter looked at his glass and drank it, and poured it

full again. His eyes had begun to shine. "Drink your drink, Ed. I know you think it isn't right—so soon, but no one'll know but you and me. Kick up the fire. I'm not sad."

Chappell went to the grate and stirred the glowing wood until lots of sparks flew up the chimney like little shining birds. Peter filled the glasses and retired to the sofa again. When Ed went back to the chair he sipped from his glass and pretended he didn't know it was filled up. His cheeks were flushing. It didn't seem so terrible, now, to be drinking. The afternoon and the death had receded into an indefinite past.

"Want some cake?" Peter asked. "There's half a dozen cakes in the pantry."

"No, I don't think I will thank you for some."

"You know," Peter confessed, "I don't think I'll eat cake again. For ten years, every time Emma was sick, people sent cakes. It was nice of 'em, of course, only now cake means sickness to me. Drink your drink."

Something happened in the room. Both men looked up, trying to discover what it was. The room was somehow different than it had been a moment before. Then Peter smiled sheepishly. "It was that mantel clock stopped. I don't think I'll start it any more. I'll get a little quick alarm clock that ticks fast. That clack-clack-clack is too mournful." He swallowed his whiskey. "I guess you'll be telling around that I'm crazy, won't you?"

Ed looked up from his glass, and smiled and nodded. "No, I will not. I can see pretty much how you feel about things. I didn't know you wore that harness and belt."

"A man ought to stand up straight," Peter said. "I'm a natural sloucher." Then he exploded: "I'm a natural fool! For twenty years I've been pretending I was a wise, good man—except for that one week a year." He said loudly, "Things have been dribbled to me. My life's been dribbled out to me. Here, let me fill your glass. I've got another bottle out in the barn, way down under a pile of sacks."

Ed held out his glass to be filled. Peter went on, "I thought how it would be nice to have my whole river flat in sweet peas. Think how it'd be to sit on the front porch and see all those acres of blue and pink, just solid. And when the wind came up over them, think of the big smell. A big smell that would almost knock you over."

"A lot of men have gone broke on sweet peas. 'Course

you get a big price for the seed, but too many things can happen to your crop."

"I don't give a damn," Peter shouted. "I want a lot of everything. I want forty acres of color and smell. I want fat women, with breasts as big as pillows. I'm hungry, I tell you, I'm hungry for everything, for a lot of everything."

Ed's face became grave under the shouting. "If you'd just take one of these, you'd get some sleep."

Peter looked ashamed. "I'm all right. I didn't mean to yell like that. I'm not just thinking these things for the first time. I been thinking about them for years, the way a kid thinks of vacation. I was always afraid I'd be too old. Or that I'd go first and miss everything. But I'm only fifty. I've got plenty of vinegar left. I told Emma about the sweet peas, but she wouldn't let me. I don't know how she made me do things," he said wonderingly. "I can't remember. She had a way of doing it. But she's gone. I can feel she's gone just like that harness is gone. I'm going to slouch, Ed—slouch all over the place. I'm going to track dirt into the house. I'm going to get a big fat housekeeper—a big fat one from San Francisco. I'm going to have a bottle of brandy on the shelf all the time."

Ed Chappell stood up and stretched his arms over his head. "I guess I'll go home now, if you feel all right. I got to get some sleep. You better wind that clock, Peter. It don't do a clock any good to stand not running."

The day after the funeral Peter Randall went to work on his farm. The Chappells, who lived on the next place, saw the lamp in his kitchen long before daylight, and they saw his lantern cross the yard to the barn half an hour before they even got up.

Peter pruned his orchard in three days. He worked from first light until he couldn't see the twigs against the sky any more. Then he started to shape the big piece of river flat. He plowed and rolled and harrowed. Two strange men dressed in boots and riding breeches came out and looked at his land. They felt the dirt with their fingers and ran a posthole digger deep down under the surface, and when they went away they took little paper bags of the dirt with them.

Ordinarily, before planting time, the farmers did a good deal of visiting back and forth. They sat on their haunches, picking up handfuls of dirt and breaking little clods between their fingers. They discussed markets and crops, recalled other years when beans had done well in a good market, and other years when field peas didn't bring enough to pay for the seed hardly. After a great number of these discussions it usually happened that all the farmers planted the same things. There were certain men whose ideas carried weight. If Peter Randall or Clark DeWitt thought they would put in pink beans and barley, most of the crops would turn out to be pink beans and barley that year; for, since such men were respected and fairly successful, it was conceded that their plans must be based on something besides chance choice. It was generally believed but never stated that Peter Randall and Clark DeWitt had extra reasoning powers and special prophetic knowledge.

When the usual visits started, it was seen that a change had taken place in Peter Randall. He sat on his plow and talked pleasantly enough. He said he hadn't decided yet what to plant, but he said it in such a guilty way that it was plain he didn't intend to tell. When he had rebuffed a few inquiries, the visits to his place stopped and the farmers went over in a body to Clark DeWitt. Clark was putting in Chevalier barley. His decision dictated the major part of the planting in the vicinity.

But because the questions stopped, the interest did not. Men driving by the forty-five acre flat of the Randall place studied the field to try to figure out from the type of work what the crop was going to be. When Peter drove the seeder back and forth across the land no one came in, for Peter had made it plain that his crop was a secret.

Ed Chappell didn't tell on him, either. Ed was a little ashamed when he thought of that night; ashamed of Peter for breaking down, and ashamed of himself for having sat there and listened. He watched Peter narrowly to see whether his vicious intentions were really there or whether the whole conversation had been the result of loss and hysteria. He did notice that Peter's shoulders weren't back and that his stomach stuck out a little. He went to Peter's house and was relieved when he saw no dirt on the floor and when he heard the mantel clock ticking away.

Mrs. Chappell spoke often of the afternoon. "You'd've thought he lost his mind the way he carried on. He just howled. Ed stayed with him part of the night, until he quieted down. Ed had to give him some whiskey to get him to sleep. But," she said brightly, "hard work is the thing to kill sorrow. Peter Randall is getting up at three o'clock every morning. I can see the light in his kitchen window from my bedroom."

The pussywillows burst out in silver drops, and the little weeds sprouted up along the roadside. The Salinas River ran dark water, flowed for a month, and then subsided into green pools again. Peter Randall had shaped his land beautifully. It was smooth and black; no clod was larger than a small marble, and under the rains it looked purple with richness.

And then the little weak lines of green stretched out across the black field. In the dusk a neighbor crawled under the fence and pulled one of the tiny plants. "Some kind of legume," he told his friends. "Field peas, I guess. What did he want to be so quiet about it for? I asked him right out what he was planting, and he wouldn't tell me."

The word ran through the farms, "It's sweet peas. The whole God-damn' forty-five acres is in sweet peas!" Men called on Clark DeWitt then, to get his opinion.

His opinion was this: "People think because you can get twenty to sixty cents a pound for sweet peas you can get rich on them. But it's the most ticklish crop in the world. If the bugs don't get it, it might do good. And then come a hot day and bust the pods and lose your crop on the ground. Or it might come up a little rain and spoil the whole kaboodle. It's all right to put in a few acres and take a chance, but not the whole place. Peter's touched in the head since Emma died."

This opinion was widely distributed. Every man used it as his own. Two neighbors often said it to each other, each one repeating half of it. When too many people said it to Peter Randall he became angry. One day he cried, "Say, whose land is this? If I want to go broke, I've got a damn good right to, haven't I?" And that changed the whole feeling. Men remembered that Peter was a good farmer. Perhaps he had special knowledge. Why, that's who those two men in boots were—soil chemists! A good many of the farmers wished they'd put in a few acres of sweet peas.

They wished it particularly when the vines spread out, when they met each other across the rows and hid the dark earth from sight, when the buds began to form and it was seen the crop was rich. And then the blooms came; forty-five acres of color, forty-five acres of perfume. It was said that you could smell them in Salinas, four miles away. Busses brought the school children out to look at them. A group of men from a seed company spent all day looking at the vines and feeling the earth.

Peter Randall sat on his porch in a rocking-chair every afternoon. He looked down on the great squares of pink and blue, and on the mad square of mixed colors. When the afternoon breeze came up, he inhaled deeply. His blue shirt was open at the throat, as though he wanted to get the perfume down next his skin.

Men called on Clark DeWitt to get his opinion now. He said, "There's about ten things that can happen to spoil that crop. He's welcome to his sweet peas." But the men knew from Clark's irritation that he was a little jealous. They looked up over the fields of color to where Peter sat on his porch, and they felt a new admiration and respect for him.

Ed Chappell walked up the steps to him one afternoon. "You got a crop there, mister."

"Looks that way," said Peter.

"I took a look. Pods are setting fine."

Peter sighed. "Blooming's nearly over," he said. "I'll hate to see the petals drop off."

"Well, I'd be glad to see 'em drop. You'll make a lot of money, if nothing happens."

Peter took out a bandana handkerchief and wiped his nose, and jiggled it sideways to stop an itch. "I'll be sorry when the smell stops," he said.

Then Ed made his reference to the night of the death. One of his eyes drooped secretly. "Found somebody to keep house for you?"

"I haven't looked," said Peter. "I haven't had time." There were lines of worry about his eyes. But who wouldn't worry, Ed thought, when a single shower could ruin his whole year's crop.

If the year and the weather had been manufactured for sweet peas, they couldn't have been better. The fog lay close to the ground in the mornings when the vines were pulled. When the great piles of vines lay safely on spread canvases, the hot sun shone down and crisped the pods for the threshers. The neighbors watched the long cotton sacks filling with round black seeds, and they went home and tried to figure out how much money Peter would make on his tremendous crop. Clark DeWitt lost a good part of his following. The men decided to find out what Peter was going to plant next year if they had to follow him around. How did he know, for instance, that this year'd be good for sweet peas? He must have some kind of special knowledge.

When a man from the upper Salinas Valley goes to San Francisco on business or for a vacation, he takes a room in the Ramona Hotel. This is a nice arrangement, for in the lobby he can usually find someone from home. They can sit in the soft chairs of the lobby and talk about the Salinas Valley.

Ed Chappell went to San Francisco to meet his wife's cousin who was coming out from Ohio for a trip. The train was not due until the next morning. In the lobby of the Ramona, Ed looked for someone from the Salinas Valley, but he could see only strangers sitting in the soft chairs. He went out to a moving picture show. When he returned, he looked again for someone from home, and still there were only strangers. For a moment he considered glancing over the register, but it was quite late. He sat down to finish his cigar before he went to bed.

There was a commotion at the door. Ed saw the clerk motion with his hand. A bellhop ran out. Ed squirmed around in his chair to look. Outside a man was being helped out of a taxicab. The bellhop took him from the driver and guided him in the door. It was Peter Randall. His eyes were glassy, and his mouth open and wet. He had no hat on his mussed hair. Ed jumped up and strode over to him.

"Peter!"

Peter was batting helplessly at the bellhop. "Let me alone," he explained. "I'm all right. You let me alone, and I'll give you two bits."

Ed called again, "Peter!"

The glassy eyes turned slowly to him, and then Peter fell into his arms. "My old friend," he cried. "Ed Chappell, my old, good friend. What you doing here? Come up to my room and have a drink."

Ed set him back on his feet. "Sure I will," he said. "I'd like a little night-cap."

"Night-cap, hell. We'll go out and see a show, or something."

Ed helped him into the elevator and got him to his room.

Peter dropped heavily to the bed and struggled up to a sitting position. "There's a bottle of whiskey in the bathroom. Bring me a drink, too."

Ed brought out the bottle and the glasses. "What you doing, Peter, celebrating the crop? You must've made a pile of money."

Peter put out his palm and tapped it impressively with a forefinger. "Sure I made money—but it wasn't a bit better than gambling. It was just like straight gambling."

"But you got the money."

Peter scowled thoughtfully. "I might've lost my pants," he said. "The whole time, all the year, I been worrying. It was just like gambling."

"Well, you got it, anyway."

Peter changed the subject, then. "I been sick," he said. "I been sick right in the taxicab. I just came from a fancy house on Van Ness Avenue," he explained apologetically. "I just had to come up to the city. I'd a busted if I hadn't come up and got some of the vinegar out of my system."

Ed looked at him curiously. Peter's head was hanging loosely between his shoulders. His beard was draggled and rough. "Peter—" Ed began, "the night Emma—passed on, you said you was going to—change things."

Peter's swaying head rose up slowly. He stared owlishly at Ed Chappell. "She didn't die dead," he said thickly. "She won't let me do things. She's worried me all year about those peas." His eyes were wondering. "I don't know how she does it." Then he frowned. His palm came out, and he tapped it again. "But you mark, Ed Chappell, I won't wear that harness, and I damn well won't ever wear it. You remember that." His head dropped forward again. But in a moment he looked up. "I been drunk," he said seriously. "I been to fancy houses." He edged out confidentially toward Ed. His voice dropped to a heavy whisper. "But it's all right, I'll fix it. When I get back, you know what I'm going to do? I'm going to put in electric lights. Emma always wanted electric lights." He sagged sideways on the bed.

Ed Chappell stretched Peter out and undressed him before he went to his own room.

Friend of the Family

BY KAY BOYLE

WHEN THEY were young they had a theater with men and women, and the shrubbery even, on wires they could shift about. They hung a curtain across half the room and set the stage up on a table in the middle. Thunder was present in a thin piece of cardboard waved till it bellowed out behind the scenes. But the best play was the one in which the glass coffin with the princess visible in it was allowed to fall. "The coffin," said the voice of one of the children, reading behind the stage, "fell and was broken into a-toms." And then the coffin was whisked off on its wire, and bits of white cardboard were cast in from the wings.

At this moment the Baron always burst into applause, clapping and shouting to stamp out the sound of his own laughter, maybe; but even then the curtain was descending, so the storm of his clamor fitted in very well.

"*Bis! Bis!*" shouted the Baron.

They learned the word from his mouth. He stood up from his chair and held his hands up far and high as he applauded. They brought out the players and jerked them at him, and at Mother, and at whoever else might be watching. A minute or two after, the Baron would go to the piano in the other room and sing the "Glowworm" song in German, the words thundering, thundering till the walls of the house fell in, and his voice went soaring away.

He had a big dark voice that filled the spaces of concert halls and made the glass sticks of the chandeliers shudder. Twice they were taken to New York, and there they heard him sing in the opera at night. The first time he wore tights and a doublet and played stormily in the darkness. The second time he looked as they knew him: in an evening suit with a white flower in his lapel. But however he dressed, he remained a foreign young man to them, luxuriant and black as a bear, making all the other young men who came to the house seem white as albinos and as tasteless.

He did not come often, only two or three times in the

year maybe; but Mother had her ostrich feather dipped bluer
and curled up fresh every time before he came. She bought
him neckties and put them away in the drawer for him: as
rich in color as she could find, because that was the way he
would have chosen them himself. He did not dress like any
man they knew. This time he wore a snow-white overcoat
of wool, and a heliotrope suit, and white spats over his
shiny shoes. He stood on the step of the Pullman car when
the train came in and he jumped off shouting before it had
so much as halted. His gloves were yellow chamois with
black backbones, and he ripped them off when he kissed
their cheeks and gave all the flowers to Mother.

"Good God, how are you all?" he said with joy, while
they stood looking speechless, because they had forgotten he
was so tall and talked so loud. He was a Bavarian, and the
Middle West was as unsuitable as the grave to him. He
walked out of the station to the car with Mother's arm in
his, and his foreign aspect like a bright cloak all around
them.

The Baron sat beside Mother on the cushions, and the
two little girls, in their patent-leather hats, sat erect on the
side seats with their backs to the others and watched him
in the strip of glass.

"I miss my own mother so much," he said, and there in
the mirror they could see him kiss Mother's hand inside and
out. She shook her blue feather at him, and his dark eyes
were shining, and his gold face was filled with alien things.

He changed into white flannels for lunch and walked boldly
out onto the terrace. His voice hummed deeply in his throat,
and his fingers danced on his open shirt, rapped quick and
hard as if striking music from a shapely barrel of sound.
He remembered everything that had been there, and what
changes they had made.

"Ah, the jump-ups here this year!" he sang out deeply to
Mother. "You know, I'll tell you something. I like it much
better. What a good idea you had, Mrs. *Mutter.*"

Even Mother's dress was changed.

"It's so hot," she said when the children saw it with delight. "It's suddenly so mild," said Mother, "that I slipped
this one on."

"But it's *new!*" said the little girls. "It's awfully pretty!"

"Yes," said Mother. "Now let's show the Baron the baby
doves."

"But what a beautiful dress!" said the Baron. "I can't

quite take my eyes off it." He caught his clean white shoe in a croquet wicket and must put out his hand and touch Mother's arm to get his balance again.

"Did you hurt yourself?" cried Mother softly, and he stood quite still, looking at her.

"Yes," said the Baron in his dark deep voice. "Yes, I have hurt myself for all my life."

He remembered the number of white doves there had been before in the autumn. The gladiola trees were blooming and they now cast a blush and a languor on the air. He remembered the exact proportion of gin and grenadine for Father's cocktail. When he came back to the table on the terrace, he rolled up his sleeves to make it, and the black silk hairs lay quiet on his arms.

"Ah, ah, ah, *ahhhhhh!*" he sang, as though practicing his scales. The silver shaker was frosting in his hands. "Here comes Mr. *Mutter* out of the car! Hello, hello, hello!" he cried. He went striding down the flight of steps in the garden as if welcoming a guest who had come to call. "Hello, hello, Mr. *Mutter!*" he shouted.

"Hello," said Father quietly. Standing beside the Baron, he looked like a small man, and all of a sudden the gray hairs seemed to spring out like magic all over his head. "When did you get here?" said Father. He had come from the office, and he had his dark-blue suit on.

"In time to make a cocktail for you!" the Baron cried out with a burst of laughter.

"You'd make a first-rate butler," said Father, but he did not smile.

When they sat down to lunch, with the little girls sitting quiet and respectful at one end of the table, the Baron began to tell them of what his own mother had meant to him. His teeth shone out like stars and he ate his food with gusto. The sun was on his face binding great wreaths of beauty to his brows.

"When you grow up, little girls," he said, "it does a terrible thing to your mother. It wipes the light right out of her sweet face and puts something else you never thought of there. Br-rr, rr-rr," said the Baron in his own peculiar language, and he shook as if the cold had struck him. "It sometimes keeps me awake at night, the awful things that one year after another put into my mother's eyes. She couldn't get used to me being in the army. She thought she could persuade everyone that I had dressed up like an

army officer just for the fun. When I'd come home to her,
she'd say: 'Now you will take off the uniform,' as if that
would make a little boy of me again!"

The Baron helped himself to the chicken and cream sauce
sown with scarlet peppers. But in spite of his interest in
this, his thoughts were elsewhere, for he was telling them
of the first time he ran away from home.

"My *Mutter,* she looked in all the cafés for two days
for me, and she went to every musical revue in town, where
she hated to be. She waited outside the opera every night,
because she couldn't bear to go inside and see the stairs
where my father dropped dead from his heart when he was
a young man of thirty-five. Think of that! Dead from
singing too loud, and eating too well, and drinking too much
wine. Now that's a fine way to pop off, Mr. *Mutter,* what
do you know about it? My God, what a wonderful look
that man left behind in my poor mother's face!"

The Baron threw aside his knife and fork in his emotion.

"My God, Mr. *Mutter!*" he cried out to Father. "Sometimes I think I could talk for the rest of my life to your
children here, saying, 'Be good, be good, be good to that
wonderful thing that God gives you for a little while!' Sometimes I think I could go down on my knees," said the Baron,
"and ask them that they be good to their wonderful little
mother."

Father wiped his lips with his napkin and he sat looking
at the Baron.

"You mean because of her resemblance to your own
mother?" Father said politely.

"My God, yes!" cried the Baron. But he picked up his
knife and fork again as though his taste for the food before
him had returned. "Here we are, living men, Mr. *Mutter,*"
he said after a moment. "But do you think that either one
of us could bring that wonderful look to Mrs. *Mutter* that
one dead man gave to my own mother's face?"

"I'm quite sure that, either alive or dead, I couldn't,"
said Father.

"And all the time she was looking for me, the poor
woman," said the Baron, "all the time I was out of the
city. I grew up overnight, and I went off with a soubrette
into the country. I——"

Father laid down his napkin and pushed his chair back
from the table.

"After all," he said, "there are children present whose development may be less precocious than yours was——"

The little girls did not lift their eyes. In a minute their father stood up and said he must be going back to the office. The Baron stood up and bowed a little over the table.

"I don't doubt I'll see you this evening," Father said.

They all watched the limousine turn and saw Father driven down the driveway, the gravel crackling slowly under the soft, elegant tires on the wheels.

"What's a soubrette?" one of the children said.

"It's a kind of a frying pan," said Mother. She looked without smiling at the Baron. "Well, what happened next?" she said. The Baron gave her a cigarette from his case and lighted it for her.

"My God. It was awful," he said.

"I should have thought it would be awfully nice," said Mother.

"Two days in the country with a—with a——" said the Baron.

"With a frying pan," said Mother, smoking. "Do, please, go on."

But the Baron jumped up, as if in anger, and started across the terrace. Suddenly he came back and stood great and broad, towering and mighty over Mother's chair.

"Two days!" he thundered at her. "Two days I kept jumping out of the window to see the trees, or the sky, or the river, or anything that tasted fresh and good!"

"Just like a musical-comedy officer!" said Mother lightly.

"Very well," said the Baron. The color ran up into his golden face. "Very well," he said, and he turned and walked away.

He went the length of the terrace and down the steps, and they could hear his white shoes crunching across the drive. The little girls, having finished their fruit, folded their napkins and followed Mother to the balustrade. There they saw the top of the Baron's head disappearing around the grape arbor's arch.

"It might be almost anywhere," Mother said to them. Her voice was soft and filled with love for them. She stood looking out over the sight of the river and the thick curve of woods above the shining bands of blue. There were no barges or ferries to spoil it just at that moment, and the current seemed swift and clean, although the city lay hidden not far beyond. "It might be almost anywhere, it's so lovely,"

Mother said, and she took the little girls' hands. "He's such
a little child," she said, "we'd better go and see."

They found the Baron on his knees looking for four-leaf
clovers; for things went in and out of his head like this,
and no anger could fix them there. Mother and the little
girls sat down and spread out their skirts on the grasses.
They saw Mother's crossed ankles and her little, high-heeled
boots, and they saw with shyness their own and each other's
bare red knees sprinkled over with yellow hair. They tried
to cover their knees, but could not. But the Baron, in any
case, was talking about the new roles he was going to sing.

In the afternoon he wrote a one-act opera for them. He
sat on the bench in the music room, rippling it out across
the keyboard: songs and ballets that charmed them and set
them to dancing because they were like so many tunes
they had heard before. All afternoon Mother sat in the window, stitching new skirts and cloaks on the puppets. In the
end it was an opera filled with humorous songs, written
out nimble and fast by the Baron's pen as he played with
the other hand, preserved for them in notes with tails and
without tails on the glazed, ruled sheets.

Mother accompanied them day after day, and in a little
while the children knew it all, could sing out the parts
without laughing, and could make the saucepan dance on
its strings. "An *opéra-comique* in one act," said the Baron,
"entitled: *The Soubrette, the Saucepan, and the Percolator.*"
He himself sang the coffee percolator's part, striking his broad
ringing chest and shouting with joy when they practiced
it together. The Soubrette was a frying pan, very shiny and
small, and Mother had stuck a piece of her own blue feather
over the painted eyes.

On the night of the performance Father sat down in the
front row; and when the curtain went up he said:

"The Soubrette looks like Mother."

"How silly!" said Mother from where she was softly playing the opening bars. The children saw her turn her head
in the candlelight and smile at the dinner guests who now
made up the audience. The scene before them was the top
of a kitchen stove and in a moment the Percolator was
jerked onto the stage, and the Baron began to sing his
stirring song.

"*Moi, le Percolator,* perka, perka, perk!" sang his rich
wondrous voice. The song was taken from the Toreador's,
but it did not matter at all. Deeply, widely rang out the

bubbling voice of the Baron from behind the tall curtain, while the silver Percolator in a purple cape strutted across the stove. "*Je perk, je perk, je perk!*" sang the Baron, and now the little Soubrette suddenly leaped upright from where she had been reclining on the coals. Her mouth was painted open for singing, and the children's voices blended and lifted together to give her speech. She uttered one phrase:

"*Quand tu es là, je ne pense qu'à ton percolating!*" and then the Baron again burst into song. His gay mouth opened wide behind the children, and his voice torrented out upon them, so close that it set their hearts to quaking. In his magic throat there swelled a breaking sorrow, a terrible, stirring sorrow that made their spines go cold with joy. Every other time and all other music had been but a preparation for this wild moment. Surely the stones and the beams of the house must fall when his voice arched up as ringing and strong as stone itself, and he called out, as though summoning someone to his side:

"*Soubrette, ma poêle à frire, je t'aime!*"

Everyone in the room burst into instantaneous applause, but in a moment, Father said in a voice that could be heard quite clearly:

"I've always liked my Bizet sung by the Italians or French. The Teutonic interpretation leaves me a little cold."

Then, like a small, passionate choir, the children's voices were softly raised in song. Behind them hummed the Baron's voice, tender, wooing as a cello, shaping them and guiding them toward love. Softly their mother played the breathless bars, and their own frail lungs went wide and piped all their mother's loveliness to beauty for the world to hear. The Frying Pan hastened across the glowing stage to the Percolator's side and melted into his embrace.

Spout to painted mouth, thus it was the Saucepan found them, and by a wonderful feat, steam exploded in fury from under his lid. He sent them clattering apart, the Soubrette's blue feather blowing in agitation. He tossed his tin cover down on the stove and minced his anger out. It was the Baron's voice again that gave vent to a pompous, testy ire; but the Baron's voice turned high in spite, running shallow, and his mouth turned up to smile.

> *Je suis une casserole pleine d'affaires,*
> *Je trouve les arts bien amers.*
> *L'Etat Civil, les Codes, la Loi,*

Sont toujours respectés, grâce à moi.
Je n'ai pas le temps de m'amuser
Car je fais la cuisine—c'est la vérité!
Je n'ai pas le temps pour quoi que ce soit!
Je suis une casserole!

The Saucepan began a *pas seul* across the stage, but suddenly Father stood up among all the laughing people.

"What is the matter?" said Mother's soft voice across the dark as she played the music.

"Haven't the time to be amused," said Father. There was a little stir of surprise among the guests.

"Don't be so silly!" Mother cried out, for now the Baron had ceased singing.

"I don't like the part that's been given me," said Father loudly. He had brought the whole performance to an end.

"But you're not the Saucepan!" cried Mother, and everybody laughed. Even the Baron behind the wings stood shaking with laughter. "Ha, ha, ha, ha, ha!" his golden notes rang out.

"My God, Mr. *Mutter!*" he called out in his thundering voice. "You don't even look like a saucepan!"

"I suppose I do!" said Father savagely from the door. "It was just something that hadn't occurred to me before!"

Sometimes at night the children remembered how the Baron looked when he was laughing, or how he threw his head up in the sun, or how his hands spread wide over the keyboard of the piano. That was the last time he ever came to the house, but they remembered him for a long time after he went away, and how Mother had lain on the bed, and how the wind or something else had moaned and sobbed at the window like a woman crying all night.

The Rumor

BY ERSKINE CALDWELL

To GEORGE WILLIAMS went the distinction of being the first to suggest making Sam Billings the new town-treasurer. The moment he made the nomination at the annual town meeting there was an enthusiastic chorus of approval that resulted in the first unanimous election in the history of Androscoggin. During the last of the meeting everybody was asking himself why no one had ever thought of Sam Billings before.

The election of Sam to the office of town-treasurer pleased everybody. He was a good business man and he was honest. Furthermore, the summer hotel property that he owned and operated on the east shore of Androscoggin Lake paid about a tenth of the town's total tax assessment, and during the season he gave employment to eighty or ninety people whose homes were in the town. After he was elected everybody wondered why they had been giving the office to crooks and scoundrels for the past twenty years or more when the public money could have been safe and secure with Sam Billings. The retiring treasurer was still unable to account to everybody's satisfaction for about eighteen hundred dollars of the town's money, and the one before him had allowed his books to get into such a tangled condition that it cost the town two hundred and fifty dollars to hire an accountant to make them balance.

Clyde Ballard, one of the selectmen, took George aside to talk to him when the meeting was over. Clyde ran one of the general stores in the village.

"You did the town a real service today," he told George. "Sam Billings is the man who should have been treasurer all the time. How did you come to think of him?"

"Well," George said, "Sam Billings was one of my dark horses. The next time we need a good selectman I'll trot another one of them out."

"George, there's nothing wrong with me as a selectman, is there?" Clyde asked anxiously.

"Well, I'm not saying there is, and I'm not saying there's not. I'm not ready to make up my mind yet. I'll wait and see if the town builds me a passable road over my way. I may want to buy me an automobile one of these days and if I do I'll want a lot of road work done between my place and the village."

Clyde nodded his head understandingly. He had heard that George Williams was kicking about his road and saying that the selectmen had better make the road commissioners take more interest in it. He shook hands with George and drove back to the village.

The summer-hotel season closed after the first week in

September and the guests usually went home to Boston and
New York Tuesday or Wednesday after Labor Day. Sam
Billings kept his hotel open until the first of October because there were many men who came down over the
weekends to play golf. In October he boarded up the windows and doors and took a good rest after working hard all
summer. It was two or three weeks after that before he
could find out what his season's profits were, because he
took in a lot of money during July and August.

That autumn, for the first time in two or three decades,
there was no one who spoke uneasily concerning the treasurer
or the town's money. Sam Billings was known to be an
honest man, and because he was a good business man everybody knew that he would keep the books accurately. All
the money collected was given to Sam. The receipt of the
money was promptly acknowledged, and all bills were paid
when presented. It would have been almost impossible to
find a complaint to make against the new treasurer.

It was not until the first real snow of the winter, which
fell for three days during the first week in January, that
anything was said about the new town-treasurer. Then overnight there was in general circulation the news that Sam
Billings had gone to Florida.

George Williams drove to the village the same afternoon
the news reached him over on the back road. He happened
to be listening to a conversation on the party line when
something was said about Sam Billings having gone to Florida, otherwise George might possibly have waited a week or
longer before somebody came by his place and told him.

He drove his horse to the village in a hurry and went
into Clyde Ballard's store. They were talking about Sam
Billings when George walked in.

George threw off his heavy coat and sat down in a chair
to warm his feet against the stove.

"Have you heard about it yet, George?" Clyde asked him.

"Sure I have, and God never made a bigger scoundrel
than Sam Billings," he answered. "I wouldn't trust him with
a half-dollar piece of my money any farther than I can
toss a steer by the tail."

"I heard you was one of Sam's principal backers," one
of the men said from the other side of the stove. "You
shouldn't talk like that about your prime candidate, George."

Clyde came up to the stove to warm his hands and light
a cigar.

"George," he said, winking at the other men around the fire, "you told me that Sam Billings was your dark-horse candidate—you must have meant to say *horse-thief*."

Everybody shouted and clapped his knees and waited for George to say something.

"I used to swear that Sam was an honest man," George began seriously, "but I didn't think then that he would turn around and run off to Florida with all the town's money in his pants. At the next election I'm going to vote to tie the town's money around my old black cow's neck. I'd never again trust an animal that walks standing up on its hind legs."

"Well, George," Clyde said, "you ain't heard it all, about Sam yet. Can you stand a little more?"

"What else did he do?" George stood up to hear better.

"He took Jenny Russell with him. You know Jenny Russell—Arthur Russell's oldest girl. I guess he's having plenty of good times with her and the town's money down in Florida. I used to think that I had good times when I was younger but Sam Billings's got me beat a mile when it comes to anything like that."

George sat down again. He filled his pipe and struck a match.

"So he made off with a woman too, did he? Well, that's what they all do when they get their hands on some money that don't belong to them. Those two things go hand-in-hand—stolen money and women."

"He picked a good-looker while he was about it," another of the men said. "He'd have to travel a far piece to find a better-looker than Jenny Russell. And if he don't have a good time with her he ought to step aside for a younger man."

George grunted contemptuously and sucked the flame into the bowl of his pipe. He remembered the time when he had had an eye on Jenny Russell himself.

"I heard it said this morning that Sam was going to have his hotel property fired so he could collect the insurance on it," Clyde said from behind the counter where he was waiting on a customer. "If he does that, the whole town assessment will have to be changed so we will be able to collect enough tax money to keep the roads repaired and the schools running."

Nobody said anything for several minutes. George glared

at each man around the stove. The raising of the tax-rate stared everybody full in the face.

Clyde came over to the stove again and stood beside it, warming his hands.

"My wife heard it said over the party line last night—" He paused and looked from face to face. Everybody in the store leaned forward to hear what Clyde was going to say. "—She heard that Sam Billings murdered one of those rich men from New York in his hotel last summer. I guess he killed him to get his money. He wouldn't stop at anything now."

"Well, I always said that Sam Billings was the biggest crook that ever lived in the town of Androscoggin," George said disgustedly. "The last time I saw Sam I thought to myself, 'Now, how in hell is Sam Billings going to keep the town's money from getting mixed up with his own?' I know now that I was right in thinking that. We ought to catch him and have him sent to the Federal prison for the rest of his life."

"He'll be a slick eel to catch," Clyde said. "Men like Sam Billings figure out their getaway months beforehand. He's probably laughing at us up here now, too. That's the way they all do."

"The Federal government knows how to catch men like Sam Billings," George said. "They can catch him if they start after him. But I don't suppose they would bother with him. We can send him to the State prison, though."

The men around the stove agreed with George. They said that if they ever got their hands on Sam they would do their best to have him sent to prison for as long a time as the law would allow.

A few days later George saw another of the selectmen and asked him about Sam Billings. George's plan of action was to get the Florida police to locate him and then have the sheriff send a deputy down to bring him back for trial. The selectman was in favor of getting Arthur Russell to have the Federal government go after Sam on the charge of taking his daughter Jenny out of the State. In that case, he explained to George, they could get Sam back without it costing the town any of its own money.

George was in favor of any plan just so long as Sam Billings was brought back and tried for stealing the money.

Later in the winter somebody told George that Sam had taken Jenny Russell and gone to Cuba with her. After that was generally known, there was nobody in the whole town who would take up for Sam or speak a word in his behalf. He had taken the town's money and made off with it. That was all there was to it.

"I never did take any stock in that Billings," George said in Clyde's store in the village. "He made so much money out of his hotel he couldn't be satisfied with what he had of his own, but had to go and take the town's money too. And if I was Arthur Russell I'd get the Federal law after him for taking Jenny off like he did. If she was my daughter and Sam Billings took her off to Florida for a good time, or wherever it was he went to, I'd get him arrested so quick it would scare the hide off his back."

"We made a big mistake when we trusted all the town's money to him," Clyde admitted. "It will take us ten years to wipe out that loss. He had almost a thousand dollars when he left."

"You were one of the fools that voted for him," George said. "It's a pity the voters ain't got more sense than they have about such things."

"If I remember correctly," Clyde retorted, "you nominated Sam Billings for town-treasurer."

George went outside and unhitched his horse. He drove home without answering Clyde Ballard.

Nothing further was heard either directly or indirectly from Sam during the remainder of the winter. There were no bills that had to be paid right away though, and the town was not yet suffering because the funds were in Sam's possession.

Early that spring, when Sam usually began getting his hotel into shape for the season that opened in June, everybody in town heard one day that he was back home. Sam Billings had been seen in the village early one morning hiring a crew of carpenters and laborers. He had always made repairs on his hotel property at the same time each year.

And Jenny Russell was back home too, and everybody knew about it the same day.

There was a crew of twenty men at work around the hotel Monday morning, getting it ready for the coming season. The boards were removed from the windows and doors, and a new boathouse was being built beside the landing-float in front of the hotel. All the unemployed men in town went to the hotel and applied for jobs, because everybody

knew that Sam Billings paid good wages and settled promptly every Saturday night.

Sam went about his business just as he had always done
each spring. No one told him of the things that had been
said about him during the past winter, and he knew nothing
about the charges that Clyde Ballard and George Williams
and practically everybody else in town had talked about all
winter.

George went to the village the first of the week and
heard that Sam was back in town for the summer. He went
into Clyde's store and sat down on the counter.

"Well, I guess the town's money is safe enough," he told
Clyde. "Sam Billings is back home, and I hear that Jenny
Russell is too."

"I heard over the party line last night that Sam bought a
big hotel down in Florida last autumn." Clyde said. "He
hired Jenny Russell to go down there with him to see that
the chamber-maids kept it clean and orderly. Jenny Russell
is a good worker, and I guess Sam figured that she was a
better supervisor than he could get anywhere else. She
keeps his hotel here clean and orderly all the time."

"Sure, Jenny is a good supervisor," said George. "There's
no better worker anywhere than Jenny Russell. I used to
think I'd hire her for my house-keeper, and maybe marry
her some day. Sure, she is a fine supervisor. Sam Billings
is a good business man and he knows the kind of help he
needs for his two high-class hotels."

"There's no sense in worrying about the town's money,"
Clyde said. "Sam Billings is an honest man."

"Sure, Sam is. There never was a more honest man alive
than Sam Billings. I've known Sam all my life. The town's
money is just as safe with him as it would be in my own
hands. Sam Billings is an honest man, Clyde."

There Was a Young Lady of Perth

BY WILLIAM SAROYAN

I sold the first issue of *Liberty* magazine. In it was the
beginning of the memoirs of George M. Cohan, and a
limerick contest, for which the first prize was an enormous

sum of money. Was it five thousand dollars, fifty thousand, or five hundred thousand? In any case, it was enough to make me stop and think about there having been a young lady of Perth.

Now, of course, I'm not unaware that most people don't remember the first issue of *Liberty* magazine, if in fact they remember the second. How could they? The magazine saw the light of day when I was not much more than eleven or twelve, or thirteen or fourteen.

Did I sell it, or did I buy it? Did I make a profit of two and a half cents, or did I throw away a nickel? Memory fails me, and while it's not as bad as if a bank had failed me, it's bad enough, because I *deal* in memory. And when memory fails me, I'm in trouble. I have either got to invent, or I have got to do research.

I can invent fair to middling, feeling an awful liar all the while, but I can't do research worth a bottle cap. I forget what I'm looking for and wind up with six or seven other things that I can't use. I don't mind inventing if there is a little aesthetic truth in it, as we say in the profession—"versimilitude," I once heard one writer say, but I can't vouch for either the spelling or the aptness. *Very similar* would have to be the words I would use, because I can spell those words and believe I know what they mean.

George M. Cohan happened to be a man I admired even more than I admired Benjamin Franklin, who was quite simply one of the truly great cutups in my life, as of course (later on, and in a different way) George M. Cohan was. I knew Ben had put up a kite and taken a chance on electrocution in order to invent electricity, and I knew he had written a boy's story called *The Autobiography of,* but the thing I liked about him was his easygoing way of getting to be a great man. Finally, they sent him to Paris as the ambassador, and he *enchanted* the French, in their own words.

And so, in that first issue of *Liberty* magazine I was eager to find out how George M. Cohan had begun his life, because George, the Yankee Doodle Dandy, was still alive and kicking. I thought it would be interesting to find out his secret of success, in case someday our paths were to cross. There was no such chance with Ben Franklin, of course.

Was the year 1924? If so, Ben had been dead for some time, and George M. was surely not much more than thirty.

Or might it have been forty? Thirty or forty, he was certainly at the height of his fame, writing plays, singing, dancing, and being an all-round American Boy, born on Independence Day. They made a movie about him, but I presumed they had done it for money, so I never saw it.

The world was different then, whether it was 1924, or a couple of years earlier, or a couple later. It was just plain different. It wasn't necessarily better, and in all probability it was worse, but an American Boy had a chance in those days, on his own, unsponsored, so to say. All he needed was willingness, wit, and vitality, and so it was great to be an American, to be under voting age, to be unknown, to have the challenge there night and day, still unmet.

Liberty magazine had a fine editorial policy, although I have forgotten precisely what it was. In the name of something, somebody meant to be an American Boy, and to make money. I envied him, although I didn't know his name. He was back of the whole thing, though, and the arrival of his magazine into my life an event of some importance.

After work, I examined the magazine from cover to cover to find out what it came to, and then I read George M. Cohan's contribution, which I found fascinating, because he was swift, confident, and talented. He was born backstage, and as soon as he could walk he went out and wowed 'em, singing, dancing, and telling jokes.

The photographs of George and his beautiful sister and his handsome father and mother were an inspiration, but in those days the theater wasn't my line, and so if I was to get started in the business of making my fame and fortune, out of the pages of *Liberty* magazine, it would have to be by winning the limerick contest, by making something out of the fact that there *was* a young lady of Perth, if in fact that was what it was, as it probably wasn't, although it was certainly the equivalent of it.

The trouble was I didn't know anything about limericks, but *Liberty* magazine gave a brief history of them, how they had originated in a place called Limerick, and the magazine also gave three or four illustrations of perfect ones. These were incredibly clever, apt, wise, and witty. Somebody from somewhere tried to do something and as a result something unexpected happened. In a way, that was a little like the story of my life up to that time, and now it was time for a change. Instead of being the subject of a limerick, I wanted to be a writer of one, I wanted to be the writer of the greatest limerick of all time, because that would mean that I would win the contest, I would win the money, and people would say, "There goes the American Boy who wrote the limerick."

I couldn't think of a second line, though. There was a young lady of Perth; who she was or what she was up to, I couldn't guess.

I kept it in mind, though. I had the first line, supplied by the magazine, and all I needed next was a second line that was so extraordinary that the rest of the lines of the limerick would fall into place and sound like perfection itself. The words that rhymed with Perth were "worth," "mirth," "birth," "dearth," "girth," and, of course, "earth" —all good usable words. There *was* an earth, there *was* a birth, there were mirth and worth and the others, and so all I really needed to do was rattle them together and throw them out like dice, for a natural. With my conscious mind, the mind that was supposed to be equal to such a challenge, equal to thought, I had little luck. "There was a young lady of Perth who didn't know what she was worth," for instance, just wasn't right.

And so I slept on it, or, to be a little more exact, it slept on me. The young lady of Perth was here, there, and everywhere, but the limerick remained incomplete, and I woke up in the morning knowing I had been in a fight and hadn't won.

That first issue of *Liberty* magazine passed from me to my brother, who also took an interest in the limerick contest, and then to my sisters, so that before the second issue of the magazine came out everybody in my family was at work trying to win fame and fortune as a limerick writer. We weren't good at it, though. I don't know who fell out first, but I know it wasn't me. I think it was my brother, who tended to be cynical about contests in general, and about theories of how easy it is to rise in the world. He said it just wasn't an overnight proposition. A man of thirteen, he believed, was a little less likely to be invited to Washington to discuss educational reform with President Harding than a man of sixteen, for instance. But a man of sixteen was less likely than a man of nineteen, and our neighborhood was pretty well stocked with nineteen-year-old American Boys who knew a thing or two about educational reform—throw out teachers who had remained stupid after considerable schooling. That was the basic educational reform principle of the neighborhood.

I noticed with regret my brother's scorn for the limerick-writing contest, and I made up my mind to be different. I made up my mind to have stick-to-itiveness, because I had heard that everybody who had ever amounted to anything had had stick-to-itiveness. I reasoned that if *they* had had it, and had *needed* it, and had won through to success on *account* of it, I was going to have it, too. Every evening when I got home from work I checked with the other contestants, only to discover, after two or three such checks, that everybody had given up. I also discovered that my persistence, or stick-to-itiveness, was being taken for a nuisance.

Somebody said, "To hell with the young lady of Perth. This is Fresno."

This amounted to nothing better than the waving of the white flag, surrender, armistice, failure, humiliation. I was flabbergasted and more determined than ever to win the contest.

There was time, the deadline was still ten or eleven days off, and I felt confident that long before the required midnight postmark of the final day I would have my limerick neatly written and on its way to *Liberty* magazine in—wherever it was. I don't believe it was in New York, or in Chicago, either. I just don't remember where it was, but it was somewhere, and this place could be reached by train mail in a matter of six or seven days. There was no airmail in those days.

One afternoon the chain on my bike broke while I was sprinting, and I was sent over the handle bars onto the pavement. Something was always happening to my bike. It wasn't holding up, but nobody ever said, "They don't make them the way they used to." The wire spokes of the wheel were always loosening, and while I had a spoke tightener, as every practical-minded messenger had, whenever I tightened a couple of loose spokes I noticed that the alignment of the wheel became unbalanced. You had to be an expert even in a thing like that.

The dive was on my head, which was at least a little protected by the blue cap of Postal Telegraph, or at any rate would have been had the cap not fallen off just before my head struck the pavement, when I needed it most.

It was quite a jolt, but, as always, I hoped there had been no witnesses, for I despised having accidents, and I resented help and sympathy.

The minute my head hit the pavement the whole winning limerick came to me, and I was stunned by the brilliance and rightness of it, the simplicity and inevitability of it, and by the fact that it had taken a foolish accident to bring the thing around. I was all set to begin committing it to memory before I forgot it when an elderly lady of Fresno hurried up and asked, as a mother or a grandmother might, "Are you all right?"

"Yes, ma'am, it's nothing, thank you." All quickly said, so she would be satisfied and move along, but no, she wanted to chat.

"Are you sure? Here, let me help you up."

Well, then I realized I was still flat on my back, so I leaped to my feet, picked up the fallen bike, and began to unwheel the chain, which had become entangled around the hub.

There was no getting away from her, or rather no getting her away from me. On and on she chatted, and of course my upbringing compelled me to answer every question respectfully.

At last I was able to walk away with my bike. It was time to commit the limerick to memory, but all I could remember was the first line again. The thing was lost.

I was still so mad that evening when I got home that my brother couldn't help noticing.

"What's the matter with you?"

"Lousy chain broke again."

I didn't want to tell him about the limerick because I was afraid he wouldn't believe me, and a younger brother hates not being believed. I'd *had* that whole limerick right after I had dived, and it was the winning one, too. I'd had it, and then that nice old lady of Fresno had come up and had made me forget it. My brother examined my head and told me there was a bump there. I told him I *knew* there was a bump there. He wasn't really satisfied with my reason for being mad, and little by little he won me over to a full confession. I was astonished that he *didn't* disbelieve me. On the contrary, he was sure that I *had* had the winning limerick and had lost it.

"The thing to do," he said, "is to get it back."

"How?"

"The same way."

"Sprint and break the chain and dive on my head? Nothing doing."

"That's how it came to you. That's how you'll get it back. If you want something badly enough, you've got to pay the price for it."

"It was an accident," I said. "I'm not going to have an accident on purpose. I don't think it's possible in the first place, and even if it were, even if I *had* another accident, how do I know what kind of limerick I'd get out of it? It might not be the winner at all."

"Suit yourself," my brother said.

Now, it never occurred to me that he was having fun, and I kept thinking about his suggestion. After supper we went out to the back yard, where our wheels were. I looked at mine, with the chain as good as new again, repaired by Frank the Portuguese bike man, from whom we had bought our bikes, secondhand, and after a moment I got on the bike real slow and easy and rode out across the empty lot adjoining our back yard, and then out onto the sidewalk of San Benito Avenue, and then out onto the pavement of M Street, and there I began to sprint. My brother came running after me, shouting, "For God's sake, I was only kidding, don't do it, you'll kill yourself."

Well, the fact is I really hadn't *meant* to do it, I had only meant to sprint, racing, going as fast as I could go, as a kind of test of the fates. The chain was strong, and it just wasn't likely to break—unless the fates wanted me to take another dive, get back the winning limerick, and be on my way to fame and fortune. I heard my brother. The memory of what it was I had a lot of—stick-to-itiveness—came back to me, and I decided I *would* do my best to make that repaired chain snap and break, after all. I raced three blocks to Ventura Avenue without luck; the chain was as strong as ever. My brother rode up on his wheel and said, "Now, look, if you really think that that's the way to get the lost limerick back, I'll do everything I can to help you."

"How?"

"I'll hold you about two feet above the pavement—that's enough—and drop you. It's safer that way."

We were riding back on M Street in any case, so we rode on up to the Rainier Brewery, a kind of Bavarian red-brick castle entangled in railroad tracks and company roads, and we rode around the brewery, closed now, finished for the day, and we discussed the problem. After a while we dismounted and sat on the steps of the brewery to discuss procedure a little further and to make sure that nobody was around. The coast was clear and procedure had been agreed upon, when Eddie Imirian and Johnny Suni came up, bouncing an old tennis ball. My brother and I were challenged to a game of handball against the brewery wall. We won 21 to 18, and then it was dark, but Eddie and Johnny wanted another game, so we played in the dark and won 21 to 12.

When we reached our house, the boys sat with us on our front porch steps and talked about school. It looked as if they never wanted to go home, but finally they did, and my brother said, "Well, how about it?"

"The tar on San Benito Avenue isn't hard enough," I said.

"Want to try the sidewalk?"

"It's *harder* than the pavement I hit."

"Whatever you say."

Well, we were both pretty tired, but it seemed to me this was a matter of stick-to-itiveness if I ever saw one, so I quickly said, "Let's try her."

My brother was holding me around the knees, about two feet over the sidewalk, and was all set to drop me on my head when my mother came out on the front porch with a pitcher of tahn on a tray. "Oh-oh," my brother said.

Well, it was now or never, so I said, "Let go."

Now, I was all set to get back the winning limerick, but my brother didn't let go.

"Why are you holding your brother that way?" my mother said.

"Just exercise," my brother said. "We take turns."

He let me down, and I took him around the knees and held him precisely as he had held me. For a moment I thought of dropping *him*, without plan, but I thought better of it and didn't.

"Come and drink tahn," my mother said.

I let him down and we went up onto the porch and drank two big glasses each of the best drink in the world. Put two cups of yogurt in a pitcher, add four or five cups of cold water, stir, and drink.

Well, the drink was great, because it helped you to know how alive you were, and what a privilege it was.

One of my sisters began to play *Dardanella* on the piano,

and the other began to sing. My brother and I listened and looked around at where we were, and then up at the sky, full of stars. It was kind of silly, in a way, living in a house like that, nothing to it really, a few boards and a little wallpaper, and us, in a whole neighborhood like that, but what could you do? The tahn was great. The air was full of something that made you know you were alive, and the sky seemed a lot like something almost as good as money in the bank.

Pretty soon my sisters came out on the porch. We all sat around and talked and told jokes and laughed. I liked it, but I kept feeling I was losing my stick-to-itiveness, and that was the one thing I couldn't afford to lose. After about an hour we went inside to close up for the night.

My brother dropped me headfirst onto my bed, but all I did was bounce. The winning limerick didn't come back. And then I dropped him, and all *he* did was bounce.

I did my best with my conscious mind, and sent in a limerick, and lost.

I read every installment of George M. Cohan's life, and I envied him. I read the winning limerick, too. It didn't come to very much.

About forty years later I reached Perth, which is on the west coast of Australia. It seemed like a nice place, something like Fresno. I saw the young lady of Perth in person. I saw her six or seven *hundred* times, as a matter of fact. I *spoke* to her six or seven times. She replied in a nice Australian accent. There was nothing suitable for a limerick in her.

She was just a nice girl.

In 1939 I met George M. Cohan in the offices of a theater in New York. He was a gentle, kindly fellow with a touch of sorrow in his eyes.

Liberty magazine changed hands a couple of times, and then gave up the ghost.

I forgot all about limericks. Also, stick-to-itiveness.

I decided that *don't-stick-to-itiveness* is a pretty usable philosophy, too, especially for a writer.

The Downfall of Fascism in Black Ankle County

BY JOSEPH MITCHELL

EVERY TIME I see Mussolini shooting off his mouth in a news reel or Göring goose-stepping in a rotogravure, I am reminded of Mr. Catfish Giddy and my first encounter with Fascism. In 1923, when I was in the ninth grade in Stonewall, North Carolina, Mr. Giddy and Mr. Spuddy Ransom organized a branch of the Knights of the Ku Klux Klan, or the Invisible Empire, which spread terror through Black Ankle County for several months. All the kids in town had seen "The Birth of a Nation," and they were fascinated by the white robes and hoods worn by the local Klansmen, and by the fiery crosses they burned at midnight on Saturdays in the vacant lot behind the Atlantic Coast Line depot. On Tuesday and Friday, the Klan's meeting nights, the kids would hide in the patch of Jerusalem-oak weeds in the rear of the Planters Bank & Trust Company and watch the Klansmen go up the back stairs to their meeting hall above the bank. Sometimes they reappeared in a few minutes, dressed in flowing white robes, and drove off mysteriously. I spent so many nights hiding in the weed patch that I failed my final examinations in algebra, the history of North Carolina, English composition, and French, and was not promoted, which I did not mind, as I had already spent two years in the ninth grade and felt at home there.

Now, when I look back on that period and reflect on the qualities of Mr. Giddy, Mr. Ransom, and their followers, I wonder why the people of Black Ankle County, particularly the people of Stonewall, stood for the Ku Klux Klan as long as they did. Traditionally, the people of Stonewall are sturdy and self-reliant. In fact, the town was named General Stonewall Jackson, North Carolina, when it was founded right after the Civil War; later the name was shortened to Stonewall. There was certainly nothing frightening about Mr. Giddy, the Führer of the local Klan. His full name was J. Raymond Giddy, but he had a mustache on his plump face which he treated with beeswax and which stuck out sharply on both sides, and consequently he was almost always referred to as Mr. Catfish Giddy, even in the columns of the weekly *Stonewall News*. He was rather proud of the nickname. He used to say, "I may not be the richest man in Black Ankle County, but I sure am the ugliest; you can't take that away from me." Mr. Giddy was a frustrated big businessman. Before he got interested in the Klan, he had organized the Stonewall Boosters and a Stonewall Chamber of Commerce, both of which died after a few meetings. He was always making speeches about big business, but he was never much of a big businessman himself. At the time he and Mr. Ransom organized the Klan he was a travelling salesman for a chewing-tobacco concern. When he returned from a trip he would never brag about how many boxes of cut plug he had sold. Instead, he would brag that the cut plug manufactured in North Carolina in one year, if laid end to end, would damn near reach to Egypt, or Australia, or the moon, or some other distant place.

"In the manufacture of chewing tobacco, my friends," he would boast, "the Tarheel State leads the whole civilized world."

He was the town orator and the town drunk. In his cups, he would walk up and down Main Street, singing. He had a bass voice and his favorite songs were "Old Uncle Bud," new verses for which he would make up as he went along, and a song about Lydia Pinkham's vegetable compound and its effect on the human race, a song he had learned when he was a young man attending a business college in Atlanta. The high-school boys and girls, drinking Coca-Colas in the Stonewall Drug Company, would run to the door and stare and giggle when Mr. Giddy got drunk and marched up Main Street. "Old Uncle Bud," he would sing, "is the jelly-roll king. Got a hump on his back from shaking that thing."

Mr. Ransom was far more frightening than Mr. Giddy. He was a gaunt, wild-eyed farmer. He was a religious fanatic, always screaming about wickedness. Even when he was dressed in his Ku Klux Klan outfit, he could easily be identified because he walked with a peculiar, hobbledehoy gait. He was a deacon in the Stonewall Jackson Baptist Church, the church I went to, and he used to ring the bell before services until he got a little too impassioned one Sunday morning and pulled the rope so hard the bell came unscrewed and fell out of the loft, landing on his left shoulder. After that accident he always walked as if his next step would be his last. Like Mr. Giddy, he had a nickname. He was christened John Knox Ransom, but he was called Mr. Spuddy because he habitually argued that the Southern farmer should quit planting cotton and tobacco and plant Irish potatoes. "Something you can eat," he would argue, smacking his palms together for emphasis. "Goodness gracious, my friends, if you can't sell your crop, you can put it on the table and eat it." One winter he tried to live on Irish potatoes and got so thin his belt wouldn't hold his pants up. His worried wife would urge him to eat some meat to get his strength back, and he would shout, "Is a mule strong? Does a mule eat meat?" His wife, who was a sensible woman, would ask meekly, "Does a mule eat Irish potatoes?"

I don't think Mr. Giddy, the drunken drummer, and Mr. Ransom, the fanatical deacon, thought very highly of each other until Mr. Giddy returned from a selling trip in the winter of 1923 with some booklets abut the Klan he had picked up in Atlanta. Mr. Giddy discreetly distributed the booklets among some of the loafers in Stonewall, and Mr. Ransom got one. After reading it, he came to the conclusion that the best way to fight wickedness, the best way to drive corn-whiskey distillers, loose women, gypsy mule traders and fortune tellers, chautauquas, and Holy Roller preachers out of Black Ankle County was to organize the Klan there.

He and Mr. Giddy got together, hired the hall over the bank, painted the windows black for the sake of secrecy, and enrolled seventeen men in the Klan. They included a tobacco auctioneer, an undertaker, a grocery clerk, an indolent house painter, and a number of farmers. The farmers were all like Mr. Ransom in that they spent less time in their fields than they did around the pot-bellied stoves of the Stonewall Hardware & General Merchandise Company, arguing about religion and politics. Most of the men joined the Klan because it gave them an excuse to get away from their wives at night and because it seemed to them to have even more mystery and ceremony than the Masons or the Woodmen of the World. The undertaker and Mr. Ransom were the only "respectable" men in it; most of the others, according to the standards of Stonewall, were either "common" or "sorry." Some were both—the house painter, for example. I once heard him summed up by an old woman in

Stonewall, who said, "He's common. Fishes in the summer and hunts in the winter, and when it rains he sits by the stove and plays checkers. He sure is one sorry man."

The fathers of some of my friends joined the Klan and gradually I learned many of the Klan secrets. I learned that the initiation fee was ten dollars and that the robe and hood cost six-fifty. A friend of mine swiped his father's Klan books. One was called "The Platform of the Invisible Empire." I persuaded him to let me have it in exchange for Zane Grey's "Riders of the Purple Sage." I still have it. On the cover is this declaration: "The Ku Klux Klan stands on a platform of 100-per-cent Americanism, white supremacy in the South, deportation of aliens, purity of womanhood, and eradication of the chain store." In the book are a number of denunciations of Catholics, Jews, Negroes, and labor unions. The kids in Stonewall spied on the Klan much as kids now play G-men and gangsters; it was a game. We were frightened by the Klansmen, but not too frightened to hide in the weed patch and watch them come and go. I remember one kid, lying beside me in the weeds, pointing to a robed figure and hoarsely whispering, "There goes Pa."

Mules are used almost exclusively instead of horses in the tobacco and cotton fields of Black Ankle County, and during the first weeks of the Klan's existence in Stonewall the members rode plough mules on their night rides about the countryside. They preferred to ride cross-country, probably because that made them feel invincible, and they couldn't use automobiles because they would quickly bog down in the sticky mud of the bottom fields and the sloblands, the black mud which gives the county its name. The mules were supplied by Mr. Ransom and by other members who were farmers. That lasted until Mr. Giddy and Mr. Ransom, as the leaders, sent to Klan headquarters in Atlanta for some white horse-robes. They draped the robes over their mules one dark night and rode out to a sawmill in a swamp to keep a rendezvous with their followers. When they galloped up on their shrouded steeds the mules of the other Klansmen got frightened; they let out angry neighs, reared back on their heels, and stampeded into the swamp with their riders. One Klansman was thrown from his mule and suffered a broken leg and three fractured ribs. After that the Klansmen gave up cross-country riding. They stuck to the highways and used automobiles. Fat Mr. Giddy undoubtedly felt out of place on the sharp back of a plough mule, anyway.

The Klansmen began their terrorism by burning fiery crosses, huge crosses made of fence rails sprinkled with kerosene, in the yards of all the Negro churches in the lower part of the county. Then they kidnapped an aged, irritable blacksmith who was celebrated for his profanity. They covered him with tar. They sprinkled chicken feathers over the tar. Then they tossed him into Bearcat Millpond. I have heard that the old blacksmith crawled out of the millpond with ten brand-new oaths. A few nights later the Klansmen went after a mentally defective woman who used to wander about the county with her fatherless children, sleeping in tobacco barns and haylofts. They flogged her, clipped her hair close to her scalp, and branded a "K" on her head. Next day a rural policeman found the bleeding, frantic woman on a ditch bank beside a country road and took her to a hospital. Later she was sent to an asylum. One night, a few weeks later, they broke into a chain grocery in Stonewall, the A. & P., and wrecked it. The same night they went to a Negro café in the Back Alley, the Negro section of Stonewall, and smashed a big, loud Edison phonograph, which the proprietor of the café had mortgaged her home to buy. Then they began threatening a quiet, lonesome Jew who lived above his dry-goods store on Main Street. Some of the members of the Klan had charge accounts, long unpaid, at his store. At the post office one night, waiting around for the evening mail to be sorted, I heard Mr. Giddy talking about him. He said, "He sits up there all night long, reading books. No telling what he's plotting." The dry-goods merchant went to the hardware store one morning at a time when some of the Klan members were sitting around the stove and bought a double-barrelled shotgun and three boxes of twelve-gauge shells. He was not threatened any more.

Late that spring it was rumored in Stonewall that the Klan had decided to do something about the corn-whiskey-distilling situation. The biggest distiller was Mr. Sledge MacKellar; he employed four men at his copper still in Pocahontas Swamp. We knew he was immune from the Klan because he was Mr. Giddy's personal bootlegger, because he was fabulously expert with a shotgun, and because he had publicly served notice on the Klan. Mr. MacKellar came out of the swamp one afternoon and said he was prepared for "the Bed-Sheets." By that time Klansmen were called "the Bed-Sheets." He said, "I'm a Democrat and I got my rights. The first time one of them Bed-Sheets sticks his head in my front gate, I'm going to take his head right off. I got a shotgun and I got it loaded and I'm just aching to pull the trigger."

We knew the distillers the Klan had in mind were the Kidney boys, and we were not surprised when we heard that a date had been set on which they were to be tarred and feathered. The Kidney boys were three drunken Irish brothers who lived in a house about two and a half miles out from Stonewall and operated a still in Big Cherokee Swamp, behind their house. Their names were Patrick, Pinky, and Francis. They drank about half the whiskey they manufactured. When they came to town that week for supplies, the clerks in the stores kidded them. "I hear the Bed-Sheets are going to call on you boys for a pot of tea Friday night," one clerk said.

The Kidney boys had a hired man, an aged Negro named Uncle Bowleg, who later worked for a relative of mine. One time Uncle Bowleg told me how the Kidney boys brought about the downfall of the Invisible Empire in Black Ankle County. There were three entrances to the Kidney house—a front door, a back door, and a side door. When they heard the Klan was planning a call on Friday night, the brothers rented three dynamite outfits from a man who made his living blasting out tree stumps. They swapped him a gallon of charcoal-cured corn whiskey for the use of the outfits. They buried three great charges of dynamite in the yard, under the three paths leading to the entrances of the house. Wires led from the buried dynamite to batteries, to which switches were attached. The Kidney boys placed the batteries in the house, beneath three windows where they could sit and watch for approaching Klansmen. They planned to throw a switch the moment the Klansmen walked up one of the paths.

That night the Kidney boys turned off all the lights and took places at the windows with the dynamite batteries and switches in their laps. Uncle Bowleg was in the house with them. The Kidneys soon got tired of staring out into the yard, waiting for Klansmen, and ordered Uncle Bowleg to fetch them a jug of whiskey and a pitcher of water. Uncle Bowleg said he was kept busy running from one Kidney to another with the whiskey. The whiskey made them happy and they began to talk, speculating on how much noise their blasts would make. "We'll blow those Bed-Sheets to Kingdom Come," said Pinky.

About ten o'clock, when the moon was high, Francis Kidney, who was guarding the side door, decided he could wait no longer. The whiskey had given him an irresistible desire to throw the switch on his battery.

"Get ready!" he shouted suddenly. "I just can't wait no longer. I'm going to test this dynamite. The Bed-Sheets won't come in by the side door, anyway."

He threw the switch and there was a blast that shook the entire lower half of Black Ankle County. It caused people to leap out of their beds. We heard the blast in my home, and I remember that my grandmother said she thought that Judgment Day or the Second Coming was at hand.

Uncle Bowleg said the blast tore up a massive longleaf pine tree in the yard of the Kidney house and threw it into the highway. Uncle Bowleg was so frightened he jumped under a bed and hid. The Kidneys ran to the front porch and looked at the great tree lying in the highway. It pleased them. They laughed and slapped each other's shoulders. They came in and poured themselves some drinks. Then Patrick and Pinky took their places again, but Francis had thrown his switch, so he lost interest and went to sleep in his chair. In about half an hour, Patrick Kidney, who was guarding the rear door, heard a rustle out in back of the house. He knew it was the wind rustling the leaves on the chinquapin bushes, but all he wanted was an excuse to throw his switch.

"I think I hear them coming!" he shouted to Pinky, who was sitting at the front door with his hand on his switch. "Get ready. I'm going to let go."

Pinky needed some excitement, too. "Throw the switch!" he yelled.

Patrick threw his switch. The blast rattled Pinky and he threw his switch, too. The blasts were almost simultaneous. The slats fell out of the bed under which Uncle Bowleg was hiding and bruised him all over. A big framed picture of the mother of the Kidney brothers fell off the wall and hit Francis on the head. The legs dropped off the kitchen range and it fell apart. The entire back porch was torn loose from the house. The blast blew up the chicken house and a barrel in which the two hounds slept. All the chickens were killed, except an old rooster, and he never crowed again. Next morning there were six dead hens on the roof of the house and dead hens and ducks were scattered all over the yard. The South Carolina line runs near the rear of the

Kidney house, and Uncle Bowleg swears that the hounds landed in South Carolina and were so shocked and outraged they never crossed back into North Carolina again. The mule's stall fell in.

"The roof fell down on that old plug," Uncle Bowleg told me, "and he bolted out into the road with the roof on his back like a saddle and galloped two miles before he felt safe enough to slow down and look around. And there was a rocking chair on the back porch and the dynamite set it to rocking. Next morning it was still rocking."

When the noise died down that night, and when things stopped falling apart, the Kidney brothers looked at each other. They were shamefaced. Suddenly they felt frightened. Without their dynamite, they felt naked and defenseless. "If the Bed-Sheets come now, we're sure done for," Francis said. His mother's picture was raising a bump on his head. All of a sudden the Kidney boys ran out of the house and made a dash for Big Cherokee Swamp, with Uncle Bowleg following. Early next morning Uncle Bowleg got hungry and went back to the house for something to eat but the Kidney boys stayed in the swamp until noon.

As a matter of fact, they would have been just as safe in their wrecked house as they were in the swamp, because the Ku Klux Klan never did show up. The Klan had postponed its scheduled call because Mr. Giddy had arrived at the hall over the bank too drunk to take any interest in Klan matters. However, while the Kidneys were still snoring in the swamp, Mr. Ransom, who hadn't been able to get any sleep because of the three strange blasts, drove into Stonewall in his Ford and picked up Mr. Giddy. Mr. Ransom was sleepy and irritable and Mr. Giddy had a bad hangover, and they were not a happy pair. They drove out to the Kidney house to see what had happened during the night. When they arrived, Uncle Bowleg was sitting in the rocking chair on the front porch, eating a plate of corn bread and molasses. Mr. Giddy and Mr. Ransom walked into the yard and looked into the three gaping holes. Uncle Bowleg watched them like a hawk.

"Spuddy," said Mr. Giddy as he peered into the hole out of which the longleaf pine had come, "that sure is a damned big hole. I sure am glad I wasn't around when those holes were dug."

"Catfish," said Mr. Ransom in a frightened voice, "somebody might of got murdered last night. It's a good thing the Klan didn't ride last night."

Uncle Bowleg said they both stared into the holes and shuddered. Then they got into the Ford and drove away rapidly. During the day all the members of the Invisible Empire took occasion to drive by the Kidney house. They also shuddered when they saw the dynamite pits.

Late that afternoon Mr. Giddy showed up on Main Street. He was drunk again. He walked down Main Street, but he didn't sing. He stopped each person he met and said, "Friend, I have resigned." "Resigned from what, Mr. Catfish?" people asked. "Don't make no difference what I resigned from," he answered. "I just want you to know I resigned." The Ku Klux Klan never held another meeting in Stonewall. In a week or two the black paint was scraped off the windows in the hall above the bank and a "For Rent" sign was hung out. One woman ripped up her husband's Klan robe and made a pillowcase out of the cloth. Others heard about it and did the same. Mrs. Catfish Giddy ripped up her husband's robe and told her friends he was so fat she found enough material in it for two pillowcases, an apron, and a tablecloth.

The French Scarecrow

BY WILLIAM MAXWELL

> *I spied John Mouldy in his cellar*
> *Deep down twenty steps of stone;*
> *In the dusk he sat a-smiling,*
> *Smiling there alone.*
> *—Walter de la Mare.*

DRIVING PAST the Fishers' house on his way out to the public road, George Martin said to himself absent-mindedly, "There's Edmund working in his garden," before he realized that it was a scarecrow. And two nights later he woke up sweating from a dream, a nightmare, which he related next day, lying tense on the analyst's couch.

"I was in this house, where I knew I oughtn't to be, and

I looked around and saw there was a door, and in order to get to it I had to pass a dummy—a dressmaker's dummy without any head."

After a considerable silence the disembodied voice with a German accent said, "Any day remnants?"

"I can't think of any," George Martin said, shifting his position on the couch. "We used to have a dressmaker's dummy in the sewing room when I was a child, but I haven't thought of it for years. The Fishers have a scarecrow in their garden, but I don't think it could be that. The scarecrow looks like Edmund. The same thin shoulders, and his clothes, of course, and the way it stands looking sadly down at the ground. It's a caricature of Edmund. One of those freak accidents. I wonder if they realize it. Edmund is not sad, exactly, but there was a period in his life when he was neither as happy or as hopeful as he is now. Dorothy is a very nice woman. Not at all maternal, I would say. At least, she doesn't mother Edmund. And when you see her with some woman with a baby, she always seems totally indifferent. Edmund was married before, and his first wife left him. Helena was selfish but likable, the way selfish people sometimes are. And where Edmund was concerned, completely heartless. I don't know why. She used to turn the radio on full blast at two o'clock in the morning, when he had to get up at six-thirty to catch a commuting train. And once she sewed a ruffle all the way around the bed he was trying to sleep in. Edmund told me once that her mother preferred her older sister, and that Helena's whole childhood had been made miserable because of it. He tried every way he could think of to please her and make her happy, and with most women that would have been enough, I suppose, but it only increased her dissatisfaction. Maybe if there had been any children . . . She used to walk up and down the road in a long red cloak, in the wintertime when there was snow on the ground. And she used to talk about New York. And it was as if she was under a spell and waiting to be delivered. Now she blames Edmund for the divorce. She tells everybody that he took advantage of her. Perhaps he did, unconsciously. Consciously, he wouldn't take advantage of a fly. I think he needs analysis, but he's very much opposed to it. Scared to death of it, in fact . . ."

Step by step, George Martin had managed to put a safe distance between himself and the dream, and he was beginning to breathe easier in the complacent viewing of someone else's failure to meet his problems squarely when the voice said, "Well—see you again?"

"I wish to Christ you wouldn't say that! As if I had any choice in the matter."

His sudden fury was ignored. A familiar hypnotic routine obliged him to sit up and put his feet over the side of the couch. The voice became attached to an elderly man with thick glasses and a round face that George would never get used to. He got up unsteadily and walked toward the door. Only when he was outside, standing in front of the elevator shaft, did he remember that the sewing room had a door opening into his mother and father's bedroom, and at one period of his life he had slept there, in a bed with sides that could be let down, a child's bed. This information was safe from the man inside—unless he happened to think of it while he was lying on the couch next time.

That evening he stopped when he came to the Fishers' vegetable garden and turned the engine off and took a good look at the scarecrow. Then, after a minute or two, afraid that he would be seen from the house, he started the car and drove on.

The Fishers' scarecrow was copied from a scarecrow in France. The summer before, they had spent two weeks as paying guests in a country house in the Touraine, in the hope that this would improve their French. The improvement was all but imperceptible to them afterward, but they did pick up a number of ideas about gardening. In the *potager*, fruit trees, tree roses, flowers, and vegetables were mingled in a way that aroused their admiration, and there was a more than ordinarily fanciful scarecrow, made out of a blue peasant's smock, striped morning trousers, and a straw hat. Under the hat the stuffed head had a face painted on it; and not simply two eyes, a nose, and a mouth but a face with a sly expression. The scarecrow stood with arms upraised, shaking its white-gloved fists at the sky. Indignant, self-centered, half crazy, it seemed to be saying: *This is what it means to be exposed to experience.* The crows were not taken in.

Effects that had needed generations of dedicated French gardeners to bring about were not, of course, to be imitated successfully by two amateur gardeners in Fairfield County in a single summer. The Fishers gave up the idea of marking off the paths of their vegetable garden with espaliered dwarf apple and pear trees, and they could see no way of having tree roses without also having to spray them, and afterwards having to eat the spray. But they did plant zinnias, marigolds, and blue pansies in with the lettuce and the peas, and they made a very good scarecrow. Dorothy made it, actually. She was artistic by inclination, and threw herself into all such undertakings with a childish pleasure.

She made the head out of a dish towel stuffed with hay, and was delighted with the blue stripe running down the face. Then she got out her embroidery thread and embroidered a single eye, gathered the cloth in the middle of the face into a bulbous nose, made the mouth leering. For the body she used a torn pair of Edmund's blue jeans she was tired of mending, and a faded blue workshirt. When Edmund, who was attached to his old clothes, saw that she had also helped herself to an Army fatigue hat from the shelf in the hall closet, he exclaimed, "Hey, don't use that hat for the scarecrow! I wear it sometimes."

"*When* do you wear it?"

"I wear it to garden in."

"You can wear some other old hat to garden in. He's got to have something on his head," she said lightly, and made the hat brim dip down over the blank eye.

"When winter comes, I'll wear it again," Edmund said to himself, "if it doesn't shrink too much, or fall apart in the rain."

The scarecrow stood looking toward the house, with one arm limp and one arm extended stiffly, ending in a gloved hand holding a stick. After a few days the head sank and sank until it was resting on the straw breastbone, and the face was concealed by the brim of the hat. They tried to keep the head up with a collar of twisted grass, but the grass dried, and the head sank once more, and in that attitude it remained.

The scarecrow gave them an eerie feeling when they saw it from the bedroom window at twilight. A man standing in the vegetable garden would have looked like a scarecrow. If he didn't move. Dorothy had never lived in the country before she married Edmund, and at first she was afraid. The black windows at night made her nervous. She heard noises in the basement, caused by the steam circulating through the furnace pipes. And she would suddenly have the feeling—even though she knew it was only her imagination—that there was a man outside, looking through the windows at them. "Shouldn't we invite him in?" Edmund would say when her glance strayed for a second. "Offer him a drink and let him sit by the fire? It's not a very nice night out."

He assumed that The Man Outside represented for her all the childish fears—the fear of the dark, of the burglar on the stairs, of what else he had no way of knowing. Nor she either, probably. The Man Outside was simply there, night after night, for about six weeks, and then he lost his power to frighten, and finally went away entirely, leaving the dark outside as familiar and safe to her as the lighted living room. It was Edmund, strangely, who sometimes, as they were getting ready for bed, went to the front and back doors and locked them. For he was aware that the neighborhood was changing, and that things were happening—cars stolen, houses broken into in broad daylight—that never used to happen in this part of the world.

The Fishers' white clapboard house was big and rambling, much added onto at one time or another, but in its final form still plain and pleasant-looking. The original house dated from around 1840. Edmund's father, who was a New York banker until he retired at the age of sixty-five, had bought it before the First World War. At that time there were only five houses on this winding country road, and two of them were farmhouses. When the Fishers came out from town for the summer, they were met at the railroad station by a man with a horse and carriage. The surrounding country was hilly and offered many handsome views, and most of the local names were to be found on old tombstones in the tiny Presbyterian churchyard. Edmund's mother was a passionate and scholarly gardener, the founder of the local garden club and its president for twenty-seven years. Her regal manner was quite unconscious, and based less on the usual foundations of family, money, etc. than on the authority with which she could speak about the culture of delphinium and lilies, or the pruning of roses. The house was set back from the road about three hundred yards, and behind it were the tennis courts, the big three-story barn, a guesthouse overlooking the pond where all the children in the neighborhood skated in winter, and, eventually, a five-car garage. Back of the pond, a wagon road went off into the woods and up onto higher ground. In the late twenties, when Edmund used to bring his school friends home for spring and fall weekends and the Easter vacation, the house

seemed barely large enough to hold them all. During the
last war, when the taxes began to be burdensome, Edmund's father sold off the back land, with the guesthouse, the
barn, and the pond, to a Downtown lawyer, who shortly
afterward sold it to a manufacturer of children's underwear.
The elder Mr. and Mrs. Fisher started to follow the wagon
road back into the woods one pleasant Sunday afternoon,
and he ordered them off his property. He was quite within
his rights, of course, but nevertheless it rankled. "In the old
days," they would say whenever the man's name was mentioned, "you could go anywhere, on anybody's land, and no
one ever thought of stopping you."

Edmund's father, working from his own rough plans and
supervising the carpenters and plumbers and masons himself, had converted the stone garage into a house, and he had
sold it to George Martin, who was a bachelor. The elder
Fishers were now living in the Virgin Islands the year round,
because of Mrs. Fisher's health. Edmund and Dorothy still
had ten acres, but they shared the cinder drive with George
and the clothing manufacturer, and, of course, had less
privacy than before. The neighborhood itself was no longer
the remote place it used to be. The Merritt Parkway had
made all the difference. Instead of five houses on the two-
and-a-half-mile stretch of dirt road, there were twenty-five,
and the road was macadamized. Cars and delivery trucks
cruised up and down it all day long.

In spite of all these changes, and in spite of the considerable difference between Edmund's scale of living and his
father's—Dorothy managed with a part-time cleaning woman where in the old days there had been a cook, a waitress,
an upstairs maid, a chauffeur, and two gardeners—the big
house still seemed to express the financial stability and social
confidence and belief in good breeding of the Age of Trel-
lises. Because he had lived in the neighborhood longer than
anyone else, Edmund sometimes felt the impulses of a host,
but he had learned not to act on them. His mother always
used to pay a call on new people within a month of their settling in, and if she liked them, the call was followed by an
invitation to the Fishers' for tea or cocktails, at which time
she managed to bring up the subject of the Garden Club.
But in the last year or so she had lived there, she had
all but given this up. Twice her call was not returned, and
one terribly nice young couple accepted an invitation to tea
and blithely forgot to come. Edmund was friendly when he

met his neighbors on the road or on the station platform, but he let them go their own way, except for George Martin, who was rather amusing, and obviously lonely, and glad of an invitation to the big house.

"I am sewed to this couch," George Martin said. "My sleeves are sewed to it, and my trousers. I could not move if I wanted to. Oedipus is on the wall over me, answering the spink-spank-sphinx, and those are pussy willows, and I do not like bookcases with glass sides that let down, and the scarecrow is gone. I don't know what they did with it, and I don't like to ask. And today *I* might as well be stuffed with straw. This dream I had last night did it. I broke two plates, and woke up unconfident and nervous and tired. I don't know what the dream means. I had three plates and I dropped two of them, and it was so vivid. It was a short dream but very vivid. I thought at first that the second plate —why *three* plates?—was all right, but while I was looking at it, the cracks appeared. When I picked it up, it gave; it came apart in my hands. It was planted with flowers, and it had openwork, and I was in a hurry, and in my hurry I dropped the plates. And I was upset. I hardly ever break anything. Last night while I was drying the glasses, I thought how I never break any of them. They're Swedish and very expensive. The plates I dreamed about were my mother's. Not actually; I *dreamed* that they were my mother's plates. I broke two things of hers when I was little. And both times it was something she had warned me about. I sat in the tea-cart playing house, and forgot and raised my head suddenly, and it went right through the glass tray. And the other was an etched-glass hurricane lamp that she prized very highly. I climbed up on a chair to reach it. And after she died, I could have thought—I don't ever remember thinking this, but I could have thought that I did something I shouldn't have, and she died. . . . Thank you, I have matches. . . . I can raise my arm. I turned without thinking. I can't figure out that dream. My stepmother was there, washing dishes at the sink, and she turned into Helena Fisher, and I woke up thinking, Ah, that's it. They're *both* my stepmothers! My stepmother never broke anything that belonged to my mother, so she must have been fond of her. They knew each other as girls. And I never broke anything that belonged to my stepmother. I only broke something that belonged to my mother. . . . Did I tell you I saw her the other day?"

"You saw someone who reminded you of your mother?"

"No, I saw Helena Fisher. On Fifth Avenue. I crossed over to the other side of the street, even though I'm still fond of her, because she hasn't been very nice to Dorothy, and because it's all so complicated, and I really didn't have anything to say to her. She was very conspicuous in her country clothes." He lit another cigarette and then said, after a prolonged silence, "I don't seem to have anything to say now, either." The silence became unbearable, and he said, "I can't think of anything to talk about."

"Let's talk about you—about this dream you had," the voice said, kind and patient as always, the voice of his father (at $20 an hour).

The scarecrow had remained in the Fishers' vegetable garden, with one arm limp and one arm stiffly extended, all summer. The corn and the tomato vines grew up around it, half obscuring it during the summer months, and then, in the fall, there was nothing whatever around it but the bare ground. The blue workshirt faded still more in the sun and rain. The figure grew frail, the straw chest settled and became a middle-aged thickening of the waist. The resemblance to Edmund disappeared. And on a Friday afternoon in October, with snow flurries predicted, Edmund Fisher went about the yard carrying in the outdoor picnic table and benches, picking up stray flowerpots, and taking one last look around for the pruning shears, the trowel, and the nest of screwdrivers that had all disappeared during the summer's gardening. There were still three or four storm windows to put up on the south side of the house, and he was about to bring them out and hang them when Dorothy, on her hands and knees in the iris bed, called to him.

"What about the scarecrow?"

"Do you want to save it?" he asked.

"I don't really care."

"We might as well," he said, and was struck once more by the lifelike quality of the scarecrow, as he lifted it out of the soil. It was almost weightless. "Did the doctor say it was all right for you to do that sort of thing?"

"I didn't ask him," Dorothy said.

"Oughtn't you to ask him?"

"No," she said, smiling at him. She was nearly three months pregnant. Moonfaced, serenely happy, and slow of movement (when she had all her life been so quick about everything), she went about now doing everything she had always done but like somebody in a dream, a sleepwalker. The clock had been replaced by the calendar. Like the gardeners in France, she was dedicated to making something grow. As Edmund carried the scarecrow across the lawn and around the corner of the house, she followed him with her eyes. Why is it, she wondered, that he can never bear to part with anything, even though it has ceased to serve its purpose and he no longer has any interest in it?

It was as if sometime or other in his life he had lost something, of such infinite value that he could never think of it without grieving, and never bear to part with anything worthless because of the thing he had had to part with that meant so much to him. But what? She had no idea, and she had given some thought to the matter. She was sure it was not Helena; he said (and she believed him) that he had long since got over any feeling he once had for her. His parents were both still living, he was an only child, and death seemed never to have touched him. Was it some early love, that he had never felt he dared speak to her about? Some deprivation? Some terrible injustice done to him? She had no way of telling. The attic and the basement testified to his inability to throw things away, and she had given up trying to do anything about either one. The same with people. At the end of a perfectly pleasant evening he would say "Oh no, it's early still. You mustn't go home!" with such fervor that even though it actually was time to go home and the guests wanted to, they would sit down, confused by him, and stay a while longer. And though the Fishers knew more people than they could manage to see, he would suddenly remember somebody he hadn't thought of or written to in a long time, and feel impelled to do something about them. Was it something that happened to him in his childhood, Dorothy asked herself. Or was it something in his temperament, born in him, a flaw in his horoscope, Mercury in an unsympathetic relation to the moon?

She resumed her weeding, conscious in a way that she hadn't been before of the autumn day, of the end of the summer's gardening, of the leaf-smoke smell and the smell of rotting apples, the hickory tree that lost its leaves before all the other trees, the grass so deceptively green, and the chill that had descended now that the sun had gone down behind the western hill.

Standing in the basement, looking at the hopeless disorder ("A place for everything," his father used to say, "and nothing in its place"), Edmund decided that it was more important to get at the storm windows than to find a place for the scarecrow. He laid it on one of the picnic-table benches, with the head toward the oil burner, and there it sprawled, like a man asleep or dead-drunk, with the line of the hipbone showing through the trousers, and one arm extended, resting on a slightly higher workbench, and one shoulder raised slightly, as if the man had started to turn in his sleep. In the dim light it could have been alive. I must remember to tell Dorothy, he thought. If she sees it like that, she'll be frightened.

The storm windows were washed and ready to hang. As Edmund came around the corner of the house, with IX in one hand and XI in the other, the telephone started to ring, and Dorothy went in by the back door to answer it, so he didn't have a chance to tell her about the scarecrow. When he went indoors, ten minutes later, she was still standing by the telephone, and from the fact that she was merely contributing a monosyllable now and then to the conversation, he knew she was talking to George Martin. George was as dear as the day was long—everybody liked him—but he had such a ready access to his own memories, which were so rich in narrative detail and associations that dovetailed into further narratives, that if you were busy it was a pure and simple misfortune to pick up the telephone and hear his cultivated, affectionate voice.

Edmund gave up the idea of hanging the rest of the storm windows, and instead he got in the car and drove to the village; he had remembered that they were out of cat food and whiskey. When he walked into the house, Dorothy said, "I've just had such a scare. I started to go down in the cellar—"

"I knew that would happen," he said, putting his hat and coat in the hall closet. "I meant to tell you."

"The basement light was burnt out," she said, "and so I took the flashlight. And when I saw the scarecrow I thought it was a man."

"Our old friend," he said, shaking his head. "The Man Outside."

"And you weren't here. I knew I was alone in the house . . ."

Her fright was still traceable in her face as she described it.

On Saturday morning, Edmund dressed hurriedly, the alarm clock having failed to go off, and while Dorothy was getting breakfast, he went down to the basement, half asleep, to get the car out and drive to the village for the cleaning woman, and saw the scarecrow in the dim light, sprawling by the furnace, and a great clot of fear seized him and his heart almost stopped beating. It lay there like an awful idiot, the realistic effect accidentally encouraged by the pair of work shoes Edmund had taken off the night before and tossed carelessly down the cellar stairs. The scarecrow had no feet—only two stumps where the trouser legs were tied at the bottom—but the shoes were where, if it had been alive, they might have been dropped before the person lay down on the bench. I'll have to do something about it, Edmund thought. We can't go on frightening ourselves like this. . . . But the memory of the fright was so real that he felt unwilling to touch the scarecrow. Instead, he left it where it was, for the time being, and backed the car out of the garage.

On the way back from the village, Mrs. Ryan, riding beside him in the front seat of the car, had a story to tell. Among the various people she worked for was a family with three boys. The youngest was in the habit of following her from room to room, and ordinarily he was as good as gold, but yesterday he ran away, she told Edmund. His mother was in town, and the older boys, with some of the neighbors' children, were playing outside with a football, and Mrs. Ryan and the little boy were in the house. "Monroe asked if he could go outside, and I bundled him up and sent him out. I looked outside once, and saw that he was playing with the Bluestones' dog, and I said, 'Monroe, honey, don't pull that dog's tail. He might turn and bite you.'" While she was ironing, the oldest boy came inside for a drink of water, and she asked him where Monroe was, and he said, "Oh, he's outside." But when she went to the door, fifteen minutes later, the older boys were throwing the football again and Monroe was nowhere in sight. The boys didn't know what had happened to him. He disappeared. All around the house was woods, and Mrs. Ryan, in a panic, called and called.

"Usually when I call, he answers immediately, but this

time there was no answer, and I went into the house and
telephoned the Bluestones, and they hadn't seen him. And
then I called the Hayeses and the Murphys, and they hadn't
seen him either, and Mr. Hayes came down, and we all
started looking for him. Mr. Hayes said only one car had
passed in the last half hour—I was afraid he had been kidnapped, Mr. Fisher—and Monroe wasn't in it. And I thought,
When his mother comes home and I have to tell her what
I've done . . . And just about that time, he answered,
from behind the hedge!"

"Was he there all the time?" Edmund asked, shifting into
second as he turned in to his own driveway.

"I don't know where he was," Mrs. Ryan said. "But he
did the same thing once before—he wandered off on me.
Mr. Ryan thinks he followed the Bluestones' dog home.
His mother called me up last night and said that he knew
he'd done something wrong. He said 'Mummy, I was bad
today. I ran off on Sadie. . . .' But Mr. Fisher, I'm
telling you, I was almost out of my mind."

"I don't wonder," Edmund said soberly.

"With woods all around the house, and as Mr. Hayes
said, climbing over a stone wall a stone could fall on him
and we wouldn't find him for days."

Ten minutes later, she went down to the basement for
the scrub bucket, and left the door open at the head of the
stairs. Edmund heard her exclaim, for their benefit, "God
save us, I've just had the fright of my life!"

She had seen the scarecrow.

The tramp that ran off with the child, of course, Edmund thought. He went downstairs a few minutes later,
and saw that Mrs. Ryan had picked the dummy up and
stood it in a corner, with its degenerate face to the wall,
where it no longer looked human or frightening.

Mrs. Ryan is frightened because of the nonexistent
tramp. Dorothy is afraid of The Man Outside. What am I
afraid of, he wondered. He stood there waiting for the oracle
to answer, and it did, but not until five or six hours later.
Poor George Martin called, after lunch, to say that he had
the German measles.

"I was sick as a dog all night," he said mournfully. "I
thought I was dying. I wrote your telephone number on a
slip of paper and put it beside the bed, in case I *did* die."

"Well, for God's sake, why didn't you call us?" Edmund
exclaimed.

"What good would it have done?" George said. "All you could have done was say you were sorry."

"Somebody could have come over and looked after you."

"No, somebody couldn't. It's very catching. I think I was exposed to it a week ago at a party in Westport."

"I had German measles when I was a kid," Edmund said. "We've both had it."

"You can get it again," George said. "I still feel terrible. . . ."

When Edmund left the telephone, he made the mistake of mentioning George's illness to Mrs. Ryan, forgetting that it was the kind of thing that was meat and drink to her.

"Has Mrs. Fisher been near him?" she asked, with quickened interest.

He shook his head.

"There's a great deal of it around," Mrs. Ryan said. "My daughter got German measles when she was carrying her first child, and she lost it."

He tried to ask if it was a miscarriage or if the child was born dead, and he couldn't speak; his throat was too dry.

"She was three months along when she had it," Mrs. Ryan went on, without noticing that he was getting paler and paler. "The baby was born alive, but it only lived three days. She's had two other children since. I feel it was a blessing the Lord took that one. If it had lived, it might have been an imbecile. You love them even so, because they belong to you, but it's better if they don't live, Mr. Fisher. We feel it was a blessing the child was taken."

Edmund decided that he wouldn't tell Dorothy, and then five minutes later he decided that he'd better tell her. He went upstairs and into the bedroom where she was resting, and sat down on the edge of the bed, and told her about George's telephone call. "Mrs. Ryan says it's very bad if you catch it while you're pregnant. . . . And she said some more."

"I can see she did, by the look on your face. You shouldn't have mentioned it to her. What did she say?"

"She said—" He swallowed. "She said the child could be born an imbecile. She also said there was a lot of German measles around. You're not worried?"

"We all live in the hand of God."

"I tell myself that every time I'm really frightened. Unfortunately that's the only time I do think it."

"Yes, I know."

Five minutes later, he came back into the room and said, "Why don't you call the doctor? Maybe there's a shot you can take."

The doctor was out making calls, and when he telephoned back, Dorothy answered, on the upstairs extension. Edmund sat down on the bottom step of the stairs and listened to her half of the conversation. As soon as she had hung up, she came down to tell him what the doctor had said.

"The shot only lasts three weeks. He said he'd give it to me if I should be exposed to the measles anywhere."

"Did he say there was an epidemic of it?"

"I didn't ask him. He said that it was commonly supposed to be dangerous during the first three months, but that the statistics showed that it's only the first two months, while the child is being formed, that you have to worry." Moonfaced and serene again, she went to put the kettle on for tea.

Edmund got up and went down to the basement. He carried the dummy outside, removed the hat and then the head, unbuttoned the shirt, removed the straw that filled it and the trousers, and threw it on the compost pile. The hat, the head, the shirt and the trousers, the gloves that were hands, he rolled into a bundle and put away on a basement shelf, in case Dorothy wanted to make the scarecrow next summer. The two crossed sticks reminded him of the comfort that Mrs. Ryan, who was a devout Catholic, had and that he did not have. The hum of the vacuum cleaner overhead in the living room, the sad song of a mechanical universe, was all the reassurance he could hope for, and it left so much (it left the scarecrow, for example) completely unexplained and unaccounted for.

The Blue-Winged Teal

BY WALLACE STEGNER

STILL IN waders, with the string of ducks across his shoulder, he stood hesitating on the sidewalk in the cold November wind. His knees were stiff from being cramped up all day in the blind, and his feet were cold. Today, all day, he had been alive; now he was back ready to be dead again.

Lights were on all up and down the street, and there was a rush of traffic and a hurrying of people past and around him, yet the town was not his town, the people passing were strangers, the sounds of evening in this place were no sounds that carried warmth or familiarity. Though he had spent most of his twenty years in the town, knew hundreds of its people, could draw maps of its streets from memory, he wanted to admit familiarity with none of it. He had shut himself off.

Then what was he doing here, in front of this poolhall, loaded down with nine dead ducks? What had possessed him in the first place to borrow gun and waders and car from his father and go hunting? If he had wanted to breathe freely for a change, why hadn't he kept right on going? What was there in this place to draw him back? A hunter had to have a lodge to bring his meat to and people who would be glad of his skill. He had this poolhall and his father, John Lederer, Prop.

He stepped out of a woman's path and leaned against the door. Downstairs, in addition to his father, he would find old Max Schmeckebier, who ran a cheap blackjack game in the room under the sidewalk. He would find Giuseppe Sciutti, the Sicilian barber, closing his shop or tidying up the rack of *Artists and Models* and *The Nudist* with which he lured trade. He would probably find Billy Hammond, the night clerk from the Windsor Hotel, having his sandwich and beer and pie, or moving alone around a pool table, whistling abstractedly, practicing shots. If the afternoon blackjack game had broken up, there would be Navy Edwards, dealer and bouncer for Schmeckebier. At this time of evening there might be a few counter customers and a cop collecting his tribute of a beer or that other tribute that Schmeckebier paid to keep the cardroom open.

And he would find, sour contrast with the bright sky and the wind of the tule marshes, the cavelike room with its back corners in darkness, would smell that smell compounded of steam heat and cue-chalk dust, of sodden butts in cuspidors, of coffee and meat and beer smells from the counter, of cigarette smoke so unaired that it darkened the walls. From anywhere back of the middle tables there would be the pervasive reek of toilet disinfectant. Back of the lunch counter his father would be presiding, throwing the pool-hall light switch to save a few cents when the place was empty, flipping it on to give an air of brilliant and success-ful use when feet came down the stairs past Sciutti's shop.

The hunter moved his shoulder under the weight of the ducks, his mind full for a moment with the image of his father's face, darkly pale, fallen in on its bones, and the pouched, restless, suspicious eyes that seemed always look-ing for someone. Over that image came the face of his mother, dead now and six weeks buried. His teeth clicked at the thought of how she had held the old man up for thirty years, kept him at a respectable job, kept him from slipping back into the poolroom Johnny he had been when she married him. Within ten days of her death he had hunted up this old failure of a poolhall.

In anger the hunter turned, thinking of the hotel room he shared with his father. But he had to eat. Broke as he was, a student yanked from his studies, he had no choice but to eat on the old man. Besides, there were the ducks. He felt somehow that the thing would be incomplete unless he brought his game back for his father to see.

His knees unwilling in the stiff waders, he went down the steps, descending into the light shining through Joe Sciutti's door, and into the momentary layer of clean bay-rum smell, talcum smell, hair-tonic smell, that rose past the still revolving barber pole in the angle of the stairs.

Joe Sciutti was sweeping wads of hair from his tile floor, and hunched over the counter beyond, their backs to the door, were Schmeckebier, Navy Edwards, Billy Ham-mond, and an unknown customer. John Lederer was behind the counter, mopping alertly with a rag. The poolroom lights were up bright, but when Lederer saw who was coming he flipped the switch and dropped the big room back into dusk.

As the hunter came to the end of the counter their heads turned toward him. "Well I'm a son of a bee," Navy Ed-wards said, and scrambled off his stool. Next to him Billy Hammond half stood up so that his pale yellow hair took a halo from the backbar lights. "Say!" Max Schmeckebier said. "Say, dot's goot, dot's pooty goot, Henry!"

But Henry was watching his father so intently he did not turn to them. He slid the string of ducks off his shoul-der and swung them up onto the wide walnut bar. They landed solidly—offering or tribute or ransom or whatever they were. For a moment it was as if this little act were private between the two of them. He felt queerly moved, his stomach tightened in suspense or triumph. Then the old man's pouchy eyes slipped from his and the old man came quickly forward along the counter and laid hands on the ducks.

He handled them as if he were petting kittens, his big white hands stringing the heads one by one from the wire. "Two spoonbill," he said, more to himself than to the others crowding around. "Shovel ducks. Don't see many of those any more. And two, no, three, hen mallards and one drake. Those make good eating."

Schmeckebier jutted his enormous lower lip. Knowing him for a stingy, crooked, suspicious little man, Henry almost laughed at the air he could put on, the air of a man of probity about to make an honest judgment in a dispute between neighbors. "I take a budderball," he said thickly. "A liddle budderball, dot is vot eats goot."

An arm fell across Henry's shoulders, and he turned his head to see the hand with red hairs rising from its pores, the wristband of a gray silk shirt with four pearl buttons. Navy Edwards' red face was close to his. "Come clean now," Navy said. "You shot 'em all sitting, didn't you, Henry?"

"I just waited till they stuck their heads out of their holes and let them have it," Henry said.

Navy walloped him on the back and convulsed himself laughing. Then his face got serious again, and he bore down on Henry's shoulder. "By God, you could've fooled me," he said. "If I'd been makin' book on what you'd bring in I'd've lost my shirt."

"Such a pretty shirt, too," Billy Hammond said.

Across the counter John Lederer cradled a little drab duck in his hand. Its neck, stretched from the carrier, hung far down, but its body was neat and plump and its feet were waxy. Watching the sallow face of his father, Henry thought it looked oddly soft.

"Ain't that a beauty, though?" the old man said. "There ain't a prettier duck made than a blue-wing teal. You can have all your wood ducks and redheads, all the flashy ones." He spread a wing until the hidden band of bright blue showed. "Pretty?" he said, and shook his head and laughed suddenly, as if he had not expected to. When he laid the duck down beside the others his eyes were bright with sentimental moisture.

So now, Henry thought, you're right in your element. You always did want to be one of the boys from the pool-room pouring out to see the elk on somebody's running board, or leaning on a bar with a schooner of beer talking baseball or telling the boys about the big German Brown somebody brought in in a cake of ice. We haven't any elk or German Browns right now, but we've got some nice ducks, a fine display along five feet of counter. And who brought them in? The student, the alien son. It must gravel you.

He drew himself a beer. Several other men had come in, and he saw three more stooping to look in the door beyond Sciutti's. Then they too came in. Three tables were going; his father had started to hustle, filling orders. After a few minutes Schmeckebier and Navy went into the cardroom with four men. The poolroom lights were up bright again, there was an ivory click of balls, a rumble of talk. The smoke-filled air was full of movement.

Still more people dropped in, kids in high school athletic sweaters and bums from the fringes of skid road. They all stopped to look at the ducks, and Henry saw glances at his waders, heard questions and answers. John Lederer's boy. Some of them spoke to him, deriving importance from con-tact with him. A fellowship was promoted by the ducks strung out along the counter. Henry felt it himself. He was so mellowed by the way they spoke to him that when the players at the first table thumped with their cues, he got off his stool to rack them up and collect their nickels. It occurred to him that he ought to go to the room and get into a bath, but he didn't want to leave yet. Instead he came back to the counter and slid the nickels toward his father and drew himself another beer.

"Pretty good night tonight," he said. The old man nodded and slapped his rag on the counter, his eyes already past Henry and fixed on two youths coming in, his mouth fixing itself for the greeting and the "Well, boys, what'll it be?"

Billy Hammond wandered by, stopped beside Henry a moment. "Well, time for my nightly wrestle with tempta-tion," he said.

"I was just going to challenge you to a game of call-shot."

"Maybe tomorrow," Billy said, and let himself out care-fully as if afraid a noise would disturb someone—a mild, gentle, golden-haired boy who looked as if he ought to be in some prep school learning to say "Sir" to grownups instead of clerking in a girlie hotel. He was the only one of the poolroom crowd that Henry half liked. He thought he understood Billy Hammond a little.

He turned back to the counter to hear his father talking with Max Schmeckebier. "I don't see how we could on this rig. That's the hell of it, we need a regular oven."

"In my room in back," Schmeckebier said. "Dot old electric range."

"Does it work?"

"Sure. Vy not? I tink so."

"By God," John Lederer said. "Nine ducks, that ought to give us a real old-fashioned feed." He mopped the counter, refilled a coffee cup, came back to the end and pinched the breast of a duck, pulled out a wing and looked at the band of blue hidden among the drab feathers. "Just like old times, for a change," he said, and his eyes touched Henry's in a look that might have meant anything from a challenge to an apology.

Henry had no desire to ease the strain that had been between them for months. He did not forgive his father the poolhall, or forget the way the old man had sprung back into the old pattern, as if his wife had been a jailer and he was now released. He neither forgot nor forgave the red-haired woman who sometimes came to the poolhall late at night and waited on a bar stool while the old man closed up. Yet now when his father remarked that the ducks ought to be drawn and plucked right away, Henry stood up.

"I could do ten while you were doing one," his father said.

The blood spread hotter in Henry's face, but he bit off what he might have said. "All right," he said. "You do them and I'll take over the counter for you."

So here he was, in the poolhall he had passionately sworn he would never do a lick of work in, dispensing Mrs. Morrison's meat pies and tamales smothered in chile, clumping behind the counter in the waders which had been the sign of his temporary freedom. Leaning back between orders, watching the Saturday night activity of the place, he half understood why he had gone hunting, and why it had seemed to him essential that he bring his trophies back here.

That somewhat disconcerted understanding was still troubling him when his father came back. The old man had put on a clean apron and brushed his hair. His pouched eyes,

brighter and less houndlike than usual, darted along the
bar, counting, and darted across the bright tables, counting
again. His eyes met Henry's, and both half smiled. Both
of them, Henry thought, were a little astonished.

Later, propped in bed in the hotel room, he put down
the magazine he had been reading and stared at the drawn
blinds, the sleazy drapes, and asked himself why he was
here. The story he had told others, and himself, that his
mother's death had interrupted his school term and he was
waiting for the new term before going back, he knew to
be an evasion. He was staying because he couldn't get
away, or wouldn't. He hated his father, hated the poolhall,
hated the people he was thrown with. He made no move
to hobnob with them, or hadn't until tonight, and yet he
deliberately avoided seeing any of the people who had been
his friends for years. Why?

He could force his mind to the barrier, but not across it.
Within a half minute he found himself reading again, div-
ing deep, and when he made himself look up from the page
he stared for a long time at his father's bed, his father's
shoes under the bed, his father's soiled shirts hanging in
the open closet. All the home he had any more was this
little room. He could not pretend that as long as he stayed
here the fragments of his home and family were held together. He couldn't fool himself that he had any function
in his father's life any more, or his father in his, unless
his own hatred and his father's uneasy suspicion were func-
tions. He ought to get out and get a job until he could go
back to school. But he didn't.

Thinking made him sleepy, and he knew what that
was, too. Sleep was another evasion, like the torpor and
monotony of his life. But he let drowsiness drift over him,
and drowsily he thought of his father behind the counter
tonight, vigorous and jovial, Mine Host, and he saw that the
usual fretful petulance had gone from his face.

He snapped off the bed light and dropped the magazine
on the floor. Then he heard the rain, the swish and hiss of
traffic in the wet street. He felt sad and alone, and he disliked the coldness of his own isolation. Again he thought
of his father, of the failing body that had once been tireless and bull-strong, of the face before it had sagged and
grown dewlaps of flesh on the square jaws. He thought of
the many failures, the jobs that never quite worked out, the

schemes that never quite paid off, and of the eyes that could not quite meet, not quite hold, the eyes of his cold son.

Thinking of this, and remembering when they had been a family and when his mother had been alive to hold them together, he felt pity, and he cried.

His father's entrance awakened him. He heard the fumbling at the door, the creak, the quiet click, the footsteps that groped in darkness, the body that bumped into something and halted, getting its bearings. He heard the sighing weight of his father's body on the other bed, his father's sighing breath as he bent to untie his shoes. Feigning sleep, he lay unmoving, breathing deeply and steadily, but an anguish of fury had leaped in him as sharp and sudden as a sudden fear, for he smelled the smells his father brought with him: wet wool, stale tobacco, liquor; and above all, more penetrating than any, spreading through the room and polluting everything there, the echo of cheap musky perfume.

The control Henry imposed upon his body was like an ecstasy. He raged at himself for the weak sympathy that had troubled him all evening. One good night, he said to himself now, staring furiously upward. One lively Saturday night in the joint and he can't contain himself, he has to go top off the evening with his girl friend. And how? A drink in her room? A walk over to some illegal afterhours bar on Rum Alley? Maybe just a trip to bed, blunt and immediate?

His jaws ached from the tight clamping of his teeth, but his orderly breathing went in and out, in and out, while the old man sighed into bed and creaked a little, rolling over, and lay still. The taint of perfume seemed even stronger now. The sow must slop it on by the cupful. And so cuddly. Such a sugar baby. How's my old sweetie tonight? It's been too long since you came to see your baby. I should be real mad at you. The cheek against the lapel, the unreal hair against the collar, the perfume like some gaseous poison tainting the clothes it touched.

The picture of his mother's bureau drawers came to him, the careless simple collection of handkerchiefs and gloves and lace collars and cuffs, and he saw the dusty blue sachet packets and smelled the faint fragrance. That was all the scent she had ever used.

My God, he said, how can he stand himself?

After a time his father began to breathe heavily, then to

snore. In the little prison of the room his breathing was
obscene—loose and bubbling, undisciplined, animal. Henry
with an effort relaxed his tense arms and legs, let himself
sink. He tried to concentrate on his own breathing, but
the other dominated him, burst out and died and whiffled
and sighed again. By now he had a resolution in him like
an iron bar. Tomorrow, for sure, for good, he would break
out of his self-imposed isolation and see Frank, see Welby.
They would lend him enough to get to the coast. Not another day in this hateful relationship. Not another night in
this room.

He yawned. It must be late, two or three o'clock. He
ought to get to sleep. But he lay uneasily, his mind tainted
with hatred as the room was tainted with perfume. He
tried cunningly to elude his mind, to get to sleep before it
could notice, but no matter how he composed himself for
blankness and shut his eyes and breathed deeply, his mind
was out again in a half minute, bright-eyed, lively as a
weasel, and he was helplessly hunted again from hiding
place to hiding place.

Eventually he fell back upon his old device.

He went into a big dark room in his mind, a room shadowy
with great half-seen tables. He groped and found a string
above him and pulled, and light fell suddenly in a bright
cone from the darker cone of the shade. Below the light
lay an expanse of dark green cloth, and this was the only
lighted thing in all that darkness. Carefully he gathered
bright balls into a wooden triangle, pushing them forward
until the apex lay over a round spot on the cloth. Quietly
and thoroughly he chalked a cue: the inlaid handle and the
smooth taper of the shaft were very real to his eyes and
hands. He lined up the cue ball, aimed, drew the cue back
and forth in smooth motions over the bridge of his left
hand. He saw the balls run from the spinning shock of
the break, and carom, and come to rest, and he hunted up
the yellow 1-ball and got a shot at it between two others.
He had to cut it very fine, but he saw the shot go true, the 1
angle off cleanly into the side pocket. He saw the cue
ball rebound and kiss and stop, and he shot the 2 in
a straight shot for the left corner pocket, putting drawers
on the cue ball to get shape for the 3.

Yellow and blue and red, spotted and striped, he shot
pool balls into pockets as deep and black and silent as the
cellars of his consciousness. He was not now quarry that

his mind chased, but an actor, a willer, a doer, a man in command. By an act of will or of flight he focused his whole awareness on the game he played. His mind undertook it with intent concentration. He took pride in little two-cushion banks, little triumphs of accuracy, small successes of foresight. When he had finished one game and the green cloth was bare he dug the balls from the bin under the end of the table and racked them and began another.

Eventually, he knew, nothing would remain in his mind but the clean green cloth traced with running color and bounced by simple problems, and sometime in the middle of an intricately planned combination shot he would pale off into sleep.

At noon, after the rain, the sun seemed very bright. It poured down from a clearing sky, glittered on wet roofs, gleamed in reflection from pavements and sidewalks. On the peaks beyond the city there was a purity of snow.

Coming down the hill, Henry noticed the excessive brightness and could not tell whether it was really as it seemed, or whether his plunge out of the dark and isolated hole of his life had restored a lost capacity to see. A slavery, or a paralysis, was ended; he had been for three hours in the company of a friend; he had been eyed with concern; he had been warmed by solicitude and generosity. In his pocket he had fifty dollars, enough to get him to the coast and let him renew his life. It seemed to him incredible that he had alternated between dismal hotel and dismal poolroom so long. He could not understand why he had not before this moved his legs in the direction of the hill. He perceived that he had been sullen and morbid, and he concluded with some surprise that even Schmeckebier and Edwards and the rest might have found him a difficult companion.

His father too. The fury of the night before had passed, but he knew he would not bend again toward companionship. That antipathy was too deep. He would never think of his father again without getting the whiff of that perfume. Let him have it; it was what he wanted, let him have it. They could part without an open quarrel, maybe, but they would part without love. They could part right now, within an hour.

Two grimy stairways led down into the cellar from the alley he turned into. One went to the furnace room, the other to the poolhall. The iron rail was blockaded with filled ashcans. Descent into Avernus, he said to himself, and went down the left-hand stair.

The door was locked. He knocked, and after some time knocked again. Finally someone pulled on the door from inside. It stuck, and was yanked irritably inward. His father stood there in his shirt sleeves, a cigar in his mouth.

"Oh," he said. "I was wondering what had become of you."

The basement air was foul and heavy, dense with the reek from the toilets. Henry saw as he stepped inside that at the far end only the night light behind the bar was on, but that light was coming from Schmeckebier's door at this end too, the two weak illuminations diffusing in the shadowy poolroom, leaving the middle in almost absolute dark. It was the appropriate time, the appropriate place, the stink of his prison appropriately concentrated. He drew his lungs full of it with a kind of passion, and he said, "I just came down to . . ."

"Who is dot?" Schmeckebier called out. He came to his door, wrapped to the armpits in a bar apron, with a spoon in his hand, and he bent, peering out into the dusk like a disturbed dwarf in an underhill cave. "John? Who? Oh, Henry. Shust in time, shust in time. It is not long now." His lower lip waggled, and he pulled it up, apparently with an effort.

Henry said, "What's not long?"

"Vot?" Schmeckebier said, and thrust his big head far out. "You forgot about it?"

"I must have," Henry said.

"The duck feed," his father said impatiently.

They stood staring at one another in the dusk. The right moment was gone. With a little twitch of the shoulder Henry let it go. He would wait awhile, pick his time. When Schmeckebier went back to his cooking, Henry saw through the doorway the lumpy bed, the big chair with a blanket folded over it, the rolltop desk littered with pots and pans, the green and white enamel of the range. A rich smell of roasting came out and mingled oddly with the chemical stink of toilet disinfectant.

"Are we going to eat in here?" he asked.

His father snorted. "How could we eat in there? Old Maxie lived in the ghetto too damn long. By God, I never saw such a boar's nest."

"Vot's duh matter? Vot's duh matter?" Schmeckebier said. His big lip thrust out, he stooped to look into the oven, and John Lederer went shaking his head up between the tables to the counter. Henry followed him, intending to make the break when he got the old man alone. But he saw the three plates set up on the bar, the three glasses of tomato juice, the platter of olives and celery, and he hesitated. His father reached with a salt shaker and shook a little salt into each glass of tomato juice.

"All the fixings," he said. "Soon as Max gets those birds out of the oven we can take her on."

Now it was easy to say, "As soon as the feed's over I'll be shoving off." Henry opened his mouth to say it, but was interrupted this time by a light tapping at the glass door beyond Sciutti's shop. He swung around angrily and saw duskily beyond the glass the smooth blond hair, the even smile.

"It's Billy," he said. "Shall I let him in?"

"Sure," the old man said. "Tell him to come in and have a duck with us."

But Billy Hammond shook his head when Henry asked him. He was shaking his head almost as he came through the door. "No thanks, I just ate. I'm full of chow mein. This is a family dinner anyway. You go on ahead."

"Got plenty," John Lederer said, and made a motion as if to set a fourth place at the counter.

"Who is dot?" Schmeckebier bowled from the back. "Who come in? Is dot Billy Hammond? Set him up a blate."

"By God, his nose sticks as far into things as his lip," Lederer said. Still holding the plate, he roared back, "Catch up with the parade, for Christ sake, or else tend to your cooking." He looked at Henry and Billy and chuckled.

Schmeckebier had disappeared, but now his squat figure blotted the lighted doorway again. "Vot? Vot you say?"

"Vot?" John Lederer said. "Vot, vot, vot? Vot does it matter vot I said? Get the hell back to your kitchen."

He was, Henry saw, in a high humor. The effect of last night was still with him. He was still playing Mine Host. He looked at the two of them and laughed so naturally that Henry almost joined him. "I think old Maxie's head is full of duck dressing," he said, and leaned on the counter. "I ever tell you about the time we came back from Reno together? We stopped off in the desert to look at a mine, and got lost on a little dirt road so we had to camp. I was trying to figure out where we were, and started looking for stars, but it was clouded over, hard to locate anything. So I ask old Maxie if he can see the Big Dipper anywhere. He thinks about that maybe ten minutes with his lip stuck out and then he says, 'I t'ink it's in duh water bucket.'"

He did the grating gutturals of Schmeckebier's speech so accurately that Henry smiled in spite of himself. His old man made another motion with the plate at Billy Hammond. "Better let me set you up a place."

"Thanks," Billy said. His voice was as polite and soft as his face, and his eyes had the ingenuous liquid softness of a girl's. "Thanks, I really just ate. You go on, I'll shoot a little pool if it's all right."

Now came Schmeckebier with a big platter held in both hands. He bore it smoking through the gloom of the pool-hall and up the steps to the counter, and John Lederer took it from him there and with a flourish speared one after another three tight-skinned brown ducks and slid them onto the plates set side by side for the feast. The one frugal light from the backbar shone on them as they sat down. Henry looked over his shoulder to see Billy Hammond pull the cord and flood a table with a sharp-edged cone of brilliance. Deliberately, already absorbed, he chalked a cue. His lips pursed, and he whistled, and whistling, bent to take aim.

Lined up in a row, they were not placed for conversation, but John Lederer kept attempting it, leaning forward over his plate to see Schmeckebier or Henry. He filled his mouth with duck and dressing and chewed, shaking his head with pleasure, and snapped off a bite of celery with a crack like a breaking stick. When his mouth was clear he leaned and said to Schmeckebier, "Ah, das schmeckt gut, hey, Maxie?"

"Ja," Schmeckebier said, and sucked grease off his lip and only then turned in surprise. "Say, you speak German?"

"Sure I speak German," Lederer said. "I worked three weeks once with an old squarehead brick mason that taught me the whole language. He taught me about sehr gut and nicht wahr and besser I bleiben right hier, and he always had his frau make me up a lunch full of kalter auf-schnitt and gemixte pickeln. I know all about German."

Schmeckebier stared a moment, grunted, and went back to his eating. He had already stripped the meat from the bones and was gnawing the carcass.

"Anyway," John Lederer said, "es schmecht God damn good." He got up and went around the counter and drew a mug of coffee from the urn. "Coffee?" he said to Henry.

"Please."

His father drew another mug and set it before him. "Maxie?"

Schmeckebier shook his head, his mouth too full for talk. For a minute, after he had set out two little jugs of cream, Lederer stood as if thinking. He was watching Billy Hammond move quietly around the one lighted table, whistling. "Look at that sucker," Lederer said. "I bet he doesn't even know where he is."

By the time he got around to his stool he was back at the German. "*Schmeckebier*," he said. "What's that mean?"

"Uh?"

"What's your name mean? Tastes beer? Likes beer?"

Schmeckebier rolled his shoulders. The sounds he made eating were like sounds from a sty. Henry was half-sickened, sitting next to him, and he wished the old man would let the conversation drop. But apparently it had to be a feast, and a feast called for chatter.

"That's a hell of a name, you know it?" Lederer said, and already he was up again and around the end of the counter. "You couldn't get into any church with a name like that." His eyes fastened on the big drooping greasy lip, and he grinned.

"Schmeckeduck, that ought to be your name," he said. "What's German for duck? Vogel? Old Max Schmeckevogel. How about number two?"

Schmeckebier pushed his plate forward and Lederer forked a duck out of the steam table. Henry did not take a second.

"You ought to have one," his father told him. "You don't get grub like this every day."

"One's my limit," Henry said.

For a while they worked at their plates. Back of him Henry heard the clack of balls hitting, and a moment later the rumble as a ball rolled down the chute from a pocket. The thin, abstracted whistling of Billy Hammond broke off, became words:

"Now Annie doesn't live here any more.
  So you're the guy that she's been waiting for?
  She told me that I'd know you by the blue of your eyes . . ."

"Talk about one being your limit," his father said. "When we lived in Nebraska we used to put on some feeds. You remember anything about Nebraska at all?"

"A little," Henry said. He was irritated at being dragged into reminiscences, and he did not want to hear how many ducks the town hog could eat at a sitting.

"We'd go out, a whole bunch of us," John Lederer said. "The sloughs were black with ducks in those days. We'd come back with a buggyful, and the womenfolks'd really put us on a feed. Fifteen, twenty, thirty people. Take a hundred ducks to fill 'em up." He was silent a moment, staring across the counter, chewing. Henry noticed that he had tacked two wings of a teal up on the frame of the backbar mirror, small, strong bows with a band of bright blue half hidden in them. The old man's eyes slanted over, caught Henry's looking at the wings.

"Doesn't seem as if we'd had a duck feed since we left there," he said. His forehead wrinkled; he rubbed his neck, leaning forward over his plate, and his eyes met Henry's in the backbar mirror. He spoke to the mirror, ignoring the gobbling image of Schmeckebier between his own reflection and Henry's.

"You remember that set of china your mother used to have? The one she painted herself? Just the plain white china with the one design on each plate?"

Henry sat stiffly, angry that his mother's name should even be mentioned between them in this murky hole, and after what had passed. Gabble, gabble, gabble, he said to himself. If you can't think of anything else to gabble about, gabble about your dead wife. Drag her through the poolroom too. Aloud he said, "No, I guess I don't."

"Blue-wing teal," his father said, and nodded at the wings tacked to the mirror frame. "Just the wings, like that. Awful pretty. She thought a teal was about the prettiest little duck there was."

His vaguely rubbing hand came around from the back of his neck and rubbed along the cheek, pulling the slack flesh and distorting the mouth. Henry said nothing, watching the pouched hound eyes in the mirror.

It was a cold, skin-tightening shock to realize that the hound eyes were cloudy with tears. The rubbing hand went over them, shaded them like a hatbrim, but the mouth below remained distorted. With a plunging movement his father was off the stool.

"Oh, God damn!" he said in a strangling voice, and went past Henry on hard, heavy feet, down the steps and past Billy Hammond, who neither looked up nor broke the sad thin whistling.

Schmeckebier had swung around. "Vot's duh matter? Now vot's duh matter?"

With a short shake of the head, Henry turned away from him, staring after his father down the dark poolhall. He felt as if orderly things were breaking and flying apart in his mind; he had a moment of white blind terror that this whole scene upon whose reality he counted was really only a dream, something conjured up out of the bottom of his consciousness where he was accustomed to comfort himself into total sleep. His mind was still full of the anguished look his father had hurled at the mirror before he ran.

The hell with you, the look had said. The hell with you, Schmeckebier, and you, my son Henry. The hell with your ignorance, whether you're stupid or whether you just don't know all you think you know. You don't know enough to kick dirt down a hole. You know nothing at all, you know less than nothing because you know things wrong.

He heard Billy's soft whistling, saw him move around his one lighted table—a well-brought-up boy from some suburban town, a polite soft gentle boy lost and wandering among pimps and prostitutes, burying himself for some reason among people who never touched his surface. Did he shoot pool in his bed at night, tempting sleep, as Henry did? Did his mind run carefully to angles and banks and englishes, making a reflecting mirror of them to keep from looking through them at other things?

Almost in terror he looked out across the sullen cave, past where the light came down in an intense isolated cone above Billy's table, and heard the lugubrious whistling that went on without intention of audience, a recurrent and deadening and only half-conscious sound. He looked toward the back, where his father had disappeared in the gloom, and wondered if in his bed before sleeping the old man worked through a routine of little jobs: cleaning the steam table, ordering a hundred pounds of coffee, jacking up the janitor about the mess in the hall. He wondered if it was possible to wash yourself to sleep with restaurant crockery, work yourself to sleep with chores, add yourself to sleep with columns of figures, as you could play yourself to sleep with a pool cue and a green table and fifteen colored balls. For

a moment, in the sad old light with the wreckage of the
duck feast at his elbow, he wondered if there was anything more to his life, or his father's life, or Billy Hammond's life, or anyone's life, than playing the careful games
that deadened you into sleep.

Schmeckebier, beside him, was still groping in the fog
of his mind for an explanation of what had happened. "Vere'd
he go?" he said, and nudged Henry fiercely. "Vot's duh
matter?"

Henry shook him off irritably, watching Billy Hammond's
oblivious bent head under the light. He heard Schmeckebier's
big lip flop and heard him sucking his teeth.

"I tell you," the guttural voice said. "I got somet'ing dot
fixes him if he feels bum."

He too went down the stairs past the lighted table and
into the gloom at the back. The light went on in his
room, and after a minute or two his voice was shouting,
"John! Say, come here, uh? Say, John!"

Eventually John Lederer came out of the toilet and they
walked together between the tables. In his fist Schmeckebier was clutching a square bottle. He waved it in front of
Henry's face as they passed, but Henry was watching his
father. He saw the crumpled face, oddly rigid, like the
face of a man in the grip of a barely controlled rage, but his
father avoided his eyes.

"Kümmel," Schmeckebier said. He set four ice cream
dishes on the counter and poured three about a third full
of clear liquor. His squinted eyes lifted and peered toward
Billy Hammond, but Henry said, on an impulse, "Let him
alone. He's walking in his sleep."

So there were only the three. They stood together a moment and raised their glasses. "Happy days," John Lederer
said automatically. They drank.

Schmeckebier smacked his lips, looked at them one after
another, shook his head in admiration of the quality of his
kümmel, and waddled back toward his room with the bottle. John Lederer was already drawing hot water to wash
the dishes.

In the core of quiet which even the clatter of crockery
and the whistling of Billy Hammond did not break into,
Henry said what he had to say. "I'll be leaving," he said.
"Probably tonight."

But he did not say it in anger, or with the cold command
of himself that he had imagined in advance. He said it

like a cry, and with the feeling he might have had on
letting go the hand of a friend too weak and too exhausted
to cling any longer to their inadequate shared driftwood in
a wide cold sea.

The Archimandrite's Niece

BY JAMES REID PARKER

MR. DEVORE stood in front of one of the windows of his
office and gazed out at the heavy fog which encompassed
the towers of Pine Street. He would have denied at any time,
but particularly on this dreary morning, that his professional
life was informed with color, and would have insisted that
this was not a matter for regret. The beauty of the law,
Mr. Devore had often remarked to Miss Deevey, as well
as to many lesser employees, was the beauty of its codified
orderliness.

Now the fog was blurring the lights across the street
and turning them into sulphur-yellow splotches in the gray
waste. Mr. Devore's office, while as orderly as even he
could wish, was hardly more cheerful than the haze beyond.
As Miss Fannie Devore must have decided when she was
choosing the fabric for her bachelor brother's window dra-
peries, anything that bordered on the frivolous would be out
of keeping with the austerity that prevailed throughout the
temple of Forbes, Hathaway, Bryan & Devore, within which
the lawyers carefully prepared Delphic advice for the nervous corporations which approached them for counsel. Mr.
Devore was awaiting a Mme. Liapchev, the protégée of
an important client.

The day before, Mrs. Herbert Kraft had talked to him
eagerly and incoherently on the telephone for twenty-
three minutes about the difficulties that beset a woman
she knew. A charming person, she said, and one whom
Mr. Devore was sure to admire and pity. Mrs. Kraft had
gone on in this vein for some time, until Mr. Devore had
begun to wonder just what minor infraction of the law the
friend could have committed. He had heard similar pream-
bles before.

"You say she is in a serious predicament and is having
trouble with the authorities?"

"With the State Department. Didn't I mention that? And it isn't Mme. Liapchev herself who is having trouble. At least, she is, but only indirectly. It's a member of her family. I haven't been able to grasp the situation very clearly myself, but she'll explain everything to you. I'd like to send her down to your office tomorrow. She's visiting us for a while. Tomorrow *will* be all right, won't it? And please try to do something for her, for my sake."

"Of course!" Mr. Devore had said warmly. The Herbert Krafts could, and did, set him whatever tasks they chose, and for an excellent reason. Forbes, Hathaway, Bryan & Devore enjoyed a substantial annual retainer for representing Mr. Kraft's various enterprises.

The morning was well under way when Miss Deevey announced, with something of a sniff, that Mme. Liapchev was calling. Mr. Devore, astutely comprehending that the sniff meant something like "I hope you're not going to fritter away the whole morning," said in a warning tone that the visitor was a friend of Mrs. Herbert Kraft and that he would see her at once.

A distinctly handsome woman came into the room. She wore black, and her manner was impressive. She was a frowningly majestic brunette, in the forties, perhaps, and not unlike Sir Joshua Reynolds' portrait of Mrs. Siddons. Mr. Devore rose and bowed courteously.

"I am Helena Nicolaevna Liapchev," she said, and they shook hands.

"How do you do?" said Mr. Devore. "I am always very happy to be of service to a friend of Mrs. Kraft's."

"God will comfort you," she said. "God will wash and refresh your soul!"

Mr. Devore was startled. His relationship with God, while correctly Episcopalian, had never been intimate. He felt toward God much as he felt toward his friends the H. Chauncey Folgers. He made a point of paying a formal call on God once or twice a year, just as he made a point of paying one or two formal calls on the Folgers. It was inconceivable that either Chauncey Folger or God would ever try to wash and refresh his soul.

"I can tell," he said, recovering as quickly as he could from his discomfiture, "I can tell from your very charming accent that you are Russian."

"You are mistaken. I am Bulgar. My husband was Bulgar, and I am obliged to have his nationality."

"Er—yes, I see," Mr. Devore said politely. "Then—ah—what *are* you? I mean, what are you by *birth*?"

"I am Slavonian," she said with pride. "Or perhaps you are accustomed to say Slovenian?" Mr. Devore responded with a vague smile. "I was born a Prebičević, in the town of Koprivinica in Croatia-Slavonia," Mme. Liapchev went on. Then her expression darkened for a moment. "My mother was Hercegovinian. I did not love my mother."

Mr. Devore tried to picture in his mind a detailed map of the Balkans, but became confused.

"My father's family was devoted to the Church," Mme. Liapchev said suddenly. "It gave many brilliant men to the Church. That is why my uncle is in such trouble. He never should have joined the Church. He should have become a political leader, but his father commanded him to turn to a spiritual life. His problem might have been even worse, of course. He might have risen in the hierarchy instead of in a brotherhood. Imagine how terrible if he had become a metropolitan or even a patriarch and then permitted his political enthusiasms to appear! He would have drawn much more attention to himself than he does as an archimandrite. But you must not misunderstand me"— Mr. Devore was trying harder than ever not to—"he should never have gone so far as to become what he is now. He certainly should not have become an archimandrite. A hegumenos, perhaps, but no more. He should have asked to be allowed to remain the Hegumenos of Enos. It is quite a small monastery, but so nice, so charmingly situated, and the gardens are very attractive. The altitude is high, and the water agrees with him. The water at St. Methodius does not agree with my uncle. It gives him—what is the word for it? I am not sure what the word for it is. It gives him—"

"Yes, yes," Mr. Devore said hastily. "I know. I quite understand. I once had a similar affliction myself in—ah—Pittsburgh."

"It is unthinkable that the Archimandrite of St. Methodius should undertake political activities in Slavonia. The Hegumenos of Enos, yes. That would have excited comparatively little comment, but the Archimandrite of St. Methodius, no!"

"No?" Mr. Devore said, looking at her in wonder.

"When I was a young girl in Koprivinica, it would have been preposterous even to imagine such a thing," Mme. Liapchev said. "And now he has disappeared! I have writ-

ten to the brotherhood, and the brotherhood has sent me
a beautiful and touching reply. It is as ignorant of my
uncle's whereabouts as I am. It is supposed that he is
in Croatia-Slavonia. He had been contemplating such a visit.
I should explain that he habitually carried papers which permitted him to enter Yugoslavia from St. Methodius. St. Methodius is in the Florina province, which is to say northwestern Greece, perhaps forty kilometres east of Albania."

"Ah, yes, northwestern Greece," said Mr. Devore, dazed
by the variety of regions that had to be taken into account.
"Forty kilometres east of Albania." He began to scribble on
a memorandum pad. "This *was* what you wanted to see me
about, wasn't it—the disappearance of this gentleman?"

"Certainly."

"Who, as I understand it, went *from* Greece *to* Yugoslavia?"

"To Croatia-Slavonia," Mme. Liapchev corrected him. "It
is the only part of Yugoslavia to which one would care to
go. In Serbia there are merely swine. I would go so far
as to say that my uncle did not even go to Croatia. You
can depend upon it—he went to Slavonia."

"You have not yet told me your uncle's name," Mr. Devore said, holding his pencil over the pad.

"His name is Cyril. The family name, as I believe I said,
is Prebičević, but my uncle is now known simply as the
Archimandrite of St. Methodius."

Mr. Devore could not help feeling that Cyril was a deceptively mild name for so troublesome an uncle, but he
was glad to record at last a piece of information that
was easy to spell. He had doubts about his rendition of a
number of the words in his visitor's deposition. When he
looked up, he noted with regret that Mme. Liapchev seemed
about to grow fervent again. There was a return of the inspired expression which he had seen when she had commended him to God.

"Who knows what may have happened to him by now?"
she said with a musical quaver. "The Drave Banovina should
be searched!"

"I presume you are speaking of a river?" Mr. Devore said,
feeling strangely divided between irritation and sympathy.

"Certainly not!" She dropped the inspired expression and
manifested a certain impatience. "I am speaking of the district that comprises what we know as Old Slavonia. Forgive

me"—she became gentle once more, and there was an alarmingly intimate quality in her voice when she was gentle—"I make the mistake of supposing that you are acquainted with my country, do I not? There are nine *banovinas*.

"Nine?" said Mr. Devore, going into a kind of trance.

"I feel sure that he is going around the countryside of the Drave Banovina, criticizing all the politicians who are not to his taste and telling the people to do dangerous things. My uncle has a habit of speaking so recklessly! On certain occasions he has been mistaken for a madman."

Mr. Devore pulled himself together. "I infer that your uncle is a highly imprudent person," he said. "We have men like that in this country, thanks to the extraordinary liberties which prevail here. Your uncle evidently uses the Church as a cloak for radicalism."

Mme. Liapchev was shocked. *"Radicalism? He is a conservative!* He was the first to demand vengeance after the Skupstina tragedy!"

Mr. Devore felt that it was time for him to assert himself. "I'm afraid I don't know anything about the—ah—the Skupstina tragedy," he said firmly.

"You don't remember it? You don't remember Punisa Racic? He fired on the Croat deputies in the Skupstina. Racic was a Montenegrin radical. Oh, it was too shocking! I shall never forget it. No one in Slavonia will ever forget it, in spite of the fact that the Croats are unbelievably inferior to the people of the Drave Banovina. At least, the deputies were not Serbs! It would have been so much better if they *had* been!"

"Quite so. And now to return to the matter we were discussing." He had no intention of enduring any more of these complications, not even for Mrs. Herbert Kraft's sake. "Perhaps he has some close friends to whom you could write."

"Friends?" Mme. Liapchev seemed to consider this a novel idea. She pondered the suggestion for a few moments and then said, "I believe there is a Dr. Hrdla in Moravia. Unless my uncle has quarrelled with him. My uncle quarrels with everyone. But Moravia—can one send letters to Moravia these day? I do not think so. No, there is no close friend to whom I could write."

"Perhaps our own State Department could help you," Mr. Devore said. Then he remembered it was with the

State Department that she was supposed to be having trouble. He gave her a puzzled look.

"The State Department!" she said with scorn. "They are stupid there. They told me I was not to bother them any more. They told me I must not come back!"

Mr. Devore understood perfectly. "When your uncle goes into"—he hesitated, but decided to be independent of geographical niceties—"into Yugoslavia, does he visit anyone in particular?"

"I have never heard him speak of anyone," she said with a shrug. "He has never mentioned anyone in his letters. His chief reason for going is to annoy the Muslim faction."

"Indeed?" Mr. Devore said with cold exasperation. He had made up his mind. "Our friend Mrs. Kraft," he continued, "is a kindhearted woman. She is always generous, but I fear impulsively so. Like so many kindhearted women" —even with his self-assurance restored, he felt it expedient to stress the tribute—"she is not always aware when obstacles *can* be surmounted and when obstacles *cannot* be surmounted. I must confess that there is absolutely nothing I can do for you. Frankly, it seems to me that the information you wish can be secured only through consular channels, with which you are probably more familiar than I am. I must ask you to tell Mrs. Kraft how sorry I am that I, in my very limited sphere, am helpless to bring such an affair as this to a successful end."

He waited uncomfortably for a display of histrionics, but none materialized. Mme. Liapchev showed no sign of anger or even of acute disappointment. She looked at him dreamily and smoothed her gloves with exquisite grace.

"You are so sympathetic," she said, either with rapt admiration or an excellent imitation of it. "So sympathetic and so *good!*"

"I—ah—I regret that I can be of no assistance to you, but surely you can understand that I am powerless."

"Yes," she said softly. "I regret it so much."

When Mme. Liapchev had departed, Mr. Devore found that he was able to relax a little. But he was afraid Mrs. Kraft's reaction would be one of chagrin and perhaps something even stronger.

He happened not to meet Mrs. Kraft until almost a month later, when they encountered each other in the lobby of Carnegie Hall. Mrs. Kraft said "Henry Devore!" in a reproachful tone. What led Mr. Devore to take heart, how-

ever, was the fact that at the same time she sounded play-
fully arch.

"I'm always picking out the perfect wife for you,
Henry," she said, "and you never give them the least little
bit of encouragement!"

A Mother's Tale

BY JAMES AGEE

THE CALF ran up the hill as fast as he could and stopped
sharp. "Mama!" he cried, all out of breath. "What *is* it!
What are they *doing!* Where are they *going!*"

Other spring calves came galloping too.

They all were looking up at her and awaiting her explanation, but she looked out over their excited eyes. As
she watched the mysterious and majestic thing they had
never seen before, her own eyes became even more than
ordinarily still, and during the considerable moment before she answered, she scarcely heard their urgent questioning.

Far out along the autumn plain, beneath the sloping
light, an immense drove of cattle moved eastward. They
were at a walk, not very fast, but faster than they could
imaginably enjoy. Those in front were compelled by those
behind; those at the rear, with few exceptions, did their
best to keep up; those who were locked within the herd
could no more help moving than the particles inside a falling rock. Men on horses rode ahead, and alongside, and behind, or spurred their horses intensely back and forth, keeping the pace steady, and the herd in shape; and from man
to man a dog sped back and forth incessantly as a shuttle,
barking, incessantly, in a hysterical voice. Now and then one
of the men shouted fiercely, and this like the shrieking of
the dog was tinily audible above a low and awesome sound
which seemed to come not from the multitude of hooves
but from the center of the world, and above the sporadic
bawlings and bellowings of the herd.

From the hillside this tumult was so distant that it only
made more delicate the prodigious silence in which the
earth and sky were held; and, from the hill, the sight was

as modest as its sound. The herd was virtually hidden in the dust it raised, and could be known, in general, only by the horns which pricked this flat sunlit dust like little briars. In one place a twist of the air revealed the trembling fabric of many backs; but it was only along the near edge of the mass that individual animals were discernible, small in a driven frieze, walking fast, stumbling and recovering, tossing their armed heads, or opening their skulls heavenward in one of those cries which reached the hillside long after the jaws were shut.

From where she watched, the mother could not be sure whether there were any she recognized. She knew that among them there must be a son of hers; she had not seen him since some previous spring, and she would not be seeing him again. Then the cries of the young ones impinged on her bemusement: "Where are they going?"

She looked into their ignorant eyes.

"Away," she said.

"Where?" they cried. "Where? Where?" her own son cried again.

She wondered what to say.

"On a long journey."

"But where *to?*" they shouted. "Yes, where *to?*" her son exclaimed, and she could see that he was losing his patience with her, as he always did when he felt she was evasive.

"I'm not sure," she said.

Their silence was so cold that she was unable to avoid their eyes for long.

"Well, not *really* sure. Because, you see," she said in her most reasonable tone, "I've never seen it with my own eyes, and that's the only way to *be* sure; *isn't* it?"

They just kept looking at her. She could see no way out.

"But I've *heard* about it," she said with shallow cheerfulness, "from those who *have* seen it, and I don't suppose there's any good reason to doubt them."

She looked away over them again, and for all their interest in what she was about to tell them, her eyes so changed that they turned and looked, too.

The herd, which had been moving broadside to them, was being turned away, so slowly that like the turning of stars it could not quite be seen from one moment to the next; yet soon it was moving directly away from them, and even during the little while she spoke and they all watched

after it, it steadily and very noticeably diminished, and
the sounds of it as well.

"It happens always about this time of year," she said
quietly while they watched. "Nearly all the men and horses
leave, and go into the North and the West."

"Out on the range," her son said, and by his voice she
knew what enchantment the idea already held for him.

"Yes," she said, "out on the range." And trying, impos-
sibly, to imagine the range, they were touched by the
breath of grandeur.

"And then before long," she continued, "everyone has
been found, and brought into one place; and then . . .
what you see, happens. All of them.

"Sometimes when the wind is right," she said more quietly, "you can hear them coming long before you can see
them. It isn't even like a sound, at first. It's more as if
something were moving far under the ground. It makes you
uneasy. You wonder, why, what in the world can *that*
be! Then you remember what it is and then you can really
hear it. And then finally, there they·all are."

She could see this did not interest them at all.

"But where are they *going?*" one asked, a little impatiently.

"I'm coming to that," she said; and she let them wait.
Then she spoke slowly but casually.

"They are on their way to a railroad."

There, she thought; that's for that look you all gave me
when I said I wasn't sure. She waited for them to ask;
they waited for her to explain.

"A railroad," she told them, "is great hard bars of metal
lying side by side, or so they tell me, and they go on and
on over the ground as far as the eye can see. And great
wagons run on the metal bars on wheels, like wagon wheels
but smaller, and these wheels are made of solid metal
too. The wagons are much bigger than any wagon you've
ever seen, as big as, big as sheds, they say, and they are
pulled along on the iron bars by a terrible huge dark machine, with a loud scream."

"Big as *sheds?*" one of the calves said skeptically.

"Big *enough*, anyway," the mother said. "I told you I've
never seen it myself. But those wagons are so big that
several of us can get inside at once. And that's exactly what
happens."

Suddenly she became very quiet, for she felt that somehow, she could not imagine just how, she had said altogether too much.

"Well, *what* happens," the son wanted to know. "What do you mean, *happens*."

She always tried hard to be a reasonably modern mother. It was probably better, she felt, to go on, than to leave them all full of imaginings and mystification. Besides, there was really nothing at all awful about what happened . . . if only one could know *why*.

"Well," she said, "it's nothing much, really. They just— why, when they all finally *get* there, why there are all the great cars waiting in a long time, and the big dark machine is up ahead . . . smoke comes out of it, they say . . . and . . . well, then, they just put us into the wagons, just as many as will fit in each wagon, and when everybody is in, why . . ." She hesitated, for again, though she couldn't be sure why, she was uneasy.

"Why then," her son said, "the train takes them away."

Hearing that word, she felt a flinching of the heart. Where had he picked it up, she wondered, and she gave him a shy and curious glance. Oh dear, she thought. I should never have even *begun* to explain. "Yes," she said, "when everybody is safely in, they slide the doors shut."

They were all silent for a little while. Then one of them asked thoughtfully, "Are they taking them somewhere they don't want to go?"

"Oh, I don't think so," the mother said. "I imagine it's very nice."

"*I* want to go," she heard her son say with ardor. "I want to go right now," he cried. "Can I, Mama? *Can* I? *Please?*" And looking into his eyes, she was overwhelmed by sadness.

"Silly thing," she said, "there'll be time enough for that when you're grown up. But what I very much hope," she went on, "is that instead of being chosen to go out on the range and to make the long journey, you will grow up to be very strong and bright so they will decide that you may stay here at home with Mother. And you, too," she added, speaking to the other little males; but she could not honestly wish this for any but her own, least of all for the eldest, strongest and most proud, for she knew how few are chosen.

She could see that what she said was not received with enthusiasm.

"But I want to go," her son said.

"Why?" she asked. "I don't think any of you realize that it's a great *honor* to be chosen to stay. A great privilege. Why, it's just the most ordinary ones are taken out onto the range. But only the very pick are chosen to stay here at home. If you want to go out on the range," she said in hurried and happy inspiration, "all you have to do is be ordinary and careless and silly. If you want to have even a chance to be chosen to stay, you have to try to be stronger and bigger and braver and brighter than anyone else, and that takes *hard work. Every day.* Do you see?" And she looked happily and hopefully from one to another. "Besides," she added, aware that they were not won over, "I'm told it's a very rough life out there, and the men are unkind.

"Don't you see," she said again; and she pretended to speak to all of them, but it was only to her son.

But he only looked at her. "Why do you want me to stay home?" he asked flatly; in their silence she knew the others were asking the same question.

"Because it's safe here," she said before she knew better; and realized she had put it in the most unfortunate way possible. "Not safe, not just that," she fumbled. "I mean . . . because here we *know* what happens, and what's going to happen, and there's never any doubt about it, never any reason to wonder, to worry. Don't you see? It's just *Home*," and she put a smile on the word, "where we all know each other and are happy and well."

They were so merely quiet, looking back at her, that she felt they were neither won over nor alienated. Then she knew of her son that he, anyhow, was most certainly not persuaded, for he asked the question she most dreaded: "Where do they go on the train?" And hearing him, she knew that she would stop at nothing to bring that curiosity and eagerness, and that tendency toward skepticism, within safe bounds.

"Nobody knows," she said, and she added, in just the tone she knew would most sharply engage them, "Not for sure, anyway."

"What do you mean, *not for sure,*" her son cried. And the oldest, biggest calf repeated the question, his voice cracking.

The mother deliberately kept silent as she gazed out over the plain, and while she was silent they all heard the last

they would ever hear of all those who were going away:
one last great cry, as faint almost as a breath; the infin-
itesimal jabbing vituperation of the dog; the solemn muttering of the earth.

"Well," she said, after even this sound was entirely lost,
"there was one who came back." Their instant, trustful
eyes were too much for her. She added, "Or so they say."

They gathered a little more closely around her, for now
she spoke very quietly.

"It was my great-grandmother who told me," she said.
"She was told it by *her* great-grandmother, who claimed
she saw it with her own eyes, though of course I can't
vouch for that. Because of course I wasn't even dreamed of
then; and Great-grandmother was so very, very old, you see,
that you couldn't always be sure she knew quite *what* she
was saying."

Now that she began to remember it more clearly, she was
sorry she had committed herself to telling it.

"Yes," she said, "the story is, there was one, *just* one,
who ever came back, and he told what happened on the
train, and where the train went and what happened after.
He told it all in a rush, they say, the last things first and
every which way, but as it was finally sorted out and gotten
into order by those who heard it and those they told it to,
this is more or less what happened:

"He said that after the men had gotten just as many of
us as they could into the car he was in, so that their sides
pressed tightly together and nobody could lie down, they
slid the door shut with a startling rattle and a bang, and
then there was a sudden jerk, so strong they might have
fallen except that they were packed so closely together, and
the car began to move. But after it had moved only a little
way, it stopped as suddenly as it had started, so that they
all nearly fell down again. You see, they were just moving up the next car that was joined on behind, to put more
of us into it. He could see it all between the boards of the
car, because the boards were built a little apart from each
other, to let in air."

Car, her son said again to himself. Now he would never
forget the word.

"He said that then, for the first time in his life, he became very badly frightened, he didn't know why. But he
was sure, at that moment, that there was something dread-
fully to be afraid of. The others felt this same great fear.

They called out loudly to those who were being put into the car behind, and the others called back, but it was no use; those who were getting aboard were between narrow white fences and then were walking up a narrow slope and the men kept jabbing them as they do when they are in an unkind humor, and there was no way to go but on into the car. There was no way to get out of the car, either: he tried, with all his might, and he was the one nearest the door.

"After the next car behind was full, and the door was shut, the train jerked forward again, and stopped again, and they put more of us into still another car, and so on, and on, until all the starting and stopping no longer frightened anybody; it was just something uncomfortable that was never going to stop, and they began instead to realize how hungry and thirsty they were. But there was no food and no water, so they just had to put up with this; and about the time they became resigned to going without their suppers (for now it was almost dark), they heard a sudden and terrible scream which frightened them even more deeply than anything had frightened them before, and the train began to move again, and they braced their legs once more for the jolt when it would stop, but this time, instead of stopping, it began to go fast, and then even faster, so fast that the ground nearby slid past like a flooded creek and the whole country, he claimed, began to move too, turning slowly around a far mountain as if it were all one great wheel. And then there was a strange kind of disturbance inside the car, he said, or even inside his very bones. He felt as if everything in him was *falling*, as if he had been filled full of a heavy liquid that all wanted to flow one way, and all the others were leaning as he was leaning, away from this queer heaviness that was trying to pull them over, and then just as suddenly this leaning heaviness was gone and they nearly fell again before they could stop leaning against it. He could never understand what this was, but it too happened so many times that they all got used to it, just as they got used to seeing the country turn like a slow wheel, and just as they got used to the long cruel screams of the engine, and the steady iron noise beneath them which made the cold darkness so fearsome, and the hunger and the thirst and the continual standing up, and the moving on and on and on as if they would never stop."

"*Didn't* they ever stop?" one asked.

"Once in a great while," she replied. "Each time they did," she said, "he thought, Oh, now *at last! At last* we can get out and stretch our tired legs and lie down! *At last* we'll be given food and water! But they never let them out. And they never gave them food or water. They never even cleaned up under them. They had to stand in their manure and in the water they made."

"Why did the train stop?" her son asked; and with somber gratification she saw that he was taking all this very much to heart.

"He could never understand why," she said. "Sometimes men would walk up and down alongside the cars, and the more nervous and the more trustful of us would call out; but they were only looking around, they never seemed to do anything. Sometimes he could see many houses and bigger buildings together where people lived. Sometimes it was far out in the country and after they had stood still for a long time they would hear a little noise which quickly became louder, and then became suddenly a noise so loud it stopped their breathing, and during this noise something black would go by, very close, and so fast it couldn't be seen. And then it was gone as suddenly as it had appeared, and the noise became small, and then in the silence their train would start up again.

"Once, he tells us, something very strange happened. They were standing still, and cars of a very different kind began to move slowly past. These cars were not red, but black with many glass windows like those in a house; and he says they were as full of human beings as the car he was in was full of our kind. And one of these people looked into his eyes and smiled, as if he liked him, or as if he knew only too well how hard the journey was.

"So by his account it happens to them, too," she said, with a certain pleased vindictiveness. "Only they were sitting down at their ease, not standing. And the one who smiled was eating."

She was still, trying to think of something; she couldn't quite grasp the thought.

"But didn't they *ever* let them out?" her son asked.

The oldest calf jeered. "Of *course* they did. He came back, didn't he? How would he ever come back if he didn't get out?"

"They didn't let them out," she said, "for a long, long time."

"How long?"

"So long, and he was so tired, he could never quite be sure. But he said that it turned from night to day and from day to night and back again several times over, with the train moving nearly all of this time, and that when it finally stopped, early one morning, they were all so tired and so discouraged that they hardly even noticed any longer, let alone felt any hope that anything would change for them, ever again; and then all of a sudden men came up and put up a wide walk and unbarred the door and slid it open, and it was the most wonderful and happy moment of his life when he saw the door open, and walked into the open air with all his joints trembling, and drank the water and ate the delicious food they had ready for him; it was worth the whole terrible journey."

Now that these scenes came clear before her, there was a faraway shining in her eyes, and her voice, too, had something in it of the faraway.

"When they had eaten and drunk all they could hold they lifted up their heads and looked around, and everything they saw made them happy. Even the trains made them cheerful now, for now they were no longer afraid of them. And though these trains were forever breaking to pieces and joining again with other broken pieces, with shufflings and clashings and rude cries, they hardly paid them attention any more, they were so pleased to be in their new home, and so surprised and delighted to find they were among thousands upon thousands of strangers of their own kind, all lifting their voices in peacefulness and thanksgiving, and they were so wonder-struck by all they could see, it was so beautiful and so grand.

"For he has told us that now they lived among fences as white as bone, so many, and so spiderishly complicated, and shining so pure, that there's no use trying even to hint at the beauty and the splendor of it to anyone who knows only the pitiful little outfittings of a ranch. Beyond these mazy fences, through the dark and bright smoke which continually turned along the sunlight, dark buildings stood shoulder to shoulder in a wall as huge and proud as mountains. All through the air, all the time, there was an iron humming like the humming of the iron bar after it has been struck to tell the men it is time to eat, and in all the air, all the time, there was that same strange kind of iron strength which makes the silence before lightning so different from all other silence.

"Once for a little while the wind shifted and blew over them straight from the great buildings, and it brought a strange and very powerful smell which confused and disturbed them. He could never quite describe this smell, but he has told us it was unlike anything he had ever known before. It smelled like old fire, he said, and old blood and fear and darkness and sorrow and most terrible and brutal force and something else, something in it that made him want to run away. This sudden uneasiness and this wish to run away swept through every one of them, he tells us, so that they were all moved at once as restlessly as so many leaves in a wind, and there was great worry in their voices. But soon the leaders among them concluded that it was simply the way men must smell when there are a great many of them living together. Those dark buildings must be crowded very full of men, they decided, probably as many thousands of them, indoors, as there were of us, outdoors; so it was no wonder their smell was so strong and, to our kind, so unpleasant. Besides, it was so clear now in every other way that men were not as we had always supposed, but were doing everything they knew how to make us comfortable and happy, that we ought to just put up with their smell, which after all they couldn't help, any more than we could help our own. Very likely men didn't like the way we smelled, any more than we liked theirs. They passed along these ideas to the others, and soon everyone felt more calm, and then the wind changed again, and the fierce smell no longer came to them, and the smell of our own kind was back again, very strong of course, in such a crowd, but ever so homey and comforting, and everyone felt easy again.

"They were fed and watered so generously, and treated so well, and the majesty and the loveliness of this place where they had all come to rest was so far beyond anything they had ever known or dreamed of, that many of the simple and ignorant, whose memories were short, began to wonder whether that whole difficult journey, or even their whole lives up to now, had ever really been. Hadn't it all been just shadows, they murmured, just a bad dream?

"Even the sharp ones, who knew very well it had all really happened, began to figure that everything up to now had been made so full of pain only so that all they had come to now might seem all the sweeter and the more glorious. Some of the oldest and deepest were even of a mind that all the puzzle and tribulation of the journey had been sent us as a kind of harsh trying or proving of our worthiness; and that it was entirely fitting and proper that we could earn our way through to such rewards as these, only through suffering, and through being patient under pain which was beyond our understanding; and that now at the last, to those who had borne all things well, all things were made known: for the mystery of suffering stood revealed in joy. And now as they looked back over all that was past, all their sorrows and bewilderment seemed so little and so fleeting that, from the simplest among them even to the most wise, they could feel only the kind of amused pity we feel toward the very young when, with the first thing that hurts them or they are forbidden, they are sure there is nothing kind or fair in all creation, and carry on accordingly, raving and grieving as if their hearts would break."

She glanced among them with an indulgent smile, hoping the little lesson would sink home. They seemed interested but somewhat dazed. I'm talking way over their heads, she realized. But by now she herself was too deeply absorbed in her story to modify it much. *Let* it be, she thought, a little impatient; it's over *my* head, for that matter.

"They had hardly before this even wondered that they were alive," she went on, "and now all of a sudden they felt they understood *why* they were. This made them–very happy, but they were still only beginning to enjoy this new wisdom when quite a new and different kind of restiveness ran among them. Before they quite knew it they were all moving once again, and now they realized that they were being moved, once more, by men, toward still some other place and purpose they could not know. But during these last hours they had been so well that now they felt no uneasiness, but all moved forward calm and sure toward better things still to come; he has told us that he no longer felt as if he were being driven, even as it became clear that they were going toward the shade of those great buildings; but guided.

"He was guided between fences which stood ever more and more narrowly near each other, among companions who were pressed ever more and more closely against each other; and now as he felt their warmth against him it was not uncomfortable, and his pleasure in it was not through any need to be close among others through anxiousness, but was a new kind of strong and gentle delight, at being so very close, so deeply of his own kind, that it seemed as if the very breath and heartbeat of each one were being exchanged through all that multitude, and each was another, and others were each, and each was a multitude, and the multitude was one. And quieted and made mild within this melting, they now entered the cold shadow cast by the buildings, and now with every step the smell of the buildings grew stronger, and in the darkening air the glittering of the fences was ever more queer.

"And now as they were pressed ever more intimately together he could see ahead of him a narrow gate, and he was strongly pressed upon from either side and from behind, and went in eagerly, and now he was between two fences so narrowly set that he brushed either fence with either flank, and walked alone, seeing just one other ahead of him, and knowing of just one other behind him, and for a moment the strange thought came to him, that the one ahead was his father, and that the one behind was the son he had never begotten.

"And now the light was so changed that he knew he must have come inside one of the gloomy and enormous buildings, and the smell was so much stronger that it seemed almost to burn his nostrils, and the smell and the somber new light blended together and became some other thing again, beyond his describing to us except to say that the whole air beat with it like one immense heart and it was as if the beating of this heart were pure violence infinitely manifolded upon violence: so that the uneasy feeling stirred in him again that it would be wise to turn around and run out of this place just as fast and as far as ever he could go. This he heard, as if he were telling it to himself at the top of his voice, but it came from somewhere so deep and so dark inside him that he could only hear the shouting of it as less than a whisper, as just a hot and chilling breath, and he scarcely heeded it, there was so much else to attend to.

"For as he walked along in this sudden and complete loneliness, he tells us, this wonderful knowledge of being one with all his race meant less and less to him, and in its place came something still more wonderful: he knew what it was to be himself alone, a creature separate and different from any other, who had never been before, and would never be again. He could feel this in his whole weight as he walked, and in each foot as he put it down and gave his weight to it and moved above it, and in every muscle as he moved, and it was a pride which lifted him up and made him feel large, and a pleasure which pierced him through. And as he began with such wondering delight to be aware of his own exact singleness in this world, he also began to understand (or so he thought) just why these fences were set so very narrow, and just why he was walking all by himself. It stole over him, he tells us, like the feeling of a slow cool wind, that he was being guided toward some still more wonderful reward or revealing, up ahead, which he could not of course imagine, but he was sure it was being held in store for him alone.

"Just then the one ahead of him fell down with a great sigh, and was so quickly taken out of the way that he did not even have to shift the order of his hooves as he walked on. The sudden fall and the sound of that sigh dismayed him, though, and something within him told him that it would be wise to look up: and there he saw Him.

"A little bridge ran crosswise above the fences. He stood on this bridge with His feet as wide apart as He could set them. He wore spattered trousers but from the belt up He was naked and as wet as rain. Both arms were raised high above his head and in both hands He held an enormous Hammer. With a grunt which was hardly like the voice of a human being, and with all His strength, He brought this Hammer down into the forehead of our friend: who, in a blinding blazing, heard from his own mouth the beginning of a gasping sigh; then there was only darkness."

Oh, this is *enough!* it's *enough!* she cried out within herself, seeing their terrible young eyes. How *could* she have been so foolish as to tell so much!

"What happened then?" she heard, in the voice of the oldest calf, and she was horrified. This shining in their eyes: was it only excitement? no pity? no fear?

"What happened?" two others asked.

Very well, she said to herself. I've gone so far; now I'll go the rest of the way. She decided not to soften it, either. She'd teach them a lesson they wouldn't forget in a hurry.

"Very well," she was surprised to hear herself say aloud.

"How long he lay in this darkness he couldn't know, but when he began to come out of it, all he knew was the most unspeakably dreadful pain. He was upside down and very slowly swinging and turning, for he was hanging by the tendons of his heels from great frightful hooks, and he has told us that the feeling was as if his hide were being torn from him inch by inch, in one piece. And then as he became more clearly aware he found that this was exactly what was happening. Knives would sliver and slice along both flanks, between the hide and the living flesh; then there was a moment of most precious relief; then red hands seized his hide and there was a jerking of the hide and a tearing of tissue which it was almost as terrible to hear as to feel, turning his whole body and the poor head at the bottom of it; and then the knives again.

"It was so far beyond anything he had ever known unnatural and amazing that he hung there through several more such slicings and jerkings and tearings before he was fully able to take it all in: then, with a scream, and a supreme straining of all his strength, he tore himself from the hooks and collapsed sprawling to the floor and, scrambling right to his feet, charged the men with the knives. For just a moment they were so astonished and so terrified they could not move. Then they moved faster than he had ever known men could—and so did all the other men who chanced to be in his way. He ran down a glowing floor of blood and down endless corridors which were hung with the bleeding carcasses of our kind and with bleeding fragments of carcasses, among blood-clothed men who carried bleeding weapons, and out of that vast room into the open, and over and through one fence after another, shoving aside many an astounded stranger and shouting out warnings as he ran, and away up the railroad toward the West.

"How he ever managed to get away, and how he ever found his way home, we can only try to guess. It's told that he scarcely knew, himself, by the time he came to this part of his story. He was impatient with those who interrupted him to ask about that, he had so much more important things to tell them, and by then he was so exhausted and so far gone that he could say nothing very clear about the little he did know. But we can realize that he must have had really tremendous strength, otherwise he couldn't have outlived the Hammer; and that strength such as his—which we simply don't see these days, it's of the olden time—is capable of things our own strongest and bravest would sicken to dream of. But there was something even stronger than his strength. There was his righteous fury, which nothing could stand up against, which brought him out of that fearful place. And there was his high and burning and heroic purpose, to keep him safe along the way, and to guide him home, and to keep the breath of life in him until he could warn us. He did manage to tell us that he just followed the railroad, but how he chose one among the many which branched out from that place, he couldn't say. He told us, too, that from time to time he recognized shapes of mountains and other landmarks, from his journey by train, all reappearing backward and with a changed look and hard to see, too (for he was shrewd enough to travel mostly at night), but still recognizable. But that isn't enough to account for it. For he has told us, too, that he simply *knew* the way; that he didn't hesitate one moment in choosing the right line of railroad, or even think of it as choosing; and that the landmarks didn't really guide him, but just made him the more sure of what he was already sure of; and that whenever he *did* encounter human beings—and during the later stages of his journey, when he began to doubt he would live to tell us, he traveled day and night—they never so much as moved to make him trouble, but stopped dead in their tracks, and their jaws fell open.

"And surely we can't wonder that their jaws fell open. I'm sure yours would, if you had seen him as he arrived, and I'm very glad I wasn't there to see it, either, even though it is said to be the greatest and most momentous day of all the days that ever were or shall be. For we have the testimony of eyewitnesses, how he looked, and it is only too vivid, even to hear of. He came up out of the East as much staggering as galloping (for by now he was so worn out by pain and exertion and loss of blood that he could hardly stay upright), and his heels were so piteously torn by the hooks that his hooves doubled under more often than not, and in his broken forehead the mark of the Hammer was like the socket for a third eye.

"He came to the meadow where the great trees made shade over the water. 'Bring them all together!' he cried out, as soon as he could find breath. 'All!' Then he drank; and then he began to speak to those who were already there: for as soon as he saw himself in the water it was as clear to him as it was to those who watched him that there was no time left to send for the others. His hide was all gone from his head and his neck and his forelegs and his chest and most of one side and a part of the other side. It was flung backward from his naked muscles by the wind of his running and now it lay around him in the dust like a ragged garment. They say there is no imagining how terrible and in some way how grand the eyeball is when the skin has been taken entirely from around it: his eyes, which were bare in this way, also burned with pain, and with the final energies of his life, and with his desperate concern to warn us while he could; and he rolled his eyes wildly while he talked, or looked piercingly from one to another of the listeners, interrupting himself to cry out, 'Believe me! Oh, believe me!' For it had evidently never occurred to him that he might not be believed, and must make this last great effort, in addition to all he had gone through for us, to make himself believed; so that he groaned with sorrow and with rage and railed at them without tact or mercy for their slowness to believe. He had scarcely what you could call a voice left, but with this relic of a voice he shouted and bellowed and bullied us and insulted us, in the agony of his concern. While he talked he bled from the mouth, and the mingled blood and saliva hung from his chin like the beard of a goat.

"Some say that with his naked face, and his savage eyes, and that beard and the hide lying off his bare shoulders like shabby clothing, he looked almost human. But others feel this is an irreverence even to think; and others, that it is a poor compliment to pay the one who told us, at such cost to himself, the true ultimate purpose of Man. Some did not believe he had ever come from our ranch in the first place, and of course he was so different from us in appearance and even in his voice, and so changed from what he might ever have looked or sounded like before, that nobody could recognize him for sure, though some were sure they did. Others suspected that he had been sent among us with his story for some mischievous and cruel purpose, and the fact that they could not imagine what this purpose might be, made them, naturally, all the more suspicious. Some believed he was actually a man, trying— and none too successfully, they said—to disguise himself as one of us; and again the fact that they could not imagine why a man would do this, made them all the more uneasy. There were quite a few who doubted that anyone who could get into such bad condition as he was in, was fit even to give reliable information, let alone advice, to those in good health. And some whispered, even while he spoke, that he had turned lunatic; and many came to believe this. It wasn't only that his story was so fantastic; there was good reason to wonder, many felt, whether anybody in his right mind would go to such trouble for others. But even those who did not believe him listened intently, out of curiosity to hear so wild a tale, and out of the respect it is only proper to show any creature who is in the last agony.

"What he told, was what I have just told you. But his purpose was away beyond just the telling. When they asked questions, no matter how curious or suspicious or idle or foolish, he learned, toward the last, to answer them with all the patience he could and in all the detail he could remember. He even invited them to examine his wounded heels and the pulsing wound in his head as closely as they pleased. He even begged them to, for he knew that before everything else, he must be believed. For unless we could believe him, wherever could we find any reason, or enough courage, to do the hard and dreadful things he told us we must do!

"It was only these things, he cared about. Only for these, he came back."

Now clearly remembering what these things were, she felt her whole being quail. She looked at the young ones quickly and as quickly looked away.

"While he talked," she went on, "and our ancestors listened, men came quietly among us; one of them shot him. Whether he was shot in kindness or to silence him is an endlessly disputed question which will probably never be settled. Whether, even, he died of the shot, or through his own great pain and weariness (for his eyes, they say, were glazing for some time before the men came), we will never be sure. Some suppose even that he may have died of his sorrow and his concern for us. Others feel that he had quite enough to die of, without that. All these things are tangled and lost in the disputes of those who love to theorize and to argue. There is no arguing about his dying words, though; they were very clearly remembered:

"*Tell them! Believe!*"

After a while her son asked, "What did he tell them to do?"

She avoided his eyes. "There's a great deal of disagreement about that, too," she said after a moment. "You see, he was so very tired."

They were silent.

"So tired," she said, "some think that toward the end, he really *must* have been out of his mind."

"Why?" asked her son.

"Because he was so tired out and so badly hurt."

They looked at her mistrustfully.

"And because of what he told us to do."

"What did he tell us to do?" her son asked again.

Her throat felt dry. "Just . . . things you can hardly bear even to think of. That's all."

They waited. "Well, *what?*" her son asked in a cold, accusing voice.

"*Each one is himself,*" she said shyly. "*Not of the herd. Himself alone.*' That's one."

"What else?"

"*Obey nobody. Depend on none.*'"

"What else?"

She found that she was moved. "*Break down the fences!*'" she said less shyly. "*Tell everybody, everywhere.*'"

"Where?"

"Everywhere. You see, he thought there must be ever so many more of us than we had ever known."

They were silent. "What else?" her son asked.

"*For if even a few do not hear me, or disbelieve me, we are all betrayed.*'"

"Betrayed?"

"He meant, doing as men want us to. Not for ourselves, or the good of each other."

They were puzzled.

"Because, you see, he felt there was no other way." Again her voice altered: "*All who are put on the range are put onto trains. All who are put onto trains meet the Man With The Hammer. All who stay home are kept here to breed others to go onto the range, and so betray themselves and their kind and their children forever.*

" 'We are brought into this life only to be victims; and there is no other way for us unless we save ourselves.'

"Do you understand?"

Still they were puzzled, she saw; and no wonder, poor things. But now the ancient lines rang in her memory, terrible and brave. They made her somehow proud. She began actually to want to say them.

" 'Never be taken,' " she said. " 'Never be driven. Let those who can, kill Man. Let those who cannot, avoid him.' "

She looked around at them.

"What else?" her son asked, and in his voice there was a rising valor.

She looked straight into his eyes. " 'Kill the yearlings,' " she said very gently. " 'Kill the calves.' "

She saw the valor leave his eyes.

"Kill us?"

She nodded. " 'So long as Man holds dominion over us,' " she said. And in dread and amazement she heard herself add, " 'Bear no young.' "

With this they all looked at her at once in such a way that she loved her child, and all these others, as never before; and there dilated within her such a sorrowful and marveling grandeur that for a moment she was nothing except her own inward whisper, "Why *I* am one alone. And of the herd, too. Both at once. All one."

Her son's voice brought her back: "Did they do what he told them to?"

The oldest one scoffed, "Would we be here, if they had?"

"They say some did," the mother replied. "Some tried. Not all."

"What did the men do to them?" another asked.

"I don't know," she said. "It was such a very long time ago."

"Do you believe it?" asked the oldest calf.

"There are some who believe it," she said.

"Do *you?*"

"I'm told that far back in the wildest corners of the range there are some of us, mostly very, very old ones, who have never been taken. It's said that they meet, every so often, to talk and just to think together about the heroism and the terror of two sublime Beings, The One Who Came Back, and The Man With The Hammer. Even here at home, some of the old ones, and some of us who are just old-fash-

ioned, believe it, or parts of it anyway. I know there are
some who say that a hollow at the center of the forehead
—a sort of shadow of the Hammer's blow—is a sign of very
special ability. And I remember how Great-grandmother used
to sing an old, pious song, let's see now, yes, 'Be not like
dumb-driven cattle, be a hero in the strife.' But there aren't
many. Not any more."

"Do *you* believe it?" the oldest calf insisted; and now she
was touched to realize that every one of them, from the
oldest to the youngest, needed very badly to be sure about
that.

"Of course not, silly," she said; and all at once she was
overcome by a most curious shyness, for it occurred to her
that in the course of time, this young thing might be bred
to her. "It's just an old, old legend." With a tender little
laugh she added, lightly, "We use it to frighten children
with."

By now the light was long on the plain and the herd
was only a fume of gold near the horizon. Behind it, dung
steamed, and dust sank gently to the shattered ground. She
looked far away for a moment, wondering. Something—it
was like a forgotten word on the tip of the tongue. She
felt the sudden chill of the late afternoon and she wondered what she had been wondering about. "Come, children," she said briskly, "it's high time for supper." And she
turned away; they followed.

The trouble was, her son was thinking, you could never
trust her. If she said a thing was so, she was probably just
trying to get her way with you. If she said a thing wasn't so,
it probably was so. But you never could be sure. Not
without seeing for yourself. I'm going to go, he told himself; I don't care *what* she wants. And if it isn't so, why
then I'll live on the range and make the great journey and
find out what *is* so. And if what she told was true, why then
I'll know ahead of time and the one *I* will charge is The
Man With The Hammer. I'll put Him and His Hammer out
of the way forever, and that will make me an even better
hero than The One Who Came Back.

So when his mother glanced at him in concern, not quite
daring to ask her question, he gave her his most docile
smile, and snuggled his head against her, and she was
comforted.

The littlest and youngest of them was doing double skips
in his effort to keep up with her. Now that he wouldn't be

interrupting her, and none of the big ones would hear and make fun of him, he shyly whispered his question, so warmly moistly ticklish that she felt as if he were licking her ear.

"What is it, darling?" she asked, bending down.

"What's a train?"

The National Pastime

BY JOHN CHEEVER

To BE an American and unable to play baseball is comparable to being a Polynesian and unable to swim. It's an impossible situation. This will be apparent to everyone, and it was to me, a country boy brought up on a farm—or, to be precise, in a country house—just outside the village of St. Botolph's, in Massachusetts. The place is called West Farm. My ancestors had lived in that village and in that house since the seventeenth century, and they had distinguished themselves as sailors and athletes. Leander, my father (his brothers were named Orpheus and Hamlet), had played shortstop for the St. Botolph's Hose Company. Although the hose-company games sometimes figured in his recollections, his memories were usually of a different order. He was nearly sixty when I was born, and he could remember the last days of St. Botolph's as a port. My grandfather had been a ship's master, and when I was a boy, our house was partly furnished with things that he had brought back from Ceylon and China. The maritime past that my father glimpsed had been glorious, full of gold and silver, full of Samoan beauties and tests of courage. Then—so he told me—box-wood had grown in our garden, and the paths had been covered once a year with pebbles that were brought from a cove near West Travertine where the stones were as round and white as pearls. In the rear wing of our house, there was a peculiar, very clean smell that was supposed to have been left there by my grandfather's Chinese servants. My father liked to recall this period of splendor, but he liked even better to recall his success as a partner in the gold-bead factory that had been built in St. Botolph's when its maritime prosperity was ended. He had gone to work as an office

boy, and his rise had been brilliant and swift. He had
business acumen, and he was convivial. He took an intense
pleasure in having the factory whistle blown. He had it
blown for all our birthdays and for his wedding anniversary,
and when my mother had guests for lunch, the whistle usually blew as the ladies sat down.

In the twenties, the gold-bead factory was mortgaged
and converted to the manufacture of table silver, and presently my father and his partner were ruined. My father
felt that he was an old man who had spent all his energy
and all his money on things that were unredeemable and vulgar,
and he was inconsolable. He went away, and my mother called
my two sisters and me to her room and told us that she was
afraid he had killed himself. He had left a note hinting at this,
and he had taken a pistol with him. I was nine years old
then, and my sisters were fourteen and fifteen. Suicide may
have been my father's intention, but he returned a few
days later and began to support the family by selling the
valuables that had come to him from the shipmaster. I had
decided to become a professional baseball player. I had
bought a Louisville Slugger, a ball, and a first baseman's
mitt. I asked my father to play catch with me one Sunday
afternoon, but he refused. My mother must have overheard
this conversation, because she called him to her room, where
they quarrelled. In a little while, he came out to the garden and asked me to throw the ball to him. What happened
then was ridiculous and ugly. I threw the ball clumsily once
or twice and missed the catches he threw to me. Then I
turned my head to see something—a boat on the river. He
threw the ball, and it got me in the nape of the neck and
stretched me out unconscious in my grandfather's ruined
garden. When I came to, my nose was bleeding and my
mouth was full of blood. I felt that I was being drowned.
My father was standing over me. "Don't tell your mother
about this" he said. When I sat up and he saw that I was
all right, he went down through the garden toward the barn
and the river.

My mother called me to her room that night after supper.
She had become an invalid and she seldom left her bed. All
the furniture in her room was white, and the rugs were
white, and there was a picture of "Jesus the Shepherd" on
the wall beside her bed. The room was getting dark, I remember, and I felt, from the tone of her voice, that we were
approaching a kind of emotional darkness I had noticed

before in our family affairs. "You must try to understand your father," she said, putting down her Bible and reaching for my hand. "He is old. He is spoiled." Then, although I don't think he was in the house, she lowered her voice to a whisper, so that we could not be overheard. "You see, some years ago his cousin Lucy Hartshorn left him a great deal of money, in trust. She was a meddlesome old lady. I guess you don't remember her. She was an antivivisectionist, and wanted to abolish the celebration of Christmas. She liked to order your father around, and she felt the family was petering out. We had Grace and Vikery then, and she left your father the money on condition that he not have any more children. He was very upset when he found out that I was *enceinte*. I wouldn't want you to know what went on. He had planned a luxurious old age—he wanted to raise pigeons and have a sailboat—and I think he sometimes sees in you the difference between what he had planned and what he has been reduced to. You'll have to try and understand." Her words made almost no impression on me at the time. I remember counting the larches outside her window while she talked to me, and looking beyond them to the faded lettering on the wall of the barn—"Boston Store: Rock Bottom Prices"—and to some pines ringed with darkness beyond the barn. The little that I knew of our family history was made up of revokable trusts, purloined wills, and dark human secrets, and since I had never seen Lucy Hartshorn, this new secret seemed to have no more to do with me than the others did.

The school I went to was an old frame building in the village, and every morning I walked two miles upriver to get there. Two of the spinster teachers were cousins of mine, and the man who taught manual training and coached athletics was the son of our garbage collector. My parents had helped him through normal school. The New England spring was in force, and one fine morning we left the gymnasium for the ball field. The instructor was carrying some baseball equipment, and as soon as I saw it, the sweet, salty taste of blood came into my mouth. My heart began to pound, my legs felt weak, and while I thought, from these symptoms, that I must be sick, I knew instinctively how to cure myself. On the way to the field, we passed an old field house that stood on some concrete posts, concealed by a scrim of rotten lattice. I began to walk slowly and when the rest of the class had passed the field house, I got down on my hands and knees and crawled through a broken place in the lattice and underneath the building. There was hardly room for me to lie there between the dirt and the sills that were covered with cobwebs. Someone had stuffed an old sneaker and a rusted watering can under the building, confident that they would never be seen again. I could hear from the field the voices of my friends choosing sides, and I felt the horror of having expelled myself from the light of a fine day, but I also felt, lying in the dirt, that the taste of blood was beginning to leave my mouth, that my heart was beginning to regulate its beating, and that the strength was returning to my legs. I lay in the dirt until the game ended and I could see, through the lattice, the players returning to school.

I felt that the fault was Leander's, and that if I could bring myself to approach him again, when he was in a better humor, he would respond humanely. The feeling that I could not assume my responsibilities as a baseball player without some help from him was deep, as if parental love and baseball were both national pastimes. One afternoon, I got my ball and mitt and went into the library, where he was taking books down from the shelves and tying them up in bundles of ten, to be taken into Boston and sold. He had been a handsome man, I think. I had heard my relations speak of how he had aged, and so I suppose that his looks had begun to deteriorate. He would have been taken for a Yankee anywhere, and he seemed to feel that his alliance to the sea was by blood as well as tradition. When he went into an oyster bar and found people who were patently not American-born eating oysters, he would be stirred. He ate quantities of fish, swam daily in the salt river, and washed himself each morning with a sea sponge, so he always smelled faintly of brine and iodine, as if he had only recently come dripping out of the Atlantic. The brilliant blue of his eyes had not faded, and the boyish character of his face—its lightness and ovalness—was intact. He had not understood the economic fragility of his world, his wife's invalidism seemed to be a manifest rebuke for the confusion of his affairs, and his mind must have been thronged with feelings of being unwanted and also feelings of guilt. The books he was preparing to sell were his father's and his grandfather's; he would rail about this later, feeling that if histrionics would not redeem him, they would at least recapture for a minute his sense of identity and pride. If I had looked closely, I might have seen a face harried with anxiety and the weaknesses of old age, but I expected him, for my sake, to regain his youth and to appear like the paternal images I had seen on calendars and in magazine advertisements.

"Will you please play catch with me, Poppa?" I asked.

"How can you ask me to play baseball when I will be dead in another month!" he said. He sighed and then said, "I won't live through the summer. Your mother has been complaining all morning. She has nothing to say to me unless she has a complaint to make. She's complaining now of pains in her feet. She can't leave her bed because of the pains in her feet. She's trying to make me more unhappy than I already am, but I have some facts to fall back on. Here, let me show you." He took down one of the many volumes in which he had recorded his life, and searched through the pages until he found what he wanted. "Your mother wore custom-made shoes from 1904 until 1908, when Mr. Schults died. He made her six, twelve, fourteen—he made her seventeen pairs of shoes in four years. Then she began buying her shoes at Nettleton's." He wet his finger and turned a page. "She never paid less than twelve dollars a pair there, and in 1908 she bought four pairs of shoes and two pairs of canvas pumps. In 1910, she bought four pairs of shoes at Nettleton's and a pair of evening slippers at Stetson's. She said the slippers pinched her feet, but we couldn't take them back because she'd worn them. In 1911, she bought three pairs of shoes at Stetson's and two at Nettleton's. In 1912, she had Henderson make her a pair of walking shoes. They cost eighteen dollars. She paid twenty-four dollars for a pair of gold pumps at Stetson's. In 1913, she bought another pair of canvas pumps, two pairs of suède shoes, golf shoes, and some beaded shoes." He looked to me for some confirmation of the unreasonableness of my mother's illness, but I hung my head and went out of the library.

The next time the class went out for baseball, I hid in a building closer to the school, where rakes and rollers and other grounds equipment were stored. This place also was dark, but there was room to stand and move and enjoy an illusion of freedom, although the light of day and the voices on the field from which I was hidden seemed like the lights and the sounds of life. I had been there only a few minutes when I heard someone approach and open

the door. I had thought it would be the old grounds keeper,
but it was a classmate of mine, who recognized, a second
after he saw me, what I was doing, and seemed—since he
was doing the same thing—delighted to have a conspirator.
I disliked him and his friends, but I couldn't have disliked
him more than I disliked the symptoms of my own panic,
for I didn't leave the building. After this, I had to hide
not only from the ball game but from my classmate. He continued to hide in the tool shed and I hid near the playing
field, in some woods behind the backstop, and chewed pieces
of grass until the period ended.

That fall, I went out for football, and I had always liked
winter sports, but in the spring, when the garbage man's
son took the balls and bats out of the chest near the door
of the gymnasium, the taste of blood in my mouth, the beating of my heart, and the weakness in my legs were keener
than ever, and I found myself stuffed in the dirt under
the track house again, with the old tennis sneaker and the
watering can, horrified that I should have chosen or should
have been made to lie in this filth when I could be walking
freely over a green field. As the season progressed, I began
to find new hiding places and to invent new ailments that
would excuse me from having to play baseball, and the feeling that Leander had the cure to my cowardice returned,
although I could not bring myself to approach him again.
He still seemed to preserve, well on the dark side of his
mind, some hard feelings about my being responsible for
the revocation of Lucy Hartshorn's trust. Several times when
I went to a movie or a dance, he locked the house up so
tight that I couldn't find any way to get in, and had to
sleep in the barn. Once, I returned in the daytime and found
the house locked. I heard him moving inside and I rang
the bell. He opened the door long enough to say, "Whatever
it is you're selling, I don't want any." Then he slammed
the door in my face. A minute later, he opened the door
again. "I'm sorry, Eben," he said. "I didn't realize it was
you."

My mother died when I was in my third year of high
school. When I graduated the following year, Leander claimed
to be too infirm to come to the ceremony, and when I
looked down from the platform into a gathering where there
were no relatives of mine, it occurred to me—without pleasure or guilt—that I had probably not been up to bat more
than three times.

My Cousin Juliana put up the money to send me to college, and I entered college feeling that my troubles with Leander and baseball were over. Both my sisters had married by then, and gone to live in the West, and I dutifully spent part of my Christmas holiday at West Farm and planned to spend all my Easter vacation there. On the morning that college closed for the spring recess, I drove with my two roommates over to Mount Holyoke, where we picked up three girls. We were planning to have a picnic somewhere along the river. When we stopped for lunch, one of my roommates went around to the back of the car and got out his camera to take a picture of the girls. Glancing into the luggage compartment, I noticed a baseball and a bat. Everyone was around in front of the car. I couldn't be seen. The ground was loose, and with my hands I dug a hole nearly a foot deep. Then I dropped the baseball into this hole and buried it.

It was late when we got into Boston, and I took the last train down to St. Botolph's. I had written Leander that I was coming, in the hope that he would not lock the house up, but when I reached there, after midnight, all the doors and windows were secured. I didn't feel like spending the night in the barn, and I broke a windowpane in the dining room and climbed in. I could hear Leander moving around upstairs, and because I felt irritated, I didn't call out to him. A few seconds later, there was an explosion in the room. Somebody had shot off a pistol and I thought I had been killed. I got to a switch and turned on the lights and saw, with a wild, crazy uprush of joy, that I was alive and unharmed. Then I saw Leander standing in the doorway with the pistol in his hand. He dropped it to the floor and, stumbling toward me, laid his head on my shoulder and wept. "Oh, Eben! Eben! Eben!" he sobbed. "I thought it was a prowler! I heard someone trying to get in! I heard the breaking glass. Forgive me, forgive me."

I remember that he was wearing a fez, and some kind of ragged and outrageous robe over his shoulders. He had, up until that year, always dressed with great simplicity and care, feeling that a sensible regard for appearances facilitated human relationships. He had always put on a dark coat for dinner, and he would never consider as acquaintances or as business associates men with grease in their hair, men with curls, men who wore pointed shoes or diamond cuff links or who put pheasant feathers in their colored hats. Age seemed to have revised these principles, and during the Easter holidays he appeared in many brilliant costumes, many of them the robes and surplices of a fraternal order that had been disbanded in the twenties. Once when I stepped into the bathroom, I found him before the full-length mirror in the ostrich-plumed hat, the cross-ribbon heavy with orders, and the ornate sword of a Poor Knight of Christ and the Temple and a Guardian of the Gates of Gaza. He often quoted from Shakespeare.

The first job I got after leaving college was at Chatfield Academy. The school was in New Hampshire—in the mountains—and I went north in the fall. I liked teaching, and the place itself seemed oddly detached and peaceful. Chimes rang at the quarter hour, the buildings were old or copied old forms, the leaves fell past the classroom windows for a month, the nights smelled of smoke, and, leaving my classroom one evening in December, I found the air full of a swift, dry snow. The school was conservative, and at its helm was old Dr. Wareham. Robust on the playing field, tearful in chapel, bull-necked and vigorous in spite of his advanced age, he was that kind of monolithic father image that used to be thought a necessity for the education of youth. After the Easter recess, I signed a contract for the following year and arranged to teach summer school. In April, I got a notice that faculty participation in the annual meeting of the board of trustees was mandatory. I asked a man at supper one night what this meant.

"Well, they come up on Friday," my colleague said, "and Wareham gives them a dinner. Then they have their annual meeting. We have demonstration classes on Saturday and they snoop around, but they're mostly intelligent and they don't make trouble. Then Saturday noon, the old troll barbecues a side of beef and we have lunch with them. After this, there's a ball game between the trustees and the faculty members. The new members are always expected to play, and you'd better be good. The old troll feels that men get to know one another best on the playing field, and he doesn't miss a trick. We had a frail art teacher here a couple of years ago who claimed to have a headache, but Wareham got him out of bed and made him play third base. He made three errors and Wareham fired him. Then, after that, there's a cocktail party at Wareham's house, with good sour-mash bourbon for the brass and sherry for the rest of us. Then they go home."

The old taste of blood came into my mouth. The appetite for the meat and potatoes I had heaped onto my plate was gone. I nevertheless gorged myself, for I seemed to have been put into a position where my only recourse was to overlook my feelings or to conceal them where this was not possible. I knew by then that a thorough inspection of the history of the problem would not alter the facts, and that the best I could bring to the situation was a kind of hollow good cheer. I told myself that the game was inconsequential, and presently I seemed to feel this. There was some gossip the next day about Dr. Wareham's seriousness about the game. The piano teacher—a tall man named Bacon—had refused to play, and somebody said that he would be fired. But I was occupied with my classwork and I nearly forgot about the annual meeting until, leaving my classroom on a Friday afternoon, I saw a large car driven by a chauffeur go around the quadrangle and stop at Dr. Wareham's house. The trustees were beginning to arrive.

After supper, I corrected papers until about eleven, when I went to bed. Something woke me at three in the morning, and I went to the open window and I looked out at the night for signs of rain before I realized that this was an old habit of childhood. Rain had meant that I would be free, for a day, of hiding under the field house or in the woods behind the backstop. And now, still half asleep, I turned my ear to the window, listening with the purest anxiety, colored by a kind of pleading, for the stir of rain beginning or the heavier sound of a settled storm. A single drop of water would have sounded like music. I knew from which quarter the rain wind might rise; I knew how cumbrously the wind would blow, how it would smell of wetness, how the storm, as it came west through the village, would make a distant roar, how the first drops would sound on the elm trees in the yard and the shrubs against the wall, how the rain would drum in the grass, how it would swell, how it would wet the kindling at the barbecue pit and disintegrate the paper bags that contained the charcoal, how it would confine the trustees to Dr. Wareham's house and prevail on one or two of them to leave before the cocktail party, and how it would first fill in the slight indentation around second base and then spread slow-

ly toward first and third, until the whole field was flooded. . . .
But I saw only a starry and windless night. I got back into
bed and, settling for the best I had—a kind of hollow good
cheer—fell asleep.

The morning was the best kind of spring weather; even
I saw this. The demonstration classes satisfied everyone,
and at noon we went over to the barbecue pit to have our
lunch with the trustees. The food seemed to stick in my
throat, but this may have been the fault of the barbecue itself, because the meat was raw and the cooking arrangements were a disappointment all around. I was still eating
my dessert when the Doctor gave the rallying cry "Into your
uniforms, men!" I put down my plate and started for the
field house, with the arm of a French instructor thrown warmly over my shoulder and in a cheerful, friendly crowd
that seemed blamelessly on their way to recapturing, or
at least to reënacting, the secure pleasures of youth.
But since the hour they returned to was one that I had
never possessed, I felt the falseness of my position. I was
handed a uniform—a gesture that seemed unalterably to be
one of parting. But it was the too large shoes, wrapped with
friction tape, that, when I bent over to lace them, gave
me the worst spasm of despair. I picked a glove out of a
box near the door and jogged out to the field.

The bleachers were full of students and faculty wives,
and Dr. Wareham was walking up and down, leading them
in singing to the band. The faculty members were first
up, facing a formidable concentration of power and wealth
in the field. The first batter got a line drive that was missed
by the bank president on first and was good for a double.
The second man up struck out, but the third man up reached
first, and the industrialist who was pitching walked the
fourth batter. I gave a yank to my cap and stepped up to
the plate, working my mouth and swallowing to clean it,
if I could, of the salty taste of blood. I kept my eye on the
ball, and when the first pitch seemed to be coming straight
over the plate, I chopped at it with all my might. I heard
the crack, I felt the vibration up my forearm, and, telling
myself that a baseball diamond, like most things, must op-
erate on a clockwise principle, I sprinted for third and
knocked down the runner who was coming in to score. I
knocked him flat, and, bending over to see if he was all

right, I heard Dr. Wareham roaring at me, "Get off the field! Get out of my sight!"

I walked back to the field house alone. The soberness of my feeling seemed almost to verge on romantic love—it seemed to make the air I walked through heavy—as if I were sick at heart for some gorgeous raven-haired woman who had been separated from me by a convulsion of nature. I took off my uniform and stood for a long time in the shower. Then I dressed and walked back across the quadrangle, where I could hear, from the open windows of the music building, Bacon playing the Chopin preludes. The music—swept with rains, with ruins, with unrequited and autumnal loves, with here and there a passage of the purest narcissism—seemed to outrage my senses, and I wanted to stop my ears. It took me an hour or so to pack, and when I carried my bags downstairs, I could still hear the cheering from the field. I drove into the village and had the tank filled with gas. At the edge of town, I wondered what direction to take, and then I turned south, for the farm.

It was six or seven when I got to St. Botolph's, and I took the precaution of calling Leander before I drove out to the house. "Hello, hello, hello!" the old man shouted. "You must have the wrong number. Oh, hello, Eben . . ." When I got to the house, I left my bags in the hall and went upstairs. Leander was in his room. "Welcome home, Eben," he said. "I was reading a little Shakespeare to the cat."

When I sat down, the arm of my chair crashed to the floor, and I let it lie there. On his thick white hair Leander still wore his fez. For clothing, he had drawn from his store of old-fashioned bathing suits one with a striped skirt. It must have been stolen, since there were some numerals stencilled on the back. He had decided some time before that the most comfortable shoes he had were some old riding boots, and he was wearing these. Pictures of lost sailboats, lost cottages, dead friends and dogs gazed down at him from the wall. He had tied a length of string between the four wooden pineapples of his high poster bed and had hung his wash there to dry. The cat and his copy of Shakespeare were on his lap. "What are your plans?" he asked.

"I've been fired," I said. "I thought I'd leave some clothes here. I think I'll go for a swim now."

"Have you any clothes I can wear?"

"You're welcome to anything I have. The bags are downstairs."

"I still swim every day," Leander said. "Every day, that is, until the first of October. Last year I went swimming through the fifteenth—the fifteenth or the sixteenth. If you'll wait a minute, I'll make sure." He got up from his chair, and, stooping a little, so the tassel of his fez hung over his brow, he walked to his journal. After consulting it, he said, "I went swimming on the fifteenth last year. I went swimming on the twenty-fifth the year before that. Of course, that was nothing to what I could do when I was younger. I went swimming on the fourth of December, the eighth of January, the second of March. I went swimming on Christmas Day, New Year's Day, the twelfth of January, and the tenth of February . . ."

After I left him to go out to the river, he went downstairs to where my bags were. An old pair of riding pants took his eye. He managed to get his legs well into them before he realized that they were too small. He tried to remove the pants and couldn't, because his legs had begun to swell. And when he tried to stand, the pants knifed him in the tendons at the back of his knees and brought him to the floor. Halfway out in the river, I could hear him roaring for help, and I swam back to shore and ran up to the house and found him moving slowly and painfully toward the kitchen, where he hoped to find a knife and cut himself free. I cut the riding breeches off him, and we drank some whiskey together, but I left in the morning for New York.

It was a good thing that I did leave, because I got a job the day I reached the city, and sailed three days later for Basra, to work for an oil company. I took the long voyage out on one of the company ships; it was five weeks after leaving New York that we stopped at Aden and another four days before we docked at Basra. It was hot. The flat volcanic ruins trembled in the heat, and the car that took me across the city to the oil-company settlement travelled through a maze of foul-smelling streets. The dormitory where I was to be quartered was like an army barracks, and when I reached it, in midafternoon, there was no one there but some Arabs, who helped me with my bags and told me the other men would be in after four, when the offices closed. When the men I shared the barracks with came in, they seemed pleased to see anyone newly arrived from the

States, and they were full of practical information about how to make a life in Basra. "We practice baseball two or three nights a week," one of them said, "and then on Sundays we play Shell or Standard Oil. We only have eleven men on the squad now, so if you could play outfield? We call ourselves the Infidels. . . ."

It was not until long after my return from Basra, long after my marriage, that Leander died, one summer afternoon, sitting in the rose garden, with a copy of "Primitive Sexual Mores" on his lap. The housekeeper found him there, and the local undertaker sent me a wire in New York. I did not feel any grief when I got the news. Alice and I had three children by then, and my life would not in any way be affected by Leander's death. I telephoned my sisters, in Denver, but neither of them felt that they could come East. The next day, I drove to St. Botolph's, and found that the undertaker had made all the arrangements. The services were to be at two. Three old cousins came out from Boston, to my surprise, and we were the only mourners. It was the kind of weather that we used to call haying weather when I lived in the valley. The fields of timothy and sweet grass had been cut, the cemetery smelled of cut hay, and while the minister was praying, I heard the sound of distant thunder and saw the daylight dim, the way the lights dim in a farmhouse during a storm. After the ceremony, I returned to the house, feeling that there would be a lot there to occupy me, but it turned out that there was not much to do. It had begun to rain. I wandered through the rooms to see if there was anything left in them. I found some whiskey. The bird cages, the three-legged tables, and the cracked soup tureens must have been refused by the junkman. I thought that there must be a will, and I went reluctantly—disconsolately, at any rate—up to Leander's room and sat uneasily in his chair. His papers were copious and bizarre, and it took me nearly two hours to find the will. He left the house and the land to my older sister. To my other sister he left the jewelry, but this was immaterial, since all the jewelry had been sold. I was mentioned. "To my changeling son, Eben," he wrote, "the author of all my misfortunes, I leave my copy of Shakespeare, a hacking cough . . ." The list was long and wicked, and although he had written it ten years earlier and although I had buried him that afternoon, I couldn't help

feeling, for a minute, that the piece of paper was evidence
of my own defeat. It was dark then, and it was still raining.
The whiskey bottle was empty and the unshaded electric
light was baneful. The old house, which had always seemed
to have an extensive life of its own, was creaking and stirring under the slender weight of the storm. The feeling that
in burying Leander I had resolved a sad story seemed
farcical, and if my reaction to his will was evidence, the
old fool had pierced the rites and ceremonies of death.
I thought desperately of my family in New York, and of
the rooms where my return was waited with anxiety and
love, but I had never been able to build any kind of
bridge from Leander's world to the worlds where I lived,
and I failed now in my efforts to remember New York.
I went downstairs to telephone my wife, but the telephone was dead, and for all I knew it might have been dis-
connected years ago. I packed my bag, turned out the lights,
threw the house key into the river, and started home.

In the years that followed, I thought now and then about
Leander and the farm, and although I had resolved to
break with these memories, they both continued to enjoy
the perfect freedom of my dreams; the bare halls of the
house, the massive granite stoop, the rain dripping from the
wooden gutters, and the mass of weeds in the garden often
surrounded me while I slept. My participation in baseball continued to be painful. I drove a ball through my
mother-in-law's parlor window—and the rest of the family,
who were intimidated, didn't understand why I should feel
so happy—but it was not enough to lay Leander's ghost,
and I still didn't like old men with white hair to be at
the helm of the ships I travelled on. Some years later—my
oldest son was nine—I took all five boys uptown to Yankee
Stadium to see their first game. It was one of the hottest days
of the year. I bought my sons food, eyeshades, pennants,
score cards, pencils, and souvenir pins, and I took the youngest two to the bathroom several times. Mantle was up in
the sixth, with a count of three and two. He fouled three
balls into the netting above the backstop and fouled the
fourth straight toward where we were sitting—a little high.
It was coming like a shot, but I made the catch—one-
handed, barehanded—and although I thought the impact had
broken some bones in my hand, the pain was followed swiftly by a sense of perfect joy. The old man and the old house

seemed at last to fall from the company and the places of my dreams, and I smelled the timothy and the sweet grass again, and saw a gravedigger hidden behind a marble angel, and the smoky, the grainy light of a thunderstorm, when the clearness of the green world—the emblazoned fields—reminds us briefly of a great freedom of body and mind. Then the boys began to argue for possession of the ball, and I gave it to the oldest one, hoping that I wouldn't have any more use for it. It would have troubled Leander to think that he would be buried in any place as distant from West Farm as Yankee Stadium, but that is where his bones were laid to rest.

The Girls in Their Summer Dresses

BY IRWIN SHAW

FIFTH AVENUE was shining in the sun when they left the Brevoort. The sun was warm, even though it was February, and everything looked like Sunday morning—the buses and the well-dressed people walking slowly in couples and the quiet buildings with the windows closed.

Michael held Frances' arm tightly as they walked toward Washington Square in the sunlight. They walked lightly, almost smiling, because they had slept late and had a good breakfast and it was Sunday. Michael unbuttoned his coat and let it flap around him in the mild wind.

"Look out," Frances said as they crossed Eighth Street. "You'll break your neck."

Michael laughed and Frances laughed with him.

"She's not so pretty," Frances said. "Anyway, not pretty enough to take a chance of breaking your neck."

Michael laughed again. "How did you know I was looking at her?"

Frances cocked her head to one side and smiled at her husband under the brim of her hat. "Mike, darling," she said.

"O.K.," he said. "Excuse me."

Frances patted his arm lightly and pulled him along a little faster toward Washington Square. "Let's not see anybody all day," she said. "Let's just hang around with each

other. You and me. We're always up to the neck with people, drinking their Scotch or drinking our Scotch; we only
see each other in bed. I want to go out with my husband all day long. I want him to talk only to me and listen
only to me."

"What's to stop us?" Michael asked.

"The Stevensons. They want us to drop by around one
o'clock and they'll drive us into the country."

"The cunning Stevensons," Mike said. "Transparent.
They can whistle. They can go driving in the country by
themselves."

"Is it a date?"

"It's a date."

Frances leaned over and kissed him on the tip of the
ear.

"Darling," Michael said, "this is Fifth Avenue."

"Let me arrange a program," Frances said. "A planned
Sunday in New York for a young couple with money to
throw away."

"Go easy."

"First let's go the Metropolitan Museum of Art," Frances
suggested, because Michael had said during the week he
wanted to go. "I haven't been there in three years and
there're at least ten pictures I want to see again. Then we
can take the bus down to Radio City and watch them
skate. And later we'll go down to Cavanagh's and get a
steak as big as a blacksmith's apron, with a bottle of
wine, and after that there's a French picture at the Film-
arte that everybody says—say, are you listening to me?"

"Sure," he said. He took his eyes off the hatless girl with
the dark hair, cut dancer-style like a helmet, who was walking past him.

"That's the program for the day," Frances said flatly.
"Or maybe you'd just rather walk up and down Fifth
Avenue."

"No," Michael said. "Not at all."

"You always look at other women," Frances said. "Everywhere. Every damned place we go."

"Now, darling," Michael said, "I look at everything. God
gave me eyes and I look at women and men and subway
excavations and moving pictures and the little flowers of
the field. I casually inspect the universe."

"You ought to see the look in your eye," Frances said,
"as you casually inspect the universe on Fifth Avenue."

"I'm a happily married man." Michael pressed her elbow tenderly. "Example for the whole twentieth century—Mr. and Mrs. Mike Loomis. Hey, let's have a drink," he said, stopping.

"We just had breakfast."

"Now listen, darling," Mike said, choosing his words with care, "it's a nice day and we both felt good and there's no reason why we have to break it up. Let's have a nice Sunday."

"All right. I don't know why I started this. Let's drop it. Let's have a good time."

They joined hands consciously and walked without talking among the baby carriages and the old Italian men in their Sunday clothes and the young women with Scotties in Washington Square Park.

"At least once a year everyone should go to the Metropolitan Museum of Art," Frances said after a while, her tone a good imitation of the tone she had used at breakfast and at the beginning of their walk. "And it's nice on Sunday. There're a lot of people looking at the pictures and you get the feeling maybe Art isn't on the decline in New York City after all—"

"I want to tell you something," Michael said very seriously. "I have not touched another woman. Not once. In all the five years."

"All right," Frances said.

"You believe that, don't you?"

"All right."

They walked between the crowded benches under the scrubby city-park trees.

"I try not to notice it," Frances said, "but I feel rotten inside, in my stomach, when we pass a woman and you look at her and I see that look in your eye and that's the way you looked at me the first time. In Alice Maxwell's house. Standing there in the living room, next to the radio, with a green hat on and all those people."

"I remember the hat," Michael said.

"The same look," Frances said. "And it makes me feel bad. It makes me feel terrible."

"Sh-h-h, please, darling, sh-h-h."

"I think I would like a drink now," Frances said.

They walked over to a bar on Eighth Street, not saying anything, Michael automatically helping her over curbstones and guiding her past automobiles. They sat near a window in the bar and the sun streamed in and there was a small, cheerful fire in the fireplace. A little Japanese waiter came over and put down some pretzels and smiled happily at them.

"What do you order after breakfast?" Michael asked.

"Brandy, I suppose," Frances said.

"Courvoisier," Michael told the waiter. "Two Courvoisiers."

The waiter came with the glasses and they sat drinking the brandy in the sunlight. Michael finished half his and drank a little water.

"I look at women," he said. "Correct. I don't say it's wrong or right. I look at them. If I pass them on the street and I don't look at them, I'm fooling you, I'm fooling myself."

"You look at them as though you want them," Frances said, playing with her brandy glass. "Every one of them."

"In a way," Michael said, speaking softly and not to his wife, "in a way that's true. I don't do anything about it, but it's true."

"I know it. That's why I feel bad."

"Another brandy," Michael called. "Waiter, two more brandies."

He sighed and closed his eyes and rubbed them gently with his finger tips. "I love the way women look. One of the things I like about New York is the battalions of women. When I first came to New York from Ohio that was the first thing I noticed, the million wonderful women, all over the city. I walked around with my heart in my throat."

"A kid," Frances said. "That's a kid's feeling."

"Guess again," Michael said. "Guess again. I'm older now, I'm a man getting near middle age, putting on a little fat and I still love to walk along Fifth Avenue at three o'clock on the east side of the street between Fiftieth and Fifty-seventh Streets. They're all out then, shopping, in their furs and their crazy hats, everything all concentrated from all over the world into seven blocks—the best furs, the best clothes, the handsomest women, out to spend money and feeling good about it."

The Japanese waiter put the two drinks down, smiling with great happiness.

"Everything is all right?" he asked.

"Everything is wonderful," Michael said.

"If it's just a couple of fur coats," Frances said, and forty-five-dollar hats—"

"It's not the fur coats. Or the hats. That's just the scenery for that particular kind of woman. Understand," he said, "you don't have to listen to this."

"I want to listen."

"I like the girls in the offices. Neat, with their eyeglasses, smart, chipper, knowing what everything is about. I like the girls on Forty-fourth Street at lunchtime, the actresses, all dressed up on nothing a week. I like the salesgirls in the stores, paying attention to you first because you're a man, leaving lady customers waiting. I got all this stuff accumulated in me because I've been thinking about it for ten years and now you've asked for it and here it is."

"Go ahead," Frances said.

"When I think of New York City, I think of all the girls on parade in the city. I don't know whether it's something special with me or whether every man in the city walks around with the same feeling inside him, but I feel as though I'm at a picnic in this city. I like to sit near the women in the theaters, the famous beauties who've taken six hours to get ready and look it. And the young girls at the football games, with their red cheeks, and when the warm weather comes, the girls in their summer dresses." He finished his drink. "That's the story."

Frances finished her drink and swallowed two or three times extra. "You say you love me?"

"I love you."

"I'm pretty, too," Frances said. "As pretty as any of them."

"You're beautiful," Michael said.

"I'm good for you," Frances said, pleading. "I've made a good wife, a good housekeeper, a good friend. I'd do any damn thing for you."

"I know," Michael said. He put his hand out and grapsed hers.

"You'd like to be free to—" Frances said.

"Sh-h-h."

"Tell the truth." She took her hand away from under his.

Michael flicked the edge of his glass with his finger. "O.K.," he said gently. "Sometimes I feel I would like to be free."

"Well," Frances said, "any time you say."

"Don't be foolish." Michael swung his chair around to her side of the table and patted her thigh.

She began to cry silently into her handkerchief, bent over just enough so that nobody in the bar would notice. "Someday," she said, crying, "you're going to make a move."

Michael didn't say anything. He sat watching the bartender slowly peel a lemon.

"Aren't you?" Frances asked harshly. "Come on, tell me. Talk. Aren't you?"

"Maybe," Michael said. He moved his chair back again. "How the hell do I know?"

"You know," Frances persisted. "Don't you?"

"Yes," Michael said after a while, "I know."

Frances stopped crying then. Two or three snuffles into the handkerchief and she put it away and her face didn't tell anything to anybody. "At least do me one favor," she said.

"Sure."

"Stop talking about how pretty this woman is or that one. Nice eyes, nice breasts, a pretty figure, good voice." She mimicked his voice. "Keep it to yourself. I'm not interested."

Michael waved to the waiter. "I'll keep it to myself," he said.

Frances flicked the corners of her eyes. "Another brandy," she told the waiter.

"Two," Michael said.

"Yes, ma'am, yes, sir," said the waiter, backing away.

Frances regarded Michael coolly across the table. "Do you want me to call the Stevensons?" she asked. "It'll be nice in the country."

"Sure," Michael said. "Call them."

She got up from the table and walked across the room toward the telephone. Michael watched her walk, thinking what a pretty gal, what nice legs.

The Death of Shorty

BY RICHARD P. BISSELL

*"Karamazov," cried Kolya, "can it be true
what's taught us in religion, that we shall all
rise again from the dead and shall live and see
each other again, all, Ilusha too?"—Dostoevski*

"Now I went and done it," Shorty thought, "here I am
about to drownd, how and the hell did I ever pull such a
dumb one as that?"

Just then his head hit the steel bottom plates of the barge
rake: *crack!* and the current shoved him around the bottom of the rake and under the barges.

"This is worse than the carnival," Shorty thought. "So
long Ma, so long boys. It's hell to die so young," and he
did so. He felt better immediately.

"It sure is one hell of a lot cooler now, and no more
worryin about which watch will get Keokuk lock. Poor
Bill, I bet he like to had a hem'rage when I went over.
Now they have got the engines stopped, and Joe and Bill
and Diamond are gettin the yawl out to look around for
me, I must be clear back to the first coupling by now, or
maybe by the boat, but I don't hear the generator, I don't
hear nothin. They can have my stuff but I hope they send
my watch belonged to Pa home. Sargent will go crazy—
oh, how he hates a drowndin on his boat. And I had no
lifejacket on after all his preachin—that will make him
even wilder. No sleep for the Captain, I'll give him bad
dreams for a week. Well, I'm down here to stay for a while
and I know one thing sure, I will never get back to that
lock. We must of been right at Victory Bend when I took
that dive. I suppose if I can get around the bend without
goin aground I will make her down past Lost Channel to
De Soto. It all depends on how much water I am drawin
by that time. If I would of ate more for supper I s'pose
I would drift a little closer to the surface in a couple of
days. If I can stay out of the weeds and them little

sloughs and cricks down by Indian Camp, maybe I can
make her around Lansing Bend about the time I am gettin
ripe. If I could get picked up there it would be handy, a
nice thing to pull on a guy out in a yawl with his girl,
but if I get past Lansing where am I—down the crick and
no paddle, nothin below there clean to Lynxville and I
would get lost in the pool sure. Maybe some duck hunters
next fall would ketch what's left of me by then; if I can
flank in at Lansing somehow and kind of bob around in
there by them fishermen's boats they will see me, more'n
likely they will be lookin for me anyways. I suppose Cap
will tell them at the lock and they will all know it from
here to Guttenberg and be on the lookout for me. That is
gonna be tough gettin past them bends and out of the
sloughs without no Pilot's License. I will look nice in a
box there on the baggage platform of the Milwaukee at
Lansing. Poor Ma. Looks like I ain't ever gonna see Beards-
town again or find out how Uncle Jim's corn come out.
They all tole me I was crazy to go roamin off on the river
when I could of worked on the farm. Funny the way I was
standin there that day watchin the flood and along comes
ole Batty Welch, but I didn't know him then, he says,
'Boy, how would you like to work on a steamboat?' I says,
'I never give it no thought.' Yes sir, that was the old
Western Belle, a beat-up little coal burner with a split
wheel. After the first time we come down the Chain of
Rocks and past Burlington Elevator and on down under
McKinley Bridge and then on down under Eads Bridge and
I see the lights of St. Louis and the boats tied up, the
Federal boats and the Streckfus boats and the old *Ralph
Hicks* rotting away and the showboat and the *Golden Eagle*
and the *Susie Hazard* and them big smokestacks up in the
air across the river at Cahokia, after that I never could go
it no longer down the corn rows. Never would be here
now layin under the tow so far from home in the Upper
Mississippi if I hadn't just a been there that day Batty
come along and he says, 'Boy, how would you like to
work on a steamboat?' Was I ever green and they sent me
to the Engineer to fetch a bucket of steam, but how
the hell did I know the difference? And the first time we
made a yawl play at Havana they made me watch the
yawl while they went uptown and got beered up. I remember it was a hot afternoon and there was a dead carp
layin on the bank where the water had gone down, and

an old boy was tryin to patch up a motorboat and I talked to him. I bet Bill will be all tore up about this, the poor bastard will figure he coulda grabbed me, I be god damned if I can figure how come I fell off that barge—I knew that lock line was there, right where it always is, laid out in bights—seems like I slipped in that loose coal on the deck. I always thought it was a lot of bull sweepin them decks off but look at me now, boys, look at me now, no more beer and no more girls—I ain't never goin to see that ole Marth no more. It grieves me when I think back on that time we was makin hay to her dad's place and we went down to the crick in the evenin, nobody never caught on. We got all mosquito bites and then we use to get in the crick and do it under the water. I wonder where Batty Welch is now, I heard he was pilot on the *Chicago Bridge,* and then again some deckhand off the *Hurley* told me he was a mate on one of the *City* boats, he took me in hand and he says, 'Boy, I'll make a deck hand out of you, and you'll be ridin these cinder throwin devils till you lay down someday and die out on the barges.' Well, I'm dead all right but I'm under the barges, not on 'em. Then when we broke up our tow there at Cottonwood Island we had barges all over the river and two down through the Burlington railroad bridge and one went down and hit the Quincy highway bridge—we was out there thirty hours and run through a couple of new coils of line and Jackie Winders fell overboard and come near to drowndin. When he was all done and had her made up and Captain Leverett had her goin up the river again we was settin there on the barges too tired to even go back to the galley for coffee, we was right abreast of Hogback Island and Batty says to me, and he give me a tailor made, he says, 'You done good, kid, you done good, you'll make a deckhand yet, even with the manure still in your shoes you're a better deckhand than some I know.' He meant that wise guy—what was his name, Ken something?—from St. Louis who was always ravin about all the big boats he been on, ole Batty couldn't stand the sight of him. I wonder if Marth is still workin there in the café. What will she think when she sees it in the paper: 'Randolph Calhoun drowned on the Upper Mississippi, an employee of the Inland Barge Line and the nephew of Jacob Randolph, route #2.' I must be clear of the boat now and them poor bastards are out in the yawl and Al is out of bed and the other deckhands they got

them up to tie the tow off, I reckon, and Bill is givin his
version of it again, the poor bastard. They got a fine chance
of findin me tonight with no life vest on and the river dark
anyways; if the *Sprague* was sunk in the middle of the
channel they couldn't find her tonight, dark as it is. Then
after the *Jane Collins* Batty took me over onto the Federal
after he got a watchman's job over there. We spent the
summer on the *James W. Good* until I fell in that empty
lease barge one night at Red Wing and was laid up—it
was nice in the hospital and they give me magazines to
read. The next season I went back on the Illinois on the
Betty Jane but the less about that season the better. Then
I got on the Federals again for two seasons and worked
for Uncle Jim in the winter. And then there was the *Transporter* from Cincinnati to Helena and ole Cap Saunders—
he was all right except when he would get on the bottle
and Flea Williams and I would stand watch together. Flea
was a comical bastard—I can laugh myself sick now thinkin of some of the rare ones he use to pull—then he got
married and went to work in a fillin station in Hannibal.
She's been a grand ole time and I'd just as soon be down
here makin friends with the catfish as of spent all my days
shovelin manure and plantin corn. I sure hope they fish me
outa here, though. I don't hanker to stay down here after
the heat wave is over. Ole Joe will be sore he got nobody to
help him with the jackknifin, I s'pose he will get Bill to
help him jackknife and leave Diamond handle the head
line and get one of the other watch to stand the stern line.
They will prob'ly pick up a deckhand up at La Crosse or
Winona or Fountain City if they can find one, some kid
out of a ice cream parlor that will last for about two locks,
maybe they can get one of them guys at Genoa on the
way down, some good deckhands around there. Well, he's
got ole Bill and Diamond anyways and they can hold up
their end any time. Here goes my chance at relief watchman
I been in line for—Al told me Sargent had me in mind for
relief man when he went on next vacation—ain't that the
roses though? Then let's see, after the *Transporter* I went
over on the dredge for a while and then on the *Mackenzie*
on the Upper Mississippi and spent the summer foolin
with that ole fuel flat and we hit the Burlington Bridge and
took half the pier right on up the river with us; the ole
Mack never even hesitated and the limestone blocks and
half the bullnosing was right on the deck of the barge. After

that I went over to the Illinois again on the *Marcia T.*, quite a comedown after the big *Mack*, and we messed with them ice cakes all winter and punched a hole in her bottom at Marseilles and all got off but the messboy—when they raised her they found the poor bastard down in the hole. Lookin for some soap powder, I suppose, when she went down. And we use to go over there to the Ace of Clubs by the landing in Joliet and play the juke box and get lit up and go out in a cab to them whorehouses when we got a chance, and then two months on the little *Mortimer Jones* in the drainage canal and a few trips down the Sag to South Chicago with one load at a time but that run gets old awful quick and I asked for transfer and got onto the new boat and we run from Joliet to Havana and every time you looked up there was some more out of the Chicago office comin aboard with their wives to see the new boat and the port captain was around all the time and Captain Ferris had to show them what a big rough tough ole boy he was and had the megaphone stuck out the pilothouse all the time. What a joke—not only that but all them landins every other day and makin up eight loads at a time, carry out all that riggin just to carry it back forty hours later and make up all over again. To make a long story short, then I tole them I had enough of it and they transferred me to the ole *Inland Coal* and yours truly is now under water for good. I don't see I can make it down to Lansing. Thank god they's plenty of fishermen around here, maybe one of them will pick me up. She's a rough go and that will be tough gettin past them bends and sloughs without no Pilot's License."

And then Shorty was clear of the barges and the towboat, but instead of rising to the surface to help make Genoa lock, he sank slowly and the current and wheel wash gently rolled him over in the soft mud at the bottom of the river.

Grandma and the Hindu Monk

BY SEYMOUR FREEDGOOD

It was only with my old Jewish grandmother that I expected trouble when Brahmachari, a Hindu monk I had met
at the University of Chicago, came to stay with us on
Wreck Lead that summer. Our parents' house in that sea-
side village was a bright, noisy, communal sort of gathering place. Located equidistant between bay and ocean—
Wreck Lead is a narrow strip of island that fronts on the
Atlantic and has its back to a smaller ocean of marshes
and bayous that separate it from Long Island proper—it
was a haven for my college friends. In the garage one of
my brothers was always building a sailboat. In the yard and
over the surrounding sand dunes our youngest brother, sometimes aided by Ernst, the police dog, waged a constant war
for survival over half a hundred neighborhood kids. Projects were always on hand—either a voyage of discovery to
an adjoining island or the launching of a new surf boat
on the beach. Against those clear Atlantic seascapes the
agreeable combination of hot sun, salt air, white beaches,
salt marshes, and interior bays made the town an exciting
place to visit and our house was always full. Josey, the
Czech cook, was never sure who might come down to breakfast any morning. Even more than our parents, whose
work took them daily to New York, it was our seventy-
year-old grandmother who ruled this precarious ménage.

Her lot was not easy. She was a pious, near-sighted old
lady who spoke chiefly Yiddish and spent most of her
time at her prayers. Out of respect for the Jewish dietary
laws and a distrust for Josey she prepared her meals in
the basement and ate them in her own room. Betweentimes
she made periodic inspections of the house. My two brothers
and I usually entertained our visitors, both New York and
local, in a small, book-lined study—which was also a re-
pository for most of the fishnets, paddles, and overnight
camping gear in the community—in the rear of the house.
An extra-large window gave it separate entrance. Sometimes,
upon getting up from table, my brothers, our house

guests, and I would retreat to this room and find that ten or twelve of our Wreck Lead associates, having finished their own suppers earlier, had come through the window and were waiting expectantly to discuss new projects—a crabbing expedition or a trip by rowboat to an overnight camping spot.

There was a fixed routine to Grandma's periodic inspections. Invariably she would poke her gray, mild old head through the door of the study and peer near-sightedly through her glasses—usually they were sunglasses—at the occupant of the nearest chair. "Where's Seymour?" she would ask. To this question there was a fixed reply. "Here I am, Grandma," would answer whoever it was who occupied the chair. She'd peer a little closer. Behind the sunglasses her eyes were misty and uncertain but whether she wore the dark lenses against the glare, or against the truth, or possibly against the glare of the truth, it was hard to say. "What time is it?" she'd want to know. "Twelve o'clock, Grandma," was the set reply. "Good," would say the little old lady. Satisfied that her eldest grandson was present and that the world was still at meridian, she'd return to her cooking or prayers.

Except for Mr. Isaacs, a local Hebrew teacher and Talmudic scholar who had recently immigrated from southeast Europe and who provided her with a special link with her past, she had few friends of her own. Isaacs would stop by frequently to give her religious counsel, find her place in her prayer book, and criticize the finer points of her dietary observances. She accepted these ministrations with the good grace of a Roman lady who, condemned to spend her life in a distant and barbarous colony, took instruction in the traditional virtues from a clever Greek slave. Grandma was indebted to, yet suspicious of, Mr. Isaacs. In her conversations with me she sometimes observed that the scholar, coming as he did from southeast Europe, must have secret ties with the Hasidim, a mystical Jewish sect which had it origin in the eighteenth-century Ukraine. Grandma was anti-Hasidic. Yet Mr. Isaacs was a solace. Mystic or not, he at least knew the Talmud. And that was more than one could say about the rabbi of the local synagogue. All *he* wanted was a new gymnasium. She was also encouraged by the fact that Mr. Isaacs, in his frequent excursions into our back room, took occasion to chide my brothers, myself, and those of our friends who were of the Jewish community

about our lack of respect for the ancestral values. He didn't
get far.

Into this household, with Grandma its titular chief, the
Hindu was easily absorbed. It's possible that three years before, when the monk—a delegate from East Bengal who
turned up in America to represent his religious order at the
World Conference of Religions at the 1933 Chicago World's
Fair—had first arrived in this country, he would have fitted
less nicely. By now, though, after a period of residence at
the University of Chicago, he had acquired more polish.
When I met him there the previous Easter, he seemed to be
just the sort of fellow who could liven up the summer at
our house. I invited him at once. It's true that his costume
was an obstacle but there was no changing that.

I still remember the shock I had when I first saw him
in it. He couldn't have been four foot six. He had an ingenuous smile and protruding, fan-shaped teeth. Around his
head was wrapped a turban, upon which a series of San-
skrit prayers had been scrawled in red and yellow crayons.
A similar cloth hung around his shoulders. Beneath it
was a gray undervest which did not entirely hide a woolen
sweater and the tops of some brown underwear. And
below all of this a white cotton skirt dropped clear to his
feet. These, mercifully, were not naked; instead he had
shod them in a pair of blue tennis shoes. Taken together,
this outfit was his version of khaddar—Indian homespun—
for adoption in northern climates. The sneakers he wore
for religious reasons; any other footwear is of leather
which would be in violation of sacred cows. I don't know
why they were blue. He also had a string of wooden prayer
beads wrapped around his neck.

Such a costume, you may be sure, takes a lot of explaining but I felt we could surmount it somehow. Besides, he
was clever and amenable and had a deliciously boyish quality. I knew that my parents, once the first shock of confron-
tation was over, would accept him as one of their sons.
Anyway, he had dietary laws of his own to observe and
I promised them and Josey that he'd prepare his own meals
and eat them in his room. As for my younger brothers, I
knew they would be amused by him. Monk or not, he
could give them a hand with their boats. It was only with
Grandma that I anticipated difficulties. She and Brahma-

chari were bound to run into each other eventually. I felt it important to prepare her.

I tried to explain to her, some months in advance, that a Hindu rabbi was coming to stay with us for the summer. Have you ever tried to make clear the facts of geography and history to an old woman whose Baedeker to the contemporary world is the first five books of the Old Testament, David's Psalms, and certain vestigial memories of a town in northeastern Europe where she spent her youth? That Brahmachari was a member of the Jewish clergy she was prepared to consider possible. Her world was full of mendicant clergymen—generally old men with beards, fur hats, and frock coats; many of them, she hinted darkly, were Hasidim. No offense to Mr. Isaacs, of course. She was even prepared to believe that Brahmachari, since he was a friend of mine, did not belong to this ragged company. A rabbi, to be sure. But just what community had I said he belonged to? India? A province of Russia, no doubt. Or further to the south?

"A little to the south," I admitted. "And maybe a bit to the east."

"Not Egypt?" she said, startled. Egypt had a special place in Grandma's world view. It was only a matter of years— or had it already been centuries?—since Moses had led us out of that wretched country. She was unkindly disposed toward the Egyptians and each spring at Passover she invented new atrocity stories about them. I sometimes had the impression that on the deeper levels of her mind Grandma felt closer to the times of the Exodus than to the European town where she had spent her youth.

"Certainly not Egypt," I said hastily.

She said she'd consult with Mr. Isaacs. Meanwhile we'd wait and see.

II

As it happened, Brahmachari was already in the house for two or three days before Grandma even noticed him. They were enjoyable if hectic days. As I had anticipated, the Hindu was absorbed into the household with a minimum of fuss. It's true that when he first drove up from the depot he was so surrounded by luggage and parcels that my parents were upset. They replied to his greeting with visible apprehension and eyed his turban, his skirts, and his shining brown face with alarm. For his part, the monk seemed to accept this as natural and tried to put them at ease.

"I am Mahanan Brata Brahmachari," he told them, in the meanwhile ordering the taxi driver to deposit his luggage on the veranda, "a Hindu mendicant from the Sri Angan Monastery, Faridpur, East Bengal. Your son has invited me to stay with you for the summer. Ay, Seymour," he said, noticing me for the first time in the crowd that by now had gathered around the taxi, "there you are. Delighted to see you. Please pay this man." His fan-shaped teeth shot through his smile with an almost disembodied brilliance as he folded his palms in front of his face and bowed to my parents in the traditional Hindu gesture of greeting. He then shook hands with my brothers, patted the police dog, and clucked sympathetically at my parents' polite but strained expressions. They were plainly worried about how they were going to explain the presence in their house of this little turbaned stranger to their friends at the Men's Club and the Ladies' Auxiliary.

No sooner had Brahmachari installed himself on the couch in the backroom study—immediately upon entering the room he had removed his sneakers and squatted down in the middle of the couch, his legs folded under him, and from this position supervised my two brothers and me as we carried in his luggage—than my parents were inside with us. In the background Josey hovered, concerned about his meals. These, it appeared, must consist entirely of vegetables. No eggs, no fish, no meat. "Not even eggs?" asked my mother. "Can Josey fix you a salad for lunch?" He agreed that a salad would be splendid and the two women bustled off, full of plans. It was apparent that he would have to do little cooking himself.

My brothers and I got on with his luggage. This consisted, in addition to three tin suitcases, of a box full of philosophy books, and a potted plant, securely wrapped in brown paper, which he asked me to unbind and set in a window seat. When my father, who was an amateur gardener, expressed interest in this rather hideous bit of shrubbery—it looked a little like the rubber plants which once were a feature of many middle-class American households, but was dwarf-sized and covered with small, dark brown beans—Brahmachari explained, waggling his finger at us from where he sat in the middle of the couch, that it was a Tulasi plant, a bush sacred to the Hindus for a reason I now forget. His abbot had given it to him when he first left India. He never traveled without it. It reminded him of home.

More people were crowding into the room to greet the Hindu but my brothers and I admitted only Mr. Isaacs. It was my hope that the Talmudic scholar would act as an intermediary between Grandma and the monk. A direct meeting, particularly on his first day at the house, seemed unwise. As for our other friends in the house and out in the yard, some of whom were tapping on the window and demanding that they be let in at once, I asked them to be patient until the monk had settled. His trip from Chicago had been tiring and he wanted to rest. Later we'd all go to the beach. A boat-launching was scheduled for that afternoon and the Hindu would come along. Meanwhile Mr. Isaacs sat down with Brahmachari on the couch.

It was soon apparent that the Hindu and the mystical Jewish scholar had hit it off. Indeed, so absorbed did these two become in each other that they seemed unaware of the tumult outside the house, where my brothers and their friends were preparing for the launching of a long, slender surf boat on which they had been working for weeks.

It's my impression that Brahmachari was comparing the attitudes toward God and salvation that obtained in his Hindu monastery with those of the Hasidic Jews. His order was devoted to Lord Krishna, he told Mr. Isaacs. This meant that it was opposed to Brahmanic formalism and put its stress on music and dancing and ecstatic union with God. As among the Hasidim there is a preference for the Psalms of David over the priestcraft and legalisms of the Mosaic testaments, so among the members of his order less attention was paid to the Vedic writings than to the Bhagavad-Gita, a song by the same Lord Krishna in praise of Himself. In short Brahmachari and Mr. Isaacs, despite their differences in cultural background, costume, and language, had much in common. In stressing the ascendancy of the poet and the musician over the legalist they were defying ancient parochialisms and giving full praise to the Lord. With much of this Mr. Isaacs agreed. He did feel, though, that Brahmachari, if he had any sense about him, should keep these opinions to himself. Grandma might hear. In fact, it was his advice to us to keep Brahmachari and Grandma apart as long as possible. God knows what would be her reaction if she learned that we were entertaining another Hasid in the house. Especially in those skirts. The issues of the spirit were beyond her. Best play it safe.

Sound as was Mr. Isaacs' advice, it was less program than circumstance that led us to act on it. The immediate occasion was the renewed uproar that now swept the yard. Evidently the boat was now ready for launching, for faces appeared at the open window, my two brothers' among them, and there was no resisting their demand. We must join them at once.

A great cheer went up from the yard a few minutes later when Brahmachari, now clad only in loin cloth covered by a bright piece of turban, and I, more conventionally clad in shorts and sunglasses, joined the launching party. There were hasty introductions but my brothers and their friends were too busy with last minute preparations for plunging the boat, a slender, canvas-covered affair, into the surf to attend to further ceremony. As their only concession to Brahmachari's status—or perhaps this was to test him—he was assigned to the bow. Huge waves coiled up in front of us as we lifted the boat to our shoulders and walked it toward the ocean. In the bow Brahmachari was already perched, a small, well constructed, brown figure, dressed in a brightly colored loin cloth and holy beads, his teeth flashing with excitement, a paddle in his hands. "All set?" I asked, looked up at him as he sat in the boat. He nodded enthusiastically. "Let's go." We lunged forward into the surf.

At Wreck Lead the idea in surf boating is to get the craft out beyond the first three rows of breakers, reverse it without capsizing, and race back in. As the first row of breakers crashed over us the Hindu disappeared. He bobbed up a moment later, his sleek head dividing the waters, still perched in the bow. We were now up to our shoulders in the water and had begun to swim alongside. A second row of breakers rolled over us but again the monk bobbed up, the boat riding lightly under him. He was now working his paddle and grinning. By the time we had survived the ocean's third assault he was definitely the skipper of the boat. "Here," he said, flashing me a brilliant smile as I crawled exhaustedly over the gunwale. He handed me a paddle. "You take the stern." A moment later with Brahmachari calling instructions from the bow seat, we were racing toward shore.

This maneuver was repeated until even my youngest brother was limp.

By the time we had returned to the house there was little feeling among any of us that the Hindu was a stranger. In one afternoon he had successfully submerged himself in the routines of the house. So far did this absorption go that when Grandma, making her six o'clock inspection, looked into the study and inquired about my whereabouts, Brahmachari—but surely he had been told about this beforehand: could he have got it wrong?—answered for me. "It's six o'clock, Grandma," he said to her. "Seymour's upstairs." I was later told that she failed to notice the discrepancy and left the room.

It's possible that this happy state of affairs might have continued indefinitely if Grandma and Brahmachari, because of their separate dietary practices, hadn't been preparing their own meals, Grandma on a stove in the basement, Brahmachari on a Bunsen burner in the now vacated garage, and eating in their rooms. They began to meet, their hands full of trays and dishes, on the stairs. After two or three days of this Grandma came up to me one afternoon in the study. Brahmachari was off somewhere with Mr. Isaacs and for once I was alone. For once also she had removed her sunglasses and seemed reasonably certain that it was I she was addressing. Who, she wanted to know, was the old colored lady who had moved into the room next to hers?

"Old colored lady, Grandma?" My grasp of Yiddish has never been perfect and I wasn't sure I had heard her correctly.

She repeated her question. Who was the old colored woman in the shawl, white skirts, beads, and kerchief who had been monopolizing Mr. Isaacs for the last few days?

"That's not a colored lady, Grandma. That's a man. It's that Hindu rabbi I told you about. Hasn't Mr. Isaacs introduced you?"

"Him!" she sniffed. "That Hasid. But he's black," she objected. "You said he's a Hindu rabbi. Can Jews be black?"

The answer to this would have called for such a lecture on the wanderings of the Jews since the burning of the first temple and their relocation in such unlikely spots as the Congo and Outer Mongolia that I decided to cut it short. "Of course they can be black. They can be any color you want. As a matter of fact," I added irrelevantly, "Brahmachari's brown. Now don't worry yourself about this, Grandma. Believe me, he's a man."

But she did worry, poor lady. I didn't realize until later how worried she must have been. Fifty years had elapsed since Grandma had come to this country but her attitudes, flexible as they may have been to start with, had long become fixed. The point of view from which she judged her children, her grandsons, our house on Wreck Lead, and her grandsons' friends was in violent contrast to the contemporary world of cultural interchange and racial transcendence. Nor was it any longer rooted, except indirectly, in the tight, exclusive, inversely aristocratic Jewry of nineteenth-century eastern Europe. Between the European world of her childhood and the transformed Long Island household in which she was spending her last days she had projected a screen upon which all social occurrences were interpreted according to their Old Testament archetypes. To her way of thinking, for example, every non-Jew was a potential raider on the caravan—Grandma in charge of one of the camel carts—which traveled interminably from Egypt to the Promised Land. In Grandma's mythical world-view the time was always Biblical—either midnight, or high noon—and the space was a limitless desert across which she and her people moved. Perhaps you've felt that her periodic inspections of our back-room study, her queries about my whereabouts, and her requests for the time were no more than the obsessive rituals of a vague old lady. Or that our replies to her questions—"Here I am, Grandma," and, "It's twelve o'clock, Grandma"—were a cruel sort of joke. Obsessiveness and cruelty were no doubt involved but it occurs to me that what she was really demanding when she asked for my whereabouts was the promise that the caravan was secure. That despite the wide open doors and windows and the crowds of strangers, no enemies had come in, no hereditary antagonists of the race.

In retrospect I now realize that for some days after our conversation she looked more harried and distraught than ever. It's true that the house was crowded that week—another boat-launching was planned—and the yard and the back room were again full of enthusiasts. This added to her rounds. Also, it had been hot and for some time she had been ailing. Her illness was diabetes, I think, although she was secretive about it. She also had a leg infection.

But I didn't know until the very moment of discovery that she had extended her patrols. Evidently she had taken on a new assignment after our talk about the monk. She began to observe him at night. Since her room adjoined his on the second floor and had access to it by an outside balcony, this wasn't hard.

The spectacle of that mild old lady creeping along the balcony after midnight to peer through a closed screen door and observe by moonlight a sleeping Hindu would be ludicrous if the eventual result hadn't been so shattering to her brave old spirit. Early one morning—it was the hour of the false dawn, I think: there was an unnatural light in my room—I was awakened by a violent tug. I rolled over, opened my eyes, and discovered that it was Grandma who was standing over my bed. She was dressed in a night shift and was barefooted and trembling with rage. "He's risen, he's risen!" she almost screamed at me.

It occurred to me that she might have been cooking all night and had eccentrically baked a cake. "What's risen?"

"The savage! The demon you brought to the house!"

I heaved to a sitting position and now realized that Mr. Isaacs was standing behind her. In the half light he looked as sleepy and bewildered as I felt. Presumably she had roused him first—he had by God's grace chosen this night of all nights to spend at the house—and had only given him time to throw his frock coat over his night shirt before rushing him to me. He too was barefooted and his beard was uncombed but he hadn't forgotten his fur hat. "The demons!" Grandma was now screaming. "Your friends, the demons!" She clutched at me savagely. There were other cries of alarm from up and down the ground-floor corridor as my father and mother, my brothers and Josey, perhaps thinking that the house had been burgled, came running from their rooms. Ernst, also aroused in the study, began to bark. I looked at Mr. Isaacs, who raised his shoulders in a shrug. "What demons, for God's sake?"

Instead of answering she grabbed me by the elbow and almost hoisted me from the bed. There was the strength of ten thousand demons in that little old woman. She then whirled on her bare feet and ran back up the stairs. Mr. Isaacs and I followed dumbly, with the rest of my family crowding behind us. "The Hindu's risen," I told them. "God knows what she means." Josey and the police dog, who now had been silenced, protected our rear. "What *does* she mean?" I whispered to Mr. Isaacs as we trailed Grandma across her bedroom and through the door to the outside balcony. "She caught him praying," he said indistinctly. "Praying?" I asked. "What's wrong with that?" Grandma had rushed on ahead and was now glaring—a fierce, stooped little figure in her white night shift—through Brahmachari's screen. "Burglars?" panted my father, who brushed past us to join her. "Where are they?" He was carrying a shotgun. A moment later we were overtaken and passed by the rest of my family, all of them in various states of undress and each of them armed—my mother with her pocketbook, my brothers with boat hooks and a fish net, and Josey with Ernst on a chain. "Well?" I asked Mr. Isaacs as we hurried over to join them. "What's wrong with praying?"

"It's the way he does it," Mr. Isaacs stuttered. "It's his dawn prayer. He shouldn't be seen." Mr. Isaacs was trembling, but whether from cold or apprehension I couldn't make out. "Speak up!" I said harshly. "What does he do?" Across the eastern horizons of Long Island there spread the soft-tinted reds and purples that herald the true dawn; then up from the eastern horizon shot the fast rising sun.

I grabbed Mr. Isaacs by the arm and pushed him through the small crowd around the screen door. "That's what scared your grandmother," the scholar said hysterically. "He does it by rising himself." Mr. Isaacs was trembling with horror. "She saw him praying four feet in the air over his bed."

Mr. Isaacs and I, our eyes straining against the screen door and our arms around Grandma, who was making inarticulate sounds, now had minds for nothing except the vision of the monk on his bed. Bolt upright in the middle of the counterpane, and dressed only in a turban, his loin cloth, and holy beads, Brahmachari was rapt in prayer. His legs were folded under him in the traditional yoga position, his eyes were shut tight and turned inward, but on his lips was a cryptic smile. In a circle around him on the counterpane he had placed his begging bowl, his cymbals, his hand drum, and the water jug, and beside him on the night table the Tulasi plant nodded and rustled in the early morning breeze. Perhaps I was deluded by what Mr. Isaacs had just told me—and nobody, not even Brahmachari, would confirm this later—but I had the distinct impression that the Hindu, at the very moment the sun had risen, had floated down from the middle of the air. At that

Grandma screamed again and lurched against me and Mr. Isaacs. As we put out our arms to support her I discovered that she had fainted dead away.

With many expressions of commiseration and sympathy we lifted Grandma up and carried her to her bed in the next room. It was into a vastly changed household that the monk descended several hours later when he came downstairs to prepare his own breakfast. The doctor had already come, examined Grandma, prescribed absolute quiet and rest, and had gone, promising to return later in the day. The virtual coma into which the old woman had lapsed after the tension at the screen door had changed into mild delirium. She was conscious, the doctor had told us, but a bit out of her head. "What's been going on around here?" he asked, looking at us queerly.

"What do you mean, Doctor?" Mr. Isaacs asked. "Did she tell you anything?" My parents and brothers were looking at each other intently.

"Well," the doctor said hesitantly, "have you got any dark-skinned people around here? Dressed in shawls and turbans?" He paused, no doubt afraid he was about to make a fool of himself. "She has the idea that you've got somebody around here that Moses was angry about. She told me that when the Jews were leaving Egypt some dark-skinned people fell on the rear of the caravan, where the sick and the old folks were, and threw rocks at them. She says that Moses was very angry and told the Jews never to speak to those people again. It's my professional opinion," the doctor concluded bravely, "that if you've got anybody like that around here, get rid of him."

Even my brothers turned pale. "Dark-skinned?" said my father. "The only one I can think of is a friend of one of my sons, a Hindu, and she couldn't mean him. India," he continued loyally, "is on the other side of the ocean from Egypt. Matter of thousands of miles. Besides, he's highly civilized. Never threw a rock at anybody." They were all looking at me sternly, though. The doctor agreed that Grandma might be suffering from shock. It was only an unaccountable swelling of her legs that disturbed him. She had suffered from this before, he knew—diabetes, perhaps—but it was now accompanied by paralysis. Temporary, of course. Keep her off her feet and under sedatives. He'd be back later.

"You and your monks," one of my brothers said gloomily.

III

It was into this hostile atmosphere that Brahmachari shortly descended. In his arms he was carrying my mother's pocketbook, as well as the fish net and the boat hooks with which my brothers had armed themselves. "Are these your properties?" he asked, smiling politely at us as we sat around the breakfast table. "I found them on the porch outside the door."

"We have no idea how they got there," my mother said stonily. She was speaking, it was clear, for the household.

"Excuse me," said Mr. Isaacs. Leaving his eggs untouched he got up from the table, took the monk by the arm, and led him out of the house. Later I saw them panbroiling some rice together over the Bunsen burner in the garage. The two oddly costumed men—Mr. Isaacs in his frock coat, fur hat, and beard, Brahmachari in a red turban and a clean skirt—were talking earnestly to each other.

The doctor's return the following morning did not ease the tension. Later that same afternoon he had briefly reappeared, stationed a nurse in Grandma's room, instructed her to keep the old lady under sedatives and to massage her legs, and had abruptly left. His only word to us was by way of warning—stay out of her room and keep the Hindu, or whatever he was, away from her. The nurse would attend to the rest.

So it was with considerable anxiety that I watched the doctor come down from Grandma's room the following morning. His own anxiety seemed even greater than mine. In fact, when my parents took hold of him at the foot of the stairs and demanded to know what the trouble was, he seemed almost incoherent. "It's all in the mind," he mumbled over and over.

"In the mind?" my father asked. "I wish you'd enlighten us on that, doctor."

The doctor, perhaps recalled to his senses by my father's tone, tried to explain. He had taken Grandma off sedatives, he told us, although the old lady was still far from well. Despite hot applications and massage, the swelling in her legs had not gone down. It was almost as if she didn't want it to go down. You get cases like that, he confided. As if the patient refused to get well. It was his suggestion that we call in a psychiatrist. He'd be glad to recommend a good man, a cousin of his who was in that line. Otherwise the old lady might be permanently bedridden.

It was at this critical juncture, with my mother in tears at the mention of a psychiatrist and my father stern, that Josey made a great outcry at the kitchen door. "No, no," she was shouting, "stay out!"

"Come on, Josey," I heard one of my brothers tell her. "It's only us and Mr. Isaacs." A moment later my two brothers, with Mr. Isaacs in the lead, appeared at the foot of the stairs. "Where've you been?" I asked them. "The doctor wants to bring a psychiatrist."

"Out in the garage," said the youngest one. "That's where Mr. Isaacs spent the night." I looked at them closely. "Anybody else in the garage?" But if they had a secret they were determined to keep it. "Could be," said my other brother. "You worried?"

Mr. Isaacs ran his hand through his thick black beard. "A psychiatrist? For the reverend dame?"

"For Grandma," my mother wept. "They think the swelling is in her head." My father, himself verging on tears, tried to console her.

"In her head, is it?" Somewhere in the scholar's beard I detected a smile. "I can well believe it. I always thought her memory was bad. But before you call a psychiatrist, and with the doctor's permission," he said, making the outraged physician a formal bow, "I wonder if I could bring in a colleague?"

My father stared at him. "A colleague? Do you have colleagues? Another Hasid, I suppose."

"You might call him that," the Talmudist said imperturbably. "A certain theologian of my acquaintance." Again followed by my brothers, who winked at me broadly as they passed, he went back to the kitchen door, opened it, and returned a moment later by himself. "I would like to introduce Dr. Mahanan B. Brahmachari, my colleague from the University of Calcutta." This time preceded by my brothers, who with the greatest solemnity were carrying his hand drum, his copper begging bowl, his brass cymbals, and the water jug, Brahmachari appeared in the downstairs foyer. He was gorgeously made up.

On his head was a ceremonial turban of transparent gauze. His body was shrouded in a toga of similar material and on his forehead and cheekbones he had daubed in yellow paste the markings of his religious order. It was plain he had come on business. "Good morning," he said, smiling at us amicably. "I've come to call on your grandmother."

"The Hindu!" cried the doctor. "Not the Hindu? Out! Out!" My mother was no less vociferous. Brahmachari's markings—they were in direct violation of the Mosaic injunction against tattooing or painting the flesh—seemed final proof. "The demons!" she cried. "It's the demons that Mamma was telling about!" But my father was more circumspect. "What did you mean?" he asked Mr. Isaacs. "You said the old lady had a bad memory. About what?"

Mr. Isaacs gestured triumphantly. "About locating herself in the Bible. It hurts me to say this," the Hebrew teacher told my parents, "but you've been wasting your money on her Hebrew lessons. Such a bad student. The worst I've had!"

It was clear that Mr. Isaacs had a point. Among the Jews, as with other groups who make use of the Old or New Testaments as the basis for their liturgical year, the sacred text is divided into portions for weekly reading. It was an old joke in our family that Grandma, whenever she became confused about the section for the week—and, according to Mr. Isaacs, this was often—would revert almost by instinct to the portion which describes the flight of the Jews from Egypt. So notorious was this habit that Mr. Isaacs sometimes referred to himself ruefully as Grandma's guide to the Promised Land. It was his hope that someday he would get her there. By some means he must teach her to follow, not her private idiosyncrasy, but the text. Finally, here was his chance. "For example," he continued, beginning to sway backward and forward in the approved manner of a Talmudist when he is about to explain anything, "she tells us that our friend Brahmachari is a member of the tribe who stoned us on our way out of Egypt. This is a plain case of mistaken identity. Or insufficient attention to text," he added in a voice that was now falling into its traditional sing-song. "Our friend Dr. Brahmachari comes from another section entirely. Examine his cymbals and drum. Are these the equipment of a man who attacks caravans? Certainly not," he answered himself. "Then what section does he come from?" He looked at us expectantly.

"St. John?" said Josey.

"Wrong Testament," Mr. Isaacs told her. He looked at the cook disapprovingly. "Try the other one."

"Look here," the doctor protested. "I can't allow this to go any further. Whose patient is she?"

But we ignored him. It was plain that Mr. Isaacs, by recasting the issue in a more favorable Biblical framework, was turning the tide in Brahmachari's direction.

"I have the Emperor Solomon in mind," said Mr. Isaacs. "Solomon, son of David, the dancing king. In the lesson we are about to give your grandmother I will try to recall to her that King Solomon, when he went about expanding his empire, took wives from all over the Orient. It will be our thesis that Brahmachari is a relic of Solomon by one of his Indian wives."

My head reeled at this preposterous interpretation of history. "For goodness sake, Brahmachari," I said, hoping to be able to appeal to the monk as a university graduate, "surely you don't believe that?"

"What's the difference what he believes?" one of my brothers said violently. "You want Grandma to get well, don't you? Trust us, we've got it figured. If one shock put her into bed, a bigger one will get her out. Providing she holds still for it," he added grimly. "Otherwise we'll have a funeral around here."

"Of course," Mr. Isaacs continued dreamily, "there's always that affair with the Queen of Sheba. It's possible that Brahmachari is a son of Solomon by the Ethiopian queen. But no," he decided cautiously, "that puts him too close to Egypt. Best play it safe."

I was staggered by the perfidy of this reasoning. "Brahmachari," I again appealed to the Hindu, "you can't go along with this?"

The monk looked me straight in the eye. "I think I can. In a poetic sense, of course. It's possible that Mr. Isaacs, in his zeal to dignify my origins, is playing a little loose with his record. But in so far as Solomon was himself sired by King David, the author of the Psalms, I accept the paternity."

"You accept the paternity? He just made it up!"

"And a nice construction it is," the monk said comfortably. "Perhaps you're not aware of the close affinities between David, the dancing king of the Hebrews, and Lord Krishna, the ecstatic deity of the Hindus, one of whose followers I am. For both, the proper method of worship is not doctrine and ritual but enthusiasm and song. You've

been asked to examine my equipment. Look at it again." He
reached over and gave the drum in the hands of one of my
brothers a smart tap. "Cymbals and drum! Aren't these the
implements of your own King David? Have you read the
Psalms? We have more of a problem in treating your
grandmother," he continued, "than giving me status in her
somewhat quixotic world-view. Beyond that, it's a problem
of convincing her that no matter what she's heard to the
contrary, she's broken no commandment by accepting a
mystic in her house. Or, as Mr. Isaacs would say, a Hasid.
A devotee of the Psalms. We feel that once she's acknowledged that religious salvation, guided though it can be by
rule and precept, has its origin not in theological doctrine
but in a spontaneous welling-up from below, from within
the person, and is furthered less by abstract argument than
by emotion, by a conversion of heart—she'll stop fighting
herself. She'll no longer identify the sources of her movement with monsters and demons. She'll get up and walk.
Even more than that," he added mischievously, "she'll get
up and dance. That will cure her." He nodded to my
parents, signaled my brothers to precede him, and with
Mr. Isaacs at his side began to mount the stairs.

"I forbid it," the doctor shouted. He tried to block the
procession. "Nurse, nurse, lock the door!" But he was too
late: in a moment the procession had swept past him and
disappeared up the stairs.

Our ears cocked, we waited for the first sound from
above. It came in a moment, preceded by a short gasp and
a scuffle which I took to be the nurse protesting and then
being thrust aside as the procession moved into Grandma's
room. Grandma's shriek, while not quite as shrill as the
one with which she had greeted the sight of Brahmachari
at prayer, had more substance. Full of violence, the sound
reverberated down the stair well.

My father shook his head. "It's those markings," he said,
nodding sagely. "I knew she wouldn't take to that paint job.
Against the Laws of Moses, you know," he informed the
doctor. To this the latter had no reply.

Then there came from upstairs a sound of such intensity
that Grandma's in comparison was the whimper of a small
girl in a hurricane. In mood, though, the sounds were reversed. Whereas Grandma's was shrill, even strident in
undertone, the new sound that emerged from her bedroom,

soul-piercing as it was, had a high, sweet, overriding quality that seemed to originate, not in the brainpan, but in the heart. It had been going on for some time, I later realized —first low and muted, as if two soft metals had been struck together, then louder and stronger and more sweetly resonant—but none of us downstairs had been truly struck by it because of the violence of Grandma's cry. When it struck us it was all at once and almost at crescendo. It had in it the sound—not that the wind makes, but that the wind means, before sunup on a clear June morning. It had in it the swell of the sea; and the echo of the conch shell that reproduces internally the sea's message. It was Brahmachari, of course, dancing like an oriental King David in front of Grandma and clashing his cymbals.

Then came silence, abrupt and absolute. The sound had stopped.

"Jesus, Mary, and Joseph," the cook said. She crossed herself.

I looked around me and saw that my parents were huddled together in a corner like two frightened children. They nodded to me and without a word we swept past the doctor and up the stairs. Outside the shut door to Grandma's bedroom the nurse was standing, her face as white as her uniform. For a moment we surrounded her as my father tried the door. It was locked. From inside the room there came fresh sounds, but this time, although hard to make out, they were human. As if from another world I heard Mr. Isaacs chanting in Hebrew. "To the chief musician," he sang. "A psalm by David. Sing unto the Lord a new song, His praise in the congregation of the pious." I also heard a drum being tapped.

Wordlessly, and with my parents still in the lead, we turned and made our way through Brahmachari's adjoining bedroom and out to the balcony. There, with my arms around my parents' shoulders and our faces pressed to her screen door, we saw Grandma for the first time since her illness. She didn't seem ill at all. Still wearing the same white night shift but with her hair and face made up—she had, in preparing for these inevitable visitors, even applied a little rouge—Grandma was propped against the pillows at the head of her bed. She seemed many years younger, and on her face there was a dazed but contented expression. At the end opposite hers on the bed Brahmachari was squatted, his legs folded under him. He had again stripped down to his

loin cloth, his turban and the holy beads, and with his
long brown fingers he was tapping on the two-headed
drum. Bolt upright in front of Grandma and with a slight
smile on his lips he weaved the upper half of his body as
he tapped. "Hari Krishna," the monk hummed. "Praise
Krishna."

She smiled at him dazedly, her cheeks flushed. Brahmachari, I now realized, had also applied the religious markings to his chest. It was at these that she was staring. Tentatively, she put a hand to her own slightly made-up face.
As he continued to tap on his drum and sway in front of
her I also noted that the large copper begging bowl was
placed on the bedspread between them. In it was the pair
of now discarded cymbals. Each no larger than the palm of
a man's hand and tied to the other by a thong that ran
through their centers, they seemed dim and inconspicuous
instruments to have produced the sounds that had drowned
out Grandma's. And on the night table beside them Brahmachari's Tulasi plant nodded and rustled in the noonday
breeze.

"A psalm by David," Mr. Isaacs chanted. The Hebrew
teacher had taken up his station in a corner of the room
and with a prayer book in front of him was singing and
rocking backward and forward. "Hallelujah," he repeated.
"Sing unto the Lord a new song, His praise in the congregation of the pious."

"What time is it, Grandma?" the monk asked. He paused
in his drumming for a moment. "Who am I?"

Her lips moved wordlessly. "King David?" she asked presently, but in a voice so timid that my parents and I, with
our faces pressed to the screen door, could hardly hear.

"Hallelujah," Mr. Isaacs chanted. "Praise Him upon the
clear-ringing cymbals. Praise Him on the high-sounding cymbals."

"It's Dr. Brahmachari, Grandma," my brother told her.
"It's the Hindu Hasid that Mr. Isaacs wants to introduce to
you. Up on your feet," he urged her. "Say hello to the
Hasid."

They slipped their hands under her shoulders and lifted
her to the floor. As she stood there between them, smiling
bashfully and still uncertain on her feet, the monk slipped
off the other side of the bed and came around to greet
her. "I am Mahanan Brata Brahmachari," he said, folding
his palms in front of his face and bowing, "a Hindu monk

from the Sri Angan Monastery, Faridpur, East Bengal. I've been invited by your grandsons to stay for the summer."

There was an instant of silence. At the church around the corner a bell struck the midday. Then Grandma came across. "Good afternoon, Dr. Brahmachari," she said in English. "Welcome to our house."

"Hallelujah," Mr. Isaacs began again but Grandma beat him to it. "Hallelujah!" she cried, wresting herself from my brothers' arms. "Let everything that hath breath praise the Lord." It was my parents' impression that she stumbled towards the Hindu but my own feeling is that she skipped. As my brothers stepped forward to grab her she turned to them with a radiant expression. "It's twelve o'clock, children," she told them. "Where's . . . ?" But before she could ask her final question I had plunged through the screen door and taken the old woman in my arms.

Madame Zilensky and the King of Finland

BY CARSON MC CULLERS

To Mr. Brook, the head of the music department at Ryder College, was due all the credit for getting Madame Zilensky on the faculty. The college considered itself fortunate; her reputation was impressive, both as a composer and as a pedagogue. Mr. Brook took on himself the responsibility of finding a house for Madame Zilensky, a comfortable place with a garden, which was convenient to the college and next to the apartment house where he himself lived.

No one in Westbridge had known Madame Zilensky before she came. Mr. Brook had seen her pictures in musical journals, and once he had written to her about the authenticity of a certain Buxtehude manuscript. Also, when it was being settled that she was to join the faculty, they had exchanged a few cables and letters on practical affairs. She wrote in a clear, square hand, and the only thing out of the ordinary in these letters was the fact that they contained an occasional reference to objects and persons altogether unknown to Mr. Brook, such as "the yellow cat in Lisbon" or "poor Heinrich." These lapses Mr. Brook put

down to the confusion of getting herself and her family
out of Europe.

Mr. Brook was a somewhat pastel person; years of Mozart
minuets, of explanations about diminished sevenths and minor
triads, had given him a watchful vocational patience. For
the most part, he kept to himself. He loathed academic fid-
dle-faddle and committees. Years before, when the music department had decided to gang together and spend the summer in Salzburg, Mr. Brook sneaked out of the arrangement
at the last moment and took a solitary trip to Peru. He had
a few eccentricities himself and was tolerant of the peculiarities of others; indeed, he rather relished the ridiculous. Often,
when confronted with some grave and incongruous situation, he would feel a little inside tickle, which stiffened
his long, mild face and sharpened the light in his gray eyes.

Mr. Brook met Madame Zilensky at the Westbridge station
a week before the beginning of the fall semester. He recognized her instantly. She was a tall, straight woman with a
pale and haggard face. Her eyes were deeply shadowed and
she wore her dark, ragged hair pushed back from her forehead. She had large, delicate hands, which were very grub-
by. About her person as a whole there was something noble
and abstract that made Mr. Brook draw back for a moment
and stand nervously undoing his cuff links. In spite of her
clothes—a long, black skirt and a broken-down old leather
jacket—she made an impression of vague elegance. With
Madame Zilensky were three children, boys between the
ages of ten and six, all blond, blank-eyed, and beautiful.
There was one other person, an old woman who turned out
later to be the Finnish servant.

This was the group he found at the station. The only luggage they had with them was two immense boxes of manuscripts, the rest of their paraphernalia having been forgotten in the station at Springfield when they changed trains.
That is the sort of thing that can happen to anyone. When
Mr. Brook got them all into a taxi, he thought the worst
difficulties were over, but Madame Zilensky suddenly tried
to scramble over his knees and get out of the door.

"My God!" she said. "I left my—how do you say?—my tick-
tick-tick——"

"Your watch?" asked Mr. Brook.

"Oh no!" she said vehemently. "You know, my tick-tick-
tick," and she waved her forefinger from side to side, pendu-
lum fashion.

"Tick-tick," said Mr. Brook, putting his hands to his fore-head and closing his eyes. "Could you possibly mean a metronome?"

"Yes! Yes! I think I must have lost it there where we changed trains."

Mr. Brook managed to quiet her. He even said, with a kind of dazed gallantry, that he would get her another one ths next day. But at the time he was bound to admit to himself that there was something curious about this panic over a metronome when there was all the rest of the lost luggage to consider.

The Zelinsky ménage moved into the house next door, and on the surface everything was all right. The boys were quiet children. Their names were Sigmund, Boris, and Sammy. They were always together and they followed each other around Indian file, Sigmund usually the first. Among themselves they spoke a desperate-sounding family Esperanto made up of Russian, French, Finnish, German, and English; when other people were around, they were strangely silent. It was not any one thing that the Zilenskys did or said that made Mr. Brook uneasy. There were just little incidents. For example, something about the Zilensky children subconsciously bothered him when they were in a house, and finally he realized that what troubled him was the fact that the Zilensky boys never walked on a rug; they skirted it single file on the bare floor, and if a room was carpeted, they stood in the doorway and did not go inside. Another thing was this: Weeks passed and Madame Zilensky seemed to make no effort to get settled or to furnish the house with anything more than a table and some beds. The front door was left open day and night, and soon the house began to take on a queer, bleak look like that of a place abandoned for years.

The college had every reason to be satisfied with Madame Zilensky. She taught with a fierce insistence. She could become deeply indignant if some Mary Owens or Bernadine Smith would not clean up her Scarlatti trills. She got hold of four pianos for her college studio and set four dazed students to playing Bach fugues together. The racket that came from her end of the department was extraordinary, but Madame Zilensky did not seem to have a nerve in her, and if pure will and effort can get over a musical idea, then Ryder College could not have done better. At night Madame Zilensky worked on her twelfth symphony. She seemed never to sleep; no matter what time of night Mr. Brook happened to look out of his sitting-room window, the light in her studio was always on. No, it was not because of any professional consideration that Mr. Brook became so dubious.

It was in late October when he felt for the first time that something was unmistakably wrong. He had lunched with Madame Zilensky and had enjoyed himself, as she had given him a very detailed account of an African safari she had made in 1928. Later in the afternoon she stopped in at his office and stood rather abstractedly in the doorway.

Mr. Brook looked up from his desk and asked, "Is there anything you want?"

"No, thank you," said Madame Zilensky. She had a low, beautiful, sombre voice. "I was only just wondering. You recall the metronome. Do you think perhaps that I might have left it with that French?"

"Who?" asked Mr. Brook.

"Why, that French I was married to," she answered.

"Frenchman," Mr. Brook said mildly. He tried to imagine the husband of Madame Zilensky, but his mind refused. He muttered half to himself, "The father of the children."

"But no," said Madame Zilensky with decision. "The father of Sammy."

Mr. Brook had a swift prescience. His deepest instincts warned him to say nothing further. Still, his respect for order, his conscience, demanded that he ask, "And the father of the other two?"

Madame Zilensky put her hand to the back of her head and ruffled up her short, cropped hair. Her face was dreamy, and for several moments she did not answer. Then she said gently, "Boris is of a Pole who played the piccolo."

"And Sigmund?" he asked. Mr. Brook looked over his orderly desk, with the stack of corrected papers, the three sharpened pencils, the ivory-elephant paperweight. When he glanced up at Madame Zilensky, she was obviously thinking hard. She gazed around at the corners of the room, her brows lowered and her jaw moving from side to side. At last she said, "We were discussing the father of Sigmund?"

"Why, no," said Mr. Brook. "There is no need to do that."

Madame Zilensky answered in a voice both dignified and final. "He was a fellow-countryman."

Mr. Brook really did not care one way or the other. He had no prejudices; people could marry seventeen times and have Chinese children so far as he was concerned. But there was something about this conversation with Madame Zilensky that bothered him. Suddenly he understood. The children didn't look at all like Madame Zilensky, but they looked exactly like each other, and as they all had different fathers, Mr. Brook thought the resemblance astonishing.

But Madame Zilensky had finished with the subject. She zipped up her leather jacket and turned away.

"That is exactly where I left it," she said, with a quick nod. "*Chez* that French."

Affairs in the music department were running smoothly. Mr. Brook did not have any serious embarrassments to deal with, such as the harp teacher last year who had finally eloped with a garage mechanic. There was only this nagging apprehension about Madame Zilensky. He could not make out what was wrong in his relations with her or why his feelings were so mixed. To begin with, she was a great globe-trotter, and her conversations were incongruously seasoned with references to far-fetched places. She would go along for days without opening her mouth, prowling through the corridor with her hands in the pockets of her jacket and her face locked in meditation. Then suddenly she would buttonhole Mr. Brook and launch out on a long, volatile monologue, her eyes reckless and bright and her voice warm with eagerness. She would talk about anything or nothing at all. Yet, without exception, there was something queer, in a slanted sort of way, about every episode she ever mentioned. If she spoke of taking Sammy to the barbershop, the impression she created was just as foreign as if she were telling of an afternoon in Bagdad. Mr. Brook could not make it out.

The truth came to him very suddenly, and the truth made everything perfectly clear, or at least clarified the situation. Mr. Brook had come home early and lighted a fire in the little grate in his sitting room. He felt comfortable and at peace that evening. He sat before the fire in his stocking feet, with a volume of William Blake on the table by his side, and he had poured himself a half-glass of apricot brandy. At ten o'clock he was drowsing cozily before the fire, his mind full of cloudy phrases of Mahler and floating half-thoughts. Then all at once, out of this delicate stupor, four words came to his mind: "The King of Finland." The words seemed familiar, but for the first moment he could not place them. Then all at once he tracked them down.

He had been walking across the campus that afternoon when Madame Zilensky stopped him and began some preposterous rigamarole, to which he had only half listened; he was thinking about the stack of canons turned in by his counterpoint class. Now the words, the inflections of her voice, came back to him with insidious exactitude. Madame Zilensky had started off with the following remark: "One day, when I was standing in front of a *pâtisserie*, the King of Finland came by in a sled."

Mr. Brook jerked himself up straight in his chair and put down his glass of brandy. The woman was a pathological liar. Almost every word she uttered outside of class was an untruth. If she worked all night, she would go out of her way to tell you she spent the evening at the cinema. If she ate lunch at the Old Tavern, she would be sure to mention that she had lunched with her children at home. The woman was simply a pathological liar, and that accounted for everything.

Mr. Brook cracked his knuckles and got up from his chair. His first reaction was one of exasperation. That day after day Madame Zilensky would have the gall to sit there in his office and deluge him with her outrageous falsehoods! Mr. Brook was intensely provoked. He walked up and down the room, then he went into his kitchenette and made himself a sardine sandwich.

An hour later, as he sat before the fire, his irritation had changed to a scholarly and thoughtful wonder. What he must do, he told himself, was to regard the whole situation impersonally and look on Madame Zilensky as a doctor looks on a sick patient. Her lies were of the guileless sort. She did not dissimulate with any intention to deceive, and the untruths she told were never used to any possible advantage. That was the maddening thing; there was simply no motive behind it all.

Mr. Brook finished off the rest of the brandy. And slowly, when it was almost midnight, a further understanding came to him. The reason for the lies of Madame Zilensky was painful and plain. All her life long Madame Zilensky had worked—at the piano, teaching, and writing those beautiful and immense twelve symphonies. Day and night she had drudged and struggled and thrown her soul into her work, and there was not much of her left over for anything else. Being human, she suffered from this lack and did what she could to make up for it. If she passed the evening bent

over a table in the library and later declared that she had
spent that time playing cards, it was as though she had
managed to do both things. Through the lies, she
lived vicariously. The lies doubled the little of her existence
that was left over from work and augmented the little rag
end of her personal life.

Mr. Brook looked into the fire, and the face of Madame
Zilensky was in his mind—a severe face, with dark, weary
eyes and delicately disciplined mouth. He was conscious of
a warmth in his chest, and a feeling of pity, protectiveness,
and dreadful understanding. For a while he was in a state
of lovely confusion.

Later on he brushed his teeth and got into his pajamas.
He must be practical. What did this clear up? That French,
the Pole with the piccolo, Bagdad? And the children, Sigmund, Boris, and Sammy—who were they? Were they really
her children after all, or had she simply rounded them up
from somewhere? Mr. Brook polished his spectacles and put
them on the table by his bed. He must come to an immediate understanding with her. Otherwise, there would exist
in the department a situation which could become most
problematical. It was two o'clock. He glanced out of his
window and saw that the light in Madame Zilensky's work-
room was still on. Mr. Brook got into bed, made terrible
faces in the dark, and tried to plan what he would say
next day.

Mr. Brook was in his office by eight o'clock. He sat
hunched up behind his desk, ready to trap Madame Zilensky
as she passed down the corridor. He did not have to wait
long, and as soon as he heard her footsteps he called out
her name.

Madame Zilensky stood in the doorway. She looked vague
and jaded. "How are you? I had such a fine night's rest,"
she said.

"Pray be seated, if you please," said Mr. Brook. "I would
like a word with you."

Madame Zilensky put aside her portfolio and leaned back
wearily in the armchair across from him. "Yes?" she asked.

"Yesterday you spoke to me as I was walking across the
campus," he said slowly. "And if I am not mistaken, I believe you said something about a pastry shop and the King
of Finland. Is that correct?"

Madame Zilensky turned her head to one side and stared
retrospectively at a corner of the window sill.

"Something about a pastry shop," he repeated.

Her tired face brightened. "But of course," she said eagerly. "I told you about the time I was standing in front of this shop and the King of Finland——"

"Madame Zilensky!" Mr. Brook cried. "There is no King of Finland."

Madame Zilensky looked absolutely blank. Then, after an instant, she started off again. "I was standing in front of Bjarne's *pâtisserie* when I turned away from the cakes and suddenly saw the King of Finland——"

"Madame Zilensky, I just told you that there is no King of Finland."

"In Helsingfors," she started off again desperately, and again he let her get as far as the King, and then no further.

"Finland is a democracy," he said. "You could not possibly have seen the King of Finland. Therefore, what you have just said is an untruth. A pure untruth."

Never afterward could Mr. Brook forget the face of Madame Zilensky at that moment. In her eyes there was astonishment, dismay, and a sort of cornered horror. She had the look of one who watches his whole interior world split open and disintegrate.

"It is a pity," said Mr. Brook with real sympathy.

But Madame Zilensky pulled herself together. She raised her chin and said coldly, "I am a Finn."

"That I do not question," answered Mr. Brook. On second thought, he did question it a little.

"I was born in Finland and I am a Finnish citizen."

"That may very well be," said Mr. Brook in a rising voice.

"In the war," she continued passionately, "I rode a motorcycle and was a messenger."

"Your patriotism does not enter into it."

"Just because I am getting out the first papers——"

"Madame Zilensky!" said Mr. Brook. His hands grasped the edge of the desk. "That is only an irrelevant issue. The point is that you maintained and testified that you saw—that you saw——" But he could not finish. Her face stopped him. She was deadly pale and there were shadows around her mouth. Her eyes were wide open, doomed, and proud. And Mr. Brook felt suddenly like a murderer. A great commotion of feelings—understanding, remorse, and unreasonable love—made him cover his face with his hands. He could not speak until this agitation in his insides quieted down, and then he said very faintly, "Yes. Of course. The King of Finland. And was he nice?"

An hour later, Mr. Brook sat looking out of the window of his office. The trees along the quiet Westbridge street were almost bare, and the gray buildings of the college had a calm, sad look. As he idly took in the familiar scene, he noticed the Drakes' old Airedale waddling along down the street. It was a thing he had watched a hundred times before, so what was it that struck him as strange? Then he realized with a kind of cold surprise that the old dog was running along backward. Mr. Brook watched the Airedale until he was out of sight, then resumed his work on the canons which had been turned in by the class in counterpoint.

The Lucid Eye in Silver Town

BY JOHN UPDIKE

THE FIRST time I visited New York City, I was thirteen and went with my father. I went to meet my Uncle Quin and to buy a book about Vermeer. The Vermeer book was my idea, and my mother's; meeting Uncle Quin was my father's. A generation ago, my uncle had vanished in the direction of Chicago and become, apparently, rich; in the last week he had come east on business and I had graduated from the eighth grade with perfect marks. My father claimed that I and his brother were the smartest people he had ever met—"go-getters," he called us, with perhaps more irony than at the time I gave him credit for—and in his visionary way he suddenly, irresistibly felt that now was the time for us to meet. New York in those days was seven dollars away; we measured everything, distance and time, in money then. World War II was almost over but we were still living in the Depression. My father and I set off with the return tickets and a five-dollar bill in his pocket. The five dollars was for the book.

My mother, on the railway platform, suddenly exclaimed, "I *hate* the Augusts." This surprised me, because we were all Augusts—I was an August, my father was an August,

Uncle Quincy was an August, and she, I had thought, was an August.

My father gazed serenely over her head and said, "You have every reason to. I wouldn't blame you if you took a gun and shot us all. Except for Quin and your son. They're the only ones of us ever had any get up and git." Nothing was more infuriating about my father than his way of agreeing.

Uncle Quin didn't meet us at Pennsylvania Station. If my father was disappointed, he didn't reveal it to me. It was after one o'clock and all we had for lunch were two candy bars. By walking what seemed to me a very long way on pavements only a little broader than those of my home town, and not so clean, we reached the hotel, which seemed to sprout somehow from Grand Central Station. The lobby smelled of perfume. After the clerk had phoned Quincy August that a man who said he was his brother was at the desk, an elevator took us to the twentieth floor. Inside the room sat three men, each in a gray or blue suit with freshly pressed pants and garters peeping from under the cuffs when they crossed their legs. The men were not quite interchangeable. One had a caterpillar-shaped moustache, one had tangled blond eyebrows like my father's, and the third had a drink in his hand—the others had drinks, too, but were not gripping them so tightly.

"Gentlemen, I'd like you to meet my brother Marty and his young son," Uncle Quin said.

"The kid's name is Jay," my father added, shaking hands with each of the two men, staring them in the eye. I imitated my father, and the moustached man, not expecting my firm handshake and stare, said, "Why, hello there, Jay!"

"Marty, would you and the boy like to freshen up? The facilities are through the door and to the left."

"Thank you, Quin. I believe we will. Excuse me, gentlemen."

"Certainly."

"Certainly."

My father and I went into the bedroom of the suite. The furniture was square and new and all the same shade of maroon. On the bed was an opened suitcase, also new. The clean, expensive smells of leather and lotion were beautiful to me. Uncle Quin's underwear looked silk and was full of fleurs-de-lis. When I was through in the lavatory, I made for the living room, to rejoin Uncle Quin and his friends.

"Hold it," my father said. "Let's wait in here."

"Won't that look rude?"

"No. It's what Quin wants."

"Now Daddy, don't be ridiculous. He'll think we've died in here."

"No he won't, not my brother. He's working some deal. He doesn't want to be bothered. I know how my brother works: he got us in here so we'd stay in here."

"*Really,* Pop. You're such a schemer." But I did not want to go in there without him. I looked around the room for something to read. There was nothing, not even a newspaper, except a shiny little pamphlet about the hotel itself. I wondered when we would get a chance to look for the Vermeer book. I wondered what the men in the next room were talking about. I wondered why Uncle Quin was so short, when my father was so tall. By leaning out of the window, I could see taxicabs maneuvering like windup toys.

My father came and stood beside me. "Don't lean out too far."

I edged out inches farther and took a big bite of the high, cold air, spiced by the distant street noises. "Look at the green cab cut in front of the yellow," I said. "Should they be making U-turns on that street?"

"In New York it's OK. Survival of the fittest is the only law here."

"Isn't that the Chrysler Building?"

"Yes, isn't it graceful though? It always reminds me of the queen of the chessboard."

"What's the one beside it?"

"I don't know. Some big gravestone. The one deep in back, from this window, is the Woolworth Building. For years it was the tallest building in the world."

As, side by side at the window, we talked, I was surprised that my father could answer so many of my questions. As a young man, before I was born, he had traveled, looking for work; this was not *his* first trip to New York. Excited by my new respect, I longed to say something to remold that calm, beaten face.

"Do you really think he meant for us to stay out here?" I asked.

"Quin is a go-getter," he said, gazing over my head. "I admire him. Anything he wanted, from little on up, he went after it. Slam. Bang. His thinking is miles ahead of mine—just like your mother's. You can feel them pull out ahead of you." He moved his hands, palms down, like two taxis, the left quickly pulling ahead of the right. "You're the same way."

"Sure, sure." My impatience was not merely embarrassment at being praised; I was irritated that he considered Uncle Quin as smart as myself. At that point in my life I was sure that only stupid people took an interest in money.

When Uncle Quin finally entered the bedroom, he said, "Martin, I hoped you and the boy would come out and join us."

"Hell, I didn't want to butt in. You and those men were talking business."

"Lucas and Roebuck and I? Now, Marty, it was nothing that my own brother couldn't hear. Just a minor matter of adjustment. Both these men are fine men. Very important in their own fields. I'm disappointed that you couldn't see more of them. Believe me, I hadn't meant for you to hide in here. Now what kind of drink would you like?"

"I don't care. I drink very little any more."

"Scotch-and-water, Marty?"

"Swell."

"And the boy? What about some ginger ale, young man? Or would you like milk?"

"The ginger ale," I said.

"There was a day, you know, when your father could drink any two men under the table."

As I remember it, a waiter brought the drinks to the room, and while we were drinking them I asked if we were going to spend all afternoon in this room. Uncle Quin didn't seem to hear, but five minutes later he suggested that the boy might like to take a look around the city—Gotham, he called it. Baghdad-on-the-Subway. My father said that that would be a once-in-a-lifetime treat for the kid. He always called me "the kid" when I was sick or had lost at something or was angry—when he felt sorry for me, in short. The three of us went down in the elevator and took a taxi ride down Broadway, or up Broadway—I wasn't sure. "This is what they call the Great White Way," Uncle Quin said several times. Once he apologized, "In daytime it's just another street." The trip didn't seem so much designed for sightseeing as for getting Uncle Quin to the Pickernut Club, a little restaurant set in a block of similar canopied places. I remember we stepped down into it and it was dark inside. A piano was playing *There's a Small Hotel.*

"He shouldn't do that," Uncle Quin said. Then he waved to the man behind the piano. "How are you, Freddie? How are the kids?"

"Fine, Mr. August, fine," Freddie said, bobbing his head and smiling and not missing a note.

"That's Quin's song," my father said to me as we wriggled our way into a dark curved seat at a round table.

I didn't say anything, but Uncle Quin, overhearing some disapproval in my silence, said, "Freddie's a first-rate man. He has a boy going to Colgate this autumn."

I asked, "Is that really your song?"

Uncle Quin grinned and put his warm broad hand on my shoulder; I hated, at that age, being touched. "I let them think it is," he said, oddly purring. "To me, songs are like young girls. They're all pretty."

A waiter in a red coat scurried up. "Mr. August! Back from the West? How are you, Mr. August?"

"Getting by, Jerome, getting by. Jerome, I'd like you to meet my kid brother, Martin."

"How do you do, Mr. Martin. Are you paying New York a visit? Or do you live here?"

My father quickly shook hands with Jerome, somewhat to Jerome's surprise. "I'm just up for the afternoon, thank you. I live in a hick town in Pennsylvania you never heard of."

"I see, sir. A quick visit."

"This is the first time in six years that I've had a chance to see my brother."

"Yes, we've seen very little of him these past years. He's a man we can never see too much of, isn't that right?"

Uncle Quin interrupted. "This is my nephew Jay."

"How do you like the big city, Jay?"

"Fine." I didn't duplicate my father's mistake of offering to shake hands.

"Why, Jerome," Uncle Quin said. "My brother and I would like to have a Scotch-on-the-rocks. The boy would like a ginger ale."

"No, wait," I said. "What kinds of ice cream do you have?"

"Vanilla and chocolate, sir."

I hesitated. I could scarcely believe it, when the cheap drugstore at home had fifteen flavors.

"I'm afraid it's not a very big selection," Jerome said.
"I guess vanilla."

"Yes, sir. One plate of vanilla."

When my ice cream came it was a golf ball in a flat silver dish; it kept spinning away as I dug at it with my spoon. Uncle Quin watched me and asked, "Is there anything especially you'd like to do?"

"The kid'd like to get into a bookstore," my father said.

"A bookstore. What sort of book, Jay?"

I said, "I'd like to look for a good book of Vermeer."

"Vermeer," Uncle Quin pronounced slowly, relishing the r's, pretending to give the matter thought. "Dutch School."

"He's Dutch, yes."

"For my own money, Jay, the French are the people to beat. We have four Degas ballet dancers in our living room in Chicago, and I could sit and look at one of them for hours. I think it's wonderful, the feeling for balance the man had."

"Yeah, but don't Degas' paintings always remind you of colored drawings? For actually *looking* at things in terms of paint, for the lucid eye, I think Vermeer makes Degas look sick."

Uncle Quin said nothing, and my father, after an anxious glance across the table, said, "That's the way he and his mother talk all the time. It's all beyond me. I can't understand a thing they say."

"Your mother is encouraging you to be a painter, is she, Jay?" Uncle Quin's smile was very wide and his cheeks were pushed out as if each held a candy.

"Sure, I suppose she is."

"Your mother is a very wonderful woman, Jay," Uncle Quin said.

It was such an embarrassing remark, and so much depended upon your definition of "wonderful," that I dug at my ice cream, and my father asked Uncle Quin about his own wife, Tessie. When we left, Uncle Quin signed the check with his name and the name of some company. It was close to five o'clock.

My uncle didn't know much about the location of bookstores in New York—his last fifteen years had been spent in Chicago—but he thought that if we went to Forty-second Street and Sixth Avenue we should find something. The cab driver let us out beside a park that acted as kind of a backyard for the Public Library. It looked so inviting, so agreeably dusty, with the pigeons and the men nodding on the benches and the office girls in their taut summer dresses, that without thinking, I led the two men into it. Shimmering buildings arrowed upward and glinted through the treetops. This was New York, I felt: the silver town. Towers of ambition rose, crystalline, within me. "If you stand here," my father said, "you can see the Empire State." I went and stood beneath my father's arm and followed with my eyes the direction of it. Something sharp and hard fell into my right eye. I ducked my head and blinked; it was painful.

"What's the trouble?" Uncle Quin's voice asked.

My father said, "The poor kid's got something into his eye. He has the worst luck that way of anybody I ever knew."

The thing seemed to have life. It bit. "Ow," I said, angry enough to cry.

"If we can get him out of the wind," my father's voice said, "maybe I can see it."

"No, now, Marty, use your head. Never fool with the eyes or ears. The hotel is within two blocks. Can you walk two blocks, Jay?"

"I'm blind, not lame," I snapped.

"He has a ready wit," Uncle Quin said.

Between the two men, shielding my eye with a hand, I walked to the hotel. From time to time, one of them would take my other hand, or put one of theirs on my shoulder, but I would walk faster, and the hands would drop away. I hoped our entrance into the hotel lobby would not be too conspicuous; I took my hand from my eye and walked erect, defying the impulse to stoop. Except for the one lid being shut and possibly my face being red, I imagined I looked passably suave. However, my guardians lost no time betraying me. Not only did they walk at my heels, as if I might topple any instant, but my father told one old bum sitting in the lobby, "Poor kid got something in his eye," and Uncle Quin, passing the desk, called, "Send up a doctor to Twenty-eleven."

"You shouldn't have done that, Quin," my father said in the elevator. "I can get it out, now that he's out of the wind. This is happening all the time. The kid's eyes are too far front."

"Never fool with the eyes, Martin. They are your most precious tool in life."

"It'll work out," I said, though I didn't believe it would. It felt like a steel chip, deeply embedded.

Up in the room, Uncle Quin made me lie down on the bed. My father, a clean handkerchief wadded in his hand so that one corner stuck out, approached me, but it hurt so much to open the eye that I repulsed him. "Don't torment me," I said, twisting my face away. "What good does it do? The doctor'll be up."

Regretfully my father put the handkerchief back into his pocket.

The doctor was a soft-handed man with little to say to anybody; he wasn't pretending to be the family doctor. He rolled my lower eyelid on a thin stick, jabbed with a Q-tip, and showed me, on the end of the Q-tip, an eyelash. He dropped three drops of yellow fluid into the eye to remove any chance of infection. The fluid stung, and I shut my eyes, leaning back into the pillow, glad it was over. When I opened them, my father was passing a bill into the doctor's hand. The doctor thanked him, winked at me, and left. Uncle Quin came out of the bathroom.

"Well, young man, how are you feeling now?" he asked.

"Fine."

"It was just an eyelash," my father said.

"*Just* an eyelash! Well I know how an eyelash can feel like a razor blade in there. But, now that the young invalid is recovered, we can think of dinner."

"No, I really appreciate your kindness, Quin, but we must be getting back to the sticks. I have an eight-o'clock meeting I should be at."

"I'm extremely sorry to hear that. What sort of meeting, Marty?"

"A church council."

"So you're still doing church work. Well, God bless you for it."

"Grace wanted me to ask you if you couldn't possibly come over some day. We'll put you up overnight. It would be a real treat for her to see you again."

Uncle Quin reached up and put his arm around his younger brother's shoulders. "Martin, I'd like that better than anything in the world. But I am solid with appointments, and I must head west this Thursday. They don't let me have a minute's repose. Nothing would please my heart better than to share a quiet day with you and Grace in your home. Please give her my love, and tell her what a wonderful boy she is raising. The two of you are raising."

My father promised, "I'll do that." And, after a little more fuss, we left.

"The child better?" the old man in the lobby called to us on the way out.

"It was just an eyelash, thank you, sir," my father said.

When we got outside, I wondered if there were any bookstores still open.

"We have no money."

"None at all?"

"The doctor charged five dollars. That's how much it costs in New York to get something in your eye."

"I didn't do it on purpose. Do you think I pulled out the eyelash and stuck it in there myself? I didn't tell you to call the doctor."

"I know that."

"Couldn't we just go into a bookstore and look a minute?"

"We haven't time, Jay."

But when we reached Pennsylvania Station, it was over thirty minutes until the next train left. As we sat on a bench, my father smiled reminiscently. "Boy, he's smart, isn't he? His thinking is sixty light-years ahead of mine."

"Whose?"

"My brother. Notice the way he hid in the bathroom until the doctor was gone? That's how to make money. The rich man collects dollar bills like the stamp collector collects stamps. I knew he'd do it. I knew it when he told the clerk to send up a doctor that I'd have to pay for it."

"Well, why *should* he pay for it? *You* were the person to pay for it."

"That's right. Why should he?" My father settled back, his eyes forward, his hands crossed and limp in his lap. The skin beneath his chin was loose; his temples seemed concave. The liquor was probably disagreeing with him. "That's why he's where he is now, and that's why I am where I am."

The seed of my anger seemed to be a desire to recall him to himself, to scold him out of being old and tired. "Well, why'd you bring along only five dollars? You might have known something would happen."

"You're right, Jay. I should have brought more."

"Look. Right over there is an open bookstore. Now if you had brought *ten* dollars——"

"Is it open? I don't think so. They just left the lights in the window on."

"What if it isn't? What does it matter to us? Anyway, what kind of art book can you get for five dollars? Color plates cost money. How much do you think a decent book of Vermeer costs? It'd be cheap at fifteen dollars, even secondhand, with the pages all crummy and full of spilled coffee." I kept on, shrilly flailing the passive and infuriating figure of my father, until we left the city. Once we were on the homeward train, my tantrum ended; it had been a kind of ritual, for both of us, and he had endured my screams complacently, nodding assent, like a midwife assisting at the birth of family pride. Years passed before I needed to go to New York again.

SELECTED BIBLIOGRAPHY

IRVING, Washington
(1783–1859). *Diedrich Knickerbocker's History of New York* (1809); *The Sketch Book* (1820); *Bracebridge Hall* (1822); *The Alhambra* (1832); *A Tour of the Prairies* (1835).

HAWTHORNE, Nathaniel
(1804–64). *Twice-Told Tales* (1837–45); *Mosses from an Old Manse* (1845); *The Scarlet Letter* (1850); *The House of the Seven Gables* (1851); *The Blithedale Romance* (1852); *The Marble Faun* (1860).

POE, Edgar Allan
(1809–49). *Tamerlane* (1827); *Poems* (1831); *Tales of the Grotesque and Arabesque* (1840); *The Murders in the Rue Morgue* (1841); *The Gold Bug* (1843); *The Purloined Letter* (1845); *Tales* (1845).

MELVILLE, Herman
(1819–91). *Typee* (1846); *Omoo* (1847); *Mardi* (1849); *Moby Dick* (1851); *Billy Budd, Foretopman* (first published 1924).

O'BRIEN, Fitz-James
(1828–62). *Collected Stories; A Gentleman from Ireland* (1854).

TWAIN, Mark (Samuel Langhorne Clemens)
(1835–1910). *The Gilded Age* (1873); *The Adventures of Tom Sawyer* (1876); *Life on the Mississippi* (1883); *The Adventures of Huckleberry Finn* (1884); *A Connecticut Yankee in King Arthur's Court* (1889).

HARTE, Francis Bret
(1836–1902). *The Luck of Roaring Camp, and Other Sketches* (1870); *Tales of the Argonauts* (1875); *An Heiress of Red Dog, and Other Sketches* (1878); *Colonel Starbottle's Client, and Some Other People* (1892).

BIERCE, Ambrose
(1842–1914?). *Tales of Soldiers and Civilians* (1891); *The Monk and the Hangman's Daughter* (1892); *Can Such Things Be?* (1893); *Fantastic Fables* (1899); *The Devil's Dictionary* (1911).

JAMES, Henry
(1843–1916). *Daisy Miller* (1878); *Washington Square* (1881); *The Portrait of a Lady* (1881); *The Wings of the Dove* (1902); *The Ambassadors* (1903); *The Golden Bowl* (1904).

FREEMAN, Mary E. Wilkins
(1852–1930). *A Humble Romance and Other Stories* (1887); *A New England Nun and Other Stories* (1891); *Jane Field* (1893); *Pembroke* (1894); *Edgewater People* (1918).

JEWETT, Sarah Orne
(1849–1909). *Deephaven* (1877); *Country By-Ways* (1881); *The King of Folly Island* (1881); *A Country Doctor* (1884); *The Country of the Pointed Firs* (1896).

WHARTON, Edith
(1862–1937). *The House of Mirth* (1905); *Ethan Frome* (1911); *The Custom of the Country* (1913); *Tales of Men and Ghosts* (1917); *The Age of Innocence* (1920).

O. HENRY (William Sidney Porter)
(1862–1910). *Cabbages and Kings* (1905); *The Four Million* (1906); *The Voice of the City* (1908); *The Gentle Grafter* (1908); *Options* (1909).

ADE, George
(1866–1944). *Fables in Slang* (1899); *People You Knew* (1903); *The Sultan of Sulu* (1902); *The College Widow* (1904); *Hand-Made Fables* (1920).

DUNNE, Finley Peter
(1867–1936). *Mr. Dooley in Peace and War* (1898); *Mr. Dooley's Philosophy* (1900); *Dissertations by Mr. Dooley* (1906); *Mr. Dooley Says* (1910).

CRANE, Stephen
(1871–1900). *Maggie: A Girl of the Streets* (1893); *The Red Badge of Courage* (1895); *The Open Boat and Other Tales* (1898); *The Monster and Other Stories* (1899); *Men, Women and Boats* (1921).

FLANDRAU, Charles Macomb
(1871–1938). *Harvard Episodes* (1897); *The Diary of a*

Freshman (1901); *Viva Mexico!* (1908); *Prejudices* (1911); *Loquacities* (1931); *Sophomores Abroad* (1935).

DREISER, Theodore
(1871–1945). *Sister Carrie* (1900); *Jennie Gerhardt* (1911); *The Financier* (1912); *The Titan* (1914); *The "Genius"* (1915); *An American Tragedy* (1925).

DAY, Clarence
(1874–1935). *This Simian World* (1920); *God and My Father* (1932); *Life With Father* (1935); *Scenes from the Mesozoic* (1935); *Life With Mother* (1936).

ANDERSON, Sherwood
(1876–1941). *Windy McPherson's Son* (1916); *Marching Men* (1917); *Winesburg, Ohio* (1919); *The Triumph of the Egg* (1921); *Poor White* (1920); *Dark Laughter* (1925); *Beyond Desire* (1932).

LONDON, Jack
(1876–1916). *The Son of the Wolf* (1900); *The Call of the Wild* (1903); *The Sea-Wolf* (1904); *White Fang* (1906); *Martin Eden* (1909); *Burning Daylight* (1910).

WILLIAMS, William Carlos
(1883–1963). *In the American Grain* (1925); *White Mule* (1937); *Paterson* (1946–51); *Collected Earlier Poems* (1951); *Autobiography* (1951); *The Build-Up* (1952).

LARDNER, Ring(gold) W.
(1885–1933). *You Know Me Al* (1916); *Gullible's Travels* (1917); *The Big Town* (1920); *How to Write Short Stories* (1924); *Round Up* (1929).

AIKEN, Conrad
(b. 1889). *The Collected Novels of Conrad Aiken* (1964); *Collected Poems* (1953); *Selected Poems* (1964); *Ushant* (1961); *The Morning Song of Lord Zero* (1963); *A Seizure of Limericks* (1964); *Collected Short Stories* (1960).

BENÉT, Stephen Vincent
(1890–1943). *John Brown's Body* (1926); *Thirteen O'Clock* (1937); *Tales Before Midnight* (1939); *The Last Circle* (1946).

PARKER, Dorothy
(b. 1893). *Not So Deep As A Well* (1936); *Laments for the Living* (1930); *After Such Pleasures* (1933); *Here Lies* (1939); *The Portable Dorothy Parker* (1944).

THURBER, James
(1894–1963). *Is Sex Necessary?* (with E. B. White, 1929); *The Seal in the Bedroom* (1932); *My Life and Hard Times* (1933);

The Middle-Aged Man on the Flying Trapeze (1935); *Let Your Mind Alone!* (1937); *The Thurber Carnival* (1945); *The Beast In Me* (1948); *Thurber Country* (1953); *Alarms and Diversions* (1957); *The Years with Ross* (1957); *Lanterns and Lances* (1961); *Credos and Curios* (1962).

McNULTY, John
(1895–1956). *Third Avenue New York* (1946); *A Man Gets Around* (1951).

COATES, Robert M.
(b. 1897). *The Outlaw Years* (1930); *The Bitter Season* (1946); *Wisteria Cottage* (1948); *All the Year Round* (1943); *The View from Here* (1960); *Beyond the Alps* (1961); *The Man Just Ahead of You* (1964).

FAULKNER, William
(1897–1962). *Mosquitoes* (1927); *The Sound and the Fury* (1929); *As I Lay Dying* (1930); *Sanctuary* (1931); *Light in August* (1932); *The Wild Palms* (1939); *Absalom, Absalom* (1951); *Go Down, Moses* (1942); *Knight's Gambit* (1949); *Requiem for a Nun* (1951); *A Fable* (1954); *Intruder in the Dust* (1948); *The Reivers* (1962).

BEMELMANS, Ludwig
(1898–1962). *My War with the United States* (1935); *Life Class* (1938); *Small Beer* (1939); *Hotel Splendide* (1941); *I Love You, I Love You, I Love You* (1942); *Now I Lay Me Down to Sleep* (1943); *The Donkey Inside* (1941); *The Best of Times* (1948); *Italian Holiday* (1961); *The Street Where the Heart Lies* (1962).

HEMINGWAY, Ernest
(1898–1961). *The Sun Also Rises* (1926); *A Farewell to Arms* (1929); *Men Without Women* (1927); *Winner Take Nothing* (1933); *To Have and Have Not* (1937); *For Whom the Bell Tolls* (1940); *The Old Man and the Sea* (1952); *A Moveable Feast* (1964).

WHITE, Elwyn Brooks
(b. 1899). *The Fox of Peapack* (1938); *Quo Vadimus? or, The Case for the Bicycle* (1939); *One Man's Meat* (1942, enlarged 1944); *Stuart Little* (1945); *Charlotte's Web* (1952); *The Second Tree from the Corner* (1954); *The Points of My Compass* (1962).

LA FARGE, Oliver
(1901–63). *Laughing Boy* (1929); *Sparks Fly Upward* (1931); *The Enemy Gods* (1937); *All the Young Men* (1935); *Raw Material* (1945).

COLLIER, John
  (b. 1901). *His Monkey Wife, or Married to a Chimp* (1930);
  Defy the Foul Fiend (1933); *Full Circle* (1933); *Presenting
  Moonshine* (1940); *The Touch of Nutmeg* (1943); *Fancies and
  Goodnights* (1951).

STEINBECK, John
  (b. 1902). *Tortilla Flat* (1935); *In Dubious Battle* (1936); *Of
  Mice and Men* (1937); *The Long Valley* (1938); *The Grapes
  of Wrath* (1939); *Cannery Row* (1944); *The Pearl* (1948);
  East of Eden (1952); *The Winter of Our Discontent* (1961);
  Travels with Charley (1962).

BOYLE, Kay
  (b. 1903). *The First Lover* (1933); *The White Horses of Vienna*
  (1936); *Avalanche* (1943); *Thirty Stories* (1946); *His Human
  Majesty* (1949); *Collected Poems* (1962); *The Smoking Mountain* (1963).

CALDWELL, Erskine
  (b. 1903). *Tobacco Road* (1932); *God's Little Acre* (1933);
  Journeyman (1935); *Tragic Ground* (1944); *A House in the
  Uplands* (1946); *Men and Women* (1961); *Jenny by Nature*
  (1961); *Close to Home* (1962); *The Last Night of Summer*
  (1963); *Around About America* (1964).

SAROYAN, William
  (b. 1908). *The Daring Young Man on the Flying Trapeze*
  (1934); *The Time of Your Life* (1939); *My Heart's in the
  Highlands* (1939); *My Name Is Aram* (1940); *The Human
  Comedy* (1942); *Hello Out There* (1942); *Here Comes There
  Goes You Know Who* (1961); *Boys and Girls Together* (1963);
  Not Dying (1963); *After Thirty Years* (1964); *One Day in the
  Afternoon of the World* (1964).

MITCHELL, Joseph
  (b. 1908). *McSorley's Wonderful Saloon* (1943); *The Bottom
  of the Harbor* (1959).

MAXWELL, William
  (b. 1908). *Bright Center of Heaven* (1934); *They Came Like
  Swallows* (1937); *The Folded Leaf* (1945); *The Heavenly
  Tenants* (1946); *Time Will Darken It* (1948); *The Chateau*
  (1961).

STEGNER, Wallace
  (b. 1909). *Remembering Laughter* (1937); *Fire and Ice* (1941);
  The Big Rock Candy Mountain (1943); *One Nation* (1945);
  Second Growth (1947); *The Preacher and the Slave* (1950);
  A Shooting Star (1961); *The Women on the Wall* (1962); *Wolf*

Willow (1962); *Beyond the Hundredth Meridian* (1962); *The Gathering of Zion* (1964).

PARKER, James Reid
(b. 1909). *Academic Procession* (1937); *Attorneys at Law* (1941); *The Merry Wives of Massachusetts* (1959).

AGEE, James
(1909–1955). *Let Us Now Praise Famous Men* (with Walker Evans) (1936); *The Morning Watch* (1951); *A Death in the Family* (1957); *Agee on Film* (1958, 1960); *Letters to Father Flye* (1962).

CHEEVER, John
(b. 1912). *The Enormous Radio* (1953); *The Wapshot Chronicle* (1957); *The Housebreaker of Shady Hill* (1958); *The Wapshot Scandal* (1964); *Some People, Places, and Things That Will Not Appear in My Next Novel* (1961); *The Brigadier and the Golf Widow* (1964).

SHAW, Irwin
(b. 1913). *Sailor off the Bremen* (1937); *Act of Faith* (1946); *The Troubled Air* (1951); *Lucy Crown* (1956); *The Young Lions* (1958); *Two Weeks in Another Town* (1960); *Selected Short Stories* (1961); *In the Company of Dolphins* (1964).

BISSELL, Richard
(b. 1913). *A Stretch on the River* (1950); *7½ Cents* (1953); *Say Darling* (1957); *Goodbye, Ava* (1960); *You Can Always Tell a Harvard Man* (1962).

FREEDGOOD, Seymour
(b. 1915).

McCULLERS, Carson
(b. 1917). *The Heart Is a Lonely Hunter* (1940); *Reflections in a Golden Eye* (1941); *The Member of the Wedding* (1946); *The Ballad of the Sad Café* (1951); *Clock Without Hands* (1961); *Sweet as a Pickle and Clean as a Pig* (1964).

UPDIKE, John
(b. 1932). *The Poorhouse Fair* (1959); *The Same Door* (1959); *Rabbit, Run* (1960); *Pigeon Feathers* (1962); *The Centaur* (1963); *Telephone Poles* (1963); *Assorted Prose* (1965); *Of the Farm* (1965).